East Grinstead

Breviary Offices

From lauds to compline inclusive, translated from the Sarum Book, and

supplemented from gallican and monastic uses

East Grinstead

Breviary Offices
From lauds to compline inclusive, translated from the Sarum Book, and supplemented from gallican and monastic uses

ISBN/EAN: 9783741176067

Manufactured in Europe, USA, Canada, Australia, Japa

Cover: Foto ©Andreas Hilbeck / pixelio.de

Manufactured and distributed by brebook publishing software (www.brebook.com)

East Grinstead

Breviary Offices

BREVIARY OFFICES.

Cambridge:
PRINTED BY J. PALMER, 23, JESUS LANE.

Breviary Offices

FROM LAUDS TO COMPLINE INCLUSIVE,

Translated from the Sarum Book,

AND SUPPLEMENTED FROM

Gallican and Monastic Uses.

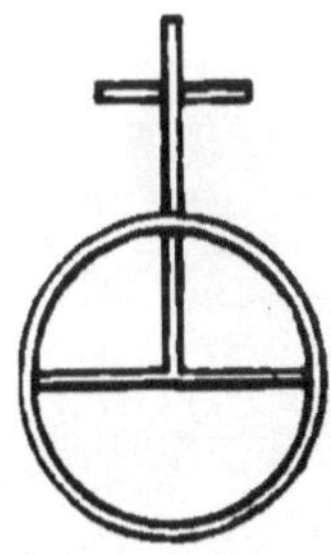

LONDON:

J. T. HAYES, LYALL PLACE, EATON SQUARE; AND
4, HENRIETTA STREET, COVENT GARDEN.
BRIGHTON: G. WAKELING, NORTH STREET.
MDCCCLXXIV.

Ut obsequium servitutis nostrae rationabile facias:
Te rogamus, audi nos.

TABLE OF CONTENTS.

THAT a community of women should offer to the English Church a new book of Offices, appears presumptuous as well as unnecessary, unless some explanation be given of the causes which led to the attempt. S. Margaret's Sisterhood, founded by the Rev. J. M. Neale, in 1854, was early provided with a Ms. translation, abridged and simplified, of the shorter Sarum Hours, and with various other offices, selected from Roman or Gallican uses, where Sarum was insufficient or apparently unsatisfactory. For although Dr. Neale considered the Sarum book as that of which the adoption was generally binding upon us, he preferred a degree of eclecticism to a servile following of the old English use, when better offices were to be found elsewhere.

Other persons, aware of our possessing many Mss., asked us to prepare a book which should supply offices yet wanting in existing manuals, and provide abundance of materials for devotion from which they might select portions suitable for use. We have thus endeavoured to respond to their request, and the present volume is the careful, but very imperfect result of our labours, containing, besides much supplementary matter, the Breviary Offices from Prime to Compline inclusive, Matins being already in course of publication separately.

In this compilation, our founder's plan has been retained; i.e. Sarum has been followed wherever possible. The Psalter, and Proper of Seasons exactly reproduce Sarum, with a few abbreviations and simplifications; except a few alterations, mentioned below.*

If it be asked why the Roman books would not suffice us, and why we should try to resuscitate a use long dead, we answer that the Gallican breviaries present us with rich and varied treasures of Scriptural applications, and mystical interpretations, which might be sought vainly in the Roman forms; and that Sarum far surpasses Rome in the dignity and variety of its daily office; in its absence of unseemly haste, (as when Rome continually replaces longer Psalms by Ps. cxvii.) and in its sedulous and hearty use of continual intercession for living and dead.†

But when we arrive at the Common and Proper of Saints, Sarum shines no more. Every one acquainted with the Roman breviary must have been struck by the excessive poverty of the Offices of the Blessed Virgin Mary, where one commonplace idea is repeated continually, with mere transposition of words, and almost the whole mass of Old Testament type and prophecy is neglected or ignored, (if not misapplied, as in the case of Ecclus. xxiv.). Sarum disappointingly

---

* The Antiphons to the Psalms are doubled at certain times, according to ordinary present use. The Christmas Eve Vesper Hymn is continued through the Octave, as in the Benedictine Breviary, instead of, as in Sarum, using *A solis ortus* both at Lauds and Vespers. The proper Office of S. Thomas of Canterbury is changed for the Common of a Martyr, the Antiphon, ℣. and ℟. to the Memorial, being all that are retained from the original. The Ants. at Vespers in Epiphany-tide are according to York, Sarum retaining the Ants. of Christmas. The Saturday Ants. after Trinity are from the Roman Breviary: because it was necessary to take the lectionary for Matins from that source, and those Ants. must agree with the lectionary of the current month. The Memorials are simplified. The Whitsun-tide Sequence at Compline is exchanged for *Veni Sancte Spiritus*. It should be added, that, also according to Dr. Neale's usage, in accordance with the present custom of the English Church, invocations of Saints and Angels are as a rule omitted, except when occurring in Psalms, Canticles, etc.

† With regard to the last assertion it may be mentioned, that, as will be seen in the body of the book, the fifteen Gradual Psalms were recited daily in Lent, with the noble Litany, "for the whole Church of God"; and that one nocturn of the Office of the Dead was to be said, whenever unhindered by Festivals, after Matins of the day. Our forefathers grudged no time nor pains in their prayers, and although it may not now be practicable for many to use them in extenso, it is as well, in these days of hurry, to have such full and leisurely Offices before our eyes.

falls to quite as low a level in this respect. Besides this, the Offices are disfigured by jingling and alliterative Antiphons, which indeed bear their testimony to the English love of the grotesque, but possess neither dignity nor beauty.

For these Offices therefore, we have drawn extensively from other sources, principally the Breviaries of Paris, Rouen, Coutances, Beauvais, Noyon; besides the Benedictine, (whose authority in England ranks next to that of Sarum). Added to which, we have drawn from the Reformed Roman Breviary, for several points of practical utility. But we have invented nothing anywhere, except one Office in the Common of Saints:—Vespers for the Sick; Matins and Lauds having been prepared long since by Dr. Neale from Card. Thomasius, who however furnishes scarce any hints for Vespers.

In the Proper of Saints, the Offices of S. Andrew, Conversion of S. Paul, Nativity of S. John Baptist, SS. Peter and Paul, Commemoration of S. Paul, S. Mary Magdalene, Holy Name, S. Michael and all Angels, (chiefly) are from Sarum. The rest are principally Gallican. In the Common of Holy-days, all the Hymns and the selection of Psalms, the Common of Apostles in Easter-tide, and through the year, are Sarum. The Common of the Blessed Virgin and the other Offices are chiefly Gallican. The Commendatory Prayers are from the Parisian and Benedictine books. The Office of the Dead is Roman.

We are at a loss to express our sense of the extreme and unwearied kindness of all to whom we have applied for that assistance, without which, our task, difficult for us in any case, would have been entirely hopeless. For advice, information, loan of valuable books, permission to reprint translated Hymns, and the translation of several expressly for this book, we return thanks to the Revs. L. Alison, R. F. Littledale, G. Moultrie, W. J. Copeland, E. Caswall, and J. D. Chambers, Esq.; and most especially to the Rev. W. J. Blew, "whose learning is only equalled by his courtesy," and who, in addition to other most important assistance, has been at the pains to draw out for this work a Sarum table of occurrence and concurrence.

We have also to acknowledge the obliging politeness with which Mr. Masters and Messrs. Novello and Co. have permitted us to reprint many of Dr. Neale's copyright Hymns.

Great pains have been taken to discover and secure the permission of the translators of the Hymns used in this book: but if any inadvertent mistake has been made in this matter, we beg to be apprised of it, in order to its correction in a future edition.

GENERAL NOTES.

Memorials. Memorials are made at Lauds and Vespers only. When the Office of any Feast or of a greater feria is superseded by that of a greater Feast, a Memorial is made of the day whose office is omitted altogether, or at first or second Vespers only. Memorials are formed thus:
(1) Antiphon to Benedictus or Magnificat from the Office which is omitted.
(2) ℣. and ℟. following the Hymn in the same Office.
(3) The Collect of the Office, preceded by *The Lord be*, etc., and *Let us pray*.
Common Memorials are set down at the beginning of the Common of Saints, to be used on those Feasts, when it may appear expedient not to use the whole Office of the Saint. They will take precedence of the Memorials in the Psalter. These Feasts are marked * in the Kalendar and in the Proper of Saints. If a Feast having its own Office set down in the Proper of Saints be commemorated by a Memorial only, such Memorial may be formed from the Proper Office, according to the rule given above. The Memorials on page 65 are said on Saturdays from Trinity to Advent exclusively. The number of Collects said at one Office must not be greater than seven, that being the number of petitions in the Lord's Prayer; therefore more than six Memorials cannot be said.

Antiphons. The Antiphons to Benedictus, Magnificat, and Nunc Dimittis are sung before and after the Canticles on all Principal and Greater Doubles. At other times the first few words only are said before the Canticle, the whole being said after. In this latter way Antiphons to Psalms are always said according to the use of Sarum. The Roman use, as being more generally practised, is followed in this book. When the words of an Antiphon are taken from the beginning of the Psalm or Canticle, they are not repeated, but the Psalm is continued from the point where the Antiphon ceased.

Collects. If the Collect be addressed to the Father, it is concluded, *Through Jesus Christ our Lord*, etc. If to the Son: *Who livest and reignest*, etc. If in the beginning of the Collect the Son has been named: *Through the same*, etc.; if the mention of the Son occurs at the end: *Who liveth and reigneth with Thee and the Holy Ghost*, etc. If the Holy Ghost has been named, in the ending is said: *In the unity of the same Holy Ghost*.

When many Collects are said, the first only shall end: *Through Jesus Christ*, etc., or otherwise, as above. The others shall be said without any ending at all, except the last; but every Collect shall have *Let us pray* before it.

Whenever Proper Collects have been supplied by the Common Prayer-book, they have here been inserted; but in cases where they were not taken from the Sarum book, translations of the Sarum Collects are supplied in brackets, except with regard to a few, the reproduction of which appeared undesirable. This note of course applies to those parts of the book only which, as stated in the Preface, are translated from the Sarum Breviary.

There are certain points in which it may seem more expedient to follow the directions of the Reformed Roman Breviary, which are clearer, less elaborate, and in more general present use. These are placed here first, for the use of those who may prefer them; it being noted that one use or the other must be wholly followed in these particulars, as there are great discrepancies between the two.

1. DIGNITY OF FEASTS. See tables of Concurrence and Occurrence.

2. DOUBLING OF ANTIPHONS. The Antiphons to the Psalms at Lauds and Vespers are doubled, as well as the Antiphons to the Canticles. The rubric in the Psalter, p. 1, accords with this use.

3. THE OFFICE OF THE DEAD. The Office of the Dead is said on the first day unhindered in every month, and on every Monday in Advent and Lent, but not in Holy Week.

4. FESTIVALS IN HOLY WEEK. Any Feast occurring on any day in Holy Week is deferred till the first day unhindered after Low Sunday.

NOTES ON CERTAIN POINTS (Sarum).

ADVENT. If any Double Feast falls on Sunday, it is transferred to Monday, and on Sunday are said first Vespers of the Feast. If on Monday, on Sunday are said first Vespers of the Feast. If on Saturday, Vespers are of the Feast, except the Saturday before Advent Sunday, when first Vespers are of Sunday. Any Feast which is the Feast of the place is not transferred, but the whole Office is said on its own day. On all Feasts in Advent a Memorial of the feria is made at Lauds and Vespers.

CHRISTMAS TIDE. Rubrics for Christmas and Epiphany are fully set down in the text, except that it is to be noted, that if the Octave of Epiphany falls on Sunday, the whole Office is of the Octave, of course with Memorial of Sunday.

If Candlemas Day falls on Sunday, the whole Office is of the Feast. If on Monday, its first Vespers are said on Sunday. If on Saturday, Vespers are of the Feast.

LENT. If the Annunciation falls on any Sunday, including Palm Sunday, it is transferred to Monday, and in this case, and also when it falls on Monday, on Sunday are said first Vespers of the Feast. If it falls on Saturday, Vespers are of Sunday.

But if it be the Feast of the place, the whole Office is said on its own day, unless it be Palm Sunday, in which case it is transferred to Monday.

If it falls on Wednesday in Holy Week, the Office is of the Feast, but its second Vespers are superseded by first Vespers of Maundy Thursday.

On Tuesday in Holy Week, the Office of the Dead is said throughout, unless prevented by a Double Feast, in which case it is said, if possible, on the day before. No Feasts are celebrated on or after Thursday in Holy Week; but Double Feasts are transferred to any convenient day after the Octave of Easter; Simple Feasts are omitted for that year.

On all Feasts in Lent, a Memorial of the Fast is made at Lauds and Vespers. Lent Compline is never altered, except that on the Feast of the Annunciation, the Hymn is sung with the proper doxology.

TENEBRÆ. Twenty four candles are set before the Altar and lighted before Matins on Maundy Thursday, according to the number of Prophets and Apostles. One is extinguished at the beginning of each Antiphon and R̰., to signify the cruelty of the Jews towards the Prophets and Apostles. While the fifth Antiphon at Lauds is being sung a light is hidden where it cannot be seen, and after the singing of the fifth Antiphon all the lights throughout the Church are extinguished. For further rubrics concerning the Tenebræ Office, see Proper of Seasons.

EASTER TIDE includes the season from Easter Day till Nones on Saturday in Whitsun Week inclusive. Any Double Feast occurring in Easter Week, or on the three days preceding, is transferred to a convenient day after the Octave. Simple Feasts are omitted for that year. This same order serves for Whitsun Week. If a Double Feast occurs on Low Sunday, it is transferred to Monday. If on Rogation Sunday, it is kept. But Simple Feasts occurring on either of these Sundays are transferred. If any Double Feast is to be kept on the morrow of Low Sunday, or of Rogation Sunday, Vespers on Sunday are of the Feast. No Memorials of ferias are made in Easter tide on any Double Feast, except when such falls on Rogation Monday or the Vigil of the Ascension, in which case Memorial is made of the Fast at Lauds only, before other Memorials. If a Simple Feast occurs on either of these days, it is observed only by a Memorial made at Lauds. The Memorials of the Resurrection are said on Sunday, whether the Office be of Sunday or of a Feast, except on the Invention of the Cross. Easter Compline does not change for Festivals, except in the doxology of the Hymn on the Annunciation.

VIGILS. [The Office of a Vigil, according to Rome, is that of the feria, with proper Collect, unless otherwise ordered in the Proper Offices. See Rubric in Common of Vigils, p. 331. If a Feast, having a Vigil, falls on Monday, the Vigil Office is said on Saturday, and no notice is taken of it on Sunday. When a Feast falls on the Vigil of another Feast, a Memorial of the Vigil is made at Lauds.] The vigils observed in Sarum are those of the Epiphany, S. John Baptist, SS. Peter and Paul, S. James, S. Lawrence, the Repose of the Blessed Virgin Mary, S. Bartholomew, SS. Simon and Jude, All Saints, S. Andrew, S. Thomas, and Christmas.

OFFICE OF THE DEAD. The Office of the Dead* is said on every feria through Advent till Christmas Eve, from the morrow of the Octave of Epiphany till Tuesday in Holy Week inclusive, and from the morrow of Trinity Sunday till Advent, with this exception, that it is never said on Double Feasts, or through their Octaves.

SIMPLE FEASTS. On Simple Feasts the Antiphons and Psalms at First Vespers are of the feria, and the Proper Office begins at the Chapter, continuing till Nones inclusive on the day following.

OCTAVES. When a Feast is kept with an Octave, the Office of the Feast, beginning at Lauds, is said for the six following days, with these exceptions:—at Lauds the five Psalms are said under the first Antiphon. The Antiphons to Benedictus and to Magnificat at Vespers are taken from among the Antiphons to Psalms at first Vespers, unless otherwise provided for. At Vespers the Psalms of the second Vespers of the day are said with the Antiphons at Lauds. The Ry. is not said.

But if Sunday falls within the Octave, at first Vespers are said Psalms of second Vespers with the first Antiphon of Lauds; all the rest as at first Vespers of the Feast, except that the Ry. is not said. Lauds is said as through the Octave. Second Vespers is said as on the Feast, except that the Ry. is not said.

On the Octave day, all is said as on the first day, except that at first Vespers the Psalms are all said under the first Antiphon; and no Ry. is said at either Vespers.

The Festivals intended to be said with Octaves, as contained in this book, besides those set down in the Psalter, are: Corpus Christi, S. John Baptist, SS. Peter and Paul, the Visitation, the Holy Name, the Repose of the Blessed Virgin Mary, All Saints.

---

* Vespers, one Nocturn, and Lauds: Noct. 1 on Monday and Thursday, Noct. 2 on Tuesday and Friday, Noct. 3 on Wednesday and Saturday: but, if festivals intervene, so arranging as, if possible, to get the 3 Nocts. said once in the course of the week.

SARUM.

Principal Doubles.

Christmas Day, the Epiphany, Easter Day, Ascension Day, Whitsun-day, Repose of Blessed Virgin Mary, Feast of the place, Dedication of Church.

Greater Doubles.

Purification, Trinity Sunday, Corpus Christi, Visitation, Holy Name, Nativity of our Lady, All Saints.

Lesser Doubles.

Feasts of S. Stephen, S. John, Ap., Holy Innocents, S. Thomas of Canterbury, Circumcision, Annunciation; Easter Monday, Tuesday and Wednesday, and Whitsun Monday, Tuesday, and Wednesday; Low Sunday, the Invention of the Cross, the Nativity of S. John Baptist, the Feast of SS. Peter and Paul, the Transfiguration, Holy Cross Day, Conception of the Blessed Virgin.

Inferior Doubles.

Feasts of S. Andrew, S. Thomas, S. Matthias, S. Gregory, S. Ambrose, S. George, S. Mark, SS. Philip and James, S. Augustine of England, S. James, S. Bartholomew, S. Augustine of Hippo, S. Matthew, S. Michael and All Angels, S. Jerome, Translation of S. Edward, S. Luke, SS. Simon and Jude.

All other Feasts are Simples.

Principal privileged Sundays.

First Sunday in Advent, Passion Sunday, Palm Sunday.

Greater Privileged Sundays.

Second, third, fourth in Advent, Septuagesima, and all after till Passion Sunday.

Lesser privileged Sundays.

Those on which a series of Matins lessons was begun:—first Sunday after the Octave of Epiphany, Sunday before Ascension Day, first Sunday after Trinity.

Inferior privileged Sundays.

All the rest, throughout the year.

Greater Ferias.

As in Rome.

ROMAN.

Doubles of the First Class.

Christmas Day, the Epiphany, Easter Day, Monday and Tuesday, Ascension-day, Whitsun-day, Monday and Tuesday, Corpus Christi, Nativity of S. John Baptist, Feast of SS. Peter and Paul, Repose of Blessed Virgin Mary, Feast of All Saints, Dedication of Church, Patron or Title of Church.

Doubles of the Second Class.

The Circumcision, Feast of the Holy Trinity, Feasts of the Purification, Annunciation, Visitation, Nativity and Conception of the Blessed Virgin; the Birthdays of the Apostles, Feasts of Evangelists, Feasts of S. Stephen, the Holy Innocents; Invention of the Cross, Feast of the Holy Name, S. Joseph, S. Lawrence, S. Michael.

Greater Doubles.

Transfiguration of our Lord, Holy Cross Day, Conversion of S. Paul, Feasts of S. John Port Latin, S. Barnabas, Beheading of S. John Baptist, Lammas Day, S. Anne, Presentation of Blessed Virgin Mary, minor Patrons.

Semi-Doubles. *

Days within Octaves. The rest are set down in the Kalendar.

All other Feasts are Simples.

GREATER SUNDAYS
Of the First Class.

First Sunday in Advent, first in Lent, Passion Sunday, Palm Sunday, Easter Day, Low Sunday, Whitsun-day, Trinity Sunday.

Of the Second Class.

Second, third, and fourth Sundays in Advent, Septuagesima, Sexagesima, and Quinquagesima Sundays; second, third, and fourth Sundays in Lent.

Greater Ferias.

Ferias in Advent and Lent, Ember Days, Rogation Monday.

* The difference between Doubles and Semi Doubles is that in the latter the Ants. to Psalms and Canticles at Lauds and Vespers are not doubled.

Roman.

TABLE I.

Occurrence.

IF THERE OCCUR ON THE SAME DAY A

	Vigil.	Greater Feria.	Simple.	Semi-Double.	Day of Octave.	Day in Octave.	Double.	Double of the 2nd Class.	Double of the 1st Class.	Ordinary Sunday.	Sunday of the 2nd Class.	Sunday of the 1st Class.
Double of the 1st Class . .	6	4	6	2	4	6	2	2	8	4	4	1
Double of the 2nd Class . .	4	4	4	2	4	6	2	8	1	4	1	1
Double	4	4	4	2	1	4	8	1	1	4	1	1
Day in Octave	4	4	4	3	3	7	3	5	5	3	3	3
Day of Octave	4	4	4	2	7	4	2	3	3	4	3	3
Semi-Double	4	4	4	8	1	4	1	1	1	1	1	1
Simple	3	3	0	3	3	3	3	3	5	3	3	3
Greater Feria	6	0	4	3	3	3	3	3	3	0	0	0
Vigil	0	5	4	3	3	3	3	3	5	0	0	0

1. Translation of the 1st, Office of the 2nd.
2. Office of the 1st, Translation of the 2nd.
3. Commemoration of the 1st, Office of the 2nd.
4. Office of the first, Commemoration of the 2nd.
5. Nothing of the 1st, Office of the 2nd.
6. Office of the 1st, nothing of the 2nd.
7. Office of the greater, Commemoration of the less.
8. Office of the greater, Translation of the less.

𝕽𝖔𝖒𝖆𝖓.

TABLE II.

Concurrence.

WHEN FIRST VESPERS OF A FEAST FALL ON THE SAME DAY AS SECOND VESPERS OF A FEAST PRECEDING.

	Day within Octave.	Octave Day.	Simple.	Semi-Double.	Lesser Double.	Greater Double.	Patron or Title of the Church.	Double of the 2nd Class.	Double of the 1st Class.	Any Sunday whatever.
Greater Sunday, or of 1st or 2nd Class	4	3	4	4	3	3	3	3	3	0
Lesser or ordinary Sunday	4	3	4	4	3	3	1	1	1	0
Double of the 1st Class	2	4	2	4	4	4	0	4	6	4
Double of the 2nd Class	4	4	4	4	4	4	3	6	3	4
Patron or Title of Church	2	4	2	4	4	4	0	4	0	4
Greater Double	4	4	4	4	4	6	1	3	1	4
Lesser Double	4	5	4	4	5	3	1	3	1	4
Semi-Double	5	3	4	5	3	3	1	1	1	5
Octave-Day	4	5	4	4	5	3	1	3	1	4
Day within Octave	0	3	4	5	3	3	1	1	1	5

1. All of the following, nothing of the preceding.
2. All of the preceding, nothing of the following.
3. All of the following, Commemoration of the preceding.
4. All of the preceding, Commemoration of the following.
5. Chapter of the following, Commemoration of the preceding.
6. All of the more worthy, Commemoration of the less worthy.

𝕾𝖆𝖗𝖚𝖒.

TABLE I.

Occurrence.

IF THERE OCCUR ON THE SAME DAY A

	Vigil.	Greater Feria.	Simple.	Octave Day.	Day in Octave.	Inferior Double.	Lesser Double.	Greater Double.	Principal Double.	Lesser or Inferior privileged Sunday.	Greater privileged Sunday.	Principal privileged Sunday.
Principal Double	6	4	6	4	6	2	2	2	8	4	4	1
Greater Double	4	4	4	4	6	2	2	8	1	4	1	1
Lesser Double	4	4	4	1	4	2	8	1	1	4	1	1
Inferior Double	4	4	4	1	4	8	1	1	1	4	1	1
Day in Octave	4	4	4	3	7	3	3	5	5	3	3	3
Octave Day	4	4	4	7	4	2	2	3	3	4	3	3
Simple	3	3	0	3	3	3	3	3	5	3	3	3
Greater Feria	6	0	4	3	3	3	3	3	3	0	0	0
Vigil	0	5	4	3	3	3	3	3	5	0	0	0

1. Translation of 1, Service of 2.
2. Service of 1, Translation of 2.
3. Commemoration of 1, Service of 2.
4. Service of 1, Commemoration of 2.
5. Nothing of 1, Service of 2.
6. Service of 1, nothing of 2.
7. Service of greater, Commemoration of less.
8. Service of greater, Translation of less.

Sarum.

TABLE II.

Concurrence.

WHEN FIRST VESPERS OF A FEAST FALL ON THE SAME DAY AS SECOND
VESPERS OF A FEAST PRECEDING.

	Simple.	Day in Octave.	Octave Day.	Inferior Double.	Lesser Double.	Greater Double.	Principal Double.	Ordinary Sunday.
Principal privileged Sunday	4	4	3	4	3	3	3	0
Greater privileged Sunday	4	4	3	4	3	3	3	0
Lesser privileged Sunday	4	4	3	4	3	3	3	0
Principal Double	2	2	4	4	4	4	6	4
Greater Double	2	4	4	4	4	6	3	4
Lesser Double	4	4	4	4	6	3	3	4
Inferior Double	4	4	4	3	5	3	3	4
Day in Octave	4	0	3	3	3	3	1	3
Octave Day	4	4	5	3	3	3	1	4

1. All of following, nothing of foregoing.
2. All of foregoing, nothing of following.
3. All of following, Commemoration of foregoing.
4. All of foregoing, Commemoration of following.
5. Chapter of following, Commemoration of foregoing.
6. All of greater, Commemoration of less.

Of Saying Office.

The bell being rung for the commencement of the Office, all rise, make the sign of the Cross, and say in silence the Lord's Prayer (and if it be so ordered, the Angelic Salutation and Creed). The officiant then begins aloud, (signing himself with the Cross,) ℣. "O God, make speed," etc., and the Office proceeds. (In Lent, all kneel till the officiant begins the ℣.) The Alleluia following the Gloria is said by all together. In Christmas and Easter tides the whole Office is said standing. At other times, those not engaged in singing are permitted to sit during the Psalms; the ferial Petitions and other Prayers are said kneeling, the priest, if present, alone standing where it is so noted in the Psalter. All stand during the recital of the three Gospel Canticles. The Hymns, when not sung, are said antiphonally. The Psalms are repeated antiphonally, whether said or sung, in this manner:—the first half of the first verse of each Psalm is said by the officiant; the whole choir joins him in the second half; after which the even verses are said on the Cantoris, and the uneven on the Decani side. But when Psalms occur amongst the Petitions, they are not so said, but the officiant says the first half of each verse, and the congregation the other half. Antiphons are said in this manner: 1. Before the Psalm or Canticle, the officiant says or sings the first two or three words alone, and the Psalm is then begun. 2. Afterwards he again begins the Ant. alone, and the choir joins in for the remainder. But when an Ant. is doubled, it is said or sung before the Psalm or Canticle according to rule 2. After, the whole is said or sung by the choir.

The manner of saying the ℟. differs at Vespers and at the Little Hours. At Vespers, the officiant says the first few words, and the choir take up the rest. At the hours, (*i. e.* Tierce, Sexts, Nones) the officiant says the whole of the first sentence, and the choir repeats it all afterwards; except in Lent, when the rule is the same as at Vespers.

The Lord's Prayer and Apostles' Creed are said wholly in silence wherever they occur in Office.

The Confessions and Absolutions are said in a low voice.

The organ is not used during Lent, except on Sundays and on Maundy Thursday.

Space does not allow us here to dwell on the spiritual meaning which underlies the whole Office, and so richly repays investigation. We conclude in the words of the "Myrroure of our Ladye": "Though this be true after the spiritual meaning, yet after the letter the changing that is in God's service from one thing to another, is ordained to let it drive away your dulness, that ye should not wax tedious and weary, but gladly and joyfully, not in vain joy, but in joy of spiritual devotion, continue in God's service. Therefore sometime ye sing, sometime ye read, sometime ye hear; now one alone, now twain together, now all. Sometime ye sit, sometime ye stand, sometime ye incline, sometime ye kneel, now toward the Altar, now toward the choir. And all to the praising of our Lord Jesus Christ; and so to exercise the body to the quickening of the soul, that all such bodily observances should not be found without cause of ghostly understanding. Now join to all this the fruit of that thing that is sung and read, and thereto the fellowship of the Angels among you in time of God's service, and most of all the marvellous and unspeakable presence of God Himself, from Whom our Lady is not far, and see whether it be not nigh another Heaven to serve and praise God in the choir."

The Kalendar.

					Dignity.	
					Sarum.	Roman.

JANUARY.

					Sarum.	Roman.
1	A	Kalendæ	Circumcision.		L. D.	D. II Cl.
2	b	iv Non.	Oct. S. Stephen.		L. D.	D.
3	c	iij Non.	Oct. S. John.		L. D.	D.
4	d	Prid. Non.	Oct. Holy Innocents.		L. D.	D.
5	e	Nonæ				
6	f	viij Idus.	Epiphany.		P. D.	D. I Cl.
7	g	vij Id.				
8	A	vj Id.	S. Lucian, P. M.*		S.	S.
9	b	v Id.				
10	c	iv Id.				
11	d	iij Id.				
12	e	Prid. Id.				
13	f	Idus.	Oct. Epiphany.	Mem. S. Hilary,	P. D.	D. I Cl.
14	g	xix Kal. Feb.		·[Bp. of Poitiers.		
15	A	xviij Kal.				
16	b	xvij Kal.				
17	c	xvi Kal.				
18	d	xv Kal.	S. Prisca, V. M.*		S.	D.
19	e	xiv Kal.				
20	f	xiij Kal.	S. Fabian, Bp. of Rome. M.*		S.	D.
21	g	xij Kal.	S. Agnes, V. M.		S.	D.
22	A	xj Kal.	S. Vincent, Deacon. M.*		S.	S. D.
23	b	x Kal.				
24	c	ix Kal.	S. Timothy, Bp. of Crete, C.*		S.	
25	d	viij Kal.	Conversion of S. Paul.		S.	G. D.
26	e	vij Kal.				
27	f	vj Kal.	S. John Chrysostom, Bp. of Constanti-		S.	D.
28	g	v Kal.	[nople, C. D.*			
29	A	iv Kal.	S. Thomas Aquinas, C. D.*		S.	D.
30	b	iij Kal.				
31	c	Prid. Kal.				

FEBRUARY.

				Dignity.	
				Sarum.	Roman.
1	d	Kalendæ	*S. Bridget of Ireland, V. A.**	S.	S.
2	e	iv Non.	𝕻urification of 𝕭. 𝖁. 𝕸ary.	G. D.	D. II Cl.
3	f	iij Non.	S. Blasius, Bp. of Sebaste, M.*	S.	D.
4	g	Prid. Non.			
5	A	Nonæ	S. Agatha, V. M.*	S.	D.
6	b	viij Idus.			
7	c	vij Id.			
8	d	vj Id.			
9	e	v Id.			
10	f	iv Id.			
11	g	iij Id.			
12	A	Prid. Id.			
13	b	Idus			
14	c	xvj Kal. Mart.	S. Valentine, P. M.*	S.	D.
15	d	xv Kal.			
16	e	xiv Kal.			
17	f	xiij Kal.			
18	g	xij Kal.			
19	A	xj Kal.			
20	b	x Kal.			
21	c	ix Kal.			
22	d	viij Kal.			
23	e	vij Kal.			
24	f	vj Kal.	𝕾. 𝕸atthias, Ap. M.	L. D.	D. II Cl.
25	g	v Kal.			
26	A	iv Kal.			
27	b	iij Kal.			
28	c	Prid. Kal.			
29					

MARCH.

					Dignity.	
					Sarum.	Roman.
1	d	Kalendæ	S. David, Bishop of Menevia, C.*		S.	D.
2	e	vj Non.	S. Chad, Bishop of Lichfield, C.*		S.	D.
3	f	v Non.				
4	g	iv Non.				
5	A	iij Non.				
6	b	Prid. Non.				
7	c	Nonæ	S. Perpetua, M., *and her Companions.**		S.	
8	d	viij Idus.				
9	e	vij Id.				
10	f	vj Id.				
11	g	v Id.				
12	A	iv Id.	S. Gregory the Great, Bp. of Rome,		L. D.	D.
13	b	iij Id.	[C. D.*			
14	c	Prid. Id.				
15	d	Idus				
16	e	xvij Kal. Apr.				
17	f	xvj Kal.	*S. Patrick, Bp. C. Apostle of Ireland.*		S.	D.
18	g	xv Kal.	S. Edward, K. M.* *S. Cyril, Bp. of*		S.	
19	A	xiv Kal.	*S. Joseph, C.* [*Jerusalem.*		S.	D. II Cl.
20	b	xiij Kal.	*S. Cuthbert, Bp. of Durham, C.**		S.	D.
21	c	xij Kal.	S. Benedict, Abbot.*		S.	D.
22	d	xj Kal.				
23	e	x Kal.				
24	f	ix Kal.				
25	g	viij Kal.	𝕬nnunciation of 𝕭. 𝖁. 𝕸ary.		L. D.	D. II Cl.
26	A	vij Kal.				
27	b	vj Kal.				
28	c	v Kal.				
29	d	iv Kal.				
30	e	iij Kal.				
31	f	Prid. Kal.				

APRIL.

				Sarum.	Roman.
1	g	Kalendæ			
2	A	iv Non.			
3	b	iij Non.	S. RICHARD, Bishop of Chichester, C.*	S.	D.
4	c	Prid. Non.	S. AMBROSE, Bishop of Milan, C.*	I. D.	L. D.
5	d	Nonæ.			
6	e	viij Idus.			
7	f	vij Id.			
8	g	vj Id.			
9	A	v Id.			
10	b	iv Id.			
11	c	iij Id.			
12	d	Prid. Id.			
13	e	Idus.			
14	f	xviij.Kal.Maij			
15	g	xvij Kal.			
16	A	xvj Kal.			
17	b	xv Kal.			
18	c	xiv Kal.			
19	d	xiij Kal.	S. ALPHEGE, Abp. of Canterbury, M.*	S.	
20	e	xij Kal.			
21	f	xj Kal.			
22	g	x Kal.			
23	A	ix Kal.	S. GEORGE, M., Patron of England.*	I. D.	D. I Cl.
24	b	viij Kal.			
25	c	vij Kal.	S. Mark, Evangelist, M.	I. D.	D. II Cl.
26	d	vj Kal.			
27	e	v Kal.			
28	f	iv Kal.			
29	g	iij Kal.			
30	A	Prid. Kal.			

MAY.

				Sarum.	Roman.
				DIGNITY.	
1	b	Kalendæ	SS. Philip and James, App. MM.	I. D.	D. II Cl.
2	c	vj Non.	*S. Athanasius, Bp. of Constantinople,*		D.
3	d	v Non.	INVENTION OF THE CROSS. [*C.**	L. D.	D. II Cl.
4	e	iv Non.			
5	f	iij Non.			
6	g	Prid. Non.	S. JOHN, Ev. Ap. Port. Latin.	S.	G. D.
7	A	Nonæ	*S. John of Beverley, Abp. of York, C.**	S.	
8	b	viij Idus.			
9	c	vij Id.			
10	d	vj Id.			
11	e	v Id.			
12	f	iv Id.			
13	g	iij Id.			
14	A	Prid. Id.			
15	b	Idus.			
16	c	xvij Kal. Junij			
17	d	xvj Kal.			
18	e	xv Kal.			
19	f	xiv Kal.	S. DUNSTAN, Abp. of Canterbury, C.*	S.	D.
20	g	xiij Kal.			
21	A	xij Kal.	*S. Helena, Matron.**	S.	D.
22	b	xj Kal.			
23	c	x Kal.			
24	d	ix Kal.			
25	e	viij Kal.	*S. Aldhelm, Bp. of Sherborne, C.**	S.	D.
26	f	vij Kal.	S. AUGUSTINE, Abp. of Canterbury, C. Apostle of England.	I. D.	D. II Cl.
27	g	vj Kal.	VENERABLE BEDE, P. C.*	S.	D.
28	A	v Kal.			
29	b	iv Kal.			
30	c	iij Kal.			
31	d	Prid. Kal.			

JUNE.

				Dignity.	
				Sarum.	Roman.
1	e	Kalendæ.	S. Nicomede, P. M.*	S.	
2	f	iv Non.			
3	g	iij Non.			
4	A	Prid. Non.			
5	b	Nonæ.	S. Boniface, Bishop of Mentz, M.*	S.	D.
6	c	viij Idus.			
7	d	vij Id.			
8	e	vj Id.			
9	f	v Id.			
10	g	iv Id.	*S. Margaret of Scotland, Q. Matron.**	S.	S. D.
11	A	iij Id.	S. Barnabas, Ap. M.	S.	G. D.
12	b	Prid. Id.			
13	c	Idus.			
14	d	xviij Kal. Julij	*S. Basil, Bishop of Cæsarea, C.**	S.	D.
15	e	xvij Kal.			
16	f	xvj Kal.			
17	g	xv Kal.			
18	A	xiv Kal.			
19	b	xiij Kal.			
20	c	xij Kal.	Translation of S. Edward, K. M.*	S.	
21	d	xj Kal.			
22	e	x Kal.	S. Alban, Protomartyr of England.	S.	G. D.
23	f	ix Kal.			
24	g	viij Kal.	Nativity of S. John Baptist.	L. D.	D. I Cl.
25	A	vij Kal.			
26	b	vj Kal.			
27	c	v Kal.			
28	d	iv Kal.			
29	e	iij Kal.	SS. Peter and Paul, App. MM.	L. D.	D. I Cl.
30	f	Prid. Kal.	*Commemoration of S. Paul.*	S.	D.

JULY.

				Dignity	
				Sarum.	Roman.
1	g	Kalendæ	*Oct. S. John Baptist.*	L. D.	D. I Cl.
2	A	vj Non.	VISITATION OF B. V. MARY.	G. D.	D. II Cl.
3	b	v Non.			
4	c	iv Non.	TRANSLATION OF S. MARTIN, Bp. C.*		
5	d	iij Non.			
6	e	Prid. Non.	*Oct. SS. Peter and Paul.*	L. D.	D. I Cl.
7	f	Nonæ.	*Translation of S. Thomas of Canter-*	L. D.	G. D.
8	g	viij Idus.	*[bury.*		
9	A	vij Id.	*Oct. Visitation.*	G. D.	D. II Cl.
10	b	vj Id.			
11	c	v Id.			
12	d	iv Id.			
13	e	iij Id.			
14	f	Prid. Idus.	*[of Winchester, C.*		
15	g	Idus.	TRANSLATION OF S. SWITHIN, Bishop	S.	D.
16	A	xvij Kal. Aug.	*Translation of S. Osmund, Bishop of*	S.	
17	b	xvj Kal.	*[Sarum, C.**		D.
18	c	xv Kal.			
19	d	xiv Kal.			
20	e	xiij Kal.	S. MARGARET OF ANTIOCH, V. M.*	S.	S.
21	f	xij Kal.			
22	g	xj Kal.	S. MARY MAGDALENE.	S.	D.
23	A	x Kal.			
24	b	ix Kal.			
25	c	viij Kal.	S. JAMES, Ap. M.	I. D.	D. II Cl.
26	d	vij Kal.	S. ANNE, Mother of B. V. Mary.*	S.	G. D.
27	e	vj Kal.			
28	f	v Kal.			
29	g	iv Kal.			
30	A	iij Kal.			
31	b	Prid. Kal.			

AUGUST.

				DIGNITY.	
				Sarum.	Roman.
1	c	Kalendæ	Lammas Day. S. PETER'S CHAINS.	S.	G. D.
2	d	iv Non.			
3	e	iij Non.			
4	f	Prid. Non.	*S. Dominic, Abbot, C.**		D.
5	g	Nonæ	*S. Oswald, K. M.**	S.	
6	A	viij Idus.	TRANSFIGURATION OF OUR LORD.	L. D.	G. D.
7	b	vij Id.	HOLY NAME OF JESUS.	G. D.	G. D.
8	c	vj Id.			
9	d	v Id.			
10	e	iv Id.	S. LAWRENCE, Deacon, M.*	S.	D. II Cl.
11	f	iij Id.			
12	g	Prid. Id.	*S. Clara, V. A.**	S.	D.
13	A	Idus.			
14	b	xix Kal. Sept.	*Oct. Holy Name.*	G. D.	G. D.
15	c	xviij Kal.	*Repose of B. V. Mary.*	P. D.	D. I Cl.
16	d	xvij Kal.			
17	e	xvj Kal.			
18	f	xv Kal.			
19	g	xiv Kal.			
20	A	xiij Kal.	*S. Bernard, C. D.**		D.
21	b	xij Kal.			
22	c	xj Kal.	*Oct. Repose of B. V. Mary.*	G. D.	G. D.
23	d	x Kal.			
24	e	ix Kal.	S. Bartholomew, Ap. M.	I. D.	D. II Cl.
25	f	viij Kal.			
26	g	vij Kal.			
27	A	vj Kal.			
28	b	v Kal.	S. AUGUSTINE, Bishop of Hippo, C. D.*	I. D.	D.
29	c	iv Kal.	BEHEADING OF S. JOHN BAPTIST.	S.	G. D.
30	d	iij Kal.			
31	e	Prid. Kal.			

| SEPTEMBER. | | | | DIGNITY. | |
				Sarum.	Roman.
1	f	Kalendæ.	S. GILES, Abbot, C.*	S.	S.
2	g	iv Non.			
3	A	iij Non.			
4	b	Prid. Non.			
5	c	Nonæ.			
6	d	viij Idus.			
7	e	vij Id.	S. EVURTIUS, Bishop of Orleans.*		
8	f	vj Id.	NATIVITY OF B. V. MARY.	G. D.	D. II Cl.
9	g	v Id.			
10	A	iv Id.			
11	b	iij Id.			
12	c	Prid. Id.			
13	d	Idus.			
14	e	xviij Kal. Oct.	EXALTATION OF THE HOLY CROSS.	L. D.	G. D.
15	f	xvij Kal.			
16	g	xvj Kal.			
17	A	xv Kal.	S. LAMBERT, Bp. of Maestricht, M.*		
18	b	xiv Kal.			
19	c	xiij Kal.			
20	d	xij Kal.			
21	e	xj Kal.	S. Matthew, Ap. Ev. M.	I. D.	D. II Cl.
22	f	x Kal.			
23	g	ix Kal.	S. Thecla, V. M.*	S.	S.
24	A	viij Kal.			
25	b	vij Kal.			
26	c	vj Kal.	S. CYPRIAN, Bp. of Carthage, M.*	S.	S. D.
27	d	v Kal.			
28	e	iv Kal.			
29	f	iij Kal.	S. Michael and all Angels.	I. D.	D. II Cl.
30	g	Prid. Kal.	S. JEROME, P. C. D.*	I. D.	D.

<table>
<tr><td colspan="6" align="center">OCTOBER.</td></tr>
<tr><td></td><td></td><td></td><td></td><td colspan="2" align="center">DIGNITY.</td></tr>
<tr><td></td><td></td><td></td><td></td><td>Sarum.</td><td>Roman.</td></tr>
<tr><td>1</td><td>A</td><td>Kalendæ.</td><td>S. REMIGIUS, Bishop of Rheims, C.*</td><td></td><td>S.</td></tr>
<tr><td>2</td><td>b</td><td>vj Non.</td><td>Holy Guardian Angels.</td><td></td><td>D.</td></tr>
<tr><td>3</td><td>c</td><td>v Non.</td><td></td><td></td><td></td></tr>
<tr><td>4</td><td>d</td><td>iv Non.</td><td>S. Francis of Assisi, Abbot, C.*</td><td></td><td>D.</td></tr>
<tr><td>5</td><td>e</td><td>iij Non.</td><td></td><td></td><td></td></tr>
<tr><td>6</td><td>f</td><td>Prid. Non.</td><td>S. FAITH, V. M.*</td><td>S.</td><td>S.</td></tr>
<tr><td>7</td><td>g</td><td>Nonæ.</td><td></td><td></td><td></td></tr>
<tr><td>8</td><td>A</td><td>viij Idus.</td><td align="right">[Companions.</td><td></td><td></td></tr>
<tr><td>9</td><td>b</td><td>vij Id.</td><td>S. DENYS, Bp. of Paris, M., and his</td><td>S.</td><td>S. D.</td></tr>
<tr><td>10</td><td>c</td><td>vj Id.</td><td>S. Paulinus, Bishop of York, C.*</td><td>S.</td><td></td></tr>
<tr><td>11</td><td>d</td><td>v Id.</td><td></td><td></td><td></td></tr>
<tr><td>12</td><td>e</td><td>iv Id.</td><td></td><td></td><td></td></tr>
<tr><td>13</td><td>f</td><td>iij Id.</td><td>TRANSLATION OF S. EDWARD, K. C.*</td><td>I. D.</td><td>D. II Cl.</td></tr>
<tr><td>14</td><td>g</td><td>Prid. Id.</td><td></td><td></td><td></td></tr>
<tr><td>15</td><td>A</td><td>Idus.</td><td>S. Theresa, V. A.*</td><td></td><td>D.</td></tr>
<tr><td>16</td><td>b</td><td>xvij Kal. Nov.</td><td></td><td></td><td></td></tr>
<tr><td>17</td><td>c</td><td>xvj Kal.</td><td>S. ETHELDRED, V. A. Q.*</td><td>S.</td><td></td></tr>
<tr><td>18</td><td>d</td><td>xv Kal.</td><td>S. Luke, Ev.</td><td>I. D.</td><td>D. II Cl.</td></tr>
<tr><td>19</td><td>e</td><td>xiv Kal.</td><td></td><td></td><td></td></tr>
<tr><td>20</td><td>f</td><td>xiij Kal.</td><td></td><td></td><td></td></tr>
<tr><td>21</td><td>g</td><td>xij Kal.</td><td></td><td></td><td></td></tr>
<tr><td>22</td><td>A</td><td>xj Kal.</td><td></td><td></td><td></td></tr>
<tr><td>23</td><td>b</td><td>x Kal.</td><td></td><td></td><td></td></tr>
<tr><td>24</td><td>c</td><td>ix Kal.</td><td></td><td></td><td></td></tr>
<tr><td>25</td><td>d</td><td>viij Kal.</td><td>SS. CRISPIN and CRISPINIAN, M.M.*</td><td>S.</td><td>D.</td></tr>
<tr><td>26</td><td>e</td><td>vij Kal.</td><td></td><td></td><td></td></tr>
<tr><td>27</td><td>f</td><td>vj Kal.</td><td></td><td></td><td></td></tr>
<tr><td>28</td><td>g</td><td>v Kal.</td><td>SS. Simon and Jude, App. MM.</td><td>I. D.</td><td>D. II Cl.</td></tr>
<tr><td>29</td><td>A</td><td>iv Kal.</td><td></td><td></td><td></td></tr>
<tr><td>30</td><td>b</td><td>iij Kal.</td><td></td><td></td><td></td></tr>
<tr><td>31</td><td>c</td><td>Prid. Kal.</td><td></td><td></td><td></td></tr>
</table>

NOVEMBER.

				Dignity.	
				Sarum.	Roman.
1	d	Kalendæ.	All Saints' Day.	G. D.	D. I Cl.
2	e	iv Non.	*All Souls' Day.*	L. D.	G. D.
3	f	iij Non.	*S. Winifred, V.M.**	S.	D.
4	g	Prid. Non.	*S. Charles Borromeo, Bp. of Milan,*		D.
5	A	Nonæ.	[*C.**		
6	b	viij Idus.	S. Leonard, C.*	S.	
7	c	vij Id.			
8	d	vj Id.	*Oct. All Saints.*	G. D.	D. I Cl.
9	e	v Id.			
10	f	iv Id.			
11	g	iij Id.	S. Martin, Bishop of Tours, M.*	S.	D.
12	A	Prid. Id.			
13	b	Idus.	S. Britius, Bp. of Tours, C.*	S.	
14	c	xviij Kal. Dec.			
15	d	xvij Kal.	S. Machutus, Bp. of Alet, C.*	S.	
16	e	xvj Kal.			
17	f	xv Kal.	S. Hugh, Bishop of Lincoln, C.*	S.	D.
18	g	xiv Kal.			
19	A	xiij Kal.	*S. Elizabeth of Hungary, Q. Matr.**	S.	D.
20	b	xij Kal.	S. Edmund, K. M.*	S.	G. D.
21	c	xj Kal.	*Presentation of B. V. Mary.**	S.	G. D.
22	d	x Kal.	S. Cecilia, V. M.*	S.	D.
23	e	ix Kal.	S. Clement, Bp. of Rome, M.*	S.	D.
24	f	viij Kal.			
25	g	vij Kal.	S. Katharine, V. M.*	S.	D.
26	A	vj Kal.			
27	b	v Kal.			
28	c	iv Kal.			
29	d	iij Kal.			
30	e	Prid. Kal.	S. Andrew, Ap. M.	I. D.	D. II Cl.

DECEMBER.

				Dignity.	
				Sarum.	Roman.
1	f	Kalendæ.			
2	g	iv Non.			
3	A	iij Non.	*S. Francis Xavier, C.**		D.
4	b	Prid. Non.			
5	c	Nonæ.			
6	d	viij Idus.	S. Nicolas, Bp. of Myra in Lycia, C.*	S.	D.
7	e	vij Id.			
8	f	vj Id.	Conception of B. V. Mary.	L. D.	D. II Cl.
9	g	v Id.			
10	A	iv Id.			
11	b	iij Id.			
12	c	Prid. Id.			
13	d	Idus.	S. Lucy, V. M.*	S.	D.
14	e	xix Kal. Jan.			
15	f	xviij Kal.			
16	g	xvij Kal.	O Sapientia.		
17	A	xvj Kal.			
18	b	xv Kal.			
19	c	xiv Kal.			
20	d	xiij Kal.			
21	e	xij Kal.	S. Thomas, Ap. M.	I. D.	D. II Cl.
22	f	xj Kal.			
23	g	x Kal.			
24	A	ix Kal.			
25	b	viij Kal.	Christmas Day.	P. D.	D. I Cl.
26	c	vij Kal.	S. Stephen, Protomartyr.	L. D.	D. II Cl.
27	d	vj Kal.	S. John, Ap. Ev.	L. D.	D. II Cl.
28	e	v Kal.	Holy Innocents.	L. D.	D. II Cl.
29	f	iv Kal.	*S. Thomas, Abp. of Canterbury, M.**	L. D.	S. D.
30	g	iij Kal.			
31	A	Prid. Kal.	S. Silvester, Bishop of Rome, C.*	S.	D.

FESTIVALS PROPER TO SCOTLAND.

		DIGNITY.	
		Sarum.	Roman.
	JANUARY.		
11.	S. DAVID, King and Confessor.	S.	
13.	S. KENTIGERN, Bishop and Confessor.	G. D.	
	FEBRUARY.		
18.	S. COLMAN, Bishop and Confessor.	S.	S. D.
	MARCH.		
11.	S. CONSTANTINE, King and Martyr.	S.	S. D.
20.	S. CUTHBERT, Bishop and Confessor.	S.	D.
	APRIL.		
1.	S. GILBERT, Bishop and Martyr.	G. D.	S. D.
20.	S. SERF, Bishop and Confessor.	S.	S. D.
	JUNE.		
9.	S. COLUMBA, Abbot and Confessor.	G. D.	G. D.
	JULY.		
6.	S. PALLADIUS, Bishop and Confessor.	L. D.	
	SEPTEMBER.		
16.	S. NINIAN, Bishop and Confessor.	G. D.	G. D.
23.	S. ADAMNAN, Abbot and Confessor.	S.	
	NOVEMBER.		
16.	Translation of S. MARGARET, Queen and Matron.	S.	
27.	S. ODE, Virgin.	S.	S. D.
30.	S. ANDREW, Apostle and Martyr, with Octave.	G. D.	D. II Cl.
	DECEMBER.		
4.	S. DROSTANE, Abbot and Confessor.	S.	

A TABLE

OF THE MOVEABLE FEASTS FOR TWENTY-SEVEN YEARS.

Year of our Lord.	The Golden Number.	The Epact.	Sunday Letter.	Sundays after Epiphany.	Septuagesima Sunday.	The First Day of Lent.	Easter Day.	Ascension Day.	Whitsun Day.	Corpus Christi.	Sundays after Trinity.	Advent Sunday.
1874	13	12	D	3	Feb. 1	Feb. 18	April 5	May 14	May 24	June 4	25	Nov. 29
1875	14	23	C	2	Jan. 24	—— 10	Mar. 28	—— 6	—— 16	May 27	26	—— 28
1876	15	4	BA	5	Feb. 13	Mar. 1	April 16	—— 25	June 4	June 15	24	Dec. 3
1877	16	15	G	3	Jan. 28	Feb. 14	—— 1	—— 10	May 20	May 31	26	—— 2
1878	17	26	F	5	Feb. 17	Mar. 6	—— 21	—— 30	June 9	June 20	23	—— 1
1879	18	7	E	4	—— 9	Feb. 26	—— 13	—— 22	—— 1	—— 12	24	Nov. 30
1880	19	18	DC	2	Jan. 25	—— 11	Mar. 28	—— 6	May 16	May 27	26	—— 28
1881	1	0	B	5	Feb. 13	Mar. 2	April 17	—— 26	June 5	June 16	23	—— 27
1882	2	11	A	4	—— 5	Feb. 22	—— 9	—— 18	May 28	—— 8	25	Dec. 3
1883	3	22	G	2	Jan. 21	—— 7	Mar. 25	—— 3	—— 13	May 24	27	—— 2
1884	4	3	FE	4	Feb. 10	—— 27	April 13	—— 22	June 1	June 12	24	Nov. 30
1885	5	14	D	3	—— 1	—— 18	—— 5	—— 14	May 24	—— 4	25	—— 29
1886	6	25	C	6	—— 21	Mar.10	—— 25	June 3	June 13	—— 24	22	—— 28
1887	7	6	B	4	—— 6	Feb. 23	—— 10	May 19	May 29	—— 9	24	—— 27
1888	8	17	AG	3	Jan. 29	—— 15	—— 1	—— 10	—— 20	May 31	26	Dec. 2
1889	9	28	F	5	Feb. 17	Mar. 6	—— 21	—— 30	June 9	June 20	23	—— 1
1890	10	9	E	3	—— 2	Feb. 19	—— 6	—— 15	May 25	—— 5	25	Nov. 30
1891	11	20	D	2	Jan. 25	—— 11	Mar. 29	—— 7	—— 17	May 28	26	—— 29
1892	12	1	CB	5	Feb. 14	Mar. 2	April 17	—— 26	June 5	June 16	23	—— 27
1893	13	12	A	3	Jan. 29	Feb. 15	—— 2	—— 11	May 21	—— 1	26	Dec. 3
1894	14	23	G	2	—— 21	—— 7	Mar. 25	—— 3	—— 13	May 24	27	—— 2
1895	15	4	F	4	Feb. 10	—— 27	April 14	—— 23	June 2	June 13	24	—— 1
1896	16	15	ED	3	—— 2	—— 19	—— 5	—— 14	May 24	—— 4	25	Nov. 29
1897	17	26	C	5	—— 14	Mar. 3	—— 18	—— 27	June 6	—— 17	23	—— 28
1898	18	7	B	4	—— 6	Feb. 23	—— 10	—— 19	May 29	—— 9	24	—— 27
1899	19	18	A	3	Jan. 29	—— 15	—— 2	—— 11	—— 21	—— 1	26	Dec. 3
1900	1	0	G	5	Feb. 11	—— 28	—— 15	—— 24	June 3	—— 14	24	—— 2

RULES to know when the Moveable Feasts and Holy-Days begin.

EASTER DAY (on which the rest depend) is always the first Sunday after the Full Moon which happens upon or next after the Twenty-first day of March; and if the Full Moon happens upon a Sunday, Easter Day is the Sunday after.

Advent Sunday is always the nearest Sunday to the Feast of S. Andrew, whether before or after.

Septuagesima Sexagesima Quinquagesima Quadragesima	Sunday is	Nine Eight Seven Six	Weeks before Easter.
Rogation Sunday Ascension Day Whitsun Day Trinity Sunday	is	Five Weeks Forty Days Seven Weeks Eight Weeks	after Easter.

Prayers that may be said privately before the Divine Office.

GRANT, O Lord, that what we sing with our lips, we may believe in our hearts, and practise in our lives; through Jesus Christ our Lord. Amen.

Prayer of the Venerable Bede.

GRANT, I entreat Thee, Almighty God, that speaking with understanding and good will, and in plainness, I may deserve to be heard by Thee: for I need Thy help in all things; so that by the gift of Thy grace, I may be enabled not unworthily to sing the words of Thy Majesty; through Jesus Christ our Lord. Amen.

GRANT, I beseech Thee, Lord God, that by the melody of this holy Psalter, my soul may be refreshed; cause me always to apply myself to Thy praises, and joyfully to come to Thy blessedness; Who livest and reignest God, world without end. Amen.

At Matins.

O LORD Jesu Christ, Son of the Living God, Who at this Matin Hour didst will to be born, to be betrayed, taken, beaten with stripes, buffeted, and spit upon for the salvation of mankind; make us, we beseech Thee, joyfully and patiently to endure injuries and reproaches for the glory of Thy Name; and so continually to keep in remembrance the memory of Thy most Sacred Passion, that we may be enabled happily to attain to the glory and fellowship of Thy Resurrection; Who livest and reignest with the Father and the Holy Ghost, God, world without end. Amen.

At Prime.

O LORD Jesu Christ, Son of the Living God, Who in the First Hour of the day wast brought before Pilate: Who, the Judge of all judges, didst yet endure the severest doom; we most devoutly beseech Thee that Thou in Thy judgment wouldest be lenient to us miserable sinners; that in the last eternal judgment we be not condemned to punishment, but may rather attain to the fellowship of Thy faithful ones in heavenly places; Who livest and reignest God, world without end. Amen.

At Tierce.

O LORD Jesu Christ, Son of the Living God, Who at the Third Hour of the day wast led forth to the pain of the Cross, for the salvation of the world; we humbly beseech Thee that by the virtue of Thy most sacred Passion, Thou wouldest blot out all our sins, and mercifully bring us to the glory of Thy blessedness; Who livest and reignest God, world without end. Amen.

At Sexts.

O LORD Jesu Christ, Son of the Living God, Who at the Sixth Hour of the day in Golgotha with great tumult didst ascend the Cross of suffering, whereon, thirsting for our salvation, Thou didst permit gall and vinegar to be given Thee to drink; we, Thy suppliants, beseech Thee that, kindling and inflaming our hearts, Thou wouldest make us to thirst for the cup of Thy Passion, and continually to find delight in Thee only, our crucified Lord; Who livest and reignest God, world without end. Amen.

At Nones.

O LORD Jesu Christ, Son of the Living God, Who at the Ninth Hour of the day, with hands extended upon the Cross, and bowing the head, didst deliver up Thy spirit to God the Father, and with the key of death didst most meritoriously unlock the gate of Paradise; grant to us, Thy suppliants, that in the hour of death Thou wouldest mercifully cause our souls to attain unto Thee, Who art the true Paradise; Who livest and reignest God, world without end. Amen.

At Vespers.

O LORD Jesu Christ, Son of the Living God, Who at the Vesper Hour of the day, being now made subject unto death, didst will to be taken down from the Cross, and (as is piously believed) to be received into the arms of Thy Mother; mercifully grant that we, casting away the burthens of our sins, may be enabled to attain even unto the presence of Thy divine Majesty; Who livest and reignest God, world without end. Amen.

At Compline.

O LORD Jesu Christ, Son of the Living God, Who at the Compline Hour rested in the sepulchre, and wast bewailed and lamented by Thy most gentle Mother, and by the other women; make us, we beseech Thee, to abound in the sorrows of Thy Passion, and with entire devotion of heart to bewail that same Passion, and to keep it ever as it were fresh in the ardent affection of our hearts; Who livest and reignest God, world without end. Amen.

PRAYERS AFTER THE DIVINE OFFICE.

PREVENT us, O Lord, in all our doings with Thy most gracious favour, and further us with Thy continual help; that in all our works begun, continued, and ended in Thee, we may glorify Thy holy Name, and finally by Thy mercy obtain everlasting life; through Jesus Christ our Lord. Amen.

TO Thee, O Lord, I commend the Service which I an unworthy sinner have offered up unto Thee. God be merciful to me, a sinner; and after Thy good knowledge and will, have pity upon me; through Jesus Christ our Lord. Amen.

ERRATA.

Page 282, line 15 from bottom, *for* March 6 *read* March 7.

" 320, " 12 from bottom, insert:

September 26. S. CYPRIAN, B.M.*

All of the Common of a Martyr, p. 217.

✠

THE PSALTER.

SUNDAY.

𝕷𝖆𝖚𝖉𝖘.

These Dominical Psalms are said at Lauds on every Sunday throughout the year, (except from Septuagesima to Easter, when certain Psalms are changed, as below,) and on all festivals.

Lauds, being said immediately after Matins, are not begun with the Invocation, &c., like the other Hours, but straightway with the Sacerdotal ℣. and ℟.

℣. The Lord is high above all people.

℟. And His glory above the heavens.

℣. O God, make speed to save us.

℟. O Lord, make haste to help us.

℣. Glory be to the Father, and to the Son, and to the Holy Ghost.

℟. As it was in the beginning, is now, and ever shall be, world without end.   Amen.

Alleluia.

[*From Septuagesima till Wednesday in Holy Week, inclusive, instead of* Alleluia *is said:*

Praise be to Thee, O Lord, King of eternal glory.]

The Antiphons are said entire both before and after each Psalm on Sundays of the first Class, and on double feasts: at other times the first words only are said before, and the whole Antiphon is said after each Psalm.

Ant. The Lord is King ✸ and hath put on glorious apparel : He hath girded Himself with strength, and His seat is from everlasting.

Psalm XCIII.   *Dominus regnavit.*

THE Lord is King, and hath put on glorious apparel : the Lord hath put on His apparel, and girded Himself with strength.

2 He hath made the round world so sure : that it cannot be moved.

3 Ever since the world began hath Thy seat been prepared : Thou art from everlasting.

4 The floods are risen, O Lord, the floods have lift up their voice : the floods lift up their waves.

5 The waves of the sea are mighty, and rage horribly : but yet the Lord, who dwelleth on high, is mightier.

6 Thy testimonies, O Lord, are very sure : holiness becometh Thine house for ever.

Glory be, etc.

Ant. The Lord is King, and hath put on glorious apparel : He hath girded Himself with strength, and His seat is from everlasting.

[*Instead of* Ps. XCIII. *is said, between Septuagesima and Easter, with Antiphon of the Season :*

Psalm LI.   *Miserere mei, Deus.*

HAVE mercy upon me, O God, after Thy great goodness : according to the multitude of Thy mercies do away mine offences.

2 Wash me throughly from my wickedness : and cleanse me from my sin.

3 For I acknowledge my faults : and my sin is ever before me.

4 Against Thee only have I sinned, and done this evil in Thy sight : that Thou mightest be justified in Thy saying, and clear when Thou art judged.

5 Behold, I was shapen in wickedness : and in sin hath my mother conceived me.

6 But lo, Thou requirest truth in the inward parts : and shalt make me to understand wisdom secretly.

7 Thou shalt purge me with hyssop, and I shall be clean : Thou shalt wash me, and I shall be whiter than snow.

8 Thou shalt make me hear of joy and gladness : that the bones which Thou hast broken may rejoice.

9 Turn Thy face from my sins : and put out all my misdeeds.

10 Make me a clean heart, O God : and renew a right spirit within me.

11 Cast me not away from Thy Presence : and take not Thy Holy Spirit from me.

12 O give me the comfort of Thy help again : and stablish me with Thy free Spirit.

13 Then shall I teach Thy ways unto the wicked : and sinners shall be converted unto Thee.

14 Deliver me from blood-guiltiness, O God, Thou that art the God of my health : and my tongue shall sing of Thy righteousness.

15 Thou shalt open my lips, O Lord : and my mouth shall show Thy praise.

16 For Thou desirest no sacrifice, else would I give it Thee : but Thou delightest not in burnt-offerings.

17 The sacrifice of God is a troubled spirit : a broken and contrite heart, O God, shalt Thou not despise.

18 O be favourable and gracious unto Sion : build Thou the walls of Jerusalem.

19 Then shalt Thou be pleased with the sacrifice of righteousness, with the burnt-offerings and oblations : then shall they offer young bullocks upon Thine altar.

Glory be, etc.]

Ant. Let us all know * that the Lord He is God : in Him let us be joyful, and exalt and praise His Name for ever.

Psalm c. *Jubilate Deo.*

O BE joyful in the Lord, all ye lands : serve the Lord with gladness, and come before His presence with a song.

2 Be ye sure that the Lord He is God : it is He that hath made us, and not we ourselves; we are His people, and the sheep of His pasture.

3 O go your way into His gates with thanksgiving, and into His courts with praise : be thankful unto Him, and speak good of His Name.

4 For the Lord is gracious, His mercy is everlasting : and His truth endureth from generation to generation.

Glory be, etc.

Ant. Let us all know that the Lord He is God : in Him let us be joyful, and exalt and praise His Name for ever.

[Instead of Ps. c. *is said, between Septuagesima and Easter, with Antiphon of the Season :*

Psalm cxviii. *Confitemini Domino.*

O GIVE thanks unto the Lord, for He is gracious : because His mercy endureth for ever.

2 Let Israel now confess that He is gracious : and that His mercy endureth for ever.

3 Let the house of Aaron now confess : that His mercy endureth for ever.

4 Yea, let them now that fear the Lord confess : that His mercy endureth for ever.

5 I called upon the Lord in trouble : and the Lord heard me at large.

6 The Lord is on my side : I will not fear what man doeth unto me.

7 The Lord taketh my part with them that help me : therefore shall I see my desire upon mine enemies.

8 It is better to trust in the Lord : than to put any confidence in man.

9 It is better to trust in the Lord : than to put any confidence in princes.

10 All nations compassed me round about : but in the Name of the Lord will I destroy them.

11 They kept me in on every side, they kept me in, I say, on every side : but in the Name of the Lord will I destroy them.

12 They came about me like bees, and are extinct even as the fire among the thorns : for in the Name of the Lord I will destroy them.

13 Thou hast thrust sore at me, that I might fall : but the Lord was my help.

14 The Lord is my strength, and my song : and is become my salvation.

15 The voice of joy and health is in the dwellings of the righteous : the right hand of the Lord bringeth mighty things to pass.

16 The right hand of the Lord hath the pre-eminence : the right hand of the Lord bringeth mighty things to pass.

17 I shall not die, but live : and declare the works of the Lord.

18 The Lord hath chastened and corrected me : but He hath not given me over unto death.

19 Open me the gates of righteousness : that I may go into them, and give thanks unto the Lord.

20 This is the gate of the Lord : the righteous shall enter into it.

21 I will thank Thee, for Thou hast heard me : and art become my salvation.

22 The same stone which the builders refused : is become the head-stone in the corner.

23 This is the Lord's doing : and it is marvellous in our eyes.

24 This is the day which the Lord hath made : we will rejoice and be glad in it.

25 Help me now, O Lord : O Lord, send us now prosperity.

26 Blessed be He that cometh in the Name of the Lord : we have wished you good luck, ye that are of the house of the Lord.

27 God is the Lord who hath shewed us light : bind the sacrifice with cords, yea, even unto the horns of the altar.

28 Thou art my God, and I will thank Thee : Thou art my God, and I will praise Thee.

29 O give thanks unto the Lord, for He is gracious : and His mercy endureth for ever.

Glory be, etc.]

Ant. As long as I live * will I magnify Thee : that I may behold Thy power and glory.

Psalm LXIII. *Deus, Deus meus.*

O GOD, Thou art my God : early will I seek Thee.

2 My soul thirsteth for Thee, my flesh also longeth after Thee : in a barren and dry land, where no water is.

3 Thus have I looked for Thee in holiness : that I might behold Thy power and glory.

4 For Thy loving-kindness is better than the life itself : my lips shall praise Thee.

5 As long as I live will I magnify Thee on this manner : and lift up my hands in Thy Name.

6 My soul shall be satisfied, even as it were with marrow and fatness : when my mouth praiseth Thee with joyful lips.

7 Have I not remembered Thee in my bed : and thought upon Thee when I was waking?

8 Because Thou hast been my helper : therefore under the shadow of Thy wings will I rejoice.

9 My soul hangeth upon Thee : Thy right hand hath upholden me.

10 These also that seek the hurt of my soul : they shall go under the earth.

11 Let them fall upon the edge of the sword : that they may be a portion for foxes.

12 But the King shall rejoice in God; all they also that swear by Him shall be commended : for the mouth of them that speak lies shall be stopped.

Here is not said Glory be, etc.

Psalm LXVII. *Deus misereatur.*

GOD be merciful unto us, and bless us : and show us the light of His countenance, and be merciful unto us;

2 That Thy way may be known upon earth : Thy saving health among all nations.

3 Let the people praise Thee, O God : yea, let all the people praise Thee.

4 O let the nations rejoice and be glad : for Thou shalt judge the folk righteously, and govern the nations upon earth.

5 Let the people praise Thee, O God : let all the people praise Thee.

6 Then shall the earth bring forth her increase : and God, even our own God, shall give us His blessing.

7 God shall bless us : and all the ends of the world shall fear Him.

Glory be, etc.

Ant. As long as I live will I magnify Thee : that I may behold Thy power and glory.

Ant. Let every creature * which is in heaven and on the earth bless the

Lord : praise Him, and magnify Him for ever.

SONG OF THE THREE CHILDREN.

Benedicite, omnia Opera.

O ALL ye Works of the Lord, bless ye the Lord : praise Him, and magnify Him for ever.

2 O ye Angels of the Lord, bless ye the Lord : O ye Heavens, bless ye the Lord.

3 O ye Waters that be above the Firmament, bless ye the Lord : O all ye Powers of the Lord, bless ye the Lord.

4 O ye Sun and Moon, bless ye the Lord : O ye Stars of Heaven, bless ye the Lord.

5 O ye Showers and Dew, bless ye the Lord : O ye Winds of God, bless ye the Lord.

6 O ye Fire and Heat, bless ye the Lord : O ye Winter and Summer, bless ye the Lord.

7 O ye Dews and Frosts, bless ye the Lord : O ye Frost and Cold, bless ye the Lord.

8 O ye Ice and Snow, bless ye the Lord : O ye Nights and Days, bless ye the Lord.

9 O ye Light and Darkness, bless ye the Lord : O ye Lightnings and Clouds, bless ye the Lord.

10 O let the earth bless the Lord : yea, let it praise Him, and magnify Him for ever.

11 O ye Mountains and Hills, bless ye the Lord : O all ye Green Things upon the earth, bless ye the Lord.

12 O ye Wells, bless ye the Lord : O ye Seas and Floods, bless ye the Lord.

13 O ye Whales, and all that move in the waters, bless ye the Lord : O all ye Fowls of the air, bless ye the Lord.

14 O all ye Beasts, and Cattle, bless ye the Lord : O ye Children of men, bless ye the Lord.

15 O let Israel bless the Lord : praise Him, and magnify Him for ever.

16 O ye Priests of the Lord, bless ye the Lord : O ye Servants of the Lord, bless ye the Lord.

17 O ye Spirits and Souls of the righteous, bless ye the Lord : O ye holy and humble Men of heart, bless ye the Lord.

18 O Ananias, Azarias, and Misael, bless ye the Lord : praise Him, and magnify Him for ever.

Instead of Glory be, etc.

Let us bless the Father, the Son, and the Holy Ghost : let us praise and exalt Him above all for ever.

Blessed art Thou, O Lord, in the firmament of heaven : and above all to be praised and glorified for ever.

Ant. Let every creature which is in heaven, and on the earth, bless the Lord : praise Him, and magnify Him for ever.

Ant. Let every thing that hath breath * praise the Lord : for He spake the word, and they were made ; He commanded, and they were created.

Ps. CXLVIII. *Laudate Dominum.*

O PRAISE the Lord of heaven : praise Him in the height.

2 Praise Him, all ye angels of His : praise Him, all His host.

3 Praise Him, sun and moon : praise Him, all ye stars and light.

4 Praise Him, all ye heavens : and ye waters that are above the heavens.

5 Let them praise the Name of the Lord : for He spake the word, and they were made ; He commanded, and they were created.

6 He hath made them fast for ever and ever : He hath given them a law which shall not be broken.

7 Praise the Lord upon earth : ye dragons, and all deeps ;

8 Fire and hail, snow and vapours : wind and storm, fulfilling His word ;

9 Mountains and all hills : fruitful trees and all cedars :

10 Beasts and all cattle : worms and feathered fowls ;

11 Kings of the earth and all people : princes and all judges of the world ;

12 Young men and maidens, old men and children, praise the Name of the Lord : for His Name only is excellent, and His praise above heaven and earth.

13 He shall exalt the horn of His people ; all His saints shall praise Him : even the children of Israel, even the people that serveth Him.

Here is not said Glory be, etc.

Psalm CXLIX.   *Cantate Domino.*

O SING unto the Lord a new song : let the congregation of saints praise Him.

2 Let Israel rejoice in Him that made him : and let the children of Sion be joyful in their King.

3 Let them praise His Name in the dance : let them sing praises unto Him with tabret and harp.

4 For the Lord hath pleasure in His people : and helpeth the meek-hearted.

5 Let the saints be joyful with glory : let them rejoice in their beds.

6 Let the praises of God be in their mouth : and a two-edged sword in their hands ;

7 To be avenged of the heathen : and to rebuke the people ;

8 To bind their kings in chains : and their nobles with links of iron.

9 That they may be avenged of them, as it is written : Such honour have all His saints.

Here is not said Glory be, etc.

Psalm CL.   *Laudate Dominum.*

O PRAISE God in His holiness : praise Him in the firmament of His power.

2 Praise Him in His noble acts : praise Him according to His excellent greatness.

3 Praise Him in the sound of the trumpet : praise Him upon the lute and harp.

4 Praise Him in the cymbals and dances : praise Him upon the strings and pipe.

5 Praise Him upon the well-tuned cymbals : praise Him upon the loud cymbals.

6 Let every thing that hath breath : praise the Lord.

Glory be, etc.

Ant. Let every thing that hath breath praise the Lord : for He spake the word, and they were made ; He commanded, and they were created.

From Epiphany to Septuagesima, and from Trinity to Advent,

CHAPTER.   Rev. vii.

B LESSING, and glory, and wisdom, and thanksgiving, and honour, and power, and might, be unto our God for ever and ever.   Amen.

R̂.   Thanks be to God.

[For Chapter at other times, see Proper of Seasons.]

After Trinity, on Sundays and all ferias.

HYMN.   *Ecce jam noctis.*

D ARKNESS is thinning, shadows are retreating,
Morning and light are coming in their beauty ;
Suppliant seek we, with an earnest outcry,
   God the Almighty.

So that our Master, having mercy on us,
May repel languor, may bestow salvation,
Granting us, Father, of Thy loving-kindness,
   Glory hereafter.

This of His mercy, ever Blessed Godhead,
Father and Son, and Holy Spirit, grant us :
Whom through the wide world celebrate for ever
   Worship and glory.

V̂.   The Lord is King.

R̂.   He hath put on glorious apparel.   Alleluia.

[For Hymns at other times, see Proper of Seasons.]

Ant. to Ben. in Proper of Seasons.

Benedictus. St. Luke i.

BLESSED be the Lord God of Israel : for He hath visited and redeemed His people ;

2 ·And hath raised up a mighty salvation for us : in the house of His servant David ;

3 As He spake by the mouth of His holy prophets : which have been since the world began ;

4 That we should be saved from our enemies : and from the hands of all that hate us ;

5 To perform the mercy promised to our forefathers : and to remember His holy covenant ;

6 To perform the oath which He sware to our forefather Abraham : that He would give us ;

7 That we being delivered out of the hand of our enemies : might serve Him without fear ;

8 In holiness and righteousness before Him : all the days of our life.

9 And thou, Child, shalt be called the Prophet of the Highest : for thou shalt go before the face of the Lord to prepare His ways ;

10 To give knowledge of salvation unto His people : for the remission of their sins,

11 Through the tender mercy of our God : whereby the day-spring from on high hath visited us ;

12 To give light to them that sit in darkness, and in the shadow of death : and to guide our feet into the way of peace.

Glory be, etc.

℣. The Lord be with you.

℟. And with thy spirit.

Let us pray.

COLLECT IN PROPER.

The Sunday Collect is said at every hour on Sunday, and through the week, *when the Office is of the Season ; except in Embertide, in Advent, on Rogation Monday : and in Lent, when the Collect changes daily.*

Sunday Memorials,

which immediately follow the Collect for the day, unless the memorial of any festival intervene, in which case the ordinary memorials yield precedence.

[For Memorials from Advent Sunday till the Octave of Epiphany, see Proper of Seasons.]

From the Octave of Epiphany till Ash-Wednesday, and after the Octave of Trinity till Advent.

MEMORIAL OF S. MARY.

Ant. Lo, Mary hath brought forth the Saviour, of whom when John saw Him, he said : Behold the Lamb of God, which taketh away the sins of the world.

℣. After child-bearing thou remainedst a Virgin.

℟. O Mother of God.

COLLECT.

O GOD, Who through the fruitful virginity of the blessed Virgin Mary, hast bestowed the rewards of eternal salvation on the human race ; grant, we beseech Thee, that she may intercede for us, through whom we have received the Author of Life, Jesus Christ our Lord. Amen.

[For Memorials from Ash-Wednesday till Whitsuntide, see Proper of Seasons.]

After the Octave of Trinity till Advent, except on Double Feasts, is said before the Memorial of S. Mary,

MEMORIAL OF THE HOLY CROSS.

Ant. It behoveth us to glory : in the Cross of our Lord Jesus Chist.

℣. All the world shall worship Thee, and sing of Thee.

℟. And praise Thy name.

COLLECT.

O GOD, Who didst ascend Thy holy Cross to enlighten the darkness of the world; may it please Thee to enlighten our hearts and bodies, Thou Saviour of the world, Who livest and reignest with the Father and the Holy Ghost, ever one God, world without end. Amen.

℣. The Lord be with you.
℞. And with thy spirit.
℣. Bless we the Lord.
℞. Thanks be to God.

FOR THE PEACE OF THE CHURCH.

Said after Lauds daily throughout the year, except on Double Feasts, and in Christmas and Easter tide.

Psalm CXXIII.

Ad Te levavi oculos meos.

UNTO Thee lift I up mine eyes : O Thou that dwellest in the heavens.

2 Behold, even as the eyes of servants look unto the hands of their masters, and as the eyes of a maiden unto the hand of her mistress : even so our eyes wait upon the Lord our God, until He have mercy upon us.

3 Have mercy upon us, O Lord, have mercy upon us : for we are utterly despised.

4 Our soul is filled with the scornful reproof of the wealthy : and with the despitefulness of the proud.

Glory be, etc.

Lord, have mercy.
Christ, have mercy.
Lord, have mercy.

Our Father:

Said silently to the end. The Priest repeats aloud :

℣. And lead us not into temptation.
℞. But deliver us from evil.
℣. O Lord, arise, help us.
℞. And deliver us for Thy Name's sake.

℣. Turn us again, O Lord God of Hosts.
℞. Show the light of Thy countenance, and we shall be whole.
℣. Hear my prayer, O Lord.
℞. And let my crying come unto Thee.
℣. The Lord be with you.
℞. And with thy spirit.

Let us pray.

O LORD, we beseech Thee, mercifully to hear the prayers of Thy Church, and grant that we, being delivered from all adversities, may serve Thee with a quiet mind; and grant us Thy peace all the days of our life; through Jesus Christ our Lord, Who liveth and reigneth with Thee and the Holy Ghost, ever One God, world without end. Amen.

MONDAY.

𝕷𝖆𝖚𝖉𝖘.

This ℣. and ℞. are said on all ferias from Epiphany to Lent, and from Trinity to Advent, when the Office is of the feria.

℣. Let Thy merciful kindness, O Lord, be upon us.
℞. As we do put our trust in Thee.
℣. O God, make speed to save us.
℞. O Lord, make haste to help us.
℣. Glory be to the Father, and to the Son : and to the Holy Ghost ;
℞. As it was in the beginning, is now, and ever shall be : world without end. Amen.

Alleluia.

[From Septuagesima to Wednesday in Holy Week,

Praise be to Thee, O Lord, King of eternal glory.]

Ant. Have mercy.

(Antiphons are never doubled on ferias.)

Psalm LI. *Miserere mei, Deus.*

HAVE mercy upon me, O God, after Thy great goodness : according to the multitude of Thy mercies, do away mine offences.

2 Wash me throughly from my wickedness : and cleanse me from my sin.

3 For I acknowledge my faults : and my sin is ever before me.

4 Against Thee only have I sinned, and done this evil in Thy sight : that Thou mightest be justified in Thy saying, and clear when Thou art judged.

5 Behold, I was shapen in wickedness : and in sin hath my mother conceived me.

6 But lo, Thou requirest truth in the inward parts : and shalt make me to understand wisdom secretly.

7 Thou shalt purge me with hyssop, and I shall be clean : Thou shalt wash me, and I shall be whiter than snow.

8 Thou shalt make me hear of joy and gladness : that the bones which Thou hast broken may rejoice.

9 Turn Thy face from my sins : and put out all my misdeeds.

10 Make me a clean heart, O God : and renew a right spirit within me.

11 Cast me not away from Thy presence : and take not Thy Holy Spirit from me.

12 O give me the comfort of Thy help again : and stablish me with Thy free Spirit.

13 Then shall I teach Thy ways unto the wicked : and sinners shall be converted unto Thee.

14 Deliver me from blood-guiltiness, O God, Thou that art the God of my health : and my tongue shall sing of Thy righteousness.

15 Thou shalt open my lips, O Lord : and my mouth shall show Thy praise.

16 For Thou desirest no sacrifice, else would I give it Thee : but Thou delightest not in burnt-offerings.

17 The sacrifice of God is a troubled spirit : a broken and contrite heart, O God, shalt Thou not despise.

18 O be favourable and gracious unto Sion : build Thou the walls of Jerusalem.

19 Then shalt Thou be pleased with the sacrifice of righteousness, with the burnt-offerings and oblations : then shall they offer young bullocks upon Thine altar.

Glory be, etc.

Ant. Have mercy : upon me, O God.

Ant. Consider.

Psalm v. *Verba mea auribus.*

PONDER my words, O Lord consider my meditation.

2 O hearken Thou unto the voice of my calling, my King and my God : for unto Thee will I make my prayer.

3 My voice shalt Thou hear betimes, O Lord : early in the morning will I direct my prayer unto Thee, and will look up.

4 For Thou art the God that hast no pleasure in wickedness : neither shall any evil dwell with Thee.

5 Such as be foolish shall not stand in Thy sight : for Thou hatest all them that work vanity.

6 Thou shalt destroy them that speak leasing : the Lord will abhor both the blood-thirsty and deceitful man.

7 But as for me, I will come into Thine house, even upon the multitude of Thy mercy : and in Thy fear

will I worship toward Thy holy temple.

8 Lead me, O Lord, in Thy righteousness, because of mine enemies : make Thy way plain before my face.

9 For there is no faithfulness in his mouth : their inward parts are very wickedness.

10 Their throat is an open sepulchre : they flatter with their tongue.

11 Destroy Thou them, O God; let them perish through their own imaginations : cast them out in the multitude of their ungodliness; for they have rebelled against Thee.

12 And let all them that put their trust in Thee rejoice : they shall ever be giving of thanks, because Thou defendest them; they that love Thy Name shall be joyful in Thee;

13 For Thou, Lord, wilt give Thy blessing unto the righteous : and with Thy favourable kindness wilt Thou defend him as with a shield.

Glory be, etc.

Ant. Consider my meditation : O Lord.

Ant. O God.

Psalm lxiii. *Deus, Deus meus*, and Psalm lxvii. *Deus misereatur*, p. 3.

Ant. O God, Thou art my God : early will I seek Thee.

Ant. Thine anger is turned away.

Song of Isaiah.

Confitebor Tibi. Is. xii.

AND in that day thou shalt say, O Lord, I will praise Thee : though Thou wast angry with me, Thine anger is turned away, and Thou comfortedst me.

2 Behold, God is my salvation; I will trust, and not be afraid : for the Lord Jehovah is my strength and my song; He also is become my salvation.

3 Therefore with joy shall ye draw water : out of the wells of salvation.

4 And in that day shall ye say, Praise the Lord, call upon His Name : declare His doings among the people, make mention that His Name is exalted.

5 Sing unto the Lord; for He hath done excellent things : this is known in all the earth.

6 Cry out and shout, thou inhabitant of Zion : for great is the Holy One of Israel in the midst of thee.

Glory be, etc.

Ant. Thine anger is turned away, O Lord : and Thou comfortedst me.

Ant. O praise.

Psalm cxlviii. *Laudate Dominum.*
Psalm cxlix. *Cantate Domino.*
Psalm cl. *Laudate Dominum*, p. 4.

Ant. O praise : the Lord of heaven.

From Epiphany to Lent, and from Trinity to Advent,

Chapter. 1 Cor. xvi.

WATCH ye, stand fast in the faith, quit you like men, be strong. Let all your things be done with charity.

℟. Thanks be to God.

From Trinity to Advent,

Hymn. *Ecce jam noctis*, p. 5.

℣. Have I not thought upon Thee when I was waking ?

℟. Because Thou hast been my helper.

[*For Hymns at other times, see Proper of Seasons.*]

Ant. to Ben. Blessed be.

Benedictus, p. 6.

Ant. Blessed be : the Lord God of Israel.

PETITIONS.

(These are not said in Christmas or Easter tide. Lauds then end as on Sunday.)

Lord, have mercy.
Christ, have mercy.
Lord, have mercy.

Our Father:

Said silently to the end. The Priest repeats aloud :

℣. And lead us not into temptation.
℟. But deliver us from evil.
℣. I said, Lord, be merciful unto me.
℟. Heal my soul, for I have sinned against Thee.
℣. Turn Thee again, O Lord, at the last.
℟. And be gracious unto, Thy servants.
℣. Let Thy merciful kindness, O Lord, be upon us.
℟. As we do put our trust in Thee.
℣. Let Thy priests be clothed with righteousness.
℟. And Thy Saints sing with joyfulness.
℣. O Lord, save the Queen.
℟. And mercifully hear us when we call upon Thee.
℣. O God, save Thy servants and handmaidens.
℟. Which put their trust in Thee.
℣. O Lord, save Thy people, and bless Thine inheritance.
℟. Govern them, and lift them up for ever.
℣. Peace be within Thy walls.
℟. And plenteousness within Thy palaces.
℣. Let us pray for the faithful departed.
℟. Eternal rest grant unto them, O Lord, and light perpetual shine upon them.
℣. Hearken unto my voice, O Lord, when I cry unto Thee.

℟. Have mercy upon me, and hear me.

Psalm li. *Miserere mei, Deus,* p. 1, *with* Glory be, etc.

[*Here follows in Lent.*

Psalm VI.   *Domine, ne in furore.*

O LORD, rebuke me not in Thine indignation : neither chasten me in Thy displeasure.
2 Have mercy upon me, O Lord, for I am weak : O Lord, heal me, for my bones are vexed.
3 My soul also is sore troubled : but, Lord, how long wilt Thou punish me ?
4 Turn Thee, O Lord, and deliver my soul : O save me for Thy mercy's sake.
5 For in death no man remembereth Thee : and who will give Thee thanks in the pit ?
6 I am weary of my groaning ; every night wash I my bed : and water my couch with my tears.
7 My beauty is gone for very trouble : and worn away because of all mine enemies.
8 Away from me, all ye that work vanity : for the Lord hath heard the voice of my weeping.
9 The Lord hath heard my petition : the Lord will receive my prayer.
10 All mine enemies shall be confounded, and sore vexed : they shall be turned back, and put to shame suddenly.
   Glory be, etc.]

(Here the reader, if a Priest, rising, stands at the step of the Sanctuary),

℣. O Lord, arise, help us.
℟. And deliver us for Thy Name's sake.
℣. Turn Thee again, O Lord God of Hosts.
℟. Show the light of Thy countenance, and we shall be whole.
℣. Hear my prayer, O Lord.
℟. And let my crying come unto Thee.
℣. The Lord be with you.
℟. And with thy spirit.

Let us pray.

COLLECT.

Ferial Memorials.

Said on all ferias, according to the rubric before Sunday Memorials, p. 6.

[For memorials from Advent Sunday till the Octave of Epiphany, see Proper of Seasons.]

From the Octave of Epiphany till Ash-Wednesday, and after the Octave of Trinity till Advent:

MEMORIAL OF S. MARY.

Ant. The Root of Jesse hath budded; a Star hath risen out of Jacob; a Virgin hath brought forth the Saviour : We praise Thee, O our God.

℣. After child-bearing thou remainedst a Virgin.

℟. O Mother of God.

COLLECT.

O GOD, Who through the fruitful virginity of the Blessed Virgin Mary hast bestowed the rewards of eternal salvation on the human race; grant, we pray Thee, that she may intercede for us, through whom we have received the Author of Life, thy Son Jesus Christ our Lord. Amen.

MEMORIAL OF ALL SAINTS.

Ant. The Saints shall be joyful with glory : they shall rejoice in their beds.

℣. Wonderful art Thou, O God, in Thy Saints.

℟. And glorious in Thy majesty.

If this ℣. has been said before in any occasional Memorial, then in this Memorial is said :

℣. The souls of the righteous are in the hand of God.

℟. And there shall no torment touch them.

COLLECT.

WE pray Thee, O Lord, let the intercession of all Thy Saints be acceptable unto Thee; and grant us forgiveness of our sins and the remedies of eternal life, through Jesus Christ our Lord. Amen.

[For Memorials from Ash-Wednesday till Whitsuntide, see Proper of Seasons.]

From Monday after the Octave of Trinity till Advent, before the Memorials of S. Mary and All Saints,

MEMORIAL OF THE HOLY CROSS.

Ant. Save us, O Christ our Saviour, by the virtue of the Holy Cross : as Thou savedst Peter in the sea; and have mercy upon us.

℣. All the world shall worship Thee, and sing of Thee.

℟. And praise Thy name.

COLLECT.

KEEP, we beseech Thee, O Lord, in perpetual peace, those whom Thou hast vouchsafed to redeem by the wood of the Holy Cross, O Saviour of the world, Who livest and reignest with the Father and the Holy Ghost, ever one God, world without end. Amen.

FOR THE PEACE OF THE CHURCH.

As at Sunday Lauds, p. 7.

℣. The Lord be with you.

℟. And with thy spirit.

℣. Bless we the Lord.

℟. Thanks be to God.

TUESDAY.

Lauds.

℣. Let Thy merciful kindness, O Lord, be upon us.

℟. As we do put our trust in Thee.

℣. O God, make speed to save us.

℟. O Lord, make haste to help us.

℣. Glory be to the Father, and to the Son : and to the Holy Ghost ;

℟. As it was in the beginning, is now, and ever shall be : world without end. Amen.

Alleluia.

[*From Septuagesima to Wednesday in Holy Week,*

Praise be to Thee, O Lord, King of eternal glory.]

Ant. According to the multitude.

Psalm li. *Miserere mei*, p. 1.

Ant. According to the multitude of Thy mercies : have mercy upon me, O God.

Ant. The help of my countenance.

Psalm XLIII. *Judica me, Deus.*

GIVE sentence with me, O God, and defend my cause against the ungodly people : O deliver me from the deceitful and wicked man.

2 For Thou art the God of my strength, why hast Thou put me from Thee : and why go I so heavily, while the enemy oppresseth me ?

3 O send out Thy light and Thy truth, that they may lead me : and bring me unto Thy holy hill, and to Thy dwelling.

4 And that I may go unto the altar of God, even unto the God of my joy and gladness : and upon the harp will I give thanks unto Thee, O God, my God.

5 Why art thou so heavy, O my soul : and why art thou so disquieted within me ?

6 O put thy trust in God : for I will yet give Him thanks, which is the help of my countenance, and my God.

Glory be, etc.

Ant. The help of my countenance : and my God.

Ant. Early.

Psalm lxiii. *Deus, Deus meus*, and Psalm lxvii. *Deus misereatur*, p. 3.

Ant. Early : will I seek Thee.

Ant. All the days of my life.

SONG OF HEZEKIAH.

Ego dixi. Isaiah xxxviii.

I SAID, in the cutting off of my days : I shall go to the gates of the grave.

2 I am deprived of the residue of my years : I said, I shall not see the Lord, even the Lord, in the land of living.

3 I shall behold man no more : with the inhabitants of the world.

4 Mine age is departed : and is removed from me as a shepherd's tent.

5 I have cut off like a weaver my life : He will cut me off with pining sickness.

6 From day even to night, wilt Thou make an end of me : I reckoned till morning that, as a lion, so will He break all my bones.

7 From day even to night wilt Thou make an end of me : like a crane or a swallow, so did I chatter ; I did mourn as a dove.

8 My eyes fail : with looking upward.

9 O Lord, I am oppressed ; undertake for me : what shall I say ? He hath both spoken unto me, and Himself hath done it.

10 I shall go softly all my years : in the bitterness of my soul.

11 O Lord, by these things men live, and in all these things is the life of my spirit : so wilt Thou recover me, and make me to live : behold, for peace I had great bitterness.

12 But Thou hast in love to my soul delivered it from the pit of corruption : for Thou hast cast all my sins behind Thy back.

13 For the grave cannot praise Thee, death cannot celebrate Thee : they that go down into the pit cannot hope for Thy truth.

14 The living, the living, he shall praise Thee, as I do this day : the father to the children shall make known Thy truth.

15 The Lord was ready to save me : therefore we will sing my songs to the stringed instruments all the days of our life in the house of the Lord.

Glory be, etc.

Ant. All the days of my life : the Lord was ready to save me.

Ant. Praise Him.

Ps. cxlviii. *Laudate Dominum.*
Ps. cxlix. *Cantate Domino.*
Ps. cl. *Laudate Dominum,* p. 4.

Ant. Praise Him : in the firmament of His power.

From Epiphany to Lent, and from Trinity to Advent,

CHAPTER. I Cor. xvi.

Watch ye, stand fast in the faith, quit you like men, be strong. Let all your things be done with charity.

R7. Thanks be to God.

From Trinity to Advent,

HYMN. *Ecce jam noctis,* p. 5.

V. Have I not thought upon Thee when I was waking?
R7. Because Thou hast been my Helper.

Ant. to Ben. And the Lord shall be to us.

Benedictus, p. 6.

Ant. And the Lord shall be to us a mighty salvation : in the house of His servant David.

PETITIONS, p. 10.

COLLECT.

FERIAL MEMORIALS, p. 11.

V. The Lord be with you.
R7. And with thy spirit.
V. Bless we the Lord.
R7. Thanks be to God.

———

WEDNESDAY.

Lauds.

V. Let Thy merciful kindness, O Lord, be upon us.
R7. As we do put our trust in Thee.
V. O God, make speed to save us.
R7. O Lord, make haste to help us.
V. Glory be to the Father, and to the Son, and to the Holy Ghost.
R7. As it was in the beginning, is now, and ever shall be, world without end. Amen.
Alleluia.

[*From Septuagesima to Wednesday in Holy Week,*

Praise be to Thee, O Lord, King of eternal glory.]

Ant. Wash me throughly.

Psalm li. *Miserere mei,* p. 1.

Ant. Wash me throughly : from my wickedness, O God.

Ant. Thou, O God.

Psalm LXV. *Te decet hymnus.*

THOU, O God, art praised in Sion : and unto Thee shall the vow be performed in Jerusalem.

2 Thou that hearest the prayer : unto Thee shall all flesh come.

3 My misdeeds prevail against me : O be Thou merciful unto our sins.

4 Blessed is the man, whom Thou choosest, and receivest unto Thee :

he shall dwell in Thy court, and shall be satisfied with the pleasures of Thy house, even of Thy holy temple.

5 Thou shalt show us wonderful things in Thy righteousness, O God of our salvation : Thou that art the hope of all the ends of the earth, and of them that remain in the broad sea.

6 Who in His strength setteth fast the mountains : and is girded about with power.

7 Who stilleth the raging of the sea : and the noise of His waves, and the madness of the people.

8 They also that dwell in the uttermost parts of the earth shall be afraid at Thy tokens : Thou that makest the outgoings of the morning and evening to praise Thee.

9 Thou visitest the earth, and blessest it : Thou makest it very plenteous.

10 The river of God is full of water : Thou preparest their corn, for so Thou providest for the earth.

11 Thou waterest her furrows, Thou sendest rain into the little valleys thereof : Thou makest it soft with the drops of rain, and blessest the increase of it.

12 Thou crownest the year with Thy goodness : and Thy clouds drop fatness.

13 They shall drop upon the dwellings of the wilderness : and the little hills shall rejoice on every side.

14 The folds shall be full of sheep : the valleys also shall stand so thick with corn, that they shall laugh and sing.

Glory be, etc.

Ant. Thou, O God : art praised in Sion.

Ant. My lips shall praise Thee.

Psalm lxiii. *Deus, Deus meus,* and Psalm lxvii. *Deus misereatur,* p. 3.

Ant. My lips shall praise Thee : as long as I live.

Ant. The Lord shall judge.

SONG OF HANNAH.

Exultavit cor meum.　ı Sam. ii.

MY heart rejoiceth in the Lord : mine horn is exalted in the Lord.

2 My mouth is enlarged over mine enemies : because I rejoice in Thy salvation.

3 There is none holy as the Lord : for there is none beside Thee : neither is there any rock like our God.

4 Talk no more : so exceeding proudly.

5 Let not arrogancy come out of your mouth : for the Lord is a God of knowledge, and by Him actions are weighed.

6 The bows of the mighty men are broken : and they that stumbled are girded with strength.

7 They that were full have hired out themselves for bread : and they that were hungry ceased.

8 So that the barren hath born seven : and she that hath many children is waxed feeble.

9 The Lord killeth, and maketh alive : He bringeth down to the grave, and bringeth up.

10 The Lord maketh poor, and maketh rich : He bringeth low, and lifteth up.

11 He raiseth up the poor out of the dust : and lifteth up the beggar from the dunghill.

12 To set them among princes : and to make them inherit the throne of glory.

13 For the pillars of the earth are the Lord's : and He hath set the world upon them.

14 He will keep the feet of His saints, and the wicked shall be silent in darkness : for by strength shall no man prevail.

15 The adversaries of the Lord shall be broken to pieces : out of heaven shall He thunder upon them.

16 The Lord shall judge the ends of the earth : and He shall give strength unto His king, and exalt the horn of His anointed.

Glory be, etc.

Ant. The Lord shall judge : the ends of the earth.

Ant. O praise God.

Psalm cxlviii. *Laudate Dominum.*
Psalm cxlix. *Cantate Domino.*
Psalm cl. *Laudate Dominum*, p. 4.

Ant. O praise God : all ye heavens.

From Epiphany to Lent, and from Trinity to Advent,

CHAPTER. 1 Cor. xvi.

WATCH ye, stand fast in the faith, quit you like men, be strong. Let all your things be done with charity.

R̃. Thanks be to God.

From Trinity to Advent,

HYMN. *Ecce jam noctis*, p. 5.

Ṽ. Have I not thought upon Thee when I was waking ?
R̃. Because Thou hast been my Helper.

Ant. to Ben. That we should be saved.

Benedictus, p. 6.

Ant. That we should be saved from our enemies, and from the hands of all that hate us : good Lord, deliver us.

PETITIONS, p. 10.

COLLECT.

FERIAL MEMORIALS, p. 11.

Ṽ. The Lord be with you.
R̃. And with thy spirit.
Ṽ. Bless we the Lord.
R̃. Thanks be to God.

THURSDAY.

Lauds.

Ṽ. Let Thy merciful kindness, O Lord, be upon us.
R̃. As we do put our trust in Thee.
Ṽ. O God, make speed to save us.
R̃. O Lord, make haste to help us.
Ṽ. Glory be to the Father, and to the Son, and to the Holy Ghost.
R̃. As it was in the beginning, is now, and ever shall be, world without end. Amen.
Alleluia.

[*From Septuagesima till Wednesday in Holy Week,*

Praise be to Thee, O Lord, King of eternal glory.]

Ant. Against Thee only.

Psalm li. *Miserere mei*, p. 1.

Ant. Against Thee only have I sinned : have mercy upon me, O God.

Ant. Lord, Thou hast been.

Psalm xc. *Domine refugium.*

LORD, Thou hast been our refuge : from one generation to another.

2 Before the mountains were brought forth, or ever the earth and the world were made : Thou art God from everlasting, and world without end.

3 Thou turnest man to destruction : again Thou sayest, Come again, ye children of men.

4 For a thousand years in Thy sight are but as yesterday : seeing that is past as a watch in the night.

5 As soon as Thou scatterest them they are even as a sleep : and fade away suddenly like the grass.

6 In the morning it is green, and groweth up : but in the evening it is cut down, dried up, and withered.

7 For we consume away in Thy displeasure : and are afraid at Thy wrathful indignation.

8 Thou hast set our misdeeds before Thee : and our secret sins in the light of Thy countenance.

9 For when Thou art angry all our days are gone : we bring our years to an end, as it were a tale that is told.

10 The days of our age are threescore years and ten; and though men be so strong that they come to fourscore years : yet is their strength then but labour and sorrow; so soon passeth it away, and we are gone.

11 But who regardeth the power of Thy wrath : for even thereafter as a man feareth, so is Thy displeasure.

12 So .teach us to number our days : that we may apply our hearts unto wisdom.

13 Turn Thee again, O Lord, at the last : and be gracious unto Thy servants.

14 O satisfy us with Thy mercy, and that soon : so shall we rejoice and be glad all the days of our life.

15 Comfort us again now after the time that Thou hast plagued us : and for the years wherein we have suffered adversity.

16 Shew Thy servants Thy work : and their children Thy glory.

17 And the glorious Majesty of the Lord our God be upon us : prosper Thou the work of our hands upon us, O prosper Thou our handy-work.

Glory be, etc.

Ant. O Lord : Thou hast been our refuge.

Ant. Have I not thought?

Psalm lxiii. *Deus, Deus meus,* and Psalm lxvii. *Deus misereatur,* p. 3.

Ant. Have I not thought upon Thee : when I was waking?

Ant. The Lord shall reign.

SONG OF MOSES.

Cantemus Domino. Exodus xv.

I WILL sing unto the Lord, for He hath triumphed gloriously : the horse and his rider hath He thrown into the sea.

2 The Lord is my strength and my song : and is become my salvation.

3 He is my God, and I will prepare Him an habitation : my father's God, and I will exalt Him.

4 The Lord is a man of war : the Lord is His Name : Pharaoh's chariots and his host hath He cast into the sea.

5 His chosen captains are drowned in the Red Sea : the depths have covered them; they sank into the bottom as a stone.

6 Thy right hand, O Lord, is become glorious in power; Thy right hand, O Lord, hath dashed in pieces the enemy : and in the greatness of Thine excellency Thou hast overthrown them that rose up against Thee.

7 Thou sentest forth Thy wrath, which consumed them as stubble : and with the blast of Thy nostrils the waters were gathered together.

8 The flood stood upright as an heap : and the depths were congealed in the heart of the sea.

9 The enemy said, I will pursue, I will overtake, I will divide the spoil : my lust shall be satisfied upon them.

10 I will draw my sword : my hand shall destroy them.

11 Thou didst blow with Thy wind, the sea covered them : they sank as lead in the mighty waters.

12 Who is like unto Thee, O Lord, among the gods : who is like unto Thee, glorious in holiness, fearful in praises, doing wonders?

13 Thou stretchedst out Thy right hand : the earth swallowed them.

14 Thou in Thy mercy : hast led forth the people which Thou hast redeemed.

15 Thou hast guided them in Thy strength : unto Thy holy habitation.

16 The people shall hear, and be afraid : sorrow shall take hold of the inhabitants of Palestina.

17 Then the dukes of Edom shall be amazed ; the mighty men of Moab, trembling shall take hold upon them : all the inhabitants of Canaan shall melt away.

18 Fear and dread shall fall upon them : by the greatness of Thine arm.

19 They shall be as still as a stone : till Thy people pass over, O Lord, till the people pass over, which Thou hast purchased.

20 Thou shalt bring them in, and plant them in the mountain of Thine inheritance : in the place, O Lord, which Thou hast made for Thee to dwell in.

21 In the sanctuary, O Lord, which Thy hands have established : the Lord shall reign for ever and ever.

22 For the horse of Pharaoh went in with his chariots and with his horsemen into the sea : and the Lord brought again the waters of the sea upon them.

23 But the children of Israel went on dry land : in the midst of the sea.

Glory be, etc.

Ant. The Lord shall reign : for ever and ever.

Ant. O praise.

Psalm cxlviii. *Laudate Dominum.*
Psalm cxlix. *Cantate Domino.*
Psalm cl. *Laudate Dominum,* p. 4.

Ant. O praise : the Lord of heaven.

From Epiphany to Lent, and from Trinity to Advent,

CHAPTER. I. Cor. xvi.

WATCH ye, stand fast in the faith, quit you like men, be strong. Let all your things be done with charity.

℟. Thanks be to God.

From Trinity to Advent,

HYMN. *Ecce jam noctis,* p. 5.

℣. Have I not thought upon Thee when I was waking ?

℟. Because Thou hast been my helper.

Ant. to Ben. Let us serve the Lord.

Benedictus, p. 6.

Ant. Let us serve the Lord in holiness : and He shall deliver us out of the hand of our enemies.

PETITIONS, p. 10.

COLLECT.

FERIAL MEMORIALS, p. 11.

℣. The Lord be with you.
℟. And with thy spirit.
℣. Bless we the Lord.
℟. Thanks be to God.

———

FRIDAY.

Lauds.

℣. Let Thy merciful kindness, O Lord, be upon us.

℟. As we do put our trust in Thee.

℣. O God, make speed to save us.

℟. O Lord, make haste to help us.

℣. Glory be to the Father, and to the Son : and to the Holy Ghost.

℟. As it was in the beginning, is now, and ever shall be : world without end. Amen.

Alleluia.

[*From Septuagesima to Wednesday in Holy Week:*

Praise be to Thee, O Lord, King of eternal glory.]

Ant. O stablish me.

Psalm li. *Miserere mei Deus*, p. 1.

Ant. O stablish me : with Thy free Spirit.

Ant. Hearken unto me.

Psalm CXLIII. *Domine, exaudi.*

HEAR my prayer, O Lord, and consider my desire : hearken unto me for Thy truth and righteousness' sake.

2 And enter not into judgement with Thy servant : for in Thy sight shall no man living be justified.

3 For the enemy hath persecuted my soul; he hath smitten my life down to the ground : he hath laid me in the darkness, as the men that have been long dead.

4 Therefore is my spirit vexed within me : and my heart within me is desolate.

5 Yet do I remember the time past; I muse upon all Thy works : yea, I exercise myself in the works of Thy hands.

6 I stretch forth my hands unto Thee : my soul gaspeth unto Thee as a thirsty land.

7 Hear me, O Lord, and that soon, for my spirit waxeth faint : hide not Thy face from me, lest I be like unto them that go down into the pit.

8 O let me hear Thy loving-kindness betimes in the morning, for in Thee is my trust : show Thou me the way that I should walk in, for I lift up my soul unto Thee.

9 Deliver me, O Lord, from mine enemies : for I flee unto Thee to hide me.

10 Teach me to do the thing that pleaseth Thee, for Thou art my God : let Thy loving Spirit lead me forth into the land of righteousness.

11 Quicken me, O Lord, for Thy Name's sake : and for Thy righteousness' sake bring my soul out of trouble.

12 And of Thy goodness slay mine enemies : and destroy all them that vex my soul; for I am Thy servant.

Glory be, etc.

Ant. Hearken unto me : for Thy truth and righteousness' sake.

Ant. God shew us.

Psalm lxiii. *Deus, Deus meus*, and Psalm lxvii. *Deus misereatur*, p. 3.

Ant. God shew us : the light of His countenance.

Ant. O Lord, I have heard.

SONG OF HABAKKUK.

Domine audivi. Habakkuk iii.

O LORD, I have heard Thy speech : and was afraid.

2 O Lord, revive Thy work : in the midst of the years.

3 In the midst of the years make known : in wrath remember mercy.

4 God came from Teman : and the Holy One from Mount Paran.

5 His glory covered the heavens : and the earth was full of His praise.

6 And His brightness was as the light : He had horns coming out of His hand.

7 And there was the hiding of His power : before Him went the pestilence.

8 And burning coals went forth at His feet : He stood and measured the earth.

9 He beheld and drove asunder the nations : and the everlasting mountains were scattered.

10 The perpetual hills did bow : His ways are everlasting.

11 I saw the tents of Cushan in affliction : and the curtains of the land of Midian did tremble.

12 Was the Lord displeased against the rivers ? was Thine anger against the rivers : was Thy wrath against the sea ;

13 That Thou didst ride upon Thine horses : and Thy chariots of salvation ?

14 Thy bow was made quite naked : according to the oaths of the tribes, even Thy word.

15 Thou didst cleave the earth with rivers : the mountains saw Thee, and trembled.

16 The overflowing of the water : passed by.

17 The deep uttered his voice : and lifted up his hands on high.

18 The sun and moon stood still in their habitation : at the light of Thine arrows they went, and at the shining of Thy glittering spear.

19 Thou didst march through the land in indignation : Thou didst thresh the heathen in anger.

20 Thou wentest forth for the salvation of Thy people : even for salvation with Thine Anointed.

21 Thou woundedst the head out of the house of the wicked : by discovering the foundation unto the neck.

22 Thou didst strike through with his staves the head of his villages : they came out as a whirlwind to scatter me.

23 Their rejoicing : was as to devour the poor secretly.

24 Thou didst walk through the sea with Thine horses : through the deep of great waters.

25 When I heard, my belly trembled : my lips quivered at the voice.

26 Rottenness entered into my bones : and I trembled in myself, that I might rest in the day of trouble.

27 When He cometh up unto the people : He will invade them with His troops.

28 Although the fig-tree shall not blossom : neither shall fruit be on the vines ;

29 The labour of the olives shall fail : and the fields shall yield no meat.

30 The flock shall be cut off from the fold : and there shall be no herd in the stalls.

31 Yet I will rejoice in the Lord : I will joy in the God of my salvation.

32 The Lord God is my strength : and He will make my feet like hinds' feet.

33 And He will make me to walk : upon mine high places.

Glory be, etc.

Ant. O Lord, I have heard Thy speech : and was afraid.

Ant. Praise Him in the cymbals.

Psalm cxlviii. *Laudate Dominum.*
Psalm cxlix. *Cantate Domino.*
Psalm cl. *Laudate Dominum*, p. 4.

Ant. Praise Him in the cymbals and dances : praise Him upon the strings and pipe.

From Epiphany to Lent, and from Trinity to Advent,

CHAPTER. 1 Cor. xvi.

WATCH ye, stand fast in the faith, quit you like men, be strong. Let all your things be done with charity.

℟. Thanks be to God.

From Trinity to Advent,

HYMN. *Ecce jam noctis*, p. 5.

℣. Have I not thought upon Thee when I was waking ?

℟. Because Thou hast been my helper.

Ant. to Ben. Through the tender mercies.

Benedictus, p. 6.

Ant. Through the tender mercies of our God : whereby the Day-spring from on high hath visited us.

PETITIONS, p. 10.

COLLECT.

FERIAL MEMORIALS. p. 11.

℣. The Lord be with you.
℞. And with thy spirit.
℣. Bless we the Lord.
℞. Thanks be to God.

SATURDAY.

𝕷𝖆𝖚𝖉𝖘.

℣. Let Thy merciful kindness, O Lord, be upon us.
℞. As we do put our trust in Thee.
℣. O God, make speed to save us.
℞. O Lord, make haste to help us.
℣. Glory be to the Father, and to the Son : and to the Holy Ghost.
℞. As it was in the beginning, is now, and ever shall be : world without end.   Amen.
Alleluia.
[*From Septuagesima to Wednesday in Holy Week :*
Praise be to Thee, O Lord, King of eternal glory.]

Ant. O be favourable.

Psalm li. *Miserere mei Deus,* p. 1.

Ant. O be favourable : and gracious unto Sion.

Ant. It is a good thing.

Psalm XCII. *Bonum est confiteri.*

IT is a good thing to give thanks unto the Lord : and to sing praises unto Thy Name, O most Highest.

2 To tell of Thy loving-kindness early in the morning : and of Thy truth in the night-season.

3 Upon an instrument of ten strings, and upon the lute : upon a loud instrument, and upon the harp.

4 For Thou, Lord, hast made me glad through Thy works : and I will rejoice in giving praise for the operations of Thy hands.

5 O Lord, how glorious are Thy works : Thy thoughts are very deep.

6 An unwise man doth not well consider this : and a fool doth not understand it.

7 When the ungodly are green as the grass, and when all the workers of wickedness do flourish : then shall they be destroyed for ever; but Thou, Lord, art the most Highest for evermore.

8 For lo, Thine enemies, O Lord, lo, Thine enemies shall perish : and all the workers of wickedness shall be destroyed.

9 But mine horn shall be exalted like the horn of an unicorn : for I am anointed with fresh oil.

10 Mine eye also shall see his lust of mine enemies : and mine ear shall hear his desire of the wicked that arise up against me.

11 The righteous shall flourish like a palm-tree : and shall spread abroad like a cedar in Libanus.

12 Such as are planted in the house of the Lord : shall flourish in the courts of the House of our God.

13 They also shall bring forth more fruit in their age : and shall be fat and well-liking.

14 That they may show how true the Lord my strength is : and that there is no unrighteousness in Him.

Glory be, etc.

Ant. It is a good thing : to give thanks unto the Lord.

Ant. All the ends of the world.

Psalm lxiii. *Deus, Deus meus,* and Psalm lxvii. *Deus misereatur,* p. 3.

Ant. All the ends of the world : shall fear Him.

Ant. The Lord shall repent.

Song of Moses.

Audite cœli. Deut. xxxii.

GIVE ear, O ye heavens, and I will speak : and hear, O earth, the words of my mouth.

2 My doctrine shall drop as the rain : my speech shall distil as the dew.

3 As the small rain upon the tender herb : and as the showers upon the grass.

4 Because I will publish : the Name of the Lord.

5 Ascribe ye greatness : unto our God.

6 He is the Rock, His work is perfect : for all His ways are judgment.

7 A God of truth and without iniquity : just and right is He.

8 They have corrupted themselves: their spot is not the spot of His children.

9 They are a perverse : and crooked generation.

10 Do ye thus requite the Lord : O foolish people and unwise?

11 Is not He thy Father that hath bought thee : hath He not made thee, and established thee?

12 Remember the days of old : consider the years of many generations.

13 Ask thy father, and he will shew thee : thy elders, and they will tell thee.

14 When the Most High divided to the nations their inheritance : when He separated the sons of Adam;

15 He set the bounds of the people : according to the number of the children of Israel.

16 For the Lord's portion is His people : Jacob is the lot of His inheritance.

17 He found him in a desert land : and in the waste howling wilderness.

18 He led him about, He instructed him : He kept him as the apple of His eye.

19 As an eagle stirreth up her nest, fluttereth over her young : spreadeth abroad her wings, taketh them, beareth them on her wings;

20 So the Lord alone did lead him : and there was no strange God with him.

21 He made him ride in the high places of the earth : that he might eat the increase of the fields.

22 And He made him suck honey out of the rock : and oil out of the flinty rock.

23 Butter of kine, and milk of sheep, with fat of lambs and rams of the breed of Basan : and goats with the fat of the kidneys of wheat, and thou didst drink the pure blood of the grape.

24 But Jeshurun waxed fat, and kicked : thou art waxen fat, thou art grown thick, thou art covered with fatness.

25 Then he forsook God Which made him : and lightly esteemed the Rock of his Salvation.

26 They provoked Him to jealousy with strange gods : with abominations provoked they Him to anger.

27 They sacrificed unto devils, not to God : to gods whom they knew not;

28 To new gods that came newly up : whom your fathers feared not.

29 Of the Rock that begat thee, thou art unmindful : and hast forgotten God that formed thee.

30 And when the Lord saw it He

abhorred them : because of the pro-
voking of His sons and of His
daughters.

31 And He said, I will hide My
Face from them : I will see what their
end shall be.

32 For they are a very froward
generation : children in whom is no
faith.

33 They have moved Me to jealousy with that which is not God :
they have provoked Me to anger with
their vanities ;

34 And I will move them to
jealousy with those that are not a
people : I will provoke them to anger
with a foolish nation.

35 For a fire is kindled in Mine
anger : and shall burn unto the lowest
hell ;

36 And shall consume the earth
with her increase : and set on fire the
foundations of the mountains.

37 I will heap mischief upon them :
I will spend Mine arrows upon them.

38 They shall be burnt with
hunger : and devoured with burning
heat, and with bitter destruction.

39 I will also send the teeth of
beasts upon them : with the poison
of serpents of the dust.

40 The sword without and terror
within shall destroy both the young
man and the virgin : the suckling
also, with the man of grey hairs.

41 I said, I would scatter them
into corners : I would make the remembrance of them to cease from
among men.

42 Were it not that I feared the
wrath of the enemy : lest their adversaries should behave themselves
strangely ;

43 And lest they should say : Our
hand is high, and the Lord hath not
done all this.

44 For they are a nation void of
counsel : neither is there any understanding in them.

45 O that they were wise, that
they understood this : that they
would consider their latter end !

46 How should one chase a thousand : and two put ten thousand to
flight ?

47 Except their Rock had sold
them : and the Lord had shut them
up.

48 For their rock is not as our
Rock : even our enemies themselves
being judges.

49 For their vine is as the vine of
Sodom : and of the fields of Go-
morrah.

50 Their grapes are grapes of gall :
their clusters are bitter.

51 Their wine is the poison of
dragons : and the cruel venom of asps.

52 Is not this laid up in store
with Me : and sealed up among My
treasures ?

53 To Me belongeth vengeance :
and recompense.

54 Their foot shall slide : in due
time.

55 For the day of their calamity
is at hand : and the things that shall
come upon them make haste.

56 For the Lord shall judge His
people : and repent Himself for His
servants ;

57 When He seeth that their
power is gone : and there is none
shut up, or left.

58 And He shall say, Where are
their gods : their rock in whom they
trusted ?

59 Which did eat the fat of their
sacrifices : and drank the wine of
their drink-offerings ?

60 Let them rise up and help you :
and be your protection.

61 See now that I, even I, am
He : and there is no god with Me.

62 I kill, and I make alive ; I
wound, and I heal : neither is there
any that can deliver out of My
hand.

63 For I lift up My hand to heaven : and say, I live for ever.

64 If I whet My glittering sword : and Mine hand take hold on judgment ;

65 I will render vengeance to Mine enemies : and will reward them that hate Me.

66 I will make Mine arrows drunk with blood : and My sword shall devour flesh.

67 And that with the blood of the slain, and of the captives : from the beginning of revenges upon the enemy.

68 Rejoice, O ye nations, with His people : for He will avenge the blood of His servants.

69 And will render vengeance to His adversaries : and will be merciful unto His land, and to His people.

Glory be, etc.

Ant. The Lord shall repent Himself : for His servants.

Ant. Praise Him.

Psalm cxlviii. *Laudate Dominum.*
Psalm cxlix. *Cantate Domino.*
Psalm cl. *Laudate Dominum,* p. 4.

Ant. Praise Him : on the well-tuned cymbals.

From Epiphany to Lent, and from Trinity to Advent,

CHAPTER. 1 Cor. xvi.

WATCH ye, stand fast in the faith, quit you like men, be strong. Let all your things be done with charity.

R7. Thanks be to God.

From Trinity to Advent,

HYMN. *Ecce jam noctis,* p. 5.

V. Have I not thought upon Thee when I was waking?

R7. Because Thou hast been my Helper.

Ant. to Ben. Guide our feet.

Benedictus, p. 6.

Ant. Guide our feet, O Lord : into the way of peace.

PETITIONS, p. 10.

COLLECT.

FERIAL MEMORIALS, p. 11.

V. The Lord be with you.
R7. And with thy spirit.
V. Bless we the Lord.
R7. Thanks be to God.

———

Prime.

Prime, and every other hour except Lauds, begin as follows, in silence :

✠ In the Name of the Father, and of the Son, and of the Holy Ghost. Amen.

Our Father, etc.

Then aloud,

✠V. O God, make speed to save us.
R7. O Lord, make haste to help us.
V. Glory be to the Father, and to the Son : and to the Holy Ghost.
R7. As it was in the beginning, is now, and ever shall be : world without end. Amen.

Alleluia.

[From Septuagesima to Wednesday in Holy Week :

Praise be to Thee, O Lord, King of eternal glory.]

HYMN. *Jam lucis orto sidere.*

NOW that the daylight fills the sky,
We lift our hearts to God on high,
That He, in all we do or say,
Would keep us free from harm to-day :

Would guard our hearts and tongues from strife;
From anger's din would hide our life;
From all ill sights would turn our eyes;
Would close our ears from vanities;

Would keep our inmost conscience pure ;
Our souls from folly would secure ;
Would bid us check the pride of sense
With due and holy abstinence.

So we, when this new day is gone,
And night in turn is drawing on,
With conscience by the world unstain'd
Shall praise His Name for victory gain'd.

All laud to God the Father be ;
All praise, Eternal Son, to Thee ;
All praise for ever, as is meet,
To God the Holy Paraclete. Amen.

[The Psalms which follow were used in the Sarum Office on Sundays and Ferias, except at Christmas and Easter tides. Prime being the correlative of Compline, as few variations were made as possible.
But for those who find the number of daily Psalms too great, the Roman use is here subjoined. And before each Psalm is indicated the day on which it is so used.
In this latter use, Glory be is said after each Psalm : in the former, after every alternate Psalm, as marked below.

Sunday. 1. Psalm liv., *Deus in nomine.* 2. Psalm cxviii., *Confitemini Domino* (changed in Lent to Psalm xciii., *Dominus regnavit*). 3. Psalm cxix., *Beati immaculati,* and *Retribue servo tuo.* 4. Psalm, *Quicunque vult.*

Daily. 1. Psalm liv., *Deus in nomine.* 3. Psalm cxix., *Beati immaculati,* and *Retribue servo tuo.*

After Psalm liv. *is said,*

Monday. 2. Psalm xxiv., *Domini est terra.*
Tuesday. 2. Psalm xxv., *Ad te, Domine, levavi.*
Wednesday. 2. Psalm xxvi., *Judica me Domine.*
Thursday. 2. Psalm xxiii., *Dominus regit me.*
Friday. 2. Psalm xxii., *Deus, Deus meus.*

On Saturdays and Festivals no intermediate Psalm, but only

1. Psalm liv., *Deus in nomine,* and 2. Psalm cxix., *Beati immaculati,* and *Retribue servo tuo.*]

ANTIPHONS.

On ordinary Sundays.

The Lord is my Shepherd : * therefore can I lack nothing.

On ordinary Ferias.

Hear my prayer, O God : * and hearken unto the words of my mouth.

On Ferias in Advent.

Come and deliver us, * O our God.

[For other Antiphons, see Proper of Seasons.]

[Or Friday only.]

Psalm XXII. *Deus, Deus meus.*

MY God, my God, look upon me ; why hast Thou forsaken me : and art so far from my health, and from the words of my complaint ?

2 O my God, I cry in the day-time, but Thou hearest not : and in the night-season also I take no rest.

3 And Thou continuest holy : O Thou worship of Israel.

4 Our fathers hoped in Thee : they trusted in Thee, and Thou didst deliver them.

5 They called upon Thee, and were holpen : they put their trust in Thee, and were not confounded.

6 But as for me, I am a worm, and no man : a very scorn of men, and the outcast of the people.

7 All they that see me laugh me to scorn : they shoot out their lips, and shake their heads, saying,

8 He trusted in God, that He would deliver Him : let Him deliver Him, if He will have Him.

9 But Thou art He that took me out of my mother's womb : Thou wast my hope, when I hanged yet upon my mother's breasts.

10 I have been left unto Thee ever since I was born : Thou art my God even from my mother's womb.

11 O go not from me, for trouble is hard at hand : and there is none to help me.

12 Many oxen are come about me : fat bulls of Basan close me in on every side.

13 They gape upon me with their mouths : as it were a ramping and a roaring lion.

14 I am poured out like water, and all my bones are out of joint : my heart also in the midst of my body is even like melting wax.

15 My strength is dried up like a potsherd, and my tongue cleaveth to my gums : and Thou shalt bring me into the dust of death.

16 For many dogs are come about me : and the counsel of the wicked layeth siege against me.

17 They pierced my hands and my feet; I may tell all my bones : they stand staring and looking upon me.

18 They part my garments among them : and cast lots upon my vesture.

19 But be not Thou far from me, O Lord : Thou art my succour, haste Thee to help me.

20 Deliver my soul from the sword : my darling from the power of the dog.

21 Save me from the lion's mouth : Thou hast heard me also from among the horns of the unicorns.

22 I will declare Thy Name unto my brethren : in the midst of the congregation will I praise Thee.

23 O praise the Lord, ye that fear Him : magnify Him, all ye of the seed of Jacob, and fear Him, all ye seed of Israel ;

24 For He hath not despised, nor abhorred, the low estate of the poor : He hath not hid His face from him, but when he called unto Him He heard him.

25 My praise is of Thee in the great congregation : my vows will I perform in the sight of them that fear Him.

26 The poor shall eat, and be satisfied : they that seek after the Lord shall praise Him; your heart shall live for ever.

27 All the ends of the world shall remember themselves, and be turned unto the Lord : and all the kindreds of the nations shall worship before Him.

28 For the kingdom is the Lord's : and He is the Governour among the people.

29 All such as be fat upon earth : have eaten, and worshipped.

30 All they that go down into the dust shall kneel before Him : and no man hath quickened his own soul.

31 My seed shall serve Him : they shall be counted unto the Lord for a generation.

32 They shall come, and the heavens shall declare His righteousness : unto a people that shall be born, whom the Lord hath made.

[Or Thursday only.]

Psalm XXIII. *Dominus regit me.*

THE Lord is my Shepherd : therefore can I lack nothing.

2 He shall feed me in a green pasture : and lead me forth beside the waters of comfort.

3 He shall convert my soul : and bring me forth in the paths of righteousness, for His Name's sake.

4 Yea, though I walk through the valley of the shadow of death, I will fear no evil : for Thou art with me; Thy rod and Thy staff comfort me.

5 Thou shalt prepare a table before me against them that trouble me : Thou hast anointed my head with oil, and my cup shall be full.

6 But Thy loving-kindness and mercy shall follow me all the days of

my life : and I will dwell in the house of the Lord for ever.

Glory be, etc.

[Or Monday only.]

Psalm xxiv. *Domini est terra.*

THE earth is the Lord's, and all that therein is : the compass of the world, and they that dwell therein.

2 For He hath founded it upon the seas : and prepared it upon the floods.

3 Who shall ascend into the hill of the Lord : or who shall rise up in His holy place?

4 Even he that hath clean hands, and a pure heart : and that hath not lift up his mind unto vanity, nor sworn to deceive his neighbour.

5 He shall receive the blessing from the Lord : and righteousness from the God of his salvation.

6 This is the generation of them that seek Him : even of them that seek thy face, O Jacob.

7 Lift up your heads, O ye gates, and be ye lift up, ye everlasting doors : and the King of Glory shall come in.

8 Who is the King of Glory : it is the Lord strong and mighty, even the Lord mighty in battle.

9 Lift up your heads, O ye gates, and be ye lift up, ye everlasting doors : and the King of Glory shall come in.

10 Who is the King of Glory : even the Lord of hosts, He is the King of Glory.

[Or Tuesday only.]

Psalm xxv. *Ad te, Domine, levavi.*

UNTO Thee, O Lord, will I lift up my soul; my God, I have put my trust in Thee : O let me not be confounded, neither let mine enemies triumph over me.

2 For all they that hope in Thee shall not be ashamed : but such as transgress without a cause shall be put to confusion.

3 Show me Thy ways, O Lord : and teach me Thy paths.

4 Lead me forth in Thy truth, and learn me : for Thou art the God of my salvation; in Thee hath been my hope all the day long.

5 Call to remembrance, O Lord, Thy tender mercies : and Thy lovingkindnesses, which have been ever of old.

6 O remember not the sins and offences of my youth : but according to Thy mercy think Thou upon me, O Lord, for Thy goodness.

7 Gracious and righteous is the Lord : therefore will He teach sinners in the way.

8 Them that are meek shall He guide in judgment : and such as are gentle, them shall He learn His way.

9 All the paths of the Lord are mercy and truth : unto such as keep His covenant, and His testimonies.

10 For Thy Name's sake, O Lord : be merciful unto my sin, for it is great.

11 What man is he, that feareth the Lord : him shall He teach in the way that He shall choose.

12 His soul shall dwell at ease : and his seed shall inherit the land.

13 The secret of the Lord is among them that fear Him : and He will shew them His covenant.

14 Mine eyes are ever looking unto the Lord : for He shall pluck my feet out of the net.

15 Turn Thee unto me, and have mercy upon me : for I am desolate, and in misery.

16 The sorrows of my heart are enlarged : O bring Thou me out of my troubles.

17 Look upon my adversity and misery : and forgive me all my sin.

18 Consider mine enemies, how many they are : and they bear a tyrannous hate against me.

19 O keep my soul, and deliver me : let me not be confounded, for I have put my trust in Thee.

20 Let perfectness and righteous dealing wait upon me : for my hope hath been in Thee.

21 Deliver Israel, O God : out of all his troubles.

Glory be, etc.

[Or Wednesday only.]

Psalm XXVI. *Judica me, Domine.*

BE Thou my Judge, O Lord, for I have walked innocently : my trust hath been also in the Lord, therefore shall I not fall.

2 Examine me, O Lord, and prove me : try out my reins and my heart.

3 For Thy loving-kindness is ever before mine eyes : and I will walk in Thy truth.

4 I have not dwelt with vain persons : neither will I have fellowship with the deceitful.

5 I have hated the congregation of the wicked : and will not sit among the ungodly.

6 I will wash my hands in innocency, O Lord : and so will I go to Thine Altar:

7 That I may show the voice of thanksgiving : and tell of all Thy wondrous works.

8 Lord, I have loved the habitation of Thy house : and the place where Thine honour dwelleth.

9 O shut not up my soul with the sinners : nor my life with the bloodthirsty;

10 In whose hands is wickedness : and their right hand is full of gifts.

11 But as for me, I will walk innocently : O deliver me, and be merciful unto me.

12 My foot standeth right : I will praise the Lord in the congregations.

[Daily.]

Psalm LIV. *Deus, in nomine.*

SAVE me, O God, for Thy Name's sake : and avenge me in Thy strength.

2 Hear my prayer, O God : and hearken unto the words of my mouth.

3 For strangers are risen up against me : and tyrants, which have not God before their eyes, seek after my soul.

4 Behold, God is my Helper : the Lord is with them that uphold my soul.

5 He shall reward evil unto mine enemies : destroy Thou them in Thy truth.

6 An offering of a free heart will I give Thee, and praise Thy Name, O Lord : because it is so comfortable.

7 For He hath delivered me out of all my trouble : and mine eye hath seen His desire upon mine enemies.

Glory be, etc.

[Or Sunday only.]

Ps. CXVIII. *Confitemini Domino.*

O GIVE thanks unto the Lord, for He is gracious : because His mercy endureth for ever.

2 Let Israel now confess, that He is gracious : and that His mercy endureth for ever.

3 Let the house of Aaron now confess : that His mercy endureth for ever.

4 Yea, let them now that fear the Lord confess : that His mercy endureth for ever.

5 I called upon the Lord in trouble : and the Lord heard me at large.

6 The Lord is on my side : I will not fear what man doeth unto me.

7 The Lord taketh my part with them that help me : therefore shall I see my desire upon my enemies.

8 It is better to trust in the Lord : than to put any confidence in man.

9 It is better to trust in the Lord : than to put any confidence in princes.

10 All nations compassed me round about : but in the name of the Lord will I destroy them.

11 They kept me in on every side, they kept me in, I say, on every side : but in the Name of the Lord will I destroy them.

12 They came about me like bees, and are extinct even as the fire among the thorns : for in the Name of the Lord I will destroy them.

13 Thou hast thrust sore at me, that I might fall : but the Lord was my help.

14 The Lord is my strength and my song : and is become my salvation.

15 The voice of joy and health is in the dwellings of the righteous : the right hand of the Lord bringeth mighty things to pass.

16 The right hand of the Lord hath the pre-eminence : the right hand of the Lord bringeth mighty things to pass.

17 I shall not die, but live : and declare the works of the Lord.

18 The Lord hath chastened and corrected me : but He hath not given me over unto death.

19 Open me the gates of righteousness : that I may go into them, and give thanks unto the Lord.

20 This is the gate of the Lord : the righteous shall enter into it.

21 I will thank Thee, for Thou hast heard me : and art become my salvation.

22 The same stone which the builders refused : is become the head-stone in the corner.

23 This the Lord's doing : and it is marvellous in our eyes.

24 This is the day which the Lord hath made : we will rejoice and be glad in it.

25 Help me now, O Lord : O Lord, send us now prosperity.

26 Blessed be He that cometh in the name of the Lord : we have wished you good luck, ye that are of the house of the Lord.

27 God is the Lord who hath showed us light : bind the sacrifice with cords, yea, even unto the horns of the altar.

28 Thou art my God, and I will thank Thee : Thou art my God, and I will praise Thee.

29 O give thanks unto the Lord, for He is gracious : and His mercy endureth for ever.

[*From Septuagesima till Easter, instead of* Psalm cxviii., Confitemini Domino, *is said* Psalm xciii., Dominus regnavit.

Psalm XCIII. *Dominus regnavit.*

THE Lord is King, and hath put on glorious apparel : the Lord hath put on His apparel, and girded Himself with strength.

2 He hath made the round world so sure : that it cannot be moved.

3 Ever since the world began hath Thy seat been prepared : Thou art from everlasting.

4 The floods are risen, O Lord, the floods have lift up their voice : the floods lift up their waves.

5 The waves of the sea are mighty, and rage horribly : but yet the Lord, Who dwelleth on high, is mightier.

6 Thy testimonies, O Lord, are very sure : holiness becometh Thine house for ever.]

[Daily.]

Psalm CXIX. *Beati immaculati.*

BLESSED are those that are undefiled in the way : and walk in the law of the Lord.

2 Blessed are they that keep His testimonies : and seek Him with their whole heart.

3 For they who do no wickedness : walk in His ways.

4 Thou hast charged : that we shall diligently keep Thy commandments.

5 O that my ways were made so direct : that I might keep Thy statutes !

6 So shall I not be confounded : while I have respect unto all Thy commandments.

7 I will thank Thee with an unfeigned heart : when I shall have learned the judgments of Thy righteousness.

8 I will keep Thy ceremonies : O forsake me not utterly.

9 Wherewithal shall a young man cleanse his way : even by ruling himself after Thy Word.

10 With my whole heart have I sought Thee : O let me not go wrong out of Thy commandments.

11 Thy words have I hid within my heart : that I should not sin against Thee.

12 Blessed art Thou, O Lord : O teach me Thy statutes.

13 With my lips have I been telling : of all the judgments of Thy mouth.

14 I have had as great delight in the way of Thy testimonies : as in all manner of riches.

15 I will talk of Thy commandments : and have respect unto Thy ways.

16 My delight shall be in Thy statutes : and I will not forget Thy Word.

Glory be, etc.

Retribue servo tuo.

O DO well unto Thy servant : that I may live, and keep Thy word.

18 Open Thou mine eyes : that I may see the wondrous things of Thy law.

19 I am a stranger upon earth : O hide not Thy commandments from me.

20 My soul breaketh out for the very fervent desire : that it hath alway unto Thy judgments.

21 Thou hast rebuked the proud : and cursed are they that do err from Thy commandments.

22 O turn from me shame and rebuke : for I have kept Thy testimonies.

23 Princes also did sit and speak against me : but Thy servant is occupied in Thy statutes.

24 For Thy testimonies are my delight : and my counsellors.

25 My soul cleaveth to the dust : O quicken Thou me, according to Thy Word.

26 I have acknowledged my ways, and Thou heardest me : O teach me Thy statutes.

27 Make me to understand the way of Thy commandments : and so shall I talk of Thy wondrous works.

28 My soul melteth away for very heaviness : comfort Thou me according unto Thy Word.

29 Take from me the way of lying : and cause Thou me to make much of Thy law.

30 I have chosen the way of truth : and Thy judgments have I laid before me.

31 I have stuck unto Thy testimonies : O Lord, confound me not.

32 I will run the way of Thy commandments : when Thou hast set my heart at liberty.

Glory be, etc.

ANTIPHONS.

On ordinary Sundays.

The Lord is my Shepherd : therefore can I lack nothing.

On ordinary Ferias.

Hear my prayer, O God : and hearken unto the words of my mouth.

On Ferias in Advent.

Come and deliver us : O our God.

CREED OF S. ATHANASIUS,

Said daily, except in Christmas and Easter tides, [but in Roman use, on Sunday only.]

ANTIPHONS.

On Sundays.

Thee, God the Father unbegotten, Thee, God the Son only-begotten, Thee, Holy Ghost, Paraclete, Holy and undivided Trinity : * with our whole heart and our lips we confess, praise and bless; to Thee be glory for ever.

In Easter tide is added, Alleluia.

On Double Feasts, except in the week following Trinity Sunday :

Thanks be to Thee, O God, thanks be to Thee, One Very Trinity : * One and Supreme Deity, and One and Holy Unity.

In Easter tide is added, Alleluia.

On all Ferias, except in the week following Trinity Sunday :

Glory to Thee, Equal Trinity, One Deity : * both before all ages, and now, and for ever.

In Easter tide is added, Alleluia.

Through the week of the Holy Trinity, whatever may be the office :

O beatific and blessed and glorious Trinity : * Father, and Son, and Holy Ghost.

Psalm. *Quicunque vult.*

WHOSOEVER will be saved : before all things it is necessary that he hold the Catholick Faith.

2 Which Faith except every one do keep whole and undefiled : without doubt he shall perish everlastingly.

3 And the Catholick Faith is this : That we worship one God in Trinity, and Trinity in Unity;

4 Neither confounding the Persons : nor dividing the Substance.

5 For there is one Person of the Father, another of the Son : and another of the Holy Ghost.

6 But the Godhead of the Father, of the Son, and of the Holy Ghost, is all one : the Glory equal, the Majesty co-eternal.

7 Such as the Father is, such is the Son : and such is the Holy Ghost.

8 The Father uncreate, the Son uncreate : and the Holy Ghost uncreate.

9 The Father incomprehensible, the Son incomprehensible : and the Holy Ghost incomprehensible.

10 The Father eternal, the Son eternal : and the Holy Ghost eternal.

11 And yet they are not three eternals : but one eternal.

12 As also there are not three incomprehensibles, nor three uncreated : but one uncreated, and one incomprehensible.

13 So likewise the Father is Almighty, the Son Almighty : and the Holy Ghost Almighty.

14 And yet they are not three Almighties : but one Almighty.

15 So the Father is God, the Son is God : and the Holy Ghost is God.

16 And yet they are not three Gods : but one God.

17 So likewise the Father is Lord, the Son Lord : and the Holy Ghost Lord.

18 And yet not three Lords : but one Lord.

19 For like as we are compelled by the Christian verity : to acknowledge every Person by Himself to be God and Lord;

20 So are we forbidden by the Catholick Religion : to say, There be three Gods, or three Lords.

21 The Father is made of none : neither created, nor begotten.

22 The Son is of the Father alone : not made, nor created, but begotten.

23 The Holy Ghost is of the Fa-

ther and of the Son : neither made, nor created, nor begotten, but proceeding.

24 So there is one Father, not three Fathers; one Son, not three Sons : one Holy Ghost, not three Holy Ghosts.

25 And in this Trinity none is afore, or after other : none is greater, or less than another.

26 But the whole three Persons are co-eternal together : and co-equal.

27 So that in all things, as is aforesaid : the Unity in Trinity, and the Trinity in Unity is to be worshipped.

28 He therefore that will be saved : must thus think of the Trinity.

29 Furthermore, it is necessary to everlasting salvation : that he also believe rightly the Incarnation of our Lord Jesus Christ.

30 For the right Faith is, that we believe and confess : that our Lord Jesus Christ, the Son of God, is God and Man.

31 God, of the Substance of the Father, begotten before the worlds : and Man, of the Substance of His Mother, born in the world;

32 Perfect God, and perfect Man : of a reasonable soul and human flesh subsisting;

33 Equal to the Father, as touching His Godhead : and inferior to the Father, as touching his Manhood.

34 Who although He be God and Man : yet He is not two, but one Christ.

35 One; not by conversion of the Godhead into flesh : but by taking of the Manhood into God;

36 One altogether; not by confusion of Substance : but by unity of Person.

37 For as the reasonable soul and flesh is one man : so God and Man is one Christ;

38 Who suffered for our salvation : descended into hell, rose again the third day from the dead.

39 He ascended into heaven, He sitteth on the right hand of the Father, God Almighty : from whence He shall come to judge the quick and the dead.

40 At whose coming all men shall rise again with their bodies : and shall give account for their own works.

41 And they that have done good shall go into life everlasting : and they that have done evil into everlasting fire.

42 This is the Catholick Faith : which except a man believe faithfully, he cannot be saved.

Glory be, etc.

ANTIPHONS.

Sunday.

Thee, God the Father unbegotten, Thee, God the Son only begotten, Thee, Holy Ghost, Paraclete, Holy and undivided Trinity : with our whole heart and our lips we confess, praise, and bless; to Thee be glory for ever.

In Easter tide is added, Alleluia.

Festal.

Thanks be to Thee, O God, thanks be to Thee, One Very Trinity : One and Supreme Deity, and One and Holy Trinity.

In Easter tide is added, Alleluia.

Ferial.

Glory to Thee, Equal Trinity, One Deity : both before all ages, and now, and for ever.

Trinity Week.

O beatific and blessed and glorious Trinity : Father, and Son, and Holy Ghost.

Chapter.

On Sundays and Doubles :

1 Tim. 1.

NOW unto the King Eternal, Immortal, Invisible, the only wise God, be honour and glory for ever and ever. Amen.

On Ferias in Christmas and Easter tides :

Is. xxxiii.

O LORD, be gracious unto us, we have waited for Thee : be Thou their arm every morning, our salvation also in the time of trouble.

On Ferias through the year :

Zech. viii.

LOVE the truth and peace, saith the Lord of hosts.

Responsory, used daily, except when otherwise marked in the Proper of Saints.

℟. Jesu Christ, Son of the living God, have mercy upon us. ℣. Thou that sittest at the right hand of the Father. ℟. Have mercy upon us. ℣. Glory be to the Father, and to the Son, and to the Holy Ghost. ℟. Jesu Christ, Son of the living God, have mercy upon us.
℣. O Lord, arise, help us.
℟. And deliver us for Thy Name's sake.

Petitions.

Said daily, except as hereafter noted.

Lord, have mercy.
Christ, have mercy.
Lord, have mercy.

Our Father :

Said silently to the end. The Priest repeats aloud :

℣. And lead us not into temptation.
℟. But deliver us from evil.

℣. O let my soul live, and it shall praise Thee.
℟. And Thy judgments shall help me.
℣. I have gone astray like a sheep that is lost.
℟. O seek Thy servant, for I do not forget Thy commandments.

I believe :

Said silently to the end. The Priest repeats aloud :

℣. The resurrection of the body.
℟. And the life everlasting.
℣. O let my mouth be filled with Thy praise.
℟. That I may sing of Thy glory and honour all the day long.
℣. Turn Thy face from my sins.
℟. And put out all my misdeeds.
℣. Make me a clean heart, O God.
℟. And renew a right spirit within me.
℣. Cast me not away from Thy presence.
℟. And take not Thy Holy Spirit from me.
℣. O give me the comfort of Thy help again.
℟. And stablish me with Thy free Spirit.
℣. Deliver me, O Lord, from the evil man.
℟. And preserve me from the wicked man.
℣. Deliver me from mine enemies, O God.
℟. Defend me from them that rise up against me.
℣. Deliver me from the wicked doers.
℟. And save me from the blood-thirsty men.
℣. So will I alway sing praise unto Thy Name.
℟. That I may daily perform my vows.
℣. Hear us, O God of our salvation.

℟. Thou that art the hope of all the ends of the earth, and of them that remain in the broad sea.

℣. O God, make speed to save. us.

℟. O Lord, make haste to help us.

℣. Holy God, Holy and Mighty, Holy and Immortal.

℟. O Lamb of God, that takest away the sins of the world, have mercy upon us.

℣. Praise the Lord, O my soul.

℟. And forget not all his benefits.

℣. Who forgiveth all thy sin.

℟. And healeth all thine infirmities.

℣. Who saveth thy life from destruction.

℟. And crowneth thee with mercy and loving-kindness.

℣. Who satisfieth thy mouth with good things.

℟. Making thee young and lusty as an eagle.

Confession and Absolution, said in a low voice.

[The Priest, if present:

I CONFESS to God Almighty, the Father, the Son, and the Holy Ghost, in the sight of the whole company of heaven, and to you, my *brethren*, that I have sinned exceedingly in thought, word, and deed, of my fault, of my own fault, of my own grievous fault; therefore I pray God to have mercy upon me, and you, my *brethren*, to pray for me.

The Choir replies:

ALMIGHTY God have mercy upon thee, forgive thee thy sins, and bring thee to everlasting life. ℟. Amen.]

The Choir.

I CONFESS to God Almighty, the Father, the Son, and the Holy Ghost, in the sight of the whole company of heaven, [and to thee, father,] that I have sinned exceedingly in thought, word, and deed, of my fault, of my own fault, of my own grievous fault; therefore I pray God to have mercy upon me, [and thee, father, to pray for me.]

[The Priest, if present:

ALMIGHTY God have mercy upon you, forgive you your sins, and bring you to everlasting life. ℟. Amen.

THE Almighty and merciful Lord grant you absolution and forgiveness of your sins, time for repentance, amendment of life, and the grace and comfort of His Holy Spirit. ℟. Amen.]

After the Confession, if there is no Priest present, the Choir says:

ALMIGHTY God have mercy upon us, forgive us our sins, and bring us to everlasting life. Amen.

℣. Wilt Thou not turn again and quicken us, O Lord?

℟. That Thy people may rejoice in Thee?

℣. Shew us Thy mercy, O Lord.

℟. And grant us Thy salvation.

℣. Vouchsafe, O Lord.

℟. To keep us this day without sin.

℣. O Lord, have mercy upon us.

℟. Have mercy upon us.

℣. O Lord, let Thy mercy lighten upon us.

℟. As our trust is in Thee.

The foregoing Petitions are said daily through the year, (except from Maundy Thursday till Low Sunday, and on All Souls' Day), then follows:

[ON SUNDAYS AND FESTIVALS:

℣. Turn us again, O Lord God of Hosts.

℟. Shew the light of Thy countenance, and we shall be whole.

℣. Hear my prayer, O Lord.

℟. And let my crying come unto Thee.

℣. The Lord be with you.

℟. And with thy spirit.

Let us pray.

COLLECT (Sunday).

O LORD, our Heavenly Father, Almighty and Everlasting God, Who hast safely brought us to the beginning of this day; defend us in the same with Thy mighty power; and grant that this day we fall into no sin, neither run into any kind of danger; but that all our doings may be ordered by Thy governance, to do always that is righteous in Thy sight; through Jesus Christ our Lord. Amen.

COLLECT (Festival).

IN this hour of this day, fill us, O Lord, with Thy mercy; that going forth in Thy strength, we may make our boast of Thee all the day long; through Jesus Christ our Lord. Amen.

℣. The Lord be with you.

℟. And with thy spirit.

℣. Bless we the Lord.

℟. Thanks be to God.]

ON FERIAS

Through the year, except in Christmas and Easter tides :

℣. Lord, hear my voice when I cry unto Thee.

℟. Have mercy upon me, and hear me.

Ps. li. *Miserere mei, Deus*, p. 1.

[*Here follows in Lent :*

Psalm XXXII. *Beati, quorum.*

BLESSED is he whose unrighteousness is forgiven : and whose sin is covered.

2 Blessed is the man unto whom the Lord imputeth no sin : and in whose spirit there is no guile.

3 For while I held my tongue : my bones consumed away through my daily complaining.

4 For Thy hand is heavy upon me day and night : and my moisture is like the drought in summer.

5 I will acknowledge my sin unto Thee : and mine unrighteousness have I not hid.

6 I said, I will confess my sins unto the Lord : and so Thou forgavest the wickedness of my sin.

7 For this shall every one that is godly make his prayer unto Thee, in a time when Thou mayest be found : but in the great water-floods they shall not come nigh him.

8 Thou art a place to hide me in, Thou shalt preserve me from trouble : Thou shalt compass me about with songs of deliverance.

9 I will inform thee, and teach thee in the way wherein thou shalt go : and I will guide thee with Mine eye.

10 Be ye not like to horse and mule, which have no understanding : whose mouths must be held with bit and bridle, lest they fall upon thee.

11 Great plagues remain for the ungodly : but whoso putteth his trust in the Lord, mercy embraceth him on every side.

12 Be glad, O ye righteous, and rejoice in the Lord : and be joyful all ye that are true of heart.

Glory be, etc.]

[*Here the reader, if a Priest, rising, stands at the step of the Sanctuary.*]

℣. O Lord, arise, help us.

℟. And deliver us for Thy Name's sake.

℣. Turn Thee again, O Lord God of hosts.

℟. Shew the light of Thy countenance, and we shall be whole.

℣. Hear my prayer, O Lord.

℟. And let my crying come unto Thee.

℣. The Lord be with you.

℟. And with thy spirit.

Let us pray.

O LORD, our heavenly Father, Almighty and everlasting God, Who hast safely brought us to the beginning of this day : defend us in the same with Thy mighty power; and grant that this day we fall into no sin, neither run into any kind of danger; but that all our doings may be ordered by Thy governance, to do always that is righteous in Thy sight; through Jesus Christ our Lord. Amen.

℣. The Lord be with you.
℟. And with thy spirit.
℣. Bless we the Lord.
℟. Thanks be to God.

OFFICE OF CHAPTER.

If the Martyrology is used, here is read the portion for the day, the reader ending with,

℣. But Thou, O Lord, have mercy upon us.
℟. Thanks be to God.
℣. Right dear in the sight of the Lord;
℟. Is the death of His Saints.
Benediction. The Lord Almighty bless us with His grace.
℟. Amen.
℣. O God, make speed to save us.
℟. O Lord, make haste to help us.
℣. Glory be to the Father, and to the Son, and to the Holy Ghost.
℟. As it was in the beginning, is now, and ever shall be : world without end. Amen.

Lord, have mercy.
Christ, have mercy.
Lord, have mercy.

Our Father:

Said silently to the end. The Priest repeats aloud :

℣. And lead us not into temptation.
℟. But deliver us from evil.
℣. Let Thy loving mercy come also unto me, O Lord.
℟. Even Thy salvation, according unto Thy word.
℣. Shew Thy servants Thy work.
℟. And their children Thy glory.
℣. And the glorious Majesty :
℟. Of the Lord our God be upon us.
℣. Prosper Thou the work of our hands upon us.
℟. O prosper Thou our handywork.

[*On Double Feasts :*

Let us pray.

ALMIGHTY and everlasting God, direct our actions according to Thy good pleasure ; that through the name of Thy beloved Son we may be found worthy to abound in good works : Who liveth and reigneth with Thee in the unity of the Holy Ghost, ever one God, world without end. Amen.

℣. The Lord be with you.
℟. And with thy spirit.
℣. Bless we the Lord.
℟. Thanks be to God.]

On ordinary Sundays and Ferias :

Let us pray.

O ALMIGHTY Lord and everlasting God, vouchsafe, we beseech Thee, to direct, sanctify, and govern both our hearts and bodies, in the ways of Thy laws, and the works of Thy commandments ; that through Thy most mighty protection, both here and ever, we may be governed and preserved in body and soul ; through Jesus Christ our Lord. Amen.

℣. The Lord be with you.
℟. And with thy spirit.
℣. Bless we the Lord.
℟. Thanks be to God.

Then, after reading the list of persons to be prayed for, is said what follows daily throughout the year, except on Double Feasts, and in Christmas and Easter tides.

Psalm CXXI. *Levavi oculos.*

I WILL lift up mine eyes unto the hills : from whence cometh my help.

2 My help cometh even from the Lord : Who hath made heaven and earth.

3 He will not suffer thy foot to be moved : and He that keepeth thee will not sleep.

4 Behold, He that keepeth Israel : shall neither slumber nor sleep.

5 The Lord Himself is thy keeper : the Lord is thy defence upon thy right hand.

6 So that the sun shall not burn thee by day : neither the moon by night.

7 The Lord shall preserve thee from all evil : yea, it is even He that shall keep thy soul.

8 The Lord shall preserve thy going out, and thy coming in : from this time forth for evermore.

Glory be, etc.

Lord, have mercy.
Christ, have mercy.
Lord, have mercy.

Our Father :

Said silently to the end. The Priest repeats aloud :

℣. And lead us not into temptation.

℟. But deliver us from evil.

℣. O Lord, shew Thy mercy upon us.

℟. And grant us Thy salvation.

℣. O God, save Thy servants and handmaidens.

℟. Which put their trust in Thee.

℣. Send them help from Thy sanctuary.

℟. And strengthen them out of Sion.

℣. Be unto them, O Lord, a tower of strength.

℟. From the face of the enemy.

℣. Let the enemy have no advantage over them.

℟. Neither the son of wickedness approach to hurt them.

℣. Hear my prayer, O Lord.

℟. And let my crying come unto Thee.

℣. The Lord be with you.

℟. And with thy spirit.

Let us pray.

ASSIST us mercifully, O Lord, in these our supplications and prayers, and dispose the way of Thy servants towards the attainment of everlasting salvation ; that, among all the changes and chances of this mortal life, they may ever be defended by Thy most gracious and ready help; through Jesus Christ our Lord. Amen.

ALMIGHTY and everlasting God, the eternal salvation of them that believe, hear us in behalf of Thy servants for whom we entreat the help of Thy compassion : that, their health being restored to them, they may return to Thee the offering of thanks in Thy Church; through Jesus Christ our Lord. Amen.

℣. Pray for a blessing.
℟. The Lord bless us.

Each person signing himself, [and the Priest, if present, making the sign of the Cross over those present,]

✠ ℣. In the Name of the Father, and, of the Son, and of the Holy Ghost.
℟. Amen.

———

Tierce.

✠ ℣. O God, make speed to save us.

℟. O Lord, make haste to help us.

℣. Glory be to the Father, and to the Son : and to the Holy Ghost.

℟. As it was in the beginning, is now, and ever shall be : world without end. Amen.

Alleluia.

[From Septuagesima to Wednesday in Holy Week,

Praise be to Thee, O Lord, King of eternal glory.]

HYMN. *Nunc Sancte nobis Spiritus.*

COME, Holy Ghost, with God the Son,
And God the Father, ever One;
Shed forth Thy grace within our breast,
And dwell with us, a ready guest.

By every pow'r, by heart and tongue,
By act and deed, Thy praise be sung;
Inflame with perfect love each sense,
That others' souls may kindle thence.

O Father, that we ask be done,
Through Jesus Christ, Thine only Son,
Who, with the Holy Ghost, and Thee,
Shall live and reign eternally. Amen.

Ant. SUNDAY. Praise and ever-lasting glory.

Ant. FERIAL. O let Thy loving mercies.

Psalm CXIX. *Legem pone.*

TEACH me, O Lord, the way of Thy statutes : and I shall keep it unto the end.

34 Give me understanding, and I shall keep Thy law : yea, I shall keep it with my whole heart.

35 Make me to go in the path of Thy commandments : for therein is my desire.

36 Incline my heart unto Thy testimonies : and not to covetousness.

37 O turn away mine eyes, lest they behold vanity : and quicken Thou me in Thy way.

38 O stablish Thy word in Thy servant : that I may fear Thee.

39 Take away the rebuke that I am afraid of : for Thy judgments are good.

40 Behold, my delight is in Thy commandments : O quicken me in Thy righteousness.

41 Let Thy loving mercy come also unto me, O Lord : even Thy salvation, according unto Thy word.

42 So shall I make answer unto my blasphemers : for my trust is in Thy word.

43 O take not the word of Thy truth utterly out of my mouth : for my hope is in Thy judgments.

44 So shall I alway keep Thy law : yea, for ever and ever.

45 And I will walk at liberty : for I seek Thy commandments.

46 I will speak of Thy testimonies also, even before kings : and will not be ashamed.

47 And my delight shall be in Thy commandments : which I have loved.

48 My hands also will I lift up unto Thy commandments, which I have loved : and my study shall be in Thy statutes.

Glory be, etc.

Memor esto servi tui.

O THINK upon Thy servant, as concerning Thy word : wherein Thou hast caused me to put my trust.

50 The same is my comfort in my trouble : for Thy word hath quickened me.

51 The proud have had me exceedingly in derision : yet have I not shrinked from Thy law.

52 For I remembered Thine everlasting judgments, O Lord : and received comfort.

53 I am horribly afraid : for the ungodly that forsake Thy law.

54 Thy statutes have been my songs : in the house of my pilgrimage.

55 I have thought upon Thy Name, O Lord, in the night-season : and have kept Thy law.

56 This I had : because I kept Thy commandments.

57 Thou art my portion, O Lord : I have promised to keep Thy law.

58 I made my humble petition in Thy presence with my whole heart : O be merciful unto me, according to Thy word.

59 I called mine own ways to remembrance : and turned my feet unto Thy testimonies.

60 I made haste, and prolonged not the time : to keep Thy commandments.

61 The congregations of the ungodly have robbed me : but I have not forgotten Thy law.

62 At midnight I will rise to give thanks unto Thee : because of Thy righteous judgements.

63 I am a companion of all them that fear Thee : and keep Thy commandments.

64 The earth, O Lord, is full of Thy mercy : O teach me Thy statutes.
Glory be, etc.

Bonitatem fecisti.

O Lord, Thou hast dealt graciously with Thy servant : according unto Thy word.

66 O learn me true understanding and knowledge : for I have believed Thy commandments.

67 Before I was troubled, I went wrong : but now have I kept Thy word.

68 Thou art good and gracious : O teach me Thy statutes.

69 The proud have imagined a lie against me : but I will keep Thy commandments with my whole heart.

70 Their heart is as fat as brawn : but my delight hath been in Thy law.

71 It is good for me that I have been in trouble : that I may learn Thy statutes.

72 The law of Thy mouth is dearer unto me : than thousands of gold and silver.

73 Thy hands have made me and fashioned me : O give me understanding, that I may learn Thy commandments.

74 They that fear Thee will be glad when they see me : because I have put my trust in Thy word.

75 I know, O Lord, that Thy judgments are right : and that Thou of very faithfulness hast caused me to be troubled.

76 O let Thy merciful kindness be my comfort : according to Thy word unto Thy servant.

77 O let Thy loving mercies come unto me, that I may live : for Thy law is my delight.

78 Let the proud be confounded, for they go wickedly about to destroy me : but I will be occupied in Thy commandments.

79 Let such as fear Thee, and have known Thy testimonies : be turned unto me.

80 O let my heart be sound in Thy statutes : that I be not ashamed.
Glory be, etc.

[*Sunday :*

Ant. Praise and everlasting glory be to God the Father, and the Son : with the Holy Paraclete, to ages of ages.

CHAPTER.　II Cor. xiii.

THE grace of the Lord Jesus Christ, and the love of God, and the communion of the Holy Ghost, be with us all. Amen.

R℣. Incline my heart unto Thy testimonies, and not to covetousness. ℣. Turn away mine eyes, lest they behold vanity, and quicken Thou me in Thy way. R℣. And not to covetousness. ℣. Glory be to the Father, and to the Son : and to the Holy Ghost. R℣. Incline my heart unto Thy testimonies, and not to covetousness.

℣. I said, Lord, be merciful unto me.

R℣. Heal my soul, for I have sinned against Thee.

℣. The Lord be with you.
R℣. And with thy spirit.

Collect of the day.

℣. The Lord be with you.
R℣. And with thy spirit.
℣. Bless we the Lord.
R℣. Thanks be to God.]

Ferial:

Ant. O let Thy loving mercies come unto me : that I may live.

CHAPTER. Jer. xvii.

HEAL me, O Lord, and I shall be healed ; save me, and I shall be saved ; for Thou art my praise.

R⁊. Heal my soul, for I have sinned against Thee. ℣. I said, Lord, be merciful unto me. R⁊. For I have sinned against Thee. ℣. Glory be to the Father, and to the Son : and to the Holy Ghost. R⁊. Heal my soul, for I have sinned against Thee.

℣. Thou hast been my succour.

R⁊. Leave me not, neither forsake me, O God of my salvation.

Petitions as at Monday Lauds, p. 10.

[*In Lent, after* Ps. LI., *Miserere, is said,*

Ps. XXXVIII. *Domine, ne in furore.*

PUT me not to rebuke, O Lord, in Thine anger : neither chasten me in Thy heavy displeasure.

2 For Thine arrows stick fast in me : and Thy hand presseth me sore.

3 There is no health in my flesh, because of Thy displeasure : neither is there any rest in my bones, by reason of my sin.

4 For my wickednesses are gone over my head : and are like a sore burthen, too heavy for me to bear.

5 My wounds stink, and are corrupt : through my foolishness.

6 I am brought into so great trouble and misery : that I go mourning all the day long.

7 For my loins are filled with a sore disease : and there is no whole part in my body.

8 I am feeble, and sore smitten : I have roared for the very disquietness of my heart.

9 Lord, Thou knowest all my desire : and my groaning is not hid from Thee.

10 My heart panteth, my strength hath failed me : and the sight of mine eyes is gone from me.

11 My lovers and my neighbours did stand looking upon my trouble : and my kinsmen stood afar off.

12 They also that sought after my life laid snares for me : and they that went about to do me evil talked of wickedness, and imagined deceit all the day long.

13 As for me, I was like a deaf man, and heard not : and as one that is dumb, who doth not open his mouth.

14 I became even as a man that heareth not : and in whose mouth are no reproofs.

15 For in Thee, O Lord, have I put my trust : Thou shalt answer for me, O Lord my God.

16 I have required that they, even mine enemies, should not triumph over me : for when my foot slipped, they rejoiced greatly against me.

17 And I, truly, am set in the plague : and my heaviness is ever in my sight.

18 For I will confess my wickedness : and be sorry for my sin.

19 But mine enemies live, and are mighty : and they that hate me wrongfully are many in number.

20 They also that reward evil for good are against me : because I follow the thing that good is.

21 Forsake me not, O Lord my God : be not Thou far from me.

22 Haste Thee to help me : O Lord God of my salvation.

Glory be, etc.]

————

Sexts.

✠ ℣. O God, make speed to save us.

R⁊. O Lord, make haste to help us.

℣. Glory be to the Father, and to the Son, and to the Holy Ghost.

R⁊. As it was in the beginning, is now, and ever shall be, world without end. Amen.

Alleluia.

[*From Septuagesima to Wednesday in Holy Week,*

Praise be to Thee, O Lord, King of eternal glory.]

HYMN. *Rector potens, verax Deus.*

O GOD of truth, O Lord of might,
  Who ord'rest time and change aright,
And send'st the early morning ray,
And light'st the glow of perfect day :

Extinguish Thou each sinful fire,
And banish every ill desire ;
And while Thou keep'st the body whole,
Shed forth Thy peace upon the soul.

O Father, that we ask be done,
Through Jesus Christ, Thine only Son ;
Who, with the Holy Ghost and Thee,
Shall live and reign eternally. Amen.

Ant. SUNDAY. Let the glory of praise.

Ant. FERIAL. Let me not.

| Psalm CXIX. *Defecit anima mea.* | *Quomodo dilexi!* |

MY soul hath longed for Thy salvation : and I have a good hope because of Thy word.

82 Mine eyes long sore for Thy word : saying, O when wilt Thou comfort me?

83 For I am become like a bottle in the smoke : yet do I not forget Thy statutes.

84 How many are the days of Thy servant : when wilt Thou be avenged of them that persecute me?

85 The proud have digged pits for me : which are not after Thy law.

86 All Thy commandments are true : they persecute me falsely; O be Thou my help.

87 They had almost made an end of me upon earth : but I forsook not Thy commandments.

88 O quicken me after Thy loving-kindness : and so shall I keep the testimonies of Thy mouth.

89 O Lord, Thy word : endureth for ever in heaven.

90 Thy truth also remaineth from one generation to another : Thou hast laid the foundation of the earth, and it abideth.

91 They continue this day according to Thine ordinance : for all things serve Thee.

92 If my delight had not been in Thy law : I should have perished in my trouble.

93 I will never forget Thy commandments : for with them Thou hast quickened me.

94 I am Thine, O save me : for I have sought Thy commandments.

95 The ungodly laid wait for me to destroy me : but I will consider Thy testimonies.

96 I see that all things come to an end : but Thy commandment is exceeding broad.

Glory be, etc.

LORD, what love have I unto Thy law : all the day long is my study in it.

98 Thou through Thy commandments hast made me wiser than mine enemies : for they are ever with me.

99 I have more understanding than my teachers : for Thy testimonies are my study.

100 I am wiser than the aged : because I keep Thy commandments.

101 I have refrained my feet from every evil way : that I may keep Thy word.

102 I have not shrunk from Thy judgments : for Thou teachest me.

103 O how sweet are Thy words unto my throat : yea, sweeter than honey unto my mouth.

104 Through Thy commandments I get understanding : therefore I hate all evil ways.

105 Thy word is a lantern unto my feet : and a light unto my paths.

106 I have sworn, and am stedfastly purposed : to keep Thy righteous judgments.

107 I am troubled above measure : quicken me, O Lord, according to Thy word.

108 Let the free-will offerings of my mouth please Thee, O Lord : and teach me Thy judgments.

109 My soul is alway in my hand : yet do I not forget Thy law.

110 The ungodly have laid a snare for me : but yet I swerved not from Thy commandments.

111 Thy testimonies have I claimed as my heritage for ever : and why? they are the very joy of my heart.

112 I have applied my heart to fulfil Thy statutes alway : even unto the end.

Glory be, etc.

Iniquos odio habui.

I HATE them that imagine evil things : but Thy law do I love.

114 Thou art my defence and shield : and my trust is in Thy word.

115 Away from me, ye wicked : I will keep the commandments of my God.

116 O stablish me according to Thy word, that I may live : and let me not be disappointed of my hope.

117 Hold Thou me up, and I shall be safe : yea, my delight shall be ever in Thy statutes.

118 Thou hast trodden down all them that depart from Thy statutes : for they imagine but deceit.

119 Thou puttest away all the ungodly of the earth like dross : therefore I love Thy testimonies.

120 My flesh trembleth for fear of Thee : and I am afraid of Thy judgments.

121 I deal with the thing that is lawful and right : O give me not over unto mine oppressors.

122 Make Thou Thy servant to delight in that which is good : that the proud do me no wrong.

123 Mine eyes are wasted away with looking for Thy health : and for the word of Thy righteousness.

124 O deal with Thy servant according unto Thy loving mercy : and teach me Thy statutes.

125 I am Thy servant, O grant me understanding : that I may know Thy testimonies.

126 It is time for Thee, Lord, to lay to Thine hand : for they have destroyed Thy law.

127 For I love Thy commandments : above gold and precious stone.

128 Therefore hold I straight all Thy commandments : and all false ways I utterly abhor.

Glory be, etc.

[*Sunday :*

Ant. Let the glory of praise resound from the lips of all to the Father, and the only-begotten Son : to the Holy Spirit let like praise be paid for ever.

CHAPTER. 1 St. John v.

THERE are Three that bear record in heaven, the Father, the Word, and the Holy Ghost : and these Three are One.

R7. O Lord, Thy word endureth for ever in heaven. V. Thy truth also remaineth from one generation to another. R7. For ever in heaven. V. Glory be to the Father, and to the Son : and to the Holy Ghost. R7. O Lord, Thy word endureth for ever in heaven.

V. The Lord is my Shepherd, therefore can I lack nothing.

R7. He shall feed me in a green pasture.

V. The Lord be with you.

R7. And with thy spirit.

Collect of the day.

V. The Lord be with you.

R7. And with thy spirit.

V. Bless we the Lord.

R7. Thanks be to God.]

Ferial :

Ant. Let me not : be disappointed of my hope.

CHAPTER. 1 Thess. v.

PROVE all things ; hold fast that which is good. Abstain from all appearance of evil.

R7. I will alway give thanks unto the Lord. V. His praise shall ever be in my mouth. R7. I will alway give thanks. V. Glory be to the Father, and to the Son : and to the Holy Ghost. R7. I will alway give thanks unto the Lord.

V. The Lord is my Shepherd, therefore shall I lack nothing.

℟. He shall feed me in a green pasture.

Petitions as at Monday Lauds, p. 10.

[*In Lent, instead of* Psalm LI., Miserere, *is said,*

Psalm LXVII. *Deus misereatur.*

GOD be merciful unto us, and bless us : and shew us the light of His countenance, and be merciful unto us ;

2 That Thy way may be known upon earth : Thy saving health among all nations.

3 Let the people praise Thee, O God : yea, let all the people praise Thee.

4 O let the nations rejoice and be glad : for Thou shalt judge the folk righteously, and govern the nations upon earth.

5 Let the people praise Thee, O God : let all the people praise Thee.

6 Then shall the earth bring forth her increase : and God, even our own God, shall give us His blessing.

7 God shall bless us : and all the ends of the world shall fear Him.

Glory be, etc.]

Nones.

✠ ℣. O God, make speed to save us.

℟. O Lord, make haste to help us.

℣. Glory be to the Father, and to the Son : and to the Holy Ghost.

℟. As it was in the beginning, is now, and ever shall be : world without end.   Amen.

Alleluia.

[*From Septuagesima to Wednesday in Holy Week,*

Praise be to Thee, O Lord, King of eternal glory.]

HYMN. *Rerum Deus tenax vigor.*

O GOD, creation's secret force,
Thyself unmov'd, all motion's source,
Who from the morn till evening's ray,
Through all its changes guid'st the day :

Grant us, when this short life is past,
The glorious evening that shall last :
That by a holy death attain'd,
Eternal glory may be gain'd.

O Father, that we ask be done,
Through Jesus Christ, Thine only Son ;
Who, with the Holy Ghost and Thee,
Shall live and reign eternally.   Amen.

Ant. SUNDAY. Of Whom and through Whom.

Ant. FERIAL. Give me understanding.

Psalm CXIX. *Mirabilia.*

THY testimonies are wonderful : therefore doth my soul keep them.

130 When Thy word goeth forth : it giveth light and understanding unto the simple.

131 I opened my mouth, and drew in my breath : for my delight was in Thy commandments.

132 O look Thou upon me, and be merciful unto me : as Thou usest to do unto those that love Thy Name.

133 Order my steps in Thy word : and so shall no wickedness have dominion over me.

134 O deliver me from the wrongful dealings of men : and so shall I keep Thy commandments.

135 Shew the light of Thy countenance upon Thy servant : and teach me Thy statutes.

136 Mine eyes gush out with water : because men keep not Thy law.

137 Righteous art Thou, O Lord : and true is Thy judgment.

138 The testimonies that Thou hast commanded : are exceeding righteous and true.

139 My zeal hath even consumed me : because mine enemies have forgotten Thy words.

140 Thy word is tried to the uttermost : and Thy servant loveth it.

141 I am small, and of no reputation : yet do I not forget Thy commandments.

142 Thy righteousness is an everlasting righteousness : and Thy law is the truth.

143 Trouble and heaviness have taken hold upon me : yet is my delight in Thy commandments.

144 The righteousness of Thy testimonies is everlasting : O grant me understanding, and I shall live.

Glory be, etc.

Clamavi in toto corde meo.

I CALL with my whole heart : hear me, O Lord, I will keep Thy statutes.

146 Yea, even unto Thee do I call : help me, and I shall keep Thy testimonies.

147 Early in the morning do I cry unto Thee : for in Thy word is my trust.

148 Mine eyes prevent the night-watches : that I might be occupied in Thy words.

149 Hear my voice, O Lord, according unto Thy loving-kindness : quicken me, according as Thou art wont.

150 They draw nigh that of malice persecute me : and are far from Thy law.

151 Be Thou nigh at hand, O Lord : for all Thy commandments are true.

152 As concerning Thy testimonies, I have known long since : that Thou hast grounded them for ever.

153 O consider mine adversity, and deliver me : for I do not forget Thy law.

154 Avenge Thou my cause, and deliver me : quicken me, according to Thy word.

155 Health is far from the ungodly : for they regard not Thy statutes.

156 Great is Thy mercy, O Lord : quicken me, as Thou art wont.

157 Many there are that trouble me, and persecute me : yet do I not swerve from Thy testimonies.

158 It grieveth me when I see the transgressors : because they keep not Thy law.

159 Consider, O Lord, how I love Thy commandments : O quicken me, according to Thy loving-kindness.

160 Thy word is true from everlasting : all the judgments of Thy righteousness endure for evermore.

Glory be, etc.

Principes persecuti sunt.

PRINCES have persecuted me without a cause : but my heart standeth in awe of Thy word.

162 I am as glad of Thy word : as one that findeth great spoils.

163 As for lies, I hate and abhor them : but Thy law do I love.

164 Seven times a day do I praise Thee : because of Thy righteous judgments.

165 Great is the peace that they have who love Thy law : and they are not offended at it.

166 Lord, I have looked for Thy saving health : and done after Thy commandments.

167 My soul hath kept Thy testimonies : and loved them exceedingly.

168 I have kept Thy commandments and testimonies : for all my ways are before Thee.

169 Let my complaint come before Thee, O Lord : give me understanding, according to Thy word.

170 Let my supplication come before Thee : deliver me, according to Thy word.

171 My lips shall speak of Thy praise : when Thou hast taught me Thy statutes.

172 Yea, my tongue shall sing of Thy word : for all Thy commandments are righteous.

173 Let Thine hand help me : for I have chosen Thy commandments.

174 I have longed for Thy saving health, O Lord : and in Thy law is my delight.

175 O let my soul live, and it shall praise Thee : and Thy judgments shall help me.

176 I have gone astray like a sheep that is lost : O seek Thy servant, for I do not forget Thy commandments.

Glory be, etc.

[Sunday.

Ant. Of Whom, and through Whom, and to Whom, are all things : to Him be glory for ever.

CHAPTER. Eph. iv.

ONE Lord, one faith, one baptism, one God and Father of all, Who is above all, and through all, and in you all, Who is blessed for ever.

R̷. I call with my whole heart : hear me, O Lord. V̷. I will keep Thy statutes. R̷. Hear me, O Lord. V̷. Glory be to the Father, and to the Son : and to the Holy Ghost. R̷. I call with my whole heart : hear me, O Lord.

V̷. O cleanse Thou me from my secret faults.

R̷. Keep Thy servant also from presumptuous sins.

V̷. The Lord be with you.

R̷. And with thy spirit.

Collect of the day.

V̷. The Lord be with you.

R̷. And with thy spirit.

V̷. Bless we the Lord.

R̷. Thanks be to God.]

Ferial.

Ant. Give me understanding : according to Thy word.

CHAPTER. Gal. vi.

BEAR ye one another's burdens, and so fulfil the law of Christ.

R̷. O deliver me, and be merciful unto me. V̷. My foot standeth right : I will praise the Lord in the congregations. R̷. And be merciful unto me. V̷. Glory be to the Father, and to the Son : and to the Holy

Ghost. R̷. O deliver me, and be merciful unto me.

V̷. O cleanse Thou me from my secret faults.

R̷. Keep Thy servant also from presumptuous sins.

Petitions as at Monday Lauds, p. 10.

[In Lent, after Ps. li. *Miserere, is said,*

Psalm CII. *Domine, exaudi.*

HEAR my prayer, O Lord : and let my crying come unto Thee.

2 Hide not Thy face from me in the time of my trouble : incline Thine ear unto me when I call ; O hear me, and that right soon.

3 For my days are consumed away like smoke : and my bones are burnt up as it were a fire-brand.

4 My heart is smitten down, and withered like grass : so that I forget to eat my bread.

5 For the voice of my groaning : my bones will scarce cleave to my flesh.

6 I am become like a pelican in the wilderness : and like an owl that is in the desert.

7 I have watched, and am even as it were a sparrow : that sitteth alone upon the house-top.

8 Mine enemies revile me all the day long : and they that are mad upon me are sworn together against me.

9 For I have eaten ashes as it were bread : and mingled my drink with weeping ;

10 And that because of Thine indignation and wrath : for Thou hast taken me up, and cast me down.

11 My days are gone like a shadow : and I am withered like grass.

12 But Thou, O Lord, shalt endure for ever : and Thy remembrance throughout all generations.

13 Thou shalt arise, and have mercy upon Sion : for it is time that Thou have mercy upon her, yea, the time is come.

14 And why ? Thy servants think upon her stones : and it pitieth them to see her in the dust.

15 The heathen shall fear Thy Name, O Lord : and all the kings of the earth Thy majesty ;

16 When the Lord shall build up Sion : and when His glory shall appear ;

17 When He turneth Him unto the prayer of the poor destitute : and despiseth not their desire.

18 This shall be written for those that come after : and the people which shall be born shall praise the Lord.

19 For He hath looked down from His sanctuary : out of the heaven did the Lord behold the earth ;

20 That He might hear the mournings of such as are in captivity : and deliver the children appointed unto death ;

21 That they may declare the Name of the Lord in Sion : and His worship at Jerusalem ;

22 When the people are gathered together : and the kingdoms also, to serve the Lord.

23 He brought down my strength in my journey : and shortened my days.

24 But I said, O my God, take me not away in the midst of mine age : as for Thy years, they endure throughout all generations.

25 Thou, Lord, in the beginning hast laid the foundation of the earth : and the heavens are the work of Thy hands.

26 They shall perish, but Thou shalt endure : they all shall wax old as doth a garment;

27 And as a vesture shalt Thou change them, and they shall be changed : but Thou art the same, and Thy years shall not fail.

28 The children of Thy servants shall continue : and their seed shall stand fast in Thy sight.

Glory be, etc.]

SUNDAY.

Vespers.

℣. O God, make speed to save us.

℟. O Lord, make haste to help us.

℣. Glory be to the Father, and to the Son, and to the Holy Ghost.

℟. As it was in the beginning, is now, and ever shall be, world without end.   Amen.

Alleluia.

[*From Septuagesima till Wednesday in Holy Week,*

Praise be to Thee, O Lord, King of eternal glory.]

Ant. Sit Thou * on my right hand : said the Lord my God.

Psalm cx.   *Dixit Dominus.*

THE Lord said unto my Lord : Sit Thou on My right hand, until I make Thine enemies Thy footstool.

2 The Lord shall send the rod of Thy power out of Sion : be Thou ruler, even in the midst among Thine enemies.

3 In the day of Thy power shall the people offer Thee free-will offerings with an holy worship : the dew of Thy birth is of the womb of the morning.

4 The Lord sware, and will not repent : Thou art a Priest for ever after the order of Melchisedech.

5 The Lord upon Thy right hand : shall wound even kings in the day of His wrath.

6 He shall judge among the heathen ; He shall fill the places with the dead bodies : and smite in sunder the heads over divers countries.

7 He shall drink of the brook in the way : therefore shall He lift up His head.

Glory be, etc.

Ant. Sit Thou on My right hand : said the Lord my God.

Ant. All His commandments * are true : they stand fast for ever and ever.

Psalm cxi.   *Confitebor tibi.*

I WILL give thanks unto the Lord with my whole heart : secretly among the faithful, and in the congregation.

2 The works of the Lord are great : sought out of all them that have pleasure therein.

3 His work is worthy to be praised, and had in honour : and His righteousness endureth for ever.

4 The merciful and gracious Lord hath so done His marvellous works : that they ought be had in remembrance.

5 He hath given meat unto them that fear Him : He shall ever be mindful of His covenant.

6 He hath showed His people the power of His works : that He may give them the heritage of the heathen.

7 The works of His hands are verity and judgment : all His commandments are true.

8 They stand fast for ever and

ever : and are done in truth and equity.

9 He sent redemption unto His people : He hath commanded His covenant for ever; holy and reverend is His Name.

10 The fear of the Lord is the beginning of wisdom : a good understanding have all they that do thereafter; the praise of it endureth for ever.

Glory be, etc.

Ant. All His commandments are true : they stand fast for ever and ever.

Ant. He hath great delight * in His commandments.

Psalm CXII. *Beatus vir.*

BLESSED is the man that feareth the Lord : he hath great delight in His commandments.

2 His seed shall be mighty upon earth : the generation of the faithful shall be blessed.

3 Riches and plenteousness shall be in his house : and his righteousness endureth for ever.

4 Unto the godly there ariseth up light in the darkness : he is merciful, loving and righteous.

5 A good man is merciful, and lendeth : and will guide his words with discretion.

6 For he shall never be moved : and the righteous shall be had in everlasting remembrance.

7 He will not be afraid of any evil tidings : for his heart standeth fast, and believeth in the Lord.

8 His heart is established, and will not shrink : until he see his desire upon his enemies.

9 He hath dispersed abroad, and given to the poor : and his righteousness remaineth for ever; his horn shall be exalted with honour.

10 The ungodly shall see it, and it shall grieve him : he shall gnash with his teeth, and consume away ; the desire of the ungodly shall perish.

Glory be, etc.

Ant. He hath great delight : in His commandments.

Ant. Blessed be the Name * of the Lord : from this time forth for evermore.

Psalm CXIII. *Laudate, pueri.*

PRAISE the Lord, ye servants : O praise the Name of the Lord.

2 Blessed be the Name of the Lord : from this time forth for evermore.

3 The Lord's Name is praised : from the rising up of the sun unto the going down of the same.

4 The Lord is high above all heathen : and His glory above the heavens.

5 Who is like unto the Lord our God, that hath His dwelling so high : and yet humbleth Himself to behold the things that are in heaven and earth ?

6 He taketh up the simple out of the dust : and lifteth up the poor out of the mire ;

7 That He may set him with the princes : even with the princes of His people.

8 He maketh the barren woman to keep house : and to be a joyful mother of children.

Glory be, etc.

Ant. Blessed be the Name of the Lord : from this time forth for evermore.

Ant. But we who live * will praise the Lord.

Psalm CXIV. *In exitu Israel.*

WHEN·Israel came out of Egypt : and the house of Jacob from among the strange people.

2 Judah was his sanctuary : and Israel his dominion.

3 The sea saw that, and fled : Jordan was driven back.

4 The mountains skipped like rams : and the little hills like young sheep.

5 What aileth thee, O thou sea, that thou fleddest : and thou Jordan, that thou wast driven back?

6 Ye mountains, that ye skipped like rams : and ye little hills like young sheep?

7 Tremble, thou earth, at the presence of the Lord : at the presence of the God of Jacob;

8 Who turned the hard rock into a standing water : and the flint stone into a springing well.

Here is not said, Glory be, etc.

Psalm cxv. *Non nobis, Domine.*

NOT unto us, O Lord, not unto us, but unto Thy Name give the praise : for Thy loving mercy, and for Thy truth's sake.

2 Wherefore shall the heathen say : Where is now their God?

3 As for our God, He is in heaven : He hath done whatsoever pleased Him.

4 Their idols are silver and gold : even the work of men's hands.

5 They have mouths, and speak not : eyes have they, and see not.

6 They have ears, and hear not : noses have they, and smell not.

7 They have hands, and handle not; feet have they, and walk not : neither speak they through their throat.

8 They that make them are like unto them : and so are all such as put their trust in them.

9 But thou, house of Israel, trust thou in the Lord : He is their succour and defence.

10 Ye house of Aaron, put your trust in the Lord : He is their helper and defender.

11 Ye that fear the Lord, put your trust in the Lord : He is their helper and defender.

12 The Lord hath been mindful of us, and He shall bless us : even He shall bless the house of Israel, He shall bless the house of Aaron.

13 He shall bless them that fear the Lord : both small and great.

14 The Lord shall increase you more and more : you and your children.

15 Ye are the blessed of the Lord : Who made heaven and earth.

16 All the whole heavens are the Lord's : the earth hath He given to the children of men.

17 The dead praise not Thee, O Lord : neither all they that go down into silence.

18 But we will praise the Lord : from this time forth for evermore. Praise the Lord.

Glory be, etc.

Ant. But we who live : will praise the Lord.

Daily from Epiphany to Septuagesima, on all Ferias from Septuagesima till the first Sunday in Lent, and daily from Trinity to Advent.

CHAPTER. II Thess. iii.

THE Lord direct your hearts into the love of God, and into the patient waiting for Christ.

℟. Thanks be to God.

On Sundays from Epiphany to Lent, and daily from Trinity to Advent,

HYMN. *Lucis Creator optime.*

O BLEST Creator of the light
Who makest the day with radiance bright,
And o'er the forming world didst call
The light from chaos first of all;

Whose wisdom joined in meet array
The morn and eve, and named them day :
Night comes with all its darkling fears,
Regard Thy people's prayers and tears.

Lest, sunk in sin, and whelmed with strife,
They lose the gift of endless life;
While thinking but the thoughts of time,
They weave new chains of woe and crime.

But grant them grace that they may strain
The heavenly gate, and prize to gain ;
Each harmful lure aside to cast,
And purge away each error past.

O Father, that we ask be done,
Through Jesus Christ, Thine only Son ;
Who, with the Holy Ghost and Thee,
Shall live and reign eternally.   Amen.

℣. Lord, let my prayer be set forth.

℟. In Thy sight as the incense.

Ant. to Magnificat, in Proper of Seasons.

[*Ferial Antiphons.*

Monday. My soul doth magnify : * the Lord.

Tuesday. My spirit hath rejoiced :* in God my Saviour.

Wednesday. O Lord my God : * Thou hast regarded my lowliness.

Thursday. He hath put down * the mighty from their seat : and hath exalted the humble and meek that confess His Christ.

Friday. God hath holpen * His servant Israel, as He promised Abraham and his seed : and He hath exalted the humble for ever.

Saturday. As in Proper.]

Magnificat.

MY soul doth magnify the Lord : and my spirit hath rejoiced in God my Saviour.

2 For He hath regarded : the lowliness of His handmaiden.

3 For behold, from henceforth : all generations shall call me blessed.

4 For He that is mighty hath magnified me : and holy is His Name.

5 And His mercy is on them that fear Him : throughout all generations.

6 He hath shewed strength with His arm : He hath scattered the proud in the imagination of their hearts.

7 He hath put down the mighty from their seat : and hath exalted the humble and meek.

8 He hath filled the hungry with good things : and the rich He hath sent empty away.

9 He remembering His mercy hath holpen His servant Israel : as He promised to our forefathers, Abraham and his seed for ever.

Glory be, etc.

℣. The Lord be with you.
℟. And with thy spirit.

Let us pray.

COLLECT.

℣. The Lord be with you.
℟. And with thy spirit.
℣. Bless we the Lord.
℟. Thanks be to God.

Sunday Memorials,

which immediately follow the Collect for the day, unless the memorial of any festival intervene, in which case the ordinary memorials yield precedence.

[*For Memorials from Advent Sunday till the Octave of Epiphany, see Proper of Seasons.*]

From the Octave of Epiphany till Ash-Wednesday :

MEMORIAL OF S. MARY.

Ant. In the Bush which Moses saw unconsumed : we recognize thy glorious virginity, O Mother of God.

℣. Thou art fairer than the children of men.

℟. Full of grace are thy lips.

COLLECT.

O GOD, Who through the fruitful virginity of the blessed Virgin Mary, hast bestowed the rewards of eternal salvation on the human race ; grant, we beseech Thee, that she may intercede for us, through whom we have received the Author of Life, Jesus Christ our Lord.   Amen.

[*For Memorials from Ash-Wednesday till Whitsuntide, see Proper of Seasons.*]

From Monday after the Octave of Trinity till Advent; except on Double Feasts,

MEMORIAL OF THE HOLY CROSS.

Ant. Save us, O Christ our Saviour, by the virtue of the Holy Cross : as Thou savedst Peter in the sea; and have mercy upon us.

℣. All the world shall worship Thee, and sing of Thee.

℟. And praise Thy name.

COLLECT.

KEEP, we beseech Thee, O Lord, in perpetual peace, those whom Thou hast vouchsafed to redeem by the wood of the Holy Cross, O Saviour of the world, Who livest and reignest with the Father and the Holy Ghost, ever one God, world without end. Amen.

MEMORIAL OF S. MARY.

As after Epiphany, p. 48.

℣. The Lord be with you.
℟. And with thy spirit.
℣. Bless we the Lord.
℟. Thanks be to God.

———

MONDAY.

Vespers.

℣. O God, make speed to save us.
℟. O Lord, make haste to help us.
℣. Glory be to the Father, and to the Son : and to the Holy Ghost.
℟. As it was in the beginning, is now, and ever shall be : world without end.   Amen.

Alleluia.

[*From Septuagesima to Wednesday in Holy Week,*

Praise be to Thee, O Lord, King of eternal glory.]

Ant. The Lord hath inclined.

Psalm CXVI.   *Dilexi, quoniam.*

I AM well pleased : that the Lord hath heard the voice of my prayer.

2 That He hath inclined His ear unto me : therefore will I call upon Him as long as I live.

3 The snares of death compassed me round about : and the pains of hell gat hold upon me.

4 I shall find trouble and heaviness, and I will call upon the Name of the Lord : O Lord, I beseech Thee, deliver my soul.

5 Gracious is the Lord, and righteous : yea, our God is merciful.

6 The Lord preserveth the simple : I was in misery, and He helped me.

7 Turn again then unto thy rest, O my soul : for the Lord hath rewarded thee.

8 And why? Thou hast delivered my soul from death : mine eyes from tears, and my feet from falling.

9 I will walk before the Lord : in the land of the living.

Glory be, etc.

Ant. The Lord hath inclined : His ear unto me.

Ant. I believed.

Psalm CXVI. 10.   *Credidi.*

I BELIEVED, and therefore will I speak; but I was sore troubled : I said in my haste, All men are liars.

11 What reward shall I give unto the Lord : for all the benefits that He hath done unto me?

12 I will receive the cup of salvation : and call upon the Name of the Lord.

13 I will pay my vows now in the presence of all His people : right dear in the sight of the Lord is the death of His saints.

14 Behold, O Lord, how that I am Thy servant : I am Thy servant, and

E

the son of Thine handmaid ; Thou hast broken my bonds in sunder.

15 I will offer to Thee the sacrifice of thanksgiving : and will call upon the Name of the Lord.

16 I will pay my vows unto the Lord, in the sight of all His people : in the courts of the Lord's house, even in the midst of thee, O Jerusalem. Praise the Lord.

Glory be, etc.

Ant. I believed : and therefore will I speak.

Ant. O praise the Lord.

Psalm CXVII. *Laudate Dominum.*

O PRAISE the Lord, all ye heathen : praise Him, all ye nations.

2 For His merciful kindness is ever more and more towards us : and the truth of the Lord endureth for ever. Praise the Lord.

Glory be, etc.

Ant. O praise the Lord : all ye heathen.

Ant. I called.

Psalm CXX. *Ad Dominum.*

W HEN I was in trouble I called upon the Lord : and He heard me.

2 Deliver my soul, O Lord, from lying lips : and from a deceitful tongue.

3 What reward shall be given or done unto thee, thou false tongue : even mighty and sharp arrows, with hot burning coals.

4 Wo is me, that I am constrained to dwell with Mesech : and to have my habitation among the tents of Kedar.

5 My soul hath long dwelt among them : that are enemies unto peace.

6 I labour for peace, but when I speak unto them thereof : they make them ready to battle.

Glory be, etc.

Ant. I called : and He heard me.

Ant. My help.

Psalm CXXI. *Levavi oculos.*

I WILL lift up mine eyes unto the hills : from whence cometh my help.

2 My help cometh even from the Lord : Who hath made heaven and earth.

3 He will not suffer thy foot to be moved : and He that keepeth thee will not sleep.

4 Behold, He that keepeth Israel : shall neither slumber nor sleep.

5 The Lord Himself is thy keeper : the Lord is thy defence upon thy right hand.

6 So that the sun shall not burn thee by day : neither the moon by night.

7 The Lord shall preserve thee from all evil : yea, it is even He that shall keep thy soul.

8 The Lord shall preserve thy going out, and thy coming in : from this time forth for evermore.

Glory be, etc.

Ant. My help : cometh even from the Lord.

Daily from Epiphany to Septuagesima ; on all Ferias from Septuagesima to the First Sunday in Lent ; and daily from Trinity to Advent,

CHAPTER. II Thess. iii., p. 47.

From Trinity to Advent,

HYMN. *Lucis Creator optime,* ℣. and ℟. p. 47.

Ferial Antiphons and Magnificat, p. 48.

[*For Chapters, Hymns, and Antiphons at other times, see Proper of Seasons.*]

PETITIONS.

These are not said in Christmas or Easter tides.

Lord, have mercy.
 Christ, have mercy.
Lord, have mercy.

Our Father:

Said silently to the end. The Priest repeats aloud:

℣. And lead us not into temptation.

℟. But deliver us from evil.

℣. I said, Lord, be merciful unto me.

℟. Heal my soul, for I have sinned against Thee.

℣. Turn Thee again, O Lord, at the last.

℟. And be gracious unto Thy servants.

℣. Let Thy merciful kindness, O Lord, be upon us.

℟. As we do put our trust in Thee.

℣. Let Thy priests be clothed with righteousness.

℟. And Thy Saints sing with joyfulness.

℣. O Lord, save the Queen.

℟. And mercifully hear us when we call upon Thee.

℣. O God, save Thy servants and handmaidens.

℟. Which put their trust in Thee.

℣. O Lord, save Thy people.

℟. And bless Thine inheritance.

℣. Peace be within Thy walls.

℟. And plenteousness within Thy palaces.

℣. Let us pray for the faithful departed.

℟. Eternal rest grant unto them, O Lord, and light perpetual shine upon them.

℣. Hearken unto my voice, O Lord, when I cry unto Thee.

℟. Have mercy upon me, and hear me.

Psalm li. *Miserere mei, Deus,* p. 1.

[*Here follows in Lent :*

Psalm cxxx. *De profundis.*

OUT of the deep have I called unto Thee, O Lord : Lord, hear my voice.

2 O let Thine ears consider well : the voice of my complaint.

3 If Thou, Lord, wilt be extreme to mark what is done amiss : O Lord, who may abide it?

4 For there is mercy with Thee : therefore shalt Thou be feared.

5 I look for the Lord; my soul doth wait for Him : in His word is my trust.

6 My soul fleeth unto the Lord : before the morning watch, I say, before the morning watch.

7 O Israel, trust in the Lord, for with the Lord there is mercy : and with Him is plenteous redemption.

8 And He shall redeem Israel : from all his sins.

Glory be, etc.]

[*Here the reader, if a Priest, rising, stands at the step of the Sanctuary.*]

℣. O Lord, arise, help us.

℟. And deliver us for Thy Name's sake.

℣. Turn us again, O Lord God of Hosts.

℟. Show the light of Thy countenance, and we shall be whole.

℣. Hear my prayer, O Lord.

℟. And let my crying come unto Thee.

℣. The Lord be with you.

℟. And with thy spirit.

Let us pray.

COLLECT.

Ferial Memorials.

[*For memorials from Advent Sunday till the Octave of Epiphany, see Proper of Seasons.*]

From the Octave of Epiphany till Ash-Wednesday,

MEMORIAL OF S. MARY.

Ant. In the Bush which Moses saw unconsumed, we recognise thy glorious virginity, O Mother of God.

℣. Thou art fairer than the children of men.

℟. Full of grace are thy lips.

COLLECT.

O GOD, Who through the fruitful virginity of the Blessed Virgin Mary hast bestowed the rewards eternal salvation on the human race; grant, we pray Thee, that she may intercede for us, through whom we have received the Author of Life, thy Son Jesus Christ our Lord. Amen.

MEMORIAL OF ALL SAINTS.

Ant. O how glorious is the Kingdom where all the Saints rejoice with Christ: they are clothed with white robes, and follow the Lamb whithersoever He goeth.

℣. Be glad, O ye righteous, and rejoice in the Lord.

℟. And be joyful, all ye that are true of heart.

If this ℣. and ℟. has been said before, then in this Memorial is said instead,

℣. The Saints shall be joyful with glory.

℟. They shall rejoice in their beds.

COLLECT.

GRANT, we beseech Thee, O Lord, that all Thy Saints may always pray for us, and vouchsafe always to hear their prayers; through Jesus Christ our Lord. Amen.

[For Memorials from Ash-Wednesday till Whitsuntide, see Proper of Seasons.]

From Monday after the Octave of Trinity till Advent,

MEMORIAL OF THE HOLY CROSS.
As at Sunday Vespers, p. 48.

MEMORIAL OF S. MARY.
As at Sunday Vespers, p. 49.

MEMORIAL OF ALL SAINTS.
As after Epiphany, above.

℣. The Lord be with you.
℟. And with thy spirit.
℣. Bless we the Lord.
℟. Thanks be to God.

TUESDAY.

Vespers.

℣. O God, make speed to save us.
℟. O Lord, make haste to help us.
℣. Glory be to the Father, and to the Son : and to the Holy Ghost.
℟. As it was in the beginning, is now, and ever shall be : world without end. Amen.
Alleluia.

[From Septuagesima till Wednesday in Holy Week,

Praise be to Thee, O Lord, King of eternal glory.]*

Ant. We will go.

Psalm CXXII. *Lætatus sum.*

I WAS glad when they said unto me : We will go into the house of the Lord.

2 Our feet shall stand in thy gates : O Jerusalem.

3 Jerusalem is built as a city : that is at unity in itself.

4 For thither the tribes go up, even the tribes of the Lord : to testify unto Israel, to give thanks unto the Name of the Lord.

5 For there is the seat of judgment : even the seat of the house of David.

6 O pray for the peace of Jerusalem : they shall prosper that love thee.

7 Peace be within thy walls : and plenteousness within thy palaces.

8 For my brethren and companions' sakes : I will wish thee prosperity.

9 Yea, because of the house of the Lord our God : I will seek to do thee good.
Glory be, etc.

Ant. We will go gladly : into the house of the Lord.

Ant. O Thou that dwellest.

Ps. CXXIII. *Ad te levavi oculos meos.*

UNTO Thee lift I up mine eyes : O Thou that dwellest in the heavens.

2 Behold, even as the eyes of servants look unto the hand of their masters, and as the eyes of a maiden unto the hand of her mistress : even so our eyes wait upon the Lord our God, until He have mercy upon us.

3 Have mercy upon us, O Lord, have mercy upon us : for we are utterly despised.

4 Our soul is filled with the scornful reproof of the wealthy : and with the despitefulness of the proud.

Glory be, etc.

Ant. O Thou that dwellest in the heavens : have mercy upon us.

Ant. Our help.

Psalm CXXIV. *Nisi quia Dominus.*

IF the Lord Himself had not been on our side, now may Israel say : if the Lord Himself had not been on our side, when men rose up against us ;

2 They had swallowed us up quick : when they were so wrathfully displeased at us.

3 Yea, the waters had drowned us : and the stream had gone over our soul.

4 The deep waters of the proud : had gone even over our soul.

5 But praised be the Lord : Who hath not given us over for a prey unto their teeth.

6 Our soul is escaped even as a bird out of the snare of the fowler : the snare is broken, and we are delivered.

7 Our help standeth in the Name of the Lord : Who hath made heaven and earth.

Glory be, etc.

Ant. Our help standeth : in the Name of the Lord.

Ant. Do well.

Psalm CXXV. *Qui confidunt.*

THEY that put their trust in the Lord shall be even as the mount Sion : which may not be removed, but standeth fast for ever.

2 The hills stand about Jerusalem : even so standeth the Lord round about His people, from this time forth for evermore.

3 For the rod of the ungodly cometh not into the lot of the righteous : lest the righteous put their hand unto wickedness.

4 Do well, O Lord : unto those that are good and true of heart.

5 As for such as turn back unto their own wickedness : the Lord shall lead them forth with the evildoers ; but peace shall be upon Israel.

Glory be, etc.

Ant. Do well, O Lord : unto those that are good and true of heart.

Ant. Then were we like.

Psalm CXXVI. *In convertendo.*

WHEN the Lord turned again the captivity of Sion : then were we like unto them that dream.

2 Then was our mouth filled with laughter : and our tongue with joy.

3 Then said they among the heathen : The Lord hath done great things for them.

4 Yea, the Lord hath done great things for us already : whereof we rejoice.

5 Turn our captivity, O Lord : as the rivers in the south.

6 They that sow in tears : shall reap in joy.

7 He that now goeth on his way weeping, and beareth forth good seed : shall doubtless come again

with joy, and bring his sheaves with him.

Glory be, etc.

Ant. Then were we like : unto them that dream.

Daily from Epiphany to Septuagesima; on all Ferias from Septuagesima to the First Sunday in Lent; and daily from Trinity to Advent,

CHAPTER. II Thess. iii., p. 47.

From Trinity to Advent,

HYMN. *Lucis Creator optime,*
℣. and ℟., p. 47.

Ferial Antiphons and Magnificat,
p. 48.

[*For Chapters, Hymns, and Antiphons at other times, see Proper of Seasons.*]

PETITIONS, p. 50.

COLLECT.

FERIAL MEMORIALS, p. 51.

℣. The Lord be with you.
℟. And with thy spirit.
℣. Bless we the Lord.
℟. Thanks be to God.

———

WEDNESDAY.

Vespers.

✠ ℣. O God, make speed to save us.

℟. O Lord, make haste to help us.
℣. Glory be to the Father, and to the Son : and to the Holy Ghost.
℟. As it was in the beginning, is now, and ever shall be : world without end. Amen.
Alleluia!

[*From Septuagesima till Wednesday in Holy Week,*

Praise be to Thee, O Lord, King of eternal glory.]

Ant. Happy is the man.

Psalm CXXVII. *Nisi Dominus.*

EXCEPT the Lord build the house : their labour is but lost that build it.

2 Except the Lord keep the city : the watchman waketh but in vain.

3 It is but lost labour that ye haste to rise up early, and so late take rest, and eat the bread of carefulness : for so He giveth His beloved sleep.

4 Lo, children and the fruit of the womb : are an heritage and gift that cometh of the Lord.

5 Like as the arrows in the hand of a giant : even so are the young children.

6 Happy is the man that hath his quiver full of them : they shall not be ashamed when they speak with their enemies in the gate.

Glory be, etc.

Ant. Happy is the man : that hath his quiver full.

Ant. Blessed are all they.

Psalm CXXVIII. *Beati omnes.*

BLESSED are all they that fear the Lord : and walk in His ways.

2 For thou shalt eat the labours of thine hands : O well is thee, and happy shalt thou be.

3 Thy wife shall be as the fruitful vine : upon the walls of thine house.

4 Thy children like the olive-branches : round about thy table.

5 Lo, thus shall the man be blessed : that feareth the Lord.

6 The Lord from out of Sion shall so bless thee : that thou shalt see Jerusalem in prosperity all thy life long.

7 Yea, that thou shalt see thy children's children : and peace upon Israel.

Glory be, etc.

Ant. Blessed are all they : that fear the Lord.

Ant. We wish you good luck.

Psalm CXXIX. *Sæpe expugnaverunt.*

MANY a time have they fought against me from my youth up : may Israel now say.

2 Yea, many a time have they vexed me from my youth up : but they have not prevailed against me.

3 The plowers plowed upon my back : and made long furrows.

4 But the righteous Lord : hath hewn the snares of the ungodly in pieces.

5 Let them be confounded and turned backward : as many as have evil will at Sion.

6 Let them be even as the grass growing upon the house-tops : which withereth afore it be plucked up;

7 Whereof the mower filleth not his hand : neither he that bindeth up the sheaves his bosom.

8 So that they who go by say not so much as, The Lord prosper you : we wish you good luck in the Name of the Lord.

Glory be, etc.

Ant. We wish you good luck : in the Name of the Lord.

Ant. Out of the deep.

Psalm CXXX. *De profundis.*

OUT of the deep have I called unto Thee, O Lord : Lord, hear my voice.

2 O let Thine ears consider well : the voice of my complaint.

3 If Thou, Lord, wilt be extreme to mark what is done amiss : O Lord, who may abide it?

4 For there is mercy with Thee : therefore shalt Thou be feared.

5 I look for the Lord; my soul doth wait for Him : in His word is my trust.

6 My soul fleeth unto the Lord : before the morning watch, I say, before the morning watch.

7 O Israel, trust in the Lord, for with the Lord there is mercy : and with Him is plenteous redemption.

8 And He shall redeem Israel : from all his sins.

Glory be, etc.

Ant. Out of the deep : have I called unto Thee, O Lord.

Ant. O Israel.

Psalm CXXXI. *Domine, non est.*

LORD, I am not high-minded : I have no proud looks.

2 I do not exercise myself in great matters : which are too high for me.

3 But I refrain my soul, and keep it low, like as a child that is weaned from his mother : yea, my soul is even as a weaned child.

4 O Israel, trust in the Lord : from this time forth for evermore.

Glory be, etc.

Ant. O Israel : trust in the Lord.

Daily from Epiphany to Septuagesima ; on all Ferias from Septuagesima to the First Sunday in Lent ; and daily from Trinity to Advent,

CHAPTER. II Thess. iii., p. 47.

From Trinity to Advent,

HYMN. *Lucis Creator optime,* ℣. and ℟., p. 47.

Ferial Antiphons and Magnificat, p. 48.

[*For Chapters, Hymns, and Antiphons at other times, see Proper of Seasons.*]

PETITIONS, p. 50.

COLLECT.

FERIAL MEMORIALS, p. 51.

℣. The Lord be with you.
℟. And with thy spirit.
℣. Bless we the Lord.
℟. Thanks be to God.

THURSDAY.

Vespers.

℣. O God, make speed to save us.
℟. O Lord, make haste to help us.
℣. Glory be to the Father, and to the Son : and to the Holy Ghost.
℟. As it was in the beginning, is now, and ever shall be : world without end. Amen.
Alleluia.

[*From Septuagesima till Wednesday in Holy Week,*

Praise be to Thee, O Lord, King of eternal glory.]

Ant. And all.

Psalm CXXXII. *Memento, Domine.*

LORD, remember David : and all his trouble;

2 How he sware unto the Lord : and vowed a vow unto the Almighty God of Jacob.

3 I will not come within the tabernacle of mine house : nor climb up into my bed;

4 I will not suffer mine eyes to sleep, nor mine eyelids to slumber : neither the temples of my head to take any rest;

5 Until I find out a place for the temple of the Lord : an habitation for the mighty God of Jacob.

6 Lo, we heard of the same at Ephrata : and found it in the wood.

7 We will go into His tabernacle : and fall low on our knees before His footstool.

8 Arise, O Lord, into Thy resting-place : Thou, and the ark of Thy strength.

9 Let Thy priests be clothed with righteousness : and let Thy saints sing with joyfulness.

10 For Thy servant David's sake : turn not away the presence of Thine Anointed.

11 The Lord hath made a faithful oath unto David : and He shall not shrink from it.

12 Of the fruit of thy body : shall I set upon thy seat.

13 If thy children will keep my covenant, and My testimonies that I shall learn them : their children also shall sit upon thy seat for evermore.

14 For the Lord hath chosen Sion to be an habitation for Himself : He hath longed for her.

15 This shall be My rest for ever : here will I dwell, for I have a delight therein.

16 I will bless her victuals with increase : and will satisfy her poor with bread.

17 I will deck her priests with health : and her saints shall rejoice and sing.

18 There shall I make the horn of David to flourish : I have ordained a lantern for Mine Anointed.

19 As for His enemies, I shall clothe them with shame : but upon Himself shall His crown flourish.

Glory be, etc.

Ant. And all : his trouble.

Ant. Behold, how good.

Psalm CXXXIII. *Ecce, quam bonum!*

BEHOLD, how good and joyful a thing it is : brethren, to dwell together in unity!

3 It is like the precious ointment upon the head, that ran down unto the beard : even unto Aaron's beard, and went down to the skirts of his clothing.

3 Like as the dew of Hermon : which fell upon the hill of Sion.

4 For there the Lord promised His blessing : and life for evermore.

Glory be, etc.

Ant. Behold : how good and joyful.

Ant. Whatsoever.

Psalm cxxxv. *Laudate nomen.*

O PRAISE the Lord, laud ye the Name of the Lord : praise it, O ye servants of the Lord ;

2 Ye that stand in the house of the Lord : in the courts of the house of our God.

3 O praise the Lord, for the Lord is gracious : O sing praises unto His Name, for it is lovely.

4 For why? the Lord hath chosen Jacob unto Himself : and Israel for His own possession.

5 For I know that the Lord is great : and that our Lord is above all gods.

6 Whatsoever the Lord pleased, that did He in heaven, and in earth : and in the sea, and in all deep places.

7 He bringeth forth the clouds from the ends of the world : and sendeth forth lightnings with the rain, bringing the winds out of His treasures.

8 He smote the first-born of Egypt : both of man and beast.

9 He hath sent tokens and wonders into the midst of thee, O thou land of Egypt : upon Pharaoh, and all his servants.

10 He smote divers nations : and slew mighty kings;

11 Sehon king of the Amorites, and Og the king of Basan : and all the kingdoms of Canaan ;

12 And gave their land to be an heritage : even an heritage unto Israel His people.

13 Thy Name, O Lord, endureth for ever : so doth Thy memorial, O Lord, from one generation to another.

14 For the Lord will avenge His people : and be gracious unto His servants.

15 As for the images of the heathen, they are but silver and gold : the work of men's hands.

16 They have mouths, and speak not : eyes have they, but they see not.

17 They have ears, and yet they hear not : neither is there any breath in their mouths.

18 They that make them are like unto them : and so are all they that put their trust in them.

19 Praise the Lord, ye house of Israel : praise the Lord, ye house of Aaron.

20 Praise the Lord, ye house of Levi : ye that fear the Lord, praise the Lord.

21 Praised be the Lord out of Sion : who dwelleth at Jerusalem.

Glory be, etc.

Ant. Whatsoever : the Lord pleased, that did He.

Ant. For His mercy.

Psalm cxxxvi. *Confitemini Domino.*

O GIVE thanks unto the Lord, for He is gracious : and His mercy endureth for ever.

2 O give thanks unto the God of all gods : for His mercy endureth for ever.

3 O thank the Lord of all lords : for His mercy endureth for ever.

4 Who only doeth great wonders : for His mercy endureth for ever.

5 Who by His excellent wisdom made the heavens : for His mercy endureth for ever.

6 Who laid out the earth above the waters : for His mercy endureth for ever.

7 Who hath made great lights : for His mercy endureth for ever.

8 The sun to rule the day : for His mercy endureth for ever;

9 The moon and the stars to govern the night : for His mercy endureth for ever.

10 Who smote Egypt with their first-born : for His mercy endureth for ever.

11 And brought out Israel from among them : for His mercy endureth for ever.

12 With a mighty hand, and stretched out arm : for His mercy endureth for ever.

13 Who divided the Red Sea in two parts : for His mercy endureth for ever.

14 And made Israel to go through the midst of it : for His mercy endureth for ever.

15 But as for Pharaoh and his host, He overthrew them in the Red Sea : for His mercy endureth for ever.

16 Who led His people through the wilderness : for His mercy endureth for ever.

17 Who smote great kings : for His mercy endureth for ever.

18 Yea, and slew mighty kings : for His mercy endureth for ever.

19 Sehon king of the Amorites : for His mercy endureth for ever.

20 And Og the king of Basan : for His mercy endureth for ever.

21 And gave away their land for an heritage : for His mercy endureth for ever.

22 Even for an heritage unto Israel His servant : for His mercy endureth for ever.

23 Who remembered us when we were in trouble : for His mercy endureth for ever.

24 And hath delivered us from our enemies : for His mercy endureth for ever.

25 Who giveth food to all flesh : for His mercy endureth for ever.

26 O give thanks unto the God of heaven : for His mercy endureth for ever.

27 O give thanks unto the Lord of lords : for His mercy endureth for ever.

Glory be, etc.

Ant. For His mercy : endureth for ever.

Ant. Sing us.

Psalm CXXXVII. *Super flumina.*

BY the waters of Babylon we sat down and wept ; when we remembered thee, O Sion.

2 As for our harps, we hanged them up : upon the trees that are therein.

3 For they that led us away captive required of us then a song, and melody, in our heaviness : Sing us one of the songs of Sion.

4 How shall we sing the Lord's song : in a strange land ?

5 If I forget thee, O Jerusalem : let my right hand forget her cunning.

6 If I do not remember thee, let my tongue cleave to the roof of my mouth : yea, if I prefer not Jerusalem in my mirth.

7 Remember the children of Edom, O Lord, in the day of Jerusalem : how they said, Down with it, down with it, even to the ground.

8 O daughter of Babylon, wasted with misery : yea, happy shall he be that rewardeth thee, as thou hast served us.

9 Blessed shall he be that taketh thy children : and throweth them against the stones.

Glory be, etc.

Ant. Sing us : one of the songs of Sion.

Daily from Epiphany to Septuagesima ; on all Ferias from Septuagesima to the First Sunday in Lent ; and daily from Trinity to Advent,

CHAPTER. II Thess. iii., p. 47.

From Trinity to Advent,

HYMN. *Lucis Creator optime,* V̓. and R̓., p. 47.

Ferial Antiphons and Magnificat, p. 48.

[*For Chapters, Hymns, and Antiphons at other times, see Proper of Seasons.*]

PETITIONS, p. 50.

COLLECT.

FERIAL MEMORIALS, p. 51.

℣. The Lord be with you.
℟. And with thy spirit.
℣. Bless we the Lord.
℟. Thanks be to God.

FRIDAY.

Vespers.

✠ ℣. O God, make speed to save us.

℟. O Lord, make haste to help us.
℣. Glory be to the Father, and to the Son : and to the Holy Ghost.
℟. As it was in the beginning, is now, and ever shall be : world without end. Amen.

Alleluia.

[*From Septuagesima to Wednesday in Holy Week,*

Praise be to Thee, O Lord, King of eternal glory.]

Ant. Before the gods.

Psalm CXXXVIII. *Confitebor tibi.*

I WILL give thanks unto Thee, O Lord, with my whole heart : even before the gods will I sing praise unto Thee.

2 I will worship toward Thy holy temple, and praise Thy Name, because of Thy lovingkindness and truth : for Thou hast magnified Thy Name, and Thy Word, above all things.

3 When I called upon Thee, Thou heardest me : and enduedst my soul with much strength.

4 All the kings of the earth shall praise Thee, O Lord : for they have heard the words of Thy mouth.

5 Yea, they shall sing in the ways of the Lord : that great is the glory of the Lord.

6 For though the Lord be high, yet hath He respect unto the lowly : as for the proud, He beholdeth them afar off.

7 Though I walk in the midst of trouble, yet shalt Thou refresh me : Thou shalt stretch forth Thy hand upon the furiousness of mine enemies, and Thy right hand shalt save me.

8 The Lord shall make good His loving kindness toward me : yea, Thy mercy, O Lord, endureth for ever : despise not then the works of Thine own hands.

Glory be, etc.

Ant. Before the gods : will I sing praise unto Thee, my God.

Ant. O Lord, Thou hast searched.

Psalm CXXXIX. *Domine, probasti.*

O LORD, Thou hast searched me out, and known me : Thou knowest my down-sitting, and mine uprising ; Thou understandest my thoughts long before.

2 Thou art about my path, and about my bed : and spiest out all my ways.

3 For lo, there is not a word in my tongue : but Thou, O Lord, knowest it altogether.

4 Thou hast fashioned me behind and before : and laid Thine hand upon me.

5 Such knowledge is too wonderful and excellent for me : I cannot attain unto it.

6 Whither shall I go then from Thy Spirit : or whither shall I go then from Thy presence?

7 If I climb up into heaven, Thou art there : if I go down to hell, Thou art there also.

8 If I take the wings of the morning : and remain in the uttermost parts of the sea ;

9 Even there also shall Thy hand

lead me : and Thy right hand shall hold me.

10 If I say, Peradventure the darkness shall cover me : then shall my night be turned to day.

11 Yea, the darkness is no darkness with Thee, but the night is as clear as the day : the darkness and light to Thee are both alike.

12 For my reins are Thine : Thou hast covered me in my mother's womb.

13 I will give thanks unto Thee, for I am fearfully and wonderfully made : marvellous are Thy works, and that my soul knoweth right well.

14 My bones are not hid from Thee : though I be made secretly, and fashioned beneath in the earth.

15 Thine eyes did see my substance, yet being imperfect : and in Thy book were all my members written ;

16 Which day by day were fashioned : when as yet there was none of them.

17 How dear are Thy counsels unto me, O God : O how great is the sum of them !

18 If I tell them, they are more in number than the sand : when I wake up I am present with Thee.

19 Wilt Thou not slay the wicked, O God ? : depart from me, ye bloodthirsty men.

20 For they speak unrighteously against Thee : and Thine enemies take Thy Name in vain.

21 Do not I hate them, O Lord, that hate Thee : and am not I grieved with those that rise up against Thee ?

22 Yea, I hate them right sore : even as though they were mine enemies.

23 Try me, O God, and seek the ground of my heart : prove me, and examine my thoughts.

24 Look well if there be any way of wickedness in me : and lead me in the way everlasting.

Glory be, etc.

Ant. O Lord, Thou hast searched me out : and known me.

Ant. Preserve me.

Psalm CXL. *Eripe me, Domine.*

DELIVER me, O Lord, from the evil man : and preserve me from the wicked man.

2 Who imagine mischief in their hearts : and stir up strife all the day long.

3 They have sharpened their tongues like a serpent : adder's poison is under their lips.

4 Keep me, O Lord, from the hands of the ungodly : preserve me from the wicked men, who are purposed to overthrow my goings.

5 The proud have laid a snare for me, and spread a net abroad with cords : yea, and set traps in my way.

6 I said unto the Lord, Thou art my God : hear the voice of my prayers, O Lord.

7 O Lord God, Thou strength of my health : Thou hast covered my head in the day of battle.

8 Let not the ungodly have his desire, O Lord : let not his mischievous imagination prosper, lest they be too proud.

9 Let the mischief of their own lips fall upon the head of them : that compass me about.

10 Let hot burning coals fall upon them : let them be cast into the fire, and into the pit, that they never rise up again.

11 A man full of words shall not prosper upon the earth : evil shall hunt the wicked person to overthrow him.

12 Sure I am that the Lord will avenge the poor : and maintain the cause of the helpless.

13 The righteous also shall give thanks unto Thy Name : and the just shall continue in Thy sight.
Glory be, etc.

Ant. Preserve me : from the wicked man.

Ant. Lord, I call.

Psalm cxli. *Domine, clamavi.*

LORD, I call upon Thee, haste Thee unto me : and consider my voice when I cry unto Thee.
2 Let my prayer be set forth in Thy sight as the incense : and let the lifting up of my hands be an evening sacrifice.
3 Set a watch, O Lord, before my mouth : and keep the door of my lips.
4 O let not mine heart be inclined to any evil thing : let me not be occupied in ungodly works with the men that work wickedness, lest I eat of such things as please them.
5 Let the righteous rather smite me friendly : and reprove me.
6 But let not their precious balms break my head : yea, I will pray yet against their wickedness.
7 Let their judges be overthrown in stony places : that they may hear my words, for they are sweet.
8 Our bones lie scattered before the pit : like as when one breaketh and heweth wood upon the earth.
9 But mine eyes look unto Thee, O Lord God : in Thee is my trust, O cast not out my soul.
10 Keep me from the snare that they have laid for me : and from the traps of the wicked doers.
11 Let the ungodly fall into their own nets together : and let me ever escape them.
Glory be, etc.

Ant. Lord, I call upon Thee : haste Thee unto me.

Ant. Thou art my portion.

Ps. CXLII. *Voce mea ad Dominum.*

I CRIED unto the Lord with my voice : yea, even unto the Lord did I make my supplication.
2 I poured out my complaints before Him : and shewed Him of my trouble.
3 When my spirit was in heaviness Thou knewest my path : in the way wherein I walked have they privily laid a snare for me.
4 I looked also upon my right hand : and saw there was no man that would know me.
5 I had no place to flee unto : and no man cared for my soul.
6 I cried unto Thee, O Lord, and said : Thou art my hope and my portion in the land of the living.
7 Consider my complaint : for I am brought very low.
8 O deliver me from my persecutors : for they are too strong for me.
9 Bring my soul out of prison, that I may give thanks unto Thy Name : which thing if Thou wilt grant me, then shall the righteous resort unto my company.
Glory be, etc.

Ant. Thou art my portion : in the land of the living.

Daily from Epiphany to Septuagesima ; on all Ferias from Septuagesima to the First Sunday in Lent ; and daily from Trinity to Advent,

CHAPTER. II Thess. iii., p. 47.

From Trinity to Advent,

HYMN. *Lucis Creator optime,*
℣. and ℟., p. 47.

Ferial Antiphons and Magnificat,
p. 48.

[*For Chapters, Hymns, and Antiphons at other times, see Proper of Seasons.*]

PETITIONS, p. 50.

COLLECT.

FERIAL MEMORIALS. p. 51.

℣. The Lord be with you.
℟. And with thy spirit.
℣. Bless we the Lord.
℟. Thanks be to God.

———

SATURDAY.

First Vespers of Sunday.

✠ ℣. O God, make speed to save us.

℟. O Lord, make haste to help us.
℣. Glory be to the Father, and to the Son : and to the Holy Ghost.
℟. As it was in the beginning, is now, and ever shall be : world without end. Amen.
Alleluia.

[*From Septuagesima to Wednesday in Holy Week :*

Praise be to Thee, O Lord, King of eternal glory.]

Ant. Blessed be * the Lord my strength.

Psalm CXLIV. *Benedictus Dominus.*

BLESSED be the Lord my strength : Who teacheth my hands to war, and my fingers to fight;
2 My hope and my fortress, my castle and deliverer, my defender in Whom I trust : Who subdueth my people that is under me.
3 Lord, what is man, that Thou hast such respect unto him : or the son of man, that Thou so regardest him?
4 Man is like a thing of nought : his time passeth away like a shadow.
5 Bow Thy heavens, O Lord, and come down : touch the mountains, and they shall smoke.
6 Cast forth Thy lightning, and tear them : shoot out Thine arrows, and consume them.
7 Send down Thine hand from above : deliver me, and take me out of the great waters, from the hand of strange children ;
8 Whose mouth talketh of vanity : and their right hand is a right hand of wickedness.
9 I will sing a new song unto Thee, O God : and sing praises unto Thee upon a ten-stringed lute.
10 Thou hast given victory unto kings : and hast delivered David Thy servant from the peril of the sword.
11 Save me, and deliver me from the hand of strange children : whose mouth talketh of vanity, and their right hand is a right hand of iniquity.
12 That our sons may grow up as the young plants : and that our daughters may be as the polished corners of the temple.
13 That our garners may be full and plenteous with all manner of store : that our sheep may bring forth thousands and ten thousands in our streets.
14 That our oxen may be strong to labour, that there be no decay : no leading into captivity, and no complaining in our streets.
15 Happy are the people that are in such a case : yea, blessed are the people who have the Lord for their God.

Glory be, etc.

Ant. Blessed be : the Lord my strength.

Ant. For ever * and ever.

Psalm CXLV. *Exaltabo te, Deus.*

I WILL magnify Thee, O God, my King : and I will praise Thy Name for ever and ever.
2 Every day will I give thanks unto Thee : and praise Thy Name for ever and ever.

3 Great is the Lord, and marvellous : there is no end of His greatness.

4 One generation shall praise Thy works unto another : and declare Thy power.

5 As for me, I will be talking of Thy worship : Thy glory, Thy praise, and wondrous works ;

6 So that men shall speak of the might of Thy marvellous acts : and I will also tell of Thy greatness.

7 The memorial of Thine abundant kindness shall be shewed : and men shall sing of Thy righteousness.

8 The Lord is gracious, and merciful : long-suffering, and of great goodness.

9 The Lord is loving unto every man : and His mercy is over all His works.

10 All Thy works praise Thee, O Lord : and Thy saints give thanks unto Thee.

11 They shew the glory of Thy kingdom : and talk of Thy power ;

12 That Thy power, Thy glory, and mightiness of Thy kingdom : might be known unto men.

13 Thy kingdom is an everlasting kingdom : and Thy dominion endureth throughout all ages.

14 The Lord upholdeth all such as fall : and lifteth up all those that are down.

15 The eyes of all wait upon Thee, O Lord : and Thou givest them their meat in due season.

16 Thou openest Thine hand : and fillest all things living with plenteousness.

17 The Lord is righteous in all His ways : and holy in all His works.

18 The Lord is nigh unto all them that call upon Him : yea, all such as call upon Him faithfully.

19 He will fulfil the desire of them that fear Him : He also will hear their cry, and will help them.

20 The Lord preserveth all them that love Him : but scattereth abroad all the ungodly.

21 My mouth shall speak the praise of the Lord : and let all flesh give thanks unto His holy Name for ever.

Glory be, etc.

Ant. For ever : and ever.

Ant. While I live * will I praise the Lord.

Psalm CXLVI. *Lauda anima mea.*

PRAISE the Lord, O my soul; while I live will I praise the Lord : yea, as long as I have any being, I will sing praises unto my God.

2 O put not your trust in princes, nor in any child of man : for there is no help in them.

3 For when the breath of man goeth forth he shall turn again to his earth : and then all his thoughts perish.

4 Blessed is he that hath the God of Jacob for his help : and whose hope is in the Lord his God ;

5 Who made heaven and earth, the sea, and all that therein is : Who keepeth His promise for ever ;

6 Who helpeth them to right that suffer wrong : Who feedeth the hungry.

7 The Lord looseth men out of prison : the Lord giveth sight to the blind.

8 The Lord helpeth them that are fallen : the Lord careth for the righteous.

9 The Lord careth for the strangers ; He defendeth the fatherless and widow : as for the way of the ungodly, He turneth it upside down.

10 The Lord thy God, O Sion, shall be King for evermore : and throughout all generations.

Glory be, etc.

Ant. While I live : will I praise the Lord.

Ant. Yea, a joyful and pleasant thing * it is to be thankful.

Psalm cxlvii. *Laudate Dominum.*

O PRAISE the Lord, for it is a good thing to sing praises unto our God : yea, a joyful and pleasant thing it is to be thankful.

2 The Lord doth build up Jerusalem : and gather together the outcasts of Israel.

3 He healeth those that are broken in heart : and giveth medicine to heal their sickness.

4 He telleth the number of the stars : and calleth them all by their names.

5 Great is our Lord, and great is His power : yea, and His wisdom is infinite.

6 The Lord setteth up the meek : and bringeth the ungodly down to the ground.

7 O sing unto the Lord with thanksgiving : sing praises upon the harp unto our God;

8 Who covereth the heaven with clouds, and prepareth rain for the earth : and maketh the grass to grow upon the mountains, and herb for the use of men;

9 Who giveth fodder unto the cattle : and feedeth the young ravens that call upon Him.

10 He hath no pleasure in the strength of an horse : neither delighteth He in any man's legs.

11 But the Lord's delight is in them that fear Him : and put their trust in His mercy.

Glory be, etc.

Ant. Yea, a joyful and pleasant thing : it is to be thankful.

Ant. Praise the Lord * O Jerusalem.

Ps. CXLVII. 12. *Lauda Hierusalem.*

PRAISE the Lord, O Jerusalem : praise thy God, O Sion.

13 For He hath made fast the bars of thy gates : and hath blessed thy children within thee.

14 He maketh peace in thy borders : and filleth thee with the flour of wheat.

15 He sendeth forth His commandment upon earth : and His word runneth very swiftly.

16 He giveth snow like wool : and scattereth the hoar-frost like ashes.

17 He casteth forth His ice like morsels : who is able to abide His frost ?

18 He sendeth out His word, and melteth them : He bloweth with His wind, and the waters flow.

19 He showeth His word unto Jacob : His statutes and ordinances unto Israel.

20 He hath not dealt so with any nation : neither have the heathen knowledge of His laws.

Glory be, etc.

Ant. Praise the Lord : O Jerusalem.

From Trinity to Advent,

CHAPTER. II Cor. i.

BLESSED be God, even the Father of our Lord Jesus Christ, the Father of mercies, and the God of all comfort; Who comforteth us in all our tribulation.

℞. Thanks be to God.

From Trinity to Advent,

HYMN. *O lux beata Trinitas.*

O TRINITY of blessed light,
O Unity of princely might,
The fiery sun now goes his way :
Shed Thou within our hearts Thy ray.

To Thee our morning song of praise,
To Thee our evening prayer we raise;
Thy glory suppliant we adore
For ever and for evermore. Amen.

℣. Let our evening prayer come up before Thee, O Lord.

℞. And let Thy mercy come down on us.

Ferial Antiphons and Magnificat,
p. 48.

[*For Chapters, Hymns, and Antiphons at other times, see Proper of Seasons.*]

℣. The Lord be with you.
℞. And with thy spirit.

Let us pray.

COLLECT.

MEMORIAL OF THE HOLY TRINITY.

Ant. Thou art our hope, our salvation, our honour : O blessed Trinity.

℣. Let us praise the Father, the Son, and the Holy Ghost.

℞. Praise and exalt Him for ever.

COLLECT.

ALMIGHTY and everlasting God, Who hast given unto us Thy servants grace by the confession of a true faith to acknowledge the glory of the eternal Trinity, and in the power of the Divine Majesty to worship the Unity; we beseech Thee, that Thou wouldest keep us stedfast in this faith, and evermore defend us from all adversities, Who livest and reignest, one God, world without end. Amen.

MEMORIAL OF THE HOLY CROSS.

Ant. O glorious Cross, O adorable Cross, O precious wood, O admirable sign : whereby the devil hath been conquered, and the world redeemed with the Blood of Christ. Alleluia.

℣. We adore Thee, O Christ, and bless Thee.

℞. For by Thy Cross Thou hast redeemed the world.

COLLECT.

O GOD, Who by the precious and life-giving Blood of Thy only-begotten Son our Lord Jesus Christ, hast willed to consecrate the standard of the Cross; grant, we pray Thee, that they who rejoice in the honour of the holy Cross, may also rejoice everywhere in Thy protection; through the same Thy Son Jesus Christ our Lord. Amen.

MEMORIAL OF S. MARY.

Ant. Thou art become fair and pleasant, O holy Mother of God : in the delights of virginity. The daughter of Sion saw her among the roses and lilies, and blessed her : the queens, and they praised her.

℣. After child-bearing thou remainedst a Virgin.

℞. O Mother of God.

COLLECT.

O God, Who through the fruitful virginity of the Blessed Virgin Mary hast bestowed the rewards of eternal salvation on the human race; grant, we pray Thee, that she may intercede for us, through whom we have received the Author of life, Thy Son Jesus Christ our Lord. Amen.

℣. The Lord be with you.
℞. And with thy spirit.
℣. Bless we the Lord.
℞. Thanks be to God.

———

Compline.

✠ ℣. Turn us, O God our Saviour.

℞. And let Thine anger cease from us.

℣. O God, make speed to save us.
℞. O Lord, make haste to help us.
℣. Glory be to the Father, and to the Son : and to the Holy Ghost.

℞. As it was in the beginning. is now, and ever shall be : world without end. Amen.

Alleluia.

[*From Septuagesima to Wednesday in Holy Week,*

Praise be to Thee, O Lord, King of eternal glory.]

Ant. Have mercy.

Psalm IV. *Cum invocarem.*

HEAR me when I call, O God of my righteousness : Thou hast set me at liberty when I was in trouble; have mercy upon me, and hearken unto my prayer.

2 O ye sons of men, how long will ye blaspheme Mine honour : and have such pleasure in vanity, and seek after leasing?

3 Know this also, that the Lord hath chosen to Himself the man that is godly : when I call upon the Lord, He will hear me.

4 Stand in awe, and sin not : commune with your own heart, and in your chamber, and be still.

5 Offer the sacrifice of righteousness : and put your trust in the Lord.

6 There be many that say : Who will shew us any good?

7 Lord, lift Thou up : the light of Thy countenance upon us.

8 Thou hast put gladness in my heart : since the time that their corn, and wine, and oil, increased.

9 I will lay me down in peace, and take my rest : for it is Thou, Lord, only, that makest me dwell in safety.

Glory be, etc.

Psalm XXXI. *In te, Domine, speravi.*

IN Thee, O Lord, have I put my trust : let me never be put to confusion, deliver me in Thy righteousness.

2 Bow down Thine ear to me : make haste to deliver me.

3 And be Thou my strong rock, and house of defence : that Thou mayest save me.

4 For Thou art my strong rock, and my castle : be Thou also my guide, and lead me for Thy Name's sake.

5 Draw me out of the net that they have laid privily for me : for Thou art my strength.

6 Into Thy hands I commend my spirit : for Thou hast redeemed me, O Lord, Thou God of truth.

Glory be, etc.

Psalm XCI. *Qui habitat.*

WHOSO dwelleth under the defence of the most High : shall abide under the shadow of the Almighty.

2 I will say unto the Lord, Thou art my hope, and my strong hold : my God, in Him will I trust.

3 For He shall deliver thee from the snare of the hunter : and from the noisome pestilence.

4 He shall defend thee under His wings, and thou shalt be safe under His feathers : His faithfulness and truth shall be thy shield and buckler.

5 Thou shalt not be afraid of any terror by night : nor for the arrow that flieth by day;

6 For the pestilence that walketh in darkness : nor for the sickness that destroyeth in the noon-day.

7 A thousand shall fall beside thee, and ten thousand at thy right hand : but it shall not come nigh thee.

8 Yea, with thine eyes shalt thou behold : and see the reward of the ungodly.

9 For Thou, Lord, art my hope : Thou hast set Thine house of defence very high.

10 There shall no evil happen unto thee : neither shall any plague come nigh thy dwelling.

11 For He shall give His angels charge over thee : to keep thee in all thy ways.

12 They shall bear thee in their hands : that thou hurt not thy foot against a stone.

13 Thou shalt go upon the lion and adder : the young lion and the dragon shalt Thou tread under Thy feet.

14 Because he hath set his love upon Me, therefore will I deliver him : I will set him up, because he hath known My Name.

15 He shall call upon Me, and I will hear him : yea, I am with him in trouble : I will deliver him, and bring him to honour.

16 With long life will I satisfy him : and shew him My salvation.

Glory be, etc.

Psalm CXXXIV. *Ecce nunc.*

BEHOLD now, praise the Lord : all ye servants of the Lord;

2 Ye that by night stand in the house of the Lord : even in the courts of the house of our God.

3 Lift up your hands in the sanctuary : and praise the Lord.

4 The Lord that made heaven and earth : give thee blessing out of Sion.

Glory be, etc.

Ant. Have mercy upon me : and hearken unto my prayer.

This Ant. is always said, unless some other be appointed in Proper of Seasons.

CHAPTER. Jer. xiv.

THOU, O Lord, art in the midst of us, and we are called by Thy Name; leave us not, O our God.

R̰. Thanks be to God.

This Chapter is always said, except from Maundy Thursday to Low Sunday, inclusive.

HYMN. *Te lucis ante terminum.*

BEFORE the ending of the day,
Creator of the world, we pray
That with Thy wonted favour, Thou
Would'st be our Guard and Keeper now.

From all ill dreams defend our eyes,
From nightly fears and fantasies;
Tread under foot our ghostly foe,
That no pollution we may know.

O Father, that we ask be done,
Through Jesus Christ, Thine only Son;
Who with the Holy Ghost and Thee,
Shall live and reign eternally. Amen.

V̰. Keep us, O Lord.

R̰. As the apple of an eye : hide us under the shadow of Thy wings.

This Hymn, V̰., and R̰. are said on ordinary Sundays and Ferias from Epiphany to Lent, and from Trinity to Christmas.

[HYMN. *Salvator mundi Domine.*

SAVIOUR of man, and Lord alone,
Who through this day hast saved Thine own,
Protect us through the coming night,
And ever save us by Thy might.

Be with us, Lord, in mercy nigh,
And spare Thy servants when they cry;
Blot out our every past offence,
And lighten Thou our darkened sense.

O let not sleep oppress the soul,
Nor Satan with his spirits foul;
Our flesh keep chaste, that it may be
An holy temple unto Thee.

To Thee, Who makest souls anew,
With heartfelt vows we humbly sue;
That pure in heart, and free from stain,
We from our beds may rise again.

All laud to God the Father be;
All praise, Eternal Son, to Thee;
All glory, as is ever meet,
To God the blessed Paraclete. Amen.

V̰. Keep us, O Lord.

R̰. As the apple of an eye : hide us under the shadow of Thy wings.

This Hymn, V̰., and R̰. are said from Christmas to the Octave of Epiphany; on Whitsun Eve, and on Thursday, Friday, and Saturday in Whitsun Week; and on all Double Feasts from Epiphany to Lent, and from Whitsuntide to Christmas, except the Feasts of Corpus Christi, the Transfiguration, and the Holy Name.

On Double Feasts, except on the Feasts of the Holy Name, of the Blessed Virgin, and of All Saints, the following Ant. is said to Nunc Dimittis:

Ant. Lord, grant us Thy light, * that being rid of the darkness of our hearts, we may come to the true light, which is Christ.]

Ferial Ant. to Nunc Dim. Save us waking.

Nunc Dimittis.

LORD, now lettest Thou Thy servant depart in peace : according
to Thy word.

2 For mine eyes have seen : Thy
salvation.

3 Which Thou hast prepared : before the face of all people ;

4 To be a light to lighten the
Gentiles : and to be the glory of Thy
people Israel.

Glory be, etc.

Ant. Save us waking, O Lord : and
guard us sleeping, that awake we
may be with Christ, and may sleep
in peace.

PETITIONS.

Lord, have mercy.
　　Christ, have mercy.
Lord, have mercy.

Our Father :

*Said silently to the end.　The Priest
repeats aloud :*

℣. And lead us not into temptation.
℟. But deliver us from evil.
℣. I will lay me down in peace.
℟. And take my rest.

I believe :

*Said silently to the end.　The Priest
repeats aloud :*

℣. The resurrection of the body.
℟. And the life everlasting.
℣. Let us bless the Father, the
Son, and the Holy Ghost.
℟. Let us praise and exalt Him
above all for ever.
℣. Blessed art Thou, O Lord, in
the firmament of heaven.
℟. And above all to be praised
and glorified for ever.
℣. May the Almighty and most
merciful Lord bless us and keep us.
℟. Amen.

*Confession and Absolution, said in a
low voice.*

[The Priest, if present :

I CONFESS to God Almighty, the
Father, the Son, and the Holy
Ghost, in the sight of the whole
company of heaven, and to you, my
brethren, that I have sinned exceedingly in thought, word, and deed, of
my fault, of my own fault, of my own
grievous fault; therefore I pray God
to have mercy upon me, and you, my
brethren, to pray for me.

The Choir replies :

ALMIGHTY God have mercy upon
thee, forgive thee thy sins, and
bring thee to everlasting life. ℟.
Amen.]

The Choir :

I CONFESS to God Almighty, the
Father, the Son, and the Holy
Ghost, in the sight of the whole
company of heaven, [and to thee,
father,] that I have sinned exceedingly
in thought, word, and deed, of my
fault, of my own fault, of my own
grievous fault; therefore I pray God
to have mercy upon me, [and thee,
father, to pray for me].

[The Priest, if present :

ALMIGHTY God have mercy upon
you, forgive you your sins, and
bring you to everlasting life. ℟.
Amen.

THE Almighty and merciful Lord
grant you absolution and forgiveness of your sins, time for repentance, amendment of life, and the
grace and comfort of His Holy Spirit.
℟. Amen.]

*After the Confession, if there is no Priest
present, the Choir says :*

ALMIGHTY God have mercy upon
us, forgive us our sins, and bring
us to everlasting life. Amen.

℣. Wilt Thou not turn again and quicken us, O Lord?

℟. That Thy people may rejoice in Thee?

℣. Shew us Thy mercy, O Lord.

℟. And grant us Thy salvation.

℣. Vouchsafe, O Lord.

℟. To keep us this day without sin.

℣. O Lord, have mercy upon us.

℟. Have mercy upon us.

℣. O Lord, let Thy mercy lighten upon us.

℟. As our trust is in Thee.

The foregoing Petitions are said daily through the year; (except from Maundy Thursday till Low Sunday, and on All Souls' Day:) then follows:

[ON SUNDAYS AND FESTIVALS:

℣. Turn us again, O Lord God of Hosts.

℟. Shew the light of Thy countenance, and we shall be whole.

℣. Hear my prayer, O Lord.

℟. And let my crying come unto Thee.

℣. The Lord be with you.

℟. And with thy spirit.

Let us pray.

LIGHTEN our darkness, we beseech Thee, O Lord: and by Thy great mercy defend us from all perils and dangers of this night; for the love of Thy only Son, our Saviour, Jesus Christ. Amen.

℣. The Lord be with you.

℟. And with thy spirit.

℣. Bless we the Lord.

℟. Thanks be to God.]

ON FERIAS

Through the year, except in Christmas and Easter tides:

℣. Lord, hear my voice when I cry unto Thee.

℟. Have mercy upon me, and hear me.

Psalm li. *Miserere*, p. 1.

[*Here follows in Lent:*

Psalm cxliii. *Domine, exaudi.*

HEAR my prayer, O Lord, and consider my desire : hearken unto me for Thy truth and righteousness' sake.

2 And enter not into judgement with Thy servant : for in Thy sight shall no man living be justified.

3 For the enemy hath persecuted my soul; he hath smitten my life down to the ground : he hath laid me in the darkness, as the men that have been long dead.

4 Therefore is my spirit vexed within me : and my heart within me is desolate.

5 Yet do I remember the time past; I muse upon all Thy works : yea, I exercise myself in the works of Thy hands.

6 I stretch forth my hands unto Thee : my soul gaspeth unto Thee as a thirsty land.

7 Hear me, O Lord, and that soon, for my spirit waxeth faint : hide not Thy face from me, lest I be like unto them that go down into the pit.

8 O let me hear Thy loving kindness betimes in the morning, for in thee is my trust : shew Thou me the way that I should walk in, for I lift up my soul unto Thee.

9 Deliver me, O Lord, from mine enemies : for I flee unto Thee to hide me.

10 Teach me to do the thing that pleaseth Thee, for Thou art my God : let Thy loving Spirit lead me forth into the land of righteousness.

11 Quicken me, O Lord, for Thy Name's sake : and for Thy righteousness' sake bring my soul out of prison.

12 And of Thy goodness slay mine enemies: and destroy all them that vex my soul; for I am Thy servant.

Glory be, etc.]

[*Here the reader, if a Priest, rising, stands at the step of the Sanctuary*].

℣. O Lord, arise, help us.

℟. And deliver us for Thy Name's sake.

℣. Turn Thee again, O Lord God of Hosts.

℟. Shew the light of Thy countenance, and we shall be whole.

℣. Hear my prayer, O Lord.

℟. And let my crying come unto Thee.

℣. The Lord be with you.

℟. And with thy spirit.

Let us pray.

LIGHTEN our darkness, we beseech Thee, O Lord, and by Thy

great mercy defend us from all perils and dangers of this night, for the love of Thy only Son, our Saviour Jesus Christ.   Amen.

℣. The Lord be with you.
℞. And with thy spirit.
℣. Bless we the Lord.
℞. Thanks be to God.

For the Peace of the Church.

Said daily throughout the year, except on Double Feasts, and in Christmas and Easter tides.

Psalm cxxiii.

Ad Te levavi oculos meos.

UNTO Thee lift I up mine eyes : O Thou that dwellest in the heavens.

2 Behold, even as the eyes of servants look unto the hands of their masters, and as the eyes of a maiden unto the hand of her mistress : even so our eyes wait upon the Lord our God, until He have mercy upon us.

3 Have mercy upon us, O Lord, have mercy upon us : for we are utterly despised.

4 Our soul is filled with the scornful reproof of the wealthy : and with the despitefulness of the proud.

Glory be, etc.

Lord, have mercy.
Christ, have mercy.
Lord, have mercy.

Our Father:
Said silently to the end.   The Priest repeats aloud :

℣. And lead us not into temptation.
℞. But deliver us from evil.
℣. O Lord, arise, help us.
℞. And deliver us for Thy Name's sake.
℣. Turn us again, O Lord God of hosts.
℞. Shew the light of Thy countenance, and we shall be whole.
℣. Hear my prayer, O Lord.
℞. And let my crying come unto Thee.
℣. The Lord be with you.
℞. And with thy spirit.

Let us pray.

O LORD, we beseech Thee, mercifully to hear the prayers of Thy Church, and grant that we, being delivered from all adversities, may serve Thee with a quiet mind; and grant us Thy peace all the days of our life; through Jesus Christ our Lord, Who liveth and reigneth with Thee and the Holy Ghost, ever One God, world without end. Amen.

℣. The Lord be with you.
℞. And with thy spirit.
℣. Bless we the Lord.
℞. Thanks be to God.

MAY the souls of the faithful, through the mercy of God, rest in peace.   Amen.

This Prayer, May the souls, etc., is said at Compline only.

Proper of Seasons.

✠

PROPER OF SEASONS.

FIRST SUNDAY IN ADVENT.

First Vespers.

CHAPTER. Is. ii.

AND it shall come to pass in the last days, that the mountain of the Lord's house shall be established in the top of the mountains, and shall be exalted above the hills; and all nations shall flow unto it.

R̃. Thanks be to God.

This R̃., Thanks be to God, is always said at all Hours, immediately after the Chapter.

R̃. Behold, the days come, saith the Lord, that I will raise unto David a righteous branch, and a king shall reign and prosper, and shall execute judgment and justice in the earth. ✳ And this is His Name whereby He shall be called. † The Lord our Righteousness. V̇. In His days Judah shall be saved, and Israel shall dwell safely. R̃. And this is His Name whereby He shall be called. V̇. Glory be to the Father, and to the Son, and to the Holy Ghost. R̃. The Lord our Righteousness.

HYMN. *Conditor alme siderum.*

CREATOR of the stars of night,
Thy people's everlasting light,
Jesu, Redeemer, save us all,
And hear Thy servants when they call.

Thou, grieving that the ancient curse
Should doom to death an universe,
Hast found the med'cine, full of grace,
To save and heal a ruin'd race.

Thou cam'st, the Bridegroom of the Bride,
As drew the world to evening tide,
Proceeding from a virgin shrine,
The spotless Victim all divine.

At Whose dread Name, majestic now,
All knees must bend, all hearts must bow;
And things celestial Thee shall own,
And things terrestrial, Lord alone.

O Thou whose coming is with dread,
To judge and doom the quick and dead,
Preserve us, while we dwell below,
From ev'ry insult of the foe.

To Him Who comes the world to free,
To God the Son, all glory be:
To God the Father, as is meet,
To God the blessed Paraclete. Amen.

V̇. Drop down, ye heavens, from above. R̃. And let the skies pour down righteousness : let the earth open, and let them bring forth salvation.

Ant. to Mag. Behold, the Name of the Lord cometh from far : for His glory filleth the whole earth.

COLLECT.

ALMIGHTY God, give us grace that we may cast away the works of darkness, and put upon us the armour of light, now in the time of this mortal life, in which Thy Son Jesus Christ came to visit us in great humility; that in the last day, when He shall come again in His glorious

Majesty to judge both the quick and dead, we may rise to the life immortal, through Him Who liveth and reigneth with Thee and the Holy Ghost, now and ever. Amen. .

[*Or this,*

RAISE up, we pray Thee, O Lord, Thy power, and come: that from the dangers which hang over us by reason of our sins, we may be shielded by Thy protection, and delivered by Thy salvation, Who livest and reignest with the Father and the Holy Ghost, ever one God, world without end. Amen.]

On this day no Memorial is said except that of S. Mary.

MEMORIAL OF S. MARY.

Ant. Hail, Mary, full of grace, the Lord is with thee : blessed art thou among women. Alleluia.

℣. There shall come forth a rod out of the stem of Jesse.

℞. And a branch shall grow out of his roots.

COLLECT.

O GOD, Who didst will that Thy Word should take flesh in the womb of the Blessed Virgin Mary, grant to Thy suppliants, that we, who believe her to be indeed the Mother of God, may be helped by her intercession before Thee; through the same Thy Son Jesus Christ our Lord, Who liveth and reigneth with Thee and the Holy Ghost, ever one God, world without end. Amen.

[*At Lauds the* MEMORIAL OF S. MARY *is said with the same* ℣., ℞., *and Collect, but with this*

Ant. The angel Gabriel was sent to the Virgin Mary : espoused to Joseph.

At the second Vespers, with this

Ant. Blessed art thou, Mary, who hast believed : for there shall be a performance of those things that were told thee from the Lord. Alleluia.

These Memorials are said on all Sundays and Festivals of nine lessons until Christmas Eve. But when the Ant., Blessed art thou, is said to Magnificat, the Ant. of the Memorial is as on Ferias :

Ant. Fear not, Mary : for thou hast found favour with God. And behold, thou shalt conceive in thy womb, and bring forth a Son. Alleluia.

[*If* O Sapientia *is begun on a Sunday, the Memorial of S. Mary at the second Vespers is the same as at the first Vespers :* Hail, Mary.]

℣. The Lord be with you.

℞. And with thy spirit.

℣. Bless we the Lord.

℞. Thanks be to God.

Compline.

Ant. to Nunc Dim. Come, O Lord, and visit us in peace, that we may rejoice before Thee with a perfect heart.

This Ant. is said daily through Advent.

Lauds.

Daily until Christmas Eve is said this Sacerdotal ℣. *and* ℞.

℣. Send, O Lord, the Lamb to the ruler of the land.

℞. From the rock of the wilderness, unto the mount of the daughter of Sion.

℣. O God, make speed, etc.

Psalms of Sunday, p. 1.

Ant. 1. In that day the mountains shall drop down new wine : and the hills shall flow with milk. Alleluia.

Ant. 2. Rejoice greatly, O daughter of Zion : shout, O daughter of Jerusalem. Alleluia.

Ant. 3. The Lord my God shall come : and all His saints with Him. And it shall come to pass in that day, that the light shall not be clear, nor dark : but at evening time it shall be light. Alleluia.

Ant. 4. Ho, every one that thirsteth, come ye to the waters. Seek ye the Lord, while He may be found. Alleluia.

Ant. 5. Behold, a great Prophet cometh, and He shall renew Jerusalem. Alleluia.

CHAPTER. Rom. xiii.

NOW it is high time to awake out of sleep: for now is our salvation nearer than when we believed.

℟. Thanks be to God.

HYMN. *Vox clara ecce intonat.*

A THRILLING voice by Jordan rings,
　Rebuking guilt and darksome things:
Vain dreams of sin and visions fly;
Christ in His might shines forth on high.

Now let each torpid soul arise,
That sunk in guilt and wounded lies;
See! the New Star's refulgent ray
Shall chase disease and sin away!

The Lamb descends from Heaven above,
To pardon sin with freest love;
For such indulgent mercy shewn,
With tearful joy our thanks we own:

That when again He shines revealed,
And trembling worlds to terror yield,
He give not sin its just reward,
But in His love protect and guard.

To Him, Who comes the world to free,
To God the Son, all glory be:
All glory, as is ever meet,
To Father and to Paraclete. Amen.

℣. A voice crying in the wilderness.

℟. Prepare ye the way of the Lord: make straight a highway for our God.

Ant. to Ben. The Holy Ghost shall come down upon thee, Mary; fear not, bearing in thy womb the Son of God. Alleluia.

Collect as at the First Vespers, p. 73.

MEMORIAL OF S. MARY, p. 74.

Prime.

(The Antiphons at the little Hours are never doubled.)

Ant. In that day * the mountains shall drop down new wine: and the hills shall flow with milk. Alleluia.

Ant. to Quicunque. Thee, God the Father, p. 30.

Tierce.

Ant. Rejoice greatly, * O daughter of Zion : shout, O daughter of Jerusalem. Alleluia.

CHAPTER. Rom. xiii.

NOW it is high time to awake out of sleep: for now is our salvation nearer than when we believed.

The Reader says ℟. Come and save us * O Lord God of Hosts. *The Choir repeats the same. The Reader says* ℣. Shew the light of Thy countenance, and we shall be whole. *Choir.* O Lord God of Hosts. *Reader.* Glory be to the Father, and to the Son, and to the Holy Ghost. *Choir.* Come and save us, O Lord God of Hosts.

The Reader says ℣. The heathen shall fear Thy Name, O Lord.

The Choir answers: ℟. And all the kings of the earth Thy majesty.

This order is to be observed in all ℟℟. at the little Hours throughout the year, out of Lent, except on Septuagesima, Sexagesima, and Quinquagesima Sundays.

Then the Reader saith the Collect of the day, preceded by

℣. The Lord be with you.
℟. And with thy spirit.

Let us pray.

Collect as at Lauds.

This Collect is said at every Hour through this day, and during the week, when the Office is of the season. And this rule is to be observed throughout the year, whether the Office be of the season, or of any Saint: the Collect said at Lauds is repeated at Tierce, Sexts, Nones, and Second Vespers, except on certain days, as hereafter noted.

Sexts.

Ant. The Lord my God shall come : * and all His saints with Him. And it shall come to pass in that day, that the light shall not be clear, nor dark : but at evening time it shall be light. Alleluia.

CHAPTER. Rom. xiii.

THE night is far spent, the day is at hand ; let us therefore cast off the works of darkness, and let us put on the armour of light.

R7. O Lord, shew Thy mercy upon us. V. And grant us Thy salvation. R7. Thy mercy upon us. V. Glory be to the Father, and to the Son : and to the Holy Ghost. R7. O Lord, shew Thy mercy upon us.

V. Remember me, O Lord, according to the favour that Thou bearest unto Thy people.

R7. O visit me with Thy salvation.

Nones.

Ant. Behold, a great Prophet cometh : and He shall renew Jerusalem. Alleluia.

CHAPTER. Rom. xiii.

LET us walk honestly as in the day ; not in rioting and drunkenness, not in chambering and wantonness, not in strife and envying. But put ye on the Lord Jesus Christ.

R7. The Lord shall arise upon thee, O Jerusalem. V. And His glory shall be seen upon thee. R7. O Jerusalem. V. Glory be to the Father, and to the Son : and to the Holy Ghost. R7. The Lord shall arise upon thee, O Jerusalem.

V. Turn us again, O Lord God of Hosts.

R7. Shew the light of Thy countenance, and we shall be whole.

Second Vespers.

CHAPTER. Rom. xiii.

NOW it is high time to awake out of sleep : for now is our salvation nearer than when we believed.

R7. Thanks be to God.

The Reader begins this R7. Thou shalt arise, O Lord. * The Choir continues :* R7. And have mercy upon Sion. *The Reader :* V. For it is time that Thou have mercy upon her, yea, the time is come. R7. And have mercy upon Sion. V. Glory be, etc. R7. Thou shalt arise, O Lord, and have mercy upon Sion.

This R7. *is said daily till* O Sapientia, *and the* R7. *at Vespers is always said in the above order.*

HYMN. *Conditor alme siderum,*
V. and R7., p. 73.

Ant. to Mag. Fear not, Mary, for thou hast found favour with God : behold, thou shalt conceive, and bring forth a Son. Alleluia.

COLLECT.

MEMORIAL OF S. MARY, p. 74.

———

Monday.

Lauds.

V. Send, O Lord, the Lamb to the ruler of the land. R7. From the rock of the wilderness to the mountain of the daughter of Sion.

CHAPTER. Jer. xxiii.

BEHOLD, the days come, saith the Lord, that I will raise unto David a righteous branch, and a King shall reign and prosper, and shall execute judgment and justice in the earth.

HYMN. *Vox clara ecce intonat,*
V. and R7., p. 75.

Ant. to Ben. The angel of the Lord brought tidings unto Mary : and she conceived of the Holy Ghost.

MEMORIAL OF S. MARY.

Ant. The Holy Ghost shall come upon thee, Mary : fear not, for thou hast in thy womb the Son of God. Alleluia.

℣. And there shall come forth a rod out of the stem of Jesse.

℟. And a branch shall grow out of his roots.

COLLECT.

O GOD, Who didst will that Thy Word should take flesh in the womb of the blessed Virgin Mary ; grant to Thy suppliants, that we, who believe her to be indeed the Mother of God, may be helped by her intercession before Thee ; through the same Thy Son Jesus Christ our Lord, Who liveth and reigneth with Thee and the Holy Ghost, ever one God, world without end. Amen.

MEMORIAL OF ALL SAINTS.

Behold the Lord shall come, and all His Saints with Him : and there shall be in that day a great light. Alleluia.

℣. Behold, the Lord shall appear on a white cloud.

℟. And with Him ten thousands of His Saints.

COLLECT.

VISIT, we beseech Thee, O Lord, and cleanse our consciences, that Thy Son our Lord Jesus Christ, when He cometh, may find in us a dwelling-place prepared for Himself ; Who liveth and reigneth with Thee and the Holy Ghost, ever one God, world without end. Amen.

At VESPERS *the* MEMORIAL OF S. MARY *is said with this*

Ant. Fear not, Mary ; for thou hast found favour with God : and behold, thou shalt conceive in thy womb, and bring forth a Son. Alleluia.

MEMORIAL OF ALL SAINTS *as at Lauds.*

These Memorials of S. Mary and of All Saints are said at Lauds and Vespers on all Ferias until Christmas Eve, except that the Memorial of All Saints is not said on or after O Sapientia.

Prime.

Ant. to Psalms. Come and deliver us : * O our God.

Ant. to Quicunque. Glory to Thee, p. 30.

Tierce.

Ant. O Lord, raise up Thy power : * and come and save us.

CHAPTER. Heb. x.

FOR yet a little while, and He that shall come will come, and will not tarry.

℟. Come and save us, O Lord God of Hosts. ℣. Shew the light of Thy countenance, and we shall be whole. ℟. O Lord God of Hosts. ℣. Glory be to the Father, and to the Son, and to the Holy Ghost. ℟. Come and save us, O Lord God of Hosts.

℣. The heathen shall fear Thy Name, O Lord.

℟. And all the kings of the earth Thy Majesty.

Sexts.

Ant. When Thou comest : * deliver us, O Lord.

CHAPTER. Is. xiii., xiv.

HER time is near to come, and her days shall not be prolonged. For the Lord will have mercy on Jacob, and will yet choose Israel.

℟. O Lord, shew Thy mercy upon us. ℣. And grant us Thy salvation. ℟. Thy mercy upon us. ℣. Glory be to the Father, and to the Son : and to the Holy Ghost. ℟. O Lord, shew Thy mercy upon us.

℣. Remember me, O Lord, according to the favour that Thou bearest unto Thy people.

℟. O visit me with Thy salvation.

Nones.

Ant. Come, O Lord, * and tarry not : do away the offences of Thy people Israel.

CHAPTER. Micah iv.

COME, and let us go up to the mountain of the Lord, and to the house of the God of Jacob; and He will teach us of His ways, and we will walk in His paths: for the law shall go forth of Zion, and the word of the Lord from Jerusalem.

R̷. The Lord shall arise upon thee, O Jerusalem. V̷. And His glory shall be seen upon thee. R̷. O Jerusalem. V̷. Glory be to the Father, and to the Son : and to the Holy Ghost. R̷. The Lord shall arise upon thee, O Jerusalem.

V̷. Turn us again, O Lord God of Hosts.

R̷. Shew the light of Thy countenance, and we shall be whole.

Vespers.

CHAPTER. Jer. xxiii.

IN His days Judah shall be saved, and Israel shall dwell safely: and this is His Name whereby He shall be called, The Lord our righteousness.

Reader : R̷. Thou shalt arise, O Lord. *Choir.* And have mercy upon Sion. V̷. For it is time that Thou have mercy upon her, yea, the time is come. R̷. And have mercy upon Sion. V̷. Glory be to the Father, and to the Son, and to the Holy Ghost. R̷. Thou shalt arise, O Lord, and have mercy upon Sion.

HYMN. *Conditor alme siderum,*
V̷. and R., p. 73.

Ant. to Mag. O Jerusalem, look about thee toward the east : and behold. Alleluia.

[*For. Ferial Vesper Memorials in Advent,*
see Lauds, p. 77.]

The Office is thus said on Ferias through Advent, except the Ants. to Benedictus *and* Magnificat, *which change as below.*

Tuesday.

Ant. to Ben. O Jerusalem, lift up thine eyes, and behold the power of the King : Lo, the Saviour shall come to loose thee from thy chain.

Ant. to Mag. Seek ye the Lord while He may be found : call ye upon Him while He is near. Alleluia.

Wednesday.

Ant. to Ben. The law shall go forth of Sion : and the word of the Lord from Jerusalem.

Ant. to Mag. One mightier than I cometh : the latchet of Whose shoes I am not worthy to unloose.

Thursday.

Ant. to Ben. Blessed art thou among women : and blessed is the fruit of thy womb.

Ant. to Mag. I will wait upon the Lord : and I will look for Him, for He is at hand. Alleluia.

Friday.

Ant. to Ben. Behold, God and man shall come forth from the house of David : to sit on the throne. Alleluia.

Ant. to Mag. Out of Egypt have I called My Son : for He shall come to save His people.

Saturday.

Ant. to Ben. Sion, fear not : behold, God cometh. Alleluia.

SECOND SUNDAY IN ADVENT.

First Vespers.

CHAPTER. Is. iv.

IN that day shall the branch of the Lord be beautiful and glorious, and the fruit of the earth shall be excellent and comely, for them that are escaped out of Israel.

Ry. The Lord shall teach us His ways, and we will walk in His paths. * For the law shall go forth of Zion, and the word of the Lord from Jerusalem. Ƴ. Come, and let us go up to the mountain of the Lord, and to the house of the God of Jacob. Ry. For the law shall go forth of Zion, and the word of the Lord from Jerusalem.

HYMN. *Conditor alme siderum*, Ƴ. and Ry., p. 73.

Ant. to Mag. The Saviour of the world shall arise as the sun : and come down into the Virgin's womb, as the showers upon the grass.

COLLECT.

BLESSED Lord, Who hast caused all holy Scriptures to be written for our learning; grant that we may in such wise hear them, read, mark, learn, and inwardly digest them, that by patience and comfort of Thy holy word, we may embrace and ever hold fast the blessed hope of everlasting life, which Thou hast given us in our Saviour Jesus Christ. Amen.

[*Or this,*

QUICKEN our hearts, O Lord, to make ready the way of Thine only-begotten Son; that being purified by His Advent, we may attain to serve Thee with pure hearts: through the same Jesus Christ our Lord. Amen.]

Lauds.

Psalms of Sunday, p. 1.

Ant. 1. Behold, the Lord shall come in the clouds of heaven : with great power. Alleluia.

Ant. 2. Zion is the city of our strength ; the Saviour hath set thereon walls and bulwarks : Open ye the gates, for God is with us. Alleluia.

Ant. 3. Behold, the Lord will appear, and will not lie : though He tarry, wait for Him, because He will surely come, He will not tarry. Alleluia.

Ant. 4. The mountains and the hills shall break forth before Him into singing : and all the trees of the field shall clap their hands, for the Lord the Governour shall come unto His everlasting kingdom. Alleluia. Alleluia.

Ant. 5. Behold, our Lord shall come with power : to enlighten the eyes of His servants. Alleluia.

CHAPTER. Rom. xv.

WHATSOEVER things were written aforetime were written for our learning, that we through patience and comfort of the scriptures might have hope.

Ry. Thanks be to God.

HYMN. *Vox clara ecce intonat.* Ƴ. and Ry. p. 75.

Ant. to Ben. Upon the throne of David, and upon His kingdom : shall He sit for ever and ever. Alleluia.

Collect as at First Vespers.

Prime.

Ant. to Psalms. Behold, the Lord shall come in the clouds of heaven : with great power. Alleluia.

Tierce.

Ant. Zion is the city of our strength ; the Saviour hath set thereon walls and bulwarks : Open ye the gates, for God is with us. Alleluia.

CHAPTER. Rom. xv.

WHATSOEVER things were written aforetime were written for our learning, that we through patience and comfort of the scriptures might have hope.

Ry. Come and save us.   p. 75.

Sexts.

Ant. Behold the Lord will appear, and will not lie : though He tarry, wait for Him, because He will surely come, He will not tarry.   Alleluia.

CHAPTER. Rom. xv.

NOW the God of patience and consolation grant you to be like-minded one toward another according to Christ Jesus : that ye may with one mind and one mouth glorify God, even the Father of our Lord Jesus Christ.

Ry. O Lord, shew Thy mercy. p. 76.

Nones.

Ant. Behold, our Lord shall come with power : to enlighten the eyes of His servants.   Alleluia.

CHAPTER. Rom. xv.

NOW the God of hope fill you with all joy and peace in believing, that ye may abound in hope, through the power of the Holy Ghost.

Ry. The Lord shall arise.   p. 76.

Second Vespers.

CHAPTER. Rom. xv.

WHATSOEVER things were written aforetime were written for our learning, that we through patience and comfort of the scriptures might have hope.

Ry. Thou shalt arise.   p. 76.

HYMN. *Conditor alme siderum.*
    V. and Ry. p. 73.

Ant. to Mag. Blessed art thou, Mary, that believedst : for there shall be a performance of those things which were told thee from the Lord. Alleluia.

Monday.

Ant. to Ben. From heaven shall come the Lord the Governour : and in His hand are honour and rule.

Ant. to Mag. Behold, the King cometh, the Lord of the earth : and He shall take away the yoke of our captivity.

Tuesday.

Ant. to Ben. The Lord shall arise upon thee, O Jerusalem : and His glory shall be seen upon thee.

Ant. to Mag. The voice of one crying in the wilderness; Prepare ye the way of the Lord : make straight a highway for our God.

Wednesday.

Ant. to Ben. Behold, I send My angel : which shall prepare Thy way before Thy face.

Ant. to Mag. O Sion, thou shalt be renewed : and see thy righteous One, Which is come unto thee.

Thursday.

Ant. to Ben. Thou art He that should come, O Lord : for Whom we look to save Thy people.

Ant. to Mag. He that cometh after me is preferred before me : Whose shoe's latchet I am not worthy to unloose.

Friday.

Ant. to Ben. Say to them that are of a fearful heart : Be strong, fear not; behold, your God will come.

Ant. to Mag. Sing unto the Lord a new song : and His praise from the end of the earth.

Saturday.

Ant. to Ben. He shall set up an ensign for the nations : and shall assemble the outcasts of Israel.

THIRD SUNDAY IN ADVENT.

First Vespers.

CHAPTER. Gen. xlix.

THE sceptre shall not depart from Judah, nor a lawgiver from between his feet, until Shiloh come; and unto Him shall the gathering of the people be.

℟. He that shall come, will come, and will not tarry. Now shall there be no more fear in thy borders. * For He is our Saviour. ℣. He will subdue our iniquities : and cast our sins into the depths of the sea. ℟. For He is our Saviour. ℣. Glory be to the Father, and to the Son, and to the Holy Ghost. ℟. For He is our Saviour.

HYMN. *Conditor alme siderum.* ℣. and ℟. p. 73.

Ant. to Mag. Before Me there was no God formed, neither shall there be after Me : for to Me every knee shall bow, and Me every tongue confess.

COLLECT.

O LORD Jesu Christ, who at Thy first coming didst send Thy messenger to prepare Thy way before Thee; grant that the ministers and stewards of Thy mysteries may likewise so prepare and make ready Thy way, by turning the hearts of the disobedient to the wisdom of the just, that, at Thy second coming to judge the world, we may be found an acceptable people in Thy sight, Who livest and reignest with the Father and the Holy Spirit, ever one God, world without end. Amen.

[Or this,

BOW down Thine ear to our prayers, O Lord, we beseech Thee; and lighten the darkness of our souls by the grace of Thy visitation; Who livest and reignest with the Father, and the Holy Ghost, ever one God, world without end. Amen.]

Lauds.

Ant. 1. The Lord will surely come, He will not tarry : and will bring to light the hidden things of darkness, and reveal Himself to all people. Alleluia.

Ant. 2. Jerusalem, rejoice with great joy : for the Saviour shall come to thee.

Ant. 3. I will place salvation in Sion : for Israel My glory. Alleluia.

Ant. 4. Every mountain and hill shall be made low, and the crooked shall be made straight : and the rough places plain. Come, O Lord, and tarry not. Alleluia.

Ant. 5. Let us live soberly, righteously, and godly : looking for that blessed hope, and the coming of the Lord.

CHAPTER. i Cor. iv.

LET a man so account of us, as of the ministers of Christ, and stewards of the mysteries of God.

℟. Thanks be to God.

HYMN. *Vox clara ecce intonat,* ℣. and ℟. p. 75.

Ant. to Ben. When John had heard in the prison the works of Christ, he sent two of his disciples : and said unto Him, Art Thou He that should come, or do we look for another?

Collect as at the First Vespers.

Prime.

Ant. to Psalms. The Lord will surely come, He will not tarry : and will bring to light the hidden things of darkness, and reveal Himself to all people. Alleluia.

Tierce.

Ant. Jerusalem, rejoice with great joy : for the Saviour shall come to thee.

CHAPTER. 1 Cor. iv.

LET a man so account of us, as of the ministers of Christ, and stewards of the mysteries of God.

R7. Come and save us. p. 75.

Sexts.

Ant. I will place salvation in Sion : for Israel My glory. Alleluia.

CHAPTER. 1 Cor. iv.

BUT with me it is a very small thing that I should be judged of you, or of man's judgment: yea, I judge not mine own self.

R7. O Lord, shew Thy mercy. p. 76.

Nones.

Ant. Let us live soberly, righteously, and godly : looking for that blessed hope, and the coming of the Lord.

CHAPTER. 1 Cor. iv.

THEREFORE judge nothing before the time, until the Lord come, who both will bring to light the hidden things of darkness, and will make manifest the counsels of the hearts : and then shall every man have praise of God.

R7. The Lord shall arise. p. 76.

Second Vespers.

CHAPTER. 1 Cor. iv.

LET a man so account of us, as of the ministers of Christ, and stewards of the mysteries of God. Moreover, it is required in stewards, that a man be found faithful.

R7. Thou shalt arise. p. 76.

Unless on, or after O Sapientia, *in which case is said,*

R7. Make haste, O Lord, tarry not : ✳ and deliver Thy people. V. Come, O Lord, tarry not, do away the offences of Thy people Israel. R7. And deliver Thy people. V. Glory be to the Father, and to the Son : and to the Holy Ghost. R7. And deliver Thy people.

HYMN. *Conditor alme siderum,*
V. and R7., p. 73.

Ant. to Mag. (*if not one of the Great Ant*s·) Go and shew John again those things which ye do hear and see : the blind receive their sight, and the lame walk, the lepers are cleansed, and the deaf hear.

The R7. of the 3rd Sunday in Advent, Make haste, O Lord, *is said daily before the Great Ant*s·, *except at the First Vespers of the 4th Sunday in Advent. On and after* O Sapientia, *the Memorial of All Saints is omitted, and no petitions are said at Vespers ; but at Compline and the other Hours they are said as usual.*

THE GREAT ANTIPHONS,
Each of which is said at Vespers on its own day.

DECEMBER 16. *O Sapientia.*

O WISDOM, Which camest forth out of the mouth of the Most High, and reachest from one end to the other, mightily and sweetly ordering all things : Come and teach us the way of prudence.

DECEMBER 17. *O Adonai.*

O LORD and Ruler of the house of Israel, Who appearedst unto Moses in a flame of fire in the bush, and gavest unto him the law in Sinai : Come and redeem us with an outstretched arm.

DECEMBER 18. *O Radix Jesse.*

O ROOT of Jesse, Who standest for an ensign of the people, at Whom kings shall shut their mouths, unto

Whom the Gentiles shall pray : Come and deliver us, and tarry not.

DECEMBER 19.   *O Clavis David.*

O KEY of David, and Sceptre of the house of Israel, Thou that openest, and no man shutteth, and shuttest, and no man openeth : Come, and loose the prisoner from the prison-house, and him that sitteth in darkness from the shadow of death.

DECEMBER 20.   *O Oriens.*

O ORIENT, Brightness of the eternal light, and Sun of righteousness : Come and lighten them that sit in darkness, and in the shadow of death.

DECEMBER 21.   *O Rex Gentium.*

O KING of the Gentiles, and their desire, the Corner-stone, Who madest both one : Come and save man, whom Thou hast made out of the dust of the earth.

DECEMBER 22.   *O Emmanuel.*

O EMMANUEL, our King and Lawgiver, the desire of all nations, and their Saviour : Come and save us, O Lord our God.

DECEMBER 23.   *O Virgo Virginum.*

O VIRGIN of virgins, how shall this be ? For neither before thee was any like thee, nor shall there be after : Daughters of Jerusalem, why marvel ye at me ? The thing which ye behold is a divine mystery.

Monday.
Lauds.

At the remaining Ferias in Advent, each Psalm at Lauds has a proper Ant.

Psalms of the Feria.

Ant. 1. Behold, the Lord shall come, the Prince of the kings of the earth : blessed are they that are prepared to go out to meet Him.

Ant. 2. When the Son of man cometh : shall He find faith on the earth ?

Ant. 3. Behold, the fulness of the time is come : wherein God hath sent forth His Son.

Ant. 4. With joy : shall ye draw water out of the wells of salvation.

Ant. 5. The Lord shall come forth from His holy place : He shall come to save His people.

Ant. to Ben. There shall come forth a rod out of the stem of Jesse : and all the earth shall be filled with the glory of the Lord ; and all flesh shall see the salvation of God.

Vespers.

Ant. to Mag. (if not a Great Ant.) Awake, awake : stand up, O Jerusalem ; loose thyself from the bands of thy neck, O captive daughter of Sion.

Tuesday.
Lauds.

Ant. 1. Behold, our Lord shall come with power : and Himself shall break the yoke of our captivity.

Ant. 2. Send, O Lord, the Lamb, the Ruler of the land : from the rock of the wilderness unto the mount of the daughter of Sion.

Ant. 3. That Thy way, O Lord, may be known upon earth : Thy saving health among all nations.

Ant. 4. Reward them, O Lord, that wait for Thee : and let Thy prophets be found faithful.

Ant. 5. The law was given by Moses : but grace and truth came by Jesus Christ.

Ant. to Ben. And thou, Bethlehem, in the land of Judah, art not the least among the princes of Judah : for out of thee shall come a Governour, that shall rule My people Israel.

Vespers.

Ant. to Mag. (if not a Great Ant.)
Let the mountains break forth with joy, and the hills with righteousness : for the Lord, the light of the world, cometh with power.

Ember Wednesday.
Lauds.

Ant. 1. Drop down, ye heavens, from above, and let the skies pour down righteousness : let the earth open, and let them bring forth salvation.

Ant. 2. The prophets did foretell : that Messiah should be born of the Virgin Mary.

Ant. 3. The spirit of the Lord is upon Me : He hath anointed Me to preach the Gospel to the poor.

Ant. 4. Behold, the Lord shall come : that He may sit among princes, and inherit the throne of His glory.

Ant. 5. Tell it out among the nations : and say ye; Behold, God our Saviour cometh.

Ant. to Ben. The angel Gabriel was sent from God : to Mary a virgin espoused to a man whose name was Joseph.

The petitions are not said at Lauds on the three Ember Days, but are said at all the other Hours, (except Vespers, if after O Sapientia.)

COLLECT.

GRANT, we beseech Thee, Almighty God, that the coming solemnity of our redemption may bestow on us all things needful to this life, and the rewards of eternal blessedness; through Jesus Christ our Lord. Amen.

This Collect is said at Lauds only. At all the other Hours is said the Collect of Sunday.

Vespers.

Ant. to Mag. (if not a Great Ant.)
How shall this be, O angel of God, seeing I know not a man ? : Hearken, Mary, Virgin of Christ, the Holy Ghost shall come upon thee, and the power of the Highest shall overshadow thee.

Thursday.
Lauds.

Ant. 1. Out of Sion shall come forth the Lord Almighty : to save His people.

Ant. 2. Turn Thee again, O Lord, a little while : and delay not to come unto Thy servants.

Ant. 3. Out of Sion shall come He that shall reign : He is our Lord Immanuel ; great is His Name.

Ant. 4. Behold, this is our God ; and I will prepare Him an habitation : my father's God, and I will exalt Him.

Ant. 5. The Lord is our lawgiver ; the Lord is our King : He will come and save us.

Ant. to Ben. The Lord our God is at hand : watch ye therefore in your hearts.

Vespers.

Ant. to Mag. (if not a Great Ant.)
Rejoice ye with Jerusalem : and be glad with her, all ye that love her for ever.

Ember Friday.
Lauds.

Ant. 1. Stand ye still : and see the salvation of the Lord with you.

Ant. 2. Unto Thee, O Lord, do I lift up my soul : come and deliver me, for unto Thee, O Lord, have I fled.

Ant. 3. Come, O Lord, and tarry not : do away the offences of Thy people Israel.

Ant. 4. God shall come from Teman, and the Holy One from mount

Paran : His brightness shall be as the light.

Ant. 5. Therefore will I look unto the Lord : I will wait for the God of my salvation.

Ant. to Ben. As soon as the voice of thy salutation sounded in mine ears : the babe leaped in my womb for joy. Alleluia.

COLLECT.

RAISE up, we pray Thee, O Lord, Thy power, and come : that they who trust in Thy loving-kindness may be delivered from all adversity : Who livest and reignest with the Father and the Holy Ghost, ever one God, world without end. Amen.

This Collect is said at Lauds only. At all the other Hours is said the Collect of Sunday.

Vespers.

Ant. to Magnificat. *A Great Ant., according to the day of the month, and so on till Christmas.*

Ember Saturday.

Lauds.

Ant. 1. The Lord shall come with great power; and all flesh shall see Him : and He shall save us.

Ant. 2. Now consider how great this Man is : Who entereth in to save His people to the uttermost.

Ant. 3. Thy messenger shall come again, O Lord : and shall prepare Thy ways.

Ant. 4. The doctrine of the Lord shall drop as the rain : and our God shall distil upon us as the dew.

Ant. 5. Prepare to meet thy God : O Israel, for He cometh.

Ant. to Ben. Every valley shall be exalted; and every mountain and hill shall be made low : and all flesh shall see the salvation of God.

COLLECT.

O GOD, Who seest that we grieve by reason of our sinfulness, mercifully grant that by Thy visitation we may be consoled : Who livest and reignest with the Father and the Holy Ghost, ever one God, world without end. Amen.

This Collect is only said at Lauds. At all the other Hours is said the Collect of Sunday.

FOURTH SUNDAY IN ADVENT.

First Vespers.

CHAPTER. Is. xxviii. Rom. ix.

BEHOLD I lay in Sion for a foundation a Stone, a tried Stone, a precious Corner-stone, a sure foundation : and whosoever believeth on Him shall not be ashamed.

R͡. The sceptre shall not depart from Judah, not a lawgiver from between his feet ; until Shiloh come* and unto Him shall the gathering of the people be. V͡. His eyes shall be fairer than wine, and His teeth whiter than milk. R͡. And unto Him shall the gathering of the people be. V͡. Glory be to the Father, and to the Son, and to the Holy Ghost. R͡. And unto Him shall the gathering of the people be.

HYMN. *Conditor alme siderum,* V͡. *and* R͡. *p. 73.*

Great Antiphon.

COLLECT.

O LORD, raise up (we pray thee) Thy power, and come among us, and with great might succour us ; that whereas, through our sins and wickedness, we are sore let and hindered in running the race that is set before us, Thy bountiful grace and mercy may speedily help and deliver us ; through the satisfaction of Thy Son our Lord, to Whom with

Thee and the Holy Ghost be honour and glory, world without end. Amen.

[*Or this,*

RAISE up, we beseech Thee, O Lord, Thy power, and come, and with great might succour us; that whereas, through our sins and wickedness we are sore let and hindered, Thy mercy may speedily deliver us; Who livest and reignest with the Father and the Holy Ghost, ever one God, world without end. Amen.]

𝕷𝖆𝖚𝖉𝖘.

Ant. 1. Blow ye the trumpet in Sion, for the day of the Lord is nigh at hand : behold, He cometh to save us. Alleluia, Alleluia.

Ant. 2. Behold, the Desire of all nations shall come : and the house of the Lord shall be filled with glory. Alleluia.

Ant. 3. The crooked shall be made straight, and the rough places plain : come, O Lord, and tarry not. Alleluia.

Ant. 4. The Lord cometh; go ye out to meet Him, saying, Great is His dominion, and of His kingdom there shall be no end : the mighty God, the everlasting Father, the Prince of peace.

Ant. 5. Thine Almighty Word, O Lord, leapeth down from Heaven : out of Thy royal throne. Alleluia.

CHAPTER. Phil. iv.

REJOICE in the Lord alway, and again I say, Rejoice. Let your moderation be known unto all men. The Lord is at hand.

HYMN. *Vox clara ecce intonat,* ℣. and ℟. p. 75.

Ant. to Ben. I am the voice of one crying in the wilderness : Make straight the way of the Lord, as said the prophet Esaias.

Collect as at First Vespers.

𝕻𝖗𝖎𝖒𝖊.

Ant. Blow ye the trumpet in Sion, for the day of the Lord is nigh at hand : behold, He cometh to save us. Alleluia.

𝕿𝖎𝖊𝖗𝖈𝖊.

Ant. Behold, the Desire of all nations shall come : and the house of the Lord shall be filled with glory. Alleluia.

CHAPTER. Phil. iv.

REJOICE in the Lord alway, and again I say, Rejoice. Let your moderation be known unto all men. The Lord is at hand.

℟. Come and save us. p. 77.

𝕾𝖊𝖗𝖙𝖘.

Ant. The crooked shall be made straight, and the rough places plain : Come, O Lord, and tarry not. Alleluia.

CHAPTER. Phil. iv.

BE careful for nothing : but in everything by prayer and supplication with thanksgiving, let your requests be made known unto God.

℟. O Lord, shew Thy mercy. p. 77.

𝕹𝖔𝖓𝖊𝖘.

Ant. Thine Almighty Word, O Lord : leapeth down from Heaven out of Thy royal throne. Alleluia.

CHAPTER. Phil. iv.

AND the peace of God, which passeth all understanding, shall keep your hearts and minds.

℟. The Lord shall arise. p. 78.

𝕾𝖊𝖈𝖔𝖓𝖉 𝖁𝖊𝖘𝖕𝖊𝖗𝖘.

CHAPTER. Phil. iv.

REJOICE in the Lord alway, and again I say, Rejoice. Let your moderation be known unto all men. The Lord is at hand.

℟. Make haste, O Lord. p. 82.

HYMN. *Conditor alme siderum,*
℣. and ℟. p. 73.
Great Antiphon.

Monday,
(If not Christmas Eve.)
Lauds.
Ants. to Psalms as on 3rd Monday in Advent, p. 83.

Ant. to Ben. The Lord saith, Repent ye : for the kingdom of heaven is at hand. Alleluia.

Tuesday,
(If not Christmas Eve.)
Lauds.
Ants. to Psalms as on 3rd Tuesday in Advent, p. 83.

Ant. to Ben. Awake, awake, put on strength : O arm of the Lord.

Wednesday,
(If not Christmas Eve.)
Lauds.
Ants. to Psalms as on 3rd Wednesday in Advent, p. 84.

Ant. to Ben. Let them give glory unto the Lord, and declare His praise in the islands : for behold, He shall come, and shall not tarry.

Thursday,
(If not Christmas Eve.)
Lauds.
Ants. to Psalms as on 3rd Thursday in Advent, p. 84.

Ant. to Ben. Comfort ye, comfort ye My people : saith the Lord.

Friday,
(If not Christmas Eve.)
Lauds.
Ants. to Psalms as on 3rd Friday in Advent, p. 84.

Ant. to Ben. The day of the Lord shall come as a thief in the night : be ye therefore also ready, for at such an hour as ye think not, the Son of man cometh.

CHRISTMAS EVE.
Lauds.
℣. To-morrow shall the wickedness of the earth be done away.
℟. And the Saviour of the world shall be King over us.
℣. O God, make speed, etc.
Psalms of the Feria.

Ant. 1. O Judah and Jerusalem, fear not, nor be dismayed; to-morrow go ye forth : for the Lord will be with you.

Ant. 2. Ye shall know this day that the Lord will come : and in the morning, then shall ye see His glory.

Ant. 3. To-morrow shall the wickedness of the earth be done away : and the Saviour of the world shall be King over us.

Ant. 4. The Word of the Lord shall be looked for as rain : and our God shall come down upon us as the dew.

Ant. 5. To-morrow ye shall have help : saith the Lord God of Hosts.

CHAPTER. Is. lxii.
FOR Sion's sake will I not hold my peace, and for Jerusalem's sake I will not rest, until the righteousness thereof go forth as brightness, and the salvation thereof as a lamp that burneth.

HYMN. *Vox clara ecce intonat,*
p. 75.

℣. Ye shall know this day that the Lord will come.

℟. And in the morning, then shall ye see His glory.

Ant. to Ben. When Mary the mother of Jesus was espoused unto Joseph, before they came together she was found with child : for That which was conceived in her, was of the Holy Ghost. Alleluia.

COLLECT.

O GOD, Who makest us glad with the yearly expectation of our redemption : grant that we, who with joy receive Thine only-begotten Son as our Redeemer, may, without fear, behold Him when He shall come to be our Judge, even Thy Son our Lord Jesus Christ; Who liveth and reigneth with Thee in the unity of the Holy Ghost, God, world without end. Amen.

℣. The Lord be with you.
℟. And with thy spirit.
℣. Bless we the Lord.
℟. Thanks be to God.

This Collect is said at every Hour of Christmas Eve. No Memorial is said on this day but that of All Saints (except it be Sunday, when the Memorial of Sunday is said before that of All Saints).

From henceforth till after the Octave of Epiphany, the Ferial Petitions are not said. There is no kneeling at any of the Hours. Ps. cxxiii., Ad te levavi, with the prayers following, at Prime, is omitted till the Sunday after the Octave of Epiphany.

Prime.

Ant. O Judah and Jerusalem, fear not, nor be dismayed; to-morrow go ye forth : for the Lord will be with you.

CHAPTER. 1 Tim. 1.

NOW unto the King eternal, immortal, invisible, the only wise God, be honour and glory for ever and ever. Amen.

℟. Jesu Christ, Son of the living God, have mercy upon us. Alleluia, Alleluia. ℣. Thou that sittest at the right hand of the Father. Alleluia. ℟. Have mercy upon us. Alleluia, Alleluia. ℣. Glory be to the Father, and to the Son, and to the Holy Ghost. ℟. Jesu Christ, Son of the living God, have mercy upon us. Alleluia, Alleluia.

Tierce.

Ant. Ye shall know this day that the Lord will come : and in the morning, then shall ye see His glory.

CHAPTER. Isa. lxii.

FOR Sion's sake will I not hold my peace, and for Jerusalem's sake I will not rest, until the righteousness thereof go forth as brightness, and the salvation thereof as a lamp that burneth.

℟. Stand ye still. Alleluia, Alleluia. ℣. And see the salvation of the Lord with you. ℟. Alleluia, Alleluia. ℣. Glory be to the Father, and to the Son, and to the Holy Ghost. ℟. Stand ye still. Alleluia, Alleluia.

℣. To-morrow ye shall have help.
℟. Saith the Lord God of Hosts.

Sexts.

Ant. To-morrow shall the wickedness of the earth be done away : and the Saviour of the world shall be King over us.

CHAPTER. Isaiah lxii.

THE Gentiles shall see Thy righteousness, and all kings Thy glory : and Thou shalt be called by a new name, which the mouth of the Lord shall name.

℟. To-morrow ye shall have help. Alleluia, Alleluia. ℣. Saith the

Lord God of Hosts. Ry. Alleluia, Alleluia. ℣. Glory be to the Father, and to the Son, and to the Holy Ghost. Ry. To-morrow ye shall have help. Alleluia, Alleluia.

℣. Ye shall know this day that the Lord will come.

Ry. And in the morning, then shall ye see His glory.

Nones.

Ant. To-morrow ye shall have help : saith the Lord God of Hosts.

CHAPTER. Is. lxii.

THOU shalt no more be termed forsaken ; neither shall thy land any more be termed desolate : but thou shalt be called Hephzi-bah, and thy land Beulah : for the Lord delighteth in thee, and thy land shall be married.

Ry. Ye shall know this day that the Lord will come. Alleluia, Alleluia. ℣. And in the morning, then shall ye see His glory. Ry. Alleluia, Alleluia. ℣. Glory be to the Father, and to the Son, and to the Holy Ghost. Ry. Ye shall know this day that the Lord will come. Alleluia, Alleluia.

℣. Stand ye still.

Ry. And see the salvation of the Lord with you.

CHRISTMAS DAY.
First Vespers.

Ant. 1. The King of peace is exalted : Whom the whole earth seeketh.

Psalm cxiii. *Laudate, pueri,* p. 46.

Ant. 2. The King of peace is exalted : higher than the kings of the earth.

Psalm cxvii. *Laudate Dominum, omnes gentes,* p. 50.

Ant. 3. Know ye that the kingdom of God is nigh at hand : Verily I say unto you, it shall not tarry.

Psalm cxlvi. *Lauda, anima mea,* p. 63.

Ant. 4. Lift up your heads : for your redemption draweth nigh.

Psalm cxlvii. *Laudate Dominum,* p. 64.

Ant. 5. The days of Mary were accomplished : that she should bring forth her first-born Son.

Psalm cxlvii. 12. *Lauda Hierusalem,* p. 64.

CHAPTER. Is. ix.

THE people that walked in darkness have seen a great light : they that dwell in the land of the shadow of death, upon them hath the light shined.

Ry. Judah and Jerusalem, fear not : * to-morrow go ye forth. ℣. For the Lord will be with you. Ry. To-morrow go ye forth. ℣. Glory be to the Father, and to the Son, and to the Holy Ghost. Ry. To-morrow go ye forth.

HYMN. *Veni Redemptor gentium.*

COME, Thou Redeemer of the earth,
Come, testify Thy Virgin birth :
All lands admire,—all times applaud ;
Such is the birth that fits a God.

Begotten of no human will,
But of the Spirit, mystic still,
The Word of God in flesh arrayed,
The promised fruit to man displayed.

The Virgin womb that burden gained,
With Virgin honour all unstained ;
The banners there of virtue glow :
God in His temple dwells below.

Proceeding from His chamber free,
The royal hall of chastity,
Giant of twofold substance, straight
His destined way He runs elate.

From God the Father, He proceeds :
To God the Father back He speeds :
Proceeds,—as far as very hell ;
Speeds back, to light ineffable.

O Equal to Thy Father, Thou :
Gird on Thy fleshly mantle now ;
The weakness of our mortal state
With deathless might invigorate.

Thy cradle here shall glitter bright,
And darkness breathe a newer light :
Where endless faith shall shine serene,
And twilight never intervene.

[*At these Vespers only, this Doxology :*

All laud to God the Father be,
All praise, eternal Son, to Thee ;
All glory, as is ever meet,
To God the blessed Paraclete. Amen.]

But through Christmas tide the following:

All honour, laud, and glory be,
O Jesu, Virgin-born, to Thee!
All glory, as is ever meet,
To Father and to Paraclete. Amen.

℣. As a bridegroom.

℟. The Lord coming out of His chamber.

Ant. to Mag. At sunrise ye shall behold the King of kings from heaven : as a bridegroom out of his chamber, proceeding from God the Father.

COLLECT.

ALMIGHTY God, Who hast given us Thy only-begotten Son to take our nature upon Him, and as at this time to be born of a pure Virgin : grant that we, being regenerate, and made Thy children by adoption and grace, may daily be renewed by Thy Holy Spirit; through the same our Lord Jesus Christ, Who liveth and reigneth with Thee and the same Spirit, ever one God, world without end. Amen.

[*Or Collect for Christmas Eve,* p. 88.]

These Vespers end with Bless we the Lord, etc., *without* Alleluia.

Compline.

Ant. to Psalms. Be ye ready, like unto men that wait for their lord : when he shall return from the wedding.

HYMN. *Salvator mundi Domine,* ℣. *and* ℟. p. 67, *with doxology as there given.*

Ant. to Nunc Dim. Watch and pray : for ye know not when the time is. Watch ye therefore, for ye know not when the Lord cometh, at even, or at midnight, or at the cock-crowing, or in the morning; lest coming suddenly He find you sleeping.

Lauds.

Immediately after the Midnight Celebration, the principal Priest, before leaving the Altar, says the Sacerdotal

℣. The Word was made flesh. Alleluia.

℟. And dwelt among us. Alleluia.

℣. O God, make speed, etc.

Psalms of Sunday.

Ant. 1. Whom saw ye, O shepherds ? say ye, tell us, who hath appeared upon earth ? : We beheld the Child, the Lord and Saviour, in the choir of angels. Alleluia, Alleluia.

Ant. 2. A maiden hath borne the King Whose name is everlasting : she hath the joy of a mother, and likewise the honour of virginity; none hath been seen like unto her, neither shall there be any such. Alleluia.

Ant. 3. The angel said unto the shepherds : Behold, I bring you good tidings of great joy; for unto you is born this day the Saviour of the world. Alleluia, Alleluia.

Ant. 4. There was with the angel a multitude of the heavenly host, praising God, and saying : Glory to God in the highest, and on earth peace, good will towards men. Alleluia.

Ant. 5. Unto us a Child is born this day : and His name shall be called the mighty God. Alleluia, Alleluia.

CHAPTER. Titus ii.

THE grace of God that bringeth salvation hath appeared to all men, teaching us that, denying ungodliness and worldly lusts, we should live soberly, righteously, and godly in this present world.

HYMN. *A solis ortus cardine.*

FROM lands that see the sun arise,
  To earth's remotest boundaries,
The Virgin-born to-day we sing,
The Son of Mary, Christ the King.

Blest Author of this earthly frame,
To take a servant's form He came,
That liberating flesh by flesh,
Whom He had made might live afresh.

In that chaste parent's holy womb
Celestial grace hath found its home :
And she, as earthly bride unknown,
Yet calls that offspring blest her own.

The mansion of the modest breast
Becomes a shrine where God shall rest:
The pure and undefiled one
Conceived in her womb the Son.

That Son, that royal Son she bore,
Whom Gabriel's voice had told afore;
Whom, in His Mother yet conceal'd,
The infant Baptist had reveal'd.

The manger and the straw He bore,
The cradle did He not abhor:
By milk in infant portions fed,
Who gives e'en fowls their daily bread.

The heavenly chorus filled the sky,
The angels sang to God on high,
What time to shepherds, watching lone,
They made creation's Shepherd known.

For that Thine Advent glory be,
O Jesu, Virgin-born, to Thee!
With Father, and with Holy Ghost,
From men and from the heavenly host.
Amen.

℣. Blessed be He that cometh in the Name of the Lord.

℞. God is the Lord Who hath shewed us light.

Ant. to Ben. Glory to God in the highest : and on earth peace, good will towards men. Alleluia, Alleluia.

Collect as at First Vespers.

[*Or this,*

GRANT, we beseech Thee, Almighty God, that we who are held under the ancient bondage of sin, may be set free by the new birth in flesh of Thine only-begotten Son; Who liveth and reigneth with Thee and the Holy Ghost, ever one God, world without end. Amen.]

MEMORIAL OF S. MARY

At the full consummation of the mystery of the Incarnation.

Ant. Behold, all things are fulfilled : which were spoken by the angel of the Virgin Mary.

℣. After child-bearing thou remainedst a Virgin.

℞. O Mother of God.

COLLECT.

O GOD, Who through the fruitful virginity of the Blessed Virgin Mary hast bestowed the rewards of eternal salvation on the human race :

grant, we pray Thee, that she may intercede for us, through whom we have received the Author of Life, Thy Son Jesus Christ our Lord. Amen.

℣. Bless we the Lord.

℞. Thanks be to God.

Bless we the Lord *is not said with* Alleluia *except at Easter.*

Prime.

The last verse of the Hymn, Jam lucis, is sung thus :

All honour, laud, and glory be,
O Jesu, Virgin-born, to Thee!
All glory, as is ever meet,
To Father and to Paraclete. Amen.

This doxology is said to all Hymns of this metre, except A solis ortus cardine, till the morrow of the Purification (except on the Feast, and through the Octave of Epiphany).

Ant. to Psalms. Whom saw ye, O shepherds? Say ye, tell us, who hath appeared upon earth? : We beheld the Child, the Lord and Saviour, in the choir of angels. Alleluia, Alleluia.

CHAPTER. 1 Tim. i.

NOW unto the King eternal, immortal, invisible, the only wise God, be honour and glory, for ever and ever. Amen.

℞. Jesu Christ, Son of the living God, have mercy upon us. Alleluia, Alleluia. ℣. Thou that didst not abhor the Virgin's womb. ℞. Have mercy upon us. Alleluia, Alleluia. ℣. Glory be to the Father, and to the Son : and to the Holy Ghost. ℞. Jesu Christ, Son of the living God, have mercy upon us. Alleluia, Alleluia.

℣. O Lord, arise, help us.

℞. And deliver us for Thy Name's sake.

This ℞. is said at Prime daily till the morrow of the Purification, except on the Feast, and through the Octave of Epiphany.

Tierce.

Ant. A maiden hath borne the King, Whose name is everlasting : She hath the joy of a mother, and likewise the honour of virginity; none hath been seen like unto her, neither shall there be any such. Alleluia.

CHAPTER. Titus ii.

THE grace of God that bringeth salvation hath appeared unto all men, teaching us that, denying ungodliness and worldly lusts, we should live soberly, righteously, and godly in this present world.

Ry. The Word was made flesh. Alleluia, Alleluia. Ꝟ. And dwelt among us. Ry. Alleluia, Alleluia. Ꝟ. Glory be to the Father, and to the Son : and to the Holy Ghost. Ry. The Word was made flesh. Alleluia, Alleluia.

Ꝟ. He shall call Me.

Ry. Thou art my Father.

Sexts.

Ant. The angel said unto the shepherds : Behold, I bring you good tidings of great joy; for unto you is born this day the Saviour of the world. Alleluia, Alleluia.

CHAPTER. Titus iii.

AFTER that the kindness and love of God our Saviour towards man appeared, not by works of righteousness which we have done, but according to His mercy He saved us.

Ry. He shall call me. Alleluia, Alleluia. Ꝟ. Thou art my Father. Ry. Alleluia, Alleluia. Ꝟ. Glory be to the Father, and to the Son : and to the Holy Ghost. Ry. He shall call me. Alleluia, Alleluia.

Ꝟ. The Lord declared.

Ry. His salvation.

Nones.

Ant. Unto us a Child is born this day : and His name shall be called the mighty God. Alleluia, Alleluia.

CHAPER. Heb. i.

GOD, Who at sundry times and in divers manners spake in time past unto the fathers by the prophets, hath in these last days spoken unto us by His Son.

Ry. The Lord declared. Alleluia, Alleluia. Ꝟ. His salvation. Ry. Alleluia, Alleluia. Ꝟ. Glory be to the Father, and to the Son : and to the Holy Ghost. Ry. The Lord declared. Alleluia, Alleluia.

Ꝟ. Blessed be He that cometh in the Name of the Lord.

Ry. God is the Lord Who hath shewed us light.

Second Vespers.

Ant. 1. In the day of Thy power * shall the people offer Thee free-will offerings with an holy worship : the dew of Thy birth is of the womb of the morning.

Psalm cx. *Dixit Dominus.*

THE Lord said unto my Lord : Sit Thou on My right hand, until I make Thine enemies Thy footstool.

2 The Lord shall send the rod of Thy power out of Sion : be Thou ruler, even in the midst among Thine enemies.

3 In the day of Thy power shall the people offer Thee free-will offerings with an holy worship : the dew of Thy birth is of the womb of the morning.

4 The Lord sware, and will not repent : Thou art a Priest for ever after the order of Melchisedech.

5 The Lord upon Thy right hand : shall wound even kings in the day of His wrath.

6 He shall judge among the heathen ; He shall fill the places with the dead bodies : and smite in sunder the heads over divers countries.

7 He shall drink of the brook in

the way : therefore shall He lift up His head.

Glory be, etc.

Ant. 2. He sent redemption * unto His people : He hath commanded His covenant for ever.

Psalm CXI. *Confitebor tibi.*

I WILL give thanks unto the Lord with my whole heart : secretly among the faithful, and in the congregation.

2 The works of the Lord are great : sought out of all them that have pleasure therein.

3 His work is worthy to be praised, and had in honour : and His righteousness endureth for ever.

4 The merciful and gracious Lord hath so done His marvellous works : that they ought to be had in remembrance.

5 He hath given meat unto them that fear Him : He shall ever be mindful of His covenant.

6 He hath shewed His people the power of His works : that He may give them the heritage of the heathen.

7 The works of His hands are verity and judgment : all His commandments are true.

8 They stand fast for ever and ever : and are done in truth and equity.

9 He sent redemption unto His people : He hath commanded His covenant for ever; holy and reverend is His Name.

10 The fear of the Lord is the beginning of wisdom : a good understanding have all they that do thereafter; the praise of it endureth for ever.

Glory be, etc.

Ant. 3. Unto the godly * there ariseth up light in the darkness : the

Lord is merciful, loving, and righteous.

Psalm CXII. *Beatus vir.*

BLESSED is the man that feareth the Lord : he hath great delight in His commandments.

2 His seed shall be mighty upon earth : the generation of the faithful shall be blessed.

3 Riches and plenteousness shall be in his house : and his righteousness endureth for ever.

4 Unto the godly there ariseth up light in the darkness : he is merciful, loving, and righteous.

5 A good man is merciful, and lendeth : and will guide his words with discretion.

6 For he shall never be moved : and the righteous shall be had in everlasting remembrance.

7 He will not be afraid of any evil tidings : for his heart standeth fast, and believeth in the Lord.

8 His heart is established, and will not shrink : until he see his desire upon his enemies.

9 He hath dispersed abroad, and given to the poor : and his righteousness remaineth for ever; his horn shall be exalted with honour.

10 The ungodly shall see it, and it shall grieve him : he shall gnash with his teeth, and consume away; the desire of the ungodly shall perish.

Glory be, etc.

Ant. 4. With the Lord * there is mercy : and with Him is plenteous redemption.

Psalm CXXX. *De profundis.*

OUT of the deep have I called unto Thee, O Lord : Lord, hear my voice.

2 O let Thine ears consider well : the voice of my complaint.

3 If Thou, Lord, wilt be extreme

to mark what is done amiss : O Lord, who may abide it ?

4 For there is mercy with Thee : therefore shalt Thou be feared.

5 I look for the Lord; my soul doth wait for Him : in His word is my trust.

6 My soul fleeth unto the Lord : before the morning watch, I say, before the morning watch.

7 O Israel, trust in the Lord, for with the Lord there is mercy : and with Him is plenteous redemption.

8 And He shall redeem Israel : from all his sins.

Glory be, etc.

Ant. 5. Of the fruit * of thy body : shall I set upon thy seat.

Psalm CXXXII. *Memento, Domine.*

LORD, remember David : and all his trouble;

2 How he sware unto the Lord : and vowed a vow unto the Almighty God of Jacob.

3 I will not come within the tabernacle of mine house : nor climb up into my bed;

4 I will not suffer mine eyes to sleep, nor mine eyelids to slumber : neither the temples of my head to take any rest;

5 Until I find out a place for the temple of the Lord : an habitation for the mighty God of Jacob.

6 Lo, we heard of the same at Ephrata : and found it in the wood.

7 We will go into His tabernacle : and fall low on our knees before His footstool.

8 Arise, O Lord, into Thy resting-place : Thou, and the ark of Thy strength.

9 Let Thy priests be clothed with righteousness : and let Thy saints sing with joyfulness.

10 For Thy servant David's sake : turn not away the presence of Thine Anointed.

11 The Lord hath made a faithful oath unto David : and He shall not shrink from it.

12 Of the fruit of thy body : shall I set upon thy seat.

13 If thy children will keep my covenant, and My testimonies that I shall learn them : their children also shall sit upon thy seat for evermore.

14 For the Lord hath chosen Sion to be an habitation for Himself : He hath longed for her.

15 This shall be My rest for ever : here will I dwell, for I have a delight therein.

16 I will bless her victuals with increase : and will satisfy her poor with bread.

17 I will deck her priests with health : and her saints shall rejoice and sing.

18 There shall I make the horn of David to flourish : I have ordained a lantern for Mine Anointed.

19 As for His enemies, I shall clothe them with shame : but upon Himself shall His crown flourish.

Glory be, etc.

These Antiphons and Psalms are said daily till the First Vespers of Epiphany.

CHAPTER. Heb. i.

GOD, Who at sundry times and in divers manners spake in time past unto the fathers by the prophets, hath in these last days spoken unto us by His Son.

R/. The Word was made flesh. Alleluia, Alleluia. V/. And dwelt among us. R/. Alleluia, Alleluia. V/. Glory be to the Father, and to the Son : and to the Holy Ghost. R/. The Word was made flesh. Alleluia, Alleluia.

V/. He shall call Me.

R/. Thou art My Father.

HYMN. *Veni Redemptor gentium,* V/. and R/. p. 89.

Ant. to Mag. To-day Christ is born, to-day our Saviour appeared; to-day angels sing upon earth, and archangels rejoice: to-day the righteous are merry and say, Glory be to God on high. Alleluia.

Collect as at First Vespers.

MEMORIAL OF S. STEPHEN.

Ant. Thou art chief in the choirs of martyrs, like unto an angel: who didst pray to God for them that stoned thee.

℣. Thou hast crowned him with glory and worship.

℟. Thou makest him to have dominion of the works of Thy hands.

COLLECT.

For S. Stephen's Day.

GRANT, O Lord, that, in all our sufferings here upon earth for the testimony of Thy truth, we may stedfastly look up to heaven, and by faith behold the glory that shall be revealed; and, being filled with the Holy Ghost, may learn to love and bless our persecutors by the example of Thy first martyr Saint Stephen, who prayed for his murderers to Thee, O blessed Jesus, Who standest at the right hand of God to succour all those that suffer for Thee, our only Mediator and Advocate. Amen.

At these Vespers, and henceforth until the morrow of the Circumcision, no Memorial is made of S. Mary, at Lauds or Vespers. No Memorial is made of All Saints.

Compline.

Ant. to Psalms. Unto us is born this day in the city of David: a Saviour, which is Christ the Lord.

HYMN. *Salvator mundi Domine, with Christmas Doxology.*

Ant. to Nunc Dim. Alleluia. The Word was made flesh; Alleluia: and dwelt among us. Alleluia, Alleluia.

Compline is thus said till the Feast of the Circumcision.

FESTIVAL OF S. STEPHEN.

Lauds.

℣. The righteous shall flourish like a palm-tree.

℟. And shall spread abroad like a cedar in Libanus.

℣. O God, make speed, etc.

Psalms of Sunday.

Ant. 1. And they stoned Stephen, calling upon God, saying: Lord, lay not this sin to their charge.

Ant. 2. The stones of the brook were sweet unto him: him doth every soul of the righteous follow.

Ant. 3. My soul hangeth upon Thee, O God: for Thy sake hath my body been stoned.

Ant. 4. Stephen saw the heavens opened; he saw and entered in: blessed is he unto whom the heavens shall be opened.

Ant. 5. Behold, I see the heavens opened: and the Son of man standing on the right hand of God.

CHAPTER. Acts vi.

AND Stephen, full of faith and power, did great wonders and miracles among the people.

HYMN. *Sancte Dei pretiose.*

SAINT of God, elect and precious,
    Protomartyr Stephen, bright
With thy love, of amplest measure,
    Shining round thee like a light,
Who to God commendedst, dying,
    Them that did thee all despite:

Glitters now the crown above thee,
    Figured in thy sacred name:
Oh! that we, who truly love thee,
    May have portion in the same;
In the dreadful day of judgment
    Fearing neither sin nor shame.

Laud to God, and might and honour,
　Who with flowers of rosy dye
Crowned thy forehead, and hath placed thee
　In the starry throne on high :
He direct us, He protect us
　From death's sting eternally.　Amen.

℣. The righteous shall grow as a lily.

℟. He shall flourish for ever before the Lord.

Ant. to Ben. The wicked thrust sore at him to give him over unto death, but he endured the stones : rejoicing that he was accounted worthy to receive the crown of glory. Alleluia.

Collect as at First Vespers, p. 95.

MEMORIAL OF THE NATIVITY.

Ant. To-day a faithful Virgin brought forth the Incarnate Word; and yet after child-bearing she abideth virgin : in whose praise let us all say, Blessed art thou among women.

℣. Blessed is He that cometh in the Name of the Lord.

℟. God is the Lord Who hath shewed us light.

COLLECT.

GRANT, we beseech Thee, Almighty God, that the new birth of Thine Only-begotten may deliver us, who by old bondage are held under the yoke of sin.　Through the same Jesus Christ our Lord.　Amen.

Prime.

Ant. And they stoned Stephen, calling upon God, saying : Lord, lay not this sin to their charge.

Tierce.

Ant. The stones of the brook were sweet unto him : him doth every soul of the righteous follow.

CHAPTER.　Acts vi.

AND Stephen, full of faith and power, did great wonders and miracles among the people.

℟. Thou hast crowned him with glory and worship. Alleluia, Alleluia.

℣. Thou makest him to have dominion of the works of Thy hands. ℟. Alleluia, Alleluia.　℣. Glory be to the Father, and to the Son, and to the Holy Ghost.　℟. Thou hast crowned him with glory and worship. Alleluia, Alleluia.

℣. Thou hast set upon his head, O Lord.

℟. A crown of pure gold.

The ℟℟. *are said with* Alleluia *daily till the morrow of the Octave of the Epiphany.*

Sexts.

Ant. My soul hangeth upon Thee, O God : for Thy sake hath my body been stoned.

CHAPTER.　Acts vii.

STEPHEN, being full of the Holy Ghost, looked up stedfastly into heaven, and saw the glory of God, and Jesus standing on the right hand of God, and said, Behold, I see the heavens opened, and the Son of man standing on the right hand of God.

℟. Thou hast set upon his head, O Lord. Alleluia, Alleluia.　℣. A crown of pure gold.　℟. Alleluia, Alleluia.　℣. Glory be the Father, and to the Son, and to the Holy Ghost.　℟. Thou hast set upon his head, O Lord.　Alleluia, Alleluia.

℣. The righteous shall flourish like a palm-tree.

℟. And shall spread abroad like a cedar in Libanus.

Nones.

Ant. Behold, I see the heavens opened : and the Son of man standing on the right hand of God.

CHAPTER.　Acts vii.

AND he kneeled down and cried with a loud voice, Lord, lay not this sin to their charge. And when he had said this, he fell asleep.

Ṛ. The righteous shall flourish like a palm-tree. Alleluia, Alleluia. Ẏ. And shall spread abroad like a cedar in Libanus. Ṛ. Alleluia, Alleluia. Ẏ. Glory be to the Father, and to the Son, and to the Holy Ghost. Ṛ. The righteous shall flourish like a palm-tree. Alleluia, Alleluia.

Ẏ. The righteous shall blossom as a lily.

Ṛ. He shall flourish for ever before the Lord.

Vespers.

Ants. and Psalms, p. 92.

CHAPTER. Acts vi.

AND Stephen, full of faith and power, did great wonders and miracles among the people.

Ṛ. They ran upon him with one accord, and cast him out of the city, praying, and saying, * Lord Jesus, receive my spirit. Ẏ. Stephen was full of the grace of God: he did great wonders among the people; he beheld the heavens opened; he saw Jesus standing at the right hand of God: and he said. Ṛ. Lord Jesus, receive my spirit. Ẏ. Glory be to God the Almighty Father, and to the King His only Son, and to the Holy Ghost, from both proceeding; as it was in the beginning, and now, and ever, and to all ages. Amen. Ṛ. Lord Jesus, receive my spirit.

HYMN. *Sancte Dei pretiose*, p. 95.

Ant. to Mag. The doors of heaven are laid open to blessed Stephen, martyr of Christ : who was first to be numbered among the saints, and is therefore triumphantly crowned in heaven.

Collect, p. 95.

MEMORIAL OF THE NATIVITY.

Ant. Light is risen upon us; because to-day the Saviour is born. Alleluia.

Ẏ. The Word was made flesh. Alleluia.

Ṛ. And dwelt among us. Alleluia.

Collect, p. 96.

MEMORIAL OF S. JOHN THE EVANGELIST.

Ant. Greatly is blessed John to be had in honour, for he lay on the Lord's bosom at the Supper.

Ẏ. Thou shalt make them princes in all lands.

Ṛ. They shall remember Thy Name, O Lord.

COLLECT
For S. John's Day.

MERCIFUL Lord, we beseech Thee to cast Thy bright beams of light upon Thy church, that it being enlightened by the doctrine of Thy blessed Apostle and Evangelist Saint John, may so walk in the light of Thy truth, that it may at length attain to the light of everlasting life; through Jesus Christ our Lord. Amen.

———

FESTIVAL OF
S. JOHN THE EVANGELIST.

Lauds.

Ẏ. Greatly is blessed John to be had in honour.

Ṛ. For he lay on the Lord's bosom at the Supper.

Ẏ. O God, make speed, etc.

Psalms of Sunday.

Ant. 1. This is the disciple which did testify and write : and we know that his testimony is true.

Ant. 2. This is My disciple : and so I will that he abide till I come.

H

Ant. 3. Behold Mine elect, whom I have chosen : I have put My Spirit upon him.

Ant. 4. There be some of them standing here, which shall not taste of death : till they see the Son of man coming in His kingdom.

Ant. 5. So I will that he abide till I come : follow thou Me.

CHAPTER. Ecclus. xv.

HE that feareth the Lord will do good ; and he that hath knowledge of the law shall obtain wisdom. And as a mother shall she meet him, and receive him as a wife married of a virgin.

HYMN. *Exultet cœlum laudibus, as in Common of Apostles.*

℣. They have declared His honour unto the heathen.

℞. And His wonders unto all people.

Ant. to Ben. This is John who leaned on the Lord's bosom at the Supper : blessed Apostle to whom were made known the secrets of heaven.

Collect of the Day, p. 97.

MEMORIAL OF THE NATIVITY.

Ant. To-day a spotless Virgin bringeth forth God, clothed in our flesh : let us all worship Him Who cometh to save us.

℣. Blessed be He that cometh in the Name of the Lord.

℞. God is the Lord Who hath shewed us light.

Collect, p. 96.

MEMORIAL OF S. STEPHEN.

Ant. And devout men carried Stephen to his burial, and made great lamentation over him.

℣. The righteous shall blossom as a lily.

℞. He shall flourish for ever before the Lord.

Collect of S. Stephen, p. 95.

Prime.

Ant. to Psalms. This is the disciple which did testify and write : and we know that his testimony is true.

Tierce.

Ant. This is My disciple : and so I will that he abide till I come.

CHAPTER. Ecclus. xv.

HE that feareth the Lord will 'do good ; and he that hath knowledge of the law shall obtain wisdom. And as a mother shall she meet him, and receive him as a wife married of a virgin.

℞. Their sound is gone out into all lands. Alleluia, Alleluia. ℣. And their words into the ends of the world. ℞. Alleluia, Alleluia. ℣. Glory be to the Father, and to the Son : and to the Holy Ghost. ℞. Their sound is gone out into all lands. Alleluia, Alleluia.

℣. Thou shalt make them princes in all lands.

℞. They shall remember Thy name, O Lord.

Sexts.

Ant. Behold Mine elect, whom I have chosen : I have put My spirit upon him.

CHAPTER. Ecclus. xv.

WITH the bread of understanding shall she feed him, and give him the water of wisdom to drink. He shall be stayed upon her, and shall not be moved ; and shall rely upon her, and shall not be confounded. She shall exalt him above his neighbours.

℞. Thou shalt make them princes in all lands. Alleluia, Alleluia. ℣. They shall remember Thy name, O Lord. ℞. Alleluia, Alleluia. ℣. Glory be to the Father, and to the

Son : and to the Holy Ghost. Ry. Thou shalt make them princes in all lands. Alleluia, Alleluia.

℣. How dear are Thy friends unto me, O God.

Ry. O how great is the sum of them.

Nones.

Ant. So I will that he abide till I come : follow thou Me.

CHAPTER. Ecclus. xv.

IN the midst of the congregation shall wisdom open his mouth; he shall find joy and a crown of gladness, and she shall cause him to inherit an everlasting name.

Ry. How dear are Thy friends unto me, O God. Alleluia, Alleluia. ℣. O how great is the sum of them. Ry. Alleluia, Alleluia. ℣. Glory be to the Father, and to the Son : and to the Holy Ghost. Ry. How dear are Thy friends unto me, O God. Alleluia, Alleluia.

℣. They have declared His honour unto the heathen.

Ry. And His wonders unto all people.

Vespers.

Ants. and Psalms, p. 92.

CHAPTER. Ecclus. xv.

HE that feareth the Lord will do good; and he that hath knowledge of the law shall obtain wisdom. And as a mother shall she meet him, and receive him as a wife married of a virgin.

Ry. This is John who leaned on the Lord's bosom at the Supper. * Alleluia, Alleluia. ℣. Blessed Apostle, to whom were made known the secrets of heaven. Ry. Alleluia, Alleluia. ℣. Glory be to the Almighty Father Unbegotten, to His Only-begotten Son, and to the Spirit the Comforter. Ry. Alleluia, Alleluia.

HYMN. *Exultet cælum laudibus,* ℣. *and* Ry., *as in Common of Apostles.*

Ant. to Mag. In the midst of the Church he opened his lips : and the Lord filled him with the spirit of wisdom and understanding. He put upon him a robe of glory. Alleluia, Alleluia.

Collect of the Day.

MEMORIAL OF THE NATIVITY.

Ant. Let us be glad, all ye faithful; our Saviour is born into the world : to-day the Son is gone forth gloriously, and virginal purity is preserved.

℣. The Word was made flesh.

Ry. And dwelt among us.

Collect, p. 96.

MEMORIAL OF S. STEPHEN.

Ant. And they stoned Stephen, calling upon God : saying, Lord, lay not this sin to their charge.

℣. Thou hast crowned him with glory and honour.

Ry. Thou hast put all things in subjection under his feet.

Collect for S. Stephen's Day, p. 95.

MEMORIAL OF THE HOLY INNOCENTS.

Ant. Innocent children by cruel Herod were slain for Christ, even children at the breast. They follow the Lamb without spot, and say alway, Glory be to Thee, O Lord.

℣. Be glad, O ye righteous, and rejoice in the Lord.

Ry. And be joyful, all ye that are true of heart.

COLLECT.

O ALMIGHTY God, Who out of the mouth of babes and sucklings hast ordained strength, and madest infants to glorify Thee by their deaths; mortify and kill all vices in us, and so strengthen us by Thy grace, that by the innocency of our lives and constancy of our faith even unto death, we may glorify Thy holy Name; through Jesus Christ our Lord. Amen.

———

FESTIVAL OF

The Holy Innocents.

Lauds.

℣. The righteous live for evermore.

℟. Their reward also is with the Lord.

Psalms of Sunday.

Ant. 1. Herod being exceeding wroth : sent forth and slew all the children that were in Bethlehem.

Ant. 2. From two years old and under : did Herod slay many children for the Lord's sake.

Ant. 3. A voice was heard in Ramah, lamentation and bitter weeping : Rachel weeping for her children.

Ant. 4. From under the throne of God all Saints cry out : Avenge our blood, O our God.

Ant. 5. Let children praise Thee, O Lord of Hosts : for by the victory Thou hast won they rejoice in their innocence.

CHAPTER. Rev. xiv.

I LOOKED, and lo, a Lamb stood on the Mount Sion, and with Him an hundred forty and four thousand, having His Father's Name written in their foreheads.

℟. Thanks be to God.

Hymn. *Rex gloriose Martyrum.*

ALL-GLORIOUS King of Martyrs Thou,
Crown of Confessors here below;
Whom, casting earthly joys away,
Thou guidest to celestial day.

O quickly bend a gracious ear,
To this our suppliant voice of prayer,
As we their sacred triumphs chant,
Forgiveness to our errors grant.

In Martyrs, victory is Thine,
In Thy Confessors, mercies shine,
Then conquer, Lord, our wickedness,
And us with loving pardon bless.

All honour, laud, and glory be,
O Jesu, Virgin-born, to Thee !
All glory, as is ever meet,
To Father and to Paraclete. Amen.

℣. The righteous Lord loveth righteousness.

℟. His countenance will behold the thing that is just.

Ant. to Ben. These are they which were not defiled with women : for they are virgins. These are they which follow the Lamb whithersoever He goeth.

Collect of the Day, p. 99.
Throughout the Octave all the Collects to Memorials are as on S. John's Day.

Memorial of the Nativity.

Ant. The Virgin Mother, knowing no man, painlessly brought forth the Saviour of the world : the holy Virgin, filled with heaven, gave nourishment to the King of Angels.

℣. Blessed be He that cometh in the Name of the Lord.

℟. God is the Lord Who hath shewed us light.

Collect, p. 96.

Memorial of S. Stephen.

Ant. The stones of the brook were sweet unto him : him doth every soul of the righteous follow.

℣. The righteous shall blossom as a lily.

℟. He shall flourish for ever before the Lord.

Collect for S. Stephen's Day, p. 95.

Memorial of S. John.

Ant. This is the disciple which did testify and write : and we know that his testimony is true.

℣. Greatly is blessed John to be had in honour.

℟. For he lay on the Lord's bosom at the Supper.

Collect for S. John's Day, p. 97.

Prime.

Ant. Herod being exceeding wroth; sent forth and slew all the children that were in Bethlehem.

Tierce.

Ant. From two years old and under: did Herod slay many children for the Lord's sake.

CHAPTER. Rev. xiv.

I LOOKED, and lo, a Lamb stood on the Mount Sion, and with Him an hundred forty and four thousand, having His Father's Name written in their foreheads.

R7. Be glad, O ye righteous, and rejoice in the Lord. Alleluia, Alleluia. V. And be joyful all ye that are true of heart. R7. Alleluia, Alleluia. V. Glory be to the Father, and to the Son : and to the Holy Ghost. R7. Be glad, O ye righteous, and rejoice in the Lord. Alleluia, Alleluia.

V. Let the righteous be glad, and rejoice before God.

R7. Let them also be merry and joyful.

Sexts.

Ant. A voice was heard in Ramah, lamentation and bitter weeping : Rachel weeping for her children.

CHAPTER. Rev. xiv.

THESE are they which were not defiled with women; for they are virgins. These are they which follow the Lamb whithersoever He goeth.

R7. Let the righteous be glad, and rejoice before God. Alleluia, Alleluia. V. Let them also be merry and joyful. R7. Alleluia, Alleluia. V. Glory be to the Father, and to the Son : and to the Holy Ghost. R7. Let the righteous be glad, and rejoice before God. Alleluia, Alleluia.

V. The souls of the righteous are in the hand of God.

R7. And there shall no torment touch them.

Nones.

Ant. From under the throne of God all Saints cry out: Avenge our blood, O our God.

CHAPTER. Rev. xiv.

THESE were redeemed from among men, being the first-fruits unto God, and to the Lamb. And in their mouth was found no guile.

R7. The souls of the righteous are in the hand of God. Alleluia, Alleluia. V. And there shall no torment touch them. R7. Alleluia, Alleluia. V. Glory be to the Father, and to the Son, and to the Holy Ghost. R7. The souls of the righteous are in the hand of God. Alleluia, Alleluia.

V. The righteous Lord loveth righteousness.

R7. His countenance will behold the thing that is just.

Vespers.

Ants. and Psalms as on Christmas Day, p. 89.

CHAPTER. Rev. xiv.

I LOOKED, and lo, a Lamb stood on the mount Sion, and with Him an hundred forty and four thousand, having His Father's Name written in their foreheads.

R7. The hundred and forty and four thousand which were redeemed from the earth : these are they which were not defiled with women, for they are virgins. * Therefore they reign with God : and the Lamb of God with them. V. These were the firstfruits among men, being redeemed unto God and to the Lamb. R7. Therefore they reign with God : and the Lamb of God with them. V. Glory be to the Father, and to the Son, and to the Holy Ghost. R7.

Therefore they reign with God: and the Lamb of God with them.

HYMN. *Rex gloriose Martyrum,* V̌. and R̂., p. 100.

Ant. to Mag. I looked, and lo, a Lamb stood on the Mount Sion : and with Him an hundred forty and four thousand, having His Father's Name written in their foreheads.

MEMORIAL OF THE NATIVITY.

Ant. A Virgin, she conceived, a Virgin she abode : a Virgin, she brought forth the King of all kings.

V̌. The Word was made flesh. Alleluia.

R̂. And dwelt among us. Alleluia.

Collect, p. 96.

MEMORIAL OF S. STEPHEN.

Ant. My soul hangeth upon Thee, O God : for Thy sake hath my body been stoned.

V̌. Thou hast crowned him with glory and worship.

R̂. Thou makest him to have dominion of the works of Thy hands.

Collect for S. Stephen's Day, p. 95.

MEMORIAL OF S. JOHN.

Ant. This is My disciple : and so I will that he abide till I come.

V̌. Greatly is blessed John to be had in honour.

R̂. For he lay on the Lord's bosom at the Supper.

Collect for S. John's Day, p. 97.

MEMORIAL OF S. THOMAS OF CANTERBURY.

Ant. The keeper of the vine fell in the vineyard : the leader in the camp, the husbandman in the field.

V̌. As corn purged in the threshing-floor.

R̂. He was carried to the heavenly garner.

COLLECT.

A LMIGHTY and eternal God, Who didst kindle the flame of Thy love in the heart of Thy holy Martyr and Bishop Thomas; give to our minds the same strength of faith and charity, that as we rejoice in his triumph, so we may profit by his example; through Jesus Christ our Lord. Amen.

———

FESTIVAL OF S. THOMAS OF CANTERBURY.

All of the Common of one Martyr Bishop, with these Memorials.

𝔏𝔞𝔲𝔡𝔰.

MEMORIAL OF THE NATIVITY.

Ant. Blessed is the womb that bare Thee, O Christ : and the paps which gave suck to the Lord and Saviour of the world. Alleluia.

V̌. Blessed be He that cometh in the Name of the Lord.

R̂. God is the Lord Who hath shewed us light.

Collect, p. 96.

MEMORIAL OF S. STEPHEN.

Ant. Stephen saw the heavens opened; he saw and entered in : blessed is he to whom the heavens shall be opened.

V̌. The righteous shall blossom as a lily.

R̂. He shall flourish for ever before the Lord.

Collect for S. Stephen's Day, p. 95.

MEMORIAL OF S. JOHN.

Ant. Behold Mine elect, whom I have chosen : I have put My Spirit upon him.

V̌. Greatly is blessed John to be had in honour.

R̂. For he lay on the Lord's bosom at the Supper.

Collect for S. John's Day, p. 97.

MEMORIAL OF
THE HOLY INNOCENTS.

Ant. They have washed their robes, and made them white in the blood of the Lamb : therefore are they before the throne of God.

℣. Wonderful art Thou in Thy Saints, O God.

℟. And glorious in Thy majesty.

Collect for Holy Innocents, p. 99.

Vespers.

MEMORIAL OF THE NATIVITY.

Ant. O Virgin Mother of God : Him Whom the whole world cannot contain, thou didst contain in thy womb.

℣. The Word was made flesh. Alleluia.

℟. And dwelt among us. Alleluia.

Collect, p. 96.

MEMORIAL OF S. STEPHEN.

Ant. Behold, I see the heavens opened : and the Son of man standing on the right hand of God.

℣. Thou hast crowned him with glory and worship.

℟. Thou makest him to have dominion of the works of Thy hands.

Collect for S. Stephen's Day, p. 95.

MEMORIAL OF S. JOHN.

Ant. There be some of them standing here which shall not taste of death : till they see the Son of man coming in His kingdom.

℣. Greatly is blessed John to be had in honour.

℟. For he lay on the Lord's bosom at the Supper.

Collect for S. John's Day, p. 97.

MEMORIAL OF
THE HOLY INNOCENTS.

Ant. They shall walk with Me in white : for they are worthy.

℣. Be glad, O ye righteous, and rejoice in the Lord.

℟. And be joyful, all ye that are true of heart.

Collect for Holy Innocents, p. 99.

———

SIXTH DAY AFTER THE NATIVITY.
(*Dec.* 30)

Lauds.

℣. The Word was made flesh. Alleluia.

℟. And dwelt among us. Alleluia.

Psalms of Sunday. The Psalms are all said under this

Ant. Whom saw ye, O shepherds ? say ye, tell us. Who hath appeared upon earth ? We beheld the Child, in a choir of angels, singing unto our Lord and Saviour. Alleluia.

CHAPTER. Gal. iv.

NOW I say that the heir, as long as he is a child, differeth nothing from a servant, though he be lord of all ; but is under tutors and governors until the time appointed of the father.

℟. Thanks be to God.

HYMN. *A solis ortus cardine,*
℣. and ℟., p. 90.

Collect for Christmas Day, p. 90.

[*Or this,*

ALMIGHTY, everlasting God, direct our ways according to Thy good pleasure ; that in the name of Thy beloved Son we may merit to abound in good works ; Who liveth and reigneth with Thee in the unity of the Holy Ghost, ever one God, world without end. Amen.

This Collect is said at Lauds only; at the other hours is said the Collect for Christmas Day.]

MEMORIAL OF THE NATIVITY.

Ant. Shepherds, tell us what ye have seen, and make known the birth of Christ : We have seen the Child wrapped in swaddling clothes, and choirs of angels praising the Saviour.

℣. He shall call Me.
℟. Thou art My Father.

Collect, p. 96.

MEMORIAL OF S. STEPHEN.

Ant. Blessed Stephen, strengthened by constant meditation in the law, was like a tree bearing fruit, planted beside living waters : and having fulfilled his course, first yielded the fruit of martyrdom in his season.

℣. The righteous shall blossom as a lily.

℟. He shall flourish for ever before the Lord.

Collect for S. Stephen's Day, p. 95.

MEMORIAL OF S. JOHN.

Ant. So I will that he abide till I come : follow thou Me.

℣. Greatly is blessed John to be had in honour.

℟. For he lay on the Lord's bosom at the Supper.

Collect for S. John's Day, p. 97.

MEMORIAL OF THE HOLY INNOCENTS.

Ant. They sung as it were a new song : before the throne.

℣. Wonderful art Thou in Thy Saints, O God.

℟. And glorious in Thy majesty.

Collect for the Holy Innocents, p. 99.

Prime, Tierce, Sexts, and Nones, as on Christmas Day.

If Sunday fall on any day but this, throughout the Octave, the Office is wholly of the Feast, with no commemoration of the Sunday: if it fall on this day, it is noticed at Matins only, and at no other Hour.

FESTIVAL OF S. SILVESTER, POPE AND CONFESSOR.

Common of a Confessor Bishop, except the Ants. and Psalms at Vespers, which are of Christmas Day, p. 92; and the Memorials, as below.

But if the Office of S. Silvester be not used, all is said as on Dec. 30, with Memorial of a Confessor Bishop, and Memorials of the Seasons, as below.

Vespers.

MEMORIAL OF THE NATIVITY.

Ant. To-day a faithful Virgin brought forth the Incarnate Word : and yet after child-bearing she abideth Virgin; in whose praise let us all say, Blessed art thou among women.

℣. The Word was made flesh.

℟. And dwelt among us.

Collect, p. 96.

MEMORIAL OF S. STEPHEN.

Ant. God made him a preacher of His commandments, and he studied to serve Him in His holy fear : having faithfully fulfilled his office, he was counted worthy to ascend into His holy hill.

℣. Thou hast crowned him with glory and worship.

℟. Thou makest him to have dominion of the works of Thy hands.

Collect for S. Stephen's Day, p. 95.

MEMORIAL OF S. JOHN.

Ant. John the Apostle and Evangelist was chosen by the Lord, being a virgin : and was loved above the rest.

℣. Thou shalt make them princes in all lands.

℟. They shall remember Thy Name, O Lord.

Collect for S. John's Day, p. 97.

MEMORIAL OF THE HOLY INNOCENTS.

Ant. Herod, being exceeding wroth : sent forth and slew all the children that were in Bethlehem.

℣. Be glad, O ye righteous, and rejoice in the Lord.

℟. And be joyful, all ye that are true of heart.

Collect for the Holy Innocents, p. 99.

Lauds.

MEMORIAL OF THE NATIVITY.

Ant. To-day a spotless Virgin bringeth forth God, clothed in our flesh : let us all worship Him Who cometh to save us.

℣. Blessed be He that cometh in the Name of the Lord.

℞. God is the Lord Who hath shewed us light.

Collect, p. 96.

MEMORIAL OF S. STEPHEN.

Ant. A shower of stones overwhelmed him, a multitude surrounded him, but he feared not : for he saw Jesus his deliverer, ready to bring him to heaven in safety.

℣. The righteous shall blossom as a lily.

℞. He shall flourish for ever before the Lord.

Collect for S. Stephen's Day, p. 95.

MEMORIAL OF S. JOHN.

Ant. As he lay on the sacred bosom of the Lord Jesus : he drank of the waters of the Gospel at their source.

℣. Greatly is blessed John to be had in honour.

℞. For he lay on the Lord's bosom at the Supper.

Collect for S. John's Day, p. 97.

MEMORIAL OF THE HOLY INNOCENTS.

Ant. From two years old and under : did Herod slay many children for the Lord's sake.

℣. Wonderful art Thou in Thy saints, O Lord.

℞. And glorious in Thy majesty.

Collect of the Holy Innocents, p. 99.

FESTIVAL OF
THE CIRCUMCISION.

First Vespers.

Ants. and Psalms as on Christmas Day.

CHAPTER. Titus ii.

THE grace of God that bringeth salvation hath appeared unto all men, teaching us that, denying ungodliness and worldly lusts, we should live soberly, righteously, and godly in this present world.

℞. The Word was made flesh. Alleluia, Alleluia. ℣. And dwelt among us. ℞. Alleluia, Alleluia. ℣. Glory be to the Father, and to the Son : and to the Holy Ghost. ℞. The Word was made flesh. Alleluia.

℣. He shall call Me.

℞. Thou art My Father.

HYMN. *A solis ortus cardine*, p. 90.

℣. As a Bridegroom.

℞. The Lord coming out of His chamber.

Ant. to Mag. He that is of the earth is earthly, and speaketh of the earth : He that cometh from heaven is above all. And what He hath seen and heard, that He testifieth ; and no man receiveth His testimony. He that hath received His testimony hath set to his seal that God is true.

COLLECT.

ALMIGHTY God, Who madest Thy blessed Son to be circumcised, and obedient to the law for man ; grant us the true circumcision of the Spirit, that, our hearts and all our members, being mortified from all worldly and carnal lusts, we may in all things obey Thy blessed will ; through the same Thy Son Jesus Christ our Lord. Amen.

[Or this,

O GOD, Who grantest us to celebrate the Octave of our Saviour's birth ;

grant, we beseech Thee, that as we are renewed by the communion of His Flesh, so we may ever be defended by His Divinity; Who liveth and reigneth with Thee and the Holy Ghost, ever one God, world without end.   Amen.]

No Memorial is said at these Vespers.

Compline.

Ant. to Psalms. When the Lord was born, the choirs of angels sang, saying : Salvation to our God, which sitteth upon the throne, and unto the Lamb.

HYMN. *Salvator mundi Domine,* ℣. and ℞., p. 67.

Ant. to Nunc Dim. Alleluia. The Word was made flesh, Alleluia; and dwelt among us.   Alleluia, Alleluia.

Compline is thus said till the Feast of the Epiphany.

Lauds.

℣. The Word was made flesh. Alleluia.

℞. And dwelt among us. Alleluia.

Psalms of Sunday.

Ant. 1.   O wonderful exchange! The Creator of mankind taking to Himself a living body, vouchsafed to be born of a Virgin : and, proceeding forth as man, made us co-heirs of His Godhead.

Ant. 2.   When Thou wast born ineffably of a Virgin, then was the Scripture fulfilled : He shall come down like the rain into a fleece of wool, to save mankind.   We praise Thee, O our God.

Ant. 3. In the burning bush which Moses saw unconsumed : we acknowledge the preservation of the glorious virginity of the Mother of God.

Ant. 4. The root of Jesse hath sprung up; the star hath come out of Jacob : a Virgin hath brought forth a Saviour.   We praise Thee, O our God.

Ant. 5. Lo, Mary hath brought forth a Saviour, of Whom, when John saw Him, he said : Behold the Lamb of God, which taketh away the sins of the world.   Alleluia.

CHAPTER. Titus ii.

THE grace of God that bringeth salvation hath appeared to all men, teaching us that, denying ungodliness and worldly lusts, we should live soberly, righteously, and godly in this present world.

℞. Thanks be to God.

HYMN. *A solis ortus cardine,* ℣. and ℞., p. 90.

Ant. to Ben. A wonderful mystery is made known.   To-day is nature to do a new thing.   God is made Man : that which was, still abideth, and that which was not, He assumed, suffering no confusion or division.

Collect as at First Vespers.

No Memorial is said at these Lauds.

Prime.

All as on Christmas Day, except the

Ant. O wonderful exchange ! The Creator of mankind taking to Himself a living body, vouchsafed to be born of a Virgin : and proceeding forth as man, made us co-heirs of His Godhead.

At Tierce, Sexts, and Nones, all as on Christmas Day, except the Antiphons ; and the Collect, which is that of the Circumcision.

Tierce.

Ant. When Thou wast born ineffably of a Virgin, then was the Scripture fulfilled : He shall come down like the rain into a fleece of wool, to save mankind.   We praise Thee, O our God.

Sexts.

Ant. In the burning bush which Moses saw unconsumed : we acknowledge the preservation of the glorious virginity of the Mother of God.

Nones.

Ant. The root of Jesse hath sprung up; the star hath come out of Jacob : a Virgin hath brought forth a Saviour. We praise Thee, O our God.

Second Vespers.

Ants. and Psalms as on Christmas Day, p. 92.

CHAPTER. Titus ii.

THE grace of God that bringeth salvation hath appeared to all men, teaching us that, denying ungodliness and worldly lusts, we should live soberly, righteously, and godly in this present world.

℟. Established is the heart of the Virgin wherein at the word of the angel she received divine mysteries : who in her chaste womb conceived Him that is fairer than the children of men. * And she, who is blessed for ever, brought forth God and man for us. ℣. The mansion of the modest breast becomes a shrine where God shall rest : the pure and undefiled one conceived in her womb the Son. ℟. And she, who is blessed for ever, brought forth God and man for us. ℣. Glory be to the Father, and to the Son : and to the Holy Ghost. ℟. And she, who is blessed for ever, brought forth God and man for us.

HYMN. *Veni Redemptor gentium,* ℣. and ℟., p. 89.

Ant. to Mag. O marvellous mystery! The womb of a Virgin who knew not man is become the unspotted temple of God : of her He taketh flesh, and to Him shall all nations come, saying, Glory be to Thee, O Lord.

MEMORIAL OF S. STEPHEN, *As on Christmas Day,* p. 95.

———

OCTAVE OF S. STEPHEN.

Lauds.

℣. Thou hast set upon his head, O Lord.

℟. A crown of pure gold.

℣. O God, make speed, etc.

Psalms of Sunday, all said under one Ant., unless the day fall on Sunday, in which case the Ants. are said as on the festival. This rule applies also to the two days following.

Ant. And they stoned Stephen, calling upon God, and saying : Lord, lay not this sin to their charge.

The rest of the Office at Lauds and all the Hours as on S. Stephen's Day, except that the ℟. is not said at Vespers, and that these Memorials are said :

At Lauds.

MEMORIAL OF S. JOHN.

Ant. As one of the streams of Paradise : the Evangelist John shed the grace of the Word of God throughout the whole world.

℣. Greatly is blessed John to be had in honour.

℟. For he lay on the Lord's bosom at the Supper.

Collect for S. John's Day, p. 97.

MEMORIAL OF
THE HOLY INNOCENTS.

Ant. A voice was heard in Ramah; lamentation and bitter weeping : Rachel weeping for her children.

℣. Wonderful art Thou in Thy Saints, O God.

℟. And glorious in Thy majesty.

Collect for the Holy Innocents, p. 99.

MEMORIAL OF S. MARY.

Ant. Behold, all things are fulfilled : which were spoken by the angel of the Virgin Mary.

℣. After child-bearing thou remainedst a virgin.

℟. O Mother of God.

Collect as in Memorial at Vespers, infra.

Vespers.

MEMORIAL OF S. JOHN.

Ant. Greatly is blessed John to be had in honour : for he lay on the Lord's bosom at the Supper.

℣. Thou shalt make them princes in all lands.

℟. They shall remember Thy Name, O Lord.

Collect for S. John's Day, p. 97.

MEMORIAL OF THE HOLY INNOCENTS.

Ant. Under the throne of God all Saints cry out : Avenge our blood, O our God.

℣. Be glad, O ye righteous, and rejoice in the Lord.

℟. And be joyful, all ye that are true of heart.

Collect for the Holy Innocents, p. 99.

MEMORIAL OF S. MARY.

Ant. When Thou wast born ineffably of a Virgin, then was the Scripture fulfilled : He shall come down like the rain into a fleece of wool to save mankind. We praise Thee, O our God.

℣. Thou art fairer than the children of men.

℟. Full of grace are Thy lips.

COLLECT.

O GOD, Who through the fruitful virginity of the blessed Virgin Mary, hast bestowed the rewards of eternal salvation on the human race; grant, we beseech Thee, that she may intercede for us, through whom we have received the Author of Life, Thy Son Jesus Christ our Lord. Amen.

OCTAVE OF S. JOHN THE EVANGELIST.

All as on S. John's Day, except that which follows :

Lauds.

Ant. to Psalms. This is the disciple which did testify and write : and we know that his testimony is true.

MEMORIAL OF THE HOLY INNOCENTS.

Ant. Let children praise Thee, O Lord of Hosts : for by the victory Thou hast won they rejoice in their innocence.

℣. Wonderful art Thou in Thy Saints, O God.

℟. And glorious in Thy majesty.

Collect for the Holy Innocents, p. 99.

MEMORIAL OF S. MARY.

Ant. Lo, Mary hath brought forth the Saviour, of Whom when John saw Him, he said : Behold, the Lamb of God, Which taketh away the sins of the world. Alleluia.

℣. After child-bearing thou remainedst a virgin.

℟. O Mother of God.

COLLECT.

O GOD, Who through the fruitful virginity of the blessed Virgin Mary, hast bestowed the rewards of eternal salvation on the human race; grant, we pray Thee, that she may intercede for us, through whom we have received the Author of Life, Thy Son Jesus Christ, our Lord. Amen.

Vespers.

The R℣. is not said.

MEMORIAL OF
THE HOLY INNOCENTS.

Ant. Innocent children by cruel Herod were slain for Christ, even children at the breast : they follow the Lamb without spot, and say alway, Glory be to Thee, O Lord.

℣. Be glad, O ye righteous, and rejoice in the Lord.

R℣. And be joyful, all ye that are true of heart.

Collect for the Holy Innocents, p. 99.
Memorial of S. Mary as at Vespers on the Octave of S. Stephen.

OCTAVE OF
THE HOLY INNOCENTS.

All as on Holy Innocents' Day, except that which follows :

Lauds.

Ant. to Psalms. Herod, being exceeding wroth : sent forth and slew all the children that were in Bethlehem.

At Lauds and Vespers the Memorial of S. Mary as on the Octave of S. John. The R℣. is not said at Vespers. At Vespers is made a

MEMORIAL OF S. EDWARD THE
CONFESSOR.

Ant. I will liken him unto a wise man : which built his house upon a rock.

℣. The Lord loved him, and beautified him with comely ornaments.

R℣. He clothed him with a robe of glory.

COLLECT.

O GOD, Who hast vouchsafed unto the blessed King Edward Thy Confessor a crown of heavenly glory ;

grant that we who commemorate him here on earth, may hereafter reign with him in heaven; through Jesus Christ our Lord, Who liveth and reigneth with Thee and the Holy Ghost, ever one God, world without end. Amen.

VIGIL OF THE EPIPHANY.

Lauds.

℣. The Word was made flesh.
R℣. And dwelt among us.
℣. O God, make speed, etc.

Sunday Psalms, all said under one Ant. whether the day be Sunday or not.

Ant. to Psalms. O wonderful exchange ! The Creator of mankind taking to Himself a living body, vouchsafed to be born of a Virgin : and, proceeding forth as man, made us co-heirs of His Godhead.

Chapter, Hymn, A solis ortus cardine, ℣. and R℣., p. 90.

Ant. to Ben. Blessed is the womb that bare Thee, O Christ : and the paps which Thou hast sucked.

COLLECT.

L IGHTEN our hearts, we beseech Thee, O Lord, by this coming Festival: that, being rid of the darkness of this world, we may come to the light of the eternal Country; through Jesus Christ our Lord. Amen.

MEMORIAL OF ALL SAINTS.

Ant. The Saints shall be joyful with glory : they shall rejoice in their beds.

℣. Wonderful art Thou in Thy Saints, O God.

R℣. And glorious in Thy majesty.

COLLECT.

W E pray Thee, O Lord, let the intercession of all Thy Saints be acceptable unto Thee; and grant to us forgiveness of our sins, and the remedies of eternal life; through Jesus Christ our Lord. Amen.

No Memorial is made of S. Mary. If this Vigil falls on a Sunday, no Memorial is made of All Saints.

MEMORIAL OF S. EDWARD THE CONFESSOR.

Ant. Well done, thou good and faithful servant : enter thou into the joy of thy Lord.

℣. The righteous shall flourish like a palm-tree.

℟. And spread abroad like a cedar in Libanus.

Collect as in Memorial at Vespers.

All at the other Hours as on the Circumcision, except the Collect, which is the same as at Lauds.

THE EPIPHANY.

First Vespers.

Ants. and Psalms as at the Second Vespers of Christmas Day, p. 92.

CHAPTER. Is. lx.

ARISE, shine; for thy Light is come, and the glory of the Lord is risen upon thee.

℟. The kings of Tharsis and of the isles shall give presents, * the kings of Arabia and Saba shall bring gifts * to the Lord God. ℣. All kings shall fall down before Him : all nations shall do Him service. ℟. The kings of Arabia and Saba shall bring gifts. ℣. Glory be to the Father, and to the Son, and to the Holy Ghost. ℟. To the Lord God.

HYMN. *Hostis Herodes impie.*

WHY, impious Herod, vainly fear,
That Christ the Saviour cometh here?
He takes not earthly realms away,
Who gives the crown that lasts for aye.

To greet His birth the wise men went,
Led by the star before them sent :
Called on by light, towards Light they press'd,
And by their gifts their God confess'd.

In holy Jordan's purest wave
The heav'nly Lamb vouchsaf'd to lave;
That He, to Whom was sin unknown,
Might cleanse His people from their own.

New miracle of power divine !
The water reddens into wine :
He spake the word; and pour'd the wave
In other streams than nature gave.

All glory, Lord, to Thee we pay
For Thine Epiphany to-day :
All glory, as is ever meet,
To Father and to Paraclete. Amen.

This Doxology is said throughout the Octave to Hymns of this metre.

℣. All they from Sheba shall come.

℟. They shall bring gold and incense, and they shall shew forth the praises of the Lord.

Ant. to Mag. When the wise men saw the star, they said one to another : This is the sign of the great King, come let us seek Him and present unto Him gifts; gold and frankincense and myrrh.

COLLECT.

O GOD, Who by the leading of a star didst manifest Thy Only-begotten Son to the Gentiles; mercifully grant that we, which know Thee now by faith, may after this life have the fruition of Thy glorious Godhead; through Jesus Christ our Lord. Amen.

MEMORIAL OF S. MARY,
As at Vespers on Octave of S. Stephen, p. 108.

Compline.

Ant. to Psalms. Thou hast appeared, O Christ : Thou, Light of Light, to Whom the wise men bring gifts. Alleluia, Alleluia, Alleluia.

HYMN. *Salvator mundi Domine,* ℣. and ℟., p. 67.

Ant. to Nunc Dim. Alleluia. All they from Sheba shall come. Alleluia : They shall bring gold and incense. Alleluia, Alleluia.

This Compline is said daily throughout the Octave.

Lauds.

℣. All they from Sheba shall come.

℟. They shall bring gold and incense, and they shall shew forth the praises of the Lord.

℣. O God, make speed, etc.

Psalms of Sunday.

Ant. 1. He, begotten before the Morning Star, and before all ages, the Lord our Saviour, to-day appeared to the world.

Ant. 2. Thy light, O Jerusalem, is come; and the glory of the Lord is risen upon thee : and the Gentiles shall come to thy light. Alleluia.

Ant. 3. When they had opened their treasures, they presented unto Him gifts : gold, and frankincense, and myrrh. Alleluia.

Ant. 4. O ye seas and floods, bless ye the Lord : O ye wells, bless ye the Lord. Alleluia.

Ant. 5. Three are the gifts which the wise men presented unto the Lord : gold, and frankincense, and myrrh, to the King, the Son of God. Alleluia.

CHAPTER. Is. lx.

ARISE, shine, for thy light is come, and the glory of the Lord is risen upon thee.

℟. Thanks be to God.

HYMN. *A Patre Unigenitus.*

FROM God the Father, Virgin-born
To us the only Son came down;
By death the font to consecrate,
The faithful to regenerate.

From highest heaven His course began,
He took the form of mortal man;
Creation by His death restored,
And shed new joys of life abroad.

Glide on, Thou glorious Sun, and bring
The gift of healing on Thy wing;
The clearness of Thy light dispense
Unto Thy people's every sense.

Abide with us, O Lord, we pray,
The gloom of night remove away;
Thy work of healing, Lord, begin,
And do away the stain of sin.

We know that Thou didst come of yore;
Thou, we believe, shalt come once more :
Thy guardian shield o'er us extend,
Thine own dear sheepfold to defend.

All glory, Lord, to Thee, we pay,
For Thine Epiphany to-day ;
All glory, as is ever meet,
To Father and to Paraclete. Amen.

℣. It is the Lord that commandeth the waters.

℟. It is the glorious God that maketh the thunder. It is the Lord that ruleth the sea.

Ant. to Ben. To-day is the Church joined to her heavenly Bridegroom; for in Jordan Christ hath washed away her sins : the wise men hasten with gifts to the royal nuptials; and by water made wine are the guests rejoiced.

Collect as at First Vespers.

MEMORIAL OF S. MARY,
As at Lauds on Octave of S. John, p. 108.

Prime.

Ant. He that is begotten before all worlds : the Lord our Saviour, hath to-day appeared to the world.

CHAPTER. 1 Tim. i.

NOW unto the King eternal, immortal, invisible, the only wise God, be honour and glory, for ever and ever. Amen.

℟. Jesu Christ, Son of the living God, have mercy upon us. Alleluia, Alleluia. ℣. Thou Who on this day didst appear to the world. ℟. Have mercy upon us. Alleluia, Alleluia. ℣. Glory be to the Father, and to the Son : and to the Holy Ghost. ℟. Jesu Christ, Son of the living God, have mercy upon us. Alleluia, Alleluia.

℣. O Lord, arise, help us.

℟. And deliver us for Thy Name's sake.

Tierce.

Ant. Thy light, O Jerusalem, is come; and the glory of the Lord is risen upon thee : and the Gentiles shall come to thy light. Alleluia.

CHAPTER. Is. lx.

ARISE, shine, for thy light is come, and the glory of the Lord is risen upon thee.

R̦. All they from Sheba shall come. Alleluia, Alleluia. V̦. They shall bring gold and incense, and they shall shew forth the praises of the Lord. R̦. Alleluia, Alleluia. V̦. Glory be to the Father, and to the Son, and to the Holy Ghost. R̦. All they from Sheba shall come. Alleluia, Alleluia.

V̦. The kings of Tharsis and of the isles shall give presents.

R̦. The kings of Arabia and Saba shall bring gifts.

Sexts.

Ant. When they had opened their treasures, they presented unto Him gifts : gold, and frankincense, and myrrh. Alleluia.

CHAPTER. Is. lx.

THE Lord shall arise upon thee, O Jerusalem, and His glory shall be seen upon thee. And the Gentiles shall come to thy light, and kings to the brightness of thy rising.

R̦. The kings of Tharsis and of the isles shall give presents. Alleluia, Alleluia. V̦. The kings of Arabia and Saba shall bring gifts. R̦. Alleluia, Alleluia. V̦. Glory be to the Father, and to the Son, and to the Holy Ghost. R̦. The kings of Tharsis and of the isles shall give presents. Alleluia, Alleluia.

V̦. O worship the Lord.

R̦. In the beauty of holiness.

Nones.

Ant. Three are the gifts which the wise men presented unto the Lord : gold, and frankincense, and myrrh, to the King, the Son of God. Alleluia.

CHAPTER. Is. lx.

ALL they from Sheba shall come ; they shall bring gold and incense, and they shall shew forth the praises of the Lord.

R̦. O worship the Lord. Alleluia, Alleluia. V̦. In the beauty of holiness. R̦. Alleluia, Alleluia. V̦. Glory be to the Father, and to the Son, and to the Holy Ghost. R̦. O worship the Lord. Alleluia, Alleluia.

V̦. Worship the Lord.

R̦. All ye angels of His.

Second Vespers.

Ants. of Lauds, p. 111, with Sunday Psalms. Vespers are thus said till the Octave.

CHAPTER. Is. lx.

ARISE, shine, for thy light is come, and the glory of the Lord is risen upon thee.

R̦. Three are the gifts which the wise men presented unto the Lord. Alleluia, Alleluia. V̦. Gold, and frankincense, and myrrh, to the King, the Son of God. R̦. Alleluia, Alleluia. V̦. Glory be to the Father, and to the Son, and to the Holy Ghost. R̦. Three are the gifts which the wise men presented unto the Lord. Alleluia, Alleluia.

V̦. All kings shall fall down before Him.

R̦. All nations shall do Him service.

HYMN. *Hostis Herodes impie,* V̦. *and* R̦. *as at First Vespers,* p. 110.

Ant. to Mag. There came wise men from the East to Bethlehem, to worship the Lord, and when they had spread their treasures they presented unto Him precious gifts : gold as to the great King, frankincense as to the true God, and myrrh for His burial. Alleluia.

MEMORIAL OF S. MARY
As at Vespers on Octave of S. Stephen,
p. 108.

FROM THE FEAST OF THE
EPIPHANY TILL THE OCTAVE.

Lauds.

℣. All they from Sheba shall come.

℟. They shall bring gold and incense, and they shall shew forth the praises of the Lord.

℣. O God, make speed, etc.

Psalms of Sunday, all said under this

Ant. He, begotten before the morning star, and before all ages : the Lord our Saviour, to-day appeared to the world.

CHAPTER, HYMN, ℣. and ℟.,
As on the Epiphany, p. 111.

The following Antiphons are said at Lauds and Vespers to Benedictus *and* Magnificat, *except on Sunday :*

Ant. 1. The star shines like a flame, and points out God, the King of kings : wise men saw it, and brought gifts to Christ the King.

Ant. 2. When the wise men saw the star, they rejoiced with exceeding great joy : and when they were come into the house, they presented unto Him gifts; gold, frankincense, and myrrh.

Ant. 3. A voice sounded from heaven, and the voice of the Father was heard, saying : This is My beloved Son, in Whom I am well pleased.

Ant. 4. The wise men, being warned of God in a dream : departed into their own country another way.

The rest as on the Feast of the Epiphany, and so until the day of the Octave, except on Sunday.

SUNDAY IN THE OCTAVE.

All as on the Feast of the Epiphany, except that which follows :

First Vespers.

MEMORIAL OF SUNDAY.

Ant. And the Child Jesus tarried behind in Jerusalem : and Joseph and His mother knew not of it.

℣. Lord, let my prayer be set forth.

℟. In Thy sight as the incense.

COLLECT.

O LORD, we beseech Thee mercifully to receive the prayers of Thy people which call upon Thee; and grant that they may both perceive and know what things they ought to do, and also may have grace and power faithfully to fulfil the same; through Jesus Christ our Lord. Amen.

MEMORIAL OF S. MARY,
As on Octave of S. Stephen, p. 108.

Lauds.

Psalms of Sunday, under this one

Ant. He, begotten before the morning star, and before all ages : the Lord our Saviour, to-day appeared to the world.

MEMORIAL OF SUNDAY.

Ant. But they, supposing Him to have been in the company, went a day's journey : and they sought Him among their kinsfolk and acquaintance.

℣. The Lord is King.

℟. He hath put on glorious apparel. Alleluia.

Collect as above.

MEMORIAL OF S. MARY,
As on Octave of S. John, p. 108.

Second Vespers.

MEMORIAL OF SUNDAY.

Ant. Son, why hast Thou thus dealt with us? behold, Thy father and I have sought Thee sorrowing : And He said unto them, How is it that ye sought Me? wist ye not that I must be about My Father's business?

℣. Lord, let my prayer be set forth.

℟. In Thy sight as the incense.

Collect as p. 113.

MEMORIAL OF S. MARY,
As on Octave of S. Stephen, p. 108.

If the Festival of any Saint falls within the Octave, it is only commemorated at Vespers and Lauds.

OCTAVE OF THE EPIPHANY.

First Vespers.

Ants. and Psalms as on Christmas Day, p. 92.

CHAPTER. Is. xxv.

O LORD, Thou art my God; I will exalt Thee, I will praise Thy Name; for Thou hast done wonderful things; Thy counsels of old are faithfulness and truth.

℟. In the form of a dove the Holy Spirit was seen. * The voice of the Father was heard, This is My Beloved Son, in Whom I am well pleased, * hear ye Him. ℣. It is the Lord that commandeth the waters, it is the glorious God that maketh the thunder. It is the Lord that ruleth the sea. ℟. The voice of the Father was heard, This is My beloved Son, in Whom I am well pleased. ℣. Glory be to the Father, and to the Son : and to the Holy Ghost. ℟. Hear ye Him.

HYMN. *Hostis Herodes impie,*
℣. and ℟., p. 110.

Ant. to Mag. The soldier baptizes the King, the servant his Lord, John the Saviour : the water of Jordan marvels, the Dove bears witness, the Father's voice is heard, This is My beloved Son.

Collect of the Epiphany, p. 110.

MEMORIAL OF S. MARY,
As on the Octave of S. John, p. 108.

Lauds.

℣. All they from Sheba shall come.

℟. They shall bring gold and incense, and they shall shew forth the praises of the Lord.

Psalms of Sunday.

Ant. 1. Our Saviour, the Second Adam, comes to baptism : to restore corrupt nature through water, girding us about with an incorruptible garment.

Ant. 2. Thee we all glorify : Who by the Holy Ghost and by fire dost purify human corruption.

Ant. 3. The Baptist trembles, and dares not touch the holy head of God : but cries with fear, Sanctify me, O my Saviour.

Ant. 4. The Saviour breaks the head of the dragon in the waters of Jordan : delivering all men from his power.

Ant. 5. To-day is declared a great mystery : for the Creator of all things hath purged our sins in Jordan.

CHAPTER. Is. xxv.

O LORD, Thou art my God; I will exalt Thee, I will praise Thy Name: for Thou hast done wonderful things; Thy counsels of old are faithfulness and truth.

HYMN. *A Patre Unigenitus,*
℣. and ℟., p. 111.

Ant. to Ben. The Lord is baptized in Jordan; John the forerunner rejoices with Him; the whole world is made glad; water is sanctified to the remission of sins : let us cry unto Him, Have mercy upon us.

MEMORIAL OF S. MARY,
As on the Octave of S. Stephen, p. 108.

Prime.

Ant. Our Saviour, the Second Adam, comes to baptism : to restore corrupt nature through water, girding us about with an incorruptible garment.

Tierce.

Ant. Thee we all glorify : Who by the Holy Ghost and by fire, dost purify human corruption.

CHAPTER. Is. xxv.

O LORD, Thou art my God; I will exalt Thee, I will praise Thy Name; for Thou hast done wonderful things; Thy counsels of old are faithfulness and truth.

Ṛ. *at all the Hours as on the Epiphany.*

Sexts.

Ant. The Baptist trembles, and dares not touch the holy head of God : but cries with fear, Sanctify me, O my Saviour.

CHAPTER. Is. xxvi.

O LORD, Thy hand is lifted up : Thou art glorified.

Nones.

Ant. To-day is declared a great mystery : for the Creator of all things hath purged our sins in Jordan.

CHAPTER. Is. xii.

WITH joy shall ye draw water out of the wells of salvation : and in that day shall ye say, Praise the Lord, call upon His Name.

Second Vespers.

Sunday Psalms, with Ants. of Lauds.
CHAPTER, HYMN, V. *and* Ṛ.,
as at First Vespers.

Ant. to Mag. The fountains of water were sanctified when Christ gloriously appeared : the nations of earth draw water with joy from the wells of salvation, for Christ our God then sanctified every creature.

Collect of the Epiphany, p. 110.

MEMORIAL OF S. MARY,
As on the Epiphany, p. 110.

If the Octave of the Epiphany falls on Saturday, the Second Vespers are of the Octave, and a memorial is made of Sunday.
The day after the Octave of the Epiphany, everything as in the Psalter, except that which follows.

These Hymns are said from the Octave of the Epiphany till the First Vespers of the First Sunday in Lent, exclusive.

Saturday.

Vespers.

HYMN. *Deus Creator omnium.*

O BLEST Creator, God most high,
Great Ruler of the starry sky,
Who, robing day with beauteous light,
Hast clothed in soft repose the night :

That sleep may wearied limbs restore,
And fit for toil and use once more;
May gently soothe the careworn breast,
And lull our anxious griefs to rest;

We thank Thee for the day now gone;
We pray Thee while the night comes on,
Help us, poor sinners, as we raise,
Our wonted offering of praise.

To Thee our hearts their music bring,
Thee our united voices sing;
To Thee our pure affections soar,
Thee may our chastened souls adore.

So when the deepening shades prevail,
And night o'er day hath dropped her veil,
Faith may no wildering darkness know,
But night with faith's own radiance glow.

From every wrongful passion free,
Our inmost hearts make sleep in Thee,
Nor let the fiend with envious snare
Our rest with sinful terrors scare.

Christ, with the Father ever one :
Spirit, of Father and of Son;
God over all, of mighty sway,
Shield us, great Trinity, we pray. Amen.

V. Let our evening prayer come up before Thee, O Lord.

Ṛ. And let Thy mercy come down on us.

SUNDAY.

Lauds.

HYMN. *Æterne rerum Conditor.*

DREAD Framer of the earth and sky,
Who dost the circling seasons give,
And all the cheerful change supply
Of alternating morn and eve :

Light of our darksome journey here,
  With days dividing night from night :
Loud crows the dawn's shrill harbinger,
  And wakens up the sunbeams bright.

Forthwith at this, the darkness chill
  Retreats before the star of morn :
And from their busy schemes of ill,
  The vagrant crews of night return.

Fresh hope, at this, the sailor cheers,
  The waves their stormy strife allay ;
The Church's Rock at this, in tears,
  Hastens to wash his guilt away.

Arise ye, then, with one accord :
  Nor longer wrapt in slumber lie ;
The cock rebukes all who their Lord
  By sloth neglect, by sin deny.

At his clear cry joy springs afresh,
  Health courses through the sick man's veins,
The dagger glides into its sheath,
  The fallen soul her faith regains.

Jesu ! look on us when we fall ;—
  One momentary glance of Thine
Can from her guilt the soul recal
  To tears of penitence divine.

Awake us from false sleep profound,
  And through our senses pour Thy light ;
Be Thy blest Name the first we sound
  At early dawn, the last at night.

Doxology till Candlemas :

All honour, laud, and glory be,
O Jesu, Virgin-born, to Thee !
All glory, as is ever meet,
To Father and to Paraclete. Amen.

After Candlemas :

All laud to God the Father be ;
All laud, eternal Son, to Thee !
All laud, as is for ever meet,
To God the Holy Paraclete. Amen.

*And the Doxology is thus said in all
Hymns, except* Deus Creator omnium,
during these seasons.

℣. *and* ℟. *to Hymns at Sunday Lauds :*

Till Septuagesima :

℣. The Lord is King.

℟. He hath put on glorious apparel. Alleluia.

From Septuagesima till Lent :

℣. Lord, Thou hast been our refuge.

℟. From one generation to another.

Vespers.

HYMN. *Lucis Creator optime,*
℣. *and* ℟., p. 47.

———

Monday.

Lauds.

HYMN. *Splendor Paternæ Gloriæ.*

THOU brightness of the Father's ray,
  True Light of light and Day of day ;
Light's fountain and eternal spring :
Thou Morn the morn illumining !

Glide in, Thou very Sun divine ;
With everlasting brightness shine :
And shed abroad on every sense
The Spirit's light and influence.

Thee, Father, let us seek aright :
The Father of perpetual light :
The Father of almighty grace :
Each wile of sin away to chase.

Our acts with courage do Thou fill :
Blunt Thou the tempter's tooth of ill :
Misfortune into good convert,
Or give us grace to bear unhurt.

Our spirits, whatsoe'er betide,
In chaste and loyal bodies guide ;
Let faith, with fervour unalloy'd,
The bane of falsehood still avoid ;

And Christ our daily food be nigh,
And faith our daily cup supply ;
So may we quaff, to calm and bless,
The Spirit's rapturous holiness.

Now let the day in joy pass on :
Our modesty like early dawn,
Our faith like noontide splendour glow,
Our souls the twilight never know.

Doxology till Candlemas :

All honour, laud, and glory be,
O Jesu, Virgin-born, to Thee !
All glory, as is ever meet,
To Father and to Paraclete. Amen.

℣. Have I not thought upon Thee when I was waking ?

℟. Because Thou hast been my helper.

After Candlemas :

All laud to God the Father be ;
All laud, eternal Son, to Thee ;
All laud, as is for ever meet,
To God the Holy Paraclete. Amen.

℣. *and* ℟. *as before Candlemas.*

Vespers.

HYMN. *Immense cæli conditor.*

O GREAT Creator of the sky,
  Who wouldest not the floods on high
With earthly waters to confound,
But mad'st the firmament their bound ;

The floods above Thou didst ordain ;
The floods below Thou didst restrain :
That moisture might attemper heat,
Lest the parch'd earth should ruin meet.

Upon our souls, good Lord, bestow
The gift of grace in endless flow :
Lest some renewed deceit or wile
Of former sin should us beguile.

Let faith discover heavenly light;
So shall its rays direct us right :
And let this faith each error chase ;
And never give to falsehood place.

Doxology till Candlemas :

All honour, laud, and glory be,
O Jesu, Virgin-born, to Thee !
All glory, as is ever meet,
To Father and to Paraclete.   Amen.

℣. Lord, let my prayer be set forth.
℟. In Thy sight as the incense.

After Candlemas :

O Father, that we ask be done,
Through Jesus Christ, Thine only Son ;
Who, with the Holy Ghost, and Thee,
Shall live and reign eternally.   Amen.

℣. and ℟. *as before Candlemas.*

Tuesday.
Lauds.

HYMN.   *Ales diei nuntius.*

THE wingèd herald of the day
Proclaims the morn's approaching ray :
And Christ the Lord our souls excites,
And so to endless life invites.

Take up thy bed, to each He cries,
Who sick, or wrapped in slumber lies :
And chaste, and just, and sober stand,
And watch : My coming is at hand.

With earnest cry, with tearful care,
Call we the Lord to hear our prayer,
While supplication, pure and deep,
Forbids each chastened heart to sleep.

Do Thou, O Christ, our slumbers wake ;
Do Thou the chains of darkness break ;
Purge Thou our former sins away,
And in our souls new light display.

All laud to God the Father be,
All laud, eternal Son, to Thee ;
All laud, as is for ever meet,
To God the Holy Paraclete.   Amen.

℣. Have I not thought upon Thee when I was waking ?

℟. Because Thou hast been my helper.

Doxology according to Rubric, p. 116.

Vespers.

HYMN.   *Telluris ingens Conditor.*

EARTH'S mighty Maker, Whose command
Rais'd from the sea the solid land ;
And drove each billowy heap away,
And bade the earth stand firm for aye :

That so with flowers of golden hue,
The seeds of each it might renew ;
And fruit-trees bearing fruit might yield,—
And pleasant pasture of the field :

Our spirit's rankling wounds efface
With dewy freshness of Thy grace :
That grief may cleanse each deed of ill,
And o'er each lust may triumph still.

Let every soul Thy law obey,
And keep from every evil way ;
Rejoice each promis'd good to win,
And flee from every mortal sin.

O Father, that we ask be done,
Through Jesus Christ, Thine only Son ;
Who, with the Holy Ghost, and Thee,
Shall live and reign eternally.   Amen.

℣. Lord, let my prayer be set forth.
℟. In Thy sight as the incense.

Doxology according to Rubric, p. 116.

Wednesday.
Lauds.

HYMN.   *Nox et tenebræ et nubila.*

HENCE, night and clouds that night-time brings,
Confus'd and dark and troubled things :
The dawn is here ; the sky grows white ;
Christ is at hand : depart from sight !

Earth's dusky veil is torn away,
Pierc'd by the sparkling beams of day :
The world resumes its hues apace,
Soon as the day-star shews its face.

But Thee, O Christ, alone we seek,
With conscience pure and temper meek :
With tears and chants we humbly pray
That Thou would'st guide us through the day.

For many a shade obscures each sense,
Which needs Thy beams to purge it thence :
Light of the morning star, illume,
Serenely shining, all our gloom !

All laud to God the Father be,
All laud, eternal Son, to Thee ;
All laud, as is ever meet,
To God the Holy Paraclete.   Amen.

℣. Have I not thought upon Thee when I was waking ?

℟. Because Thou hast been my helper.

Doxology according to Rubric, p. 116.

Vespers.

HYMN.   *Cæli Deus sanctissime.*

O GOD, Whose hand hath spread the sky
And all its shining hosts on high,
And painting it with fiery light,
Made it so beauteous and so bright :

Thou, when the Wednesday was begun,
Didst frame the circle of the sun,
And set the moon for ordered change,
And planets for their wider range :

To night and day, by certain line,
Their varying bounds Thou didst assign ;
And gav'st a signal, known and meet,
For months begun and months complete.

Enlighten Thou the hearts of men ;
Polluted souls make pure again ;
Unloose the bands of guilt within ;
Remove the burden of our sin.

O Father, that we ask be done,
Through Jesus Christ, Thine only Son ;
Who, with the Holy Ghost and Thee,
Shall live and reign eternally.   Amen.

℣. Lord, let my prayer be set forth.
℟. In Thy sight as the incense.

Doxology according to Rubric, p. 116.

— — —

Thursday.

𝕷𝖆𝖚𝖉𝖘.

HYMN.   *Lux ecce surgit aurea.*

BEHOLD the golden dawn arise;
The paling night forsakes the skies :
Those shades that hid the world from view,
And us to dangerous error drew.

May this new day be calmly past,
May we keep pure while it shall last ;
Nor let our lips from truth depart,
Nor dark designs engage the heart.

So may the day speed on ; the tongue
No falsehood know, the hands no wrong :
Our eyes from wanton gaze refrain ;
No guilt our guarded bodies stain.

For God All-seeing from on high
Surveys us with a watchful eye ;
Each day our ev'ry act He knows,
From early dawn to evening's close.

All laud to God the Father be ;
All laud, eternal Son, to Thee ;
All laud, as is for ever meet,
To God the Holy Paraclete.   Amen.

℣. Have I not thought upon Thee when I was waking?

℟. Because Thou hast been my helper.

Doxology according to Rubric, p. 116.

𝖁𝖊𝖘𝖕𝖊𝖗𝖘.

HYMN.   *Magnæ Deus potentiæ.*

ALMIGHTY God, Who from the flood
Didst bring to light a twofold brood ;
Part in the firmament to fly,
And part in ocean depths to lie :

Appointing fishes in the sea,
And fowls in open air to be ;
That each, by origin the same,
Its separate dwelling-place might claim :

Grant that Thy servants, by the tide
Of blood and water purified,
No guilty fall from Thee may know,
Nor death eternal undergo.

Let none despair through sin's distress ;
Be none puffed up with boastfulness ;
That contrite hearts be not dismayed,
Nor haughty souls in ruin laid.

O Father, that we ask be done,
Through Jesus Christ, Thine only Son ;
Who, with the Holy Ghost and Thee,
Shall live and reign eternally.   Amen.

℣. Lord, let my prayer be set forth.
℟. In Thy sight as the incense.

Doxology according to Rubric, p. 116.

— — —

Friday.

𝕷𝖆𝖚𝖉𝖘.

HYMN.   *Æterna cœli gloria.*

ETERNAL glory of the sky,
Blest hope of frail humanity,
The Father's sole-begotten One,
Yet born a spotless Virgin's Son :

Uplift us with Thine arm of might,
And let our hearts rise pure and bright ;
And ardent in God's praises, pay
The thanks we owe Him every day.

The day-star's rays are glittering clear,
And tells that day itself is near ;
The shadows of the night depart ;
Thou, Holy Light, illume the heart !

Within our senses ever dwell,
And worldly darkness thence expel :
Long as the days of life endure,
Preserve our souls devout and pure.

The faith that first must be possessed,
Root deep within our inmost breast :
And joyous hope in second place ;
Then charity, Thy greatest grace.

All laud to God the Father be ;
All laud, eternal Son, to Thee ;
All laud, as is for ever meet,
To God the Holy Paraclete.   Amen.

℣. Have I not thought upon Thee when I was waking?

℟. Because Thou hast been my helper.

Doxology according to Rubric, p. 116.

Vespers.

HYMN. *Plasmator hominis Deus.*

MAKER of men! from heaven Thy throne
Who orderest all things, God alone;
By Whose decree the teeming earth
To reptile and to beast gave birth:

The mighty forms that fill the land,
Instinct with life at Thy command,
Thou gav'st subdued to humankind
For service in their rank assigned.

From all Thy servants chase away
Whate'er of thought impure to-day
Hath mingled with the heart's intent,
Or with the actions hath been blent.

In heaven Thine endless joys bestow,
But grant Thy gifts of grace below:
From chains of strife our souls release;
Bind fast the gentle bands of peace.

O Father, that we ask be done,
Through Jesus Christ, Thine only Son;
Who, with the Holy Ghost and Thee,
Shall live and reign eternally. Amen.

℣. Lord, let my prayer be set forth.
℟. In Thy sight as the incense.

Doxology according to Rubric, p. 116.

Saturday.

Lauds.

HYMN. *Aurora jam spargit polum.*

DAWN sprinkles all the east with light;
Day o'er the earth is gliding bright;
Morn's glittering rays their course begin;
Farewell to darkness and to sin.

Each phantom of the night depart,
Each thought of guilt forsake the heart:
Let every ill that darkness brought
Beneath its shade now come to nought.

So that last morning, dread and great,
Which we with trembling hope await,
With blessed light for us shall glow,
Who chant the song we sang below,—

All laud to God the Father be;
All laud, eternal Son, to Thee;
All laud, as is for ever meet,
To God the Holy Paraclete. Amen.

℣. Have I not thought upon Thee
when I was waking?
℟. Because Thou hast been my
helper.

Doxology according to Rubric, p. 116.

MEMORIALS

*Said from the Octave of Epiphany till
Ash-Wednesday.*

Lauds.

MEMORIAL OF S. MARY,
Daily.

Ant. The root of Jesse hath budded; a star hath risen out of Jacob:
a Virgin hath brought forth the Saviour. We praise Thee, O our God.

℣. After child-bearing thou remainedst a Virgin.
℟. O Mother of God.

COLLECT.

O GOD, Who through the fruitful
virginity of the blessed Virgin
Mary hast bestowed the rewards of
eternal salvation on the human race:
grant, we pray Thee, that she may
intercede for us, through whom we
have received the Author of Life, Thy
Son Jesus Christ our Lord. Amen.

MEMORIAL OF ALL SAINTS,
On Ferias and Simple Feasts only.

Ant. The Saints shall be joyful
with glory: they shall rejoice in their
beds.

℣. Wonderful art Thou in Thy
Saints, O God.
℟. And glorious in Thy Majesty.

COLLECT.

WE pray Thee, O Lord, let the intercession of all Thy Saints be
acceptable unto Thee; and grant to
us forgiveness of our sins, and the
remedies of eternal life; through
Jesus Christ our Lord. Amen.

*When the ℣. Wonderful, etc., is said in
the Office of Lauds, at the Memorial of
All Saints is said instead:*

℣. The souls of the righteous are
in the hand of God.
℟. And there shall no torment
touch them.

Vespers.

MEMORIAL OF S. MARY,
Daily.

Ant. In the bush which Moses saw unconsumed : we recognise thy glorious virginity, O Mother of God.

℣. Thou art fairer than the children of men.

℟. Full of grace are thy lips.

Collect as at Lauds.

MEMORIAL OF ALL SAINTS,
On Ferias and Simple Feasts only.

Ant. O how glorious is the kingdom where all the Saints rejoice with Christ : they are clothed with white robes, and follow the Lamb whithersoever He goeth.

℣. Be glad, O ye righteous, and rejoice in the Lord.

℟. And be joyful, all ye that are true of heart.

Collect as at Lauds.

When the ℣. *Be glad, etc., is said in the Office of Vespers, in the Memorial of All Saints is said instead :*

℣. The Saints shall be joyful with glory.

℟. They shall rejoice in their beds.

———

SECOND SUNDAY AFTER THE EPIPHANY.

First Vespers.

Ant. to Mag. My sins, O Lord, are stuck fast in me like arrows : but do Thou heal me by the remedies of penitence, before the wounds become corrupt.

COLLECT.

ALMIGHTY and everlasting God, Who dost govern all things in heaven and earth ; mercifully hear the supplications of Thy people, and grant us Thy peace all the days of our life ; through Jesus Christ our Lord. Amen.

Lauds.

Ant. to Ben. There was a marriage in Cana of Galilee : and the Mother of Jesus was there. And Jesus also was called.

Second Vespers.

Ant. to Mag. And when they wanted wine, Jesus saith unto them : Fill the waterpots with water ; and it was made wine.

———

THIRD SUNDAY AFTER THE EPIPHANY.

First Vespers.

Ant. to Magnificat as on the Second Sunday after the Epiphany.

COLLECT.

ALMIGHTY and everlasting God, mercifully look upon our infirmities, and in all our dangers and necessities stretch forth Thy right hand to help and defend us ; through Jesus Christ our Lord. Amen.

Lauds.

Ant. to Ben. When He was come down from the mountain, great multitudes followed Him. And behold, there came a leper and worshipped Him, saying : Lord, if Thou wilt, Thou canst make me clean. And Jesus put forth His hand, and touched him, saying, I will ; be thou clean.

Second Vespers.

Ant. to Mag. Lord, my servant lieth at home sick of the palsy, grievously tormented : and Jesus saith unto him, I will come and heal him.

———

FOURTH SUNDAY AFTER THE EPIPHANY.

First Vespers.

Ant. to Magnificat as on the Second Sunday after the Epiphany.

COLLECT.

O GOD, Who knowest us to be set in the midst of so many and great dangers, that by reason of the frailty of our nature we cannot always stand upright: grant to us such strength and protection, as may support us in all dangers, and carry us through all temptations; through Jesus Christ our Lord. Amen.

Lauds.

Ant. to Ben. And when He was entered into a ship, His disciples followed Him. And behold, there arose a great tempest in the sea, insomuch that the ship was covered with the waves : but He was asleep. And His disciples came to Him, and awoke Him, saying, Lord, save us, we perish.

Second Vespers.

Ant. to Mag. He arose, and rebuked the winds and the sea : and there was a great calm.

FIFTH SUNDAY AFTER THE EPIPHANY.

First Vespers.

Ant. to Magnificat *as on the Second Sunday after the Epiphany.*

COLLECT.

O LORD, we beseech Thee to keep Thy Church and household continually in Thy true religion; that they who do lean only upon the hope of Thy heavenly grace, may evermore be defended by Thy mighty power; through Jesus Christ our Lord. Amen.

Lauds.

Ant. to Ben. Sir, didst not thou sow good seed in thy field? from whence then hath it tares? He said unto them, An enemy hath done this.

Second Vespers.

Ant. to Mag. Gather ye together first the tares, and bind them in bundles to burn them : but gather the wheat into my barn.

SIXTH SUNDAY AFTER THE EPIPHANY.

First Vespers.

Ant. to Magnificat *as on the Second Sunday after the Epiphany.*

COLLECT.

O GOD, Whose blessed Son was manifested that He might destroy the works of the devil, and make us the sons of God, and heirs of eternal life; grant us, we beseech Thee, that, having this hope, we may purify ourselves, even as He is pure; that, when He shall appear again with power and great glory, we may be made like unto Him in His eternal and glorious kingdom; where with Thee, O Father, and Thee, O Holy Ghost, He liveth and reigneth, ever one God, world without end. Amen.

Lauds.

Ant. to Ben. Immediately after the tribulation of those days shall the sun be darkened, and the moon shall not give her light, and the stars shall fall from heaven, and the powers of the heavens shall be shaken.

Second Vespers.

Ant. to Mag. Then shall appear the sign of the Son of Man in heaven : and then shall all the tribes of the earth mourn.

SEPTUAGESIMA SUNDAY.

From henceforth till Easter, Alleluia is not said. In its place at the beginning of each Hour is said :

Praise be to Thee, King of eternal glory.

First Vespers.

CHAPTER. 1 Cor. xi.

KNOW ye not, that they which run in a race run all, but one receiveth the prize? So run that ye may obtain.

℟. Thus the heavens and the earth were finished, and all the host of them: and on the seventh day God ended His work which He had made, * and He rested from all His work which He had made. ℣. And God saw every thing that He had made, and behold, it was very good. ℟. And He rested from all His work which He had made. ℣. Glory be to the Father, and to the Son, and to the Holy Ghost. ℟. Thus the heavens and the earth were finished, and all the host of them: and on the seventh day God ended all His work which He had made; and He rested from all His work which He had made.

HYMN. *Deus Creator omnium*, p. 115.

Ant. to Mag. And the Lord God planted a garden eastward in Eden: and there He put the man whom He had formed.

COLLECT.

O LORD, we beseech Thee favourably to hear the prayers of Thy people; that we, who are justly punished for our offences, may be mercifully delivered by Thy goodness, for the glory of Thy Name; through Jesus Christ our Saviour, Who liveth and reigneth with Thee and the Holy Ghost, ever one God, world without end. Amen.

Lauds.

Psalms of Sunday, as below.

Ant. 1. Have mercy upon me, O God: wash me throughly from my wickedness, for against Thee only have I sinned.

Psalm li. *Miserere mei Deus.*

Ant. 2. I will thank Thee: for Thou hast heard me.

Psalm cxviii. *Confitemini Domini.*

Ant. 3. O God, my God, early will I seek Thee: because Thou hast been my helper.

Psalm lxiii., *Deus, Deus meus*, and Psalm lxvii., *Deus misereatur.*

Ant. 4. Blessed art Thou, O God, in the firmament of heaven: and above all to be praised and glorified for ever.

Psalm. *Benedicite, omnia opera.*

Ant. 5. O praise: the Lord of heaven.

Psalm. cxlvii. *Laudate Dominum*, etc.

These are the Sunday Psalms from henceforth till Easter.

CHAPTER. 1 Cor. ix.

KNOW ye not, that they which run in a race run all, but one receiveth the prize? So run that ye may obtain.

℟. Thanks be to God.

HYMN. *Æterne rerum Conditor,* ℣. and ℟. p. 115.

Ant. to Ben. The kingdom of heaven is like unto a man that is an householder: which went out early in the morning to hire labourers into his vineyard, saith the Lord.

Prime.

Ant. And when he had agreed with the labourers for a penny a-day: he sent them into his vineyard.

Psalm xciii., Dominus regnavit, *is said at Prime from henceforth till Easter, instead of* Psalm cxviii., Confitemini Domino.

Tierce.

Ant. And he went out about the third hour, and saw others standing idle in the market-place, and said unto them: Go ye also into the vineyard, and whatsoever is right I will give you.

CHAPTER. I Cor. xi.

KNOW ye not, that they which run in a race run all, but one receiveth the prize? So run that ye may obtain.

℞. Thou hast been my succour, [*here the Choir take up*] leave me not. ℣. Neither forsake me, O God of my salvation. ℞. Leave me not. ℣. Glory be to the Father, and to the Son : and to the Holy Ghost. ℞. Thou hast been my succour, leave me not.

℣. I said, Lord, be merciful unto me.

℞. Heal my soul, for I have sinned against Thee.

Sexts.

Ant. Why stand ye here all the day idle? : They say unto him, Because no man hath hired us.

CHAPTER. I Cor. ix.

AND every man that striveth for the mastery is temperate in all things : now they do it to obtain a corruptible crown, but we an incorruptible.

℞. Thou wast my hope * when I hanged yet upon my mother's breasts. ℣. I have been left unto Thee ever since I was born : Thou art my God even from my mother's womb. ℞. When I hanged yet upon my mother's breasts. ℣. Glory be to the Father, and to the Son : and to the Holy Ghost. ℞. Thou wast my hope, when I hanged yet upon my mother's breasts.

℣. The Lord is my Shepherd, therefore can I lack nothing.

℞. He shall feed me in a green pasture.

Nones.

Ant. The householder said to his labourers : Why stand ye here all the day idle? They say unto him, Because no man hath hired us. He saith unto them, Go ye also into the vineyard; and whatsoever is right, that shall ye receive.

CHAPTER. I Cor. x.

MOREOVER, brethren, I would not that ye should be ignorant, how that all our fathers were under the cloud, and all passed through the sea; and were all baptized unto Moses in the cloud and in the sea.

℞. O cleanse Thou me * from my secret faults. ℣. Keep Thy servant also from presumptuous sins. ℞. From my secret faults. ℣. Glory be to the Father, and to the Son : and to the Holy Ghost. ℞. O cleanse Thou me from my secret faults.

℣. Thou hast been my succour.

℞. Leave me not, neither forsake me, O God of my salvation.

Second Vespers.

CHAPTER. I Cor. ix.

KNOW ye not, that they which run in a race run all, but one receiveth the prize? So run, that ye may obtain.

℞. Thanks be to God.

HYMN. *Lucis Creator optime,* ℣. and ℞. p. 47.

Ant. to Mag. So when even was come, the lord of the vineyard saith unto his steward : Call the labourers, and give them their hire.

If the Purification falls on Septuagesima or Sexagesima Sunday, the Office is of the feast, with memorial of the Sunday.

Ants. to Benedictus *and* Magnificat *for the current week when the Office is of the feria.*

Ant. 1. Call the labourers : and give them their hire, saith the Lord.

Ant. 2. But the lord of the vineyard answered one of them, and said,

Friend, I do thee no wrong : didst thou not agree with me for a penny? Take that thine is, and go thy way.

Ant. 3. Friend, I do thee no wrong: didst not thou agree with me for a penny? Take that thine is, and go thy way.

Ant. 4. Take that thine is, and go thy way : for I am good, saith the Lord.

Ant. 5. Is it not lawful for me to do what I will with mine own? : Is thine eye evil, because I am good? saith the Lord.

Ant. 6. The first shall be last, and the last first : for many are called, but few chosen, saith the Lord.

Ant. 7. So the last shall be first, and the first last : for many are called, but few chosen, saith the Lord.

SEXAGESIMA SUNDAY.

First Vespers.

CHAPTER. II Cor. xi.

YE suffer fools gladly, seeing ye yourselves are wise. For ye suffer if a man bring you into bondage, if a man devour you, if a man take of you, if a man exalt himself, if a man smite you on the face.

Ry. Noah, seeking to know if the waters were abated, sent forth a dove, and lo, in her mouth was an olive-leaf plucked off, when she * returned unto him into the ark. Vy. The dove, bearing in her mouth the sign of God's mercy. Ry. Returned unto him into the ark. Vy. Glory be to the Father, and to the Son : and to the Holy Ghost. Ry. She returned unto him into the ark.

HYMN. *Deus Creator omnium,* Vy. and Ry., p. 115.

Ant. to Ben. And God said unto Noah : I do set My bow in the cloud, and it shall be for a token of a covenant between Me and the earth.

COLLECT.

O LORD God, Who seest that we put not our trust in any thing that we do; mercifully grant that by Thy power we may be defended against all adversity : through Jesus Christ our Lord.　Amen.

Lauds.

Psalms as on Septuagesima Sunday.

Ant. 1. According to the multitude of Thy mercies : do away mine offences.

Ant. 2. Thou art my God, and I will thank Thee : Thou art my God, and I will praise Thee.

Ant. 3. Early will I seek Thee : that I might behold Thy power.

Ant. 4. Praise Him : and magnify Him for ever.

Ant. 5. O praise the Lord of heaven : praise Him, all ye angels of His.

CHAPTER. II Cor. xi.

YE suffer fools gladly, seeing ye yourselves are wise. For ye suffer if a man bring you into bondage, if a man devour you, if a man take of you, if a man exalt himself, if a man smite you on the face.

Ry. Thanks be to God.

HYMN. *Æterne rerum Conditor,* Vy. and Ry., p. 115.

Ant. to Ben. When much people were gathered together, and were come to Him out of every city, He spake by a parable : A sower went out to sow his seed.

Prime.

Ant. And other fell on good ground, and sprang up, and bare fruit an hundred-fold : and other some sixty-fold.

Tierce.

Ant. The seed fell on good ground: and brought forth fruit with patience.

CHAPTER. II Cor. xi.

YE suffer fools gladly, seeing ye yourselves are wise. For ye suffer if a man bring you into bondage, if a man devour you, if a man take of you, if a man exalt himself, if a man smite you on the face.

R̷. Thou hast been. p. 123.

Sexts.

Ant. When Jesus had said these things, He cried : He that hath ears to hear, let him hear.

CHAPTER. II Cor. xii.

I KNEW a man in Christ, above fourteen years ago, (whether in the body I cannot tell; or whether out of the body I cannot tell : God knoweth;) such an one caught up to the third heaven.

R̷. Thou wast my hope, p. 123.

Nones.

Ant. Unto you it is given to know the mysteries of the kingdom of God : but to others in parables, saith Jesus to His disciples.

CHAPTER. II Cor. xii.

A ND I knew such a man, (whether in the body or out of the body I cannot tell : God knoweth :) how that he was caught up into paradise, and heard unspeakable words, which it is not lawful for a man to utter.

R̷. O cleanse Thou me. p. 123.

Second Vespers.

CHAPTER. II Cor. xi.

YE suffer fools gladly, seeing ye yourselves are wise. For ye suffer if a man bring you into bondage, if a man devour you, if a man take of you, if a man exalt himself, if a man smite you on the face.

R̷. Thanks be to God.

HYMN. *Lucis Creator optime,*
 ℣. and R̷., p. 47.

Ant. to Mag. They, which in an honest and good heart keep the word of God : bring forth fruit with patience.

Ants. to Benedictus *and* Magnificat *for the week, when the Service is of the Feria.*

Ant. 1. The seed is the word of God, but the Sower is Christ : he that heareth Him abideth for ever.

Ant. 2. But that on the good ground are they, which in an honest and good heart : having heard the word, keep it, and bring forth fruit with patience.

Ant. 3. If ye desire to be truly rich : love the true riches.

Ant. 4. If ye seek the height of true honour : hasten with all speed to the heavenly country.

QUINQUAGESIMA SUNDAY.

First Vespers.

CHAPTER. I Cor. xiii.

THOUGH I speak with the tongues of men and of angels, and have not charity, I am become as sounding brass, or a tinkling cymbal.

R̷. When Abraham returned from the slaughter of the three kings, there met him Melchisedec, king of Salem, bringing forth bread and wine. * And he was the priest of the most high God, and he blessed him. ℣. Blessed be Abraham of the most high God. R̷. And he was the priest of the most high God, and he blessed him. ℣. Glory be to the Father, and to the Son, and to the Holy Ghost. R̷. And he was the priest of the most high God, and he blessed him.

HYMN. *Deus Creator omnium,*
 ℣. and R̷., p. 115.

Ant. to Mag. When Abraham abode in the plain of Mamre, he saw three men coming down by the way : he beheld three, and adored One.

COLLECT.

O LORD, Who hast taught us that all our doings without charity are nothing worth : send Thy Holy Ghost, and pour into our hearts that most excellent gift of charity, the very bond of peace and of all virtues, without which whosoever liveth is counted dead before Thee ; grant this for Thine only Son Jesus Christ's sake. Amen.

[*Or this,*

WE beseech Thee, O Lord, mercifully to hear our prayers : that we, being loosed from the chains of our sins, may be preserved from all adversities; through Jesus Christ our Lord.   Amen.]

Lauds.

Psalms as on Septuagesima Sunday.

Ant. 1. Turn Thy face, O Lord, from my sins : and put out all my misdeeds.

Ant. 2. The Lord is my strength, and my song : and is become my salvation.

Ant. 3. Have I not thought upon Thee, when I was waking? : because Thou hast been my helper.

Ant. 4. Let us bless the Father, and the Son : with the Holy Ghost.

Ant. 5. Young men and maidens, old men and children : praise the Name of the Lord.

CHAPTER. 1 Cor. xiii.

THOUGH I speak with the tongues of men and of angels, and have not charity, I am become as sounding brass, or a tinkling cymbal.

R̷. Thanks be to God.

HYMN. *Æterne rerum conditor,* ℣. and R̷., p. 115.

Ant to Ben. Behold, we go up to Jerusalem : and all things that are written by the prophets concerning the Son of man shall be accomplished.

Prime.

Ant. to Psalms. As Jesus was come nigh unto Jericho : the blind man cried to him that he might receive his sight.

Tierce.

Ant. As the Lord passed by, the blind man cried unto Him : Thou Son of David, have mercy upon me.

CHAPTER. 1 Cor. xiii.

THOUGH I speak with the tongues of men and of angels, and have not charity, I am become as sounding brass, or a tinkling cymbal.

R̷. Thou hast been. p. 123.

Sexts.

Ant. The blind man sat by the way, and cried : Have mercy upon me.

CHAPTER. 1 Cor. xiii.

CHARITY suffereth long, and is kind ; charity envieth not: charity vaunteth not itself, is not puffed up, doth not behave itself unseemly, seeketh not her own.

R̷. Thou wast my hope.   p. 123.

Nones.

Ant. The blind man cried so much the more : that the Lord would give him light.

CHAPTER. 1 Cor. xiii.

CHARITY is not easily provoked, thinketh no evil ; rejoiceth not in iniquity, but rejoiceth in the truth.

R̷. O cleanse Thou me.   p. 123.

Second Vespers.

CHAPTER. 1 Cor. xiii.

THOUGH I speak with the tongues of men and of angels, and have not charity, I am become as sounding brass, or a tinkling cymbal.

℟. Thanks be to God.

HYMN. *Lucis Creator optime,*
℣. and ℟., p. 47.

Ant. to Mag. And Jesus stood, and commanded him to be brought unto Him, and asked him, saying, What wilt thou that I should do unto thee? And he said, Lord, that I may receive my sight : and Jesus said unto him, Receive thy sight; thy faith hath saved thee. And immediately he received his sight, and followed Him, glorifying God.

On this following Monday is to be said the Office of the Blessed Virgin : if this be not done, the Ants. for Tuesday must be used on both days.

———

Tuesday.

Ant. to Ben. What wilt thou : that I should do unto thee?

Ant. to Mag. All the people, when they saw it : gave praise unto God.

———

ASH-WEDNESDAY,
The Head of the Fast.

Lauds.

Ants. and Psalms of the Feria.

CHAPTER. Joel ii.

TURN ye even unto Me, saith the Lord, with all your heart, and with fasting, and with weeping, and with mourning : and rend your hearts, and not your garments, saith the Lord Almighty.

This Chapter is said daily, at Ferial Lauds, till Passion Sunday.

COLLECT.

ALMIGHTY and everlasting God, Who hatest nothing that Thou hast made, and dost forgive the sins of all them that are penitent; create and make in us new and contrite hearts, that we worthily lamenting our sins, and acknowledging our wretchedness, may obtain of Thee, the God of all mercy, perfect remission and forgiveness; through Jesus Christ our Lord. Amen.

[*Or this,*

GRANT, we beseech Thee, O Lord, to Thy faithful people, that the holy solemnities of the fast may begin with due reverence, and continue with sure devotion; through Jesus Christ our Lord. Amen.]

The same Collect is said at every Hour of this day.

MEMORIAL OF PENITENTS.

Ant. Turn ye even unto Me, saith the Lord, with all your heart, and with fasting, and with weeping, and with mourning.

℣. We have sinned with our fathers.

℟. We have done amiss, and dealt wickedly.

COLLECT.

O LORD, we beseech Thee, mercifully hear our prayers, and spare all those who confess their sins unto Thee; that they, whose consciences by sin are accused, by Thy merciful pardon may be absolved; through Christ our Lord. Amen.

Prime and the other Hours as usual.
The Hours are thus said till the First Sunday in Lent, except that the Collect and Ants. to Benedictus and Magnificat are changed.

Vespers.

Ant. to Mag. Lay up for yourselves treasures in heaven : where neither moth nor rust doth corrupt.

MEMORIAL OF PENITENTS.

Ant. Who knoweth if the Lord will return and repent : and leave a blessing behind Him?

℣. O Lord, deal not with us after our sins.

℞. Neither reward us after our iniquities.

COLLECT.

O LORD, we beseech Thee, mercifully hear our prayers, and spare all those who confess their sins unto Thee; that they, whose consciences by sin are accused, by Thy merciful pardon may be absolved; through Christ our Lord. Amen.

The Office for this day is not to be changed for any Feast whatever.

From this day till Maundy Thursday, on Double Feasts, there shall always be solemn Memorials of the Fast at both Vespers and at Lauds. From this day till the morrow of Low Sunday, there shall be no Office or Memorial for Simple Feasts. The Memorials of Penitents are said as on this day at Lauds and Vespers till Wednesday in Holy Week.

Thursday.

Lauds.

All of the Feria, except that which follows.

Chapter as on Wednesday.

Ant. to Ben. Lord, my servant lieth at home sick of the palsy, grievously tormented : Verily, I say unto thee, I will come and heal him.

[COLLECT.

GOD, Who art offended by sin, and appeased by penitence; mercifully regard the prayers of Thy suppliant people, and turn away the scourges of Thy wrath, which by our sins we have deserved; through Jesus Christ our Lord. Amen.]

Vespers.

All of the Feria, except that which follows.

Ant. to Mag. Lord, I am not worthy that Thou shouldest come under my roof : but speak the word only, and my servant shall be healed.

[COLLECT.

SPARE, O Lord, spare Thy people; that, having been justly chastised by Thy scourging, they may be relieved by Thy tender mercy; through Jesus Christ our Lord. Amen.]

Friday.

Lauds.

Ant. to Ben. When thou doest alms : let not thy left hand know what thy right hand doeth.

[COLLECT.

WE beseech Thee, O Lord, of Thy loving favour, that we may persevere in the fast we have begun, and with pure minds perform our bodily observance; through Jesus Christ our Lord. Amen.]

Vespers.

Ant. to Mag. But thou, when thou prayest, enter into thy closet : and when thou hast shut thy door, pray to thy Father.

[COLLECT.

DEFEND Thy people, O Lord, and graciously protect them from all sin; whereas no adversity may harm, if no wickedness have dominion over them; through Jesus Christ our Lord. Amen.]

Saturday.

Lauds.

Ant. to Ben. Wherefore have we fasted, and Thou seest not? : wherefore have we afflicted our soul, and Thou takest no knowledge?

[COLLECT.

BE present, O Lord, to our supplications; and grant that with devout service we may celebrate this holy fast, instituted for the health and saving of our souls and bodies; through Jesus Christ our Lord. Amen.]

FIRST SUNDAY IN LENT.

First Vespers.

CHAPTER. II Cor. vi.

WE then beseech you also that ye receive not the grace of God in vain. (For He saith, I have heard thee in a time accepted, and in the day of salvation have I succoured thee.)

℞. Let us amend those things wherein we have ignorantly sinned; lest, suddenly prevented by the day of death, we seek place of repentance, and find it not : Hear, Lord, and have mercy : for we have sinned against Thee. ℣. We have sinned with our fathers : we have done amiss, and dealt wickedly. ℞. Hear, Lord, and have mercy : for we have sinned against Thee. ℣. Glory be to the Father, and to the Son : and to the Holy Ghost. ℞. Hear, Lord, and have mercy : for we have sinned against Thee.

HYMN. *Ex more docti mystico.*

THE fast, as taught by holy lore,
We keep in solemn course once more :
The fast to all men known, and bound
In forty days of yearly round.

The law and seers that were of old
In divers ways this Lent foretold,
Which Christ, all seasons' King and Guide,
In after ages sanctified.

More sparing therefore let us make
The words we speak, the food we take,
Our sleep and mirth,—and closer barred
Be every sense in holy guard.

In prayer together let us fall,
And cry for mercy, one and all,
And weep before the Judge's feet,
And His avenging wrath entreat.

Thy grace have we offended sore
By sins, O God, which we deplore,
But pour upon us from on high,
O pardoning One, Thy clemency.

Remember Thou, though frail we be,
That yet Thine handiwork are we;
Nor let the honour of Thy Name
Be by another put to shame.

Forgive the sin that we have wrought;
Increase the good that we have sought;
That we at length, our wanderings o'er,
May please Thee here and evermore.

Grant, O Thou blessed Trinity,
Grant, O Essential Unity,
That this our fast of forty days
May work our profit and Thy praise. Amen.

℣. He shall give His angels charge over thee.

℞. To keep thee in all thy ways.

This Hymn, ℣., and ℞. are said at Vespers daily, till the Third Sunday in Lent.

Ant. to Mag. Behold, now is the accepted time; behold, now is the day of salvation : let us then in all things approve ourselves as the servants of God, in much patience, in watchings, in fastings; by love unfeigned.

COLLECT.

O LORD, Who for our sake didst fast forty days and forty nights; give us grace to use such abstinence, that, our flesh being subdued to the Spirit, we may ever obey Thy godly motions, in righteousness and true holiness, to Thy honour and glory, Who livest and reignest with the Father and the Holy Ghost, one God, world without end. Amen.

[*Or this,*

O GOD, Who dost purify Thy Church by the yearly observance of Lent: grant to Thy family that those things which they seek of Thee by abstinence, they may follow up by good works; through Jesus Christ our Lord. Amen.]

Compline.

Ant. to Psalms. The light of Thy countenance hath sealed us, O Lord : Thou hast put gladness in my heart.

CHAPTER. Jer. xiv.

THOU, O Lord, art in the midst of us, and we are called by Thy Name; leave us not, O our God.

Ry. In peace: *The Choir proceeds:* in the very same : I will sleep and I will rest. Vy. I will not suffer mine eyes to sleep, nor mine eyelids to slumber. Ry. I will sleep and I will rest. Vy. Glory be to the Father, and to the Son : and to the Holy Ghost. Ry. In peace, in the very same, I will sleep and I will rest.

HYMN. *Christe qui lux esset dies.*

O CHRIST, Who art the Light and Day,
Who driv'st the clouds of night away;
The very Light of Light art Thou,
Preaching glad tidings here below.

We pray Thee, holy Lord, our Light,
Defend us in this coming night;
Grant us a perfect rest in Thee,
A quiet night from perils free.

Let not dull slumber quell the soul,
Nor Satan with his spirits foul;
Nor let our flesh consent begin
To make us in Thy presence sin.

Grant that our eyes due sleep may take,
Our hearts to Thee be e'er awake;
May Thy right hand defend and guide
Thy servants who in Thee confide.

Look down, O Lord, our strong defence,
Repress our foes' proud insolence;
Direct Thy people in all good,
The purchase of Thy precious Blood.

Remember us, O Lord, we pray,
Pent in this cumb'ring frame of clay;
Thou Who dost e'er our souls defend,
Be with us, our eternal Friend.

All laud to God the Father be;
All praise, eternal Son, to Thee;
All glory, as is ever meet,
To God the blessed Paraclete. Amen.

Vy. Keep us.

Ry. As the apple of an eye, hide us under the shadow of Thy wings.

Ant. to Nunc Dim. When thou seest the naked, cover thou him : and hide not thyself from thine own flesh. Then shall thy light break forth as the morning, and the glory of the Lord shall be thy rereward.

Here follow the Prayers, p. 68.
On all Ferias is said after Psalm li.,
    Psalm cxliii., Domine exaudi.

This Compline is said daily till the 3rd Sunday in Lent.

Lauds.

Vy. He hath delivered me.

Ry. From the snare of the hunter, and from the sharp word.

Psalms as on Septuagesima Sunday.

Ant. 1. Make me a clean heart, O God : and renew a right spirit within me.

Ant. 2. Help me now, O Lord : O Lord, send us now prosperity.

Ant. 3. As long as I live will I magnify Thee on this manner : and lift up my hands in Thy Name.

Ant. 4. In a contrite heart and an humble spirit let us be accepted by Thee, O Lord : and so let our sacrifice be in Thy sight this day, and let it please Thee, O Lord God.

Ant. 5. Praise Him, all ye heavens : and ye waters that are above the heavens.

CHAPTER. II Cor. vi.

WE then beseech you also that ye receive not the grace of God in vain. (For He saith, I have heard thee in a time accepted, and in the day of salvation have I succoured thee.)

Ry. Thanks be to God.

HYMN. *Audi benigne Conditor.*

O MAKER of the world, give ear!
Accept the prayer, and own the tear,
Towards Thy seat of mercy sent,
In this most holy fast of Lent.

Each heart is manifest to Thee :
Thou knowest our infirmity :
Forgive Thou then each soul that fain
Would seek to Thee, and turn again.

Our sins are manifold and sore;
But pardon them that sin deplore;
And, for Thy Name's sake, make each soul,
That feels and owns its languor, whole.

So mortify we every sense
By grace of outward abstinence,
That from each stain and spot of sin
The soul may keep her fast within.

Grant, O Thou blessed Trinity,
Grant, O Essential Unity,
That this our fast of forty days
May work our profit and Thy praise. Amen.

℣. His faithfulness and truth shall be thy shield and buckler.

℟. Thou shalt not be afraid for any terror by night.

This Hymn, ℣., and ℟. are said at Lauds daily, till the Third Sunday in Lent.

Ant. to Ben. Then was Jesus led up of the Spirit into the wilderness to be tempted of the devil : and when He had fasted forty days and forty nights, He was afterwards an hungered.

Collect as at First Vespers.

Prime.

Ant. to Psalms. And when Jesus had fasted forty days and forty nights : He was afterwards an hungered.

Tierce.

Ant. Man shall not live by bread alone : but by every word that proceedeth out of the mouth of God.

CHAPTER. II Cor. vi.

WE then beseech you also that ye receive not the grace of God in vain. (For He saith, I have heard thee in a time accepted, and in the day of salvation have I succoured thee.)

℟. Make me : *The Choir proceeds :* A companion of all them that fear Thee : and keep Thy commandments. ℣. O look Thou upon me, and be merciful unto me, as Thou usest to do unto those that love Thy Name. ℟. And keep Thy commandments. ℣. Glory be to the Father, and to the Son : and to the Holy Ghost. ℟. And keep Thy commandments.

℣. I will say unto the Lord, Thou art my hope, and my strong hold.

℟. My God, in Him will I trust.

Sexts.

Ant. Then the devil taketh Him up into the holy city, and setteth Him on a pinnacle of the temple, and saith unto Him : If Thou be the Son of God, cast Thyself down.

CHAPTER. II Cor. vi.

BEHOLD, now is the accepted time; behold, now is the day of salvation. Giving no offence in any thing, that the ministry be not blamed.

℟. Refrain : *The Choir proceeds :* my feet from every evil way : that I may keep Thy word. ℣. I have not shrunk from Thy judgments, for Thou teachest me. ℟. That I may keep Thy word. ℣. Glory be to the Father, and to the Son : and to the Holy Ghost. ℟. Refrain my feet from every evil way, that I may keep Thy word.

℣. He shall deliver thee from the snare of the hunter.

℟. And from the noisome pestilence.

Nones.

Ant. Get thee behind me, Satan : thou shalt not tempt the Lord thy God.

CHAPTER. II Cor. vi.

IN all things approving ourselves as the ministers of God : in much patience, in fastings, by the armour of righteousness.

℟. Let Thy : *The Choir proceeds :* loving mercy come also : unto me, O Lord. ℣. When Thy word goeth forth, it giveth understanding. ℟. Unto me, O Lord. ℣. Glory be to the Father, and to the Son : and to the Holy Ghost. ℟. Let Thy loving mercy come also unto me, O Lord.

℣. He shall defend thee under His wings.

℟. And thou shalt be safe under His feathers.

Second Vespers.

CHAPTER. II Cor. vi.

WE then beseech you also that ye receive not the grace of Go...

vain. (For He saith, I have heard thee in a time accepted, and in the day of salvation have I succoured thee.)

℞. Be Thou for us, O Lord : *The Choir proceeds :* a strong tower. ℣. Against the enemy. ℞. A strong tower. ℣. Glory be to the Father, and to the Son : and to the Holy Ghost. ℞. Be Thou for us, O Lord, a strong tower.

HYMN. *Ex more docti mystico,* ℣. and ℞., p. 129.

Ant. to Mag. Then the devil leaveth Him : and behold, angels came and ministered unto Him.

———

Monday.
Lauds.

℣. He shall deliver thee from the snare of the hunter.

℞. And from the noisome pestilence.

This ℣. and ℞. is said daily at Ferial Lauds.

Ants. and Psalms of the Feria.

CHAPTER. Joel ii.

TURN ye even unto Me, saith the Lord, with all your heart, and with fasting, and with weeping, and with mourning. And rend your hearts, and not your garments, and turn unto the Lord your God.

℞. Thanks be to God.

HYMN. *Audi benigne Conditor,* ℣. and ℞., p. 130.

Ant. to Ben. Come, ye blessed of My Father : inherit the kingdom prepared for you from the foundation of the world.

Then are said the Ferial Petitions; and Psalm vi., Domine, ne in furore, is said after Psalm li., Miserere. After every Hour in Lent, when the Office is of the Feria, one of the seven Penitential Psalms is said, according to order, after

Psalm li., except at Sexts, when Psalm lxvii., Deus misereatur, is said alone, instead of Psalm li. And if a Double Feast follow on the morrow, then at Nones the three last Penitential Psalms shall be said. And so in like manner on Saturdays.

[COLLECT.

TURN us, O God of our salvation; and, that the Lenten fast may profit us, instruct our souls with heavenly doctrine; through Jesus Christ our Lord. Amen.]

Prime.

Ant. As I live, saith the Lord God, I have no pleasure in the death of the wicked : but that the wicked turn from his way and live.

After Psalm li. is said Psalm xxxii. Beati quorum.

Tierce.

Ant. Let us chasten ourselves : in much patience, by the armour of the righteousness of God.

CHAPTER. Joel ii.

TURN unto the Lord your God; for He is gracious and merciful; slow to anger, and of great kindness, and repenteth Him of the evil.

℞. Make me a companion of all them that fear Thee : and keep Thy commandments. ℣. O look Thou upon me, and be merciful unto me, as Thou usest to do unto those that love Thy Name. ℞. And keep Thy commandments. ℣. Glory be to the Father, and to the Son : and to the Holy Ghost. ℞. Make me a companion of all them that fear Thee, and keep Thy commandments.

℣. I will say unto the Lord, Thou art my hope, and my strong hold.

℞. My God, in Him will I trust.

After Psalm li. is said Psalm xxxviii., Domine ne in furore.

From this day till the Wednesday before Easter inclusive, when the Office is of the Feria, are said, after Tierce, the fifteen Gradual Psalms, for all the people of God, with Litany, as in Common of Saints.

Sexts.

Ant. Let us chasten ourselves : in much patience and fastings, by the armour of righteousness.

CHAPTER. Is. lv.

LET the wicked forsake his way, and the unrighteous man his thoughts : and let him return unto the Lord, and He will have mercy upon him, and to our God, for He will abundantly pardon.

R̷. Refrain my feet from every evil way, that I may keep Thy word. V̷. I have not shrunk from Thy judgments, for Thou teachest me. R̷. That I may keep Thy word. V̷. Glory be to the Father, and to the Son : and to the Holy Ghost. R̷. Refrain my feet from every evil way, that I may keep Thy word.

V̷. He shall deliver thee from the snare of the hunter.

R̷. And from the noisome pestilence.

Instead of Psalm li. *is said* Psalm lxvii., Deus misereatur.

Nones.

Ant. The days of penitence are come to us : for the redemption of sins, and the salvation of souls.

CHAPTER. Is. lviii.

DEAL thy bread to the hungry, and bring the poor that are cast out to thy house : when thou seest the naked, cover thou him ; and hide not thyself from thine own flesh, saith the Lord Almighty.

R̷. Let Thy loving mercy come also unto me, O Lord. V̷. When Thy word goeth forth, it giveth understanding. R̷. Unto me, O Lord.

V̷. Glory be to the Father, and to the Son : and to the Holy Ghost. R̷. Let Thy loving mercy come also unto me, O Lord.

V̷. He shall defend thee under His wings.

R̷. And thou shalt be safe under His feathers.

After Psalm li. *is said* Psalm cii., Domine exaudi.

Vespers.

Ants. and Psalms of the Feria.

CHAPTER. Ezekiel xviii.

THE soul that sinneth, it shall die. The son shall not bear the iniquity of the father, neither shall the father bear the iniquity of the son, saith the Lord Almighty.

R̷. Be Thou for us, O Lord : *The Choir proceeds :* a strong tower. V̷. Against the enemy. R̷. A strong tower. V̷. Glory be to the Father, and to the Son : and to the Holy Ghost. R̷. Be Thou for us, O Lord, a strong tower.

HYMN. *Ex more docti mystico,* V̷. and R̷., p. 129.

Ant. to Mag. Inasmuch as ye have done it unto one of the least of these My brethren : ye have done it unto Me, saith the Lord.

After Psalm li. *is said* Psalm cxxx. De profundis.

[COLLECT.

LOOSE, we beseech Thee, O Lord, the bands of our sins ; and graciously turn from us those things which by reason of our iniquities we have deserved ; through Jesus Christ our Lord. Amen.]

The Day Hours are thus said till the 3rd Sunday in Lent, except the daily change of Collect, and Ant. *to* Benedictus *and* Magnificat.

Tuesday.
Lauds.

Ant. to Ben. And Jesus went into the temple, and began to cast out them that sold and bought in the temple : and overthrew the tables of the money-changers, and the seats of them that sold doves.

[COLLECT.

LOOK, O Lord, upon Thy family, and grant that our souls may so desire Thee as to glow with Thy light, while they are chastened by mortification of the flesh; through Jesus Christ our Lord. Amen.]

Vespers.

Ant. to Mag. Jesus went out of the city to Bethany : and there He taught them the things concerning the kingdom of God.

[COLLECT.

LET our prayers come up before Thee, O Lord; and do Thou drive all iniquity from Thy Church; through Jesus Christ our Lord. Amen.]

Ember Wednesday.
Lauds.

Ant. to Ben. An evil and adulterous generation seeketh after a sign : and there shall no sign be given to it, but the sign of the prophet Jonas.

[COLLECT.

WE beseech Thee, O Lord, hear our prayers; and stretch forth the right hand of Thy Majesty to be our defence against all our enemies; through Jesus Christ our Lord. Amen.]

Vespers.

Ant. to Mag. For as Jonas was three days and three nights in the whale's belly : so shall the Son of man be three days and three nights in the heart of the earth.

[COLLECT.

ENLIGHTEN our souls, we beseech Thee, O Lord, with the light of Thy glory; that we may see what things are to be done, and may attain to do such as are righteous; through Jesus Christ our Lord. Amen.]

Thursday.
Lauds.

Ant. to Ben. If ye continue in My word, then are ye My disciples indeed : and ye shall know the truth, and the truth shall make you free.

[COLLECT.

ALMIGHTY, Everlasting God, Who hast appointed fasting and alms-giving as the seal of our repentance; grant us ever to be devoted to Thee in body and soul; through Jesus Christ our Lord. Amen.]

Vespers.

Ant. to Mag. I proceeded forth and came from God : neither came I of Myself, but He sent Me.

[COLLECT.

GRANT, we beseech Thee, O Lord, to Thy Christian people, that they may act according to that which they they profess, and love the heavenly gift which they are wont to receive; through Jesus Christ our Lord. Amen.]

Ember Friday.
Lauds.

Ant. to Ben. An angel went down at a certain season into the pool : and troubled the water, and healed one.

[COLLECT.

BE favourable to Thy people, O Lord; and graciously comfort with Thy tender succour those whom Thou fillest with devotion to Thee; through Jesus Christ our Lord. Amen.]

Vespers.

Ant. to Mag. He that made me whole, the Same said unto me : Take up thy bed, and walk in peace.

[COLLECT.

HEAR us, O merciful God, and shed the light of Thy grace on our hearts; through Jesus Christ our Lord. Amen.]

Ember Saturday.

Lauds.

Ant. to Ben. Jesus took His disciples, and went up into a mountain : and was transfigured before them.

[COLLECT.

WE beseech Thee, O Lord, to look favourably on Thy people, and mercifully turn from them the scourges of Thy wrath; through Jesus Christ Thy Son our Lord. Amen.]

SECOND SUNDAY IN LENT.

First Vespers.

CHAPTER. 1 Thess. iv.

WE beseech you, brethren, and exhort you by the Lord Jesus, that as ye have received of us how ye ought to walk, and to please God, so ye would abound more and more.

Ry. God give thee of the dew of heaven, and the fatness of the earth. Let people serve thee : be lord over thy brethren. ℣. And let thy mother's sons bow down to thee. Ry. Be lord over thy brethren. ℣. Glory be to the Father, and to the Son : and to the Holy Ghost. Ry. God give thee of the dew of heaven, and the fatness of the earth. Let people serve thee : be lord over thy brethren.

HYMN. *Ex more docti mystico,* ℣. and Ry., p. 129.

Ant. to Mag. Lord, it is good for us to be here : if Thou wilt, let us make here three tabernacles; one for Thee, and one for Moses, and one for Elias.

COLLECT.

ALMIGHTY God, Who seest that we have no power of ourselves to help ourselves; keep us both outwardly in our bodies, and inwardly in our souls; that we may be defended from all adversities which may happen to the body, and from all evil thoughts which may assault and hurt the soul; through Jesus Christ our Lord. Amen.

Lauds.

℣. He shall deliver thee from the snare of the hunter.

Ry. And from the noisome pestilence.

Ant. 1. Thou shalt open my lips, O Lord : and my mouth shall shew Thy praise.

Ant. 2. The right hand of the Lord hath the pre-eminence : the right hand of the Lord bringeth mighty things to pass.

Ant. 3. My God, Thou hast been : my helper.

Ant. 4. Let us sing the song of the three children : which they sang in the fiery furnace, blessing the Lord.

Ant. 5. He hath made them fast for ever and ever : He hath given them a law which shall not be broken.

CHAPTER. 1 Thess. iv.

WE beseech you, brethren, and exhort you by the Lord Jesus, that as ye have received of us how ye ought to walk, and to please God, so ye would abound more and more.

Ry. Thanks be to God.

HYMN. *Audi benigne Conditor,* ℣. and Ry., p. 130.

Ant. to Ben. Jesus went thence,

and departed into the coasts of Tyre and Sidon : And behold, a woman of Canaan came out of the same coasts, and cried unto Him, saying, Have mercy on me, O Lord, Thou Son of David.

Collect as at First Vespers.

Prime.

Ant. And His disciples came and besought Him, saying : Send her away; for she crieth after us.

Tierce.

Ant. I am not sent but unto the lost sheep of the house of Israel : saith the Lord.

CHAPTER. 1 Thess. iv.

WE beseech you, brethren, and exhort you by the Lord Jesus, that as ye have received of us how ye ought to walk, and to please God, so ye would abound more and more.

R̲ỵ. Make me. p. 132.

Sexts.

Ant. O woman, great is thy faith : be it unto thee even as thou wilt.

CHAPTER. 1 Thess. iv.

FOR this is the will of God, even your sanctification, that ye should abstain from fornication ; that every one of you should know how to possess his vessel in sanctification and honour.

R̲ỵ. Refrain my feet. p. 133.

Nones.

Ant. Said I not unto thee, that if thou wouldest believe : thou shouldest see greater things than these?

CHAPTER. 1 Thess. iv.

THIS is the will of God : that no man go beyond and defraud his brother in any matter ; because that the Lord is the avenger of all such,

as we have also forewarned you, and testified.

R̲ỵ. Let Thy loving mercy. p. 133.

Second Vespers.

CHAPTER. 1 Thess. iv.

WE beseech you, brethren, and exhort you by the Lord Jesus, that as ye have received of us how ye ought to walk, and to please God, so ye would abound more and more.

R̲ỵ. Be Thou for us. p. 133.

HYMN. *Ex more docti mystico,* Ỵ. and R̲ỵ., p. 129.

Ant. to Mag. Jesus said unto the woman of Canaan, It is not meet to take the children's bread, and to cast it to dogs. And she said, Truth, Lord : yet the dogs eat of the crumbs which fall from their master's table. Then Jesus answered and said unto her, O woman, great is thy faith : be it unto thee even as thou wilt.

Collect as at First Vespers.

———

Monday.

Lauds.

Ant. to Ben. I am the Same : that I said unto you from the beginning.

[COLLECT.

GRANT, we beseech Thee, Almighty God, that Thy family, which afflicteth itself by abstinence from food, may, following after righteousness, fast from sin ; through Jesus Christ our Lord. Amen.]

Vespers.

Ant. to Mag. He that sent Me is with Me : the Father hath not left Me alone ; for I do always those things that please Him.

[COLLECT.

BE present to our supplications, O Almighty God, and pour Thy wonted mercy on those whom Thou grantest to trust Thy loving-kindness; through Jesus Christ our Lord. Amen.]

Tuesday.
𝕷𝖆𝖚𝖉𝖘.

Ant. to Ben. One is your Master: Which is in heaven, saith the Lord.

[COLLECT.

GRACIOUSLY perfect in us, we beseech Thee, O Lord, the observance of this holy season; that those things by Thy guidance we have learned, by Thy operation we may fulfil; through Jesus Christ our Lord. Amen.]

𝖁𝖊𝖘𝖕𝖊𝖗𝖘.

Ant. to Mag. He that is greatest among you shall be your servant: and whosoever shall exalt himself shall be abased, saith the Lord.

[COLLECT.

BE propitious, we beseech Thee, O Lord, to our supplications, and heal the sickness of our souls: that, receiving remission, we may alway rejoice in Thy blessing; through Jesus Christ our Lord. Amen.]

Wednesday.
𝕷𝖆𝖚𝖉𝖘.

Ant. to Ben. Behold we go up to Jerusalem : and the Son of Man shall be betrayed to be crucified.

[COLLECT.

WE beseech Thee, O Lord, favourably behold Thy people; and as Thou biddest us cease from carnal food, so grant us likewise to cease from sin; through Jesus Christ our Lord. Amen.]

𝖁𝖊𝖘𝖕𝖊𝖗𝖘.

Ant. to Mag. To sit on My right hand, and on My left, is not Mine to give : but it shall be given to them for whom it is prepared of My Father.

[COLLECT.

O GOD, Restorer and Lover of innocence, direct the hearts of Thy servants unto Thee; that kindled with the fervour of Thy spirit, we may be found strong in faith, and sound in works; through Jesus Christ our Lord. Amen.]

Thursday.
𝕷𝖆𝖚𝖉𝖘.

Ant. to Ben. I receive not testimony of men : but these things I say, that ye might be saved.

[COLLECT.

GRANT us, we beseech Thee, O Lord, the help of Thy grace; that being duly intent on fasting and prayer, we may be delivered from our ghostly and bodily enemies; through Jesus Christ our Lord. Amen.]

𝖁𝖊𝖘𝖕𝖊𝖗𝖘.

Ant. to Mag. The same works that I do, bear witness of Me : that the Father hath sent Me.

[COLLECT.

BE present, O Lord, to Thy servants: grant perpetual mercy to them that call on Thee, that to them that acknowledge Thee their Author and Governour Thy blessings may be restored and preserved; through Jesus Christ our Lord. Amen.]

Friday.
𝕷𝖆𝖚𝖉𝖘.

Ant. to Ben. He will miserably destroy those wicked men : and will let out His vineyard to other husbandmen, which shall render Him the fruits in their seasons.

[COLLECT.

GRANT, we beseech Thee, Almighty God, that, cleansed by the sacred fast, we may attain with pure hearts to the holy feast which lies before us; through Jesus Christ our Lord. Amen.]

Vespers.

Ant. to Mag. When they sought to lay hands on Him : they feared the multitude, because they took Him for a Prophet.

[COLLECT.

GRANT, we beseech Thee, O Lord, to Thy people health both of body and mind : that, holding fast by good works, they may be defended through the protection of Thy might; for the sake of Jesus Christ our Lord. Amen.]

———

Saturday.

Lauds.

Ant. to Ben. I will arise, and go to my father, and will say unto him : make me as one of Thy hired servants.

[COLLECT.

GRANT, we beseech Thee, O Lord, Thy blessing to our fasts, that the chastening of our flesh may work the quickening of our spirits ; through Jesus Christ our Lord. Amen.]

———

THIRD SUNDAY IN LENT.

First Vespers.

CHAPTER. Eph. v.

BE ye therefore followers of God, as dear children ; and walk in love, as Christ also hath loved us, and hath given Himself for us, an offering and a sacrifice to God for a sweet-smelling savour.

Ry. And Joseph was brought down to Egypt, and the Lord was with him, and he was a prosperous man. Ꙩ. The Lord shewed him mercy, and that which he did, the Lord made it to prosper. Ry. And he was a prosperous man. Ꙩ. Glory be to the Father, and to the Son : and to the Holy Ghost. Ry. And Joseph was brought down to Egypt, and the Lord was with him, and he was a prosperous man.

HYMN. *Ecce tempus idoneum.*

LO ! now is our accepted day,
The med'cine, purging sin away ;
Where'er our lives have wrought offence,
By thought and word, by deed and sense.

For God, the merciful and true,
Hath spared His people hitherto ;
Nor us and ours, with searching eyes,
Destroyed for our iniquities.

Him therefore now, with earnest care,
And contrite fast, and tear and prayer,
And works of mercy and of love,
We pray for pardon from above :

That from pollution making whole,
With virtues He may deck each soul,
And join us, in the heavenly place,
To angel cohorts by His grace.

O Father, that we ask be done,
Through Jesus Christ, Thine only Son ;
Who, with the Holy Ghost and Thee,
Shall live and reign eternally. Amen.

Ꙩ. He shall give His angels charge over thee.

Ry. To keep thee in all thy ways.

This Hymn, Ꙩ., and Ry. are said at Vespers daily till Passion Sunday.

Ant. to Mag. The father gave to his penitent son the first robe, and a ring ; and putting shoes on his feet, he held a great feast : we too have in baptism our first robe, and the ring is the sign of faith.

COLLECT.

WE beseech Thee, Almighty God, look upon the hearty desires of Thy humble servants, and stretch forth the right hand of Thy Majesty to be our defence against all our enemies; through Jesus Christ our Lord. Amen.

Compline.

All as p. 129, till

Ant. to Nunc Dim. In the midst of life we are in death ; of whom may we seek for succour but of Thee, O Lord, Who for our sins art justly displeased : Yet, O Lord God most holy, O Lord most mighty, O holy and most merciful Saviour, deliver us not into the bitter pains of eternal death.

Compline is thus said till Passion Sunday.

On Saturdays and Sundays, and at both Complines of Double Feasts, after Nunc Dimittis *and its Antiphon, is added,*

℣. Cast us not away in the time of age: forsake us not when our strength faileth us, O Lord.

℟. Yet, O Lord God most holy, O Lord most mighty, O holy and most merciful Saviour, deliver us not into the bitter pains of eternal death.

℣. Shut not Thy merciful ears to our prayer.

℟. O Lord most mighty, O holy and most merciful Saviour, deliver us not into the bitter pains of eternal death.

℣. Thou that knowest, Lord, the secrets of our hearts; spare our sins.

℟. O holy and most merciful Saviour, deliver us not into the bitter pains of eternal death.

Lauds.

℣. He shall deliver thee from the snare of the hunter.

℟. And from the noisome pestilence.

Ant. 1. O be favourable and gracious unto Sion: build Thou the walls of Jerusalem.

Ant. 2. The Lord is on my side: I will not fear what man doeth unto me.

Ant. 3. God be merciful unto us: and bless us.

Ant. 4. The fire forgat his own virtue: that Thy servants might be delivered unhurt.

Ant. 5. Praise Him, sun and moon: for His Name only is excellent.

CHAPTER. Eph. v.

BE ye therefore followers of God, as dear children: and walk in love,

us Christ also hath loved us, and hath given Himself for us, an offering and a sacrifice to God for a sweet-smelling savour.

℟. Thanks be to God.

HYMN. *Jesu quadragenariæ.*

JESU, the Law and Pattern, whence
Our forty days of abstinence,
Who souls to save, that else had died,
This sacred fast hast ratified;

That so to Paradise once more
Might abstinence preserv'd restore
Them that had lost its fields of light
Through crafty wiles of appetite:

Be present now, be present here,
And mark Thy Church's falling tear,
And own the grief that fills her eyes
In mourning her iniquities.

Oh by Thy grace be pardon won
For sins that former years have done;
And let Thy mercy guard us still
From crimes that threaten future ill.

That by the fast we offer here,
Our annual sacrifice sincere,
To Paschal gladness at the end,
Set free from guilt, our souls may tend.

O Father, that we ask be done,
Through Jesus Christ, Thine only Son;
Who, with the Holy Ghost and Thee,
Shall live and reign eternally. Amen.

℣. His faithfulness and truth shall be thy shield and buckler.

℟. Thou shalt not be afraid for any terror by night.

This Hymn, ℣., and ℟. are said at Lauds till Passion Sunday.

Ant. to Ben. Jesus was casting out a devil, and it was dumb: and it came to pass, when the devil was gone out, the dumb spake; and the people wondered.

Collect as at First Vespers.

Prime.

Ant. If I, by the finger of God, cast out devils: no doubt the kingdom of God is come upon you.

Tierce.

Ant. When a strong man armed keepeth his palace: his goods are in peace.

CHAPTER. Eph. v.

BE ye therefore followers of God, as dear children: and walk in love, as Christ also hath loved us, and hath given Himself for us, an offering and a sacrifice to God for a sweet-smelling savour.

℞. It is good for me: *The Choir proceeds:* that I have been in trouble: the law of Thy mouth is dearer unto me than thousands of gold and silver. ℣. Thy hands have made me, and fashioned me : O give me understanding, that I may learn Thy commandments. ℞. The law of Thy mouth is dearer unto me than thousands of gold and silver. ℣. Glory be to the Father, and to the Son, and to the Holy Ghost. ℞. It is good for me that I have been in trouble: the law of Thy mouth is dearer unto me than thousands of gold and silver.

℣. I will say unto the Lord, Thou art my hope and my strong hold.

℞. My God, in Him will I trust.

Sexts.

Ant. He that is not with Me is against Me : and he that gathereth not with Me scattereth.

CHAPTER. Eph. v.

BUT fornication, and all uncleanness, or covetousness, let it not be once named amongst you, as becometh saints.

℞. I am Thy servant : O grant me understanding. ℣. That I may know Thy testimonies. ℞. O grant me understanding. ℣. Glory be to the Father, and to the Son : and to the Holy Ghost. ℞. I am Thy servant, O grant me understanding.

℣. He shall deliver thee from the snare of the hunter.

℞. And from the noisome pestilence.

Nones.

Ant. When the unclean spirit is gone out of a man : he walketh through dry places, seeking rest and finding none.

CHAPTER. Eph. v.

FOR this ye know, that no whoremonger, nor unclean person, nor covetous man, who is an idolater, hath any inheritance in the kingdom of Christ, and of God.

℞. Seven times a day do I praise Thee : O Lord, confound me not. ℣. I have gone astray like a sheep that is lost : O seek Thy servant, for I do not forget Thy commandments. ℞. O Lord, confound me not. ℣. Glory be to the Father, and to the Son : and to the Holy Ghost. ℞. Seven times a day do I praise Thee : O Lord, confound me not.

℣. He shall defend thee under His wings.

℞. And thou shalt be safe under His feathers.

Second Vespers.

CHAPTER. Eph. v.

BE ye therefore followers of God, as dear children ; and walk in love, as Christ also hath loved us, and hath given Himself for us, an offering and a sacrifice to God for a sweet-smelling savour.

℞. Bring my soul out of prison : that I may give thanks unto Thy Name, O Lord. ℣. I had no place to flee unto, and no man cared for my soul. ℞. That I may give thanks unto Thy Name, O Lord. ℣. Glory be to the Father, and to the Son : and to the Holy Ghost. ℞. Bring my soul out of prison : that I may give thanks unto Thy Name, O Lord.

HYMN. *Ecce tempus idoneum,*
℣. and ℞. p. 138.

Ant. to Mag. A certain woman of the company lifted up her voice, and said unto Him, Blessed is the womb that bare Thee, and the paps which Thou hast sucked : but He said, Yea, rather, blessed are they that hear the word of God, and keep it.

———

Monday.

𝕷𝖆𝖚𝖉𝖘.

℣. He shall deliver thee from the snare of the hunter.

℞. And from the noisome pestilence.

CHAPTER. Joel ii.

TURN ye even unto Me, saith the Lord, with all your heart, and with fasting, and with weeping, and with mourning. And rend your hearts, and not your garments, and turn unto the Lord our God.

℞. Thanks be to God.

HYMN. *Jesu quadragenariæ,* ℣. and ℞., p. 139.

Ant. to Ben. Verily I say unto you : No prophet is accepted in his own country.

[COLLECT.

WE beseech Thee, O Lord, mercifully to pour Thy grace into our hearts : that as we abstain from bodily food, so likewise we may restrain our senses from evil excesses ; through Jesus Christ our Lord. Amen.]

𝕻𝖗𝖎𝖒𝖊.

Ant. As I live, saith the Lord God, I have no pleasure in the death of the wicked : but that the wicked turn from his way and live.

𝕿𝖎𝖊𝖗𝖈𝖊.

Ant. Let us chasten ourselves : in much patience, by the armour of the righteousness of God.

CHAPTER. Is. i.

WASH you, make you clean : put away the evil of your doings from before Mine eyes : cease to do evil ; learn to do well.

℞. It is good for me : that I have been in trouble : the law of Thy mouth is dearer unto me than thousands of gold and silver. ℣. Thy hands have made me and fashioned me : O give me understanding, that I may learn Thy commandments. ℞. The law of Thy mouth is dearer unto me than thousands of gold and silver. ℣. Glory be to the Father, and to the Son, and to the Holy Ghost. ℞. It is good for me that I have been in trouble : the law of Thy mouth is dearer unto me than thousands of gold and silver.

℣. I will say unto the Lord, Thou art my hope and my strong hold.

℞. My God, in Him will I trust.

𝕾𝖊𝖝𝖙𝖘.

Ant. Let us chasten ourselves : in much patience and fastings, by the armour of righteousness.

CHAPTER. Is. i.

SEEK judgment, relieve the oppressed, judge the fatherless, plead for the widow. Come now, and let us reason together, saith the Lord.

℞. I am Thy servant : O grant me understanding. ℣. That I may know Thy testimonies. ℞. O grant me understanding. ℣. Glory be to the Father and to the Son : and to the Holy Ghost. ℞. I am Thy servant, O grant me understanding.

℣. He shall deliver thee from the snare of the hunter.

℞. And from the noisome pestilence.

𝕹𝖔𝖓𝖊𝖘.

Ant. The days of penitence are

come to us : for the redemption of sins, and the salvation of souls.

CHAPTER. Is. i.

THOUGH your sins be as scarlet, they shall be as white as snow; though they be red like crimson, they shall be as wool.

R̷. Seven times a day do I praise Thee : O Lord, confound me not. V̷. I have gone astray like a sheep that is lost : O seek Thy servant, for I do not forget Thy commandments. R̷. O Lord, confound me not. V̷. Glory be to the Father, aud to the Son : and to the Holy Ghost. R̷. Seven times a day do I praise Thee : O Lord, confound me not.

V̷. He shall defend thee under His wings.

R̷. And thou shalt be safe under His feathers.

Vespers.

CHAPTER. Ezek. xviii.

THE soul that sinneth, it shall die. The son shall not bear the iniquity of the father, neither shall the father bear the iniquity of the son.

R̷. Bring my soul * out of prison : that I may give thanks unto Thy Name, O Lord. V̷. I had no place to flee unto, and no man cared for my soul. R̷. That I may give thanks unto Thy Name, O Lord. V̷. Glory be to the Father, and to the Son : and to the Holy Ghost. R̷. Bring my soul out of prison : that I may give thanks unto Thy Name, O Lord.

HYMN. *Ecce tempus idoneum,* V̷. and R̷. p. 138.

Ant. to Mag. But Jesus passing through the midst of them : went His way.

[COLLECT.

LET Thy mercy lighten upon us, we beseech Thee, O Lord; that whereas we are in danger by reason of our sins,

we may be rescued by Thy protection, and saved by Thy deliverance; through Jesus Christ our Lord. Amen.]

The Ferial Hours are thus said till Passion Sunday, except the daily changes of Collects and Antiphons to Benedictus and Magnificat; and the Responsary at Vespers, which changes after the fourth Sunday.

Tuesday.

Lauds.

Ant. to Ben. If two of you shall agree on earth as touching anything that they shall ask : it shall be done for them of My Father, Which is in heaven, saith the Lord.

[COLLECT.

HEAR us, Almighty and gracious God, and mercifully bestow upon us the gift of healthful temperance; through Jesus Christ our Lord. Amen.]

Vespers.

Ant. to Mag. Where two or three are gathered together in My Name : there am I in the midst of them, saith the Lord.

[COLLECT.

DEFEND us, O Lord, by Thy protection, and ever keep us from all sin; through Jesus Christ our Lord. Amen.]

Wednesday.

Lauds.

Ant. to Ben. Hear and understand the traditions : which the Lord gave unto you.

[COLLECT.

GRANT us, we beseech Thee, O Lord, that being taught by healthful fasts, and abstaining from noxious vices, we may the more readily obtain Thy favour; through Jesus Christ our Lord. Amen.]

Vespers.

Ant. to Mag. To eat with un-washen hands : defileth not a man.

[COLLECT.

GRANT, we beseech Thee, Almighty God, that we who seek the grace of Thy protection, being delivered from all evils, may serve Thee with a quiet mind ; through Jesus Christ our Lord. Amen.]

Thursday.
Lauds.

Ant. to Ben. Labour not for the meat which perisheth : but for that meat which endureth unto everlasting life.

[COLLECT.

GRANT, we beseech Thee, Almighty God, that the holy devotion of our fasts may purify us and make us accept-able before Thy Majesty ; through Jesus Christ our Lord. Amen.]

Vespers.

Ant to Mag. The Bread of God is He which cometh down from heaven : and giveth life unto the world.

[COLLECT.

LET Thy heavenly favour, we beseech Thee, O Lord, magnify Thy people that is under Thee, and make them ever to cleave to Thy commandments; through Jesus Christ our Lord. Amen.]

Friday.
Lauds.

Ant. to Ben. Sir, I perceive that Thou art a Prophet : Our fathers worshipped in this mountain.

[COLLECT.

LET Thy gracious favour, we beseech Thee, O Lord, accompany our fast, that, as in our bodies we abstain from food, so in our souls we may fast from

vices ; through Jesus Christ our Lord. Amen.]

Vespers.

Ant. to Mag. True worshippers shall worship the Father : in spirit and in truth.

[COLLECT.

GRANT, we beseech Thee, Almighty God, that we who trust in Thy pro-tection, may by Thy help overcome all things adverse; through Jesus Christ our Lord. Amen.]

Saturday.
Lauds.

Ant. to Ben. Jesus stooped down and wrote on the ground : He that is without sin among you, let him first cast a stone at her.

[COLLECT.

GRANT, we beseech Thee, Almighty God, that we, who afflict ourselves by abstinence from food, may, follow-ing after righteousness, fast from sin ; through Jesus Christ our Lord. Amen.]

FOURTH SUNDAY IN LENT.

First Vespers.

CHAPTER. Gal. iv.

IT is written, that Abraham had two sons, the one by a bond-maid, the other by a free-woman. But he who was of the bond-woman was born after the flesh ; but he of the free-woman was by promise.

Ry. Hear, O Israel, the command-ments of the Lord, and write them in thy heart as in a book : and I will give thee the land that floweth with milk and honey. Ꝟ. Beware, therefore, and hearken unto My voice, and I will be an enemy unto thine enemies. Ry. And I will give thee the land that floweth with milk and honey. Ꝟ. Glory be to the Father, and to the

Son : and to the Holy Ghost. Ry. And I will give thee the land that floweth with milk and honey.

HYMN. *Ecce tempus idoneum,* ℣. and Ry., p. 138.

Ant. to Mag. Woman, hath no man condemned thee? No man, Lord : Neither do I condemn thee; go, and sin no more.

COLLECT.

GRANT, we beseech Thee, Almighty God, that we, who for our evil deeds do worthily deserve to be punished, by the comfort of Thy grace may mercifully be relieved; through our Lord and Saviour Jesus Christ. Amen.

Lauds.

℣. He shall deliver thee from the snare of the hunter.

Ry. And from the noisome pestilence.

Ant. 1. Then shalt Thou be pleased with the sacrifice of righteousness : if Thou wilt turn Thy face from my sins.

Ant. 2. It is better to trust in the Lord : than to put any confidence in princes.

Ant. 3. God, even our own God, shall give us His blessing : God shall bless us.

Ant. 4. Thou art mighty, O Lord, to save us from the hand of death : deliver us, O God of Israel.

Ant. 5. Kings of the earth and all people : praise the Name of the Lord.

CHAPTER. Gal. iv.

IT is written, that Abraham had two sons, the one by a bond-maid, the other by a free-woman. But he who was of the bond-woman was born after the flesh; but he of the free-woman was by promise.

Ry. Thanks be to God.

HYMN. *Jesu quadragenariæ,* ℣. and Ry., p. 139.

Ant. to Ben. Jesus went over the sea of Galilee. And a great multitude followed Him : because they saw His miracles which He did. And the passover, a feast of the Jews, was nigh.

Prime.

Ant. And Jesus went up into a mountain, and there He sat with His disciples : And the passover, a feast of the Jews, was nigh.

Tierce.

Ant. And Jesus took the loaves, and when He had given thanks, He distributed to the disciples : and the disciples to them that were set down; and likewise of the fishes as much as they would.

CHAPTER. Gal. iv.

IT is written, that Abraham had two sons, the one by a bond-maid, the other by a free-woman. But he who was of the bond-woman was born after the flesh; but he of the free-woman was by promise.

Ry. It is good for me. p. 140.

Sexts.

Ant. With five loaves and two fishes : the Lord fed men in number about five thousand.

CHAPTER. Gal. iv.

REJOICE, thou barren that bearest not; break forth and cry, thou that travailest not : for the desolate hath many more children than she which hath an husband.

Ry. I am Thy servant. p. 140.

Nones.

Ant. The Lord filled five thousand men : with five loaves and two fishes.

CHAPTER. Gal. iv.

NOW we, brethren, as Isaac was, are the children of promise. But as then he that was born after the flesh persecuted him that was born after the Spirit; even so it is now. Nevertheless, what saith the Scripture?   Cast out the bond-woman and her son.

R7. Seven times a day.   p. 142.

Second Vespers.

CHAPTER.   Gal. iv.

IT is written, that Abraham had two sons, the one by a bond-maid, the other by a free-woman.   But he who was of the bond-woman was born after the flesh; but he of the free-woman was by promise.

R7. The Lord made them eat the increase of the fields : they sucked honey out of the rock, and oil out of the flinty rock.   V̂. He fed them also with the finest wheat-flour : and with honey out of the stony rock did He satisfy them.   R7. They sucked honey out of the rock, and oil out of the flinty rock.   V̂. Glory be to the Father, and to the Son : and to the Holy Ghost.   R7. They sucked honey out of the rock, and oil out of the flinty rock.

HYMN.   *Ecce tempus idoneum,* V̂. and R7., p. 138.

Ant. to Mag.   Then those men, when they had seen the miracle that Jesus did, said : This is of a truth that Prophet that should come into the world.

Monday.
Lauds.

Ant. to Ben.   Take these things hence, saith the Lord : make not My Father's House an house of merchandise.

[COLLECT.

GRANT, we beseech Thee, Almighty God, that we, yearly observing this holy season with devotion, may please

Thee both in body and mind; through Jesus Christ our Lord.   Amen.]

Vespers.

CHAPTER.   Ezek. xviii.

THE soul that sinneth, it shall die. The son shall not bear the iniquity of the father, neither shall the father bear the iniquity of the son.

R7. The Lord made them.   p. 145.
This R7. is used on Ferias till Passion Sunday.

Ant. to Mag.   Destroy this temple, saith the Lord; and in three days I will raise it up : but He spake of the temple of His body.

[COLLECT.

WE beseech Thee, O Lord, mercifully hear our supplications, and grant that we, to whom Thou hast given an hearty desire to pray, may obtain the help of Thy defence; through Jesus Christ our Lord.   Amen.]

———

Tuesday.
Lauds.

Ant. to Ben.   Ye seek to kill Me : a Man that hath told you the truth.

[COLLECT.

GRANT, we beseech Thee, O Lord, that the observance of this holy fast may avail to the increase of holiness, and the continual bestowal of Thy loving-kindness; through Jesus Christ our Lord.   Amen.]

Vespers.

Ant. to Mag.   I have done one work, and ye all marvel : because I have made a man every whit whole on the Sabbath-day.

[COLLECT.

WE beseech Thee, O Lord, have mercy on Thy people, and graciously grant us breathing-space among the tribulations under which we labour; through Jesus Christ our Lord.   Amen.]

Wednesday.

𝕷𝖆𝖚𝖉𝖘.

Ant. to Ben. Master, who did sin: this man, or his parents, that he was born blind? : Jesus answered, Neither hath this man sinned, nor his parents; but that the works of God should be made manifest in him.

[COLLECT.

GOD, Who through fasting dost grant rewards to righteous men, and pardon to sinners, have mercy on Thy suppliants, and let the confession of our guilt obtain remission of our sins; through Jesus Christ our Lord. Amen.]

𝖁𝖊𝖘𝖕𝖊𝖗𝖘.

Ant. to Mag. A Man that is called Jesus put clay upon mine eyes : and I washed, and do see.

[COLLECT.

LET Thy merciful ears, O Lord, be open to the prayers of Thy humble servants, and that they may obtain their petitions, make them to ask such things as shall please Thee; through Jesus Christ our Lord. Amen.]

———

Thursday.

𝕷𝖆𝖚𝖉𝖘.

Ant. to Ben. The Father loveth the Son : and sheweth Him all things that Himself doeth.

[COLLECT.

GRANT, we beseech Thee, Almighty God, that being chastened by fasting we may be gladdened by devotion, and that our earthly affections being tempered, we may more readily attain to heavenly things; though Jesus Christ our Lord. Amen.]

𝖁𝖊𝖘𝖕𝖊𝖗𝖘.

Ant. to Mag. As the Father raiseth up the dead and quickeneth them : even so the Son quickeneth whom He will.

[COLLECT.

O GOD, the Teacher and Governour of Thy people, drive out those sins which assault them; that they may ever be pleasing in Thy sight, and safe under Thy protection; through Jesus Christ our Lord. Amen.]

———

Friday.

𝕷𝖆𝖚𝖉𝖘.

Ant. to Ben. Our friend Lazarus sleepeth : but I go, that I may awake him out of sleep.

[COLLECT.

O GOD, Who renewest the world by ineffable Sacraments, grant, we beseech Thee, that Thine eternal counsels may avail to the welfare of Thy Church, and that it be not left destitute of Thy temporal help; through Jesus Christ our Lord. Amen.]

𝖁𝖊𝖘𝖕𝖊𝖗𝖘.

Ant. to Mag. Lord, if Thou hadst been here, Lazarus had not died : By this time he stinketh, for he hath been dead four days.

[COLLECT.

GRANT, we beseech Thee, Almighty God, that we, who, owning our weakness, trust in Thy strength, may ever rejoice in Thy protection; through Jesus Christ our Lord. Amen.]

———

Saturday.

𝕷𝖆𝖚𝖉𝖘.

Ant. to Ben. I am the Light of the world : he that followeth Me shall not walk in darkness, but shall have the light of life, saith the Lord.

[COLLECT.

WE beseech Thee, O Lord, let our devout affections bring forth fruit by the help of Thy grace; through Jesus Christ our Lord. Amen.]

PASSION SUNDAY.

First Vespers.

From Passion Sunday till the morrow of Low Sunday no Feasts are to be kept, except solemn Doubles, and these only till Maundy Thursday. If any Double Feast fall on this or the following Saturday, Vespers are to be of the Sunday, with solemn Memorial of the Feast.

CHAPTER. Lament. iii.

O LORD, Thou hast pleaded the causes of my soul; Thou hast redeemed my life.

R̸. The ungodly compassed me about, and scourged me without a cause: but Thou, O Lord, my Defender, avenge Thou me. ℣. For trouble is hard at hand, and there is none to help me. R̸. But Thou, O Lord, my Defender, avenge Thou me. Glory be, etc. *is not said, but the* R̸. *is repeated.* The ungodly compassed me about, and scourged me without a cause: but Thou, O Lord, my Defender, avenge Thou me.

[The Reader repeats this R̸. *as far as the colon only: the Choir then takes it up, and finishes it. And this order is observed in all* R̸R̸. *of Passion-tide.]*

At the verse in the following Hymn, O Cross, our one reliance, hail: *the Choir turns to the Altar, and so continues till the beginning of* Magnificat.

HYMN. *Vexilla Regis prodeunt.*

THE Royal Banners forward go;
　The Cross shines forth in mystic glow;
Where He in flesh, our flesh Who made,
Our sentence bore, our ransom paid:

Where deep for us the spear was dy'd,
Life's torrent rushing from His side,
To wash us in that precious flood
Where mingled Water flow'd, and Blood.

Fulfill'd is all that David told
In true prophetic song of old;
Amidst the nations, God, saith he,
Hath reign'd and triumph'd from the Tree.

O Tree of beauty, Tree of light!
O Tree with royal purple dight!
Elect on whose triumphal breast
Those holy limbs should find their rest:

On whose dear arms, so widely flung,
The weight of this world's ransom hung:
The price of human kind to pay,
And spoil the spoiler of his prey:

O Cross, our one reliance, hail!
This holy Passion-tide avail
To give fresh merit to the saint,
And pardon to the penitent.

To Thee, eternal Three in One,
Let homage meet by all be done:
Whom by the Cross Thou dost restore,
Preserve and govern evermore! Amen.

℣. They gave me gall to eat.

R̸. And when I was thirsty they gave me vinegar to drink.

This Hymn, ℣., *and* R̸. *are said at Vespers daily, till Wednesday in Holy Week, inclusive.*

Ant. to Mag. I am One that bear witness of Myself: and the Father that sent Me beareth witness of Me.

COLLECT.

WE beseech Thee, Almighty God, mercifully to look upon Thy people; that by Thy great goodness they may be governed and preserved evermore, both in body and soul; through Jesus Christ our Lord. Amen.

Compline.

Ant. to Psalms. Have mercy upon me: and hearken unto my prayer.

CHAPTER. Jer. xiv.

THOU, O Lord, art in the midst of us, and we are called by Thy Name; leave us not, O our God.

R̸. Into Thy hands I commend my spirit. ℣. For Thou hast redeemed me, O Lord, Thou God of Truth. R̸. Into Thy hands I commend my spirit.

HYMN. *Cultor Dei memento.*

SERVANT of Christ, remember
　The font's Baptismal dew;
Remember thy renewal
　In Confirmation too.

When at the call of slumber
　Thou seekest needful rest,
Let then the Cross's symbol
　Sign both thy heart and breast.

The Cross repels all evil,
　The Cross makes darkness flee,
A mind by this sign hallowed,
　Unstable cannot be.

Away, ye wandering phantoms,
　Away, all evil dreams,
Away, thou arch deceiver,
　With all thy subtle schemes.

And thou, O crafty serpent,
　Who seek'st by many an art,
And many a guileful winding,
　To vex the quiet heart:

Depart, for Christ is present;
　Since Christ is here, give place;
And let the sign thou ownest
　Thy ghostly legions chase.

And though awhile the body
　In sleep may lie reclin'd,
Yet Christ, in very slumber,
　Shall fill the Christian mind.

All laud to God the Father,
　All laud to God the Son;
To God the Holy Spirit
　Be equal honour done.　Amen.

℣. Keep us.

℟. As the apple of an eye, hide us under the shadow of Thy wings.

Ant. to Nunc Dim. O King, glorious among Thy saints, Who art ever to be praised, and yet art ineffable: Thou, Lord, art in the midst of us, and we are called by Thy Name: leave us not, O our God: and in the day of Judgment vouchsafe to number us amongst Thy saints, O blessed King.

℣. O blessed King, govern Thy servants in the right way.

℟. Among Thy saints, O blessed King.

℣. By holy fasts to amend our sinful lives.

℟. O blessed King, govern Thy servants in the right way.

℣. To duly keep Thy Paschal Feast.

℟. Among Thy saints, O blessed King.

Compline is said thus till Maundy Thursday, except that the ℣℣. and ℟℟. after the Ant. are not said on Ferias.
Petitions as p. 68.

Lauds.

℣. Draw nigh unto my soul and save it.

℟. O deliver me because of mine enemies.

Ant. 1. O Lord, behold my affliction : for the enemy hath magnified himself.

Ant. 2. I called upon the Lord in trouble : and the Lord heard me at large.

Ant. 3. O Lord, Thou hast pleaded the causes of my soul : Thou hast redeemed my life, O Lord my God.

Ant. 4. O My people, what have I done unto Thee? and wherein have I wearied Thee? : testify against Me.

Ant. 5. Shall evil be recompensed for good? : for they have digged a pit for my soul.

CHAPTER. Heb. ix.

CHRIST being come an High-Priest of good things to come, by a greater and more perfect tabernacle, not made with hands, that is to say, not of this building; neither by the blood of goats and calves, but by His own blood He entered in once into the holy place, having obtained eternal redemption for us.

℟. Thanks be to God.

HYMN. *Lustra sex qui jam peracta.*

THIRTY years among us dwelling,
　His appointed time fulfill'd,
Born for this, He meets His Passion,
　For that this He freely will'd:
On the Cross the Lamb is lifted,
　Where His life-blood shall be spill'd.

He endur'd the nails, the spitting,
　Vinegar, and spear, and reed;
From that holy Body broken
　Blood and Water forth proceed:
Earth, and stars, and sky, and ocean,
　By that flood from stain are freed.

Faithful Cross! above all other,
　One and only noble Tree;
None in foliage, none in blossom,
　None in fruit thy peers may be;
Sweetest wood and sweetest iron!
　Sweetest weight is hung on thee.

Bend thy boughs, O Tree of glory!
  Thy relaxing sinews bend;
For awhile the ancient rigour,
  That thy birth bestow'd, suspend;
And the King of Heavenly Beauty
  On thy bosom gently tend.

Thou alone wast counted worthy
  This world's ransom to uphold;
For a shipwreck'd race preparing
  Harbour, like the ark of old:
With the sacred Blood anointed
  From the smitten Lamb that roll'd.

To the Trinity be glory
  Everlasting, as is meet;
Equal to the Father, equal
  To the Son and Paraclete;
Trinal Unity, Whose praises
  All created things repeat. Amen.

℣. Deliver me from mine enemies, O God.

℞. Defend me from them that rise up against me.

Ant. to Ben. Which of you convinceth Me of sin? and if I say the truth, why do ye not believe Me?: He that is of God heareth God's words; ye therefore hear them not, because ye are not of God.

Collect as at First Vespers.

Prime.

Ant. I have not a devil: but I honour My Father, saith the Lord.

Till Wednesday in Holy Week, instead of ℞. *to the Chapter, at Prime is said,*

℣. O Lord, arise, help us.

℞. And deliver us for Thy mercy's sake.

Tierce.

Ant. I seek not Mine own glory: there is One that seeketh and judgeth.

Chapter. Heb. ix.

CHRIST being come an High-Priest of good things to come, by a greater and more perfect tabernacle, not made with hands, that is to say, not of this building; neither by the blood of goats and calves, but by His own blood He entered in once into the holy place, having obtained eternal redemption for us.

℞. Deliver my soul from the sword: my darling from the power of the dog. ℣. Deliver me, O Lord, from the evil man: and preserve me from the wicked man. ℞. My darling from the power of the dog. ℞. Deliver my soul from the sword: my darling from the power of the dog.

℣. Save me from the lion's mouth.

℞. Thou hast heard me also from among the horns of the unicorns.

Sexts.

Ant. Verily, verily, I say unto you: If a man keep My saying, he shall never see death.

Chapter. Heb. ix.

FOR if the blood of bulls and of goats, and the ashes of an heifer sprinkling the unclean, sanctifieth to the purifying of the flesh; how much more shall the blood of Christ, Who, through the eternal Spirit, offered Himself without spot to God, purge your conscience from dead works to serve the living God?

℞. Save me from the lion's mouth: Thou hast heard me also from among the horns of the unicorns. ℣. Deliver my soul from the sword, my darling from the power of the dog. ℞. Thou hast heard me also from among the horns of the unicorns. ℞. Save me from the lion's mouth: Thou hast heard me also from among the horns of the unicorns.

℣. O shut not up my soul with the sinners.

℞. Nor my life with the bloodthirsty.

Nones.

Ant. Your father Abraham rejoiced to see My day: and he saw it, and was glad.

Chapter. Heb. ix.

AND for this cause He is the Mediator of the new testament, that by means of death, for the redemption of the transgressions that were under the first testament, they which are called might receive the promise of eternal inheritance.

R̷. Princes have persecuted me without a cause, but my heart standeth in awe of Thy word. I am glad of Thy word. ℣. As one that findeth great spoils. R̷. I am glad of Thy word. R̷. Princes have persecuted me without a cause, but my heart standeth in awe of Thy word. I am glad of Thy word.

℣. Deliver me, O Lord, from the evil man.

R̷. And preserve me from the wicked man.

Second Vespers.

CHAPTER. Heb. ix.

CHRIST being come an High Priest of good things to come, by a greater and more perfect tabernacle, not made with hands, that is to say, not of this building; neither by the blood of goats and calves, but by His own blood He entered in once into the holy place, having obtained eternal redemption for us.

R̷. How long shall mine enemies triumph over me? : consider and hear me, O Lord my God. ℣. For if I be cast down, they that trouble me will rejoice at it. But I have hoped in Thy mercy. R̷. Consider and hear me, O Lord my God. R̷. How long shall mine enemies triumph over me? : consider and hear me, O Lord my God.

HYMN. *Vexilla regis prodeunt*, ℣. and R̷., p. 147.

Ant. to Mag. Verily, verily, I say unto you, Before Abraham was, I am : Then the Jews took up stones to cast at Jesus ; but Jesus hid Himself, and went out of the temple.

Monday.

Lauds.

℣. Draw nigh unto my soul, and save it.

R̷. O deliver me, because of mine enemies.

Ants. and Psalms of the Feria.

CHAPTER. Jer. xi.

THE Lord hath given Me knowledge of it, and I know it : then Thou shewedst me their doings. But I was like a lamb or an ox that is brought to the slaughter.

R̷. Thanks be to God.

HYMN. *Lustra sex qui jam peracta*, ℣. and R̷., p. 148.

Ant. to Ben. In the last day, that great day of the feast, Jesus stood and cried, saying : If any man thirst, let him come unto Me and drink.

[COLLECT.

SANCTIFY, we beseech Thee, O Lord, our fast, and mercifully grant us forgiveness of all our sins ; through Jesus Christ our Lord. Amen.]

Prime.

Ant. to Psalms. The ungodly are minded to do me some mischief : and my heart is disquieted within me.

Tierce.

Ant. O Lord, Thou hast pleaded the causes of my soul : Thou hast redeemed my life.

CHAPTER. Is. l.

I HID not my face from shame and spitting. For the Lord God will help Me : therefore shall I not be confounded.

R̷. Deliver my soul. p. 149.

Sext.

Ant. O My people, what have I done unto thee? : and wherein have I wearied thee? testify against Me.

CHAPTER. Is. l.

FOR the Lord God will help me; therefore shall I not be coufounded: therefore have I set my face like a flint, and I know that I shall not be ashamed.

R̸. Save me. p. 149.

Nones.

Ant. Shall evil be recompensed for good? : for they have digged a pit for My soul.

CHAPTER. Jer. xvii.

LET them be confounded that persecute me, but let not me be confounded; let them be dismayed, but let not me be dismayed: bring upon them the day of evil, and destroy them with double destruction, O Lord our God.

R̸. Princes have persecuted. p. 150.

Vespers.

Ants. and Psalms of the Feria.

CHAPTER. Lament. iii.

O LORD, Thou hast pleaded the causes of my soul: Thou hast redeemed my life.

R̸. How long shall mine enemies triumph over me? consider and hear me, O Lord my God. ℣. For if I be cast down, they that trouble me will rejoice at it. But I have hoped in Thy mercy. R̸. Consider and hear me, O Lord my God. R̸. How long shall mine enemies triumph over me? consider and hear me, O Lord my God.

HYMN. *Verilla Regis prodeunt,* ℣. and R̸., p. 147.

Ant. to Mag. If any man thirst, let him come unto Me, and drink : and out of his belly shall flow rivers of living water.

[COLLECT.

GRANT, we beseech Thee, O Lord, to Thy people the spirit of truth and peace; that they may acknowledge Thee with their whole soul, and devoutly perform those things which are pleasing unto Thee; through Jesus Christ our Lord. Amen.]

The Hours are said thus through the week, except the changes of Collects, and of Ants. to Benedictus and Magnificat.

Tuesday.

Lauds.

Ant. to Ben. My time is not yet come : but your time is alway ready.

[COLLECT.

LET our fasts, we beseech Thee, O Lord, be pleasing in Thy sight, that by expiation of our guilt we may obtain Thy mercy; through Jesus Christ our Lord. Amen.]

Vespers.

Ant. to Mag. Go ye up unto this feast : I go not yet up, for My time is not yet full come.

[COLLECT.

GRANT, we beseech Thee, O Lord, that the company of Thy servants may persevere in the performance of Thy will, so that Thy kingdom may increase upon the earth in our days; through Jesus Christ our Lord. Amen.]

Wednesday.

Lauds.

Ant. to Ben. My sheep hear My voice : and I know them.

[COLLECT.

O GOD of mercy, lighten the hearts of Thy faithful people by this holy fast, and as Thou hast given them an hearty desire to pray, so graciously hearken to their supplications; through Jesus Christ our Lord. Amen.]

Vespers.

Ant. to Mag. Many good works

have I shewed you : for which of these works do ye stone Me?

[COLLECT.

LET the mercy we hope for, come down on Thy suppliant servants, O Lord, we beseech Thee; and of Thy heavenly bounty grant them to ask such things as be right, and also to receive the same; through Jesus Christ our Lord. Amen.]

Thursday.

Lauds.

Ant. to Ben. Why trouble ye the woman? : for she hath wrought a good work upon Me.

[COLLECT.

GRANT, we beseech Thee, Almighty God, that the dignity of human nature, being wounded by excess, may be restored by the practice of healing self-denial; through Jesus Christ our Lord. Amen.]

Vespers.

Ant. to Mag. In that she hath poured this ointment on My body : she did it for My burial.

[COLLECT.

BE favourable, we beseech Thee, O Lord, to Thy people, that eschewing those things which are displeasing unto Thee, they may rather be filled with the delights of Thy commandments; through Jesus Christ our Lord. Amen.]

Friday.

Lauds.

Ant. to Ben. Now the day of the feast drew nigh, and the chief priests and scribes sought how they might kill Jesus : but they feared the people.

[COLLECT.

WE beseech Thee, O Lord, mercifully to pour the help of Thy grace into our hearts; that, subduing our sins by voluntary chastisement, we may rather mortify ourselves in this life, than be condemned to eternal torments; through Jesus Christ our Lord. Amen.]

Vespers.

Ant. to Mag. The chief priests and the scribes sought how they might take Him by craft, and put Him to death : but they said, Not on the feast day, lest there be an uproar of the people.

[COLLECT.

GRANT us, we beseech Thee, O Lord, pardon of sins and increase of piety; and, that Thou mayest multiply Thy gifts upon us, make us more ready to the fulfilment of Thy commands; through Jesus Christ our Lord. Amen.]

Saturday.

Lauds.

Ant. to Ben. With desire have I desired : to eat this Passover with you before I suffer.

[COLLECT.

LET Thy consecrated people, O Lord, increase in the spirit of devotion; that, being exercised in holy acts, we may become more pleasing to Thy majesty, and be filled more abundantly with Thy gifts; through Jesus Christ our Lord. Amen.]

PALM SUNDAY.

First Vespers.

Ants. and Psalms as in the Psalter.

CHAPTER. Phil. ii.

LET this mind be in you, which was also in Christ Jesus: Who, being in the form of God, thought it not robbery to be equal with God: but made Himself of no reputation, and took upon Him the form of a servant.

℟. The ungodly. p. 147.

HYMN. *Vexilla Regis prodeunt*, ℣. and ℟., p. 147.

Ant. to Mag. And now, O Father, glorify Thou Me with Thine own self: with the glory which I had with Thee before the world was.

COLLECT.

ALMIGHTY and everlasting God, Who, of Thy tender love towards mankind, hast sent Thy Son, our Saviour Jesus Christ, to take upon Him our flesh, and to suffer death upon the Cross, that all mankind should follow the example of His great humility; mercifully grant, that we may both follow the example of His patience, and also be made partakers of His resurrection; through the same Jesus Christ our Lord. Amen.

Lauds.

℣. Draw nigh unto my soul, and save it.

℟. O deliver me because of mine enemies.

Ant. 1. The Lord God will help me : therefore shall I not be confounded.

Ant. 2. They kept me in on every side, they kept me in, I say, on every side : but in the Name of the Lord will I destroy them.

Ant. 3. Give sentence with me, O God : for Thou, Lord, art mighty.

Ant. 4. Let them be confounded that persecute me : but let not me be confounded, O Lord God.

Ant. 5. With faithful angels and children may we be found : singing, Hosanna in the highest to the Conqueror of death.

CHAPTER. Phil. ii.

LET this mind be in you, which was also in Christ Jesus : Who, being in the form of God, thought it not robbery to be equal with God; but made Himself of no reputation, and took upon Him the form of a servant.

℟. Thanks be to God.

HYMN. *Lustra sex qui jam peracta*, ℣. and ℟., p. 148.

Ant. to Ben. And the great multitude that came together to the feast day, cried unto the Lord : Blessed is He that cometh in the Name of the Lord : Hosanna in the highest.

Collect as at Vespers.

Prime.

Ant. to Psalms. Hosanna to the Son of David. Blessed is the King of Israel that cometh in the Name of the Lord : Hosanna in the highest.

Tierce.

Ant. The children of the Hebrews cast their garments in the way, and cried, saying : Hosanna to the Son of David; blessed is He that cometh in the Name of the Lord.

CHAPTER. Phil. ii.

LET this mind be in you, which was also in Christ Jesus : Who, being in the form of God, thought it not robbery to be equal with God; but made Himself of no reputation, and took upon Him the form of a servant.

℟. He hath put my brethren far from me, and mine acquaintance are verily estranged from me. ℣. My lovers and my neighbours did stand looking upon my trouble. ℟. Mine acquaintance are verily estranged from me. ℟. He hath put my brethren far from me, and mine acquaintance are verily estranged from me.

℣. Deliver my soul from the sword.

℟. My darling from the power of the dog.

Sexts.

Ant. The children of the Hebrews, taking branches of palm, went out to meet the Lord, crying and saying : Hosanna in the highest.

CHAPTER. Phil. ii.

HE humbled Himself, and became obedient unto death, even the death of the Cross.

Ry. Give heed to me, O Lord, and hearken to the voice of them that contend with me : Shall evil be recompensed for good? for they have digged a pit for my soul. ℣. Remember that I stood before Thee to speak good for them, and to turn away Thy wrath from them. Ry. Shall evil be recompensed for good? for they have digged a pit for my soul. Ry. Give heed to me, O Lord, and hearken to the voice of them that contend with me : Shall evil be recompensed for good? for they have digged a pit for my soul.

℣. Save me from the lion's mouth.

Ry. Thou hast heard me also from among the horns of the unicorns.

Nones.

Ant. All men praise Thy Name together, and say : Blessed is He that cometh in the Name of the Lord; Hosanna in the highest.

CHAPTER. Phil. ii.

WHEREFORE God also hath highly exalted Him, and given Him a Name which is above every name; that at the Name of Jesus every knee should bow, of things in heaven, and things in earth, and things under the earth.

Ry. Save me, O God : for the waters are come in, even unto my soul. And hide not Thy face from Thy servant: for I am in trouble. O haste Thee, and hear me. ℣. Draw nigh unto my soul, and save it : O deliver me because of mine enemies. Ry. For I am in trouble. O haste Thee, and hear me. Ry. Save me, O

God, for the waters are come in, even unto my soul. And hide not Thy face from Thy servant: for I am in trouble. O haste Thee, and hear me.

℣. O shut not up my soul with the sinners.

Ry. Nor my life with the bloodthirsty.

Second Vespers.

Ants. and Psalms as in the Psalter.

CHAPTER. Phil. ii.

LET this mind be in you, which was also in Christ Jesus: Who, being in the form of God, thought it not robbery to be equal with God; but made Himself of no reputation, and took upon Him the form of a servant.

Ry. The chief priests consulted that they might put Lazarus also to death : because that by reason of him many of the Jews went away, and believed on Jesus. ℣. The people therefore that was with Him when He called Lazarus out of his grave, and raised him from the dead, bare record. Ry. Because that by reason of him many of the Jews went away, and believed on Jesus. Ry. The chief priests consulted that they might put Lazarus also to death: because that by reason of him many of the Jews went away, and believed on Jesus.

HYMN. *Vexilla Regis prodeunt,* ℣. *and* Ry., p. 147.

Ant. to Mag. The multitude come with flowers and palms to meet the Redeemer, and give due homage to the triumphant Victor. The lips of the Gentiles proclaim the Son of God, and in the praise of Christ voices chant through the heavens, Hosanna.

Collect as at First Vespers.

MONDAY IN HOLY WEEK.

Lauds.

Psalms of the Feria.

Ant. 1. I hid not My face : from shame and spitting.

Ant. 2. Awake, O sword : against them that disperse the flock.

Ant. 3. So they weighed for My price thirty pieces of silver : that I was prised at of them.

Ant. 4. Water flowed over Mine head : then I said, I am cut off. I called upon Thy Name, O Lord.

Ant. 5. Behold, O Lord, the lips of them that rise up against Me : and their devices.

HYMN. *Lustra sex qui jam peracta,* ℣. and ℟., p. 148.

CHAPTER. Jer. xi.

THE Lord hath given Me knowledge of it and I know it: then Thou shewedst Me their doings. I was like a lamb or an ox that is brought to the slaughter.

℟. Thanks be to God.

Ant. to Ben. Thou couldest have no power at all against Me : except it were given thee from above.

[COLLECT.

GRANT, we beseech Thee, Almighty God, that we who faint in adversity by reason of our infirmity, may be refreshed by intercession of the Passion of Thine Only-begotten Son; Who liveth and reigneth with Thee and the Holy Ghost, ever one God, world without end. Amen.]

Prime.

Ant. The ungodly are minded to do me some mischief : and my heart is disquieted within me.

Tierce.

Ant. O Lord, Thou hast pleaded the causes of my soul : Thou hast redeemed my life.

CHAPTER. Is. l.

I GAVE My back to the smiters, and My cheeks to them that plucked off the hair: I hid not My face from shame and spitting. For the Lord God will help Me; therefore shall I not be confounded.

℟. He hath put my brethren far from me, and : mine acquaintance are verily estranged from me. ℣. My lovers and my neighbours did stand looking upon my trouble. ℟. Mine acquaintance are verily estranged from me. ℟. He hath put my brethren far from me, and : mine acquaintance are verily estranged from me.

℣. Deliver my soul from the sword.

℟. My darling from the power of the dog.

Sexts.

Ant. O My people, what have I done unto thee? : and wherein have I wearied thee? testify against Me.

CHAPTER. Is. l.

FOR the Lord God will help me; therefore shall I not be confounded: therefore have I set my face like a flint, and I know that I shall not be ashamed.

℟. Give heed to me, O Lord, and hearken to the voice of them that contend with me : Shall evil be recompensed for good? for they have digged a pit for my soul. ℣. Remember that I stood before Thee to speak good for them. ℟. Shall evil be recompensed for good? for they have digged a pit for my soul. ℟. Give heed to me, O Lord, and hearken to the voice of them that contend with me : Shall evil be recompensed for good? for they have digged a pit for my soul.

℣. Save me from the lion's mouth.

℟. Thou hast heard me also from among the horns of the unicorns.

Nones.

Ant. Shall evil be recompensed for good : for they have digged a pit for My soul.

CHAPTER. Jer. xvii.

LET them be confounded that persecute Me, but let not Me be confounded; let them be dismayed, but let not Me be dismayed : bring upon them the day of evil, and destroy them with double destruction.

R̷. Save me, O God : for the waters are come in, even unto my soul. And hide not Thy face from Thy servant : For I am in trouble. O haste Thee, and hear me. V̷. Draw nigh unto my soul, and save it : O deliver me, because of mine enemies. R̷. For I am in trouble. O haste Thee, and hear me. R̷. Save me, O God, for the waters are come in, even unto my soul. And hide not Thy face from Thy servant : For I am in trouble. O haste Thee, and hear me.

V̷. O shut not up my soul with the sinners.

R̷. Nor my life with the bloodthirsty.

Vespers.

Ants. and Psalms of the Feria.

CHAPTER. Lam. iii.

O LORD, Thou hast pleaded the causes of my soul: Thou hast redeemed my life.

R̷. The chief priests consulted that they might put Lazarus also to death : because that by reason of him many of the Jews went away, and believed on Jesus. V̷. The people therefore that was with Him when He called Lazarus out of his grave, and raised him from the dead, bare record. R̷. Because that by reason of him many of the Jews went away, and believed on Jesus. R̷. The chief priests consulted that they might put Lazarus also to death : because that by reason of

him many of the Jews went away, and believed on Jesus.

HYMN. *Vexilla Regis prodeunt,* V̷. and R̷., p. 147.

[COLLECT.

HELP us, O God of our salvation, and grant us to come with joy to the celebration of the blessings whereby Thou hast vouchsafed to restore us; through Jesus Christ our Lord. Amen.]

The Hours are thus said till Wednesday inclusive, Collects and Antiphons being changed as usual.

TUESDAY IN HOLY WEEK.

Lauds.

Psalms of the Feria.

Ant. 1. Hide not Thy face from me, for I am in trouble : O haste Thee, and hear me.

Ant. 2. Defend my cause against the ungodly people : O deliver me from the deceitful and wicked man.

Ant. 3. I cried by reason of mine affliction to the Lord : and He heard me out of the belly of hell.

Ant. 4. O Lord, I am oppressed; undertake for me : for I know not what I shall say to mine enemies.

Ant. 5. The wicked said; let us oppress the poor righteous man : because he is clean contrary to our doings.

Ant. to Ben. No man taketh My life from Me : but I lay down My life, that I might take it again.

[COLLECT.

ALMIGHTY, everlasting God, grant us so to celebrate the mysteries of the Lord's Passion, that we may merit to obtain mercy; through the same Jesus Christ our Lord. Amen.]

Vespers.

Ant. to Mag. I sat daily with you teaching in the temple, and ye laid no hold on Me : and now, being scourged, ye lead Me to be crucified.

[COLLECT.

LET Thy mercy, O Lord, cleanse us from all corruption of the old man, and enable us to put on the new man; through Jesus Christ our Lord. Amen.]

WEDNESDAY IN HOLY WEEK.

Lauds.

On and after this day, no feast is noticed; Double feasts are transferred till after the Octave of Easter.

Psalms of the Feria.

Ant. 1. Deliver me from blood-guiltiness, O Lord, Thou that art the God of my health : and my tongue shall sing of Thy righteousness.

Ant. 2. I heard the defaming of many, fear on every side : but the Lord is with me as a mighty terrible one.

Ant. 3. These also that seek the hurt of my soul : they shall go under the earth.

Ant. 4. All mine enemies have heard of my trouble : they are glad that Thou hast done it.

Ant. 5. Bind, O Lord, the kings of the heathen in chains : and their nobles with links of iron.

Ant. to Ben. Simon, sleepest thou? : couldest thou not watch with Me one hour?

[COLLECT.

GRANT, we beseech Thee, Almighty God, that we who are continually afflicted by reason of our trespasses, may be delivered by the Passion of Thine Only-begotten Son; Who liveth and reigneth with Thee and the Holy Ghost, ever one God, world without end. Amen.]

Vespers.

CHAPTER. Is. liii.

ALL we like sheep have gone astray; we have turned every one to his own way; and the Lord hath laid on Him the iniquity of us all. He was oppressed, and He was afflicted, yet He opened not His mouth.

℞. The ungodly. p. 147.

Ant. to Mag. I sat daily with you teaching in the temple, and ye laid no hold on Me : and now, being scourged, ye lead Me to be crucified.

COLLECT.

ALMIGHTY God, we beseech Thee graciously to behold this Thy family, for which our Lord Jesus Christ was contented to be betrayed, and given up into the hands of wicked men, and to suffer death upon the Cross; Who now liveth and reigneth with Thee and the Holy Ghost, ever One God, world without end. Amen.

At these Vespers no Petitions are said, neither is the Altar censed, nor are any Memorials said, by reason of the solemnity of the Lord's Supper.

Compline is said as p. 147, the Petitions being said, as on Sundays, without Psalm li. Psalm cxxi. is not said after Compline from this day till the 1st Sunday after Trinity, inclusive.

MAUNDY THURSDAY.

Lauds.

The Sacerdotal ℣. and ℞. are omitted, and the first Antiphon is begun at once, and so on the two nights following. The Psalms are said without Glory be, etc., from this time till the First Vespers of Easter.

Ant. 1. Thou wilt be justified in Thy saying : and clear when Thou art judged.

Ant. 2. He is brought as a lamb to the slaughter : He openeth not His mouth.

Ant. 3. Mine heart within me is broken : all my bones shake.

Ant. 4. He was made strong in Thy strength : and in Thy holy comfort, O Lord.

Ant. 5. Surely He hath borne our griefs : and carried our sorrows.

(After the repetition of the 5th Ant., all the lights in the Church are put out.)

Ant. to Ben. Now he that betrayed Him gave them a sign, saying : Whomsoever I shall kiss, that same is He : hold Him fast.

After the repetition of the Ant. :

℣. Lord, have mercy. ℟. Lord, have mercy. ℣. Lord, have mercy. ℟. Christ became obedient unto death. ℣. Christ, have mercy. ℟. Who didst come to suffer for us. ℣. Christ, have mercy. ℟. Who, stretching forth Thy hands upon the Cross, didst draw all unto Thee. ℣. Christ, have mercy. ℟. Who by the prophet didst foretel, O Death, I will be thy death. ℣. Lord, have mercy. ℟. Christ the Lord became obedient unto death. ℣. Lord, have mercy. ℟. Lord, have mercy. ℣. Lord, have mercy. ℟. O Lord, have mercy upon us. ℣. Christ the Lord became obedient unto death. ℟. Even the death of the Cross.

Then the Lord's Prayer shall be said in silence, kneeling, after which Psalm li., Miserere, *shall be said in a low voice, without* Glory be, etc., *and followed immediately by the Collect, as at previous Vespers, without* The Lord be with you, or, Let us pray. *Nor is anything further said after the Collect, but all rise (and the senior person present striking on the book three times, a light is brought).*

The Petitions, etc. are not said from henceforth till after Trinity. No Memorials till after Low Sunday.

At Prime, and at the other Hours on this and the two days following, the ℣℣., ℟℟., *and Hymns are omitted at the beginning of Office, and immediately after the Lord's Prayer, is begun the Ant. to Psalms.*

Prime.

Ant. Christ became obedient for us unto death : even the death of the Cross.

Psalm liv., *Deus in nomine tuo.*
Psalm cxix., *Beati immaculati* and *Retribue servo tuo.*

℣. The Lord be with you.
℟. And with thy spirit.

Let us pray.

Collect as at Wednesday Vespers.

℣. The Lord be with you.
℟. And with thy spirit.
℣. Bless we the Lord.
℟. Thanks be to God.

Prime thus ends, and Tierce, Sexts, and Nones are said in like manner with their own Psalms.
Chapter is said on this day.

Vespers.

On this day Vespers shall be sung festively in Choir.

Ant. 1. I will receive the cup of salvation : and call upon the Name of the Lord.

Psalm cxvi. 10. *Credidi*, p. 49.

Ant. 2. I labour for peace, but when I speak unto them thereof : they make them ready to battle.

Psalm cxx. *Ad Dominum*, p. 50.

Ant. 3. Keep me, O Lord : from the hands of the ungodly.

Psalm cxl. *Eripe me Domine*, p. 60.

Ant. 4. Keep me from the snare that they have laid for me : and from the traps of the wicked doers.

Psalm cxli. *Domine clamavi*, p. 61.

Ant. 5. I looked also upon my right hand : and saw that there was no man that would know me.

Psalm cxlii. *Voce mea ad Dominum*, p. 61.

Ant. to Mag. And as they were eating, Jesus took bread : and blessed it, and brake it, and gave it to the disciples.

℣. The Lord be with you.

℟. And with thy spirit.

Collect as on Wednesday: and so these Vespers end.

Compline.

Ant. Christ became obedient for us unto death : even the death of the Cross.

Psalm iv.   *Cum invocarem.*
Psalm xxxi.   *In te Domine.*
Psalm cxxxiv.   *Ecce nunc.*
Nunc Dimittis.

(*All without* Glory be, *etc., and all said under one Ant.*)

℣. The Lord be with you.

℟. And with thy spirit.

Let us pray.

COLLECT.

ALMIGHTY God, we beseech Thee graciously to behold this Thy family, for which our Lord Jesus Christ was contented to be betrayed, and given up into the hands of wicked men, and to suffer death upon the Cross ; Who now liveth and reigneth with Thee and the Holy Ghost, ever one God, world without end.   Amen.

℣. The Lord be with you.

℟. And with thy spirit.

℣. Bless we the Lord.

℟. Thanks be to God.

GOOD FRIDAY.

Lauds.

Psalms of the Feria.

Ant. 1. God spared not His own Son : but delivered Him up for us all.

Ant. 2. My spirit is vexed within me : and my heart within me is desolate.

Ant. 3. The thief spake to the thief : We receive the due reward of our deeds, but this Man hath done nothing amiss.

Ant. 4. When I am in heaviness : I will think upon God.

Ant. 5. Lord, remember me : when Thou comest in Thy kingdom.

Ant. to Ben. And they set up over His head, His accusation written : Jesus of Nazareth, King of the Jews.

The rest as at Lauds on Maundy Thursday, except that the Collect ends without Who now liveth, etc.

Prime and the other Hours are said as on Maundy Thursday, except that all kneel from the first beginning of the Ant. throughout each Office.

After the repetition of the Ant. is said the Lord's Prayer and the Collect as at Lauds, without The Lord be with you, or, Let us pray. And so each Office ends.

Chapter is not said on this, and the following day.

Vespers.

Vespers are not sung on this day, but are said in a low voice before the Altar till Ant. to Magnificat, which, as well as Magnificat, is said aloud by the Choir. All is as on Maundy Thursday, till

Ant. to Mag. Now there stood by the Cross of Jesus His Mother.

After the repetition of the Ant. to Magnificat, is said the Lord's Prayer and Psalm li., Miserere, without Glory be, etc. Then the Priest says the Collect audibly, as at the other Hours, and so Vespers end.

Compline.

All as on Maundy Thursday, except that at the first words of the Antiphon, and thenceforth, all kneel.

After the repetition of the Antiphon is said the Lord's Prayer, and Psalm li., Miserere, without Glory be, etc., all kneeling.

All ℣℣. and ℟℟. are omitted. Compline ends with the

COLLECT.

ALMIGHTY God, we beseech Thee graciously to behold this Thy

family, for which our Lord Jesus Christ was contented to be betrayed, and to be given up into the hands of wicked men, and to suffer death upon the Cross. Amen.

EASTER EVE.
Lauds.

Psalms of the Feria, except the Canticle, which is the Song of Hezekiah, Ego dixi, p. 12.

Ant. 1. O death, I will be thy plagues : O grave, I will be thy destruction.

Ant. 2. Give heed, all ye people : and behold My sorrow.

Ant. 3. All ye that pass by, behold and see : if there be any sorrow like unto My sorrow.

Ant. 4. From the gates of hell : deliver My soul, O Lord.

Ant. 5. They shall mourn for Him, as one mourneth for his only son : because the innocent Lord is slain.

Ant. to Ben. Women sitting by the sepulchre : mourned for the Lord with weeping.

The rest as at Lauds on Maundy Thursday, except the
COLLECT.

GRANT, O Lord, that as we are baptized into the death of Thy blessed Son our Saviour Jesus Christ, so by continual mortifying our corrupt affections we may be buried with Him ; and that through the grave and gate of death, we may pass to our joyful resurrection ; for His merits, Who died, and was buried, and rose again for us, Thy Son Jesus Christ our Lord. Amen.

[Or else the Collect of Thursday, ending without Who now liveth, etc.]
The Hours are said in a low voice, and as on Good Friday.

EASTER DAY.
First Vespers.
Vespers begin at once, with

Ant. Alleluia, Alleluia, Alleluia, Alleluia.

Psalm CXVII. *Laudate Dominum omnes gentes.*

O PRAISE the Lord, all ye heathen : praise Him, all ye nations.

2 For His merciful kindness is ever more and more towards us : and the truth of the Lord endureth for ever. Praise the Lord.

Glory be, etc.

Ant. Alleluia, Alleluia, Alleluia, Alleluia.

Ant. to Mag. In the end of the Sabbath, as it began to dawn toward the first day of the week : came Mary Magdalene and the other Mary to see the sepulchre. Alleluia.

℣. The Lord be with you.
℞. And with thy spirit.

Let us pray.
Collect as at Lauds.

[*Or this,*

POUR into our hearts, O Lord, the spirit of Thy love ; that we, whom Thou hast satisfied with Paschal sacraments, may of Thy mercy be made one in heart ; through Jesus Christ our Lord, Who liveth and reigneth with Thee, in the unity of the Holy Ghost, ever one God, world without end. Amen.]

℣. The Lord be with you.
℞. And with thy spirit.
℣. Bless we the Lord.
℞. Thanks be to God.

[*At Lauds and Vespers add* Alleluia.]
So end all Hours till Low Sunday.

Compline.
The usual Invocation is made in silence : the Office begins thus :

℣. O God, make speed to save us.
℞. O Lord, make haste to help us.

℣. Glory be to the Father, etc.
℞. As it was, etc.
Alleluia.

Ant. to Psalms. Alleluia, Alleluia, Alleluia, Alleluia.

Psalm iv. *Cum invocarem.*
Psalm xxxi. *In te Domine.*
Psalm cxxxiv. *Ecce nunc.*
Nunc Dimittis.

(*Each with* Glory be, etc., *and all said under one Ant.*)

[*After, but not on, this day, here follows, through the week, after the repetition of the Ant.:*

Gradual. This is the day which the Lord hath made : we will rejoice and be glad in it.
℣. In Thy Resurrection, O Christ.
℞. Let heaven and earth rejoice.]
℣. The Lord be with you.
℞. And with thy spirit.

Let us pray.

COLLECT.

ALMIGHTY God, Who through Thine Only-begotten Son Jesus Christ, hast overcome death, and opened unto us the gate of everlasting life: we humbly beseech Thee, that as by Thy special grace preventing us, Thou dost put into our minds good desires, so by Thy continual help we may bring the same to good effect; through Jesus Christ our Lord, Who liveth and reigneth with Thee and the Holy Ghost, ever one God, world without end. Amen.

℣. The Lord be with you.
℞. And with thy spirit.
℣. Bless we the Lord.
℞. Thanks be to God.

Lauds.

℣. In Thy Resurrection, O Christ.
℞. Let heaven and earth rejoice. Alleluia.
This ℣. and ℞. is said every day at Lauds till Ascension Day.

℣. O God, make speed to save us.
℞. O Lord, make haste to help us.
℣. Glory be to the Father, etc.
℞. As it was, etc.
Alleluia.

Psalms of Sunday.

Ant. 1. The Angel of the Lord descended from heaven : and rolled back the stone from the door, and sat upon it. Alleluia, Alleluia.
Ant. 2. And, behold, there was a great earthquake : for the Angel of the Lord descended from heaven. Alleluia.
Ant. 3. His countenance was like lightning : and his raiment white as snow. Alleluia, Alleluia.
Ant. 4. And for fear of him the keepers did shake : and became as dead men. Alleluia.
Ant. 5. And the Angel answered and said unto the women, Fear not ye : for I know that ye seek Jesus. Alleluia.

Then immediately, without Hymn or Chapter :

℣. The Lord is risen from the sepulchre.
℞. Who hung for our sakes upon the tree. Alleluia.
Ant. to Ben. And very early in the morning, the first day of the week : they came unto the sepulchre at the rising of the sun. Alleluia.

COLLECT.

ALMIGHTY God, Who through Thy Only-begotten Son Jesus Christ hast overcome death, and opened unto us the gate of everlasting life; we humbly beseech Thee, that, as by Thy special grace preventing us Thou dost put into our minds good desires, so by Thy continual help we may bring the same to good effect: through Jesus Christ our Lord, Who liveth and reigneth with Thee and the Holy Ghost, ever one God, world without end. Amen.

℣. Bless we the Lord.　Alleluia.
℟. Thanks be to God.　Alleluia.

Alleluia is said with this ℣. and ℟. till Trinity.

Prime.

The Offices, except Vespers, now begin as usual, but no Hymns are said till the First Vespers of Low Sunday.

Ant. to Psalms. The Angel of the Lord descended from heaven : and came and rolled back the stone from the door, and sat upon it.　Alleluia, Alleluia.

Psalm liv. *Deus in nomine tuo.*
Psalm cxviii. *Confitemini.*
Psalm cxix. *Beati immaculati* and *Retribue servo tuo.*

After the repetition of the Ant. immediately follows the

Gradual. This is the day which the Lord hath made : we will rejoice and be glad in it.
℣. The Lord is risen.
℟. As He said unto you.　Alleluia.
℣. The Lord be with you.
℟. And with thy spirit.

Let us pray.

Collect as at Lauds.

℣. Bless we the Lord.
℟. Thanks be to God.

Prime is thus said till Low Sunday, except that, through the week, Psalm cxviii. is omitted.

Chapter is said.

Tierce.

Ant. And, behold, there was a great earthquake : for the Angel of the Lord descended from heaven. Alleluia.
Gradual. This is the day which the Lord hath made : we will rejoice and be glad in it.
℣. The Lord is risen indeed.
℟. And hath appeared unto Simon. Alleluia.

Collect as at Lauds.

Sexts.

Ant. His countenance was like lightning : and his raiment white as snow.　Alleluia.
Gradual. This is the day which the Lord hath made : we will rejoice and be glad in it.
℣. The Lord is risen from the sepulchre.
℟. Who hung for our sakes upon the tree.　Alleluia.

Nones.

Ant. And for fear of him the keepers did shake : and became as dead men.　Alleluia.
Gradual. This is the day which the Lord hath made : we will rejoice and be glad in it.
℣. In Thy Resurrection, O Christ.
℟. Let heaven and earth rejoice. Alleluia.

Tierce, Sexts, and Nones, are thus said through the week, with change of Collect, according to the day.

Second Vespers.

Vespers begin thus :

℣. Lord, have mercy.
℟. Christ, have mercy.
℣. Lord, have mercy.

Ant. Alleluia, Alleluia, Alleluia, Alleluia.

Psalms of Sunday.

After repetition of the Antiphon, follows the

Gradual. This is the day which the Lord hath made : we will rejoice and be glad in it.
℣. O give thanks unto the Lord, for He is gracious : because His mercy endureth for ever.
℟. Alleluia.
℣. Let us keep the feast with the unleavened bread of sincerity and truth.
℟. Alleluia.

℣. The Lord is risen.

℞. As He said unto you. Alleluia.

Ant. to Mag. And when they looked, they saw that the stone was rolled away : for it was very great. Alleluia.

Collect as at Lauds.

[*Or this,*

GRANT, we beseech Thee, Almighty God, that we, who celebrate the solemnities of the Lord's Resurrection, by the invocation of Thy Spirit may rise from spiritual death ; through the same Jesus Christ our Lord. Amen.]

℣. The Lord is risen from the sepulchre.

℞. Who hung for our sakes upon the tree. Alleluia.

MEMORIAL OF S. MARY.

Ant. I went down into the garden of nuts to see the fruits of the valley, and to see whether the vines flourished, and the pomegranates budded : return, return, O Shulamite ; return, return, that we may look upon thee. Alleluia.

℣. Thou art the holy Mother of God.

℞. O Ever Virgin Mary. Alleluia.

COLLECT.

WE beseech Thee, O Lord, pour Thy grace into our hearts ; that, as we have known the Incarnation of Thy Son Jesus Christ by the message of an Angel, so by His Cross and Passion we may be brought unto the glory of His Resurrection ; through the same Jesus Christ our Lord. Amen.

This Memorial is said daily at Vespers through this week.

℣. Bless we the Lord. Alleluia.

℞. Thanks be to God. Alleluia.

Vespers are thus said through the week, except the Graduals, Ants. to Magnificat, and Collects.

EASTER MONDAY.

Lauds.

℣. In Thy Resurrection, O Christ.

℞. Let heaven and earth rejoice. Alleluia.

On this day, and through the week, the Sunday Psalms are said under this one

Ant. The Angel of the Lord descended from heaven : and rolled back the stone from the door, and sat upon it. Alleluia.

Ant. to Ben. What manner of communications are these that ye have one with another, as ye walk, and are sad ? Alleluia : And the one of them, whose name was Cleophas, answering, said unto Him, Art Thou only a stranger in Jerusalem, and hast not known the things which are come to pass there in these days ? Alleluia. And He said unto them, What things ? And they said unto Him, Concerning Jesus of Nazareth, Who was a Prophet mighty in deed and word, before God and all the people. Alleluia.

Collect of Sunday.

[*Or this,*

GOD, Who by the Easter solemnity hast bestowed healing on the world, continue, we beseech Thee, to Thy people Thy heavenly gifts ; that they may attain to perfect freedom, and advance towards life eternal ; through our Lord Jesus Christ. Amen.]

MEMORIAL OF S. MARY.

Ant. My soul failed when He spake ; I sought Him, but I could not find Him ; I called Him, but He gave me no answer : The watchmen that went about the city found me, they wounded me : the keepers of the walls took away my veil from me. Alleluia.

℣., ℞., *and Collect as at Sunday Vespers. This Memorial is said daily at Lauds through this week.*

Lauds are thus said through the week, except the changes of Collects and Ants. to Benedictus.

No notice is taken of any feast or fast during this week, because all Saints arose in Christ, and the feast of Christ's Resurrection is common to all Saints. A Double Feast so occurring is transferred to the first vacant day after the Octave. And this order holds good for the Octave of Whitsun Day.

No Petitions are said at any Hour, except Prime and Compline, till Trinity. On and after Low Sunday they are said at those two Hours.

Vespers.

As on Sunday, except that which follows:

Gradual. This is the day which the Lord hath made : we will rejoice and be glad in it.

℣. Let Israel now confess that He is gracious, and that His mercy endureth for ever.

℟. Alleluia.

℣. Did not our heart burn within us concerning Jesus : while He talked with us by the way?

℟. Alleluia.

℣. The Lord is risen from the sepulchre. Alleluia.

℟. Who hung for our sakes upon the tree. Alleluia.

Ant. to Mag. Did not our heart burn within us concerning Jesus : while He talked with us by the way? Alleluia.

Collect of Sunday.

[*Or this,*

GRANT, we beseech Thee, Almighty God, that we who are bowed down under the weight of our sins, by this Paschal feast may be delivered from all evils that beset us; through Jesus Christ Thy Son our Lord. Amen.]

———

EASTER TUESDAY.

Lauds.

Ant. to Ben. Jesus Himself stood in the midst of them, and saith unto them : Peace be unto you. Alleluia, Alleluia.

Collect of Sunday.

[*Or this,*

GOD, Who dost ever multiply Thy Church with new offspring; grant to Thy servants that as they have received Thy Sacrament in faith, they may hold it fast in life; through our Lord Jesus Christ. Amen.]

Vespers.

Gradual. This is the day which the Lord hath made : we will rejoice, and be glad in it.

℣. Let them give thanks whom the Lord hath redeemed, and delivered from the hand of the enemy; and gathered them out of the lands.

℟. Alleluia.

℣. The Lord Jesus arose and stood in the midst of His disciples, and said unto them, Peace be unto you.

℟. Alleluia.

℣. The Lord is risen from the sepulchre.

℟. Who hung for our sakes upon the tree.

Ant. to Mag. Behold My hands and My feet : that it is I Myself. Alleluia, Alleluia.

Collect of Sunday.

[*Or this,*

GRANT, we beseech Thee, Almighty God, that we who keep the solemnity of the Easter feast, may always live in the grace of holiness; through Jesus Christ our Lord. Amen.]

———

Wednesday.

Lauds.

Ant. to Ben. Cast the net on the

right side of the ship : and ye shall find. Alleluia.

Collect of Sunday.

[*Or this,*

GOD, Who makest us glad with the yearly solemnity of our Lord's Resurrection; mercifully grant that through our temporal feasts we may attain to eternal joys; through the same Jesus Christ our Lord. Amen.]

Vespers.

Gradual. This is the day which the Lord hath made : we will rejoice, and be glad in it.

℣. The right hand of the Lord bringeth mighty things to pass : the right hand of the Lord hath the pre-eminence.

℞. Alleluia.

℣. The Lord arose, and met the women, saying, All hail; and they came and held Him by the feet.

℞. Alleluia.

℣. The Lord is risen from the sepulchre. Alleluia.

℞. Who hung for our sakes upon the tree. Alleluia.

Ant. to Mag. This is now the third time that Jesus shewed Himself : after that He was risen from the dead. Alleluia.

Collect of Sunday.

[*Or this,*

GRANT, we beseech Thee, Almighty God, that the marvellous mystery of this Easter festivity may bring us peace in this world, and, in the world to come, eternal life; through our Lord Jesus Christ. Amen.]

————

Thursday.

Lauds.

Ant. to Ben. Mary stood without at the sepulchre weeping : and seeth two angels in white sitting, the one at the head, the other at the feet,

where the body of Jesus had lain. Alleluia.

Collect of Sunday.

[*Or this,*

GOD, Who hast gathered together divers nations in the confession of Thy Name; grant that they who are regenerate by baptism may be one in inward faith, and in outward devotion; through our Lord Jesus Christ. Amen.]

Vespers.

Gradual. This is the day which the Lord hath made : we will rejoice, and be glad in it.

℣. The same stone which the builders refused : is become the head-stone in the corner. This is the Lord's doing : and it is marvellous in our eyes.

℞. Alleluia.

℣. In the day of My resurrection, saith the Lord, I will go before you into Galilee.

℞. Alleluia.

℣. The Lord is risen from the sepulchre.

℞. Who hung for our sakes upon the tree.

Ant. to Mag. They have taken away my Lord, and I know not where they have laid Him : If thou hast borne Him hence, tell me. Alleluia. And I will take Him away. Alleluia.

Collect of Sunday.

[*Or this,*

GOD, Who hast granted us to celebrate the Paschal mystery with free hearts; teach us to fear that which displeaseth Thee, and to love that which Thou commandest; through our Lord Jesus Christ. Amen.]

————

Friday.

Lauds.

Ant. to Ben. Then the eleven disciples went away into Galilee : and when they saw Him, they worshipped Him. Alleluia.

Collect of Sunday.

[Or this,

ALMIGHTY, everlasting God, Who hast given the Easter mystery for the reconciliation of the human race; grant to our souls, that what we profess with our lips we may shew forth with our lives; through our Lord Jesus Christ. Amen.]

Vespers.

Gradual. This is the day which the Lord hath made : we will rejoice, and be glad in it.

℣. Blessed be He that cometh in the Name of the Lord : God is the Lord Who hath shewed us light.

℞. Alleluia.

℣. Tell it out among the heathen that the Lord reigneth from the tree.

℞. Alleluia.

℣. The Lord is risen from the sepulchre.

℞. Who hung for our sakes upon the tree.

Ant. to Mag. All power is given unto Me : in heaven and earth. Alleluia.

Collect of Sunday.

[Or this,

O GOD, by Whom redemption cometh, and adoption is bestowed; grant to the works of Thy hands, that being born anew in Christ, they may attain to their eternal heritage and to true liberty; through Jesus Christ our Lord. Amen.]

Saturday.

Lauds.

Ant. to Ben. So they ran both together : and the other disciple did outrun Peter, and came first to the sepulchre. Alleluia.

Collect of Sunday.

[Or this,

GRANT, we beseech Thee, Almighty God, that we, who have reverently passed through the Easter feast, may thereby attain to eternal joys; through Jesus Christ our Lord. Amen.]

On this day, at every Hour, Alleluia is said before and after the words, This is the day, *etc.*

Low Sunday.

First Vespers.

℣. O God, make speed, etc.

Ant. Alleluia, Alleluia, Alleluia, Alleluia.

Psalms of the Feria.

CHAPTER. Rom. vi.

CHRIST being raised from the dead, dieth no more; death hath no more dominion over Him. For in that He liveth, He liveth unto God.

℞. Thanks be to God.

HYMN. *Chorus novæ Hierusalem.*

YE Choirs of New Jerusalem!
To sweet new strains attune your theme;
The while we keep, from care releas'd,
With sober joy our Paschal feast.

When Christ, unconquer'd Lion, first
The Dragon's chains by rising burst:
And while with living voice He cries,
The dead of other ages rise.

Engorg'd in former years, their prey
Must death and hell restore to-day:
And many a captive soul, set free,
With Jesus leaves captivity.

Right gloriously He triumphs now,
Worthy to Whom should all things bow:
And joining heav'n and earth again
Links in one commonweal the twain.

And we, as these His deeds we sing,
His suppliant soldiers, pray our King,
That in His palace, bright and vast,
We may keep watch and ward at last.

Long as unending ages run,
To God the Father laud be done,
To God the Son our equal praise,
And God the Holy Ghost, we raise. Amen.

℣. Abide with us.

℞. For it is toward evening, and the day is far spent. Alleluia.

Ant. to Mag. Now when Jesus was risen early the first day of the week : He appeared first unto Mary Magdalene, out of whom He had cast seven devils. Alleluia.

COLLECT.

ALMIGHTY Father, Who hast given Thine only Son to die for our sins, and to rise again for our justification ; grant us so to put away the leaven of malice and wickedness, that we may always serve Thee in pureness of living and truth ; through the merits of the same Thy Son Jesus Christ our Lord. Amen.

[*Or this,*

GRANT, we beseech Thee, Almighty God, that we who have passed through the Paschal feast, by Thy grace may hold firmly thereby in heart and life ; through Jesus Christ our Lord. Amen.]

MEMORIAL OF S. MARY, p. 163.

This Memorial is said at First Vespers of Sunday till the Ascension.

The First Vespers of Sunday are thus said till the Ascension, except the changes of Collect and Ant. to Magnificat.

Compline.

Compline begins as usual with

℣. Turn us, etc.

Ant. to Psalms. Alleluia, Alleluia, Alleluia, Alleluia.

Psalm iv. *Cum invocarem.*
Psalm xxxi. *In te Domine.*
Psalm xci. *Qui habitat.*
Psalm cxxxiv. *Ecce nunc.*

CHAPTER. Jer. xiv., *as in Psalter.*

℟. Thanks be to God.

HYMN. *Jesu Salvator seculi.*

JESU, Who brought'st redemption nigh,
  Word of the Father, God most High ;
O Light of Light, to man unknown,
And watchful Guardian of Thine own ;

Thy hand Creation made and guides ;
Thy wisdom time from time divides :
By this world's cares and toils opprest,
O give our weary bodies rest.

That while in frames of sin and pain
A little longer we remain,
Our flesh may here in such wise sleep,
That watch with Christ our souls may keep.

O free us, while we dwell below,
From insults of our ghostly foe,
That he may ne'er victorious be
O'er them that are redeemed by Thee.

We pray Thee, King with glory deck'd,
In this our Paschal joy, protect,
From all that death would fain effect,
Thy ransom'd flock, Thine own elect.

To Thee Who, dead, again dost live,
All glory, Lord, Thy people give ;
All glory, as is ever meet,
To Father and to Paraclete. Amen.

These two last verses are said at the end of all Hymns of this metre, till Ascension, except at Saturday Vespers.

℣. Keep us.

℟. As the apple of an eye, hide us under the shadow of Thy wings.

Ant. to Nunc Dim. Alleluia. The Lord is risen. Alleluia : As He said. Alleluia, Alleluia.

Petitions, p. 68.

Compline is thus said till the Ascension, except that the Christmas Doxology is used on any Feast of the Blessed Virgin.

Lauds.

Sac. ℣. *and* ℟., *Ants. and Psalms,* p. 161.

CHAPTER. 1 St. John v.

WHATSOEVER is born of God overcometh the world ; and this is the victory that overcometh the world, even our faith.

℟. Thanks be to God.

HYMN. *Sermone blando Angelus.*

WITH gentle voice the Angel gave
  The women tidings at the grave ;
"Forthwith your Master shall ye see :
He goes before to Galilee."

And while with fear and joy they pressed
To tell these tidings to the rest,
Their Lord, their living Lord, they meet,
And see His form, and kiss His feet.

Th' eleven, when they hear, with speed
To Galilee forthwith proceed ;
That there they may behold once more
The Lord's dear face, as oft afore.

In this our bright and Paschal day
The sun shines out with purer ray :
When Christ, to earthly sight made plain,
The glad Apostles see again.

The wounds, the riven wounds, He shews
Of that His flesh with light that glows,
In loud accord, both far and nigh,
The Lord's arising testify.

O Christ, the King, Who lov'st to bless,
Do Thou our hearts and souls possess;
To Thee our praise that we may pay,
To Whom our laud is due, for aye.

We pray Thee, King with glory deck'd,
In this our Paschal joy protect,
From all that death would fain effect,
Thy ransomed flock, Thine own elect.

To Thee Who, dead, again dost live,
All glory, Lord, Thy people give;
All glory, as is ever meet,
To Father and to Paraclete. Amen.

℣. The Lord hath risen from the sepulchre.

℟. Who hung for our sakes upon the tree. Alleluia.

Ant. to Ben. Then the same day at evening, being the first day of the week, when the doors were shut where the disciples were assembled : Jesus stood in the midst, and saith unto them, Peace be unto you. Alleluia.

MEMORIAL OF THE RESURRECTION.

Ant. And very early in the morning, the first day of the week : they came unto the sepulchre at the rising of the sun. Alleluia.

℣. The Lord is risen indeed.

℟. And hath appeared to Simon. Alleluia.

COLLECT.

ALMIGHTY God, Who through Thy Only-begotten Son Jesus Christ hast overcome death, and opened unto us the gate of everlasting life; we humbly beseech Thee, that, as by Thy special grace preventing us Thou dost put into our minds good desires, so by Thy continual help we may bring the same to good effect; through Jesus Christ our Lord, Who liveth and reigneth with Thee and the Holy Ghost, ever one God, world without end. Amen.

This Memorial is said at Lauds on Sunday till the Ascension.

The Sunday Memorials supersede those for Double Feasts if any such occur on, or concur with, Sunday.

A Double Feast occurring on Low Sunday is to be deferred, but not so on the Sundays following, except Rogation Sunday.

Prime.

HYMN. *Jam lucis orto sidere,*
     with Easter Doxology.

Ant. to Psalms. The Angel of the Lord descended from heaven : and came and rolled back the stone from the door, and sat upon it. Alleluia.

Psalm liv. *Deus in nomine tuo.*
Psalm cxix. *Beati immaculati* and *Retribue servo tuo.*

Ant. Thanks be to Thee, O God, thanks be to Thee, One Very Trinity : One and Supreme Deity, and One and Holy Unity. Alleluia.

Psalm. *Quicunque vult.*

CHAPTER. 1 Tim. i.

NOW unto the King Eternal, Immortal, Invisible, the only wise God, be honour and glory for ever and ever. Amen.

℟. Jesus Christ, Son of the living God, have mercy upon us. Alleluia, Alleluia. ℣. Thou Who hast risen from the dead. Alleluia. ℟. Have mercy upon us. Alleluia, Alleluia. ℣. Glory be to the Father, and to the Son : and to the Holy Ghost. ℟. Jesu Christ, Son of the living God, have mercy upon us. Alleluia.

This ℟. is used daily till the Ascension.

℣. O Lord, arise, help us.

℟. And deliver us for Thy Name's sake.

Petitions, p. 32.

Tierce.

HYMN. *Nunc sancte nobis Spiritus,*
     with Easter Doxology.

Ant. And, behold, there was a great earthquake : for the Angel of the Lord descended from heaven. Alleluia.

CHAPTER. 1 S. John v.

WHATSOEVER is born of God overcometh the world ; and this is the victory that overcometh the world, even our faith.

R7. The Lord is risen. Alleluia, Alleluia. V. As He said. R7. Alleluia. V. Glory be to the Father, and to the Son : and to the Holy Ghost. R7. The Lord is risen. Alleluia, Alleluia.

V. The Lord is risen indeed.

R7. And hath appeared to Simon. Alleluia.

Collect as at First Vespers.

Sexts.

HYMN. *Rector potens verax Deus, with Easter Doxology.*

Ant. His countenance was like lightning : and his raiment white as snow. Alleluia.

CHAPTER. 1 S. John v.

WHO is he that overcometh the world, but he that believeth that Jesus is the Son of God? This is He that came by water and blood, even Jesus Christ.

R7. The Lord is risen indeed. Alleluia, Alleluia. V. And hath appeared to Simon. R7. Alleluia. V. Glory be to the Father, and to the Son : and to the Holy Ghost. R7. The Lord is risen indeed. Alleluia, Alleluia.

V. The Lord is risen from the sepulchre.

R7. Who hung for our sakes upon the tree. Alleluia.

Nones.

HYMN. *Rerum Deus tenax vigor, with Easter Doxology.*

Ant. And for fear of him the keepers did shake : and became as dead men. Alleluia.

CHAPTER. 1 S. John v.

AND there are three that bear witness in earth, the spirit, and the water, and the blood : and these three agree in one.

R7. The Lord is risen from the sepulchre. Alleluia, Alleluia. V. Who hung for our sakes upon the tree. R7. Alleluia. V. Glory be to the Father, and to the Son : and to the Holy Ghost. R7. The Lord is risen from the sepulchre. Alleluia, Alleluia.

V. In Thy Resurrection, O Christ.

R7. Let heaven and earth rejoice. Alleluia.

Second Vespers.

Ant. Alleluia, Alleluia, Alleluia, Alleluia.

CHAPTER. 1 S. John v.

WHATSOEVER is born of God overcometh the world : and this is the victory that overcometh the world, even our faith.

R7. Thanks be to God.

HYMN. *Ad Cænam Agni providi.*

THE Lamb's high banquet we await,
In snow-white robes of royal state :
And now, the Red Sea's channel past,
To Christ our Prince we sing at last.

Upon the Altar of the Cross,
His body hath redeem'd our loss :
And tasting of His roseate blood,
Our life is hid with Him in God.

That Paschal eve God's arm was bar'd :
The devastating Angel spar'd :
By strength of hand our hosts went free
From Pharaoh's ruthless tyranny.

Now Christ, our Paschal Lamb, is slain,
The Lamb of God that knows no stain,
The true Oblation offer'd here,
Our own unleaven'd Bread sincere.

O Thou, from Whom hell's monarch flies,
O great, O very Sacrifice,
Thy captive people are set free,
And endless life restor'd in Thee.

For Christ, arising from the dead,
From conquer'd hell victorious sped :
And thrust the tyrant down to chains,
And Paradise for man regains.

We pray Thee, King with glory deck'd,
In this our Paschal joy protect,
From all that death would fain effect,
Thy ransomed flock, Thine own elect.

To Thee Who, dead, again dost live,
All glory, Lord, Thy people give;
All glory, as is ever meet,
To Father and to Paraclete.   Amen.

℣. Abide with us.

℟. For it is toward evening, and the day is far spent.   Alleluia.

Ant. to Mag. And after eight days came Jesus, the doors being shut, and stood in the midst, and said : Peace be unto you.   Alleluia.

MEMORIAL OF THE RESURRECTION.

Ant. And when they looked, they saw that the stone was rolled away : for it was very great.   Alleluia.

℣. The Lord is risen.

℟. As He said unto you. Alleluia.

Collect, p. 168.

This Memorial is said at Vespers on Sundays till Ascension.

Until Ascension the Hours are said as on Low Sunday, with these exceptions : the Vesper Psalms change according to the Feria, though the Lauds Psalms continue to be those of Sunday. The Psalms at all Offices are said under this Ant., Alleluia, Alleluia, Alleluia, Alleluia. The Ants. to Benedictus and Magnificat change daily. The Chapter and Collect at each Office, except Prime, change weekly.

Prime is said with the usual Petitions, the Psalms, and Responsary as on Sunday, Quicunque vult being said on the Ferias, with Ant. Glory to Thee, p. 30.

Ants. to Benedictus *and* Magnificat *for the week :*

1. Thomas, because thou hast seen Me, thou hast believed : blessed are they that have not seen, and yet have believed.   Alleluia.

2. And many other signs truly did Jesus in the presence of His disciples; Alleluia : which are not written in this book.   Alleluia.

3. But these are written that ye might believe that Jesus is the Christ, the Son of God : and that believing ye might have life through His Name. Alleluia.

Ferial Memorials,

From this time till Ascension.

At Lauds.

MEMORIAL OF THE CROSS.

Ant. The Crucified hath risen from the dead : He hath redeemed us. Alleluia, Alleluia.

℣. Tell it out among the heathen.

℟. That the Lord reigneth from the tree.   Alleluia.

COLLECT.

GOD, Who for our sake didst will that Thy Son should undergo the suffering of the Cross to drive away from us the power of the enemy; grant to us Thy servants that we may ever live in the joys of His Resurrection; through the same Jesus Christ our Lord.   Amen.

MEMORIAL OF S. MARY.

Ant. The gate of Paradise was closed to all by Eve : and by Mary it is again set open.   Alleluia.

℣. After child-bearing thou remainedst a Virgin.

℟. O Mother of God.   Alleluia.

COLLECT.

WE beseech Thee, O Lord, pour Thy grace into our hearts; that as we have known the Incarnation of Thy Son Jesus Christ by the message of an Angel, so by His Cross and Passion we may be brought to the glory of His Resurrection; through the same Thy Son Jesus Christ our Lord.   Amen.

MEMORIAL OF ALL SAINTS.

Ant. Thy Saints, O Lord, shall flourish as a lily; Alleluia : And they shall be as the odour of balsam before Thee. Alleluia.

℣. The voice of joy and health.

℟. Is in the dwellings of the righteous. Alleluia.

COLLECT.

GRANT, we beseech Thee, Almighty God, that in the Resurrection of Thy Son our Lord Jesus Christ with all the Saints we may truly receive a portion; Who liveth and reigneth with Thee and the Holy Ghost, ever one God, world without end. Amen.

On Ferias and simple feasts at Vespers.

MEMORIAL OF THE CROSS.

Ant. He hath endured the holy Cross Who burst the bars of hell: He is girded with power. He rose on the third day. Alleluia,

℣., ℟., *and Collect, as at Lauds.*

MEMORIAL OF S. MARY,
As at Lauds.

MEMORIAL OF ALL SAINTS.

Ant. In the heavenly kingdom is the dwelling of the Saints. Alleluia: And their rest in eternity. Alleluia.

℣., ℟., *and Collect, as at Lauds.*

Festibal Memorials,

Used on Double Feasts till Ascension, except on Sunday, at both Vespers, and at Lauds.

Lauds.

MEMORIAL OF THE RESURRECTION.

Ant. The Lord is risen from the sepulchre : Who hung for our sakes upon the tree. Alleluia.

℣. The Lord is risen.

℟. As He said to you. Alleluia.

Collect, p. 161.

Vespers.

Ant. Go quickly, and tell His disciples that He is risen from the dead. Alleluia.

℣. The Lord is risen indeed.

℟. And hath appeared to Simon. Alleluia.

Collect, p. 161.

SECOND SUNDAY AFTER EASTER.
First Vespers.
As p. 166, till

Ant. to Mag. Thou art worthy, O Lord, to receive glory, and honour, and power, for Thou hast created all things, and for Thy pleasure they are, and were created : Salvation to our God, Which sitteth upon the throne, and unto the Lamb. Alleluia.

COLLECT.

ALMIGHTY God, Who hast given Thine only Son to be unto us both a sacrifice for sin, and also an ensample of godly life; give us grace that we may always most thankfully receive that His inestimable benefit, and also daily endeavour ourselves to follow the blessed steps of His most holy life; through the same Jesus Christ our Lord. Amen.

[*Or this,*

O GOD, Who by the humiliation of Thy Son didst raise a fallen world, grant perpetual joy to Thy faithful people; that those Whom Thou hast delivered from the danger of eternal death, may be made partakers of eternal joys; through the same Jesus Christ our Lord. Amen.]

Lauds.

Ant. The Angel of the Lord descended from heaven : and came and rolled back the stone from the door, and sat upon it. Alleluia, Alleluia.

The Psalms are all said under this Ant.

CHAPTER. 1 S. Pet. ii.

CHRIST also suffered for us, leaving us an example, that ye should follow His steps: Who did no si-

neither was guile found in His mouth.

℟. Thanks be to God.

Hymn. *Sermone blando Angelus,* ℣. and ℟., p. 167.

Ant. to Ben. I am the good Shepherd Who feed My sheep : I lay down My life for My sheep. Alleluia, Alleluia.

Prime.

As p. 168.

Tierce.

As p. 168, *except*

CHAPTER. 1 S. Pet. ii.

CHRIST also suffered for us, leaving us an example, that ye should follow His steps : Who did no sin, neither was guile found in His mouth.

Sexts.

As p. 169, *except*

CHAPTER. 1 S. Pet. ii.

BUT He committed Himself to Him that judgeth righteously : Who His own self bare our sins in His own body on the tree ; by Whose stripes ye were healed.

Nones.

As p. 169, *except*

CHAPTER. 1 S. Pet. ii.

FOR ye were as sheep going astray : but are now returned unto the Shepherd and Bishop of your souls.

Second Vespers.

As p. 169, *except*

CHAPTER. 1 S. Pet. ii.

CHRIST also suffered for us, leaving us an example, that ye should follow His steps : Who did no sin, neither was guile found in His mouth.

Ant. to Mag. I am the Shepherd of the sheep. I am the Way and the Truth : I am the good Shepherd, and know My sheep, and am known of Mine. Alleluia, Alleluia.

Ants. to Benedictus *and* Magnificat *for the week :*

1. The good Shepherd : giveth His life for the sheep. Alleluia.

2. As the Father knoweth Me, even so know I the Father : and I lay down My life for the sheep. Alleluia.

3. But the hireling, whose own the sheep are not, seeth the wolf coming, and leaveth the sheep and fleeth : and the wolf catcheth them, and scattereth the sheep. Alleluia.

4. And other sheep I have, which are not of this fold : them also I must bring, and they shall hear My voice ; and there shall be one fold under one Shepherd. Alleluia.

THIRD SUNDAY AFTER EASTER.

First Vespers.

As p. 166, *except*

Ant. to Mag. I am Alpha and Omega, the First and the Last : I am the Root and Offspring of David, and the bright and morning Star. Alleluia.

COLLECT.

ALMIGHTY God, Who shewest to them that be in error the light of Thy truth, to the intent that they may return into the way of righteousness ; grant unto all them that are admitted into the fellowship of Christ's religion, that they may eschew those things that are contrary to their profession, and follow all such things as are agreeable to the same ; through our Lord Jesus Christ. Amen.

Lauds.

Ant. to Psalms, p. 171.

CHAPTER. 1 S. Pet. ii.

DEARLY beloved, I beseech you as strangers and pilgrims, abstain from fleshly lusts, which war against the soul.

℟. Thanks be to God.

Ant. to Ben. Jesus said to His disciples, A little while and ye shall not see Me : and again a little while and ye shall Me : because I go to the Father. Alleluia, Alleluia.

Prime.

As p. 168.

Tierce.

CHAPTER. 1 S. Pet. ii.

DEARLY beloved, I beseech you as strangers and pilgrims, abstain from fleshly lusts, which war against the soul.

Sexts.

CHAPTER. 1 S. Pet. ii.

SUBMIT yourselves to every ordinance of man for the Lord's sake: whether it be to the king, as supreme; or unto governours, as unto them that are sent by him, for the punishment of evil doers, and for the praise of them that do well.

Nones.

CHAPTER. 1 S. Pet. ii.

FOR so is the will of God, that with well-doing ye may put to silence the ignorance of foolish men.

Second Vespers.

CHAPTER. 1 S. Pet. ii.

DEARLY beloved, I beseech you as strangers and pilgrims, abstain from fleshly lusts, which war against the soul.

Ant. to Mag. What is this that He saith, A little while? Alleluia : We cannot tell what He saith. Alleluia.

Ants. to Benedictus *and* Magnificat *for the week :*

1. Verily, verily, I say unto you, that ye shall weep and lament. Alleluia. But the world shall rejoice : and ye shall be sorrowful, but your sorrow shall be turned into joy. Alleluia.

2. Sorrow hath filled your hearts : but your joy no man taketh from you. Alleluia.

3. I will see you again, and your heart shall rejoice : and your joy no man taketh from you. Alleluia.

FOURTH SUNDAY AFTER EASTER.

First Vespers.

As p. 166, *except*

Ant. to Mag. Great and marvellous are Thy works, Lord God Almighty; just and true are Thy ways, Thou King of Saints : Who shall not fear Thee, O Lord, and glorify Thy Name? for Thou only art holy; for all nations shall come and worship before Thee; for Thy judgments are made manifest. Alleluia.

COLLECT.

O ALMIGHTY God, Who alone canst order the unruly wills and affections of sinful men; grant unto Thy people, that they may love the thing which Thou commandest, and desire that which Thou dost promise; that so, among the manifold changes of the world, our hearts may surely there be fixed, where true joys are to be found; through Jesus Christ our Lord. Amen.

Lauds.

Ant. to Psalms, p. 171.

CHAPTER. S. James i.

EVERY good gift and every perfect gift is from above, and cometh down from the Father of lights, with Whom is no variableness, neither shadow of turning.

Ṛ. Thanks be to God.

Ant. to Ben. I go my way to Him that sent Me : But, because I have said these things unto you, sorrow hath filled your heart. Alleluia.

Prime.

As p. 168.

Tierce.

CHAPTER. S. James i.

EVERY good gift and every perfect gift is from above, and cometh down from the Father of lights, with Whom is no variableness, neither shadow of turning.

Sexts.

CHAPTER. S. James i.

LET every man be swift to hear, slow to speak, slow to wrath.

Nones.

CHAPTER. S. James i.

WHEREFORE lay apart all filthiness and superfluity of naughtiness, and receive with meekness the engrafted word, which is able to save your souls.

Second Vespers.

CHAPTER. S. James i.

EVERY good gift and every perfect gift is from above, and cometh down from the Father of lights, with Whom is no variableness, neither shadow of turning.

Ant. to Mag. I tell you the truth; it is expedient for you that I go away : for if I go not away, the Comforter will not come unto you. Alleluia.

Ants. to Benedictus and Magnificat for the week :

1. I have yet many things to say unto you, but ye cannot bear them now : Howbeit, when He, the Spirit of truth, is come, He will guide you into all truth. Alleluia.

2. When He, the Spirit of truth, is come, He will guide you into all truth : and He will shew you things to come. Alleluia.

3. He shall glorify Me : for He shall receive of Mine, and shall shew it unto you. Alleluia.

ROGATION SUNDAY.

First Vespers.

As p. 166, *except*

Ant. to Mag. Great and marvellous are Thy works, Lord God Almighty; just and true are Thy ways, Thou King of Saints : Who shall not fear Thee, O Lord, and glorify Thy Name? for Thou only art holy; for all nations shall come and worship Thee, for Thy judgments are made manifest. Alleluia.

COLLECT.

O LORD, from Whom all good things do come; grant to us Thy humble servants, that by Thy holy inspiration we may think those things that be good, and by Thy merciful guiding may perform the same: through our Lord Jesus Christ. Amen.

Lauds.

Ant. 1. The Angel of the Lord descended from heaven, and rolled back the stone from the door, and sat upon it. Alleluia, Alleluia.

Ant. 2. And, behold, there was a great earthquake : for the Angel of the Lord descended from heaven. Alleluia.

Ant. 3. His countenance was like lightning : and his raiment white as snow. Alleluia, Alleluia.

Ant. 4. And for fear of him the keepers did shake : and became as dead men. Alleluia.

Ant. 5. And the angel answered and said unto the women, Fear not ye : for I know that ye seek Jesus. Alleluia.

CHAPTER. S. James i.

BE ye doers of the word, and not hearers only, deceiving your own selves. For if any be a hearer of the word, and not a doer, he is like unto a man beholding his natural face in a glass.

Ant. to Ben. Hitherto have ye asked nothing in My Name : ask, and ye shall receive. Alleluia.

Prime.

All as p. 168.

Tierce.

CHAPTER. S. James i.

BE ye doers of the word, and not hearers only, deceiving your own selves. For if any be a hearer of the word, and not a doer, he is like unto a man beholding his natural face in a glass.

Sexts.

CHAPTER. S. James i.

BUT whoso looketh into the perfect law of liberty, and continueth therein, he being not a forgetful hearer, but a doer of the work, this man shall be blessed in his deed.

Nones.

CHAPTER. S. James i.

PURE religion and undefiled before God and the Father is this, To visit the fatherless and widows in their affliction, and to keep himself unspotted from the world.

Second Vespers.

CHAPTER. S. James i.

BE ye doers of the word, and not hearers only, deceiving your own selves. For if any be a hearer of the word, and not a doer, he is like unto a man beholding his natural face in a glass.

Ant. to Mag. Ask, and ye shall receive, that your joy may be full : for the Father Himself loveth you, because ye have loved Me, and have believed. Alleluia.

ROGATION MONDAY.

Lauds.

CHAPTER. S. James v.

CONFESS your faults one to another, and pray one for another, that ye may be healed. The effectual fervent prayer of a righteous man availeth much.

Ant. to Ben. Ask, and it shall be given you; seek, and ye shall find : knock, and it shall be opened unto you. Alleluia.

Collect of Sunday.

[Or this,

GRANT, we beseech Thee, Almighty God, that we who in our afflictions trust to Thy mercy, may by Thy protection be guarded from all adversities; through our Lord Jesus Christ. Amen.]

At all the other Hours are said the Chapter and Collect of Rogation Sunday. If any Double Feast occurs on this or the following day, the Feast is kept, with memorial of the fast at Lauds only.

On this day are to be said Vespers of the Blessed Virgin, with full service on the morrow, except a Double Feast occur : no memorial of the fast or of any Saint, but only of the Resurrection. If this be not observed, let the Ant. to Magnificat on both days be as here set down for Tuesday, and the rest of the Tuesday Office as on Monday.

ROGATION TUESDAY.

Vespers.

Ant. to Mag. Lo, now speakest Thou plainly, and speakest no proverb : Now are we sure that Thou knowest all things, and needest not that any man should ask Thee; by this we believe that Thou camest forth from God. Alleluia.

Collect of Sunday.

VIGIL OF THE ASCENSION.

Lauds.

CHAPTER. Acts iv.

AND the multitude of them that believed were of one heart and of one soul: neither said any of them that ought of the things which he possessed was his own; but they had all things common.

Ant. to Ben. And now, O Father, glorify Thou Me with Thine own self: with the glory which I had with Thee before the world was. Alleluia.

[COLLECT.

GRANT, we beseech Thee, Almighty God, that the intention of our hearts may ever tend to that place whither Thine Only-begotten Son our Lord, the Author of this coming solemnity, hath entered in; and as we press thereunto by faith, so grant us to attain to the same by holy conversation; through the same Jesus Christ our Lord. Amen.]

This Collect is said at every Hour on this day.

Memorial of S. MARY and of ALL SAINTS, p. 170.

No Memorial of the CROSS is made till after the 1st Sunday after Trinity.

Tierce.

CHAPTER. Acts iv.

AND the multitude of them that believed were of one heart and of one soul: neither said any of them that ought of .the things which he possessed was his own; but they had all things common.

Sexts.

CHAPTER. Acts iv.

AND with great power gave the apostles witness of the resurrection of the Lord Jesus: and great grace was upon them all.

Nones.

CHAPTER. Acts iv.

AS many as were possessors of lands or houses sold them, and brought the prices of the things that were sold, and laid them down at the apostles' feet: and distribution was made unto every man according as he had need.

If a Double Feast occur on this vigil, it is not transferred, and a memorial of the vigil is made at Lauds. But at Vespers no memorial is made of the feast.

THE ASCENSION OF OUR LORD JESUS CHRIST.

First Vespers.

Ant. I will not leave you comfortless. Alleluia : I go and will come to you. Alleluia. And your heart shall rejoice. Alleluia, Alleluia.

Psalms of the Feria.

CHAPTER. Acts i.

THE former treatise have I made, O Theophilus, of all that Jesus began both to do and teach, until the day in which He was taken up, after that He through the Holy Ghost had given commandments unto the apostles whom He had chosen.

℟. Let not your heart be troubled; I go to the Father, and when I am taken up from you, I will send you; Alleluia : the Spirit of truth; and your heart shall rejoice. Alleluia. ℣. I will pray the Father: and He shall give you another Comforter. ℟. The Spirit of truth: and your heart shall rejoice. Alleluia. ℣. Glory be to the Father, and to the Son : and to the Holy Ghost. ℟. Alleluia.

HYMN. *Æterne Rex altissime.*

ETERNAL Monarch, King most high,
Whose blood hath brought redemption nigh,
By Whom the death of death was wrought,
And conqu'ring grace's battle fought :

Ascending to the Throne of might,
And seated at the Father's right,
All power in heav'n is Jesu's own,
That here His Manhood had not known.

That so, in Nature's triple frame,
Each heavenly and each earthly name,
And things in hell's abyss abhorr'd,
May bend the knee and own Him Lord.

Yea, angels tremble when they see
How chang'd is our humanity,
That flesh hath purg'd what flesh had stain'd,
And God, the flesh of God, hath reign'd.

Be Thou our Joy and Thou our Guard,
Who art to be our great Reward :
Our glory and our boast in Thee,
For ever and for ever be !

All glory, Lord, to Thee we pay.
Ascending o'er the stars to-day ;
All glory, as is ever meet,
To Father and to Paraclete. Amen.

These two last verses are said at the end of all Hymns of this metre till Whitsun-tide.

℣. Christ going up on high.
℟. Led captivity captive. Alleluia.

This Hymn is said daily till Whitsun Eve.

Ant. to Mag. Father, I have manifested Thy Name unto the men which Thou gavest Me : I pray for them, I pray not for the world. And now I come to Thee. Alleluia.

Collect as at the following Lauds [or of the Vigil.]

Compline.

Ant. to Psalms. Alleluia, Alleluia, Alleluia, Alleluia.

HYMN. *Jesu nostra Redemptio.*

JESU, Redemption all divine,
Whom here we love, for Whom we pine,
God, working out creation's plan,
And, in the latter time, made Man ;

What love of Thine was that, which led
To take our woes upon Thy head,
And pangs and cruel death to bear,
To ransom us from death's despair !

To Thee hell's gate gave ready way,
Demanding there his captive prey :
And now, in pomp and victor's pride,
Thou sittest at the Father's side.

Let very mercy force Thee still
To spare us, conquering all our ill ;
And, granting that we ask, on high
With Thine own face to satisfy.

Be Thou our Joy and Thou our Guard,
Who art to be our great Reward :
Our glory and our boast in Thee,
For ever and for ever be !

All glory, Lord, to Thee we pay,
Ascending o'er the stars to-day ;
All glory, as is ever meet,
To Father and to Paraclete. Amen.

℣. Keep us.
℟. As the apple of an eye, hide us under the shadow of Thy wings.

Ant. to Nunc Dim. Alleluia. Christ going up on high. Alleluia : Led captivity captive. Alleluia, Alleluia.

Lauds.

℣. I ascend to My Father, and your Father.
℟. And to My God, and your God. Alleluia.

Psalms of Sunday.

Ant. 1. Ye men of Galilee, why stand ye gazing up into heaven? : This same Jesus, Which is taken up from you into heaven, shall so come. Alleluia.

Ant. 2. And while they looked steadfastly toward heaven as He went up : they said, Alleluia.

Ant. 3. While He blessed them, He was parted from them : and carried up into heaven. Alleluia.

Ant. 4. Exalt ye the King of kings : and sing praises to God. Alleluia.

Ant. 5. While they beheld, He was taken up : and a cloud received Him into heaven. Alleluia.

CHAPTER. Acts i.

THE former treatise have I made, O Theophilus, of all that Jesus began both to do and to teach, until the day in which He was taken up, after that He through the Holy Ghost had given commandments unto the Apostles whom He had chosen.

HYMN. *Tu Christe nostrum gaudium.*

THOU, Christ, Who art our joy alone,
  Abiding on the heavenly throne,
Throughout the earth Thy sway extends,
And earth-born joys Thy victory ends.

Therefore we pray Thee, of Thy grace,
From all our sins to turn Thy face :
And lift our hearts by Thy dear love
To rest with Thee in realms above.

That when before our dazzled sight
Thy judgment cloud glows red and bright,
Our sins' award be done away,
And our lost crowns restored for aye.

Be Thou our Joy and Thou our Guard,
Who art to be our great Reward :
Our glory and our boast in Thee
For ever and for ever be !

All glory, Lord, to Thee we pay,
Ascending o'er the stars to-day ;
All glory, as is ever meet,
To Father and to Paraclete. Amen.

℣. God is gone up with a merry noise.

℞. And the Lord with the sound of the trumpet. Alleluia.

Ant. to Ben. I ascend unto My Father, and your Father : and to My God, and your God. Alleluia.

COLLECT.

GRANT, we beseech Thee, Almighty God, that like as we do believe Thy Only-begotten Son our Lord Jesus Christ to have ascended into the heavens : so we may also in heart and mind thither ascend, and with Him continually dwell, Who liveth and reigneth with Thee and the Holy Ghost, one God, world without end. Amen.

Prime.

Ant. Ye men of Galilee, why stand ye gazing up into heaven ? : This same Jesus, Which is taken up from you into heaven, shall so come. Alleluia.

Psalm liv. *Deus in nomine.*
Psalm cxix. *Beati immaculati* and *Retribue servo Tuo.*

Ant. to Ps., Quicunque. Thanks be to Thee, p. 30.

CHAPTER. 1 Tim. i.

NOW unto the King Eternal, Immortal, Invisible, the only wise God, be honour and glory for ever and ever. Amen.

℞. Jesu Christ, Son of the living God, have mercy upon us. Alleluia, Alleluia. ℣. Thou that sittest at the right hand of God the Father. Alleluia, Alleluia. ℞. Have mercy upon us. Alleluia, Alleluia. ℣. Glory be to the Father, and to the Son : and to the Holy Ghost. ℞. Jesu Christ, Son of the living God, have mercy upon us. Alleluia, Alleluia.

℣. O Lord, arise, help us.

℞. And deliver us for Thy Name's sake.

Tierce.

Ant. And while they looked steadfastly toward heaven as He went up : they said, Alleluia.

CHAPTER. Acts i.

THE former treatise have I made, O Theophilus, of all that Jesus began both to do and teach, until the day in which He was taken up, after that He through the Holy Ghost had given commandments unto the apostles whom He had chosen.

℞. Thou hast set Thy glory, O Lord. Alleluia, Alleluia. ℣. Above the heavens. R7. Alleluia, Alleluia. V. Glory be to the Father, and to the Son : and to the Holy Ghost. R7. Thou hast set Thy glory, O Lord. Alleluia, Alleluia.

V. God is gone up with a merry noise.

R7. And the Lord with the sound of the trumpet. Alleluia.

Sexts.

Ant. While He blessed them, He was parted from them : and carried up into heaven. Alleluia.

CHAPTER. Acts i.

HE being assembled together with them, commanded them that they should not depart from Jerusalem, but wait for the promise of the Father, which, saith He, ye have heard of Me.

R7. God is gone up with a merry noise. Alleluia, Alleluia. V. And the Lord with the sound of the trumpet. R7. Alleluia, Alleluia. V. Glory be to the Father, and to the Son : and to the Holy Ghost. R7. God is gone up with a merry noise. Alleluia, Alleluia.

V. Christ going up on high.

R7. Led captivity captive. Alleluia.

Nones.

Ant. While they beheld, He was taken up : and a cloud received Him into heaven. Alleluia.

CHAPTER. Acts i.

FOR John truly baptized with water; but ye shall be baptized with the Holy Ghost not many days hence.

R7. Christ going up on high. Alleluia, Alleluia. V. Led captivity captive. R7. Alleluia, Alleluia. V. Glory be to the Father, and to the Son : and to the Holy Ghost. R7.

Christ going up on high. Alleluia, Alleluia.

V. I ascend to My Father, and your Father.

R7. To My God, and your God. Alleluia.

Second Vespers.

Ant. Ye men of Galilee, why stand ye gazing up into heaven ? : This same Jesus, Which is taken up from you into heaven, shall so come. Alleluia, Alleluia.

Psalms of Sunday.

CHAPTER. Acts i.

THE former treatise have I made, O Theophilus, of all that Jesus began both to do and teach, until the day in which He was taken up, after that He through the Holy Ghost had given commandments unto the apostles whom He had chosen.

R7. Go ye into all the world and preach, saying; Alleluia : He that believeth and is baptized shall be saved. Alleluia, Alleluia, Alleluia. V. But the Comforter, Which is the Holy Ghost, Whom the Father will send in My Name, He shall teach you all things, and bring all things to your remembrance, whatsoever I have said unto you. R7. He that believeth and is baptized shall be saved. Alleluia, Alleluia, Alleluia. V. Glory be to the Father, and to the Son : and to the Holy Ghost. R7. Alleluia, Alleluia, Alleluia.

HYMN. *Æterne Rex altissime,* V. and R7., p. 177.

Ant. to Mag. O King of glory, Lord of strength, Who on this day ascendedst a conqueror above all heavens : leave us not orphans, but send us the promise of the Father, the Spirit of truth. Alleluia.

Collect as at Lauds.

The Hours are thus said, except on Sun-

day, till the Octave, except that the Ants. to Benedictus and Magnificat change daily, and that the Psalms at Lauds are said under one Ant., as below.

Friday.
𝕷𝖆𝖚𝖉𝖘.

Ant. to Psalms. Ye men of Galilee, why stand ye gazing up into heaven? : This same Jesus, Which is taken up from you into heaven, shall so come. Alleluia.

Ant. to Ben. Go ye into all the world, and preach the Gospel to every creature. Alleluia : He that believeth and is baptized shall be saved. Alleluia. But he that believeth not shall be damned. Alleluia.

Collect of Ascension Day.

𝖁𝖊𝖘𝖕𝖊𝖗𝖘.

Ant. to Mag. I will pray the Father : and He shall give you another Comforter. Alleluia.

No Memorials of the Cross, of S. Mary, or of All Saints, are said through this Octave.

If a Double Feast occur, it is kept with Memorial of the Ascension at both Vespers and Lauds. If on Sunday, it is kept with Memorial of the Sunday preceding that of the Ascension.

Saturday.
𝕷𝖆𝖚𝖉𝖘.

Ant. to Ben. If I go not away, the Comforter will not come unto you : but if I depart, I will send Him unto you. Alleluia.

SUNDAY AFTER THE ASCENSION.
𝖋𝖎𝖗𝖘𝖙 𝖁𝖊𝖘𝖕𝖊𝖗𝖘.

All of the Ascension, nothing of the Sunday, except

Ant. to Mag. After the Lord had spoken unto them, He was received up into heaven : and sat down at the right hand of God. Alleluia.

Collect as at Lauds, [or Collect of the Ascension.]

𝕷𝖆𝖚𝖉𝖘.

Psalms of Sunday, under this one

Ant. Ye men of Galilee, why stand ye gazing up into heaven? : This same Jesus, Which is taken up from you into heaven, shall so come. Alleluia, Alleluia.

CHAPTER. 1 S. Pet. iv.

BE ye therefore sober, and watch unto prayer. And above all things have fervent charity among yourselves : for charity shall cover the multitude of sins.

R̷. Thanks be to God.

Ant. to Ben. When the Comforter is come, Whom I will send unto you from the Father : even the Spirit of truth, Which proceedeth from the Father, He shall testify of Me. Alleluia.

COLLECT.

O GOD the King of glory, Who hast exalted Thine only Son Jesus Christ with great triumph unto Thy kingdom in heaven; we beseech Thee, leave us not comfortless; but send to us Thine Holy Ghost to comfort us, and exalt us unto the same place whither our Saviour Christ is gone before, Who liveth and reigneth with Thee and the Holy Ghost, one God, world without end. Amen.

[Or this,

ALMIGHTY, everlasting God, grant that our wills may alway be devoted to Thee, and that we may alway serve Thy Majesty with a pure heart; through our Lord Jesus Christ. Amen.]

MEMORIAL OF THE ASCENSION.

Ant. I ascend to My Father, and

your Father : to My God, and your God. Alleluia.

℣. Christ going up on high.

℟. Led captivity captive. Alleluia.

Collect of the Ascension.

All at Prime, Tierce, Sexts, and Nones, as on Ascension Day, except these Chapters and the Collect.

Tierce.

CHAPTER. 1 S. Pet. iv.

BUT the end of all things is at hand: be ye therefore sober, and watch unto prayer. And above all things have fervent charity among yourselves: for charity shall cover the multitude of sins.

Sexts.

CHAPTER. 1 S. Pet. iv.

USE hospitality one to another without grudging. As every man hath received the gift, even so minister the same one to another, as good stewards of the manifold grace of God.

Nones.

CHAPTER. 1 S. Pet. iv.

IF any man minister, let him do it as of the ability which God giveth : that God in all things may be glorified through Jesus Christ.

Second Vespers.

CHAPTER. 1 S. Pet. iv.

BE ye therefore sober, and watch unto prayer. And above all things have fervent charity among yourselves: for charity shall cover the multitude of sins.

Ant. to Mag. But these things have I told you : that when the time shall come, ye may remember that I told you of them. Alleluia.

Collect as at Lauds.

MEMORIAL OF THE ASCENSION.

Ant. O King of glory, Lord of strength, Who on this day ascendedst a conqueror above all heavens : leave us not orphans, but send us the promise of the Father, the Spirit of truth. Alleluia.

℣. God is gone up with a merry noise.

℟. And the Lord with the sound of the trumpet. Alleluia.

Collect of the Ascension.

Monday.

Lauds.

Ant. to Ben. And they went forth, and preached everywhere : the Lord working with them, and confirming the word with signs following. Alleluia, Alleluia.

Collect of the Ascension.

Vespers.

Ant. to Mag. Go ye into all the world, and preach the gospel to every creature. Alleluia : He that believeth and is baptized shall be saved. Alleluia. But he that believeth not shall be damned. Alleluia.

Tuesday.

Lauds.

Ant. to Ben. I will pray the Father : and He shall give you another Comforter. Alleluia.

Vespers.

Ant. to Mag. If I go not away, the Comforter will not come unto you : but if I depart, I will send Him unto you. Alleluia.

Wednesday.

Ant. to Benedictus *as on Monday.*

OCTAVE OF THE ASCENSION.

First Vespers.

All as on the Feast of the Ascension, and so at every Hour of this day; except that the Chapter at Second Vespers is said without R̃. *If it be held expedient, the Sunday Collect is used instead of that of the Ascension, but no other change shall be made.*

If a Double Feast occur in or on the Octave, the Office is to be of the Feast, with Memorial of the Season.

Friday.

Lauds.

Ant. to Psalms. Alleluia, Alleluia, Alleluia, Alleluia.

Psalms of the Feria.

This Ant. is used et every Hour. All else as on the previous Sunday, with Sunday Collect, and so at all the Hours.

Vespers.

Psalms of the Feria.

The rest as on the previous Sunday, as p. 170. Memorials of S. MARY and of ALL SAINTS are said at Lauds and Vespers.

WHITSUN EVE.

Lauds.

Ỹ. I ascend to My Father, and your Father.

R̃. To My God and your God. Alleluia.

Ant. Alleluia, Alleluia, Alleluia, Alleluia.

Psalms of Sunday.

CHAPTER. Acts xix.

AND it came to pass, that, while Apollos was at Corinth, Paul having passed through the upper coasts came to Ephesus: and finding certain disciples, he said unto them, Have ye received the Holy Ghost since ye believed? And they said unto him, We have not so much as heard whether there be any Holy Ghost.

HYMN. *Tu Christe nostrum gaudium,* Ỹ. *and* R̃., *p.* 178.

Ant. to Ben. If ye love Me, keep My commandments : Alleluia, Alleluia, Alleluia.

[COLLECT.

GRANT, we beseech Thee, Almighty God, that the brightness of Thy glory may shine upon us, and cause the illumination of the Holy Spirit to shed the light of Thy light upon them that are born again by Thy grace; through Jesus Christ our Lord, Who liveth and reigneth with Thee in the unity of the same Spirit, one God, world without end. Amen.]

This Collect is said at every Hour of this day. Memorials of S. MARY and of ALL SAINTS, as p. 170. At all the Hours are said Easter Alleluias (four Alleluias) as Ants. to Psalms, with R̃R̃. *and* ỸỸ. *of the Ascension.*

Tierce.

CHAPTER. Acts xix.

AND it came to pass, that, while Apollos was at Corinth, Paul having passed through the upper coasts came to Ephesus: and finding certain disciples, he said unto them, Have ye received the Holy Ghost since ye believed? And they said unto him, We have not so much as heard whether there be any Holy Ghost.

Sexts.

CHAPTER. Acts xix.

JOHN verily baptized with the baptism of repentance, saying unto the people, that they should believe on Him which should come after him, that is, on Christ Jesus.

Nones.

CHAPTER. Acts xix.

PAUL went into the synagogue, and spake boldly for the space of three months, disputing and persuading the things concerning the kingdom of God.

If any Feast occur on this day, its Office is wholly omitted, except it be a Double, in which case it is kept after Trinity Sunday.

WHITSUN DAY.

First Vespers.

Ant. to Psalms. Come, Holy Ghost, fill the hearts of Thy faithful people, and kindle in them the fire of Thy love : Who, through diversity of many tongues, hast gathered the Gentiles into the unity of the faith. Alleluia, Alleluia, Alleluia.

Psalms of the Feria.

CHAPTER. Acts ii.

WHEN the day of Pentecost was fully come, they were all with one accord in one place.

R7. The apostles did speak with other tongues. Alleluia : The wonderful works of God. Alleluia. V. They were all filled with the Holy Ghost, and began to speak. R7. The wonderful works of God. Alleluia. V. Glory be to the Father, and to the Son : and to the Holy Ghost. R7. Alleluia.

HYMN. *Jam Christus astra ascenderat.*

NOW Christ, ascending whence He came,
Had mounted o'er the starry frame ;
The Holy Ghost on man to pour,
As God the Father's promise bore.

The solemn time was drawing nigh,
Replete with heavenly mystery,
On seven days' sevenfold circles borne,
That first and blessed Whitsun-morn.

When the third hour shone all around,
There came a rushing mighty sound,
And told the apostles, while in prayer,
That, as 'twas promis'd, God was there.

Forth from the Father's light it came,
That beautiful and kindly flame :
To fill, with fervour of His word,
The spirits faithful to their Lord.

Thou once in every holy breast
Didst bid indwelling grace to rest :
This day our sins, we pray, release,
And in our time, O Lord, give peace.

To God the Father, God the Son,
And God the Spirit, praise be done ;
And Christ the Lord upon us pour
The Spirit's gift for evermore. Amen.

These two last verses are said at the end of all Hymns of this metre till Trinity : except Veni Creator, *which takes the last verse only.*

V. The Spirit of the Lord filleth the world.

R7. And That which containeth all things hath knowledge of the voice. Alleluia.

Ant. to Mag. If a man love Me, he will keep My words, and My Father will love him : and We will come unto him, and make Our abode with him. Alleluia.

COLLECT.

GOD, Who as at this time didst teach the hearts of Thy faithful people, by the sending to them the light of Thy Holy Spirit : grant us by the same Spirit to have a right judgment in all things, and evermore to rejoice in His holy comfort ; through the merits of Christ Jesus our Saviour, Who liveth and reigneth with Thee, in the unity of the same Spirit, one God, world without end. Amen.

Compline.

Ant. to Psalms. Alleluia, Alleluia, Alleluia, Alleluia.

CHAPTER. Jer. xiv., p. 68.

HYMN. *Salvator mundi Domine,* V. and R7., p. 67.

On the four days following is said instead,

HYMN. *Veni sancte Spiritus.*

COME, thou holy Paraclete,
And from Thy celestial seat,
Send Thy light and brilliancy :

Father of the poor, draw near,
Giver of all gifts, be here :
  Come, the soul's true radiancy :

Come, of Comforters the best,
Of the soul the sweetest guest,—
  Come in toil refreshingly :

Thou in labour rest most sweet,
Thou art shadow from the heat,
  Comfort in adversity.

O Thou Light, most pure and blest,
Shine within the inmost breast
  Of Thy faithful company.

Where Thou art not, man hath nought ;
Every holy deed and thought
  Comes from Thy divinity.

What is soiled, make Thou pure ;
What is wounded, work its cure ;
  What is parched, fructify ;

What is rigid, gently bend ;
What is frozen, warmly tend ;
  Strengthen what goes erringly.

Fill Thy faithful who confide
In Thy power to guard and guide,
  With Thy sevenfold mystery.

Here Thy grace and virtue send ;
Grant salvation in the end,
  And in heaven felicity. Amen. Alleluia.

Ant. to Nunc Dim. Alleluia. The Spirit the Comforter. Alleluia : shall teach you all things. Alleluia.

Lauds.

℣. When Thou lettest Thy breath go forth, they shall be made.
℟. And Thou shalt renew the face of the earth. Alleluia.

Psalms of Sunday.

Ant. 1. When the day of Pentecost was fully come : they were all with one accord in one place. Alleluia.

Ant. 2. The Spirit of the Lord : filleth the world. Alleluia.

Ant. 3. They were all filled with the Holy Ghost : and began to speak. Alleluia.

Ant. 4. O ye wells and all that move in the waters : say unto God, Alleluia.

Ant. 5. The apostles did speak with other tongues : the wonderful works of God. Alleluia, Alleluia, Alleluia.

CHAPTER. Acts ii.

WHEN the day of Pentecost was fully come, they were all with one accord in one place.
℟. Thanks be to God.

HYMN. *Impleta gaudent viscera.*

BREATHED on by God the Holy Ghost,
  The breasts, which He hath filled, rejoice,
And of His wondrous deeds they boast
In languages of diverse voice.

And to the men of every race,
Barbarian, Latin, and the Greek,
While wondering eyes upon them gaze,
In each one's dialect they speak.

Then Jewry, trusting not the sign,
And by malicious hate enticed,
Reproaches, as but full of wine,
The holy messengers of Christ.

But Peter hastes with mighty deeds,
Of power miraculous to teach,
And with the words of Joel pleads
Against the falsehood of their speech.

Thou once in every holy breast
Didst bid indwelling grace to rest :
This day our sins, we pray, release,
And in our time, O Lord, give peace.

To God the Father, God the Son,
And God the Spirit, praise be done ;
And Christ the Lord upon us pour
The Spirit's gift for evermore. Amen.

℣. The apostles did speak with other tongues.
℟. The wonderful works of God. Alleluia.

Ant. to Ben. Receive ye the Holy Ghost : whosoever sins ye remit, they are remitted unto them. Alleluia.

Prime.

Ant. When the day of Pentecost was fully come : they were all with one accord in one place. Alleluia.

The rest as on Ascension Day.

Tierce.

HYMN. *Veni Creator Spiritus.*

COME, Holy Ghost, our souls inspire,
  And lighten with celestial fire :
Thou the anointing Spirit art,
Who dost Thy sevenfold gifts impart.

Thy blessed unction from above
Is comfort, life, and fire of love :
Enable with perpetual light
The dulness of our blinded sight.

Anoint and cheer our soilèd face,
With the abundance of Thy grace;
Keep far our foes, give peace at home:
Where Thou art Guide, no ill can come.

Teach us to know the Father, Son,
And Thee, of both, to be but One;
That through the ages all along,
This may be our endless song:

To God the Father, God the Son,
And God the Spirit, praise be done;
And Christ the Lord upon us pour
The Spirit's gift for evermore. Amen.

This Hymn is said instead of Nunc
sancte nobis, *on Monday, Tuesday,
and Wednesday, in this week, but on
the other days the latter Hymn is said
as usual.*

Ant. The Spirit of the Lord :
filleth the world. Alleluia.

CHAPTER. Acts ii.

WHEN the day of Pentecost was
fully come, they were all with
one accord in one place.

R7. They were all filled with the
Holy Ghost. Alleluia, Alleluia. V.
And began to speak. R7. Alleluia,
Alleluia. V. Glory be to the Father,
and to the Son : and to the Holy
Ghost. R7. They were all filled with
the Holy Ghost. Alleluia, Alleluia.

V. The apostles did speak with
other tongues.

R7. The wonderful works of God.
Alleluia.

Sexts.

Ant. They were all filled with the
Holy Ghost : and began to speak.
Alleluia.

CHAPTER. Acts ii.

AND suddenly there came a sound
from heaven, as of a rushing
mighty wind, and it filled all the
house where they were sitting.

R7. The apostles did speak with
other tongues. Alleluia, Alleluia.
V. The wonderful works of God.
R7. Alleluia, Alleluia. V. Glory be
to the Father, and to the Son : and to
the Holy Ghost. R7. The apostles

did speak with other tongues. Alleluia, Alleluia.

R7. The Spirit of the Lord filleth
the world.

R7. And That which containeth all
things hath knowledge of the voice.
Alleluia.

Nones.

Ant. The apostles did speak with
other tongues : the wonderful works
of God. Alleluia.

CHAPTER. Acts ii.

AND there appeared unto them
cloven tongues, like as of fire,
and It sat upon each of them.

R7. The Spirit of the Lord filleth
the world. Alleluia, Alleluia. V.
And That which containeth all things
hath knowledge of the voice. R7.
Alleluia, Alleluia. V. Glory be to
the Father, and to the Son : and to
the Holy Ghost. R7. The Spirit of
the Lord filleth the world. Alleluia,
Alleluia.

V. When Thou lettest Thy breath
go forth they shall be made.

R7. And Thou shalt renew the
face of the earth. Alleluia.

Second Vespers.

Ant. When the day of Pentecost
was fully come : they were all with
one accord in one place. Alleluia.

Psalms of Sunday.

CHAPTER. Acts ii.

THE multitude came together, and
were confounded, because that
every man heard them speak in his
own language.

R7. The Holy Ghost proceeding
from the throne, invisibly entered
the hearts of the apostles, with a
new token of hallowing : that in
their mouths all manner of new
tongues should spring up. Alleluia.
V. The fire of God came upon them,
not burning, but enlightening; and

bestowed on them gifts and graces. Ry. That in their mouths all manner of new tongues should spring up. V. Glory be to the Father, and to the Son : and to the Holy Ghost. Ry. Alleluia.

HYMN. *Beata nobis gaudia.*

BLEST joys for mighty wonders wrought
The year's revolving orb has brought,
What time the Holy Ghost in flame
Upon the Lord's disciples came.

The quivering fire their heads bedewed,
In cloven tongues' similitude,
That eloquent their words might be,
And fervid all their charity.

In varying tongues the Lord they praised,
The gathering people stood amazed ;
And whom the Comforter Divine
Inspired, they mocked as full of wine.

These things were done in type to-day,
When Easter-tide had worn away,
The number told which once set free
The captive at the jubilee.

Thy servants, falling on their face,
Beseech Thy mercy, God of grace,
To send us from Thy heavenly seat
The blessings of the Paraclete.

Thou once in every holy breast
Didst bid indwelling grace to rest :
This day our sins, we pray, release,
And in our time, O Lord, give peace.

To God the Father, God the Son,
And God the Spirit, praise be done ;
And Christ the Lord upon us pour
The Spirit's gift for evermore. Amen.

V. The Spirit of the Lord filleth the world.

Ry. And That which containeth all things hath knowledge of the voice. Alleluia.

This Hymn, V., and Ry. are said daily till the First Vespers of Trinity Sunday.

Ant. to Mag. To-day are fulfilled the days of Pentecost; to-day the Holy Ghost appeared in fire to the disciples, and bestowed on them gifts of graces : He sent them into all the world to preach and to testify; he that believeth and is baptized shall be saved. Alleluia.

Collect as at Lauds.

———

WHITSUN MONDAY.

Lauds.

Ant. When the day of Pentecost was fully come : they were all with one accord in one place. Alleluia.

Psalms of Sunday.

CHAPTER. Acts ii.

AND suddenly there came a sound from heaven as of a rushing mighty wind, and it filled all the house where they were sitting.

Ry. Thanks be to God.

HYMN. *Impleta gaudent viscera,* V. and Ry., p. 184.

Ant. to Ben. God so loved the world, that He gave His Only-begotten Son : that whosoever believeth in Him should not perish, but have everlasting life. Alleluia.

Ant. to Benedictus *changes daily,* [*also the Collect*].

Collect for Whitsun Day.

[*Or this,*

GOD, Who didst bestow the Holy Spirit on Thine Apostles : grant to Thy people the fruit of their devout petitions, that they to whom Thou hast given faith may also receive peace ; through Jesus Christ Thine only Son our Lord, Who liveth and reigneth with Thee, in the unity of the same Spirit, ever one God, world without end. Amen.

This Collect is said at every Hour on this day only ;] *the Ants., RyRy., and VV., as on Whitsun Day ; and this order is observed through the week, each day having its own Collect and Ants. to Benedictus and Magnificat; the Chapters at the Little Hours being said as on this day. The Ry. is omitted at Vespers.*

Tierce.

CHAPTER. Acts ii.

AND suddenly there came a sound from heaven as of a rushing mighty wind, and it filled all the house where they were sitting.

Sexts.

CHAPTER. Acts ii.

AND there appeared unto them cloven tongues, like as of fire, and It sat upon each of them.

Nones.

CHAPTER. Acts ii.

AND they were all filled with the Holy Ghost, and began to speak with other tongues, as the Spirit gave them utterance.

Vespers.

Ant. to Mag. For God sent not His Son into the world to condemn the world : but that the world through Him might be saved. Alleluia.

Collect as at Lauds.

WHITSUN TUESDAY.

Lauds.

Ant. to Ben. Verily, verily, I say unto you, He that entereth not by the door into the sheep-fold, but climbeth up some other way, the same is a thief and a robber : but he that entereth in by the door is the shepherd of the sheep. Alleluia.

[COLLECT.

LET the might of Thy Holy Spirit be present with us, we beseech Thee, O Lord, that it may mercifully purge our hearts, and guard us from all adversities; through Jesus Christ our Lord, Who liveth and reigneth with Thee, in the unity of the same Spirit, one God, world without end. Amen.]

Vespers.

Ant. to Mag. I am the Door, saith the Lord : by Me if any man enter in, he shall be saved, and shall go in and out, and find pasture. Alleluia.

Collect as at Lauds.

Wednesday.

Lauds.

Ant. to Ben. Verily, verily, I say unto you : He that believeth on Me hath everlasting life. Alleluia, Alleluia.

[COLLECT.

WE beseech Thee, O Lord, let the Comforter Which proceedeth from Thee lighten our hearts, and lead us into all truth, according to the promise of Thy Son, Who liveth and reigneth with Thee, in the unity of the same Spirit, ever one God, world without end. Amen.]

Vespers.

Ant. to Mag. I am the living Bread which came down from heaven : if any man eat of this Bread he shall live for ever; and the Bread that I will give is My Flesh, which I will give for the life of the world. Alleluia, Alleluia.

Collect as at Lauds.

Thursday.

Lauds.

Ant. to Ben. Jesus called His twelve disciples together, and gave them power and authority over all devils, and to cure diseases : aud He sent them to preach the kingdom of God, and to heal the sick. Alleluia, Alleluia.

[COLLECT.

GRANT, we beseech Thee, Almighty and merciful God, that Thy Holy Spirit, coming into our hearts, may make them fit temples for His glory to inhabit; through our Lord Jesus Christ, Who liveth and reigneth with Thee, in the unity of the same Spirit, ever one God, world without end. Amen.]

Vespers.

Ant. to Mag. The twelve departed, and went through the towns, preaching the gospel, and healing everywhere. Alleluia, Alleluia.

Collect as at Lauds.

Friday.

𝕷𝖆𝖚𝖉𝖘.

Ant. to Ben. And it came to pass on a certain day, as He was teaching, that there were Pharisees and doctors of the law sitting by, which were come out of every town of Galilee, and Judea, and Jerusalem : and the power of the Lord was present to heal them. Alleluia, Alleluia.

[COLLECT.

GRANT to Thy Church, we beseech Thee, O merciful God, that being gathered together in the Holy Spirit, it may be vexed by no incursions of the enemy ; through our Lord Jesus Christ, Who liveth and reigneth with Thee, in the unity of the same Spirit, ever one God, world without end. Amen.]

Ant. to Mag. And the sick of the palsy took up that whereon he lay, glorifying God : and they were all amazed, and glorified God. Alleluia.

Collect as at Lauds.

Saturday.

𝕷𝖆𝖚𝖉𝖘.

Ant. to Ben. Now when the sun was setting, all they that had any sick with divers diseases brought them unto Jesus : and He laid His hands on every one of them, and healed them. Alleluia.

[COLLECT.

WE beseech Thee, O Lord, mercifully to pour Thy Spirit into our hearts ; that, as we are created by His wisdom, so we may be governed by His providence ; through our Lord Jesus Christ, Who liveth and reigneth with Thee, in the unity of the same Spirit, ever one God, world without end. Amen.]

When the septiform Feast of Pentecost has been completed in seven days, on the eighth day, that is, the first Sunday after Whitsun Day, shall be held full service of the Holy Trinity.

TRINITY SUNDAY.

𝕱𝖎𝖗𝖘𝖙 𝖁𝖊𝖘𝖕𝖊𝖗𝖘.

Ant. 1. Glory be to Thee, co-equal Trinity, One God before all worlds began : and now and ever, and to ages of ages.

Psalm cxiii. *Laudate pueri*, p. 46.

Ant. 2. Praise and perpetual glory be to God, the Father, the Son, and the Holy Ghost : now and ever, and to ages of ages.

Psalm cxvii. *Laudate Dominum*, p. 50.

Ant. 3. Glory and praise resound from the lips of all to the Father, to the Only-begotten Son : and like praise for ever to the Holy Ghost.

Psalm cxlvi. *Lauda, anima mea*, p. 63.

Ant. 4. For ever from all lips let praise resound to God the Father, and the Only-begotten Son, and Thee, O Holy Ghost.

Psalm cxlvii. *Laudate Dominum*, p. 64.

Ant. 5. Of Whom, and through Whom, and in Whom, are all things : to Him be glory for ever.

Psalm cxlvii. 12. *Lauda Hierusalem,* p. 64.

CHAPTER. II Cor. xiii.

THE grace of our Lord Jesus Christ, and the love of God, and the communion of the Holy Ghost, be with you all. Amen.

Ry. Blessing and honour, and glory and power, be to the Trinity in Unity, and to the Unity in Trinity : to everlasting ages. Ȳ. Light unfading be the perpetual glory of the Trinity in Unity. Ry. To everlasting ages. Ȳ. Glory be to the Father, and to the-

Son : and to the Holy Ghost. ℣. To everlasting ages.

HYMN. *Adesto Sancta Trinitas.*

BE present, Holy Trinity;
Like splendour, and one Deity :
Of things above, and things below,
Beginning that no end shall know.

Thee all the armies of the sky
Adore, and laud, and magnify :
While Nature, in her triple frame,
For ever sanctifies Thy Name.

And we, too, thanks and homage pay,
Thine own adoring flock to-day ;
O join to that celestial song
The praises of our suppliant throng!

Light, sole and one, we Thee confess,
With triple praise we rightly bless ;
Alpha and Omega we own,
With every spirit round Thy throne.

To Thee, O Unbegotten One,
And Thee, O Sole-begotten Son,
And Thee, O Holy Ghost, we raise
Our equal and eternal praise. Amen.

℣. Let us bless the Father, the Son, and the Holy Ghost.

℞. Let us praise and exalt Him above all for ever.

Ant. to Mag. Thanks be to Thee, O God; thanks be to Thee, One Very Trinity : One and Supreme Deity, Holy and One Unity.

COLLECT.

ALMIGHTY and Everlasting God, Who hast given unto us Thy servants grace by the confession of a true faith to acknowledge the glory of the Eternal Trinity, and in the power of the Divine Majesty to worship the Unity ; we beseech Thee, that Thou wouldest keep us stedfast in this faith, and evermore defend us from all adversities, Who livest and reignest, One God, world without end. Amen.

Compline.

Ant. to Psalms. Have mercy upon me : and hearken unto my prayer.

HYMN. *Salvator mundi Domine,* p. 67.

Ant. to Nunc Dim. Lord, grant us Thy light : that being rid of the darkness of our hearts, we may come to the true Light, which is Christ.

Compline is thus said for this and the three following days.

Lauds.

℣. Blessed art Thou, O Lord, in the firmament of heaven.

℞. And above all to be praised and glorified for ever.

Psalms of Sunday.

Ant. 1. O Holy and blessed and glorious Trinity : Father, and Son, and Holy Ghost. ℣. To Thee be praise, to Thee be glory, to Thee be thanksgiving.

Ant. 2. O Holy and blessed and glorious Trinity : Father, and Son, and Holy Ghost. ℣. Have mercy, have mercy, have mercy upon us.

Ant. 3. O Very, supreme, everlasting Trinity : Father, and Son, and Holy Ghost. ℣. To Thee be praise, to Thee be glory, to Thee be thanksgiving.

Ant. 4. O Very, supreme, everlasting Trinity : Father, and Son, and Holy Ghost. ℣. Have mercy, have mercy, have mercy upon us.

Ant. 5. Thee duly praise, Thee adore : Thee glorify, all Thy creatures, O blessed Trinity. ℣. To Thee be praise, to Thee be glory, to Thee be thanksgiving.

CHAPTER. Rom. xi.

O THE depth of the riches both of the wisdom and knowledge of God! For of Him and through Him, and to Him, are all things : to Whom be glory for ever. Amen.

HYMN. *O Pater sancte, mitis atque pie.*

O HOLY Father, merciful and loving ;
O Jesu Christ, the only Son Eternal ;
O Spirit blest, our spirits sweetly moving,
One God supernal.

O Trine, thrice hallowed, Unity unshaken,
Godhead most mighty ; good, all goodness giving,

Light of the Angels, health of the forsaken,
    Hope of all living.
Thee, all things worship, which Thou hast
    created :
All Thy creation, Lord, in Thee rejoices.
We too, will worship Thee with hearts elated;
    O hear our voices.
Glory to Thee, Whose might all might ex-
    celleth,
One in Three Persons, Thee Whom nought
    can sever,
Thee, song beseemeth, Thee, with Whom
    praise dwelleth,
    Ever and ever. Amen.

℣. Blessed be the Name of the Lord.

℟. From this time forth for ever-more.

Ant. to Ben. Blessed be the Creator and Preserver of all things : the Holy and Undivided Trinity, now and ever, and to ages of ages.

Prime.

Ant. O Holy, blessed, and glorious Trinity, Father, and Son, and Holy Ghost : to Thee be praise, to Thee be glory, to Thee be thanksgiving.

Ps. liv. Deus in nomine, Ps. cxix. Beati *and* Retribue, Ps. Quicunque, *all said under this Ant. ℟. as on the Ascension.*

Tierce.

Ant. O Holy, blessed and glorious Trinity, Father, and Son, and Holy Ghost : have mercy, have mercy, have mercy upon us.

CHAPTER. Rom. xi.

O THE depth of the riches both of the wisdom and knowledge of God! For of Him and through Him, and to Him, are all things ; to Whom be glory for ever. Amen.

℟. Let us bless the Father, the Son, and the Holy Ghost. Alleluia, Alleluia. ℣. Let us praise and exalt Him above all for ever. ℟. Alleluia, Alleluia. ℣. Glory be to the Father, and to the Son : and to the Holy Ghost. ℟. Let us bless the Father,

the Son, and the Holy Ghost. Al-leluia, Alleluia.

℣. Blessed art Thou, O Lord, in the firmament of heaven.

℟. And above all to be praised and glorified for ever.

Sexts.

Ant. O Very, supreme, everlasting Trinity : Father, and Son, and Holy Ghost, to Thee be praise, to Thee be glory, to Thee be thanksgiving.

CHAPTER. i S. John v.

THERE are Three that bear record in heaven, the Father, the Word, and the Holy Ghost : and these Three are One.

℟. Blessed art Thou, O Lord, in the firmament of heaven. Alleluia, Alleluia. ℣. And above all to be praised and glorified for ever. ℟. Alleluia, Alleluia. ℣. Glory be to the Father, and to the Son : and to the Holy Ghost. ℟. Blessed art Thou, O Lord, in the firmament of heaven. Alleluia, Alleluia.

℣. By the Word of the Lord were the heavens made.

℟. And all the hosts of them by the Breath of His mouth.

Nones.

Ant. Thee duly praise, Thee adore, Thee glorify all Thy creatures, O blessed Trinity : To Thee be praise, to Thee be glory, to Thee be thanks-giving.

CHAPTER. Eph. iv.

THERE is one Lord, one faith, one baptism, one God and Father of all, Who is above all, and through all, and in you all.

℟. By the Word of the Lord were the heavens made. Alleluia, Alleluia. ℣. And all the host of them by the Breath of His mouth. ℟. Alleluia, Alleluia. ℣. Glory be to the Father, and to the Son : and to the Holy

Ghost. ℟. By the Word of the Lord were the heavens made. Alleluia, Alleluia.

℣. Blessed be the Name of the Lord.

℟. From this time forth for evermore.

Second Vespers.

Ants. of Lauds.

Psalms of Sunday.

CHAPTER. Rom. xi.

O THE depth of the riches both of the wisdom and knowledge of God! For of Him, and through Him, and to Him are all things: to Whom be glory for ever. Amen.

℟. Let us bless the Father, and the Son, and the Holy Ghost. Alleluia, Alleluia. ℣. Praise Him and magnify Him for ever. ℟. Alleluia, Alleluia. ℣. Glory be to the Father, and to the Son : and to the Holy Ghost. ℟. Let us bless the Father, and the Son, and the Holy Ghost. Alleluia, Alleluia.

HYMN. *Adesto Sancta Trinitas,* ℣. *and* ℟*., p. 189.*

Ant. to Mag. Thee, O God, Father Unbegotten, Thee, Son Only-begotten, Thee, Holy Ghost, Comforter, Holy and undivided Trinity : with our whole heart and with our mouth we confess, and praise, and bless; to Thee be glory for ever.

Collect as at First Vespers.

Except a Double Feast, or the vigil of S. John Baptist occur, this same Office is said on the next three days in commemoration of the Trinity.

———

Wednesday.

First Vespers

OF THE FESTIVAL OF

CORPUS CHRISTI.

See Office of Blessed Sacrament in Common of Holy Days, p. 206.

If any Double Feast occur on this Wednesday a Memorial of it is made at the First Vespers of Corpus Christi: if any such occur on the feast itself, it is transferred to the first day in the Octave not similarly occupied. The Office of Corpus Christi is said throughout the Octave, even on Sunday, except a Double Feast occur, in which case the feast is kept, with Memorial of Corpus Christi.

———

FIRST SUNDAY AFTER TRINITY.

(SUNDAY IN THE OCTAVE OF CORPUS CHRISTI.)

The Office is wholly of the festival, with Memorial of Sunday at both Vespers and at Lauds.

First Vespers.

Ant. And the child Samuel ministered unto the Lord before Eli : and the word of the Lord was precious in those days.

℣. Let our evening prayer come up before Thee, O Lord.

℟. And let Thy mercy come down on us.

COLLECT.

O GOD, the Strength of all them that put their trust in Thee; mercifully accept our prayers; and because through the weakness of our mortal nature we can do no good thing without Thee, grant us the help of Thy grace, that in keeping of Thy commandments we may please Thee, both in will and deed; through Jesus Christ our Lord. Amen.

Lauds.

Ant. Father Abraham, have mercy on me : and send Lazarus that he may dip the tip of his finger in water, and cool my tongue.

℣. The Lord is King.

℟. He hath put on glorious apparel. Alleluia.

Collect as at First Vespers.

Second Vespers.

Ant. Son, remember that thou in thy lifetime receivedst thy good things : and likewise Lazarus evil things.

℣. Lord, let my prayer be set forth.

℟. In Thy sight as the incense.

Collect as at First Vespers.

After the Octave of Corpus Christi, all as in the Psalter at every Hour.

———

Second Sunday after Trinity.

First Vespers.

Ant. to Mag. And all Israel from Dan even unto Beersheba knew : that Samuel was established to be a prophet of the Lord.

Collect.

O LORD, Who never failest to help and govern them whom Thou dost bring up in Thy stedfast fear and love; keep us, we beseech Thee, under the protection of Thy good providence, and make us to have a perpetual fear and love of Thy holy Name; through Jesus Christ our Lord. Amen.

Lauds.

Ant. to Ben. A certain man made a great supper, and bade many : and sent his servant at supper-time to say to them that were bidden, Come, for all things are now ready. Alleluia.

Second Vespers.

Ant. to Mag. Go out quickly into the streets and lanes of the city : and bring in hither the poor, and the maimed, and the halt, and the blind, that my house may be filled. Alleluia.

———

Third Sunday after Trinity.

First Vespers.

Ant. to Mag. So David prevailed over the Philistine with a sling and with a stone : in the Name of the Lord.

Collect.

O LORD, we beseech Thee, mercifully to hear us; and grant that we, to whom Thou hast given an hearty desire to pray, may by Thy mighty aid be defended and comforted in all dangers and adversities; through Jesus Christ our Lord. Amen.

Lauds.

Ant. to Ben. What man of you having an hundred sheep, if he lose one of them : doth not leave the ninety and nine in the wilderness, and go after that which is lost, until he find it ? Alleluia.

Second Vespers.

Ant. to Mag. What woman having ten pieces of silver, if she lose one piece : doth not light a candle, and sweep the house, and seek diligently till she find it ? Alleluia.

———

Fourth Sunday after Trinity.

First Vespers.

Ant. to Mag. Ye mountains of Gilboa, let there be no dew, neither let there be rain upon you; for there the shield of the mighty is vilely cast away, the shield of Saul, as though he had not been anointed with oil : How are the mighty fallen in the midst of the battle! O Jonathan, thou wast slain in thine high places. Saul and Jonathan were lovely and pleasant in their lives, and in their deaths they were not divided.

COLLECT.

O GOD, the protector of all that trust in Thee, without Whom nothing is strong, nothing is holy; increase and multiply upon us Thy mercy; that, Thou being our ruler and guide, we may so pass through things temporal, that we finally lose not the things eternal; grant this, O heavenly Father, for Jesus Christ's sake our Lord. Amen.

Lauds.

Ant. to Ben. Be ye therefore merciful : as your Father also is merciful, saith the Lord.

Second Vespers.

Ant. to Mag. Judge not, and ye shall not be judged : for with the same measure that ye mete withal, it shall be measured to you again.

———

FIFTH SUNDAY AFTER TRINITY.

First Vespers.

Ant. to Mag. I beseech Thee, O Lord, do away the iniquity of Thy servant : for I have done very foolishly.

COLLECT.

GRANT, O Lord, we beseech Thee, that the course of this world may be so peaceably ordered by Thy governance, that Thy Church may joyfully serve Thee in all godly quietness; through Jesus Christ our Lord. Amen.

Lauds.

Ant. to Ben. And Jesus entered into one of the ships : and sat down, and taught the people. Alleluia.

Second Vespers.

Ant. to Mag. Master, we have toiled all the night, and have taken nothing : nevertheless, at Thy word I will let down the net.

SIXTH SUNDAY AFTER TRINITY.

First Vespers.

Ant. to Mag. Zadok the priest and Nathan the prophet, anointed Solomon king in Gihon : and all the people came up and rejoiced, and said, God save king Solomon.

COLLECT.

O GOD, Who hast prepared for them that love Thee such good things as pass man's understanding; pour into our hearts such love towards Thee, that we, loving Thee above all things, may obtain Thy promises, which exceed all that we can desire; through Jesus Christ our Lord. Amen.

Lauds.

Ant. to Ben. Ye have heard that it was said by them of old time, Thou shalt not kill : and whosoever shall kill, shall be in danger of the judgment.

Second Vespers.

Ant. to Mag. If thou bring thy gift to the altar, and there rememberest that thy brother hath ought against thee : leave there thy gift before the altar, and go thy way, first be reconciled to thy brother, and then come and offer thy gift. Alleluia.

———

SEVENTH SUNDAY AFTER TRINITY.

First Vespers.

Ant. to Mag. When the Lord would take up Elijah into heaven by a whirlwind, Elisha cried : My father, my father, the chariot of Israel and the horsemen thereof.

COLLECT.

LORD of all power and might, Who art the author and giver of all good things; graft in our hearts the love of Thy Name, increase in us true religion, nourish us with all goodness, and of Thy great mercy keep us in the same; through Jesus Christ our Lord. Amen.

Lauds.

Ant. to Ben. I have compassion on the multitude, because they have now been with Me three days, and have nothing to eat : and if I send them away fasting to their own houses, they will faint by the way. Alleluia.

Second Vespers.

Ant. to Mag. And Jesus took the seven loaves, and gave thanks, and brake, and gave to His disciples to set before them : and they did set them before the people. Alleluia.

EIGHTH SUNDAY AFTER TRINITY.

First Vespers.

Ant. to Mag. And Jehoash did that which was right in the sight of the Lord : all his days, wherein Jehoiada the priest instructed him.

COLLECT.

O GOD, Whose never-failing providence ordereth all things both in heaven and earth; we humbly beseech Thee to put away from us all hurtful things, and to give us those things which be profitable for us; through Jesus Christ our Lord. Amen.

Lauds.

Ant. to Ben. Beware of false prophets, which come to you in sheep's clothing : but inwardly they are ravening wolves. Ye shall know them by their fruits.

Second Vespers.

Ant. to Mag. Not every one that saith unto Me, Lord, Lord, shall enter into the kingdom of heaven : but he that doeth the will of My Father Which is in heaven. Alleluia.

NINTH SUNDAY AFTER TRINITY.

First Vespers.

Ant. to Mag. I beseech Thee, O Lord, remember now, how I have walked before Thee in truth and with a perfect heart : and have done that which is good in Thy sight.

COLLECT.

GRANT to us, Lord, we beseech Thee, the spirit to think and do always such things as be rightful; that we, who cannot do any thing that is good without Thee, may by Thee be enabled to live according to Thy will; through Jesus Christ our Lord. Amen.

Lauds.

Ant. to Ben. And his lord called him, and said unto him, How is it that I hear this of thee? : Give an account of thy stewardship. Alleluia.

Second Vespers.

Ant. to Mag. What shall I do? for my lord taketh away from me the stewardship: I cannot dig, to beg I am ashamed : I am resolved what to do, that, when I am put out of the stewardship, they may receive me into their houses.

TENTH SUNDAY AFTER TRINITY.

First Vespers.

Ant. to Mag. Wisdom hath builded her house, she hath hewn out her seven pillars : she hath sent forth her maidens, she crieth upon the highest places of the city.

COLLECT.

LET Thy merciful ears, O Lord, be open to the prayers of Thy humble servants; and that they may obtain their petitions, make them to ask such things as shall please Thee; through Jesus Christ our Lord. Amen.

Lauds.

Ant. to Ben. And when He was come near, He beheld the city, and wept over it, saying, If thou hadst known! : For the days shall come upon thee, that thine enemies shall cast a trench about thee, and compass thee round, and keep thee in on every side, and shall lay thee even with the ground, because thou knewest not the time of thy visitation. Alleluia.

Second Vespers.

Ant. to Mag. It is written, My house is the house of prayer : but ye have made it a den of thieves. And He taught daily in the temple.

———

ELEVENTH SUNDAY AFTER TRINITY.

First Vespers.

Ant. to Mag. I dwell in high places : and my throne is in a cloudy pillar.

COLLECT.

O GOD, Who declarest Thy almighty power most chiefly in shewing mercy and pity; mercifully grant unto us such a measure of Thy grace, that we, running the way of Thy commandments, may obtain Thy gracious promises, and be made partakers of Thy heavenly treasure; through Jesus Christ our Lord. Amen.

Lauds.

Ant. to Ben. Two men went up into the temple to pray; the one a Pharisee, and the other a publican : This man went down to his house justified rather than the other. Alleluia.

Second Vespers.

Ant. to Mag. And the publican, standing afar off, would not lift up so much as his eyes unto heaven, but smote upon his breast, saying : God be merciful to me a sinner.

TWELFTH SUNDAY AFTER TRINITY.

First Vespers.

Ant. to Mag. All wisdom cometh from the Lord : and is with Him for ever.

COLLECT.

A LMIGHTY and everlasting God, Who art always more ready to hear than we to pray, and art wont to give more than either we desire, or deserve: pour down upon us the abundance of Thy mercy; forgiving us those things whereof our conscience is afraid, and giving us those good things which we are not worthy to ask, but through the merits and mediation of Jesus Christ, Thy Son, our Lord. Amen.

Lauds.

Ant. to Ben. Jesus, departing from the coasts of Tyre and Sidon, came unto the sea of Galilee : through the midst of the coasts of Decapolis. Alleluia.

Second Vespers.

Ant. to Mag. He hath done all things well : He maketh both the deaf to hear, and the dumb to speak.

———

THIRTEENTH SUNDAY AFTER TRINITY.

First Vespers.

Ant. to Mag. My son, keep thy father's commandment, and forsake not the law of thy mother : bind them continually upon thy heart.

COLLECT.

A LMIGHTY and merciful God, of Whose only gift it cometh that Thy faithful people do unto Thee true and laudable service; grant, we beseech Thee, that we may so faithfully serve Thee in this life, that we fail not finally to attain Thy heavenly promises; through the merits of Jesus Christ our Lord. Amen.

Lauds.

Ant. to Ben. A certain man went down from Jerusalem to Jericho, and fell among thieves : which stripped him of his raiment, and wounded him, and departed, leaving him half dead.

Second Vespers.

Ant. to Mag. Which now of these three, thinkest thou, was neighbour unto him that fell among the thieves?: And he said, He that shewed mercy on him. Go, and do thou likewise. Alleluia.

FOURTEENTH SUNDAY AFTER TRINITY.

First Vespers.

Ant. to Mag. In all this, Job sinned not with his lips : nor charged God foolishly.

COLLECT.

ALMIGHTY and everlasting God, give unto us the increase of faith, hope, and charity; and, that we may obtain that which Thou dost promise, make us to love that which Thou dost command; through Jesus Christ our Lord. Amen.

Lauds.

Ant. to Ben. And as He entered into a certain village, there met Him ten men that were lepers, which stood afar off : and they lifted up their voices, and said, Jesus, Master, have mercy on us.

Second Vespers.

Ant. to Mag. Were there not ten cleansed? but where are the nine? There are not found that returned to give glory to God, save this stranger : Arise, go thy way, thy faith hath made thee whole. Alleluia.

FIFTEENTH SUNDAY AFTER TRINITY.

First Vespers.

Ant. to Mag. Remember not, Lord, our offences, nor the offences of our forefathers : neither take Thou vengeance on our sins.

COLLECT.

KEEP, we beseech Thee, O Lord, Thy Church with Thy perpetual mercy; and, because the frailty of man without Thee cannot but fall, keep us ever by Thy help from all things hurtful, and lead us to all things profitable to our salvation; through Jesus Christ our Lord. Amen.

Lauds.

Ant. to Ben. Take no thought, saying, What shall we eat? or what shall we drink? : for your heavenly Father knoweth that ye have need of all these things. Alleluia.

Second Vespers.

Ant. to Mag. Seek ye first the kingdom of God, and His righteousness : and all these things shall be added unto you. Alleluia.

SIXTEENTH SUNDAY AFTER TRINITY.

First Vespers.

Ant. to Mag. But the Almighty Lord hath disappointed them : by the hand of a woman.

COLLECT.

O LORD, we beseech Thee, let Thy continual pity cleanse and defend Thy Church; and, because it cannot continue in safety without Thy succour, preserve it evermore by Thy help and goodness; through Jesus Christ our Lord. Amen.

Lauds.

Ant. to Ben. Jesus went into a city called Nain : and behold, there was a dead man carried out, the only son of his mother.

Second Vespers.

Ant. to Mag. And there came a fear on all, and they glorified God, saying : That a great prophet is risen up among us, and that God hath visited His people.

SEVENTEENTH SUNDAY AFTER TRINITY.

First Vespers.

Ant. to Mag. O Lord, Lord, the King Almighty, the whole world is in Thy power : and there is none that can gainsay Thee.

COLLECT.

LORD, we pray Thee, that Thy grace may always prevent and follow us, and make us continually to be given to all good works; through Jesus Christ our Lord. Amen.

Lauds.

Ant. to Ben. And Jesus spake unto the lawyers and Pharisees, saying, Is it lawful to heal on the Sabbath-day? : And they held their peace. And He took him, and healed him, and let him go.

Second Vespers.

Ant. to Mag. When thou art bidden to a wedding; go and sit down in the lowest room; that, when he that bade thee cometh, he may say unto thee, Friend, go up higher : then shalt thou have worship in the presence of them that sit at meat with thee. Alleluia.

EIGHTEENTH SUNDAY AFTER TRINITY.

First Vespers.

Ant. to Mag. God open your hearts in His law and commandments : and send you peace.

COLLECT.

LORD, we beseech Thee, grant Thy people grace to withstand the temptations of the world, the flesh, and the devil, and with pure hearts and minds to follow Thee the only God; through Jesus Christ our Lord. Amen.

Lauds.

Ant. to Ben. Master, which is the great commandment in the law? : Jesus said unto him, Thou shalt love the Lord thy God with all thy heart. Alleluia.

Second Vespers.

Ant. to Mag. What think ye of Christ? whose Son is He? They say unto Him, The Son of David : He saith unto them, How then doth David in spirit call Him Lord, saying, The Lord said unto my Lord, Sit Thou on My right hand?

NINETEENTH SUNDAY AFTER TRINITY.

First Vespers.

Ant. to Mag. When the sun shone upon the shields of gold : the mountains glistered therewith.

COLLECT.

O GOD, forasmuch as without Thee we are not able to please Thee; mercifully grant, that Thy Holy Spirit may in all things direct and rule our hearts; through Jesus Christ our Lord. Amen.

Lauds.

Ant. to Ben. Jesus said unto the sick of the palsy : Son, be of good cheer, thy sins be forgiven thee.

Second Vespers.

Ant. to Mag. But when the multitude saw it, they marvelled, and glorified God : Who had given such power unto men.

TWENTIETH SUNDAY AFTER TRINITY.

First Vespers.

Ant. to Mag. And all Israel made great lamentation for Judas, saying : How is the valiant man fallen, that delivered Israel !

COLLECT.

O ALMIGHTY and most merciful God, of Thy bountiful goodness keep us, we beseech Thee, from all things that may hurt us; that we, being ready both in body and soul, may cheerfully accomplish those things that Thou wouldest have done; through Jesus Christ our Lord. Amen.

Lauds.

Ant. to Ben. Tell them which are bidden, Behold, I have prepared my dinner : come unto the marriage. Alleluia.

Second Vespers.

Ant. to Mag. The wedding is ready, but they who were bidden were not worthy : go ye therefore into the highways, and as many as ye shall find, bid to the marriage. Alleluia.

TWENTY-FIRST SUNDAY AFTER TRINITY.

First Vespers.

Ant. to Mag. The Lord hear your prayers, and be at one with you : and never forsake you in time of trouble.

COLLECT.

GRANT, we beseech Thee, merciful Lord, to Thy faithful people pardon and peace, that they may be cleansed from all their sins, and serve Thee with a quiet mind: through Jesus Christ our Lord. Amen.

Lauds.

Ant. to Ben. There was a certain nobleman, whose son was sick at Capernaum : when he heard that Jesus was come out of Judæa into Galilee, he besought Him that He would come down and heal his son.

Second Vespers.

Ant. to Mag. So the father knew that it was at the same hour, in the which Jesus said unto him : Thy son liveth ; and himself believed, and his whole house.

TWENTY-SECOND SUNDAY AFTER TRINITY.

First Vespers.

Ant. to Mag. O Lord, Lord God, fearful and strong, the only and gracious King, the only giver of all things : preserve Thine own portion and sanctify it.

COLLECT.

LORD, we beseech Thee to keep Thy household the Church in continual godliness; that through Thy protection it may be free from all adversities, and devoutly given to serve Thee in good works, to the glory of Thy Name; through Jesus Christ our Lord. Amen.

Lauds.

Ant. to Ben. And the lord commanded payment to be made. The servant therefore fell down and worshipped him, saying : Lord, have patience with me, and I will pay thee all.

Second Vespers.

Ant. to Mag. O thou wicked servant, I forgave thee all that debt, because thou desiredst me : shouldest not thou also have had compassion on thy fellow-servant, even as I had pity on thee ? Alleluia.

TWENTY-THIRD SUNDAY AFTER TRINITY.

First Vespers.

Ant. to Mag. I saw the Lord sitting upon a throne high and lifted up : and His train filled the temple ; the whole earth was full of His glory.

COLLECT.

O GOD, our refuge and strength, Who art the author of all godliness ; be ready, we beseech Thee, to hear the devout prayers of Thy Church ; and grant that those things which we ask faithfully we may obtain effectually ; through Jesus Christ our Lord. Amen.

Lauds.

Ant. to Ben. Master, we know that Thou art true : and teachest the way of God in truth. Alleluia.

Second Vespers.

Ant. to Mag. Render therefore unto Cæsar the things which are Cæsar's : and unto God the things that are God's. Alleluia.

TWENTY-FOURTH SUNDAY AFTER TRINITY.

First Vespers.

Ant. to Mag. How doth the city sit solitary that was full of people ? she that was great among the na-

tions : and there is none to comfort her, but only Thou, O God.

COLLECT.

O LORD, we beseech Thee, absolve Thy people from their offences ; that through Thy bountiful goodness we may all be delivered from the bands of those sins, which by our frailty we have committed ; grant this, O heavenly Father, for Jesus Christ's sake, our blessed Lord and Saviour. Amen.

Lauds.

Ant. to Ben. While Jesus spake these things unto John's disciples, behold, there came a certain ruler, and worshipped Him, saying : My daughter is even now dead ; but come and lay Thy hand upon her, and she shall live.

Second Vespers.

Ant. to Mag. Daughter, be of good comfort, thy faith hath made thee whole : and the woman was made whole from that hour.

TWENTY-FIFTH SUNDAY AFTER TRINITY.

First Vespers.

Ant. to Mag. I have set watchmen upon thy walls, O Jerusalem : which shall never hold their peace day nor night.

COLLECT.

STIR up, we beseech Thee, O Lord, the wills of Thy faithful people ; that they, plenteously bringing forth the fruit of good works, may of Thee be plenteously rewarded ; through Jesus Christ our Lord. Amen.

Lauds.

Ant. to Ben. When Jesus then lift up His eyes, and saw a great company come unto Him, He saith unto Philip,

Whence shall we buy bread that these may eat? : (And this He said to prove him; for He Himself knew what He would do.)

Second Vespers.

Ant. to Mag. Then those men, when they had seen the miracle that Jesus did, said : This is of a truth that Prophet that should come into the world.

If there be any more Sundays before Advent Sunday, the Service of some of those Sundays that were omitted after the Epiphany shall be taken in to supply so many as are here wanting. And if there be fewer, the overplus may be omitted : provided that this last Collect, with the Antiphons to Benedictus and Magnificat, shall always be used upon the Sunday next before Advent. But if a Double Feast occur on the last Sunday before Advent, the Office is of the Feast, with the above Ants. and Collect, as Memorials of the Sunday.

EMBER-TIDE IN SEPTEMBER.

Wednesday.

Lauds.

Ant. to Ben. This kind goeth not out : save by prayer and fasting.

Ferial Petitions, p. 10.

COLLECT.

WE beseech Thee, O Lord, let the remedies of Thy mercy strengthen our frailty; that, whereinsoever it hath decayed, by Thy clemency it may be restored; through our Lord Jesus Christ. Amen.

This Collect is said at every Hour of this day only, till Vespers. At Vespers, if the Office is of the Feria, the Ferial Petitions are said with the Sunday Collect.

Friday.

Lauds.

Ant. to Ben. A woman, in the city, which was a sinner, stood at the feet of the Lord behind Him : and began to wash His feet with tears, and did wipe them with the hairs of her head, and kissed His feet, and anointed them with the ointment.

Ferial Petitions, p. 10.

COLLECT.

GRANT, we beseech Thee, Almighty God, that by the holy observance of this yearly devotion, we may please Thee in body and mind : through our Lord Jesus Christ. Amen.

This Collect is said till Vespers of this day only. At Vespers, if the Office is of the Feria, the Ferial Petitions are said, with the Sunday Collect.

Saturday.

Lauds.

Ant. to Ben. Lighten, O Lord, them that sit in darkness : and guide our feet into the way of peace, O God of Israel.

Ferial Petitions, p. 10.

COLLECT.

ALMIGHTY, everlasting God, Who by healthful continence dost restore both body and soul; we humbly entreat Thy Majesty, that being well pleased by the deprecation of our devout fasting, Thou wouldst grant us present and future help; through our Lord Jesus Christ. Amen.

This Collect is said till Vespers of this day only.

Common of Saints.

✠

I. COMMON OF HOLY DAYS.
II. OCCASIONAL OFFICES.

✠

I. COMMON OF HOLY DAYS.

Every Ant. and R̃. is said with Alleluia in Easter-tide.

COMMON MEMORIALS OF SAINTS
Said at First Vespers and Lauds.

OF A MARTYR.

Vespers.

Ant. Behold, God is my salvation; I will trust and not be afraid : for the Lord Jehovah is my strength and my song; He also is become my salvation.

Ṽ. In God have I put my trust.

R̃. I will not be afraid what man can do unto me.

COLLECT.

WE beseech Thee, O Lord, (blessed *N.*, Thy Martyr interceding,) grant us constancy in Thy faith and truth, that being grounded in divine love, we may be moved from its perfection by no temptations; through Jesus Christ our Lord. Amen.

If a Bishop :

COLLECT.

O GOD, Whose grace elected blessed *N.* Thy Bishop to the Priesthood, Whose learning instructed him in preaching, Whose power strengthened him in perseverance; grant us, after his pattern, to instruct Thy people by our lives, and to strengthen them by our patience; through Jesus Christ our Lord. Amen.

If a Priest, not a Bishop :

COLLECT.

O GOD, from Whom cometh constant faith, and Whose strength is made perfect in weakness; grant, we beseech Thee, that (by the pattern and the prayers of blessed *N.*, Thy Priest and Martyr,) the horrors of persecution and terrors of death may be overcome through the confession of Thy Name; through Jesus Christ our Lord. Amen.

Lauds.

Ant. Verily, verily, I say unto you, Except a corn of wheat fall into the ground and die, it abideth alone : but if it die, it bringeth forth much fruit.

Ṽ. The righteous shall blossom as a lily.

R̃. He shall flourish for ever before the Lord.

Collect as at First Vespers.

OF A BISHOP AND CONFESSOR.

Vespers.

Ant. He chose him out of all men living to offer sacrifices unto the Lord : incense and a sweet savour, for his people.

℣. Blessed is the man whom Thou choosest and receivest unto Thee.

℟. He shall dwell in Thy courts.

COLLECT.

ALMIGHTY, everlasting God, Who makest us glad by this festival of blessed *N.*, Thy Confessor and Bishop, we humbly beseech Thy clemency, that the pious prayers of him whose feast we celebrate may avail to obtain for us the remedies of eternal life; through Jesus Christ our Lord. Amen.

Lauds.

Ant. Well done, good and faithful servant; thou hast been faithful over a few things, I will make thee ruler over many things: enter thou into the joy of thy Lord.

℣. The righteous shall blossom as a lily.

℟. He shall flourish for ever before the Lord.

COLLECT.

O GOD, Who providest for Thy people with tenderness, and governest them with love; and Who dost so value them as to set ministers to rule over them in Thy stead; give, we pray Thee, (blessed *N.*, [Thy Bishop] interceding,) the Spirit of wisdom to those whom Thou hast appointed to preside over Thy Church, that from the welfare of the holy sheep may spring the everlasting joy of the shepherds; through Jesus Christ our Lord, Who liveth and reigneth with Thee, in the unity of the Holy Ghost, One God, world without end. Amen.

OF A DOCTOR.

Vespers.

Ant. God giveth wisdom unto the wise, and knowledge to them that know understanding : He revealeth the deep and secret things; He knoweth what is in darkness, and the light dwelleth with Him.

℣., ℟., *and Collect of a* Confessor Bishop, p. 204, *or of a* Confessor, p. 205.

Lauds.

Ant. I thank Thee, and praise Thee, O Thou God of my fathers : Who hast given me wisdom and might.

℣., ℟., *and Collect of a* Confessor Bishop, p. 204, *or of a* Confessor, p. 205.

OF AN ABBOT OR MONK.

Vespers.

If an Abbot :

Ant. Get thee out of thy country, and from thy kindred : and come into the land which I shall shew thee.

℣. His seed shall be mighty upon earth.

℟. The generation of the faithful shall be blessed.

If not an Abbot :

Ant. Thou hast left thy father and thy mother, and the land of thy nativity : the Lord recompense thy work, and a full reward be given thee of the Lord God of Israel, under Whose wings thou art come to trust.

℣. Under the shadow of Thy wings shall be my refuge.

℟. Until this tyranny be overpast.

COLLECT.

O GOD, Who didst grant to blessed *N.* the Abbot, [or Monk,] to imitate Christ in his poverty, and with humble heart to follow Him to the end: grant to all who have entered on the path of Thy commandments, neither to look back, nor err in the way, but, hasting to Thee without stumbling, to attain eternal life; through the same Jesus Christ our Lord. Amen.

Lauds.

If an Abbot:

Ant. Behold, I and the children whom the Lord hath given me: are for signs and for wonders in Israel from the Lord of hosts, Which dwelleth in Mount Sion.

℣. Come ye children, and hearken unto me.

℟. I will teach you the fear of the Lord.

If not an Abbot:

Ant. The Lord is my portion, saith my soul: therefore will I hope in Him.

℣. I cried to Thee, O Lord, and said, Thou art my hope.

℟. And my stronghold.

COLLECT.

ALMIGHTY, everlasting God, bestowing exceeding great rewards on those who for Thy sake trample on earthly things; grant us by the example and intercession of blessed *N.*, whose departure we this day celebrate, to despise all temporal things, and with our whole heart to hasten unto things eternal; through Jesus Christ our Lord. Amen.

———

OF A CONFESSOR NOT A BISHOP.

Vespers.

Ant. The Lord will shew who are His and who is holy: even him whom He hath chosen, will He cause to come near unto Him.

℣. Mine eyes look upon such as are faithful in the land.

℟. That they may dwell with Me.

If a Priest:

COLLECT.

O GOD, Who makest us glad with the yearly solemnity of blessed *N.*, Thy Confessor, mercifully grant that as we venerate his nativity, so we may imitate his actions; through Jesus Christ our Lord. Amen.

If not a Priest:

COLLECT.

GRANT, we beseech Thee, O Lord God, (blessed *N.* interceding,) that Thy people may walk in Thy love: through Jesus Christ our Lord. Amen.

Lauds.

If a Priest:

Ant. He wrought that which was good and right, and truth before the Lord his God: and in every work that he began, he did it with all his heart, and prospered.

℣. Send out Thy light and Thy truth, that they may lead me.

℟. And bring me unto Thy holy hill, and to Thy dwelling.

Collect as at Vespers.

If not a Priest:

Ant. He that doeth truth, cometh to the light: that his deeds may be made manifest that they are wrought in God.

℣. Look well if there be any way of wickedness in me.

℟. And lead me in the way everlasting.

Collect as at Vespers.

———

OF A VIRGIN AND MARTYR.

Vespers.

Ant. The kingdom of heaven is like unto a net, that was cast into the sea, and gathered of every kind: which, when it was full, they drew to shore, and gathered the good into vessels, but cast the bad away.

℣. Full of grace are thy lips.

℟. Because God hath blessed thee for ever.

Collect.

HEAR us, O God of our salvation, that as we rejoice in the feast of blessed *N.*, Thy Virgin [and Martyr]; so of Thy mercy we may be taught the spirit of devotion; through Jesus Christ our Lord. Amen.

Lauds.

Ant. When the Bridegroom came, the wise virgins, being ready : went in with Him to the marriage.

℣. The virgins that be her fellows shall bear her company.

℟. And shall be brought unto Thee.

Collect as at Vespers.

Of a Virgin not Martyr, the Memorial is the same, except that in the Collect the words, and Martyr, are omitted.

Of a Matron.

Vespers.

Ant. My heart rejoiceth in the Lord : my mouth is enlarged, because I rejoice in Thy salvation.

℣. O turn away mine eyes, lest they behold vanity.

℟. And quicken Thou me in Thy way.

Collect.

O GOD of mercy, enlighten the hearts of Thy faithful people, and (blessed *N.* [Thy Martyr] interceding,) make us to despise things earthly, and love things heavenly; through Jesus Christ our Lord. Amen.

Lauds.

Ant. The prayer of the humble : pierceth the clouds.

℣. I humbled my soul with fasting.

℟. And my prayer shall turn into mine own bosom.

Collect as at Vespers.

Office of the Blessed Sacrament.
(Corpus Christi).

This Office may be used on any Thursday in the year, if unhindered by a Vigil or Double Feast, except in Advent and Lent. Alleluia is omitted in the ℟. of the Little Hours, etc., except in the Octave of Corpus Christi, and in Eastertide.

First Vespers.

Ant. 1. Christ the Lord, a Priest for ever after the order of Melchisedec : offered bread and wine.

Psalm cx. *Dixit Dominus,* p. 45.

Ant. 2. The merciful Lord hath given meat to them that fear Him : in remembrance of His mercy.

Psalm cxi. *Confitebor tibi,* p. 45.

Ant. 3. I will receive the cup of salvation : and offer the sacrifice of thanksgiving.

Psalm cxvi. 10. *Credidi,* p. 49.

Ant. 4. Let the children of the church be as the olive-branches : round about the table of the Lord.

Psalm cxxviii. *Beati omnes,* p. 54.

Ant. 5. The Lord Who maketh peace in the borders of the church : filleth thee with the flour of wheat.

Psalm cxlvii. 12. *Lauda Hierusalem,* p. 64.

Chapter. 1 Cor. xi.

FOR I have received of the Lord that which also I delivered unto you, That the Lord Jesus the same night in which He was betrayed, took bread, and when He had given thanks, He brake it, and said, Take, eat: This is My Body, which is broken for you: this do in remembrance of Me. After the same manner also He took the

cup, when He had supped, saying,
This cup is the new testament in My
Blood: this do ye, as oft as ye drink
it, in remembrance of Me.

℟. A certain man made a great
supper, and sent his servants at
supper-time to say to them that were
bidden, Come, for all things are now
ready. ℣. Come, eat of my bread,
and drink of the wine which I have
mingled. ℟. For all things are now
ready. ℣. Glory be to the Father,
and to the Son : and to the Holy
Ghost. ℟. For all things are now
ready.

HYMN. *Pange, lingua, gloriosi.*

OF the glorious Body telling,
  O my tongue, its mysteries sing;
And the Blood, all price excelling,
  Which for this world's ransoming,
In a generous womb once dwelling,
  He shed forth, the Gentiles' King.

Given for us, for us descending
  Of a Virgin to proceed,
Man with man in converse blending,
  Scattered He the gospel seed :
Till His sojourn drew to ending,
  Which He closed in wond'rous deed.

At the last great Supper seated,
  Circled by His brethren's band,
All the Law required, completed
  In the feast its statutes planned,
To the Twelve Himself He meted
  For their food with His own hand.

Word made Flesh, by word He maketh
  Very bread His Flesh to be :
Man in wine Christ's Blood partaketh,
  And if senses fail to see,
Faith alone the true heart maketh
  To behold the mystery.

Therefore we, before it bending,
  This great Sacrament adore :
Types and shadows have their ending
  In the new rite evermore.
Faith, our outward sense amending,
  Maketh good defects before.

Honour, laud, and praise addressing
  To the Father and the Son,
Might ascribe we, virtue, blessing,
  And eternal benison,
Holy Ghost, from Both progressing,
  Equal laud to Thee be done ! Amen.

℣. Thou didst give them Bread
from heaven.

℟. Containing in Itself all sweetness. [Alleluia.]

And so throughout the Octave of Corpus

*Christi, is added Alleluia to all the
proper versicles of the Blessed Sacrament. At the other versicles it is not
added, except in Easter tide.*

Ant. to Mag. O how sweet is Thy
Spirit, O Lord, Who, to shew Thy
loving kindness to Thy children :
givest most sweet Bread from heaven,
fillest the hungry with good things
and sendest the scornful and the rich
empty away. [Alleluia.] ·

COLLECT.

O GOD, Who under a wonderful
  Sacrament hast left unto us a
memorial of Thy Passion; grant
us, we beseech Thee, so to adore the
mysteries of Thy Body and Blood,
that we may evermore feel within
ourselves the fruit of Thy redemption, Who livest and reignest with
the Father in the unity of the Holy
Spirit, one God, world without end.
Amen.

Compline.

*As in the Psalter on Festivals, except the
Ant. to* Nunc Dimittis. *The Hymn,*
Salvator mundi Domine, *is said with
proper doxology, p. 208.*

Ant. to Nunc Dim. [Alleluia.] The
Bread that I will give, [Alleluia] : is
My Flesh, which I will give for the
life of the world. [Alleluia, Alleluia.]

*This Ant. is said throughout the Octave of
Corpus Christi, even on the Feasts of
Saints.*

Lauds.

℣. I have eaten my honeycomb
with my honey.

℟. I have drunk my wine with
my milk. [Alleluia.]

Psalms of Sunday.

Ant. 1. Wisdom hath builded her
house, she hath mingled her wine :
she hath also furnished her table.
[Alleluia.]

Ant. 2. With the food of angels
Thou didst nourish Thy people : and

didst give them Bread from heaven. [Alleluia.]

Ant. 3. Rich is the Bread of Christ : and He giveth delicacies unto kings. [Alleluia.]

Ant. 4. The holy priests offer incense and bread : unto the Lord. [Alleluia.]

Ant. 5. To him that overcometh will I give the hidden manna : and a new name. [Alleluia.]

CHAPTER. 1 Cor. xi.

FOR I have received of the Lord that which also I delivered unto you, That the Lord Jesus the same night in which He was betrayed, took bread, and when He had given thanks, He brake it, and said, Take, eat: This is My Body, which is broken for you: this do in remembrance of Me. After the same manner also He took the cup, when He had supped, saying, This cup is the new testament in My Blood: this do ye, as oft as ye drink it, in remembrance of me.

R̶. Thanks be to God.

HYMN. *Verbum supernum prodiens.*

THE Word of God proceeding forth,
　Yet leaving not the Father's side,
And going to His work on earth,
　Had reached at length life's eventide.

By a disciple to be given
　To rivals, for His Blood athirst:
Himself, the very Bread of heaven,
　He gave to His disciples first.

He gave Himself in either kind,
　His precious Flesh ; His precious Blood ;
Of flesh and blood is man combined,
　And He of man would be the Food.

In birth, man's fellow man was He ;
　His Meat, while sitting at the board ;
He died, his Ransomer to be ;
　He reigns, to be his great Reward.

O saving Victim, slain to bless,
　Who op'st the heavenly gate to all :
The attacks of many a foe oppress ;
　Give strength in strife, and help in fall.

To God, the Three in One, ascend
　All thanks and praise for evermore ;
He grant the life that shall not end,
　Upon the heavenly country's shore. Amen.

V̶. He maketh peace in thy borders.

R̶. And filleth thee with the flour of wheat. [Alleluia.]

Ant. to Ben. I am the Living Bread which came down from heaven : if any man eat of this Bread he shall live for ever. [Alleluia.]

Collect as at First Vespers.

Prime.

The Hymn is to end with this Doxology, as well as all Hymns of the same metre, throughout the Office, except the Hymn, Verbum supernum :

　All honour, laud, and glory be,
　O Jesu, Virgin-born, to Thee,
　All glory, as is ever meet,
　To Father, and to Paraclete. Amen.

Ant. to Psalms. Wisdom hath builded her house, she hath mingled her wine : she hath also furnished her table. [Alleluia.]

R̶. to Chapter.

R̶. Jesu Christ, Son of the Living God : have mercy upon us. V̶. Thou Who wast born of the Virgin Mary. R̶. Have mercy upon us. V̶. Glory be to the Father, and to the Son, and to the Holy Ghost. R̶. Jesu Christ, Son of the Living God, have mercy upon us.

Tierce.

Ant. With the food of angels Thou didst nourish Thy people : and didst give them Bread from heaven. [Alleluia.]

CHAPTER. 1 Cor. xi.

FOR I have received of the Lord that which also I delivered unto you, That the Lord Jesus, the same night in which He was betrayed, took bread, and when He had given thanks, He brake it, and said, Take, eat: This is My Body, which is broken for you: this do in remembrance of Me. After the same manner also He took the cup, when He had supped, saying, This cup is the new testament in

My Blood: this do ye, as oft as ye drink it, in remembrance of Me.

R̰. Thou didst give them * Bread from heaven. [Alleluia, Alleluia.] V̰. So man did eat angels' food. R̰. [Alleluia, Alleluia.] V̰. Glory be to the Father, and to the Son, and to the Holy Ghost. R̰. Thou didst give them Bread from heaven. [Alleluia, Alleluia.]

V̰. He fed them with the finest wheat flour.

R̰. And with honey out of the stony rock did He satisfy them. [Alleluia.]

*When Alleluia is omitted, the repetition of the R̰. at the Hours begins at *.*

Sexts.

Ant. Rich is the Bread of Christ: and He giveth delicacies to kings. [Alleluia.]

CHAPTER. 1 Cor. xi.

AS often as ye eat this Bread and drink this Cup, ye do shew the Lord's death till He come.

R̰. He fed them * with the finest wheat-flour. [Alleluia, Alleluia.] V̰. And with honey out of the stony rock did He satisfy them. R̰. [Alleluia, Alleluia.] V̰. Glory be to the Father, and to the Son, and to the Holy Ghost. R̰. He fed them with the finest wheat-flour. [Alleluia, Alleluia.]

V̰. Thou bringest Bread out of the earth.

R̰. And Wine that maketh glad the heart of man. [Alleluia.]

Nones.

Ant. To him that overcometh will I give the hidden manna: and a new name. [Alleluia.]

CHAPTER. 1 Cor. xi.

THEREFORE whosoever shall eat this Bread, and drink this Cup of the Lord unworthily, shall be guilty

of the Body and Blood of the Lord. But let a man examine himself, and so let him eat of that Bread, and drink of that Cup.

R̰. Thou bringest Bread * out of the earth. [Alleluia, Alleluia.] V̰. And Wine that maketh glad the heart of man. R̰. [Alleluia, Alleluia.] V̰. Glory be to the Father, and to the Son, and to the Holy Ghost. R̰. Thou bringest Bread out of the earth. [Alleluia, Alleluia.]

V̰. He maketh Thy borders peace.

R̰. And filleth thee with the flour of wheat. [Alleluia.]

Second Vespers.

As the First Vespers, except the

Ant. to Mag. O Sacred Feast, wherein Christ is received, the remembrance of His Passion is maintained: the soul is filled with grace, and a pledge of future glory is given us. [Alleluia.]

———

COMMON
OF THE BLESSED VIRGIN MARY.

First Vespers.

Ant. 1. As the lily among thorns: so is my love among the daughters.

Psalm cxiii. *Laudate pueri*, p. 46.

Ant. 2. Behold, thou art fair, my love: thou hast dove's eyes.

Psalm cxvii. *Laudate Dominum*, p. 50.

Ant. 3. A fountain of gardens, a well of living waters: and streams from Lebanon.

Psalm cxlvi. *Lauda, anima mea*, p. 63.

Ant. 4. The eye marvelleth at the beauty: of the whiteness thereof.

Psalm cxlvii. *Laudate Dominum*, p. 64.

Ant. 5. How fair and pleasant art thou: O love, for delights!

Psalm cxlvii. 12. *Lauda Hierusalem*, p. 64.

CHAPTER. Isa. vii.

BEHOLD, a Virgin shall conceive, and bear a Son, and shall call His Name, Immanuel.

℟. Thy renown went forth among the heathen for thy beauty : for it was perfect through My comeliness which I had put upon thee, saith the Lord God. ℣. Hail, full of grace, the Lord is with thee. ℟. For it was perfect through My comeliness which I had put upon thee, saith the Lord God. ℣. Glory be to the Father, and to the Son, and to the Holy Ghost. ℟. Thy renown went forth among the heathen for thy beauty : for it was perfect through My comeliness which I had put upon thee, saith the Lord God.

HYMN. *Quem terra, pontus, sidera.*

THE God Whom earth, and sea, and sky
Adore, and laud, and magnify—
Who o'er their threefold fabric reigns,
The Virgin's spotless womb contains.

The God, Whose will by moon and sun
And all things in due course is done,
Is borne upon a Maiden's breast,
By fullest heavenly grace possess'd.

How blest that Mother, in whose shrine
The great Artificer Divine,
Whose hand contains the earth and sky,
Vouchsaf'd, as in His ark, to lie !

Blest, in the message Gabriel brought ;
Blest, by the work the Spirit wrought ;
From whom the Great Desire of earth
Took human flesh and human birth.

All honour, laud, and glory be,
O Jesu, Virgin-born, to Thee !
All glory, as is ever meet,
To Father and to Paraclete. Amen.

This Doxology is said throughout the day to Hymns of this metre.

℣. Full of grace are thy lips.

℟. Because God hath blessed thee for ever.

Ant. to Mag. Thou art the exaltation of Jerusalem : thou art the great glory of Israel ; thou art the great rejoicing of our nation.

COLLECT.

WE beseech Thee, O Lord, mercifully pour Thy grace into our hearts ; and, (most holy Mary, Mother of God, interceding) sanctify our bodies in chastity, and our souls in humility and charity ; through Jesus Christ our Lord. Amen.

Compline.

As set down in the Psalter on Festivals, except that which follows :

Ant. to Psalms. Blessed is the womb that bare Thee, O Christ : and the paps which thou hast sucked.

Ant. to Nunc Dimittis, *except on the Annunciation :*

We glorify the holy Mother of God : because of her Christ was born.

Lauds.

℣. I will give thanks unto Thee, O Lord, among the people.

℟. For Thy mercy is greater than the heavens.

Psalms of Sunday.

Ant. 1. My Beloved is mine, and I am His : He feedeth among the lilies.

Ant. 2. In thee, and in thy Seed : shall all the families of the earth be blessed.

Ant. 3. He was born in her : and the most High shall stablish her.

Ant. 4. Blessed art thou of the most high God : above all the women upon the earth.

Ant. 5. The daughters saw her, and blessed her : the queens, and they praised her.

CHAPTER. Gal. iv.

WHEN the fulness of time was come, God sent forth His Son, made of a woman, made under the law, to redeem them that were under the law.

HYMN. *O gloriosa virginum.*

O GLORIOUS Virgin, throned in rest
Amidst the starry host above,
Who gavest nurture from thy breast
To God, with pure maternal love :

What we had lost through sinful Eve
  The Blossom sprung from thee restores;
And granting bliss to souls that grieve,
  Unbars the everlasting doors.

O gate, through which hath passed the King:
  O hall, whence light shone through the
    gloom;
The ransomed nations praise and sing,
  Life given from the virgin womb.

All honour, laud, and glory be,
O Jesu, Virgin-born, to Thee;
All glory, as is ever meet,
To Father and to Paraclete. Amen.

℣. Thy name shall be called of God for ever.

℟. The peace of righteousness.

Ant. to Ben. Loose thyself from the bands of thy neck, O captive daughter of Sion. For thus saith the Lord : My people shall know My Name : they shall know in that day that I am He that doth speak : behold, it is I.

Prime.

Ant. My Beloved is mine, and I am His : He feedeth among the lilies.

Tierce.

Ant. In thee, and in thy Seed : shall all the families of the earth be blessed.

CHAPTER. Gal. iv.

WHEN the fulness of time was come, God sent forth His Son, made of a woman, made under the law, to redeem them that were under the law.

℟. God is in the midst of her : therefore shall she not be removed. ℣. God shall help her, and that right early. ℟. Therefore shall she not be removed. ℣. Glory be to the Father, and to the Son, and to the Holy Ghost. ℟. God is in the midst of her : therefore shall she not be removed.

℣. In His time shall the righteous flourish.

℟. Yea, and abundance of peace, so long as the moon endureth.

Sexts.

Ant. He was born in her : and the most High shall stablish her.

CHAPTER. Cant. vi.

WHO is she that looketh forth as the morning, fair as the moon, clear as the sun, and terrible as an army with banners?

℟. In His time : shall the righteous flourish. ℣. Yea, and abundance of peace, so long as the moon endureth. ℟. The righteous shall flourish. ℣. Glory be to the Father, and to the Son, and to the Holy Ghost. ℟. In His time : shall the righteous flourish.

℣. Upon Thy right hand did stand the queen.

℟. In a vesture of gold, wrought about with divers colours.

Nones.

Ant. The daughters saw her, and blessed her : the queens, and they praised her.

CHAPTER. Gen. xxii.

THY Seed shall possess the gate of His enemies; and in thy Seed shall all the nations of the earth be blessed.

℟. Upon Thy right hand : did stand the queen. ℣. In a vesture of gold, wrought about with divers colours. ℟. Did stand the queen. ℣. Glory be to the Father, and to the Son, and to the Holy Ghost. ℟. Upon Thy right hand : did stand the queen.

℣. The Lord loveth the gates of Sion.

℟. More than all the dwellings of Jacob.

Second Vespers.

Ant. 1. My Beloved is mine, and I am His : He feedeth among the lilies.

Psalm cx. *Dixit Dominus*, p. 92.

Ant. 2. In thee, and in thy Seed :

shall all the families of the earth be blessed.

Psalm cxi. *Confitebor*, p. 92.

Ant. 3. He was born in her : and the most High shall stablish her.

Psalm cxii. *Beatus vir*, p. 93.

Ant. 4. Blessed art thou of the most high God : above all the women upon the earth.

Psalm cxxx. *De profundis*, p. 93.

Ant. 5. The daughters saw her, and blessed her : the queens, and they praised her.

Psalm cxxxii. *Memento, Domine*, p. 94.

CHAPTER. Ecclus. xxiv.

I am the mother of fair love, and fear, and knowledge, and holy hope.

HYMN. *Quem terra, pontus, sidera,* ℣. and ℟., p. 210.

Ant. to Mag. Thou art all fair, my love : there is no spot in thee.

In Easter tide : Ant. to Mag. Thy Son liveth. Alleluia : and is Governour over all the land. Alleluia, Alleluia.

——

Of one or more Apostles or Evangelists in Easter tide,

(*That is to say, from* LOW SUNDAY *to* TRINITY SUNDAY, *exclusive.*)

First Vespers.

Ant. to Psalms. Light perpetual shall shine upon Thy Saints, O Lord : and an eternity of time. Alleluia.

Psalms of the Feria.

The Chapter at the First Vespers, and those at all the Hours, are of the Proper, if there be any ; if not, of the Common of Apostles through the year.

℟. Her Nazarites were made bright. Alleluia ; they gave their glory to God. Alleluia : They were whiter than milk : Alleluia. Alleluia. ℣. Their sound is gone out into all lands, and their words unto the end of the world. ℟. They were whiter than milk. Alleluia, Alleluia. ℣. Glory be to the Father, and to the Son, and to the Holy Ghost. ℟. Alleluia, Alleluia.

HYMN. *Tristes erant Apostoli.*

TH' Apostles' hearts were full of pain,
For their dear Lord so lately slain,
That Lord His servants' wicked train
With bitter scorn had dared arraign.

We pray Thee, King with glory deck'd,
In this our Paschal joy protect,
From all that death would fain effect,
Thy ransomed flock, Thine own elect.

To Thee Who, dead, again dost live,
All glory, Lord, Thy people give ;
All glory, as is ever meet,
To Father and to Paraclete. Amen.

If in Ascension-tide, instead of the last two verses is said :

Be Thou our Joy, and Thou our Guard,
Who art to be our great Reward :
Our glory and our boast in Thee,
For ever and for ever be !

All glory, Lord, to Thee we pay,
Ascending o'er the stars to-day ;
All glory, as is ever meet,
To Father and to Paraclete. Amen.

℣. Then were the disciples glad.

℟. When they saw the Lord. Alleluia.

Ant. to Mag. Daughters of Jerusalem, come and behold the Martyr with the crown, wherewith the Lord crowned Him, in the day of solemnity and gladness.

This Ant. is to be said in Easter-tide for one or many Martyrs or Confessors, not changing the word Martyr to the plural, because it refers to Christ.

Collect of the Proper.

(*Easter Compline is not changed.*)

Lauds.

℣. The voice of joy and health.

℟. Is in the dwelling of the righteous. Alleluia.

Psalms of Sunday.

Ant. 1. Thy Saints, O Lord, shall flourish as a lily. Alleluia : as the odour of balsam shall they be before Thee. Alleluia.

Ant. 2. Ye holy and righteous, rejoice in the Lord. Alleluia : God hath chosen you to be His inheritance. Alleluia.

Ant. 3. Within the veil Thy Saints, O Lord, cry : Alleluia, Alleluia, Alleluia.

Ant. 4. O ye spirits and souls of the righteous : bless ye the Lord. Alleluia, Alleluia.

Ant. 5. In the kingdom of heaven is the habitation of the Saints. Alleluia : Their rest is eternal. Alleluia.

Chapter according to direction at First Vespers, p. 212.

HYMN. *Claro Paschali gaudio.*

IN this our bright and Paschal day
  The sun shines out with purer ray ;
When Christ, to earthly sight made plain,
The glad Apostles see again.

The wounds, the riven wounds He shows
In that His flesh with light that glows,
With public voice both far and nigh
The Lord's arising testify.

O Christ, the King, Who lov'st to bless,
Do Thou our hearts and souls possess ;
To Thee our praise that we may pay,
To Whom our laud is due for aye.

We pray Thee, King with glory deck'd,
In this our Paschal joy protect,
From all that death would fain effect,
Thy ransomed flock, Thine own elect.

To Thee Who, dead, again dost live,
All glory, Lord, Thy people give :
All glory, as is ever meet,
To Father and to Paraclete. Amen.

In Ascension tide, the Doxology is altered as at Vespers, p. 212.

℣. Rejoice in the Lord, ye righteous.

℟. For it becometh well the just to be thankful. Alleluia.

Ant. to Ben. Light eternal shall shine upon Thy Saints, O Lord : and an eternity of time. Alleluia, Alleluia, Alleluia.

Prime.

Ant. Thy Saints, O Lord, shall flourish as a lily. Alleluia : as the odour of balsam shall they be before Thee. Alleluia.

Tierce.

Ant. Ye holy and righteous, rejoice in the Lord. Alleluia : God hath chosen you to be His inheritance. Alleluia.

Chapter according as directed, p. 212.

℟. Your sorrow : Alleluia, Alleluia. ℣. Shall be turned into joy. ℟. Alleluia, Alleluia. ℣. Glory be to the Father, and to the Son, and to the Holy Ghost. ℟. Your sorrow : Alleluia, Alleluia.

℣. Right dear in the sight of the Lord.

℟. Is the death of His Saints. Alleluia.

Sexts.

Ant. Within the veil Thy Saints, O Lord, cry : Alleluia, Alleluia, Alleluia.

Chapter according as directed, p. 212.

℟. Right dear in the sight of the Lord : Alleluia, Alleluia. ℣. Is the death of His Saints. ℟. Alleluia, Alleluia. ℣. Glory be to the Father, and to the Son, and to the Holy Ghost. ℟. Right dear in the sight of the Lord. Alleluia, Alleluia.

℣. Rejoice in the Lord, ye righteous.

℟. For it becometh well the just to be thankful. Alleluia.

Nones.

Ant. In the kingdom of heaven is the habitation of the Saints. Alleluia : Their rest is eternal. Alleluia.

Chapter according as directed, p. 212.

℟. Rejoice in the Lord, ye righteous : Alleluia, Alleluia. ℣. For it becometh well the just to be thankful. ℟. Alleluia, Alleluia. ℣. Glory be to the Father, and to the Son, and to the Holy Ghost. ℟. Rejoice in the Lord, ye righteous : Alleluia, Alleluia.

℣. The voice of joy and health.

℟. Is in the dwellings of the righteous. Alleluia.

Second Vespers.

Ants. of Lauds, with Psalms of the Second Vespers of Common of Apostles, p. 216. The rest as at First Vespers of this Office, p. 212.

OF A MARTYR OR CONFESSOR IN EASTER TIDE.

All as of the Common throughout the year, (or Proper, if there be any,) except that which follows;

First Vespers.

Ant. to Psalms. Light perpetual shall shine upon Thy Saints, O Lord : and an eternity of time. Alleluia.

And if a Martyr, ℟. to Chapter.

℟. Daughters of Jerusalem, come and behold the Martyr with the crown wherewith the Lord crowned Him : in the day of solemnity and gladness. Alleluia. ℣. For He hath made fast the bars of thy gates, and hath blessed thy children within thee. ℟. In the day of solemnity and gladness. Alleluia. ℣. Glory be to the Father, and to the Son, and to the Holy Ghost. ℟. Daughters of Jerusalem, come and behold the Martyr with the crown wherewith the Lord crowned Him in the day of solemnity and gladness. Alleluia.

After the Hymn :

℣. Your sorrow.

℟. Shall be turned into joy. Alleluia.

Lauds.

Ant. to Ben. (if a Martyr). Daughters of Jerusalem, come and behold the Martyr with the crown : wherewith the Lord crowned Him in the day of solemnity and gladness. Alleluia.

OF ONE OR MORE APOSTLES OR EVANGELISTS THROUGH THE YEAR, EXCEPT IN EASTER TIDE.

First Vespers.

Psalms of the Feria.

Ant. Be ye strong in battle, and fight with the old serpent : so shall ye receive an eternal kingdom. Alleluia.

After Septuagesima, at the end of this Antiphon, instead of Alleluia, is said, Saith the Lord. But at the end of other Antiphons, usually ending with Alleluia, is said, For evermore.

CHAPTER. Eph. ii.

NOW therefore ye are no more strangers and foreigners, but fellow-citizens with the saints, and of the household of God; and are built upon the foundation of the apostles and prophets.

℟. Who are these that fly as a cloud : and as the doves to their windows? ℣. They were purer than snow, they were whiter than milk, they were more ruddy in body than rubies. ℟. And as the doves to their windows. ℣. Glory be to the Father, and to the Son, and to the Holy Ghost. ℟. Who are these that fly as a cloud : and as the doves to their windows?

HYMN. *Annue Christe.*

O CHRIST, Thou Lord of worlds !
    Thine ear to hear us bow
On this the festival
Of Thine Apostle [*or,* Apostles] now :
That all the weary load
Of many a foul offence
May, as we sing his [their] praise,
Be lost in penitence.

Redeemer ! save Thy work,
Thy noble work of grace,
Sealed with the holy light
That beameth from Thy face :
Nor suffer them to fall
To Satan's wiles a prey,
For whom Thou didst on earth
Death's costly ransom pay.

Pity Thy flock, enthralled
By sin's captivity;
Forgive each guilty soul,
And set the bondmen free:
And those Thou hast redeemed
With Thine Own precious Blood,
Grant to rejoice with Thee,
Thou Monarch kind and good.

O Jesu, Saviour blest
And gracious Lord, to Thee,
All glory, virtue, power,
And laud and empire be:
The Father with like praise,
And Spirit we adore;
With Whom Thou reignest God,
For ages evermore. Amen.

℣. Their sound is gone out into all lands.

℞. And their words unto the ends of the world.

Ant. to Mag. (if none Proper). Blessed are ye, when men shall hate you, and when they shall separate you from their company, and shall reproach you, and cast out your name as evil, for the Son of man's sake : Rejoice ye in that day, and leap for joy ; for, behold, your reward is great in heaven.

Collect of the Vigil, if any ; if not, that of the Feast.

Lauds.

℣. Thou hast given an heritage.

℞. Unto those that fear Thy Name, O Lord.

Psalms of Sunday.

Ant. 1. This is My commandment, that ye love one another : as I have loved you.

Ant. 2. Greater love hath no man than this : that a man lay down his life for his friends.

Ant. 3. Ye are My friends : if ye do whatsoever I command you.

Ant. 4. Blessed are the pure in heart : for they shall see God.

Ant. 5. In your patience : possess ye your souls.

CHAPTER. Eph. ii.

NOW therefore ye are no more strangers and foreigners, but fellow-citizens with the saints, and of the household of God ; and are built upon the foundation of the apostles and prophets.

℞. Thanks be to God.

HYMN.   *Exultet cœlum laudibus.*

LET the round world with songs rejoice,
Let heaven return the joyful voice ;
All, mindful of the Apostles' fame,
Earth, sky, their Sovereign's praise proclaim !

Thou, at Whose word they bore the light
Of gospel truth o'er heathen night,
Still unto us that light impart,
To glad our eyes and cheer our heart.

Thou, at Whose will to them was given
The key that shuts and opens heaven,
Our chains unbind, our loss repair,
And grant us grace to enter there.

Thou, at Whose will they preached the word
Which cured disease, which health conferred,
To us its healing power prolong,
The weak support, confirm the strong.

That when Thy Son again shall come,
And speak the world's unerring doom,
He may with them pronounce us blest,
And place us in Thy endless rest.

All laud to God the Father be ;
All laud, Eternal Son, to Thee ;
All laud, as is for ever meet,
To God the Holy Paraclete. Amen.

℣. And all men that see it shall say, This hath God done.

℞. For they shall perceive that it is His work.

Ant. to Ben. (if none Proper.) They will deliver you up to the councils, and they will scourge you in their synagogues : and ye shall be brought before governours and kings for My sake, for a testimony against them and the Gentiles.

Collect of the Proper.

Prime.

Ant. This is My commandment : that ye love one another, as I have loved you.

Tierce.

Ant. Greater love hath no man than this : that a man lay down his life for his friends.

CHAPTER. Eph. ii.

NOW therefore ye are no more strangers and foreigners, but fellow-citizens with the saints, and of the household of God; and are built upon the foundation of the apostles and prophets.

℟. Their sound is gone out : into all lands. ℣. And their words into the ends of the world. ℟. Into all lands. ℣. Glory be to the Father, and to the Son, and to the Holy Ghost. ℟. Their sound is gone out : into all lands.

℣. Thou shalt make them princes in all lands.

℟. They shall remember Thy Name, O Lord.

Sexts.

Ant. Ye are My friends : if ye do whatsoever I command you.

CHAPTER. Acts v.

BY the hands of the apostles were many signs and wonders wrought among the people : but the people magnified them.

℟. Thou shalt make them princes : in all lands. ℣. They shall remember Thy Name, O Lord. ℟. In all lands. ℣. Glory be to the Father, and to the Son, and to the Holy Ghost. ℟. Thou shalt make them princes : in all lands.

℣. Exceedingly honoured are Thy friends, O Lord.

℟. Exceedingly strengthened in their principality.

Nones.

Ant. In your patience : possess ye your souls.

CHAPTER. Acts v.

AND they departed from the presence of the council, rejoicing that they were counted worthy to suffer shame for His Name.

℟. Exceedingly honoured : are Thy friends, O Lord. ℣. Exceedingly strengthened in their principality. ℟. Are Thy friends, O Lord. ℣. Glory be to the Father, and to the Son : and to the Holy Ghost. ℟. Exceedingly honoured are Thy friends, O Lord.

℣. All men that see it shall say, This hath God done.

℟. For they shall perceive that it is His work.

Second Vespers.

Ant. 1. The Lord sware, and will not repent : thou art a priest for ever.

Psalm cx. *Dixit Dominus*, p. 45.

Ant. 2. That He may set him with the princes : even with the princes of His people.

Psalm cxiii. *Laudate pueri*, p. 46.

Ant. 3. Thou hast broken my bonds in sunder : I will offer to Thee the sacrifice of thanksgiving.

Psalm cxvi. 10. *Credidi*, p. 49.

Ant. 4. He that now goeth on his way weeping : and beareth forth good seed.

Psalm cxxvi. *In convertendo*, p. 53.

Ant. 5. Exceedingly honoured are Thy friends, O Lord : exceedingly strengthened in their principality.

Psalm cxxxix. *Domine probasti*, p. 59.

CHAPTER. Eph. ii.

NOW therefore ye are no more strangers and foreigners, but fellow-citizens with the saints, and of the household of God ; and are built upon the foundation of the apostles and prophets.

℟. The fellow-citizens of the Apostles and the servants of God advance to-day : bearing torches, and enlightening their country, to give peace to the Gentiles : and to deliver the people of the Lord. ℣. Hear, Lord, our prayer, who ask the rewards of eternal life, whilst they bear in their hands the sheaves of righteousness, and joyfully come forward to-day. ℟. Bearing torches, and enlightening their country, to give peace to the Gentiles. ℣. Glory be to the Father, and to the Son, and to the Holy Ghost. ℟. And to deliver the people of the Lord.

HYMN. *Exultet cœlum laudibus,* ℣. and ℟., p. 215.

Ant. to Mag. In the regeneration when the Son of man shall sit in the throne of His glory : ye also shall sit upon twelve thrones, judging the twelve tribes of Israel.

———

OF A MARTYR THROUGH THE YEAR.

First Vespers.

Ant. to Psalms. Blessed is the man that endureth temptation : for when he is tried, he shall receive the crown of life, which the Lord hath promised to them that love Him.

Psalms of the Feria.

CHAPTER. Josh. i.

HAVE not I commanded thee ? Be strong, and of a good courage; be not afraid, neither be thou dismayed : for the Lord thy God is with thee.

℟. Thou therefore endure hardness as a good soldier of Jesus Christ : and if a man also strive for mastery, yet is he not crowned except he strive lawfully. ℣. Be thou valiant and fight the Lord's battles. ℟. And if a man also strive for mastery, yet is he not crowned except he strive lawfully. ℣. Glory be to the Father, and to the Son : and to the Holy Ghost. ℟. Thou therefore endure hardness as a good soldier of Jesus Christ : and if a man also strive

for mastery, yet is he not crowned except he strive lawfully.

HYMN. *Sanctorum meritis,* p. 220.

℣. In God have I put my trust.

℟. I will not be afraid what man can do unto me.

Ant. to Mag. Behold, God is my salvation; I will trust, and not be afraid : for the Lord Jehovah is my strength and my song; He also is become my salvation.

COLLECT.

(If no Proper.)

WE beseech Thee, O Lord (blessed *N.,* Thy Martyr, interceding,) grant us constancy in Thy faith and truth; that, being grounded in Divine love, we may be moved from its perfection by no temptations; through Jesus Christ our Lord. Amen.

If a Bishop :

COLLECT.

O GOD, Whose grace elected blessed *N.,* Thy Bishop, to the Priesthood, Whose learning instructed him in preaching, Whose power strengthened him in perseverance : grant us, after his pattern, to instruct Thy people by our lives, and to strengthen them by our patience; through Jesus Christ our Lord. Amen.

If a Priest not a Bishop :

COLLECT.

O GOD, from Whom cometh constant faith, and Whose strength is made perfect in weakness; grant, we beseech Thee, that, (by the pattern and the prayers of blessed *N.* Thy Priest and Martyr,) the horrors of persecution, and the terrors of death, may be overcome through the confession of Thy Name; through Jesus Christ our Lord. Amen.

Lauds.

℣. Thou hast crowned him, O Lord.

℟. With glory and honour.

Psalms of Sunday.

Ant. 1. Whosoever therefore shall confess Me before men : him will I confess also before My Father.

Ant. 2. He that followeth Me shall not walk in darkness : but shall have the light of life, saith the Lord.

Ant. 3. If any man serve Me, let him follow Me; and where I am, there shall also My servant be : if any man serve Me, him will My Father honour.

Ant. 4. The Lord is good, a stronghold in the day of trouble : and He knoweth them that trust in Him.

Ant. 5. Father, I will that where I am : there also may My servant be.

CHAPTER. Rev. iii.

HE that overcometh, the same shall be clothed in white raiment; and I will not blot out his name out of the book of life, but I will confess his name before My Father, and before His angels.

HYMN. *Deus tuorum militum,* p. 219.

℣. The righteous shall blossom as a lily.

℟. He shall flourish for ever before the Lord.

Ant. to Ben. Verily, verily, I say unto you, Except a corn of wheat fall into the ground and die, it abideth alone : but if it die, it bringeth forth much fruit.

Prime.

Ant. Whosoever therefore shall confess Me before men : him will I confess also before My Father.

Tierce.

Ant. He that followeth Me shall not walk in darkness : but shall have the light of life, saith the Lord.

CHAPTER. Rev. iii.

HE that overcometh, the same shall be clothed in white raiment; and I will not blot out his name out of the book of life, but I will confess his name before My Father, and before His angels.

℟. In God is my health : and my glory. ℣. The rock of my might, and in God is my trust. ℟. And my glory. ℣. Glory be to the Father, and to the Son, and to the Holy Ghost. ℟. In God is my health : and my glory.

℣. Though an host of men were laid against me, yet shall not my heart be afraid.

℟. And though there rose up war against me, yet will I put my trust in Him.

Sexts.

Ant. If any man serve Me, let him follow Me; and where I am, there shall also My servant be: if any man serve Me, him will My Father honour.

CHAPTER. Wisdom x.

WISDOM defended him from his enemies, and kept him safe from those that lay in wait, and in a sore conflict she gave him the victory; that he might know that godliness is stronger than all.

℟. Though an host of men were laid against me : yet shall not my heart be afraid. ℣. And though there rose up war against me, yet will I put my trust in Him. ℟. Yet shall not my heart be afraid. ℣. Glory be to the Father, and to the Son, and to the Holy Ghost. ℟. Though an host of men were laid against me : yet shall not my heart be afraid.

℣. The Lord is on my side.

℟. I will not fear what man doeth unto me.

Nones.

Ant. Father, I will that where I am : there also may My servant be.

CHAPTER. Ecclus. xlv.

THE Lord clothed him with a robe of glory, and set a crown of pure gold upon his head.

℟. The Lord is : on my side. ℣. I will not fear what man doeth unto me. ℟. On my side. ℣. Glory be to the Father, and to the Son, and to the Holy Ghost. ℟. The Lord is : on my side.

℣. Thou, Lord, hast holpen me.

℟. And comforted me.

Second Vespers.

Psalms of the Feria.

Ant. 1. Whosoever therefore shall confess Me before men : him will I confess also before My Father Which is in heaven.

Ant. 2. Esteeming the reproach of Christ greater riches : he had respect unto the recompense of the reward.

Ant. 3. I have fought a good fight, I have finished my course : I have kept the faith.

Ant. 4. Henceforth there is laid up for me a crown of righteousness : which the Lord, the righteous Judge, shall give me at that day.

Ant. 5. I know Whom I have believed : and am persuaded that He is able to keep that which I have committed unto Him against that day.

CHAPTER. Is. xli.

THEY that war against thee shall be as nothing, and as a thing of nought. For I the Lord thy God will hold thy right hand, saying unto thee, Fear not, I will help thee.

℣. Be thou faithful unto death, and I will give thee a crown of life : He that overcometh shall not be hurt of the second death. ℣. Strive for the truth unto death, and the Lord shall fight for thee. ℟. He that overcometh shall not be hurt of the second death. ℣. Glory be to the Father, and to the Son, and to the Holy Ghost. ℣. Be thou faithful unto death, and I will give thee a crown of life : He that overcometh shall not be hurt of the second death.

HYMN. *Deus tuorum militum.*

O GOD, Thy soldiers' Crown and Guard,
 And their exceeding great reward,
From all transgressions set us free,
Who sing Thy Martyr's victory.

The pleasures of the world he spurn'd,
From sin's pernicious lures he turn'd;
He knew their joys imbued with gall,
And thus he reach'd Thy heav'nly hall.

For Thee thro' many a woe he ran,
In many a fight he play'd the man;
For Thee his blood he dar'd to pour,
And thence hath joy for evermore.

We therefore pray Thee, full of love,
Regard us from Thy Throne above :
On this Thy Martyr's triumph-day,
Wash ev'ry stain of sin away.

O Father, that we ask be done,
Through Jesus Christ, Thine only Son :
Who, with the Holy Ghost, and Thee,
Shall live and reign eternally. Amen.

℣. The righteous shall blossom as a lily.

℟. He shall flourish for ever before the Lord.

Ant. to Mag. Daughters of Jerusalem, come and behold the Martyr with the crown wherewith the Lord crowned Him : in the day of solemnity and gladness.

———

OF MANY MARTYRS THROUGH THE YEAR.

First Vespers.

Ant. His servants shall serve Him : and they shall see His face; and His Name shall be in their foreheads.

Psalms of the Feria.

CHAPTER. S. James i.

MY brethren, count it all joy when ye fall into divers temptations; knowing this, that the trying of your faith worketh patience. But let patience have her perfect work.

R̂. Round about Thee, O Lord, is a light that never fails : where Thou hast built most bright mansions : there rest the souls of the Saints. V̂. Light perpetual shall shine upon Thy Saints, O Lord, and an eternity of time. R̂. Where Thou hast built most bright mansions. V̂. Glory be to the Father, and to the Son, and to the Holy Ghost. R̂. There rest the souls of the Saints.

HYMN. *Sanctorum meritis.*

THE triumphs of the Saints,
  Blessed for evermore,
Their love that never faints,
  The toils they bravely bore,—
For these the Church to-day
Pours forth her joyous lay,—
These victors win the noblest bay.

They, whom this world of ill,
  While it yet held, abhorr'd :
Its with'ring flowers that still
  They spurn'd with one accord:
They knew them short-liv'd all,
And followed at Thy call,
King Jesu, to Thy heavenly hall.

For Thee all pangs they bare,
  Fury and mortal hate,
The cruel scourge to tear,
  The hook to lacerate;
But vain their foes' intent :
For, every torment spent,
Their valiant spirits stood unbent.

Like sheep their blood they pour'd :
  And without groan or tear,
They bent before the sword
  For that their King most dear :
Their souls, serenely blest,
In patience they possessed,
And looked in hope towards their rest.

What tongue may here declare,
  Fancy or thought descry,
The joys Thou dost prepare
  For these Thy Saints on high !
Empurpled in the flood
Of their victorious blood,
They won the laurel from their God.

To Thee, O Lord, Most High,
  One in Three Persons still,
To pardon us we cry,
  And to preserve from ill :

Here give Thy servants peace ;
Hereafter glad release,
And pleasures that shall never cease. Amen.

V̂. Wonderful art Thou in Thy Saints, O God.

R̂. And glorious in Thy majesty.

Ant. to Mag. In heaven rejoice the souls of the Saints, who followed the footsteps of Christ : and because for His love they shed their blood, therefore with Christ they shall reign for ever.

COLLECT.

ALMIGHTY, everlasting God, grant us worthily to venerate Thy holy Martyrs, *M.* and *N.*, that so we may be delivered from the dangers of this world, and be made worthy of eternal joy; through Jesus Christ our Lord. Amen.

For many Martyrs, being Bishops or Priests :

COLLECT.

ALMIGHTY, everlasting God, Who didst kindle the fire of Thy love in the hearts of Thy holy Martyrs and Bishops (*or* Priests) *M.* and *N.*: give to our hearts the strength of the same faith and charity, that we may profit by the example of those in whose triumphs we rejoice; through Jesus Christ our Lord. Amen.

Lauds.

V̂. For the righteous shall live for evermore.

R̂. And their reward is with the most High.

Psalms of Sunday.

Ant. 1. But the souls of the righteous are in the hand of God : and there shall no torment touch them.

Ant. 2. With the palm they attained to the kingdom : the Saints received the crown of beauty from the hand of the Lord.

Ant. 3. The bodies of the Saints

are buried in peace : and their names shall live for ever.

Ant. 4. O ye Martyrs of the Lord, bless ye the Lord : praise Him and magnify Him for ever.

Ant. 5. Let the Saints be joyful with glory : let them rejoice in their beds.

CHAPTER. S. James i.

MY brethren, count it all joy when ye fall into divers temptations; knowing this, that the trying of your faith worketh patience. But let patience have her perfect work.

HYMN. *Rex gloriose Martyrum,* p. 100.

℣. The Lord God looketh upon us.

℞. And in truth hath comfort in us.

Ant. to Ben. Theirs is the kingdom of heaven who despised the life of this world : and have gained a reward in the kingdom, and have washed their robes in the Blood of the Lamb.

[*Or this,*

Ant. They have washed their robes : and made them white in the Blood of the Lamb.]

COLLECT.

O GOD, the unseen strength of them that fight, be present, we beseech Thee, when we pray; that we, who on this day, celebrate the glorious triumph of Thy holy Martyrs, *M.* and *N.*, may be protected, by their assistance, from all things hurtful to our souls; through Jesus Christ our Lord. Amen.

[*Or this,*

ALMIGHTY, everlasting God, Who kindlest the fire of Thy love in the hearts of Thy Saints, give to our souls the same strength of faith and charity; that, as we rejoice in the victories of Thy Martyrs, *N.* and his companions, so we may profit by their ex-

amples; through Jesus Christ our Lord. Amen.]

Prime.

Ant. But the souls of the righteous are in the hand of God : and there shall no torment touch them.

Tierce.

Ant.. With the palm they attained to the kingdom : the Saints received the crown of beauty from the hand of the Lord.

CHAPTER. S. James i.

MY brethren, count it all joy when ye fall into divers temptations; knowing this, that the trying of your faith worketh patience. But let patience have her perfect work.

℞. The Lord preserveth : the souls of His Saints. ℣. He shall deliver them from the hand of the ungodly. ℞. The souls of His Saints. ℣. Glory be to the Father, and to the Son, and to the Holy Ghost. ℞. The Lord preserveth : the souls of His Saints.

℣. He shall speak peace unto His people.

℞. And to His Saints.

Sexts.

Ant. The bodies of the Saints are buried in peace : and their names shall live for ever.

CHAPTER. Wisd. x.

WISDOM brought them through the Red Sea, and led them through much water : but drowned their enemies, and cast them up out of the bottom of the deep.

℞. He shall speak peace : unto His people. ℣. And to His Saints. ℞. Unto His people. ℣. Glory be to the Father, and to the Son : and to the Holy Ghost. ℞. He shall speak peace : unto His people.

℣. The souls of the righteous are in the hand of God.

℟. And' there shall no torment touch them.

Nones.

Ant. Let the Saints be joyful with glory : let them rejoice in their beds.

CHAPTER. Isa. ix.

THEY joy before Thee according to the joy in harvest, and as men rejoice when they divide the spoil.

℟. The souls of the righteous are : in the hand of God. ℣. And there shall no torment touch them. ℟. In the hand of God. ℣. Glory be to the Father, and to the Son, and to the Holy Ghost. ℟. The souls of the righteous are : in the hand of God.

℣. They shall come again with joy.

℟. And bring their sheaves with them.

Second Vespers.

Psalms of the Feria.

Ant. 1. I saw under the altar the souls of them that were slain for the word of God : and for the testimony which they held.

Ant. 2. They stood before the throne, and before the Lamb : clothed with white robes, and palms in their hands.

Ant. 3. These are they which came out of great tribulation, and have washed their robes : and made them white in the Blood of the Lamb.

Ant. 4. Therefore are they before the throne of God, and serve Him day and night in His temple : and He that sitteth on the throne shall dwell among them.

Ant. 5. They shall hunger no more, neither thirst any more : neither shall the sun light on them, nor any heat.

CHAPTER. Wisd. iii.

AND in the time of their visitation they shall shine, and run to and fro like sparks among the stubble. They shall judge the nations, and have dominion over the people, and their Lord shall reign for ever.

℟. God forbid that we should forsake the Lord : to serve other gods. ℣. To us there is but one God, the Father, of Whom are all things, and we in Him ; and one Lord Jesus Christ, by Whom are all things, and we by Him. ℟. To serve other gods. ℣. Glory be to the Father, and to the Son, and to the Holy Ghost. ℟. God forbid that we should forsake the Lord : to serve other gods.

HYMN. *Sanctorum meritis,*
℣. and ℟., p. 220.

Ant. to Mag. God shall wipe away : all tears from their eyes.

Collect as at Lauds.

———

OF A BISHOP AND CONFESSOR

THROUGH THE YEAR.

First Vespers.

Ant. Wisdom brought the righteous man through the Red Sea : and led him through much water.

Psalms of the Feria.

CHAPTER. Heb. v.

NO man taketh this honour unto himself, but he that is called of God, as was Aaron.

℟. My covenant was with him : of life and peace. ℣. And I gave them to him for the fear wherewith he feared Me. ℟. Of life and peace. ℣. Glory be to the Father, and to the Son : and to the Holy Ghost. ℟. My covenant was with him : of life and peace.

HYMN. *Iste Confessor.*

HE, the Confessor of the Lord, with triumph,
Whom through the wide world celebrate
the faithful,
He on this day through tribulation enter'd
Heavenly mansions.

Pious and prudent, continent and humble,
Sober he was, and gentle of behaviour,
While in his frame dwelt, animate with action,
Earthly existence.

Wherefore our choir, with willing hymns and
anthems,
Here, on his feast day, doth him fitting honour;
That in his glory we may have our portion,
Ever and ever.

Glory and virtue, honour and salvation,
Be unto Him that, sitting in the highest,
Ordereth meetly earth, and sky, and ocean,
'Onely and Trinal. Amen.

℣. Blessed is the man whom Thou
choosest and receivest unto Thee.

℟. He shall dwell in Thy courts.

Ant. to Mag. He chose him out of
all men living to offer sacrifices to the
Lord : incense, and a sweet savour,
for His people.

COLLECT.

ALMIGHTY, everlasting God, Who
makest us glad by this festival of
blessed *N.*, Thy Confessor and Bishop,
we humbly beseech Thy clemency
that the pious prayers of him whose
office we celebrate may avail to obtain
for us the remedies of eternal life;
through Jesus Christ our Lord. Amen.

[Or this,

GRANT, we beseech Thee, Almighty
God, that as we venerate the solemnity of blessed *N.*, Thy Confessor and
Bishop, so it may avail to our devotion;
through Jesus Christ our Lord. Amen.]

Lauds.

℣. Praise the Lord, ye house of
Aaron.

℟. Praise the Lord, ye house of
Levi.

Psalms of Sunday.

Ant. 1. I am the Door : by Me if
any man enter in, he shall be saved,
and shall go in and out, and find
pasture.

Ant. 2. In glory was there none
like unto him : who kept the law of
the most High.

Ant. 3. That faithful and wise
steward : whom his Lord shall make
ruler over His household.

Ant. 4. Blessed is that servant :
whom the Lord when He cometh
shall find watching.

Ant. 5. Good and faithful servant :
enter thou into the joy of thy Lord.

CHAPTER. S. John x.

HE that entereth in by the door is
the shepherd of the sheep. To
him the porter openeth; and the
sheep hear his voice : and he calleth
his own sheep by name, and leadeth
them out.

HYMN. *Jesu Redemptor omnium.*

JESU, the world's Redeemer, hear!
Thy Bishops' fadeless crown, draw near!
Accept with gentler love to-day
The prayers and praises that we pay!

The day that crowned with deathless fame
This meek Confessor of Thy Name,
Whose yearly feast, in solemn state,
Thy faithful people celebrate.

The world, and all its boasted good,
As vain and passing, he eschewed;
And therefore, with angelic bands,
In endless joys for ever stands.

Grant then that we, O gracious God,
May follow in the steps he trod;
And freed from ev'ry stain of sin,
As he hath won, may also win.

To Thee, O Christ, our loving King,
All glory, praise, and thanks we bring :
All glory, as is ever meet,
To Father and to Paraclete. Amen.

℣. The righteous shall blossom as
a lily.

℟. He shall flourish for ever before
the Lord.

Ant. to Ben. Well done, good and
faithful servant; thou hast been
faithful over a few things, I will
make thee ruler over many things :
enter thou into the joy of thy Lord.

COLLECT.

O GOD, Who providest for Thy
people with tenderness, and
governest them with love; and Who

dost so value them as to set ministers to rule over them in Thy stead; give, we pray Thee, (blessed *N.*, Thy Bishop interceding), the spirit of wisdom to them whom Thou hast appointed to preside over Thy Church, that from the welfare of the holy sheep may spring the everlasting joy of the shepherds; through Jesus Christ our Lord, Who liveth and reigneth with Thee in the unity of the Holy Ghost, one God, world without end. Amen.

[*Or this,*

O GOD, the Light of the faithful, and Shepherd of souls, Who hast set blessed *N.* to be a Bishop in the Church, that he might feed Thy sheep by word, and form them by example; grant us, by his intercession, to keep the faith which he taught, and to follow the way which his example directed; through Jesus Christ our Lord. Amen.]

Prime.

Ant. I am the Door : by Me if any man enter in, he shall be saved, and shall go in and out, and find pasture.

Tierce.

Ant. In glory was there none like unto him : who kept the law of the most High.

CHAPTER. S. John x.

HE that entereth in by the door is the shepherd of the sheep. To him the porter openeth : and the sheep hear his voice : and he calleth his own sheep by name, and leadeth them out.

R͡. I have set thee a watchman unto the house of Israel : therefore thou shalt hear the word at My mouth, and warn them from Me. V͡. Remember how thou hast received and heard, and hold fast. R͡. Therefore thou shalt hear the word at My mouth, and warn them from Me. V͡. Glory be to the Father, and to the Son, and to the Holy Ghost. R͡. I have set thee a watchman unto the house of Israel : therefore thou shalt hear the word at My mouth, and warn them from Me.

V͡. He led them forth by the right way.

R͡. That they might go to the city where they dwelt.

Sexts.

Ant. That faithful and wise steward : whom his Lord shall make ruler over His household.

CHAPTER. Jer. iii.

I WILL bring you to Sion, and I will give you pastors according to Mine heart, which shall feed you with knowledge and understanding.

R͡. He led them forth : by the right way. V͡. That they might go to the city where they dwelt. R͡. By the right way. V͡. Glory be to the Father, and to the Son, and to the Holy Ghost. R͡. He led them forth : by the right way.

V͡. The Lord guided the righteous man in right paths.

R͡. And shewed him the kingdom of God.

Nones.

Ant. Good and faithful servant : enter thou into the joy of thy Lord.

CHAPTER. Ecclus. xlv.

HE made him glorious in the sight of kings, and gave him a commandment for his people.

R͡. The Lord guided the righteous man : in right paths. V͡. And shewed him the kingdom of God. R͡. In right paths. V͡. Glory be to the Father, and to the Son, and to the Holy Ghost. R͡. The Lord guided the righteous man in right paths.

℣. We that are Thy people and sheep of Thy pasture.

℞. Will give Thee thanks for ever.

Second Vespers.

Psalms of the Feria.

Ant. 1. I will raise Me up a faithful priest : that shall do according to that which is in Mine heart and in My mind.

Ant. 2. Go unto the altar and offer thy sin-offering : and make an atonement for thyself, and for the people.

Ant. 3. He shall have the covenant : of an everlasting priesthood.

Ant. 4. Go in this thy might, and thou shalt save Israel : have not I sent thee?

Ant. 5. My covenant was with him of life and peace : and I gave them to him for the fear wherewith he feared Me.

Chapter. Ecclus. xlv.

HE chose him out of all men living to offer sacrifices to the Lord, incense, and a sweet savour, for a memorial, to make reconciliation for His people.

℞. I have laid help : upon one that is mighty. ℣. I have exalted one chosen out of the people. ℞. Upon one that is mighty. ℣. Glory be to the Father, and to the Son, and to the Holy Ghost. ℞. I have laid help : upon one that is mighty.

Hymn. *Iste Confessor*, p. 223.

Ant. to Mag. Let Thy priests, O Lord God, be clothed with salvation : and let Thy Saints rejoice in goodness.

___

Of a Doctor.

The Office is of a Confessor. Bishop, *or a* Confessor, *as the case may be, excepting the Ants. to* Magnificat *and* Benedictus.

Both Vespers.

Ant. to Mag. God giveth wisdom unto the wise, and knowledge to them that know understanding : He revealeth the deep and secret things ; He knoweth what is in the darkness, and the light dwelleth with Him.

Lauds.

Ant. to Ben. I thank Thee, and praise Thee, O Thou God of my fathers : Who hast given me wisdom and might.

___

Of an Abbot or Monk.

First Vespers.

Ant. to Psalms. Escape for thy life : look not behind thee, escape lest thou be consumed.

Psalms of the Feria.

Chapter. ii Cor. vi.

WHEREFORE come out from among them, and be ye separate, saith the Lord, and touch not the unclean thing; and I will receive you, and will be a Father unto you, and ye shall be My sons and daughters, saith the Lord Almighty.

℞. Thou art my defence and shield, and my trust is in Thy word : Away from me, ye wicked, I will keep the commandments of my God. ℣. Master, I will follow Thee whithersoever Thou goest. ℞. Away from me, ye wicked, I will keep the commandments of my God. ℣. Glory be to the Father, and to the Son, and to the Holy Ghost. ℞. Thou art my defence and shield, and my trust is in Thy word : Away from me, ye wicked, I will keep the commandments of my God.

Hymn. *Rex gloriose Martyrum*, p. 100.

If an Abbot :

℣. His seed shall be mighty upon earth.

℞. The generation of the faithful shall be blessed.

Ant. to Mag. Get thee out of thy country, and from thy kindred : and come into the land which I shall shew thee.

But if not an Abbot :

℣. Under the shadow of Thy wings shall be my refuge.

℟. Until this tyranny be overpast.

Ant. to Mag. Thou hast left thy father and thy mother, and the land of thy nativity : the Lord recompense thy work, and a full reward be given thee of the Lord God of Israel, under Whose wings thou art come to trust.

Lauds.

℣. O ye holy and humble men of heart, bless ye the Lord.

℟. Praise Him and magnify Him for ever.

Psalms of Sunday.

Ant. 1. I will make with them a covenant of peace, and they shall dwell safely in the wilderness, and sleep in the woods : and I will make them and the places round about My hill a blessing.

Ant. 2. We wept when we remembered thee, O Sion : how shall we sing the Lord's song in a strange land?

Ant. 3. I have put off the clothing of prosperity, and put upon me the sackcloth of my prayer : I will cry unto the Everlasting in my days. And joy is come unto me from the Holy One.

Ant. 4. Then judgment shall dwell in the wilderness : and the work of righteousness shall be peace, and the effect of righteousness, quietness, and assurance for ever.

Ant. 5. Let us go forth therefore unto Him without the camp, bearing His reproach : for here we have no continuing city, but we seek one to come.

CHAPTER. Is. li.

THE Lord shall comfort Sion : He will comfort all her waste places ; and He will make her wilderness like Eden, and her desert like the garden of the Lord ; joy and gladness shall be found therein, thanksgiving, and the voice of melody.

HYMN. *Iste Confessor*, p. 223.

If an Abbot :

℣. Come, ye children, and hearken unto me.

℟. I will teach you the fear of the Lord.

Ant. to Ben. Behold, I and the children whom the Lord hath given me are for signs and for wonders in Israel : from the Lord of hosts, which dwelleth in Mount Sion.

COLLECT.

O GOD, Who didst grant to blessed *N.*, the Abbot, to imitate Christ in His poverty, and with humble heart to follow Him to the end; grant to all who have entered on the path of Thy commandments, neither to look back nor to err in the way, but hasting to Thee without stumbling, to attain eternal life, through the same Thy Son Jesus Christ our Lord. Amen.

If not an Abbot :

℣. I cried to Thee, O Lord, and said, Thou art my hope.

℟. And my stronghold.

Ant. to Ben. The Lord is my portion, saith my soul : therefore will I hope in Him.

COLLECT.

ALMIGHTY, Everlasting God, bestowing exceeding great rewards on those who for Thy sake trample on earthly things ; grant us, by the example and intercession of blessed *N.*, whose departure we this day celebrate, to despise all temporal things, and with our whole heart to hasten unto things eternal; through Jesus Christ our Lord. Amen.

Prime.

Ant. I will make with them a covenant of peace, and they shall dwell safely in the wilderness, and sleep in the woods : and I will make them, and the places round about My hill a blessing.

Tierce.

Ant. We wept when we remembered thee, O Sion : how shall we sing the Lord's song in a strange land?

CHAPTER. Is. lvii.

THUS saith the high and lofty One that inhabiteth eternity, Whose Name is Holy: I dwell in the high and holy place, with him also that is of a contrite and humble spirit, to revive the spirit of the humble, and to revive the heart of the contrite ones.

Ry. Come, My people, enter thou into thy chambers, hide thyself as it were for a little moment : until the indignation be overpast. Ꝟ. Come ye apart into a desert place, and rest awhile. Ry. Until the indignation be overpast. Ꝟ. Glory be to the Father, and to the Son, and to the Holy Ghost. Ry. Come, My people, enter thou into thy chambers, hide thyself as it were for a little moment : until the indignation be overpast.

Ꝟ. I had rather be a doorkeeper in the house of my God.

Ry. Than to dwell in the tents of ungodliness.

Sexts.

Ant. I have put off the clothing of prosperity, and put upon me the sackcloth of my prayer : I will cry unto the Everlasting in my days.

And joy is come unto me from the Holy One.

CHAPTER. Heb. xii.

NOW no chastening for the present seemeth to be joyous, but grievous : nevertheless, afterward it yieldeth the peaceable fruit of righteousness unto them which are exercised thereby.

Ry. I would rather be : a doorkeeper in the house of my God. Ꝟ. Than to dwell in the tents of ungodliness. Ry. A door-keeper in the house of my God. Ꝟ. Glory be to the Father, and to the Son, and to the Holy Ghost. Ry. I would rather be a door-keeper : in the house of my God.

Ꝟ. Thy statutes have been my songs.

Ry. In the house of my pilgrimage.

Nones.

Ant. Let us go forth therefore unto Him without the camp, bearing his reproach : for here we have no continuing city, but we seek one to come.

CHAPTER. Ecclus. li.

BEHOLD with your eyes, how that I have had but little labour, and have gotten unto me much rest.

Ry. Thy statutes have been : my songs. Ꝟ. In the house of my pilgrimage. Ry. My songs. Ꝟ. Glory be to the Father, and to the Son, and to the Holy Ghost. Ry. Thy statutes have been : my songs.

Ꝟ. Seven times a day do I praise Thee.

Ry. Because of Thy righteous judgments.

Second Vespers.

Psalms of the Feria.

Ant. 1. They shall not be confounded : that put their trust in Thee.

Ant. 2. As dying, and behold we live; as sorrowful, yet alway rejoicing : as having nothing, and yet possessing all things.

Ant. 3. All of one mind, having compassion one of another : loving to the brethren, pitiful, courteous.

Ant. 4. Here have we no continuing city : but we seek one to come.

Ant. 5. I will sacrifice unto Thee with the voice of thanksgiving : I will pay that I have vowed.

CHAPTER. Deut. vii.

THE Lord thy God, He is God, the faithful God, Which keepeth covenant and mercy with them that love Him and keep His commandments, to a thousand generations.

R︢. Thanks be to God.

HYMN. *Rex gloriose Martyrum,*
p. 100.

If an Abbot :

V︢. The righteous shall flourish like a palm-tree.

R︢. And shall spread abroad like a cedar in Libanus.

Ant. to Mag. Ye that follow after righteousness, ye that seek the Lord : look unto your father, for I called him alone, and blessed him, and increased him.

If not an Abbot :

V︢. They shall flourish in the courts of the House of our God.

R︢. That they may shew how true the Lord my strength is.

Ant. to Magnificat *as at First Vespers,*
p. 226.

———

OF A CONFESSOR NOT A BISHOP.

First Vespers.

Psalms of the Feria.

Ant. 1. He that putteth his trust in Me shall possess the land : and shall inherit My holy mountain.

Ant. 2. The Name of the Lord is a strong tower : the righteous runneth into it and is safe.

Ant. 3. The blessing of the Lord is in the reward of the godly : and suddenly He maketh His blessing to flourish.

Ant. 4. Lord, Thou deliveredst unto me five talents : behold, I have gained beside them five talents more.

Ant. 5. And they that know Thy Name will put their trust in Thee : for Thou, Lord, hast never failed them that seek Thee.

CHAPTER. Ecclus. ii.

YE that fear the Lord, wait for His mercy; and go not aside, lest ye fall. Ye that fear the Lord, believe Him; and your reward shall not fail. Ye that fear the Lord, hope for good, and for everlasting joy and mercy.

R︢. They that fear the Lord will not disobey His word : and they that love Him will keep His ways. V︢. Love is the fulfilling of the law. R︢. They that love Him will keep His ways. V︢. Glory be to the Father, and to the Son, and to the Holy Ghost. R︢. They that fear the Lord will not disobey His word : and they that love Him will keep His ways.

HYMN. *Iste Confessor,* p. 223.

If a Priest :

V︢. Mine eyes look upon such as are faithful in the land.

R︢. That they may dwell with Me.

Ant. to Mag. The Lord will shew who are His and who is holy : even him whom He hath chosen will He cause to come near unto Him.

COLLECT.

O GOD, Who makest us glad with the yearly solemnity of blessed *N.,* Thy Confessor, mercifully grant that as we venerate his nativity, so we may imitate his actions; through Jesus Christ our Lord. Amen.

If not a Priest :

℣. They that love Thy Name shall be joyful in Thee.

℟. For Thou, Lord, wilt give Thy blessing to the righteous.

Ant. to Mag. They that put their trust in Him shall understand the truth : and such as be faithful in love shall abide with Him.

COLLECT.

GRANT, we beseech Thee, O Lord God, (blessed *N.*, interceding,) that Thy people may walk in Thy love; through Jesus Christ our Lord. Amen.

Lauds.

℣. O ye servants of the Lord, bless ye the Lord.

℟. Praise Him and magnify Him for ever.

Psalms of Sunday.

Ant. 1. Before the Lord which chose me : I will yet be more vile than thus, and will be base in mine own sight.

Ant. 2. Well done, good and faithful servant; thou hast been faithful over a few things, I will make thee ruler over many things : enter thou into the joy of thy Lord.

Ant. 3. As for me, I will behold Thy presence in righteousness : and when I awake up after Thy likeness, I shall be satisfied with it.

Ant. 4. It is a great glory : to follow the Lord.

Ant. 5. They that wait upon the Lord shall renew their strength : they shall run, and not be weary; they shall walk, and not faint.

CHAPTER. Ecclus. xxxi.

BLESSED is the rich that is found without blemish, and hath not gone after gold. Who is he? and we will call him blessed : for wonder-

ful things hath he done among his people.

HYMN. *Rex gloriose Martyrum,* p. 100.

If a Priest :

℣. Send out Thy light and Thy truth that they may lead me.

℟. And bring me unto Thy holy hill, and to Thy dwelling.

Ant. to Ben. He wrought that which was good and right, and truth, before the Lord his God : and in every work that he began, he did it with all his heart, and prospered.

If not a Priest :

℣. Look well if there be any way of wickedness in me.

℟. And lead me in the way everlasting.

Ant. to Ben. He that doeth truth, cometh to the light : that his deeds may be made manifest that they are wrought in God.

Prime.

Ant. Before the Lord which chose me : I will yet be more vile than thus, and will be base in mine own sight.

Tierce.

Ant. Well done, good and faithful servant; thou hast been faithful over a few things, I will make thee ruler over many things : enter thou into the joy of thy Lord.

CHAPTER. Ecclus. xxxi.

BLESSED is the rich that is found without blemish, and hath not gone after gold. Who is he? and we will call him blessed; for wonderful things hath he done among his people.

℟. I am a companion of : all them that fear Thee. ℣. And keep Thy commandments. ℟. All them that fear Thee. ℣. Glory be to the Father, and to the Son, and to the Holy

Ghost. ℣. I am a companion of : all them that fear Thee.

℣. Thy word is a lantern unto my feet.

℞. And a light unto my paths.

Sexts.

Ant. As for me, I will behold Thy presence in righteousness : and when I awake up after Thy likeness, I shall be satisfied with it.

CHAPTER. Gal. vi.

WHATSOEVER a man soweth, that shall he also reap. For he that soweth to his flesh shall of the flesh reap corruption; but he that soweth to the Spirit shall of the Spirit reap life everlasting.

℞. Thy word is a lantern : unto my feet. ℣. And a light unto my paths. ℞. Unto my feet. ℣. Glory be to the Father, and to the Son, and to the Holy Ghost. ℞. Thy word is a lantern : unto my feet.

℣. Thy righteousness is an everlasting righteousness.

℞. And Thy law is the truth.

Nones.

Ant. They that wait upon the Lord shall renew their strength : they shall run, and not be weary; they shall walk, and not faint.

CHAPTER. II Cor. xii.

I TAKE pleasure in infirmities, in reproaches, in necessities, in persecutions, in distresses for Christ's sake: for when I am weak, then am I strong.

℞. Thy righteousness : is an everlasting righteousness. ℣. And Thy law is the truth. ℞. An everlasting righteousness. ℣. Glory be to the Father, and to the Son, and to the Holy Ghost. ℞. Thy righteousness is : an everlasting righteousness.

℣. O take not the word of Thy truth utterly out of my mouth.

℞. For my hope is in Thy judgments.

Second Vespers.

Psalms of the Feria.

Ant. 1. Behold an Israelite indeed : in whom is no guile.

Ant. 2. I will look unto the Lord; I will wait for the God of my salvation : my God will hear me.

Ant. 3. A perfect and an upright man : one that feareth God, and escheweth evil.

Ant. 4. He will bring me forth to the light : and I shall behold His righteousness.

Ant. 5. For Thy sake have I suffered reproof, shame hath covered my face : for the zeal of Thine house hath even eaten me.

CHAPTER. II Cor. iii.

WE all, with open face beholding as in a glass the glory of the Lord, are changed into the same image from glory to glory, even as by the Spirit of the Lord.

HYMN. *Iste Confessor,*
℣. and ℞., p. 223.

Ant. to Magnificat, *as at First Vespers.*

———

OF A VIRGIN AND MARTYR.

First Vespers.

Ant. This is the wise virgin, whose lamp was ready when the Bridegroom came : she went in with the Lord to the wedding.

Psalms of the Feria.

CHAPTER. Ecclus. li.

THEN lifted I up my supplication from the earth, O Lord my God, and prayed for deliverance from death.

℞. The kingdoms of the earth and all the glory of the world I despised for the love of my Lord Jesus Christ : Whom I have seen, Whom I have loved, in Whom I have believed, Whom I have desired. ℣. My heart is inditing of a good matter. I speak of the things which I have made unto the King. ℟. Whom I have seen, Whom I have loved, in Whom I have believed, Whom I have desired. ℣. Glory be to the Father, and to the Son, and to the Holy Ghost. ℟. The kingdoms of this earth, and all the glory of the world I despised for the love of my Lord Jesus Christ, Whom I have seen, Whom I have loved, in Whom I have believed, Whom I have desired.

HYMN. *Virginis proles opifexque matris.*

CHILD of the Virgin, Maker of Thy Mother,
  Virgin-engendered, of the Virgin Son,
Virgin is she of whom we sing another
      Victory won.

[Double the palm of triumph which she beareth,
  Strove she to vanquish woman's fear of death :
Quelled now the hand of death and hell appeareth
      Her feet beneath.

Death won no conquest, nor the thousand terrors,
  Kindred of death—fierce torments bravely borne :
Gave she her blood : that blood the radiance mirrors
      Of life's new morn.]

When she pleads for us, at her sweet petition,
  That we may sing with conscience pure of sin,
From debt of guilt O grant us Thy remission,
      And peace within.

Glory to Thee, O Father, Son, and Spirit,
  Glory co-equal on the Throne on high,
Equal in power, in unity of merit,
      Eternally. Amen.

℣. Full of grace are thy lips.

℟. Because God hath blessed thee for ever.

Ant. to Mag. The kingdom of heaven is like unto a net, that was cast into the sea, and gathered of every kind : which when it was full, they drew to shore, and gathered the good into vessels, but cast the bad away.

COLLECT.

HEAR us, O God of our salvation, that as we rejoice in the feast of blessed *N.*, Thy Virgin [and Martyr;] so of Thy mercy we may be taught the spirit of devotion ; through Jesus our Lord. Amen.

Lauds.

℣. God hath given her the help of His countenance.

℟. God is in the midst of her, therefore shall she not be removed.

Psalms of Sunday.

Ant. 1. This is the wise virgin : whom the Lord found watching.

Ant. 2. This is a wise virgin : and of the number of the prudent.

Ant. 3. This is a virgin holy and glorious : for the Lord of all things hath chosen her.

Ant. 4. I bless Thee, O Father of my Lord Jesus Christ : because, through Thy Son, the fire of temptation is extinguished round about me.

Ant. 5. Come, bride of Christ, receive the crown : which the Lord hath prepared for thee for ever.

CHAPTER. Ecclus. li.

THEN lifted I up my supplication from the earth, O Lord my God, and prayed for deliverance from death.

℟. Thanks be to God.

HYMN. *Jesu, corona Virginum.*

JESU, the Virgins' Crown, do Thou
  Accept us, as in prayer we bow ;
Born of that Virgin, whom alone
The mother and the maid we own.

Amongst the lilies Thou dost feed,
With virgin choirs accompanied ;
With glory decked, the spotless brides
Whose bridal gifts Thy love provides.

They, wheresoe'er Thy footsteps bend,
With hymns and praises still attend ;
In blessed troops they follow Thee,
With dance, and song, and melody.

We pray Thee therefore to bestow
Upon our senses here below,
Thy grace, that so we may endure
From taint of all corruption pure.

All laud to God the Father be :
All laud, Eternal Son, to Thee :
All laud, as is for ever meet,
To God the Holy Paraclete. Amen.

℣. The virgins that be her fellows shall bear her company.

℞. And shall be brought unto Thee.

Ant. to Ben. When the Bridegroom came, the wise virgins : being ready, went in with Him to the marriage.

Collect as at the First Vespers.

Prime.

Ant. This is a wise virgin : whom the Lord found watching.

Tierce.

Ant. This is a wise virgin : and of the number of the prudent.

CHAPTER. Ecclus. li.

THEN lifted I up my supplication from the earth, O Lord my God, and prayed for deliverance from death.

℞. Full of grace : are thy lips. ℣. Because God hath blessed thee for ever. ℞. Are thy lips. ℣. Glory be to the Father, and to the Son, and to the Holy Ghost. ℞. Full of grace : are thy lips.

℣. In thy glory and thy beauty.

℞. Go forth, proceed, and reign.

Sexts.

Ant. This is a virgin, holy and glorious : for the Lord of all things hath chosen her.

CHAPTER. Ecclus. li.

I WILL praise Thy Name continually, and will sing praise with thanksgiving; because my prayer was heard.

℞. In thy glory : and thy beauty. ℣. Go forth, proceed, and reign. ℞. In thy beauty. ℣. Glory be to the Father, and to the Son, and to the Holy Ghost. ℞. In thy glory : and thy beauty.

℣. God hath given her the help of His countenance.

℞. God shall help her, and that right early.

Nones.

Ant. Come, bride of Christ, receive the crown : which the Lord hath prepared for thee for ever.

CHAPTER. Ecclus. li.

THOU savedst me from destruction, and deliveredst me from the evil time : therefore will I give thanks, and praise Thee, and bless Thy Name, O Lord.

℞. God hath given her : the help of His countenance. ℣. God shall help her, and that right early. ℞. The help of His countenance. ℣. Glory be to the Father, and to the Son, and to the Holy Ghost. ℞. God hath given her : the help of His countenance.

℣. The virgins that be her fellows shall bear her company.

℞. And shall be brought unto Thee.

Second Vespers.

Ant. to Psalms. This is the wise virgin : whom the Lord found watching.

CHAPTER. Ecclus. li.

THEN lifted I up my supplication from the earth, O Lord my God, and prayed for deliverance from death.

℞. Thanks be to God.

Hymn, ℣. and ℞., and Ant. to Magnificat as at First Vespers.

[*On the Feasts of* S. AGNES, S. AGATHA, *and* S. KATHARINE, *these Chapters.*

Both Vespers, Lauds, and Tierce.

CHAPTER. Ecclus. li.

I WILL thank Thee, O Lord and King, and praise Thee, O God, my

Saviour: I do give praise unto Thy Name. For Thou art my defender and helper, and hast preserved my body from destruction.

Sexts.

CHAPTER. Ecclus. li.

MY soul praised the Lord, even unto death, and my life was near to hell.

Nones.

Chapter as of the Common.]

OF A VIRGIN NOT MARTYR.

The Office is the same, except the Chapters, the second and third verses of the Hymn at Vespers being omitted.

Both Vespers, Lauds, and Tierce.

CHAPTER. II Cor. x.

HE that glorieth, let him glory in the Lord. For not he that commendeth himself is approved, but whom the Lord commendeth.

Sexts.

CHAPTER. II Cor. xi.

I AM jealous over you with godly jealousy: for I have espoused you to one husband, that I may present you as a chaste virgin to Christ.

Nones.

CHAPTER. Wisdom vii. viii.

VICE shall not prevail against wisdom. Wisdom reacheth from one end to another mightily: and sweetly doth she order all things.

OF A MATRON.

First Vespers.

Ant: to Psalms. Help me, which have no other help but Thee, O Lord: Who knowest that I hate the glory of the unrighteous.

CHAPTER. Prov. xxxi.

WHO can find a virtuous woman? for her price is far above rubies. The heart of her husband doth safely trust in her, so that he shall have no need of spoil.

HYMN. *Ad cœnam Agni providi.*

TO share the Lamb's high marriage rites,
　The Father matron-guests invites:
How blest is she who hears the call,
And seeks to keep the festival!

O'er all the Church her praise be told,
Whom Jesu's grace has made so bold,
To choose with Him the better part,
On Him alone to fix the heart.

The wound of love her spirit felt,
And on the earth no longer dwelt;
But strove to climb the rugged way,
That leads to joys that ne'er decay.

The flesh to tame, her daily care;
Her daily banquet, holy prayer;
Awaiting, in the realms above,
The Lamb's eternal feast of love.

Vouchsafe that we, O gracious God,
May follow in the steps she trod;
And, free from every stain of sin,
As she hath won, may also win.

All praise to God the Father be;
All praise, Eternal Son, to Thee;
Whom with the Spirit we adore,
For ever and for evermore. Amen.

℣. O turn away mine eyes, lest they behold vanity.

℟. And quicken Thou me in Thy way.

Ant. to Mag. My heart rejoiceth in the Lord : my mouth is enlarged, because I rejoice in Thy salvation.

COLLECT.

O GOD of mercy, enlighten the hearts of Thy faithful people, and (blessed *N.,* [Thy Martyr,] interceding) make us to despise things earthly, and love things heavenly; through Jesus Christ our Lord. Amen.

If the Office be of a Matron not Martyr, the words, Thy Martyr, *are omitted from the Collect.*

Lauds.

℣. I will praise Thy Name for evermore.

R̷. For great is Thy mercy toward me.

Psalms of the Feria.

Ant. 1. As the sun when it ariseth in the high heaven : so is the beauty of a good woman in the ordering of her house.

Ant. 2. A virtuous woman rejoiceth her husband : and he shall fulfil the years of his life in peace.

Ant. 3. A silent and loving woman : is a gift from the Lord.

Ant. 4. She openeth her mouth with wisdom : and in her tongue is the law of kindness.

Ant. 5. She departed not from the temple : but served God with fastings and prayers night and day.

CHAPTER. 1 S. Pet. iii.

YE wives, be subject to your own husbands, that, if any obey not the word, they also may without the word be won by the conversation of the wives; while they behold your chaste conversation coupled with fear.

R̷. Thanks be to God.

HYMN. *Hæc rite mundi gloria.*

THE world and all its boasted good
   As vain and passing she eschewed;
And therefore with angelic bands,
In endless joys for ever stands.

Grant then that we, O gracious God,
May follow in the steps she trod;
And, freed from every stain of sin,
As she hath won, may also win.

To Thee, O Christ, our loving King,
All glory, praise, and thanks, we bring;
All glory, as is ever meet,
To Father and to Paraclete. Amen.

V̷. I humbled my soul with fasting.

R̷. And my prayer shall turn into mine own bosom.

Ant. to Ben. The prayer of the humble pierceth the clouds : he will not depart till the Most High shall behold.

Collect as at First Vespers.

Prime.

Ant. As the sun when it ariseth in the high heavens : so is the beauty of a good woman in the ordering of her house.

Tierce.

Ant. A virtuous woman rejoiceth her husband : and he shall fulfil the years of his life in peace.

CHAPTER. Acts ii.

ON my handmaidens I will pour out in those days of my Spirit; and they shall prophesy. And I will shew wonders in heaven above, and signs in the earth beneath.

R̷. Teach me to do the thing that pleaseth Thee : for Thou art my God. V̷. Let Thy loving Spirit lead me forth into the land of righteousness. R̷. For Thou art my God. V̷. Glory be to the Father, and to the Son, and to the Holy Ghost. R̷. Teach me to do the thing that pleaseth Thee : for Thou art my God.

V̷. I will take heed to my ways, that I offend not in my tongue.

R̷. I will keep my mouth as it were with a bridle.

Sexts.

Ant. A silent and loving woman : is a gift from the Lord.

CHAPTER. Tobit x.

AND he said to his daughter, Honour thy father and thy mother-in-law, which are now thy parents : that I may hear good report of thee.

R̷. I will take heed to my ways : that I offend not in my tongue. V̷. I will keep my mouth as it were with a bridle. R̷. That I offend not in my tongue. V̷. Glory be to the Father, and to the Son, and to the Holy Ghost. R̷. I will take heed to my ways : that I offend not in my tongue.

℣. I waited patiently for the Lord, and He inclined unto me.

℟. And heard my calling.

Nones.

Ant. She departed not from the temple : but served God with fastings and prayers night and day.

CHAPTER. Ecclus. xl.

CHILDREN and the building of a city continue a man's name : but a blameless wife is counted above them both.

℟. I waited patiently for the Lord : and He inclined unto me. ℣. And heard my calling. ℟. And He inclined unto me. ℣. Glory be to the Father, and to the Son, and to the Holy Ghost. ℟. I waited patiently for the Lord : and He inclined unto me.

℣. O come hither, and behold the works of God.

℟. Who holdeth our soul in life.

Second Vespers.

Psalms of the Feria.

Ant. 1. Favour is deceitful and beauty is vain : but a woman that feareth the Lord, she shall be praised.

Ant. 2. There was none that gave her an ill word : for she feared the Lord greatly.

Ant. 3. She looketh well to the ways of her household : and eateth not the bread of idleness.

Ant. 4. She hath brought up children, lodged strangers, washed the saints' feet : relieved the afflicted, and diligently followed every good work.

Ant. 5. Her children rise up, and call her blessed : her husband also, and he praiseth her.

Chapter, Hymn, Ad cænam Agni providi, ℣. *and* ℟., *as at First Vespers,* p. 233.

Ant. to Mag. Strength and honour are her clothing ; and she shall rejoice in time to come : give her of the fruit of her hands, and let her own works praise her in the gates.

Collect as at First Vespers.

ANNIVERSARY OF THE DEDICATION OF A CHURCH.

First Vespers.

Psalms of the Feria.

Ant. 1. Is not the Lord your God with you? Set your heart and your soul to seek the Lord your God : arise therefore, and build ye the sanctuary of the Lord God.

Ant. 2. The house that is to be builded for the Lord must be exceeding magnifical, of fame and of glory throughout all countries : I will therefore now make preparation for it.

Ant. 3. Great is our God above all gods : But who is able to build Him an house?

Ant. 4. Seeing the heaven of heavens cannot contain Him : who am I then, that I should build Him an house?

Ant. 5. The most high Lord : hath commanded that I should build Him an house.

CHAPTER. Ezekiel xxxvii.

THUS saith the Lord : Moreover I will make a covenant of peace with them; it shall be an everlasting covenant with them : and I will place them, and multiply them, and will set My sanctuary in the midst of them for evermore. My tabernacle also shall be with them.

℟. All that is in the heaven and in the earth is Thine, O Lord; and of Thine own have we given Thee : O Lord our God, all this store that we have prepared to build Thee an house for Thy Holy Name cometh of Thine hand. ℣. Who hath first given to the Lord, and it shall be recompensed unto him again? R̶. O Lord our God, all this store that we have prepared to build Thee an house for Thy Holy Name cometh of Thine hand. V̶. Glory be to the Father, and to the Son, and to the Holy Ghost. R̶. O Lord our God, all this store that we have prepared to build Thee an house for Thy Holy Name cometh of Thine hand.

HYMN. *Urbs beata Hierusalem.*

BLESSED city, heavenly Salem,
  Vision dear of peace and love,
Who, of living stones upbuilded,
  Art the joy of heaven above,
And, with angel cohorts circled,
  As a bride to earth dost move!

From celestial realms descending,
  Ready for the nuptial bed,
To His presence, decked with jewels,
  By her Lord shall she be led;
All her streets, and all her bulwarks,
  Of pure gold are fashioned.

Bright with pearls her portal glitters!
  It is open evermore;
And, by virtue of His merits,
  Thither faithful souls may soar,
Who for Christ's dear Name, in this world
  Pain and tribulation bore.

Many a blow and biting sculpture
  Polished well those stones elect,
In their places now compacted
  By the heavenly Architect,
Who therewith hath willed for ever
  That His palace should be decked.

Laud and honour to the Father;
  Laud and honour to the Son;
Laud and honour to the Spirit;
  Ever Three, and ever One:
Consubstantial, Co-eternal,
  While unending ages run. Amen.

V̶. The hill of Sion is a fair place, the joy of the whole earth.

R̶. God is well known in her palaces.

Ant. to Mag. My house shall be built in Jerusalem : and the Lord shall yet comfort Sion, and shall yet choose Jerusalem.

COLLECT.

O GOD, Who year by year renewest the consecration day of this Thy holy temple, and bringest us again in safety to Thy holy mysteries; hear the prayers of Thy people, and grant that whosoever entereth this temple to ask for blessings, may rejoice in their fulfilment; through Jesus Christ our Lord, Who liveth and reigneth with Thee and the Holy Ghost, world without end. Amen.

Compline.

Ant. to Psalms. May Thine eyes be open toward this house night and day : and hearken Thou to the supplication of Thy people.

HYMN. *Salvator mundi Domine,*
  p. 67, *with this Doxology :*

Praise to the Father and the Son;
To Thee, blest Spirit, praise be done:
Whose holy unction hath restored
Our hearts as temples to the Lord. Amen.

This Doxology is said to all Hymns of the same metre throughout the Octave.

Ant. to Nunc Dim. I will fill this house with glory : and in this place will I give peace.

Lauds.

V̶. O sing unto the Lord a new song.

V̶. Let the congregation of Saints praise Him.

Psalms of Sunday, except the Canticle.

Ant. 1. The house of God is the Church of the living God : the pillar and ground of the truth.

Ant. 2. Christ's house are we : if we hold fast the confidence and the rejoicing of the hope firm unto the end.

Ant. 3. To whom coming, as unto a living stone, chosen of God and precious : ye also, as lively stones, are built up a spiritual house.

Ant. 4. In whom all the building fitly framed together groweth unto an holy temple in the Lord : in whom ye also are builded together for an habitation of God through the Spirit.

SONG OF TOBIT.

Tobit xiii. *Jerusalem civitas Dei.*

O JERUSALEM, the holy city : He will scourge thee for thy children's works, and will have mercy again on the sons of the righteous.

2 Give praise to the Lord, for He is good; and praise the everlasting King, that His tabernacle may be builded in thee again with joy : and let Him make joyful there in thee for ever those that are miserable.

3 Many nations shall come from far to the name of the Lord God with gifts in their hands, even gifts to the King of heaven : all generations shall praise Thee with great joy.

4 Cursed are all they which hate Thee : and blessed shall all be which love Thee for ever.

5 Rejoice and be glad for the children of the just : for they shall be gathered together, and shall bless the Lord of the just.

6 O blessed are they which love thee, for they shall rejoice in thy peace : blessed are they which have been sorrowful for all thy scourges : for they shall rejoice for thee, when they have seen all thy glory, and shall be glad for ever.

7 Let my soul bless God : the great King.

8 For Jerusalem shall be built up with sapphires, and emeralds, and precious stone : thy walls and towers and battlements with pure gold.

9 And the streets of Jerusalem shall be paved : with beryl and carbuncle and stones of Ophir.

10 And all her streets shall say, Alleluia : and they shall praise Him, saying, Blessed be God, which hath extolled it for ever.

Ant. 5. Ye are God's building, I have laid the foundation : let every man take heed how he buildeth thereupon, for the foundation is Jesus Christ.

CHAPTER. ii Chron. vii.

NOW have I chosen and sanctified this house, that My Name may be there for ever : and Mine eyes and Mine heart shall be there perpetually.

R̰. Thanks be to God.

HYMN. *Angulare fundamentum.*

CHRIST is made the sure Foundation,
    And the precious Corner-stone,
Who, the two-fold walls surmounting,
    Binds them closely into one :
Holy Sion's help for ever,
    And her confidence alone.

All that dedicated city,
    Dearly loved by God on high,
In exultant jubilation
    Pours perpetual melody ;
God the One, and God the Trinal,
    Singing everlastingly.

To this Temple, where we call Thee,
    Come, O Lord of Hosts, to day !
With Thy wonted loving kindness
    Hear Thy people as they pray ;
And Thy fullest benediction
    Shed within its walls for aye.

Here vouchsafe to all Thy servants
    That they supplicate to gain :
Here to have and hold for ever
    Those good things their prayers obtain :
And hereafter in Thy glory
    With Thy blessed ones to reign.

Laud and honour to the Father ;
    Laud and honour to the Son ;
Laud and honour to the Spirit ;
    Ever Three, and ever One :
Consubstantial, co-eternal,
    While unending ages run. Amen.

℣. Holiness becometh.
R̰. Thine house for ever.

Ant. to Ben. He ordained, that the days of the dedication of the altar should be kept in their season from year to year by the space of eight days : with mirth and gladness. Alleluia.

Prime.

Ant. The house of God is the Church of the living God : the pillar and ground of the truth.

R̰. Jesu Christ, Son of the living God, have mercy upon us. ℣. Thou Who dost honour Thine own place.

℟. Have mercy upon us. ℣. Glory be to the Father, and to the Son, and to the Holy Ghost. ℟. Jesu Christ, Son of the living God, have mercy upon us.

Tierce.

Ant. Christ's house are we : if we hold fast the confidence and rejoicing of the hope firm unto the end.

CHAPTER. Jer. vii.

HEAR the word of the Lord, all ye of Judah, that enter in at these gates to worship the Lord. Thus saith the Lord of hosts, the God of Israel, Amend your ways and your doings, and I will cause you to dwell in this place.

℟. I will come into Thine house : even upon the multitude of Thy mercy. Alleluia, Alleluia. ℣. In Thy fear will I worship toward Thy holy temple. ℟. Alleluia, Alleluia. ℣. Glory be to the Father, and to the Son, and to the Holy Ghost. ℟. I will come into Thine house : even upon the multitude of Thy mercy. Alleluia, Alleluia.

℣. I will go into Thine house with burnt offerings.

℟. And will pay Thee my vows.

[*Through the Octave,* Alleluia *is omitted, and the* ℟. *is taken up at the colon, and so at the other Hours.*]

Sexts.

Ant. Great is our God above all gods : but who is able to build Him an house?

CHAPTER. Lev. xxvi.

YE shall keep My sabbaths, and reverence My sanctuary : I am the Lord.

℟. Blessed is the man : whom Thou choosest and receivest unto Thee. Alleluia, Alleluia. ℣. He shall dwell in Thy court. ℟. Alleluia, Alleluia. ℣. Glory be to the Father,

and to the Son, and to the Holy Ghost. ℟. Blessed is the man : whom Thou choosest and receivest unto Thee. Alleluia, Alleluia.

℣. Blessed are they that dwell in Thy house.

℟. They will be alway praising Thee.

Nones.

Ant. Ye are God's building, I have laid the foundation : let every man take heed how he buildeth thereupon, for the foundation is Jesus Christ.

CHAPTER. II Chron. xx.

WE stand before this house, and in Thy presence, (for Thy name is in this house,) and cry unto Thee in our affliction, then Thou wilt hear and help.

℟. He shall be satisfied : with the pleasures of Thy house. Alleluia, Alleluia. ℣. Even of Thy holy temple. ℟. Alleluia, Alleluia. ℣. Glory be to the Father, and to the Son, and to the Holy Ghost. ℟. He shall be satisfied : with the pleasures of Thy house. Alleluia, Alleluia.

℣. O how amiable are Thy dwellings, Thou Lord of hosts.

℟. My soul hath a desire and longing to enter into the courts of the Lord.

Second Vespers.

Ant. 1. One of the seven angels carried me away in the spirit : and shewed me that great city, the holy Jerusalem, descending out of heaven from God.

Psalm cxxii. *Lætatus sum,* p. 52.

Ant. 2. And the building of the wall of it was of jasper : and the city was pure gold, like unto clear glass.

Psalm cxxiv. *Nisi quia Dominus,* p. 53.

Ant. 3. I saw no temple therein :

for the Lord God Almighty and the Lamb are the temple of it.

Psalm cxxxii. *Memento, Domine*, p. 56.

Ant. And the city had no need of the sun, neither of the moon to shine in it : for the glory of God did lighten it, and the Lamb is the light thereof.

Psalm cxxxvii. *Super flumina*, p. 58.

Ant. 5. There shall in no wise enter into it any thing that defileth, neither whatsoever worketh abomination or maketh a lie : but they which are written in the Lamb's book of life.

Psalm cxlvii. 12. *Lauda Hierusalem*, p. 64.

CHAPTER. 1 Cor. vi.

WHAT? know ye not that your body is the temple of the Holy Ghost which is in you, which ye have of God, and ye are not your own?

HYMN. *Urbs beata Hierusalem,* V. and R̊., *as at First Vespers*, p. 236.

Ant. to Mag. Make straight paths for your feet : for ye are come unto the city of the living God, the heavenly Jerusalem. Wherefore receiving a kingdom which cannot be moved : serve God with reverence and godly fear.

On Sunday in the Octave, the Office of Sunday is said, with Memorial of the Octave at both Vespers and Lauds. But if the Dedication Feast falls on Sunday, the Office of Dedication is said, with Memorial of Sunday, at both Vespers and Lauds. On the Octave the Office is said as on the first day.

✠

II. OCCASIONAL OFFICES.

Gradual Psalms.

[Here is set down, in case it be preferred:
The Roman Use.

The Gradual Psalms are said on every Wednesday in Lent before Matins in Choir, except on the concurrence of a Double Festival; out of Choir they are to be said as occasion serves.

The first five Psalms, Psalm cxx., Ad Dominum, Psalm cxxi., Levavi oculos, Psalm cxxii., Lætatus sum, Psalm cxxiii., Ad te levavi oculos meos, *and* Psalm cxxiv., Nisi quia Dominus, *are said without Antiphon, and without Glory be, etc. At the end of the last is said:*

℣. Eternal rest : grant unto them, O Lord. ℟. And light perpetual : shine on them.

Then is said kneeling :

Our Father :

Silently to the end. The reader repeats :

℣. And lead us not into temptation. ℟. But deliver us from evil. ℣. From the gates of hell. ℟. Deliver their souls, O Lord. ℣. May they rest in peace. ℟. Amen. ℣. Hear my prayer, O Lord. ℟. And let my crying come unto Thee. ℣. The Lord be with you. ℟. And with thy spirit.

Let us pray.
Collect.

HAVE mercy, O Lord, upon the souls of Thy servants, and of Thine handmaidens, and of all the faithful departed : and loose them from all bonds of sin; that they may obtain an inheritance among Thy Saints in the glory of the First Resurrection; through Christ our Lord. Amen.

Then follow Psalm cxxv., Qui confidunt, Psalm cxxvi., In convertendo, Psalm cxxvii., Nisi Dominus, Psalm cxxviii., Beati omnes, *and* Psalm cxxix., Sæpe expugnaverunt; *each with* Glory be, etc.

Then is said kneeling :

Lord, have mercy.
Christ, have mercy.
Lord, have mercy.

Our Father :

Silently to the end. The reader repeats :

℣. And lead us not into temptation. ℟. But deliver us from evil. ℣. O think upon Thy congregation. ℟. Whom Thou hast purchased and redeemed of old. ℣. Hear my prayer, O Lord. ℟. And let my crying come unto Thee. ℣. The Lord be with you. ℟. And with thy spirit.

Let us pray.
Collect.

O GOD, Whose nature and property is ever to have mercy and to forgive, receive our humble petitions; and though we be tied and bound with the chain of our sins, yet let the pitifulness of Thy great mercy loose us; for the honour of Jesus Christ, our Mediator and Advocate. Amen.

Then follow Psalm cxxx., De profundis, Psalm cxxxi., Domine non est, Psalm cxxxii., Memento Domine, Psalm cxxxiii., Ecce quam bonum, *and* Psalm cxxxiv., Ecce nunc; *each with* Glory be, etc.

Then is said kneeling:

Lord, have mercy.
Christ, have mercy.
Lord, have mercy.

Our Father:

Silently to the end. The reader repeats:

℣. And lead us not into temptation. ℟. But deliver us from evil. ℣. O Lord, save Thy servants. ℟. That put their trust in Thee. ℣. Hear my prayer, O Lord. ℟. And let my crying come unto Thee. ℣. The Lord be with you. ℟. And with thy spirit.

Let us pray.

COLLECT.

STRETCH forth, O Lord, to Thy servants and to thine handmaidens, the arm of Thy heavenly help: that they may both seek Thee with their whole heart, and also may obtain of Thee such things as they ask; through Christ our Lord. Amen.]

SARUM USE.

Psalm cxx. *Ad Dominum.*

WHEN I was in trouble I called upon the Lord: and He heard me.

2 Deliver my soul, O Lord, from lying lips: and from a deceitful tongue.

3 What reward shall be given or done unto thee, thou false tongue: even mighty and sharp arrows, with hot burning coals.

4 Wo is me, that I am constrained to dwell with Mesech: and to have my habitation among the tents of Kedar.

5 My soul hath long dwelt among them: that are enemies unto peace.

6 I labour for peace, but when I speak unto them thereof: they make them ready to battle.

Glory be, etc.

Psalm cxxi. *Levavi oculos.*

I WILL lift up mine eyes unto the hills: from whence cometh my help.

2 My help cometh even from the Lord: Who hath made heaven and earth.

3 He will not suffer thy foot to be moved: and He that keepeth thee will not sleep.

4 Behold, He that keepeth Israel: shall neither slumber nor sleep.

5 The Lord Himself is thy keeper: the Lord is thy defence upon thy right hand;

6 So that the sun shall not burn thee by day: neither the moon by night.

7 The Lord shall preserve thee from all evil: yea, it is even He that shall keep thy soul.

8 The Lord shall preserve thy going out, and thy coming in: from this time forth for evermore.

Glory be, etc.

Psalm cxxii. *Lætatus sum.*

I WAS glad when they said unto me: We will go into the house of the Lord.

2 Our feet shall stand in thy gates: O Jerusalem.

3 Jerusalem is built as a city: that is at unity in itself.

4 For thither the tribes go up, even the tribes of the Lord: to testify unto Israel, to give thanks unto the Name of the Lord.

5 For there is the seat of judgment: even the seat of the house of David.

6 O pray for the peace of Jerusalem: they shall prosper that love thee.

7 Peace be within thy walls : and plenteousness within thy palaces.

8 For my brethren and companions' sakes : I will wish thee prosperity.

9 Yea, because of the house of the Lord our God : I will seek to do thee good.

Glory be, etc.

Psalm cxxiii. *Ad te levavi oculos meos.*

UNTO Thee lift I up mine eyes : O Thou that dwellest in the heavens.

2 Behold, even as the eyes of servants look unto the hand of their masters, and as the eyes of a maiden unto the hand of her mistress : even so our eyes wait upon the Lord our God, until He have mercy upon us.

3 Have mercy upon us, O Lord, have mercy upon us : for we are utterly despised.

4 Our soul is filled with the scornful reproof of the wealthy : and with the despitefulness of the proud.

Glory be, etc.

Psalm cxxiv. *Nisi quia Dominus.*

IF the Lord Himself had not been on our side, now may Israel say : if the Lord Himself had not been on our side, when men rose up against us ;

2 They had swallowed us up quick : when they were so wrathfully displeased at us.

3 Yea, the waters had drowned us : and the stream had gone over our soul.

4 The deep waters of the proud : had gone even over our soul.

5 But praised be the Lord : Who hath not given us over for a prey unto their teeth.

6 Our soul is escaped even as a bird out of the snare of the fowler : the snare is broken, and we are delivered.

7 Our help standeth in the name of the Lord : Who hath made heaven and earth.

Glory be, etc.

Psalm cxxv. *Qui confidunt.*

THEY that put their trust in the Lord, shall be even as the mount Sion : which may not be removed, but standeth fast for ever.

2 The hills stand about Jerusalem : even so standeth the Lord round about His people, from this time forth for evermore.

3 For the rod of the ungodly cometh not into the lot of the righteous : lest the righteous put their hand unto wickedness.

4 Do well, O Lord : unto those that are good and true of heart.

5 As for such as turn back unto their own wickedness : the Lord shall lead them forth with the evil doers, but peace shall be upon Israel.

Glory be, etc.

Psalm cxxvi. *In convertendo.*

WHEN the Lord turned again the captivity of Sion : then were we like unto them that dream.

2 Then was our mouth filled with laughter : and our tongue with joy.

3 Then said they among the heathen : The Lord hath done great things for them.

4 Yea, the Lord hath done great things for us already : whereof we rejoice.

5 Turn our captivity, O Lord : as the rivers in the south.

6 They that sow in tears : shall reap in joy.

7 He that now goeth on his way weeping, and beareth forth good seed : shall doubtless come again with joy, and bring his sheaves with him.

Glory be, etc.

Psalm cxxvii. *Nisi Dominus.*

EXCEPT the Lord build the house : their labour is but lost that build it.

2 Except the Lord keep the city : the watchman waketh but in vain.

3 It is but lost labour that ye haste to rise up early, and so late take rest, and eat the bread of carefulness : for so He giveth His beloved sleep.

4 Lo, children and the fruit of the womb : are an heritage and gift that cometh of the Lord.

5 Like as the arrows in the hand of a giant : even so are the young children.

6 Happy is the man that hath his quiver full of them : they shall not be ashamed when they speak with their enemies in the gate.

Glory be, etc.

Psalm cxxviii. *Beati omnes.*

BLESSED are all they that fear the Lord : and walk in His ways.

2 For thou shalt eat the labours of thine hands : O well is thee, and happy shalt thou be.

3 Thy wife shall be as the fruitful vine : upon the walls of thine house.

4 Thy children like the olive-branches : round about thy table.

5 Lo, thus shall the man be blessed : that feareth the Lord.

6 The Lord from out of Sion shall so bless thee : that thou shalt see Jerusalem in prosperity all thy life long.

7 Yea, that thou shalt see thy children's children : and peace upon Israel.

Glory be, etc.

Psalm cxxix. *Sæpe expugnaverunt.*

MANY a time have they fought against me from my youth up : may Israel now say.

2 Yea, many a time have they vexed me from my youth up : but they have not prevailed against me.

3 The plowers plowed upon my back : and made long furrows.

4 But the righteous Lord : hath hewn the snares of the ungodly in pieces.

5 Let them be confounded and turned backward : as many as have evil will at Sion.

6 Let them be even as the grass growing upon the house-tops : which withereth afore it be plucked up.

7 Whereof the mower filleth not his hand : neither he that bindeth up the sheaves his bosom.

8 So that they who go by say not so much as, The Lord prosper you : we wish you good luck in the Name of the Lord.

Glory be, etc.

Psalm cxxx. *De profundis.*

OUT of the deep have I called unto Thee, O Lord : Lord, hear my voice.

2 O let Thine ears consider well : the voice of my complaint.

3 If Thou, Lord, wilt be extreme to mark what is done amiss : O Lord, who may abide it ?

4 For there is mercy with Thee : therefore shalt Thou be feared.

5 I look for the Lord, my soul doth wait for Him : in His word is my trust.

6 My soul fleeth unto the Lord : before the morning watch, I say, before the morning watch.

7 O Israel, trust in the Lord, for with the Lord there is mercy : and with Him is plenteous redemption.

8 And He shall redeem Israel : from all his sins.

Glory be, etc.

Psalm cxxxi. *Domine, non est.*

LORD, I am not high-minded : I have no proud looks.

2 I do not exercise myself in great matters : which are too high for me.

3 But I refrain my soul, and keep it low, like as a child that is weaned from his mother : yea, my soul is even as a weaned child.

4 O Israel, trust in the Lord : from this time forth for evermore.

Glory be, etc.

Psalm cxxxii. *Memento, Domine.*

LORD, remember David : and all his trouble.

2 How he sware unto the Lord : and vowed a vow unto the Almighty God of Jacob;

3 I will not come within the tabernacle of mine house : nor climb up into my bed;

4 I will not suffer mine eyes to sleep, nor mine eye-lids to slumber : neither the temples of my head to take any rest,

5 Until I find out a place for the temple of the Lord : an habitation for the mighty God of Jacob.

6 Lo, we heard of the same at Ephrata : and found it in the wood.

7 We will go into His tabernacle : and fall low on our knees before His footstool.

8 Arise, O Lord, into Thy resting place : Thou, and the ark of Thy strength.

9 Let Thy priests be clothed with righteousness : and let Thy saints sing with joyfulness.

10 For Thy servant David's sake : turn not away the presence of Thine Anointed.

11 The Lord hath made a faithful oath unto David : and He shall not shrink from it;

12 Of the fruit of thy body : shall I set upon thy seat.

13 If thy children will keep My covenant, and My testimonies that I shall learn them : their children also shall sit upon thy seat for evermore.

14 For the Lord hath chosen Sion to be an habitation for Himself : He hath longed for her.

15 This shall be My rest for ever : here will I dwell, for I have a delight therein.

16 I will bless her victuals with increase : and will satisfy her poor with bread.

17 I will deck her priests with health : and her saints shall rejoice and sing.

18 There shall I make the horn of David to flourish : I have ordained a lantern for Mine anointed.

19 As for his enemies, I shall clothe them with shame : but upon himself shall his crown flourish.

Glory be, etc.

Psalm cxxxiii. *Ecce, quam bonum.*

BEHOLD, how good and joyful a thing it is : brethren, to dwell together in unity.

2 It is like the precious ointment upon the head, that ran down unto the beard : even unto Aaron's beard, and went down to the skirts of his clothing.

3 Like as the dew of Hermon : which fell upon the hill of Sion.

4 For there the Lord promised His blessing : and life for evermore.

Glory be, etc.

Psalm cxxxiv. *Ecce nunc.*

BEHOLD now, praise the Lord : all ye servants of the Lord;

2 Ye that by night stand in the house of the Lord : even in the courts of the house of our God.

3 Lift up your hands in the sanctuary : and praise the Lord.

4 The Lord that made heaven and earth : give thee blessing out of Sion.

Glory be, etc.

LITANY.

Which follows the Gradual Psalms according to the use of Sarum.

LORD, have mercy.
  Christ, have mercy.
  Lord, have mercy.
O Christ, hear us.
  O Christ, graciously hear us.

O God the Father, of heaven,
O God the Son, Redeemer of the world,
O God the Holy Ghost,
O holy Trinity, One God,

Have mercy upon us.

Be merciful : spare us, good Lord.

From all evil,
From the snares of the devil,
From eternal damnation,
From the dangers threatening our sins,
From the assaults of evil spirits,
From the spirit of fornication,
From the desire of vain glory,
From all impurity of soul and body,
From anger and hatred and all ill-will,
From impure thoughts,
From blindness of heart,
From lightning and tempest,
From sudden and unprepared death,
By the mystery of Thy holy Incarnation,
By Thy Nativity,
By Thy holy Circumcision,
By Thy Baptism,
By Thy Fasting,
By Thy Cross and Passion,
By Thy precious Death,
By Thy glorious Resurrection,
By Thy wonderful Ascension,
By the grace of the Holy Ghost, the Comforter,

Good Lord, deliver us.

In the hour of death : help us, good Lord.
In the day of judgment : deliver us, good Lord.

We sinners : beseech Thee to hear us.
That Thou wouldest give us peace,
That Thy mercy and pity may keep us,
That Thou wouldest rule and defend Thy Church,
That Thou wouldest keep the Bishops and all Orders of the Church in holy religion,
That Thou wouldest give peace, true concord and victory to our kings and princes,
That Thou wouldest keep the congregations of all the faithful in Thy holy service,
That Thou wouldest keep all Christian people redeemed with Thy precious Blood,
That Thou wouldest reward all our benefactors with eternal blessings,
That Thou wouldest deliver our souls and the souls of our kinsfolk from eternal damnation,
That Thou wouldest give and preserve the fruits of the earth,
That Thou wouldest again cast the eyes of Thy mercy upon us,
That Thou wouldest make the obedience of our service reasonable,
That Thou wouldest raise our minds to heavenly desires,
That Thou wouldest look upon and lighten the miseries of the poor and of captives,
That Thou wouldest give eternal rest to all the faithful departed,
That Thou wouldest hear us,

We beseech Thee to hear us.

Son of God : we beseech Thee to hear us.
O Lamb of God, That takest away the sins of the world,
  Hear us, good Lord.
O Lamb of God, That takest away the sins of the world,

Spare us, good Lord.

O Lamb of God, That takest away the sins of the world,

Have mercy upon us.

Lord, have mercy.

Christ, have mercy.

Lord, have mercy.

Our Father.

℣. And lead us not into temptation. ℟. But deliver us from evil. ℣. Shew us Thy mercy, O Lord. ℟. And grant us Thy salvation. ℣. Let Thy loving mercy come also unto us, O Lord. ℟. Even Thy salvation, according unto Thy word. ℣. We have sinned with our fathers. ℟. We have done amiss, and dealt wickedly. ℣. O Lord, deal not with us after our sins. ℟. Neither reward us after our iniquities. ℣. Let us pray for all orders of the Church. ℟. Let Thy priests be clothed with righteousness, and Thy saints sing with joyfulness. ℣. For our brethren and sisters. ℟. My God, save Thy servants and handmaidens, which put their trust in Thee. ℣. For all Christian people. ℟. Save Thy people, O Lord, and give Thy blessing unto Thine inheritance; feed them, and set them up for ever. ℣. Peace be within Thy walls. ℟. And plenteousness within Thy palaces. ℣. May the souls of Thy servants and handmaidens rest in peace. ℟. Amen. ℣. Hear my prayer, O Lord. ℟. And let my crying come unto Thee. ℣. The Lord be with you. ℟. And with thy spirit.

Let us pray.

COLLECTS.

O GOD, Whose nature and property is ever to have mercy and to forgive, receive our humble petitions; and though we be tied and bound with the chain of our sins, yet let the pitifulness of Thy great mercy loose us.

ALMIGHTY and everlasting God, Who alone workest great marvels: send down upon our Bishops, and Curates, and all congregations committed to their charge, the healthful Spirit of Thy grace: and that they may truly please Thee, pour upon them the continual dew of Thy blessing.

WE beseech Thee, Almighty God, that Thy servant, our Sovereign, N., who has received from Thy mercy the government of this realm, may also receive the increase of all virtues, and being adorned therewith, may both shun the depths of sin, and overcome *his* enemies; and, being filled with grace, may be found worthy to come to Thee, the Truth and the Life, and be acceptable in Thy sight.

O GOD, Who by the grace of the Holy Ghost hast poured the gifts of charity into the hearts of Thy faithful people: grant unto Thy servants and Thy handmaidens for whom we entreat Thy mercy, health both of soul and body; that they may love Thee with all their strength, and may work out with unreserved affection the things that are well-pleasing unto Thee.

O GOD, from Whom all holy desires, all good counsels, and all just works do proceed; give unto Thy servants that peace which the world cannot give; that both our hearts may be set to obey Thy commandments, and also that by Thee we, being defended from the fear of our enemies, may pass our time in rest and quietness.

WE beseech Thee, O Lord, graciously to shew us Thine ineffable mercy, that Thou mayest both deliver us from all our sins, and set us free from the punishments which they deserve.

O GOD the Creator and Redeemer of all the faithful, grant to the souls of Thy servants and hand-maidens remission of all their sins: that the pardon they have always desired, by pious supplications may be obtained.

WE beseech Thee, O Lord, in Thy compassion to unloose the chains of our sins, and by the intercession of Mary, the blessed and glorious and ever Virgin Mother of God, and of all Saints, keep us Thy servants, and the whole Catholic Church, in all sanctity; and purge from their vices those joined to us by kindred or friend-ship, or in the confession of the faith, and adorn them with virtues; grant us peace and safety; drive away from our friends all enemies visible and in-visible, and keep them from sickness; grant charity to our enemies, and to all Thy faithful, living and departed, life in the land of the living, and eternal rest; through Jesus Christ our Lord, Who liveth and reigneth with Thee and the Holy Ghost, ever one God, world without end. Amen.

The Penitential Psalms.

According to the Sarum use, the seven Penitential Psalms are said daily in Lent, one at each Office with Psalm li., Miserere. *But before a Festival in Lent, at Nones of the Vigil, the three last Psalms are said, namely,* Psalm cii., Domine exaudi, Psalm cxxx., De profundis, *and* Psalm cxliii., Domine ex-audi; *that they may be completed before the First Vespers of the Festival.*

They are appointed to be said consecutively, after Sexts on Ash-Wednesday, before the blessing of ashes, and the ejection of penitents; after Nones on Maundy Thursday, at the reconciliation of peni-tents; and on Rogation Monday after Nones.

[According to the Roman use, which some may prefer, the seven Psalms are not said daily, but only on Fridays in Lent, with Litany, after Lauds. (The Sarum Litany, p. 245, may thus be used.)

The earlier part of the Sarum Ash-Wed-nesday Office is here subjoined, in order to form a Penitential Office for use when occasion shall serve.]

Ant. Remember not.

[*Against Anger.*]

Psalm vi. *Domine, ne in furore.*

O LORD, rebuke me not in Thine indignation : neither chasten me in Thy displeasure.

2 Have mercy upon me, O Lord, for I am weak : O Lord, heal me, for my bones are vexed.

3 My soul also is sore troubled : but, Lord, how long wilt Thou punish me?

4 Turn Thee, O Lord, and deliver my soul : O save me for Thy mercy's sake.

5 For in death no man remem-bereth Thee : and who will give Thee thanks in the pit?

6 I am weary of my groaning; every night wash I my bed : and water my couch with my tears.

7 My beauty is gone for very trouble : and worn away because of all mine enemies.

8 Away from me, all ye that work vanity : for the Lord hath heard the voice of my weeping.

9 The Lord hath heard my peti-tion : the Lord will receive my prayer.

10 All mine enemies shall be con-founded, and sore vexed : they shall be turned back, and put to shame suddenly.

Glory be, etc.

[*Against Pride.*]

Psalm xxxi. *Beati, quorum.*

BLESSED is he whose unrighteous-ness is forgiven : and whose sin is covered.

2 Blessed is the man unto whom the Lord imputeth no sin : and in whose spirit there is no guile.

3 For while I held my tongue : my bones consumed away through my daily complaining.

4 For Thy hand is heavy upon me day and night : and my moisture is like the drought in summer.

5 I will acknowledge my sin unto Thee : and mine unrighteousness have I not hid.

6 I said, I will confess my sin unto the Lord : and so Thou forgavest the wickedness of my sin.

7 For this shall every one that is godly make his prayer unto Thee, in a time when Thou mayest be found : but in the great water-floods they shall not come nigh him.

8 Thou art a place to hide me in, Thou shalt preserve me from trouble : Thou shalt compass me about with songs of deliverance.

9 I will inform thee, and teach thee in the way wherein thou shalt go : and I will guide thee with mine eye.

10 Be ye not like to horse and mule, which have no understanding : whose mouths must be held with bit and bridle, lest they fall upon thee.

11 Great plagues remain for the ungodly : but whoso putteth his trust in the Lord, mercy embraceth him on every side.

12 Be glad, O ye righteous, and rejoice in the Lord : and be joyful, all ye that are true of heart.

Glory be, etc.

[*Against Gluttony.*]

Ps. xxxviii. *Domine, ne in furore.*

PUT me not to rebuke, O Lord, in Thine anger : neither chasten me in Thy heavy displeasure.

2 For Thine arrows stick fast in me : and Thy hand presseth me sore.

3 There is no health in my flesh, because of Thy displeasure : neither is there any rest in my bones, by reason of my sin.

4 For my wickednesses are gone over my head : and are like a sore burden, too heavy for me to bear.

5 My wounds stink and are corrupt : through my foolishness.

6 I am brought into so great trouble and misery : that I go mourning all the day long.

7 For my loins are filled with a sore disease : and there is no whole part in my body.

8 I am feeble, and sore smitten : I have roared for the very disquietness of my heart.

9 Lord, Thou knowest all my desire : and my groaning is not hid from Thee.

10 My heart panteth, my strength hath failed me : and the sight of mine eyes is gone from me.

11 My lovers and my neighbours did stand looking upon my trouble : and my kinsmen stood afar off.

12 They also that sought after my life laid snares for me : and they that went about to do me evil talked of wickedness, and imagined deceit all the day long.

13 As for me, I was like a deaf man, and heard not : and as one that is dumb, who doth not open his mouth.

14 I became even as a man that heareth not : and in whose mouth are no reproofs.

15 For in Thee, O Lord, have I put my trust : Thou shalt answer for me, O Lord my God.

16 I have required that they, even mine enemies, should not triumph over me : for when my foot slipped, they rejoiced greatly against me.

17 And I, truly, am set in the plague : and my heaviness is ever in my sight.

18 For I will confess my wicked-ness : and be sorry for my sin.

19 But mine enemies live, and are mighty : and they that hate me wrongfully are many in number.

20 They also that reward evil for good are against me : because I follow the thing that good is.

21 Forsake me not, O Lord my God : be not Thou far from me.

22 Haste Thee to help me : O Lord God of my salvation.

Glory be, etc.

[*Against Lust.*]

Psalm li. *Miserere mei Deus.*

HAVE mercy upon me, O God, after Thy great goodness : according to the multitude of Thy mercies do away mine offences.

2 Wash me throughly from my wickedness : and cleanse me from my sin.

3 For I acknowledge my faults : and my sin is ever before me.

4 Against Thee only have I sinned, and done this evil in Thy sight : that Thou mightest be justified in Thy saying, and clear when Thou art judged.

5 Behold, I was shapen in wickedness : and in sin hath my mother conceived me.

6 But lo, Thou requirest truth in the inward parts : and shalt make me to understand wisdom secretly.

7 Thou shalt purge me with hyssop, and I shall be clean : Thou shalt wash me, and I shall be whiter than snow.

8 Thou shalt make me hear of joy and gladness : that the bones which Thou hast broken may rejoice.

9 Turn Thy face from my sins : and put out all my misdeeds.

10 Make me a clean heart, O God : and renew a right spirit within me.

11 Cast me not away from Thy presence : and take not Thy Holy Spirit from me.

12 O give me the comfort of Thy help again : and stablish me with Thy free Spirit.

13 Then shall I teach Thy ways unto the wicked : and sinners shall be converted unto Thee.

14 Deliver me from blood-guiltiness, O God, Thou that art the God of my health : and my tongue shall sing of Thy righteousness.

15 Thou shalt open my lips, O Lord : and my mouth shall shew Thy praise.

16 For Thou desirest no sacrifice, else would I give it Thee : but Thou delightest not in burnt-offerings.

17 The sacrifice of God is a troubled spirit : a broken and contrite heart, O God, shalt Thou not despise.

18 O be favourable and gracious unto Sion : build Thou the walls of Jerusalem.

19 Then shalt Thou be pleased with the sacrifice of righteousness, with the burnt offerings and oblations : then shall they offer young bullocks upon Thine altar.

Glory be, etc.

[*Against Avarice.*]

Psalm cii. *Domine, exaudi.*

HEAR my prayer, O Lord : and let my crying come unto Thee.

2 Hide not Thy face from me in the time of my trouble : incline Thine ear unto me when I call; O hear me, and that right soon.

3 For my days are consumed away like smoke : and my bones are burnt up as it were a fire-brand.

4 My heart is smitten down, and withered like grass : so that I forget to eat my bread.

5 For the voice of my groaning : my bones will scarce cleave to my flesh.

6 I am become like a pelican in the wilderness : and like an owl that is in the desert.

7 I have watched, and am even as it were a sparrow : that sitteth alone upon the house-top.

8 Mine enemies revile me all the day long : and they that are mad upon me are sworn together against me.

9 For I have eaten ashes as it were bread : and mingled my drink with weeping ;

10 And that because of Thine indignation and wrath : for Thou hast taken me up, and cast me down.

11 My days are gone like a shadow : and I am withered like grass.

12 But Thou, O Lord, shalt endure for ever : and Thy remembrance throughout all generations.

13 Thou shalt arise, and have mercy upon Sion : for it is time that Thou have mercy upon her, yea, the time is come.

14 And why ? Thy servants think upon her stones : and it pitieth them to see her in the dust.

15 The heathen shall fear Thy Name, O Lord : and all the kings of the earth Thy majesty ;

16 When the Lord shall build up Sion : and when His glory shall appear ;

17 When He turneth Him unto the prayer of the poor destitute : and despiseth not their desire.

18 This shall be written for those that come after : and the people which shall be born shall praise the Lord.

19 For He hath looked down from His sanctuary : out of the heaven did the Lord behold the earth ;

20 That He might hear the mournings of such as are in captivity : and deliver the children appointed unto death ;

21 That they may declare the Name of the Lord in Sion : and His worship at Jerusalem ;

22 When the people are gathered together : and the kingdoms also, to serve the Lord.

23 He brought down my strength in my journey : and shortened my days.

24 But I said, O my God, take me not away in the midst of mine age : as for Thy years, they endure throughout all generations.

25 Thou, Lord, in the beginning hast laid the foundation of the earth : and the heavens are the work of Thy hands.

26 They shall perish, but Thou shalt endure : they all shall wax old as doth a garment ;

27 And as a vesture shalt Thou change them, and they shall be changed : but Thou art the same, and Thy years shall not fail.

28 The children of Thy servants shall continue : and their seed shall stand fast in Thy sight.

Glory be, etc.

[*Against Envy.*]

Psalm cxxx. *De profundis.*

OUT of the deep have I called unto Thee, O Lord : Lord, hear my voice.

2 O let Thine ears consider well : the voice of my complaint.

3 If Thou, Lord, wilt be extreme to mark what is done amiss : O Lord, who may abide it ?

4 For there is mercy with Thee : therefore shalt Thou be feared.

5 I look for the Lord ; my soul doth wait for Him : in His word is my trust.

6 My soul fleeth unto the Lord : before the morning watch, I say, before the morning watch.

7 O Israel, trust in the Lord, for with the Lord there is mercy : and with Him is plenteous redemption.

8 And He shall redeem Israel : from all his sins.
Glory be, etc.

[*Against Sloth.*]

Psalm cxliii. *Domine, exaudi.*

HEAR my prayer, O Lord, and consider my desire : hearken unto me for Thy truth and righteousness' sake.

2 And enter not into judgment with Thy servant : for in Thy sight shall no man living be justified.

3 For the enemy hath persecuted my soul; he hath smitten my life down to the ground : he hath laid me in the darkness, as the men that have been long dead.

4 Therefore is my spirit vexed within me : and my heart within me is desolate.

5 Yet do I remember the time past; I muse upon all Thy works : yea, I exercise myself in the works of Thy hands.

6 I stretch forth my hands unto Thee : my soul gaspeth unto Thee as a thirsty land.

7 Hear me, O Lord, and that soon, for my spirit waxeth faint : hide not Thy face from me, lest I be like unto them that go down into the pit.

8 O let me hear Thy loving-kindness betimes in the morning, for in Thee is my trust : shew Thou me the way that I should walk in, for I lift up my soul unto Thee.

9 Deliver me, O Lord, from mine enemies : for I flee unto Thee to hide me.

10 Teach me to do the thing that pleaseth Thee, for Thou art my God : let Thy loving Spirit lead me forth into the land of righteousness.

11 Quicken me, O Lord, for Thy Name's sake : and for Thy righteousness' sake bring my soul out of trouble.

12 And of Thy goodness slay mine enemies : and destroy all them that vex my soul; for I am Thy servant.
Glory be, etc.

Ant. Remember not, Lord, our offences, nor the offences of our forefathers; neither take Thou vengeance of our sins : spare us, good Lord, spare Thy people, whom Thou hast redeemed with Thy most precious blood, and be not angry with us for ever.

Lord, have mercy.
Christ, have mercy.
Lord, have mercy.

Our Father :

Silently to the end. The Priest repeats aloud :

℣. And lead us not into temptation. ℟. But deliver us from evil. ℣. O God, save Thy servants and handmaidens. ℟. Who put their trust in Thee. ℣. Send them help, O Lord, from the sanctuary. ℟. And strengthen them out of Sion. ℣. Help us, O God of our salvation. ℟. And for the glory of Thy Name deliver us; and be merciful unto our sins, for Thy Name's sake. ℣. Hear my prayer, O Lord. ℟. And let my crying come unto Thee. ℣. The Lord be with you. ℟. And with thy spirit.

Let us pray.

COLLECTS.

O LORD, we beseech Thee, mercifully hear our prayers, and spare all those that confess their sins unto Thee; that they whose consciences by sin are accused, by Thy merciful pardon may be absolved.

WE beseech Thee, O Lord, inspire Thy servants with saving grace, that their hearts may be melted by true contrition, and Thine anger turned away by due repentance.

GRANT, we beseech Thee, O Lord our God, that these Thy penitent servants may be continually mindful of their purification; and that they may bring the same to good effect, let the grace of Thy presence ever prevent and follow them.

LET Thy compassion, O Lord, we beseech Thee, prevent these Thy servants, that all their iniquities may be blotted out by Thy ready forgiveness.

O LORD, hear our supplications, and shew forth Thy loving mercy to Thy servants; heal their wounds, and forgive their sins, that they, being separated from Thee by no iniquities, may ever hold fast unto Thee their Lord.

O LORD, Who in Thy mercy art not wearied by our sin, but dost accept our penitence; look, we beseech Thee, upon Thy servants who confess that they have grievously sinned against Thee; for to Thee it pertaineth to absolve offences, and pardon sinners, and Thou hast said that Thou wouldest not the death of a sinner, but his repentance. Grant therefore, O Lord, that these Thy servants may keep unto Thee the vigil of penitence here, and amending their ways, may hereafter give Thee thanks for eternal joys.

O GOD, Whose pardon all men need, remember Thy servants and handmaidens; and because through the deceitfulness and frailty of their mortal bodies they are despoiled of virtue, and have done amiss in many things, we beseech Thee, pardon them who confess, spare them who entreat; that they who by their deserts are accused, by Thy mercy may be saved; through Jesus Christ our Lord, Who liveth and reigneth with Thee and the Holy Ghost, ever one God, world without end. Amen.

INTERCESSORY OFFICE FOR THE SICK.

This Office has only First Vespers, Matins, and Lauds.

Vespers.

Ant. 1. I am the Lord : that healeth thee.

Psalm cxxi. *Levavi oculos*, p. 50.

Ant. 2. It is the Lord : let Him do what seemeth Him good.

Psalm cxxiii. *Ad te levavi*, p. 53.

Ant. 3. Let us return unto the Lord, for He hath torn, and He will heal us : He hath smitten, and He will bind us up.

Psalm cxlii. *Voce mea*, p. 61.

Ant. 4. My strength : shall be made perfect in weakness.

Psalm cxlvi. *Lauda anima mea*, p. 63.

Ant. 5. Into Thy hands : I commend my spirit.

Psalm cxlvii. *Laudate Dominum*, p. 64.

CHAPTER. Is. xxxiii.

THE inhabitant shall not say, I am sick : the people that dwell therein shall be forgiven their iniquity.

R̸. What I do thou knowest not now: but thou shalt know hereafter. V̸. I will bring the blind by a way that they knew not. R̸. But thou shalt know hereafter. V̸. Glory be to the Father, and to the Son, and to the Holy Ghost. R̸. What I do thou knowest not now: but thou shalt know hereafter.

HYMN. *Christe, cœlestis medicina Patris.*

CHRIST, from the Father sent to bring us healing,
Truest Physician, stronger than the grave,
Look on Thy people suppliantly kneeling,
Hearken and save.

Lo, unto Thee we humbly make petition,
For all whom sickness grieveth with its pain,
In mercy from their suffering condition
Lift them again.

Thou Who didst quickly cure of burning fever
  Peter's wife's mother and the noble's son,
Of the centurion's servant the reliever,
  Mightiest One;

Heal soul and body, give Thy perfect curing
  Unto those causes whence diseases spring;
Let not the gnawing pangs we are enduring
  Uselessly sting.

Vigour upon Thy drooping people sending,
  Thy full salvation ever on them pour;
Grant, as of old, to feeble ones amending;
  Help and restore.

Hearken, O God, in pity to our crying,
  Aid all for whom to Thee we make com-
    plaint,
Be Thy refreshment felt by each one lying
    Weary and faint.

Banish each pang which makes the body
    perish,
  Bid every throe of agony be still,
Let welcome health the tortured members
    cherish;
    Strengthen from ill.

So that on earth, by suffering's sharp training,
  Counted with them whom Thou in love dost
    try,
We may attain where Thou, O Lord, art
    reigning,
    Crowned upon high.

℣. Mine Angel is with you.

℞. And I Myself caring for your
souls.

Ant. to Mag. God shall wipe away
all tears from their eyes : and there
shall be no more death, neither sorrow, nor crying, neither shall there
be any more pain; for the former
things are passed away.

COLLECT.

O GOD of heavenly might, Who by
  the power of Thy command
drivest away every weakness and
every infirmity from the bodies of
men : mercifully help Thy *servant*
[or *handmaid*], that freed from *his*
sickness, and restored to health, *he*
may with renewed strength bless Thy
holy Name; through Jesus Christ
our Lord, Who liveth and reigneth
with Thee and the Holy Ghost, ever
one God, world without end. Amen.

𝕷𝖆𝖚𝖉𝖘.

℣. The grave cannot praise Thee,
death cannot celebrate Thee.

℞. The living, the living, he shall
praise Thee, as I do this day.

*Psalms of Sunday, except the Canticle,
  which is the* Song of Hezekiah, p. 12.

Ant. 1. Lord, my servant lieth at
home, sick of the palsy : Verily, I
say unto thee, I will come and heal
him.

Ant. 2. It is neither new moon
nor sabbath : She said, It shall be
well.

Ant. 3. Lord, I am not worthy
that Thou shouldest come under my
roof : but speak the word only, and
my servant shall be healed.

Ant. 4. Go and wash in Jordan
seven times : and thy flesh shall come
again to thee, and thou shalt be clean.

Ant. 5. Whatsoever ye shall ask
the Father in My Name : He will
give it you.

CHAPTER. Acts xix.

A ND God wrought special miracles
  by the hands of Paul : so that
from his body were brought unto the
sick handkerchiefs or aprons, and the
diseases departed from them, and the
evil spirits went out of them.

℞. Thanks be to God.

HYMN. *Lustra sex qui jam peracta,*
    ℣. *and* ℞., p. 148.

Ant. to Ben. He will surely come
out to me : and call on the Name of
his God, and recover the leper.

Collect as at Vespers.

ORDER FOR THE COMMENDATION OF
A SOUL BEFORE DEATH.

First is said a short Litany, as follows :

Lord, have mercy,
  Christ, have mercy.
Lord, have mercy.

Be merciful : spare *him*, good Lord.
Be merciful : help *him*, good Lord.
Be merciful : deliver *him*, good
Lord.

From Thy wrath,
From an evil death,
From the power of the devil,
From the pains of hell,
By Thy Nativity,
By Thy Cross and Passion,
By Thy Death and Burial,
By Thy glorious Resurrection,
By Thy wonderful Ascension,
By the grace of the Holy Ghost, the Comforter,
In the Day of Judgment,

Good Lord, deliver him.

We sinners : beseech Thee to hear us.

That Thou wouldest spare *him* : we beseech Thee to hear us, good Lord.

Lord, have mercy.
Christ, have mercy.
Lord, have mercy.

While the soul is in its agony, is said :

(1)

DEPART, Christian soul, out of this world; in the Name of God the Father Almighty, Who created thee: in the Name of Jesus Christ, the Son of the Living God, Who suffered for thee; in the Name of the Holy Ghost, Who regenerated thee. Thus, when thou shalt have departed from the body, mayest thou have an entrance to Mount Sion, the city of the living God, the heavenly Jerusalem, and to an innumerable company of Angels, and to the general assembly of the Church of the first-born which are written in heaven. Let God arise, and let His enemies be scattered; let the powers of darkness flee before Him; nor let them dare to assault a lamb, redeemed by the precious blood of Christ. Christ, Who suffered His agony for thee, preserve thee now in this agony of death. Christ, Who died on the Cross for thee, preserve thee from everlasting death. He, the good Shepherd, acknowledge His own

lamb and set thee in the fold of His elect. He give thee to see thy Redeemer face to face, and, being present with Him, to behold with happy eyes the full manifestation of the truth for ever and ever. Amen.

(2)

O MERCIFUL God, O gracious God, O God Who according to the multitude of Thy mercies dost blot out the sins of the penitent, and by the grace of remission dost remove the guilt of past transgressions, mercifully look upon this Thy *servant, N.,* and hear *him,* who with entire and hearty confession hath implored the pardon of all *his* sins. Renew in *him,* O most tender Father, whatsoever has been corrupted through earthly frailty, or injured by the fraud of the devil ; and bring *him,* a member of the body of the Church, into the unity of the Redeemed. Have compassion on *his* groaning, O Lord, have compassion on *his* tears ; and since *he* trusteth only in Thy mercy, admit *him* to the sacrament of Thy reconciliation ; through Christ our Lord. Amen.

[Instead of Prayers (1) and (2), may be said the following :

I COMMEND thee, dearest *brother,* to Almighty God, and commit thee to Him, Whose creature thou art ; that when thou shalt have paid the debt of mankind by death, thou mayest return to thy Maker, Who formed thee from the dust of the earth. When, therefore, thy soul shall depart from the body, may the resplendent host of Angels hasten to thee ; may the judicial council of Apostles come to thee ; may the triumphant army of white-robed Martyrs meet thee ; may the white and ruddy band of Confessors encompass thee ; may the choir of joyful Virgins receive thee ; and may the love of the blessed rest in the bosom of the Patriarchs enfold thee. May Christ Jesus appear to thee with a mild and gracious countenance, and may He assign thee to be one of those who ever stand before Him. Mayest thou know nothing of the horror of darkness, of the flames of hell, of racking torments. May the most hateful adversary and his spirits give way before thee; may he tremble at thine approach with accompanying Angels, and flee away into the vast chaos of eternal night. Let God arise, and let His enemies be scattered, and let them also that hate Him flee before Him; as the smoke vanisheth, let them vanish, and as wax melteth before the fire, so let the sinners perish before God. And let the righteous be glad and rejoice before God. Let then the legions of hell be confounded and brought to shame, and let not the ministers of Satan dare to hinder thy way. May Christ, Who was crucified for thee, deliver thee from torment; may Christ, Who vouchsafed to die for thee, deliver thee from death; may Christ, the Son of the living God, place thee in the ever verdant pastures of His Paradise, and may He, the true Shepherd, number thee amongst His sheep. May He absolve thee from all thy sins, and may He assign thee a portion at His right hand among His elect. Mayest thou see thy Redeemer face to face, and standing before Him for ever, behold with happy eyes the open vision of the truth. And placed thus among the hosts of the blessed, mayest thou enjoy the sweetness of divine contemplation for ever and ever. Amen.]

Let us pray.

RECEIVE Thy *servant*, O Lord, into the place of salvation, hoped for from Thy mercy. R7, Amen.

Deliver *his* soul, O Lord, from all the perils of hell, from the dangers of suffering, and from all tribulation. R7. Amen.

Deliver *his* soul, O Lord, as Thou didst deliver Enoch and Elias from the common death of the world. R7. Amen.

Deliver *his* soul, O Lord, as Thou didst deliver Noah from the flood. R7. Amen.

Deliver *his* soul, O Lord, as Thou didst deliver Abraham from Ur of the Chaldees. R7. Amen.

Deliver *his* soul, O Lord, as Thou didst deliver Job out of his sufferings. R7. Amen.

Deliver *his* soul, O Lord, as Thou didst deliver Isaac from being sacrificed by the hand of his father Abraham. R7. Amen.

Deliver *his* soul, O Lord, as Thou didst deliver Lot from Sodom and the flames of fire. R7. Amen.

Deliver *his* soul, O Lord, as Thou didst deliver Moses from the hand of Pharaoh, king of Egypt. R7. Amen.

Deliver *his* soul, O Lord, as Thou didst deliver Daniel from the lions' den. R7. Amen.

Deliver *his* soul, O Lord, as Thou didst deliver the three children from the fiery furnace, and from the hand of an unrighteous king. R7. Amen.

Deliver *his* soul, O Lord, as Thou didst deliver Susanna from false witness. R7. Amen.

Deliver *his* soul, O Lord, as Thou didst deliver David from the hand of king Saul, and from the hand of Goliath. R7. Amen.

Deliver *his* soul, O Lord, as Thou didst deliver Peter and Paul from prison. R7. Amen.

And, as Thou didst deliver Thy most blessed Virgin and Martyr Thecla from three most horrible torments, so deign to deliver the soul of this Thy *servant*, and make *him* to enjoy with Thee the blessedness of heaven. R7. Amen.

Let us pray.

TO Thee, O Lord, we commend the soul of Thy *servant*; and we pray Thee, O Lord Jesus Christ, Saviour of the world, that Thou wouldest not delay to place *him* in the bosom of the Patriarchs, for whom Thou didst mercifully descend into this earth. Acknowledge, O Lord, Thy creature, not created by strange gods, but by Thee, the only true and living God; for there is none other God beside Thee, O Lord, and none that can do as Thou doest. Make the soul of Thy *servant*, O Lord, joyful in Thy presence, and remember not *his* former sins and excesses, which the violence or heat of evil desires excited; for although *he* hath sinned, yet *he* hath not denied the Father, the Son, and the Holy Spirit, but hath believed, and had a zeal for God within *him*, and hath worshipped God Who made all things. R̺. Amen.

Let us pray.

REMEMBER not, O Lord, we pray Thee, the sins and ignorances of *his* youth, but according to Thy great mercy remember *him* in the brightness of Thy glory. May the heavens be opened unto *him*, may the Angels be gathered unto *him;* receive, O Lord, Thy *servant* into Thy kingdom. May holy Michael the Archangel receive *him*, who attained to be the prince of the heavenly warfare. May the holy Angels of God meet *him* on the way, and lead *him* into the city of the heavenly Jerusalem. May blessed Peter the Apostle receive *him*, to whom the keys of the heavenly kingdom were given by God. May holy Paul assist *him*, who was counted worthy to be a vessel of election. May holy John, the chosen Apostle of God, intercede for *him*, to whom heavenly secrets were revealed. May all the holy Apostles pray for *him*, to whom the power of binding and loosing was given by the Lord. May all the Saints of God intercede for *him*, who for the Name of Christ bore pain in this world; that *he*, delivered from the bands of the flesh, may be counted worthy to come to the glory of the heavenly kingdom, being presented by the same Thy Son our Lord Jesus Christ, Who liveth and reigneth with Thee and the Holy Ghost, ever one God, world without end. Amen.

If the soul continue in its agony, that which follows, or any part of it, may be said.

Ps. iii. *Domine, quid multiplicati?*

LORD, how are they increased that trouble me : many are they that rise against me.

2 Many one there be that say of my soul : There is no help for him in his God.

3 But Thou, O Lord, art my defender : Thou art my worship, and the lifter up of my head.

4 I did call upon the Lord with my voice : and He heard me out of His holy hill.

5 I laid me down and slept, and rose up again : for the Lord sustained me.

6 I will not be afraid for ten thousands of the people : that have set themselves against me round about.

7 Up, Lord, and help me, O my God : for Thou smitest all mine enemies upon the cheek-bone; Thou hast broken the teeth of the ungodly.

8 Salvation belongeth unto the Lord : and Thy blessing is upon Thy people.

Glory be, etc.

Lord, have mercy.
Christ, have mercy.
Lord, have mercy.
Our Father.

℣. And lead us not into temptation. R̺. But deliver us from evil. ℣. Save me, O God. R̺. For the waters are come in, even unto my soul. ℣. Take me out of the mire that I sink not. R̶. O let me be delivered from them that hate me, and out of the deep waters. V̶. Let not the water-flood drown me, neither let the deep swallow me up. R̶. And let not the pit shut her mouth upon me. V̶. Awake, and stand up to judge my quarrel. R̶. Avenge Thou my cause, my God and my Lord. V̶. Shew some token upon me for good, that they who hate me may see it and be ashamed. R̶. Because Thou, Lord, hast holpen me, and comforted me. V̶. The Lord be with you. R̶. And with thy spirit.

Let us pray.

ONLY-BEGOTTEN and Beloved Son of the Living God, Who for the redemption of the world didst vouchsafe to be born in a manger, to be set at nought of the Jews, to be betrayed by Judas with a kiss, to be bound with fetters, to be led as a lamb to the slaughter, to be torn with scourges, to be defiled with spitting, to be crowned with thorns, to be fastened to the Cross, to be reckoned among the transgressors, to die in agony: we beseech Thee that by these Thy most holy sufferings, and by Thy Cross and Death, Thou wouldest vouchsafe to deliver Thy *servant* from the pains of hell, and to bring *him* into that place whither Thou didst bring the thief that was crucified with Thee; Who livest and reignest with the Father and the Holy Ghost, ever one God, world without end. Amen.

The Passion of our Lord Jesus Christ according to the Four Evangelists.

JESUS taketh with Him Peter and James and John, and began to be sore amazed and very heavy: and saith unto them, My soul is exceeding sorrowful unto death, tarry ye here and watch with Me. And He went a little farther and fell on His face and prayed, saying, O My Father, if it be possible, let this cup pass from Me; nevertheless, not as I will, but as Thou wilt. And there appeared an Angel unto Him from heaven, strengthening Him. He went away again the second time and prayed, saying, Abba, Father, all things are possible unto Thee, take away this cup from Me: nevertheless, not what I will, but what Thou wilt. And being in an agony, He prayed more earnestly, and His sweat was as it were great drops of blood, falling down to the ground.

Psalm lxx. *Deus in adjutorium.*

HASTE Thee, O God, to deliver me : make haste to help me, O Lord.

2 Let them be ashamed and confounded that seek after my soul : let them be turned backward and put to confusion that wish me evil.

3 Let them for their reward be soon brought to shame : that cry over me, There, there.

4 But let all those that seek Thee be joyful and glad in Thee : and let all such as delight in Thy salvation say alway, The Lord be praised.

5 As for me, I am poor and in misery : haste Thee unto me, O God.

6 Thou art my helper, and my redeemer : O Lord, make no long tarrying.

Glory be, etc.

V̶. Hear my prayer, O God, and hide not Thyself from my petition. R̶. Take heed unto me, and hear me. V̶. My heart is disquieted within me. R̶. And the fear of death is fallen upon me. V̶. Fearfulness and trembling are come upon me. R̶. And an horrible dread hath overwhelmed me. V̶. But my hope hath been in Thee, O Lord. R̶. I have said, Thou art my God, my time is in Thy hand. V̶. Lighten mine eyes, that I sleep not in death. R7. Lest mine enemy say, I have prevailed against him. V7. O keep my soul and deliver me. R7. Let me not be confounded, for I have put my trust in Thee. V7. The Lord be with you. R7. And with thy spirit.

Let us pray.

LORD Jesus Christ, we humbly beseech Thy mercy, by that Thy sorrow of soul, even unto death, and by the agony which, when Thy Passion was at hand, Thou didst endure when Thy sweat was, as it were, great drops of blood falling down to the ground, deliver this Thy *servant*, now surrounded by the agony of death : guard *him* in this hour against all assaults of the devil : deliver *him* from the terrors of approaching death : and because *he* fears through the remembrance of *his* sin, bid *him* be of good courage, through the abundance of Thy mercy; Who livest and reignest with the Father and the Holy Ghost, ever one God, world without end. Amen.

Psalm cxlii. *Voce mea ad Dominum.*

I CRIED unto the Lord with my voice : yea, even unto the Lord did I make my supplication.

2 I poured out my complaints before Him : and shewed Him of my trouble.

3 When my spirit was in heaviness Thou knewest my path : in the way wherein I walked have they privily laid a snare for me.

4 I looked also upon my right hand : and saw there was no man that would know me.

5 I had no place to flee unto : and no man cared for my soul.

6 I cried unto Thee, O Lord, and said ; Thou art my hope, and my portion in the land of the living.

7 Consider my complaint : for I am brought very low.

8 O deliver me from my persecutors : for they are too strong for me.

9 Bring my soul out of prison, that I may give thanks unto Thy Name : which thing if Thou wilt grant me, then shall the righteous resort unto my company.

Glory be, etc.

V7. Look upon my adversity and misery. R7. And forgive me all my sin. V7. Thou, O Lord God, art full of compassion and mercy, longsuffering, plenteous in goodness and truth. R7. Turn Thee then unto me, and have mercy upon me. V7. Forsake me not, O Lord my God. R7. Be not Thou far from me. V7. O that I had wings like a dove. R7. Then would I flee away and be at rest. V7. Let me die the death of the righteous. R7. And let my last end be like his.

Let us pray.

LORD Jesus Christ, Who by the mouth of Thy prophet didst say, I have loved thee with an everlasting love, therefore with loving-kindness have I drawn thee : we beseech Thee by the love wherewith Thou hast loved us, that Thou wouldest vouchsafe to offer and to shew forth to God the Father for the soul of this Thy *servant*, all the bitterness of the Passion which Thou didst endure upon the Cross, and deal with *him* at this hour, not as *his* sins have deserved, but as Thy Death hath merited; Who livest and reignest with the Father and the Holy Ghost, ever one God, world without end. Amen.

These Psalms and Prayers having been finished, (or before they are finished, if the moment of the soul's departure be at hand), let there be read over the dying person that which follows of the Passion of our Lord Jesus Christ :

AND one of the malefactors which were hanged railed on Him, saying, If Thou be Christ, save Thyself and us. But the other answering, rebuked him, saying, Dost not thou fear God, seeing thou art in the same condemnation? and we indeed justly: for we receive the due reward of our deeds: but this Man hath done nothing amiss. And he said unto Jesus, Lord, remember me when Thou comest into Thy kingdom. And Jesus said unto him, Verily I say unto thee, To-day shalt thou be with me in paradise. And it was about the sixth hour, and there was a darkness over all the earth until the ninth hour. And about the ninth hour Jesus cried with a loud voice, saying, Eli, Eli, lama sabachthani? that is to say, My God, My God, why hast Thou forsaken me? After this, Jesus knowing that all things were now accomplished, that the scripture might be fulfilled saith, I thirst. Now there was set a vessel full of vinegar: and they filled a spunge with vinegar, and put it upon hyssop, and put it to His mouth. When Jesus therefore had received the vinegar, He said, It is finished. And when He had cried with a loud voice, He said, Father, into Thy hands I commend my spirit: and having said thus, He gave up the ghost.

Let us pray.

BE mindful, O most loving Jesu, of that hour, in which, hanging on the Cross Thou didst cry, My God, My God, why hast Thou forsaken Me? And again, Father, into Thy hands I commend My Spirit: and having said this, didst give up the ghost. By that Thy most precious Death, which was our life, we pray Thee not to forsake this Thy *servant*, who hath none other helper beside Thee; but vouchsafe to receive *his* spirit and to cause *him* to enter into Thy kingdom, where *he* may love Thee and the Father and the Holy Ghost, with perpetual love, and together with Thy Saints and elect, may tell of Thy loving-kindness for ever and ever. Amen.

[*If the agony of death still continues, these Psalms, or any of them, may be said:*

Psalm xxii. *Deus, Deus meus*, p. 24.
Psalm liv. *Deus, in nomine tuo*, p. 27.
Psalm xci. *Qui habitat*, p. 66.
Psalm cxxxix. *Domine, probasti me*, p. 59.]

As soon as the soul has departed, is said:

℞. In Thee, O Lord, have I put my trust, let me never be put to confusion; make haste to deliver me. Into Thy hands I commend my spirit: Thou hast redeemed me, O Lord, Thou God of truth; cause the light of Thy countenance to shine upon Thy *servant*. ℣. Lord Jesus: receive my spirit. ℞. Thou hast redeemed me, O Lord, Thou God of Truth; cause the light of Thy countenance to shine upon Thy *servant*.

Lord, have mercy.
Christ, have mercy.
Lord, have mercy.

Our Father.

℣. Enter not into judgment with Thy servant, O Lord. ℞. For in Thy sight shall no man living be justified. ℣. O deliver not the soul of Thy turtle dove into the hand of the enemy. ℞. And forget not the congregation of the poor for ever. ℣. Hear my prayer, O Lord. ℞. And let my crying come unto Thee.

Let us pray.

TO Thee, O Lord, we commend Thy *servant* whom Thou hast taken from the world; and as Thou hast delivered *him* from the contagion of mortality, so be Thou pleased to give *him* a portion and an inheritance among Thy Saints, Who livest and reignest with the Father and the Holy Ghost, ever one God, world without end. Amen.

[*Or, instead of the above Versicles and Prayers:*

Ry. Come, holy ones, hasten, angels of the Lord: receiving *his* soul: and presenting it before the face of the Most High. Vy. May Christ, Who called thee, receive thee; and may angels lead thee into Abraham's bosom. Ry. Receiving *his* soul. Vy. Eternal rest grant unto *him*, O Lord: and light perpetual shine on *him*. Ry. Presenting it before the face of the Most High.

Lord, have mercy.
Christ, have mercy.
Lord, have mercy.
Our Father.

Vy. And lead us not into temptation. Ry. But deliver us from evil. Vy. Eternal rest grant unto *him*, O Lord. Ry. And light perpetual shine upon *him*. Vy. From the gates of hell. Ry. Deliver *his* soul, O Lord. Vy. May *he* rest in peace. Ry. Amen. Vy. Hear my prayer, O Lord. Ry. And let my crying come unto Thee. Vy. The Lord be with you. Ry And with thy spirit.

Let us pray.

TO Thee, O Lord, we commend the soul of Thy *servant*, *N.*, that dead unto the world, it may live unto Thee; and the sins which *he* has committed through the frailty of this earthly life, do Thou mercifully blot out by Thy pitying forgiveness; through Christ our Lord. Amen.]

OFFICE OF THE DEAD.

Here follows the Roman Rubric: for the Sarum Order, see General Rubrics.
[*This is said, except in Easter tide, on the first day of every month, not hindered by a Double Feast, in which case it is said on the first day not so hindered. But in Advent and Lent, on every Monday not so hindered, except in Holy Week. In Choirs it is said after the Office of the day, i. e., Vespers after Vespers, and Matins after Lauds of the day, unless the use of the place be different: out of Choir it is said as occasion serves.*]

Vespers
begin at once with the

Ant. I will walk before the Lord: in the land of the living.

Psalm cxvi.   *Dilexi, quoniam.*

I AM well pleased: that the Lord hath heard the voice of my prayer;

2 That He hath inclined His ear unto me: therefore will I call upon Him as long as I live.

3 The snares of death compassed me round about: and the pains of hell gat hold upon me.

4 I shall find trouble and heaviness, and I will call upon the Name of the Lord: O Lord, I beseech Thee, deliver my soul.

5 Gracious is the Lord and righteous: yea, our God is merciful.

6 The Lord preserveth the simple: I was in misery, and He helped me.

7 Turn again then unto thy rest, O my soul: for the Lord hath rewarded thee.

8 And why? Thou hast delivered my soul from death: mine eyes from tears, and my feet from falling.

9 I will walk before the Lord: in the land of the living.

At the end of every Psalm and Canticle is said:

Eternal rest: grant unto them, O Lord.

And light perpetual: shine upon them.

Ant. I will walk before the Lord: in the land of the living.

Ant. Wo is me : that I am constrained to dwell with Mesech.

Psalm cxx. *Ad Dominum.*

WHEN I was in trouble I called upon the Lord : and He heard me.

2 Deliver my soul, O Lord, from lying lips : and from a deceitful tongue.

3 What reward shall be given or done unto thee, thou false tongue : even mighty and sharp arrows, with hot burning coals.

4 Wo is me, that I am constrained to dwell with Mesech : and to have my habitation among the tents of Kedar.

5 My soul hath long dwelt among them : that are enemies unto peace.

6 I labour for peace, but when I speak unto them thereof : they make them ready for battle.

Eternal rest, etc.

Ant. Wo is me : that I am constrained to dwell with Mesech.

Ant. The Lord shall preserve thee from all evil : yea, it is even He that shall keep thy soul.

Psalm cxxi. *Levavi oculos.*

I WILL lift up mine eyes unto the hills : from whence cometh my help.

2 My help cometh even from the Lord : Who hath made heaven and earth.

3 He will not suffer thy foot to be moved : and He that keepeth thee will not sleep.

4 Behold, He that keepeth Israel : shall neither slumber nor sleep.

5 The Lord Himself is thy keeper : the Lord is thy defence upon thy right hand.

6 So that the sun shall not burn thee by day : neither the moon by night.

7 The Lord shall preserve thee from all evil : yea, it is even He that shall keep thy soul.

8 The Lord shall preserve thy going out, and thy coming in : from this time forth for evermore.

Eternal rest, etc.

Ant. The Lord shall preserve thee from all evil : yea, it is even He that shall keep thy soul.

Ant. If Thou, Lord, wilt be extreme to mark what is done amiss : O Lord, who may abide it?

Psalm cxxx. *De profundis.*

OUT of the deep have I called unto Thee, O Lord : Lord, hear my voice.

2 O let Thine ears consider well : the voice of my complaint.

3 If Thou, Lord, wilt be extreme to mark what is done amiss : O Lord, who may abide it?

4 For there is mercy with Thee : therefore shalt Thou be feared.

5 I look for the Lord; my soul doth wait for Him : in His word is my trust.

6 My soul fleeth unto the Lord : before the morning watch, I say, before the morning watch.

7 O Israel, trust in the Lord, for with the Lord there is mercy : and with Him is plenteous redemption.

8 And He shall redeem Israel : from all his sins.

Eternal rest, etc.

Ant. If Thou, Lord, wilt be extreme to mark what is done amiss : O Lord, who may abide it?

Ant. Despise not then : the works of Thine own hands.

Psalm cxxxviii. *Confitebor tibi.*

I WILL give thanks unto Thee, O Lord, with my whole heart : even before the gods will I sing praise Thee.

2 I will worship toward Thy holy temple, and praise Thy Name, because of Thy loving-kindness and truth : for Thou hast magnified Thy Name, and Thy word, above all things.

3 When I called upon Thee, Thou heardest me : and enduedst my soul with much strength.

4 All the kings of the earth shall praise Thee, O Lord : for they have heard the words of Thy mouth.

5 Yea, they shall sing in the ways of the Lord : that great is the glory of the Lord.

6 For though the Lord be high, yet hath He respect unto the lowly : as for the proud, He beholdeth them afar off.

7 Though I walk in the midst of trouble, yet shalt Thou refresh me : Thou shalt stretch forth Thy hand upon the furiousness of mine enemies, and Thy right hand shall save me.

8 The Lord shall make good His loving-kindness toward me : yea, Thy mercy, O Lord, endureth for ever; despise not then the works of Thine own hands.

Eternal rest, etc.

Ant. Despise not then : the works of Thine own hands.

℣. I heard a voice from heaven, saying unto me.

℞. Blessed are the dead, which die in the Lord.

Ant. to Mag. All that the Father giveth Me, shall come unto Me : and him that cometh unto Me I will in no wise cast out.

The Prayers following are said kneeling, and so likewise at Lauds :

Our Father, *in silence.* ℣. And lead us not into temptation. ℞. But deliver us from evil.

Psalm cxlvi., Lauda, anima mea, *at Vespers, as also Psalm cxxx., De profundis, at the end of Lauds, is not said on All Souls' Day, nor on the day* of a death or burial. At other times it is always said.

Psalm cxlvi. *Lauda, anima mea.*

PRAISE the Lord, O my soul; while I live will I praise the Lord : yea, as long as I have any being, I will sing praises unto my God.

2 O put not your trust in princes, nor in any child of man : for there is no help in them.

3 For when the breath of man goeth forth he shall turn again to his earth : and then all his thoughts perish.

4 Blessed is he that hath the God of Jacob for his help : and whose hope is in the Lord his God.

5 Who made heaven and earth, the sea, and all that therein is : Who keepeth His promise for ever;

6 Who helpeth them to right that suffer wrong : Who feedeth the hungry.

7 The Lord looseth men out of prison : the Lord giveth sight to the blind.

8 The Lord helpeth them that are fallen : the Lord careth for the righteous.

9 The Lord careth for the strangers; He defendeth the fatherless and widow : as for the way of the ungodly, He turneth it upside down.

10 The Lord thy God, O Sion, shall be King for evermore : and throughout all generations.

Eternal rest, etc.

℣. From the gates of hell. ℞. Deliver their souls, O Lord. ℣. May they rest in peace. ℞. Amen. ℣. Hear my prayer, O Lord. ℞. And let my crying come unto Thee. ℣. The Lord be with you. ℞. And with thy spirit.

[*When the corpse is present, both at Vespers and Lauds, is said the greater Collect.*

O GOD, Whose property is ever to have mercy and to spare: we suppliants intreat Thee for the soul of Thy *servant* [or *handmaiden*] *N.*, which to-day Thou hast called to depart from this world: that Thou wouldest not deliver it into the hands of the enemy, nor forget it finally, but command it to be received by the holy Angels, and led into the land of the living; and whereas it hath hoped and believed in Thee, may it be found worthy to rejoice in the society of Thy Saints; through Jesus Christ Thy Son our Lord.]

COLLECTS.

GOD, Who among apostolic Priests hast raised up Thy servants to the dignity of the Episcopate [*or* Priesthood], mercifully grant them a share in their blessed companionship for ever.

GOD, Who art the Giver of pardon, and the Lover of human salvation; we pray Thy mercy, that, Blessed Mary, ever Virgin, and all Thy Saints interceding, Thou wouldest grant to all the brethren, neighbours, and benefactors of our congregation, to attain the fellowship of everlasting blessedness.

GOD, the Creator and Redeemer of all the faithful, grant to the souls of Thy servants and handmaidens remission of all their sins: that the pardon they have always desired, by pious supplications, may be obtained; Who livest and reignest to ages of ages. R̠. Amen.

But on All Souls' Day, when this last Prayer is said alone, it is ended thus:

Who livest and reignest with God the Father, in the unity of the Holy Spirit, God, throughout all ages.

On the Day of a Burial.
COLLECT.

WE beseech Thee, O Lord, deliver the soul of Thy *servant* [or *handmaid*,] *N.*, that, dead to the world, it may live unto Thee: and that which *he* hath committed by frailty of the flesh in *his* human conversation, wipe away by the grace of Thy most merciful loving-kindness; through Jesus Christ our Lord, Who liveth and reigneth with Thee and the Holy Ghost, ever one God, world without end. Amen.

On the Anniversary of that Day.
COLLECT.

GOD, Who art the Lord of mercies, grant to the souls of Thy servants and handmaidens, the anniversary of whose burial we commemorate, a place of refreshment, the quiet of beatitude, and the glory of light; through our Lord Jesus Christ. Amen.

If the Anniversary of one only, it is said in the singular number.

For a Bishop or Priest deceased.
COLLECT.

GOD, Who among apostolic Priests, etc., *as above.*

For Brethren, Friends, and Benefactors.
COLLECT.

GOD, Who art the Giver, etc., *as above.*

For Father and Mother.
COLLECT.

O GOD, Who didst command us to honour our father and mother: graciously have mercy on the souls of *my father and mother*, and cause *me* to see *them* in the joy of eternal glory; through Jesus Christ our Lord, Who liveth and reigneth with Thee and the Holy Ghost, ever one God, world without end. Amen.

If for many, it is said: the souls of our parents; *and* us *is substituted for* me.
If for a father only: the soul of my, *or,* our father.
If for a mother only: the soul of my, *or,* our mother.

For a Man Departed.

COLLECT.

INCLINE Thine ear, O Lord, to our prayers who humbly entreat Thy mercy: that Thou wouldest grant to Thy servant *N.*, whom Thou hast called from this world, a place in the land of peace and light, and wouldest call him to the companionship of Thy Saints; through Jesus Christ our Lord, Who liveth and reigneth with Thee and the Holy Ghost, ever one God, world without end. Amen.

For a Woman Departed.

COLLECT.

WE beseech Thee, O Lord, of Thy pity, have mercy on the soul of Thy handmaid, *N.*, and as Thou hast freed her from the contagion of mortality, so be Thou pleased to give her a portion and an inheritance among Thine elect; through Jesus Christ our Lord, Who liveth and reigneth with Thee and the Holy Ghost, ever one God, world without end. Amen.

℣. Eternal rest grant unto them, O Lord. ℟. And light perpetual shine upon them. ℣. May they rest in peace. ℟. Amen.

Lauds

are begun at once with

Ant. The bones which Thou hast humbled: shall rejoice.

Psalm li. *Miserere mei Deus.*

HAVE mercy upon me, O God after Thy great goodness: according to the multitude of Thy mercies do away mine offences.

2 Wash me throughly from my wickedness: and cleanse me from my sin.

3 For I acknowledge my faults: and my sin is ever before me.

4 Against Thee only have I sinned, and done this evil in Thy sight: that Thou mightest be justified in Thy saying, and clear when Thou art judged.

5 Behold, I was shapen in wickedness: and in sin hath my mother conceived me.

6 But lo, Thou requirest truth in the inward parts: and shalt make me to understand wisdom secretly.

7 Thou shalt purge me with hyssop, and I shall be clean: Thou shalt wash me, and I shall be whiter than snow.

8 Thou shalt make me hear of joy and gladness: that the bones which Thou hast broken may rejoice.

9 Turn Thy face from my sins: and put out all my misdeeds.

10 Make me a clean heart, O God: and renew a right spirit within me.

11 Cast me not away from Thy presence: and take not Thy Holy Spirit from me.

12 O give me the comfort of Thy help again: and stablish me with Thy free Spirit.

13 Then shall I teach Thy ways unto the wicked: and sinners shall be converted unto Thee.

14 Deliver me from blood-guiltiness, O God, Thou that art the God of my health: and my tongue shall sing of Thy righteousness.

15 Thou shalt open my lips, O Lord: and my mouth shall shew Thy praise.

16 For Thou desirest no sacrifice, else would I give it Thee: but Thou delightest not in burnt-offerings.

17 The sacrifice of God is a troubled spirit: a broken and contrite heart, O God, shalt Thou not despise.

18 O be favourable and gracious unto Sion: build Thou the walls of Jerusalem.

19 Then shalt Thou be pleased with the sacrifice of righteousness,

with the burnt-offerings, and oblations : then shall they offer young bullocks upon Thine altar.

Eternal rest, etc.

Ant. The bones which Thou hast humbled : shall rejoice.

Ant. Hear, Lord, my prayer : unto Thee shall all flesh come.

Psalm lxv. *Te decet hymnus.*

THOU, O God, art praised in Sion : and unto Thee shall the vow be performed in Jerusalem.

2 Thou that hearest the prayer : unto Thee shall all flesh come.

3 My misdeeds prevail against me : O be Thou merciful unto our sins.

4 Blessed is the man whom Thou choosest, and receivest unto Thee : he shall dwell in Thy court, and shall be satisfied with the pleasures of Thy house, even of Thy holy temple.

5 Thou shalt shew us wonderful things in Thy righteousness, O God of our salvation : Thou that art the hope of all the ends of the earth, and of them that remain in the broad sea.

6 Who in His strength setteth fast the mountains : and is girded about with power.

7 Who stilleth the raging of the sea : and the noise of his waves, and the madness of the people.

8 They also that dwell in the uttermost parts of the earth shall be afraid at Thy tokens : Thou that makest the out-goings of the morning and evening to praise Thee.

9 Thou visitest the earth, and blessest it : Thou makest it very plenteous.

10 The river of God is full of water : Thou preparest their corn, for so Thou providest for the earth.

11 Thou waterest her furrows, Thou sendest rain into the little valleys thereof : Thou makest it soft with the drops of rain, and blessest the increase of it.

12 Thou crownest the year with Thy goodness : and Thy clouds drop fatness.

13 They shall drop upon the dwellings of the wilderness : and the little hills shall rejoice on every side.

14 The folds shall be full of sheep : the valleys also shall stand so thick with corn, that they shall laugh and sing.

Eternal rest, etc.

Ant. Hear, Lord, my prayer : unto Thee shall all flesh come.

Ant. Thy right hand : hath upholden me, O Lord.

Psalm lxiii. *Deus, Deus meus.*

O GOD, Thou art my God : early will I seek Thee.

2 My soul thirsteth for Thee, my flesh also longeth after Thee : in a barren and dry land where no water is.

3 Thus have I looked for Thee in holiness : that I might behold Thy power and glory.

4 For Thy loving kindness is better than the life itself : my lips shall praise Thee.

5 As long as I live will I magnify Thee on this manner : and lift up my hands in Thy Name.

6 My soul shall be satisfied even as it were with marrow and fatness : when my mouth praiseth Thee with joyful lips.

7 Have I not remembered Thee in my bed : and thought upon Thee when I was waking?

8 Because Thou hast been my helper : therefore under the shadow of Thy wings will I rejoice.

9 My soul hangeth upon Thee : Thy right hand hath upholden me.

10 These also that seek the hurt of my soul : they shall go under the earth.

11 Let them fall upon the edge of the sword : that they may be a portion for foxes.

12 But the King shall rejoice in God ; all they also, that swear by Him shall be commended : for the mouth of them that speak lies shall be stopped.

Here is not said Eternal rest.

Psalm lxvii. *Deus misereatur.*

GOD be merciful unto us, and bless us : and shew us the light of His countenance, and be merciful unto us ;

2 That Thy way may be known upon earth : Thy saving health among all nations.

3 Let the people praise Thee, O God : yea, let all the people praise Thee.

4 O let the nations rejoice and be glad : for Thou shalt judge the folk righteously, and govern the nations upon earth.

5 Let the people praise Thee, O God : let all the people praise Thee.'

6 Then shall the earth bring forth her increase : and God, even our own God, shall give us His blessing.

7 God shall bless us : and all the ends of the world shall fear Him.

Eternal rest, etc.

Ant. Thy right hand : hath upholden me, O Lord.

Ant. From the gates of hell : deliver my soul, O Lord.

Song of Hezekiah.

Ego dixi. Isaiah xxxviii.

I SAID, in the cutting off of my days : I shall go to the gates of the grave.

2 I am deprived of the residue of my years : I said, I shall not see the Lord, even the Lord, in the land of living.

3 I shall behold man no more : with the inhabitants of the world.

4 Mine age is departed : and is removed from me as a shepherd's tent.

5 I have cut off like a weaver my life : He will cut me off with pining sickness.

6 From day even to night wilt Thou make an end of me : I reckoned till morning that, as a lion, so will He break all my bones.

7 From day even to night wilt Thou make an end of me : like a crane or a swallow so did I chatter ; I did mourn as a dove.

8 My eyes fail : with looking upward.

9 O Lord, I am oppressed ; undertake for me : what shall I say ? He hath both spoken unto me, and Himself hath done it.

10 I shall go softly all my years : in the bitterness of my soul.

11 O Lord, by these things men live, and in all these things is the life of my spirit : so wilt Thou recover me, and make me to live : behold, for peace I had great bitterness.

12 But Thou hast in love to my soul delivered it from the pit of corruption : for Thou hast cast all my sins behind Thy back.

13 For the grave cannot praise Thee, death cannot celebrate Thee : they that go down into the pit cannot hope for Thy truth.

14 The living, the living, he shall praise Thee, as I do this day : the father to the children shall make known Thy truth.

15 The Lord was ready to save me : therefore we will sing my songs to the stringed instruments all the days of our life in the house of the Lord.

Eternal rest, etc.

Ant. From the gates of hell : deliver my soul, O Lord.

Ant. Let every spirit : praise the Lord.

Psalm cxlviii. *Laudate Dominum.*

O PRAISE the Lord of heaven : praise Him in the height.

2 Praise Him, all ye angels of His : praise Him, all His host.

3 Praise Him, sun and moon : praise Him, all ye stars and light.

4 Praise Him, all ye heavens : and ye waters that are above the heavens.

5 Let them praise the Name of the Lord : for He spake the word, and they were made ; He commanded, and they were created.

6 He hath made them fast for ever and ever : He hath given them a law which shall not be broken.

7 Praise the Lord upon earth : ye dragons, and all deeps ;

8 Fire and hail, snow and vapours : wind and storm, fulfilling His word ;

9 Mountains and all hills : fruitful trees and all cedars ;

10 Beasts and all cattle : worms and feathered fowls ;

11 Kings of the earth and all people : princes and all judges of the world.

12 Young men and maidens, old men and children, praise the Name of the Lord : for His Name only is excellent, and His praise above heaven and earth.

13 He shall exalt the horn of His people ; all His saints shall praise Him : even the children of Israel, even the people that serveth Him.

Here is not said Eternal rest.

Psalm cxlix. *Cantate Domino.*

O SING unto the Lord a new song : let the congregation of saints praise Him.

2 Let Israel rejoice in Him that made him : and let the children of Sion be joyful in their King.

3 Let them praise His Name in the dance : let them sing praises unto Him with tabret and harp.

4 For the Lord hath pleasure in His people : and helpeth the meek-hearted.

5 Let the saints be joyful with glory : let them rejoice in their beds.

6 Let the praises of God be in their mouth : and a two-edged sword in their hands :

7 To be avenged of the heathen : and to rebuke the people :

8 To bind their kings in chains : and their nobles with links of iron.

9 That they may be avenged of them, as it is written : Such honour have all His saints.

Here is not said Eternal rest.

Psalm cl. *Laudate Dominum.*

O PRAISE God in His holiness : praise Him in the firmament of His power.

2 Praise Him in His noble acts : praise Him according to His excellent greatness.

3 Praise Him in the sound of the trumpet : praise Him upon the lute and harp.

4 Praise Him in the cymbals and dances : praise Him upon the strings and pipe.

5 Praise Him upon the well-tuned cymbals : praise Him upon the loud cymbals.

6 Let every thing that hath breath : praise the Lord.

Eternal rest, etc.

Ant. Let every spirit : praise the Lord.

℣. I heard a voice from heaven saying unto me.

℟. Blessed are the dead which die in the Lord.

Ant. to Ben. I am the Resurrection and the Life : he that believeth in Me, though he were dead, yet shall he live, and whosoever liveth and believeth in Me, shall never die.

Our Father.

Psalm cxxx., *De profundis*, p. 261, [*or* Psalm cxlv., *Exaltabo te Deus*, p. 62.]
Petitions and Collects as at Vespers.

ITINERARY.

Ant. Into the way of peace : and prosperity, the Almighty and merciful Lord direct *our* steps : and the Angel Raphael go with *us* in the way, that with peace, safety, and joy, *we* may return home.

Benedictus, p. 6.

Lord, have mercy.
Christ, have mercy.
Lord, have mercy.

Our Father.

℣. And lead us not into temptation. ℟. But deliver us from evil. ℣. O God, save Thy *servants*. ℟. Who put *their* trust in Thee. ℣. Send *us* help from the Sanctuary. ℟. And strengthen *us* out of Sion. ℣. Be unto *us*, O Lord, a tower of strength. ℟. From the face of the enemy. ℣. Let the enemy have no advantage over *us*. ℟. Neither the son of wickedness approach to hurt *us*. ℣. Blessed be the Lord this day. ℟. The God of *our* salvation make *our* journey prosperous. ℣. Shew *us* Thy ways, O Lord. ℟. And teach *us* Thy paths. ℣. O that my ways were made so direct. ℟. That I might keep Thy statutes. ℣. The crooked shall be made straight. ℟. And the rough places plain. ℣. God shall give His Angels charge over thee. ℟. To keep thee in all thy ways. ℣. Hear my prayer, O Lord. ℟. And let my crying come unto Thee. ℣. The Lord be with you. ℟. And with thy spirit.

Let us pray.

COLLECTS.

O GOD, Who leddest the children of Israel on dry land through the midst of the sea, and by the leading of a star didst shew the three Magi the way to come to Thee ; grant us, we beseech Thee, a prosperous journey and a tranquil time, that, Thy holy Angel accompanying us, we may safely reach the place whither we go, and finally attain the haven of everlasting salvation.

O GOD, Who didst bring Abraham Thy servant from Ur of the Chaldees, and didst keep him in safety through all the ways of his pilgrimage ; we beseech Thee that Thou wouldest protect *us* Thy *servants*. Be to *us*, O Lord, in setting forth, a support, in the way a consolation, in heat a shadow, in rain and cold a covering, in weariness a chariot, in adversity a support, in slippery places a staff, in shipwreck a port ; that, Thou being our Leader, we may prosperously reach the place whither we go, and at length return in safety to our home.

ASSIST us mercifully, O Lord, in these our supplications and prayers, and dispose the way of Thy servants towards the attainment of everlasting salvation ; that among all the changes and chances of this mortal life, they may ever be defended by Thy most gracious and ready help.

GRANT, we beseech Thee, Almighty God, that Thy family may walk in the way of salvation, and, following the counsels of blessed John the forerunner, may safely come to Him Whom he foretold, Thy Son Jesus Christ our Lord, Who liveth and reigneth with Thee and the Holy Ghost, ever one God, world without end. Amen.

℣. Let *us* go forth in peace.
℟. In the Name of the Lord. Amen.

Proper of Saints.

✠

PROPER OF SAINTS.

S. Andrew, Apostle and
Martyr.

First Vespers.

Ant. to Psalms. One of the two which
heard John speak, and followed Jesus :
was Andrew, Simon Peter's brother.
Alleluia.

Psalms of the Feria.

Chapter. Rom. x.

FOR with the heart man believeth
unto righteousness, and with the
mouth confession is made unto salvation.
For the Scripture saith, Whosoever believeth on Him shall not be ashamed.

Ry. The man of God was being led to
crucifixion : but the people cried with a
loud voice, saying : his innocent blood
is condemned without cause. V̆. And
when they led him to be crucified, there
was a great concourse of the people,
crying out, and saying. Ry. His innocent blood is condemned without cause.
V̆. Glory be to the Father, and to the
Son, and to the Holy Ghost. Ry. His
innocent blood is condemned without
cause.

Hymn. *Annue Christe*, p. 214.

V̆. The Lord loved Andrew.
Ry. In the odour of sweetness.

Ant. to Mag. Jesus, walking by the
sea of Galilee, saw Peter and Andrew
his brother : and saith unto them, Follow
Me, and I will make you fishers of
men : and they straightway left their
nets, and followed Him.

Collect.

ALMIGHTY God, Who didst give
such grace unto Thy holy Apostle
Saint Andrew, that he readily obeyed
the calling of Thy Son Jesus Christ, and
followed Him without delay ; grant unto
us all, that we, being called by Thy
holy word, may forthwith give up ourselves obediently to fulfil Thy holy commandments ; through the same Jesus
Christ our Lord. Amen.

If in Advent, Memorial of the Feria.

Compline.

As in the Psalter, p. 67.

Lauds.

V̆. The Lord loved Andrew.
Ry. In the odour of sweetness.

Psalms of Sunday.

Ant. 1. Hail, precious Cross : receive
the disciple of Him Who hung on thee,
my Master Christ.

Ant. 2. Blessed Andrew prayed, saying : O Lord, King of eternal glory, receive me who hang in torture.

Ant. 3. Lord, suffer not me Thy servant to be parted from Thee : it is time
that Thou commend my body to the
earth.

Ant. 4. Safely and joyfully I come
unto Thee : do Thou likewise with joy
receive me.

Ant. 5. Lord, Thou didst cast into hell him who persecuted the righteous man : and on the tree of the Cross Thou wast the leader of the righteous.

CHAPTER. Rom. x., *as at First Vespers.*

℞. Thanks be to God.

HYMN. *Exultet cœlum laudibus,* p. 215.

Ant. to Ben. Grant us the just man : restore us the holy man, slay not the man dear to God, just, meek, and pious.

If in Advent, Memorial of the Feria.

Prime.

Ant. to Psalms. Hail, precious Cross : receive the disciple of Him Who hung on thee, my Master Christ.

Tierce.

Ant. Blessed Andrew prayed, saying : O Lord, King of eternal glory, receive me who hang in torture.

CHAPTER. Rom. x., *as at First Vespers.*

℞℞. *of the Common of Apostles,* p. 216.

Sexts.

Ant. Lord, suffer not me Thy servant to be parted from Thee : it is time that Thou commend my body to the earth.

CHAPTER. Rom. x.

FOR there is no difference between the Jew and the Greek : for the same Lord over all is rich unto all that call upon Him.

℞℞. *of the Common of Apostles,* p. 216.

Nones.

Ant. Lord, Thou didst cast into hell him who persecuted the righteous man : and on the tree of the Cross Thou wast the leader of the righteous.

CHAPTER. Rom. x.

FOR whosoever shall call upon the Name of the Lord shall be saved.

℞℞. *of the Common of Apostles,* p. 216.

Second Vespers.

Ants. of Lauds, p. 271. *Psalms of the Common,* p. 216.

CHAPTER. Rom. x., *as at First Vespers.*

℞. I have stretched forth my hands all day long unto a disobedient and gainsaying people : who walk in no good way, but do after their own lusts. ℣. The God to Whom vengeance belongeth hath lifted up Himself. He hath arisen to judge the earth, and to reward the proud after their own deserving. ℞. Who walk in no good way, but do after their own lusts. ℣. Glory be to the Father, and to the Son, and to the Holy Ghost. ℞. Who walk in no good way, but do after their own lusts.

HYMN. *Exultet cœlum,* p. 215.

Ant. to Mag. O Lord Jesus Christ, good Master, receive my spirit in peace : for it is now time that I come ; and I long to behold Thee.

If in Advent, Memorial of the Feria.

FEASTS OF DECEMBER.

[*On the first day unhindered is said the Office of the Dead.*]

[December 3.

FESTIVAL OF ST. FRANCIS XAVIER, CONFESSOR.*

All of the Common of a Confessor not a Bishop, p. 238, *except the* COLLECT.

GOD, Who didst will to gather to Thy Church the nations of India, by the preaching and miracles of blessed Francis ; mercifully grant that as we venerate his glorious merits, so we may imitate the pattern of his virtue ; through Jesus Christ our Lord. Amen.

Memorial of the Feria at both Vespers and at Lauds.]

December 6.

FESTIVAL OF S. NICOLAS, BISHOP.*

All of the Common of a Bishop and Confessor, p. 222.

Memorial of the Feria at both Vespers and at Lauds.

December 8.

FESTIVAL OF THE CONCEPTION OF THE BLESSED VIRGIN MARY.

First Vespers.

Ant. 1. There shall come a Star out of Jacob : and a Sceptre shall rise out of Israel.

Psalm cxiii. *Laudate pueri*, p. 46.

Ant. 2. The ark went upon the face of the waters : and the waters prevailed exceedingly upon the earth.

Psalm cxvii. *Laudate Dominum*, p. 50.

Ant. 3. The Lord Himself shall give you a sign : Behold, a Virgin shall conceive, and bear a son.

Psalm cxlvi. *Lauda, anima mea*, p. 63.

Ant. 4. When she which travaileth hath brought forth : then the remnant of his brethren shall return unto the children of Israel.

Psalm cxlvii. *Laudate Dominum*, p. 64.

Ant. 5. The same is the woman : whom the Lord hath pointed out for my Master's Son.

Psalm cxlvii. 12. *Lauda Hierusalem*, p. 64.

CHAPTER. Jer. xxiii.

BEHOLD, the days come, saith the Lord, that I will raise unto David a righteous branch, and a king shall reign, and prosper, and shall execute judgment and justice in the earth.

Ry. Thus saith the Lord that made thee, and formed thee from the womb: I will pour My Spirit upon thy Seed, and My blessing upon thine Offspring. Ꝟ. That holy Thing which shall be born of thee shall be called the Son of God. Ry. I will pour My spirit upon Thy Seed, and My blessing upon thine Offspring. Ꝟ. Glory be to the Father, and to the Son, and to the Holy Ghost. Ry. Thus saith the Lord that made thee, and formed thee from the womb: I will pour My Spirit upon thy Seed, and My blessing upon thine Offspring.

HYMN. *Quem terra, pontus, sidera*, p. 210.

Ꝟ. This is God's hill, in the which it pleaseth Him to dwell.

Ry. Yea, the Lord will abide in it for ever.

Ant. to Mag. The work is great, for the palace is not for men : but for the Lord God.

COLLECT.

WE beseech Thee, O Lord, to bestow the gift of heavenly grace upon Thy servants : that as the Nativity of the Blessed Virgin was the dawn of our salvation, so the celebration of her Conception may bring us increase of peace ; through Jesus Christ Thy Son our Lord, Who liveth and reigneth with Thee and the Holy Ghost, ever one God, world without end. Amen.

Memorial of the Feria.

Compline.

As in the Common of the Blessed Virgin Mary, p. 210.

Lauds.

Ꝟ. The Lord shall come down like the rain into a fleece of wool.

Ry. Even as the drops that water the earth.

Psalms of Sunday.

Ant. 1. Who is she that looketh forth as the morning : fair as the moon, clear as the sun ?

Ant. 2. My dove, my undefiled is but one : she is the only one of her mother, she is the choice one of her that bare her.

Ant. 3. The daughters saw her and blessed her : yea, the queens, and they praised her.

Ant. 4. Arise, and come away, O my dove : let me see thy countenance.

Ant. 5. How fair and how pleasant art thou : O love, for delights.

CHAPTER. Baruch v.

FOR God will shew thy brightness unto every country under heaven. For thy name shall be called of God for ever, The peace of righteousness, and the glory of God's worship.

Ry. Thanks be to God.

HYMN. *O gloriosa Virginum,*
      ℣. and ℟., p. 210.

Ant. to Ben. For behold, darkness shall cover the earth, and gross darkness the people : but the Lord shall arise upon thee.

Memorial of the Feria.

Prime.

Ant. Who is she that looketh forth as the morning : fair as the moon, clear as the sun ?

The ℟. is said with this

℣. Thou Who wast born of the Virgin Mary.

Tierce.

Ant. My dove, my undefiled, is but one : she is the only one of her mother, she is the choice one of her that bare her.

CHAPTER. Baruch v.

FOR God will shew thy brightness unto every country under heaven. For thy name shall be called of God for ever, The peace of righteousness, and the glory of God's worship.

℟. Mercy and truth are met together : righteousness and peace have kissed each other. ℣. Yea, the Lord shall shew loving kindness, and our land shall give her increase. ℟. Righteousness and peace have kissed each other. ℣. Glory be to the Father, and to the Son, and to the Holy Ghost. ℟. Mercy and truth are met together : righteousness and peace have kissed each other.

℣. His salvation is nigh them that fear Him.

℟. That glory may dwell in our land.

Sexts.

Ant. The daughters saw her and blessed her : yea, the queens, and they praised her.

CHAPTER. Ecclus. xxiv.

HE that made me caused my tabernacle to rest, and said, Let thy dwelling be in Jacob, and thine inheritance in Israel.

℟. His salvation : is nigh them that fear Him. ℣. That glory may dwell in our land. ℟. Nigh them that fear Him. ℣. Glory be to the Father, and to the Son, and to the Holy Ghost. ℟. His salvation : is nigh them that fear Him.

℣. Out of the earth truth hath flourished.

℟. And righteousness hath looked down from heaven.

Nones.

Ant. How fair and how pleasant art thou : O love, for delights.

CHAPTER. Is. xli. .

I HAVE chosen thee, and not cast thee away. Fear thou not, for I am with thee.

℟. Out of the earth : truth hath flourished. ℣. And righteousness hath looked down from heaven. ℟. Truth hath flourished. ℣. Glory be to the Father, and to the Son, and to the Holy Ghost. ℟. Out of the earth : truth hath flourished.

℣. So shall the King have pleasure in thy beauty.

℟. For He is thy Lord God, and worship thou Him.

Second Vespers.

Psalms as at Second Vespers of Christmas Day, p. 92.

Ant. 1. Sing and rejoice, O daughter of Sion : for lo, I come, and I will dwell in the midst of thee, saith the Lord.

Ant. 2. The King of Israel, even the Lord : is in the midst of thee.

Ant. 3. As the light of the morning when the sun riseth : even a morning without clouds.

Ant. 4. He will rejoice over thee with joy : He will rest in His love, He will joy over thee with singing.

Ant. 5. Many nations shall be joined unto the Lord in that day, and shall be My people : and I will dwell in the midst of thee.

CHAPTER. Rev. xxi.

BEHOLD, the tabernacle of God is with men, and He will dwell with them, and they shall be His people, and God Himself shall be with them, and be their God.

R̂. Thanks be to God.

HYMN. *Quem pontus, terra, sidera,* p. 210.

Ant. to Mag. Out of thee shall He come forth unto Me that is to be Ruler in Israel : Whose goings forth have been from of old, from everlasting. And this Man shall be the peace.

Memorial of the Feria.

December 13.

FESTIVAL OF S. LUCY, VIRGIN AND MARTYR.*

All of the Common of a Virgin Martyr, p. 230, except :

Both Vespers.

Ant. to Mag. I bless Thee, Father of my Lord Jesus Christ : for by Thy Son Thou hast extinguished the flames around me.

Lauds.

Ant. to Ben. In thy patience thou possessedst thy soul, Lucy, bride of Christ : thou hatedst the things that are in the world, and dost glow among the angels ; resisting unto blood thou didst overcome the enemy.

Memorial of the Feria at both Vespers and at Lauds.

December 21.

FESTIVAL OF S. THOMAS, APOSTLE AND MARTYR.

All of the Common of Apostles, p. 214, till the

Ant. to Mag. O Christ, Who didst vouchsafe to be touched by Thomas Didymus, hear our prayers : and help us in our sorrows, nor condemn us with the wicked, when Thou shalt come to judge.

COLLECT.

ALMIGHTY and everliving God, Who for the more confirmation of the faith didst suffer Thy holy Apostle Thomas to be doubtful in Thy Son's Resurrection ; grant us so perfectly, and without all doubt, to believe in Thy Son Jesus Christ, that our faith in Thy sight may never be reproved. Hear us, O Lord, through the same Jesus Christ, to Whom, with Thee and the Holy Ghost, be all honour and glory, now and for evermore. Amen.

MEMORIAL OF ADVENT.

Ant. O Orient, Brightness of the Eternal Light, and Sun of Righteousness : come, and lighten them that sit in darkness, and in the shadow of death.

V̂. Drop down, ye heavens, from above.

R̂. And let the skies pour down righteousness : let the earth open, and let them bring forth salvation.

Collect of the week.

Lauds.

All of the Common of an Apostle, p. 215, except :

MEMORIAL OF ADVENT.

Ant. Fear not : for on the fifth day our Lord shall come to you.

V̂. A voice crying in the wilderness.

R̂. Prepare ye the way of the Lord : make straight a highway for our God.

At the Lesser Hours, all of the Common, p. 215.

Second Vespers.

All of the Common, till Ant. to Magnificat, as at First Vespers.

MEMORIAL OF ADVENT.

Ant. O King of the Gentiles, and their Desire, the Corner-stone, Who madest both one : come, and save man, whom Thou hast made out of the dust of the earth.

V̂. Drop down, ye heavens, from above.

R̂. And let the skies pour down

righteousness : let the earth open, and let them bring forth salvation.

Collect of the week.

FEASTS OF JANUARY.

[*On the first day unhindered is said the Office of the Dead.*]

January 8.

FESTIVAL OF S. LUCIAN, PRIEST AND MARTYR.

Memorial of a Martyr, p. 203.

January 13.

FESTIVAL OF S. HILARY, BISHOP AND CONFESSOR.

Memorial of a Confessor Bishop, p. 203.

January 18.

FESTIVAL OF S. PRISCA, VIRGIN AND MARTYR.*

All of the Common of a Virgin Martyr, p. 230.

January 20.

FESTIVAL OF S. FABIAN, BISHOP AND MARTYR.*

All of the Common of a Martyr, p. 217, *except that which follows :*

First Vespers.

Ant. to Mag. The Lord chose a man out of the people, and gave him the glory of the Eternal Vision : Let us celebrate the solemnity of Fabian the Martyr. Joy be in heaven, and on earth peace to men of good will : Alleluia, Alleluia.

COLLECT.

GOD, Who didst strengthen Thy blessed Martyr Fabian with the power of constancy in suffering : grant us by his example, for love of Thee, to despise the wealth of this world, and fear none of its adversity ; through Jesus Christ our Lord. Amen.

Lauds.

Ant. to Ben. Blessed art thou, and happy shalt thou be, O noble Martyr : for with the Saints thou shalt rejoice, and with the Angels shalt exult for ever.

January 21.

FESTIVAL OF S. AGNES, VIRGIN AND MARTYR.

All of the Common of a Virgin Martyr, p. 230, except that which follows :

First Vespers.

Ant. to Mag. Blessed Agnes standing in the midst of the flames, stretched out her hands and said, I pray to Thee, O tremendous and eternal Father, Who by Thy blessed Son hast saved me from shame : lo! I come to Thee, Whom I have loved, Whom I have sought, Whom I have always desired.

COLLECT.

ALMIGHTY and eternal God, Who hast chosen the weak things of the world to confound the things which are mighty; grant, we beseech Thee, that by the commemoration of Thy holy Virgin and Martyr Agnes we may glory in Thy power; through Jesus Christ our Lord, Who liveth and reigneth with Thee and the Holy Ghost, ever one God, world without end. Amen.

[MEMORIAL OF S. FABIAN.

Not to be used if his full Office have not been said on the previous day.

Ant. Behold, thy name is written in the book of life : and thy memorial shall endure for ever.

℣. O God, wonderful art Thou in Thy Saints.

℟. And glorious in Thy Majesty.

Collect of S. Fabian.]

Lauds.

Ant. to Ben. Blessed Agnes, standing in the midst of the flames, stretched out her hands and prayed, saying, Almighty, tremendous, and worshipful God, I bless Thee, and glorify Thy Name for ever.

January 22.

FESTIVAL OF S. VINCENT, DEACON AND MARTYR.*

All of the Common of a Martyr, p. 217, except that which follows:

First Vespers.

Ant. to Mag. Let us humbly commemorate this day, on which Vincent, the unvanquished Martyr of Christ : having vanquished the tyrant, gained the palm of victory, and joyfully entered heaven.

MEMORIAL OF S. AGNES.

Ant. Lo, that which I longed for, I now behold; that which I hoped for, I now possess : to Him I am joined in heaven; Whom with entire devotion I loved on earth.

℣. Full of grace are thy lips.

℟. Because God hath blessed thee for ever.

Collect of S. Agnes.

Lauds.

Ant. to Ben. Behold, O unvanquished Vincent, He for whose name thou didst faithfully strive : hath laid up a crown for thee in heavenly places.

Second Vespers.

Ant. to Mag. Let praise be given therefore to the most high God : and let the sounding organ blend with the sweetness of angel voices.

———

[January 24.

FESTIVAL OF S. TIMOTHY.*

All of the Common of a Bishop and Confessor, p. 222.]

———

January 25.

FESTIVAL OF THE CONVERSION OF S. PAUL.

First Vespers.

Ant. to Psalms. Suddenly there shined round about him a light from heaven :

and he fell to the earth, and heard a voice saying unto him, Saul, Saul, why persecutest thou Me ? And he said, Who art Thou, Lord ? And the Lord said, I am Jesus of Nazareth, Whom thou persecutest; it is hard for thee to kick against the pricks.

Psalms of the Feria.

CHAPTER. Acts ix.

AND Saul, yet breathing out threatenings and slaughter against the disciples of the Lord, came near Damascus, and suddenly there shined round about him a light from heaven.

℟. Let us celebrate the conversion of Saint Paul the Apostle : He, on this day, being a persecutor, was made a chosen vessel. ℣. Let Angels rejoice, and Archangels exult, and the sons of God shout for joy in heaven. ℟. He, on this day, being a persecutor, was made a chosen vessel. ℣. Glory be to the Father, and to the Son, and to the Holy Ghost. ℟. He, on this day, being a persecutor, was made a chosen vessel.

HYMN. *Annue Christe,* ℣. and ℟., p. 214.

Ant. to Mag. The Lord chose one out of the people, and gave him the glory of the Eternal Vision : let us celebrate the Conversion of Saint Paul.

COLLECT.

O GOD, Who, through the preaching of the blessed Apostle Saint Paul, hast caused the light of the gospel to shine throughout the world; grant, we beseech Thee, that we, having his wonderful conversion in remembrance, may shew forth our thankfulness unto Thee for the same, by following the holy doctrine which he taught; through Jesus Christ our Lord. Amen.

Compline.

As in the Psalter, p. 67.

Lauds.

℣. Thou hast given an heritage.

℟. Unto those that fear Thy Name, O Lord.

Psalms of Sunday.

Ant. 1. Saul, which is also called Paul, the great preacher, being strengthened by God : mightily convinced the Jews, shewing that this is the Christ, the Son of the Living God.

Ant. 2. And Ananias went his way and entered into the house, and putting his hands on him, said : Hail, brother, the Lord, even Jesus that appeared unto thee in the way as thou camest, hath sent me, that thou mightest receive thy sight, and be filled with the Holy Ghost.

Ant. 3. And Ananias put his hands on him, and straightway there fell from his eyes as it had been scales : and he received sight forthwith and was baptized. And when he had received meat he was strengthened; then was he certain days with the disciples that were at Damascus.

Ant. 4. Among the Apostles last in calling, first in preaching ; he fell down a most cruel persecutor, and arose a most faithful preacher : O Lord, as his words teach us of Thee, so let him avail to bring us to Thee.

Ant. 5. Paul entered into the synagogue, and preached Jesus to the Jews, affirming that this is Christ : but all that heard him were amazed.

CHAPTER. Acts ix.

AND Saul, yet breathing out threatenings and slaughter against the disciples of the Lord, came near Damascus : aud suddenly there shined round about him a light from heaven.

Ry. Thanks be to God.

HYMN. *Exultet cælum laudibus,*
 V. *and* Ry., p. 215.

Ant. to Ben. Let us celebrate the Conversion of Saint Paul the Apostle ; for to-day he that had been a persecutor became a chosen vessel : let Angels rejoice and Archangels exult, and praise in heaven the Son of God.

Prime.

Ant. to Psalms. Saul, which is also called Paul, the great preacher, being strengthened by God : mightily convinced the Jews, shewing that this is the Christ, the Son of the Living God.

Ant. to Quicunque. Thee duly praise, Thee adore, Thee glorify : all Thy creatures, O blessed Trinity.

Tierce.

Ant. And Ananias went his way, and entered into the house, and putting his hands on him, said : Hail, brother, the Lord, even Jesus, that appeared unto thee in the way as thou camest, hath sent me, that thou mightest receive thy sight, and be filled with the Holy Ghost.

CHAPTER. Acts ix.

AND Saul, yet breathing out threatenings and slaughter against the disciples of the Lord, came near Damascus, and suddenly there shined round about him a light from heaven.

Ry. Ry. *of the Common of Apostles,* p. 216.

Sexts.

Ant. And Ananias put his hands on him, and straightway there fell from his eyes as it had been scales : and he received sight forthwith, and was baptized. And when he had received meat, he was strengthened. Then was he certain days with the disciples that were at Damascus.

CHAPTER. Acts ix.

BUT the Lord said unto him, Go thy way, for he is a chosen vessel unto Me, to bear My Name before the Gentiles, and kings, and the children of Israel.

Ry. Ry. *of the Common of Apostles,* p. 216.

Nones.

Ant. Paul entered into the synagogue and preached Jesus to the Jews, affirming that this is Christ : but all that heard him were amazed.

CHAPTER. Acts ix.

AND Ananias went his way, and entered into the house, and putting his hands on him, said, Brother Saul, the Lord, even Jesus, that appeared unto thee in the way as thou camest, hath sent me that thou mightest receive thy sight, and be filled with the Holy Ghost.

R/R/. *of the Common of Apostles*, p. 216.

Second Vespers.

Antiphons of Lauds, p. 278.

Psalms of the Common of Apostles, p. 216.

CHAPTER. Acts ix.

AND Saul, yet breathing out threatenings and slaughter against the disciples of the Lord, came near Damascus: and suddenly there shined round about him a light from heaven.

R/. Thanks be to God.

HYMN. *Exultet cœlum laudibus*, V/. and R/., p. 215.

Ant. to Mag. But when it pleased God, Who separated me from my mother's womb, and called me by His grace, to reveal His Son to me, that I might preach Him among the heathen : immediately I conferred not with flesh and blood.

January 27.

FESTIVAL OF S. JOHN CHRYSOSTOM, BISHOP, CONFESSOR, AND DOCTOR.*

All of the Common of a Bishop and Confessor, p. 222.

January 29.

FESTIVAL OF S. THOMAS AQUINAS, CONFESSOR AND DOCTOR.*

All of the Common of a Confessor and Doctor, p. 225.

FEASTS OF FEBRUARY.

[*On the first day unhindered is said the Office of the Dead.*]

February 1.

FESTIVAL OF S. BRIDGET, VIRGIN.*

All of the Common of a Virgin, p. 233.

February 2.

FESTIVAL OF THE PURIFICATION OF THE BLESSED VIRGIN MARY.

First Vespers.

Psalms as at Second Vespers of Christmas Day, p. 92.

Ant. 1. Rejoice greatly, O daughter of Sion, behold thy King cometh unto thee : He is just, and having salvation.

Ant. 2. The Desire of all nations shall come : and I will fill this house with glory, saith the Lord of hosts.

Ant. 3. The glory of this latter house shall be greater than that of the former, saith the Lord of hosts : and in this place will I give peace, saith the Lord of hosts.

Ant. 4. Then shall the offering of Judah and Jerusalem be pleasant unto the Lord : as in the days of old.

Ant. 5. Open ye the gates : that the righteous nation which keepeth the truth may enter in.

CHAPTER. Mal. iii.

BEHOLD, I will send My messenger, and he shall prepare the way before Me: and the Lord, whom ye seek, shall suddenly come to His temple, even the Messenger of the covenant, whom ye delight in; behold, He shall come, saith the Lord of hosts.

R/. Sing unto the Lord, for He hath done excellent things; cry out, and shout, thou inhabitant of Sion : for great is the Holy One of Israel in the midst of thee.   V/. For yet a little while, and He that shall come, will come, and will not tarry.   R/. Great is the Holy One of Israel in the midst of thee.   V/. Glory be to the Father, and to the Son, and to the Holy Ghost.   R/. Sing unto the Lord, for He hath done marvellous things; cry out, and shout, thou inhabitant of Sion : for great is the Holy One of Israel in the midst of thee.

HYMN. *Quod chorus vatum.*

THAT which of old the reverend choir of prophets
Sang, by the Holy Spirit's inspiration,
Now is fulfilled in Mary, Virgin Mother,
    Of our salvation.

Him, Lord of earth, and God of highest
    heaven,
She both conceived and bare, a Maid unstained,
And after childbirth still a stainless Virgin
        Ever remained.

Thee, then, we laud in canticles of triumph,
Mary, thou Mother of the King eternal,
Who now art glowing in the heavenly kingdom
        With light supernal.

Now unto God be majesty and worship,
Glory and might, and praise all praise excell-
    ing,
Who on the throne of heaven's eternal glory
        Ever is dwelling. Amen.

℣. It was revealed unto him by the
Holy Ghost.

℟. That he should not see death,
until he had seen the Lord's Christ.

Ant. to Mag. Sing, O daughter of
Sion : the Lord thy God in the midst of
thee is mighty ; He will save.

Collect.

ALMIGHTY and everliving God, we
humbly beseech Thy Majesty : that
as Thy Only-begotten Son was this day
presented in the temple in substance of
our flesh, so we may be presented unto
Thee, with pure and clean hearts, by the
same Thy Son Jesus Christ our Lord.
Amen.

Compline.

*As in Common of the Blessed Virgin
Mary, p. 210.*

Lauds.

℣. I waited patiently for the Lord.

℟. And He inclined unto me, and
heard my calling.

Psalms of Sunday.

Ant. 1. Simeon was just and devout,
waiting for the consolation of Israel :
and the Holy Ghost was upon him.

Ant. 2. It was revealed unto him by
the Holy Ghost : that he should not see
death, until he had seen the Lord's
Christ.

Ant. 3. Simeon took up the Child in
his arms : and blessed God.

Ant. 4. Lord, now lettest Thou Thy
servant depart in peace : according to
Thy word.

Ant. 5. For mine eyes have seen Thy
salvation : which Thou hast prepared
be... ...ce of all people.

Chapter. Mal. iii.

BEHOLD, I will send My messenger,
and he shall prepare the way before
Me ; and the Lord, whom ye seek, shall
suddenly come to His temple, even the
messenger of the covenant, whom ye
delight in : behold, He shall come, saith
the Lord of hosts.

Hymn. *O gloriosa Virginum,*
℣. and ℟., p. 210.

℣. We wait for Thy loving-kindness,
O Lord.

℟. In the midst of Thy temple.

Ant. to Ben. The old man held the
Child, but the old man was ruled by the
Child whom the Virgin bare : and after
Child-bearing she remained a Virgin,
and worshipped Him whom she bare.

Prime.

Ant. Simeon was just and devout,
waiting for the consolation of Israel :
and the Holy Ghost was upon him.

℟. *to Chapter as on Christmas Day*, p. 91.

Tierce.

Ant. It was revealed unto him by the
Holy Ghost : that he should not see death,
until he had seen the Lord's Christ.

Chapter. Mal. iii.

BEHOLD, I will send My messenger,
and he shall prepare the way before
Me : and the Lord, whom ye seek, shall
suddenly come to His temple, even the
messenger of the covenant, whom ye
delight in : behold, He shall come, saith
the Lord of hosts.

℟. The same stone which the builders refused * is become the head stone of
the corner : Alleluia, Alleluia. ℣. This
is the Lord's doing, and it is marvellous
in our eyes. ℟. Alleluia, Alleluia.
℣. Glory be to the Father, and to the
Son, and to the Holy Ghost. ℟. The
same stone which the builders refused *
is become the head stone of the corner ;
Alleluia, Alleluia.

℣. He hath put a new song in my
mouth.

℟. Even a thanksgiving unto our God.

*If after Septuagesima, Alleluia is omitted,
and the ℟. is divided at *.*

Sexts.

Ant. Simeon took up the Child in his arms : and blessed God.

CHAPTER. Is. xlix.

THEY shall know that I am the Lord; for they shall not be ashamed that wait for Me.

R7. He hath put * a new song in my mouth : Alleluia, Alleluia. V. Even a thanksgiving unto our God. R7. Alleluia, Alleluia. V. Glory be to the Father, and to the Son, and to the Holy Ghost. R7. He hath put * a new song in my mouth. Alleluia, Alleluia.

V. I will declare Thy righteousness.

R7. In the great congregation.

Nones.

Ant. Lord, now lettest Thou Thy servant depart in peace : according to Thy word.

CHAPTER. Heb. x.

WHEN He cometh into the world He saith, Sacrifice and offering Thou wouldest not, Then said I, Lo, I come.

R7. I will declare * Thy righteousness : Alleluia, Alleluia. V. In the great congregation. R7. Alleluia, Alleluia. V. Glory be to the Father, and to the Son, and to the Holy Ghost. R7. I will declare * Thy righteousness. Alleluia, Alleluia.

V. Let them now that fear the Lord confess.

R7. That His mercy endureth for ever.

Second Vespers.

Antiphons of Lauds, p. 280.

Psalms as at Second Vespers of Christmas Day, p. 92.

CHAPTER. Eph. v.

CHRIST also hath loved us, and hath given Himself for us; an offering and a sacrifice to God for a sweet-smelling savour.

R7. The glory of the Lord came into the house by the way of the gate whose prospect is toward the east : and, behold, the glory of the Lord filled the house.

V. Christ, by a tabernacle not made with hands, entered into the holy place. R7. And behold, the glory of the Lord filled the house. V. Glory be to the Father, and to the Son, and to the Holy Ghost. R7. The glory of the Lord came into the house by the way of the gate whose prospect is toward the east : and behold, the glory of the Lord filled the house.

HYMN. *Lætabundus.*

FULL of gladness,
    Let our faithful Choir be singing
      Alleluia.
Monarch's Monarch
From unspotted Maiden springing :
      Alleluia.

Him the Holy Virgin bore,
Wonderful and Counsellor,
      Sun from star had spring :
Sun, that never knoweth night :
Star, for ever shining bright,
      Ever glittering.

As a star a ray most fair,
Thus the Virgin also bare,
      Like in form, the Child ;
Nor the star by that its ray,
Nor the Virgin any way
      By the Birth defiled.

Now conforms the cedar tall
To the hyssop of the wall
      In our vale of tears :
He, God's Word and Essence, came
To assume our mortal frame,
      And with man appears.

Though Isaiah had foreshewn,
Though the Synagogue had known,
Yet the truth she will not own,
      Still remaining blind :
If she do her prophets wrong,
If she will not hear their throng,
Still she may, in Gentile song,
      Seek the deed, and find.

Turn, Judæa, and repent,
Credit thine Old Testament :
Why upon destruction bent,
      Miserable race ?
Whom its oracles foretold,
Born to save the world, behold ;
Him a Virgin's arms enfold,
      Full of truth and grace. Amen.

Or HYMN, *Quod chorus vatum*, p. 279.

V. We wait for Thy loving kindness, O God.

R7. In the midst of Thy temple.

Ant. to Mag. The Lord is in His holy temple : let all the earth keep silence before Him.

February 3.

FESTIVAL OF S. BLAISE, BISHOP AND MARTYR.*

All of the Common of a Martyr, p. 217.

February 5.

FESTIVAL OF S. AGATHA, VIRGIN AND MARTYR.*

All of the Common of a Virgin Martyr, except that which follows :

First Vespers.

Ant. to Mag. Agatha, holy virgin of noble race : suffered a glorious passion for the sake of Christ.

COLLECT.

O GOD, Who among the other miracles of Thy power hast bestowed the crown of martyrdom even on the weaker sex; mercifully grant, that as we celebrate the birthday of Thy blessed Martyr Agatha, so by her example we may come to Thee; through Jesus Christ our Lord. Amen.

Lauds.

Ant. to Ben. But I, being helped of the Lord, will constantly confess Him : for He hath saved me, and comforted me.

Second Vespers.

Ant. to Mag. Agatha most joyfully and gloriously went to prison as it were to a banquet : and commended her sufferings to her Lord.

On all Festivals throughout Lent, Memorials of the Feria are to be said at both Vespers and Lauds.

February 14.

FESTIVAL OF S. VALENTINE, BISHOP AND MARTYR.*

All of the Common of a Martyr, p. 217.

February 24.

FESTIVAL OF S. MATTHIAS, APOSTLE AND MARTYR.

All of the Common of Apostles, p. 214, except the

COLLECT.

O ALMIGHTY God, Who into the place of the traitor Judas didst choose Thy faithful servant Matthias to be of the number of the twelve Apostles; grant that Thy Church, being always preserved from false Apostles, may be ordered and guided by faithful and true pastors; through Jesus Christ our Lord. Amen.

FEASTS OF MARCH.

[*On the first day unhindered is said the Office of the Dead.*]

March 1.

FESTIVAL OF S. DAVID, ARCHBISHOP.*

All of the Common of a Confessor Bishop, p. 222.

March 2.

FESTIVAL OF S. CHAD, BISHOP.*

All of the Common of a Confessor Bishop, p. 222.

March 6.

FESTIVAL OF S. PERPETUA, MATRON, [AND HER COMPANIONS].*

All of the Common of a Matron, p. 233, except the

COLLECT.

O GOD, strength of them that strive, and palm of Martyrs, Who didst confirm Thy handmaid Perpetua and her companions with wonderful courage against the fierceness of their torments: we pray Thee, that as Thou dost gladden us by their triumph, so Thou wouldest ever defend us at their supplication; through Jesus Christ our Lord. Amen.

March 12.

FESTIVAL OF S. GREGORY, BISHOP AND CONFESSOR.*

All of the Common of a Confessor Bishop, p. 222.

[March 17.

FESTIVAL OF S. PATRICK, BISHOP AND CONFESSOR.*

All of the Common of a Confessor Bishop, p. 222, except the

COLLECT.

GOD, Who didst vouchsafe to send Thy Confessor and Bishop Patrick to preach Thy glory to the nations, grant by his merits and intercessions, that those things which Thou teachest us to do, of Thy mercy we may have power to perform; through Jesus Christ our Lord. Amen.]

[March 18.*

FESTIVAL OF S. CYRIL, BISHOP AND CONFESSOR.*

All of the Common of a Bishop and Confessor, p. 222.]

On the same day :

S. EDWARD, KING.*

Memorial of a Confessor, from Common Memorials, p. 205, with this

COLLECT.

O GOD, Ruler of an eternal kingdom, mercifully look upon Thy family; and as Thou didst vouchsafe to glorify Thy Martyr Edward with heavenly gifts, so grant us likewise to attain eternal felicity; through Jesus Christ our Lord. Amen.

[March 19.

FESTIVAL OF S. JOSEPH, CONFESSOR.

First Vespers.

Ant. to Psalms. Jacob begat Joseph, the husband of Mary, of whom was born Jesus : that was called Christ.

Psalms of the Feria.

CHAPTER. Prov. ii.

HE keepeth the paths of judgment, and preserveth the way of His saints. Then shalt thou understand righteousness, and judgment, and equity; yea, every good path.

R̷. The beloved of the Lord shall dwell in safety by Him : and the Lord shall cover him all the day long, and he shall dwell between His shoulders. V̷. A faithful and wise servant, whom his lord hath made ruler over his household. R̷. And the Lord shall cover him all the day long, and he shall dwell between His shoulders. V̷. Glory be to the Father, and to the Son, and to the Holy Ghost. R̷. The beloved of the Lord shall dwell in safety by Him : and the Lord shall cover him all the day long, and he shall dwell between His shoulders.

HYMN. *Te Joseph celebrent agmina cælitum.*

JOSEPH, pure spouse of that immortal Bride,
Who shines in ever-virgin glory bright,
Through all the Christian climes thy praise be sung;
   Through all the realms of light.

Thine arms embraced thy Maker newly born;
With Him to Egypt's desert didst thou flee;
Him in Jerusalem did seek and find;
   O grief, O joy for thee.

Grant us, great Trinity, with this Thy Saint,
Unto the starry mansions to attain;
There, with glad tongues, Thy praise to celebrate
   In one eternal strain.

V̷. Exceeding glad shall he be.
R̷. Of Thy salvation, O Lord.
Ant. to Mag. Take this Child : and nurse It for Me.

COLLECT.

O LORD, Who didst appoint blessed Joseph to be the foster-father of Thine only - begotten Son, and the guardian of His Virgin Mother: keep us, we beseech Thee, under Thy perpetual care; through the same Jesus Christ our Lord. Amen.

Compline.

As in the Psalter, p. 67.

Lauds.

℣. I have set God alway before me.

℟. He is on my right hand, therefore I shall not fall.

Psalms of Sunday.

Ant. 1. And when they had fulfilled the days, as they returned, the child Jesus tarried behind in Jerusalem : and Joseph and His mother knew not of it.

Ant. 2. But they, supposing Him to have been in the company, went a day's journey : and they sought Him among their kinsfolk and acquaintance.

Ant. 3. And when they found Him not, they turned back again to Jerusalem : seeking Him.

Ant. 4. And it came to pass, that after three days they found Him in the temple : sitting in the midst of the doctors, both hearing them, and asking them questions.

Ant. 5. And His mother said unto Him, Son, why hast Thou thus dealt with us ? : behold, Thy father and I have sought Thee sorrowing.

CHAPTER. Prov. xxviii., xxvii.

A FAITHFUL man shall abound with blessings : he that waiteth on his master shall be honoured.

℟. Thanks be to God.

HYMN. *Rex gloriose martyrum*, p. 100.

℣. My soul, be thou joyful in the Lord.

℟. It shall rejoice in His salvation.

Ant. to Ben. And He went down with them, and came to Nazareth : and was subject unto them.

Collect as at First Vespers.

Prime.

Ant. And when they had fulfilled the days, as they returned, the child Jesus tarried behind in Jerusalem : and Joseph and His mother knew not of it.

Tierce.

Ant. But they, supposing Him to have been in the company, went a day's journey : and they sought Him among their kinsfolk and acquaintance.

Chapter as at Lauds.

℟. Seek the Lord : and His face. ℣. Seek His face evermore. ℟. Seek the Lord. ℣. Glory be to the Father, and to the Son, and to the Holy Ghost. ℟. Seek the Lord : and His face.

℣. I am like a green olive-tree in the house of my God.

℟. And my hope is in the tender mercy of God.

Sexts.

Ant. And when they found Him not, they turned back again to Jerusalem : seeking Him.

CHAPTER. Ecclus. xlv.

H E was beloved of God and of men, whose memorial was blessed. He sanctified him in his faithfulness and meekness, and chose him out of all men.

℟. I am like a green olive tree : in the house of my God. ℣. And my hope is in the tender mercy of God. ℟, In the house of my God. ℣. Glory be to the Father, and to the Son, and to the Holy Ghost. ℟. I am like a green olive tree : in the house of my God.

℣. I sought the Lord, and He heard me.

℟. Yea, He delivered me out of all my fear.

Nones.

Ant. And His mother said unto Him, Son, why hast Thou thus dealt with us ? : behold, Thy father and I have sought Thee sorrowing.

CHAPTER. Wisd. i.

I N simplicity of heart seek Him. For He will be found of them that tempt Him not : and sheweth Himself unto such as do not distrust Him.

℟. I sought the Lord : and He heard me. ℣. Yea, He delivered me out of all my fear. ℟. And He heard me. ℣. Glory be to the Father, and to the Son, and to the Holy Ghost. ℟. I sought the Lord : and He heard me.

℣. Riches and plenteousness shall be in his house.

℟. And his righteousness endureth for ever.

Second Vespers.

Ants. of Lauds, p. 284.

Psalms of the Feria.

CHAPTER. Wisd. x.

WISDOM guided the righteous man in right paths, shewed him the kingdom of God, and gave him knowledge of holy things, made him rich in his travails, and multiplied the fruit of his labours.

℟. Thanks be to God.

HYMN. *Te Joseph celebrent*, ℣. and ℟. p. 283.

Ant to Mag. Blessed is that servant : whom his lord when he cometh shall find so doing.]

———

[March 20.

FESTIVAL OF S. CUTHBERT, BISHOP AND CONFESSOR.*

All of the Common of a Confessor Bishop, p. 222.]

———

March 21.

FESTIVAL OF S. BENEDICT, ABBOT.*

All of the Common of an Abbot, p. 225.

[*The Antiphons are said throughout with Alleluia on all Feasts occurring in Easter tide.*]

———

March 25.

FESTIVAL OF THE ANNUNCIATION OF THE BLESSED VIRGIN MARY.

First Vespers.

Ant. to Psalms. Drop down, ye heavens from above, and let the skies pour down righteousness : let the earth open, and let them bring forth the Saviour. [Alleluia.]

Psalms of the Feria.

CHAPTER. Dan. ix.

SEVENTY weeks are determined upon thy people and upon thy holy city, to finish the transgression, and to make an end of sins, and to make reconciliation for iniquity, and to bring in everlasting righteousness, and to seal up the vision and prophecy, and to anoint the most High.

℟. Hear ye now, O house of David : behold, a Virgin shall conceive, and bear a Son, and shall call His Name Emmanuel. ℣. He will dwell with them, and they shall be His people, and God Himself shall be with them, and be their God. ℟. Behold, a Virgin shall conceive, and bear a Son, and shall call His Name Emmanuel. ℣. Glory be to the Father, and to the Son, and to the Holy Ghost. ℟. Hear ye now, O house of David : behold, a Virgin shall conceive, and bear a Son, and shall call His Name Emmanuel.

HYMN. *Quem terra, pontus, sidera*, p. 210.

℣. Thou shalt arise and have mercy upon Sion.

℟. For it is time that Thou have mercy upon her. [Alleluia.]

Ant. to Mag. O that Thou wouldest rend the heavens, that Thou wouldest come down : behold, see, we beseech Thee, we are all Thy people. [Alleluia.]

COLLECT.

WE beseech Thee, O Lord, pour Thy grace into our hearts; that, as we have known the Incarnation of Thy Son Jesus Christ by the message of an Angel, so by His Cross and Passion we may be brought unto the glory of His Resurrection; through the same Jesus Christ our Lord. Amen.

Compline.

As in the Common, p. 210. But if this Feast falls in Lent, no change is made from the Lent Compline, except that the proper Doxology is said at the end of the Hymn.

Lauds.

℣. He remembered us when we were in trouble.

℞. For His mercy endureth for ever. [Alleluia.]

Psalms of Sunday.

Ant. 1. In the beginning was the word, and the Word was with God : and the Word was God. [Alleluia.]

Ant. 2. All things were made by Him : and without Him was not any thing made that was made. [Alleluia.]

Ant. 3. He was in the world, and the world was made by Him : and the world knew Him not. [Alleluia.]

Ant. 4. As many as received Him, to them gave He power to become the sons of God : even to them that believe on His Name. [Alleluia.]

Ant. 5. And the Word was made flesh : and dwelt among us, and we beheld His glory. [Alleluia.]

CHAPTER. Is. lxii.

LIFT up a standard for the people. Behold, the Lord hath proclaimed unto the end of the world, Say ye to the daughter of Sion, Behold, thy salvation cometh ; behold, His reward is with Him, and His work before Him.

℞. Thanks be to God.

HYMN. *O gloriosa Virginum,*
℣. and ℞., p. 210.

Ant. to Ben. The dayspring from on high hath visited us : to give light to them that sit in darkness, and in the shadow of death. [Alleluia.]

Prime.

Ant. In the beginning was the Word, and the Word was with God : and the Word was God. [Alleluia.]

The ℞. is said with this

℣. Thou Who wast born of the Virgin Mary.

Tierce.

Ant. All things were made by Him : and without Him was not any thing made that was made. [Alleluia.]

CHAPTER. Isa. lxii.

LIFT up a standard for the people. Behold, the Lord hath proclaimed unto the end of the world, Say ye to the daughter of Sion, Behold, thy salvation cometh ; behold, His reward is with Him, and His work before Him.

℞. *of the Common,* p. 211.

Sexts.

Ant. He was in the world, and the world was made by Him : and the world knew Him not. [Alleluia.]

Chapter and ℞. as in the Common, p. 211.

Nones.

Ant. And the Word was made flesh : and dwelt among us, and we beheld His glory. [Alleluia.]

Chapter and ℞. as in the Common, p. 211.

Second Vespers.

Antiphons of Lauds, p. 286.

Psalms of the Common, p. 211.

CHAPTER. Is. lii.

BREAK forth into joy, sing together, ye waste places of Jerusalem : for the Lord hath comforted His people, He hath redeemed Jerusalem. The Lord hath made bare His holy arm in the eyes of all the nations.

℞. The Lord hath made a faithful oath unto David, and He shall not shrink from it : Of the fruit of thy body shall I set upon thy seat. ℣. As He spake to our forefathers, Abraham and his seed for ever. ℞. Of the fruit of thy body shall I set upon thy seat. ℣. Glory be to the Father, and to the Son, and to the Holy Ghost. ℞. The Lord hath made a faithful oath unto David, and He shall not shrink from it : Of the fruit of thy body, shall I set upon thy seat.

HYMN. *Quem terra, pontus, sidera,* p. 210.

Ant. to Mag. How beautiful upon the mountains are the feet of him that bringeth good tidings : that publisheth salvation. [Alleluia.]

FEASTS OF APRIL.

[On the first day unhindered is said the Office of the Dead.]

April 3.

FESTIVAL OF S. RICHARD, BISHOP AND CONFESSOR.*

All of the Common of a Confessor Bishop, p. 222.

April 4.

FESTIVAL OF S. AMBROSE, BISHOP AND DOCTOR.*

All of the Common of a Confessor Bishop, p. 222.

April 19.

FESTIVAL OF S. ALPHEGE, ARCH-BISHOP AND MARTYR.*

All of the Common of a Martyr, p. 217.

April 23.

FESTIVAL OF S. GEORGE, MARTYR.*

All of the Common of a Martyr in Easter tide, p. 214.

April 25.

FESTIVAL OF S. MARK, EVANGELIST AND MARTYR.

All of the Common of an Apostle in Easter tide, p. 212, except the Chapters and Collect.

First Vespers.

CHAPTER. Eph. iv.

UNTO every one of us is given grace, according to the measure of the gift of Christ. Wherefore He saith, When He ascended up on high, He led captivity captive, and gave gifts unto men.

Lauds.

Chapter as at First Vespers.

Tierce.

Chapter as at First Vespers.

Sexts.

CHAPTER. Eph. iv.

HE that descended is the same that ascended up far above all heavens, that He might fill all things.

Nones.

CHAPTER. Eph. iv.

AND He gave some Apostles, and some Prophets, and some Evangelists, and some pastors and teachers; for the perfecting of the saints.

Second Vespers.

Chapter as at First Vespers.

COLLECT.

O ALMIGHTY God, Who hast instructed Thy holy Church with the heavenly doctrine of Thy Evangelist Saint Mark; give us grace, that, being not like children, carried away with every blast of vain doctrine, we may be established in the truth of Thy holy Gospel; through Jesus Christ our Lord. Amen.

FEASTS OF MAY.

[On the first day unhindered is said the Office of the Dead.]

May 1.

FESTIVAL OF SS. PHILIP AND JAMES.

First Vespers.

Ant. I go to prepare a place for you; but I will see you again. Alleluia : and your heart shall rejoice. Alleluia, Alleluia.

Psalms of the Feria.

CHAPTER. Wisd. v.

THEN shall the righteous man stand in great boldness before the face of such as have afflicted him, and made no account of his labours.

R̰., HYMN, *Tristes erant,* V̰. and R̰., as in the Common, p. 212.

Ant. to Mag. Have I been so long time with you, and yet hast thou not known Me, Philip? : He that hath seen Me hath seen the Father. Alleluia.

COLLECT.

O ALMIGHTY God, Whom truly to know is everlasting life; grant us perfectly to know Thy Son Jesus Christ to be the Way, the Truth, and the Life; that, following the steps of Thy holy Apostles, Saint Philip and Saint James, we may steadfastly walk in the way that leadeth to eternal life; through the same Thy Son Jesus Christ our Lord,

Memorial of the Resurrection, p. 171.

Compline.

As in the Psalter, p. 67.

Lauds.

℣. He was known of them.
℟. In breaking of bread. Alleluia.

Psalms of Sunday.

Ant. 1. Lord, shew us the Father : and it sufficeth us. Alleluia.

Ant. 2. Philip, he that hath seen Me : hath seen the Father. Alleluia.

Ant. 3. I am the Way, the Truth, and the Life : no man cometh to the Father, but by Me. Alleluia.

Ant. 4. O ye spirits and souls of the righteous : bless ye the Lord. Alleluia.

Ant. 5. If ye abide in Me, and My words abide in you : ye shall ask what ye will, and it shall be done unto you. Alleluia.

CHAPTER. Wisd. v.

THEN shall the righteous man stand in great boldness before the face of such as have afflicted him, and made no account of his labours.
℟. Thanks be to God.

HYMN. *Claro Paschali gaudio,* ℣. *and* ℟. *as in the Common of Apostles in Easter tide,* p. 212.

Ant. to Ben. Let not your heart be troubled, ye believe in God, believe also in Me : in My Father's house are many mansions. Alleluia.

Memorial of the Resurrection, p. 171.

Prime.

Ant. Lord, shew us the Father : and it sufficeth us. Alleluia.

Tierce.

Ant. He that hath seen Me : hath seen the Father. Alleluia.

CHAPTER. Wisd. v.

THEN shall the righteous man stand in great boldness before the face of such as have afflicted him, and made no account of his labours.
℟. Then were the disciples glad : Alleluia, Alleluia. ℣. When they saw the Lord. ℟. Alleluia, Alleluia. ℣. Glory be to the Father, and to the Son, and to the Holy Ghost. ℟. Then were the disciples glad : Alleluia, Alleluia.
℣. Lord, shew us the Father.
℟. And it sufficeth us. Alleluia.

Sexts.

Ant. I am the Way, the Truth, and the Life : no man cometh to the Father, but by Me. Alleluia.

CHAPTER. Acts iv.

AND with great power gave the Apostles witness of the resurrection of the Lord Jesus : and great grace was upon them all.
℟. Lord, shew us the Father : Alleluia, Alleluia. ℣. And it sufficeth us. ℟. Alleluia, Alleluia. ℣. Glory be to the Father, and to the Son, and to the Holy Ghost. ℟. Lord, shew us the Father : Alleluia, Alleluia.
℣. Let not your heart be troubled.
℟. Neither let it be afraid. Alleluia.

Nones.

Ant. If ye abide in Me, and My words abide in you : ye shall ask what ye will, and it shall be done unto you. Alleluia.

CHAPTER. Acts iv.

AND they departed from the council, rejoicing that they were counted worthy to suffer shame for His Name.

℟. Let not your heart be troubled: Alleluia, Alleluia. ℣. Neither let it be afraid. ℟. Alleluia, Alleluia. ℣. Glory be to the Father, and to the Son, and to the Holy Ghost. ℟. Let not your heart be troubled : Alleluia, Alleluia.

℣. He was known of them.

℟. In breaking of bread. Alleluia.

Second Vespers.

Ants. of Lauds with Psalms of the Common of Apostles.

Chapter. Wisd. v.

THEN shall the righteous man stand in great boldness before the face of such as have afflicted him, and made no account of his labours.

℟., Hymn, *Tristes erant,* ℣. and ℟., *as in the Common,* p. 212.

Ant. to Mag. If ye had known Me, ye should have known My Father also : and from henceforth ye know Him, and have seen Him. Alleluia.

[May 2.

Festival of S. Athanasius, Bishop and Confessor.

All of the Common of a Confessor Bishop, except the

Collect.

GRANT, we beseech Thee, Almighty God, that as blessed Athanasius set forth the excellency of Thy word, so we may duly comprehend and rightly profit by the same; through Jesus Christ our Lord. Amen.]

May 3.

Festival of the Invention of the Cross.

First Vespers.

Ant. to Psalms. The tree of the field shall yield her fruit, and they shall know that I am the Lord : when I have broken the bands of their yoke.

Psalms of the Feria.

Chapter. Is. xi.

AND He shall set up an ensign for the nations, and shall assemble the outcasts of Israel, and gather together the outcasts of Judah from the four corners of the earth.

℟. In the midst of the city was the tree of life : and the leaves of the tree were for the healing of the nations: and there shall be no more curse. Alleluia, Alleluia. ℣. And though the living Lord be angry with us a little while, yet shall He be at one again with His servants. ℟. And the leaves of the tree were for the healing of the nations. Alleluia, Alleluia. ℣. Glory be to the Father, and to the Son, and to the Holy Ghost. ℟. And there shall be no more curse. Alleluia, Alleluia.

Hymn. *Vexilla Regis prodeunt,* p. 147, (*in the penultimate verse the word* Passion *is changed to* festal.)

℣. He shall drink of the brook in the way.

℟. Therefore shall He lift up His head. Alleluia.

Ant. to Mag. In that day there shall be a root of Jesse, which shall stand for an ensign of the people; to it shall the Gentiles seek : and His rest shall be glorious. Alleluia.

Collect.

O GOD, Who in the glorious discovery of the saving Cross didst set forth the marvels of Thy Passion ; grant that by the ransom paid on the tree of life, we may attain to the rewards of eternal life; Who livest and reignest with the Father and the Holy Ghost, ever one God, world without end. Amen.

Compline.

As in the Psalter, p. 67.

Lauds.

℣. The sign of the Cross shall appear in heaven.

℟. When the Lord shall come to judge the world. Alleluia.

Psalms of Sunday.

Ant. 1. O mighty work of love : death died, when Life died upon the wood. Alleluia.

Ant. 2. Save us, O our Saviour, by the power of the Cross : Thou Who savedst Peter on the sea, have mercy upon us. Alleluia.

Ant. 3. Blessed is the wood : whereby righteousness cometh. Alleluia.

Ant. 4. Let us glory in the Cross : of our Lord Jesus Christ. Alleluia.

Ant. 5. By the sign of the Cross : deliver us from our enemies, O our God. Alleluia.

CHAPTER. Gen. xxii.

ABRAHAM took the wood of the burnt offering, and laid it upon Isaac, his son. And Isaac spake unto his father, and said, Behold the fire and the wood : but where is the lamb for a burnt offering? And Abraham said, My son, God will provide.

R7. Thanks be to God.

HYMN. *Lustra sex*, p. 148.

V. Tell it out among the heathen.

R7. That the Lord hath reigned from the tree. Alleluia.

Ant. to Ben. Hail, glorious Cross : which alone wast counted worthy to bear the Lord, the King of Heaven. Alleluia.

Prime.

Ant. O mighty work of love : death died, when Life died upon the wood. Alleluia.

Tierce.

Ant. Save us, O our Saviour, by the power of the Cross : Thou Who savedst Peter on the sea, have mercy upon us. Alleluia.

Chapter as at Lauds.

R7. We adore and bless Thee, O Christ : Alleluia, Alleluia. V. Because by Thy holy Cross Thou hast redeemed the world. R7. Alleluia, Alleluia. V. Glory be to the Father, and to the Son, and to the Holy Ghost. R7. We adore and bless Thee, O Christ : Alleluia, Alleluia.

V. The sign of the Cross shall appear in heaven.

R7. When the Lord shall come to judge the world. Alleluia.

Sexts.

Ant. Blessed is the wood : whereby righteousness cometh. Alleluia.

CHAPTER. Heb. ii.

FOR it became Him, for Whom are all things, and by Whom are all things, in bringing many sons unto glory, to make the Captain of their salvation perfect through sufferings.

R7. The sign of the Cross shall appear in heaven : Alleluia, Alleluia. V. When the Lord shall come to judge the world. R7. Alleluia, Alleluia. V. Glory be to the Father, and to the Son, and to the Holy Ghost. R7. The sign of the Cross shall appear in heaven : Alleluia, Alleluia.

V. Tell it out among the heathen.

R7. That the Lord reigneth from the tree. Alleluia.

Nones.

Ant. By the sign of the Cross : deliver us from our enemies, O our God. Alleluia.

CHAPTER. Eph. iii.

THAT Christ may dwell in your hearts by faith : that ye, being rooted and grounded in love, may be able to comprehend with all saints what is the breadth, and length, and depth, and height; and to know the love of Christ, which passeth knowledge, that ye might be filled with all the fulness of God.

R7. Tell it out among the heathen : Alleluia, Alleluia. V. That the Lord reigneth from the tree. R7. Alleluia, Alleluia. V. Glory be to the Father, and to the Son, and to the Holy Ghost. R7. Tell it out among the heathen : Alleluia, Alleluia.

V. We adore and bless Thee, O Christ.

R7. Because by Thy holy Cross Thou hast redeemed the world. Alleluia, Alleluia.

Second Vespers.

Ants. of Lauds.

Psalms of Sunday.

Chapter as at Lauds.

HYMN. *Vexilla regis prodeunt,*
℣. and ℟., p. 147.

Ant. to Mag. He who burst the bars of hell, endured the Holy Cross : He is girded with power. He rose on the third day. Alleluia.

——

May 6.

FESTIVAL OF S. JOHN PORT-LATIN.

First Vespers.

Psalms of the Feria.

Ant. to Psalms. For Thou savedst me from destruction, and deliveredst me from the evil time : therefore will I give thanks, and praise Thee, and bless Thy Name, O Lord. Alleluia.

CHAPTER. Is. xliii.

THUS saith the Lord, Fear not; I have redeemed thee, thou art Mine : when thou passest through the waters, I will be with thee; and through the rivers, they shall not overflow thee; when thou walkest through the fire, thou shalt not be burned, neither shall the flame kindle upon thee.

HYMN. *Tristes erant Apostoli,* p. 212.

℣. In God have I put my trust.

℟. I will not fear what man can do unto me. Alleluia.

Ant. to Mag. Jesus saith to James and John, Ye shall indeed drink of the cup that I drink of : and be baptized with the baptism that I am baptized with. Alleluia.

COLLECT.

O GOD, Who with the oil of holy gladness didst anoint blessed John a companion in the tribulation and patience of the Lord Jesus : grant us, according to his pattern, so to rejoice in the fellowship of Christ's Passion, that we may rejoice abundantly in the revelation of His glory; Who liveth and reigneth with Thee and the Holy Ghost, ever one God, world without end. Amen.

Compline.

As in the Psalter, p. 67.

Lauds.

℣. They had almost made an end of me upon earth.

℟. But I forsook not Thy commandments. Alleluia.

Psalms of Sunday.

Ant. 1. I, John, am your companion in tribulation : and in the kingdom and patience of Jesus Christ. Alleluia.

Ant. 2. I was in the isle that is called Patmos : for the word of God, and for the testimony of Jesus Christ. Alleluia.

Ant. 3. I heard a great voice, as of a trumpet, saying, I am Alpha and Omega, the first and the last : and, What thou seest, write in a book, and send unto the seven churches. Alleluia.

Ant. 4. And the Angel said unto me : Thou must prophecy again before many peoples, and nations, and tongues, and kings. Alleluia.

Ant. 5. I, John, saw these things and heard them : and he saith unto me, Seal not the sayings of the prophecy of this book; for the time is at hand. Alleluia.

CHAPTER. Rev. xix.

AND I fell at his feet to worship him. And he said unto me, See thou do it not : I am thy fellowservant, and of thy brethren that have the testimony of Jesus : worship God : for the testimony of Jesus is the spirit of prophecy.

℟. Thanks be to God.

HYMN. *Claro Paschali gaudio,* p. 213.

℣. In a barren and dry land have I looked for Thee, my God.

℟. That I might behold Thy power and glory. Alleluia.

Ant. to Ben. Therefore that disciple whom Jesus loved saith unto Peter : It is the Lord. Alleluia, Alleluia.

Prime.

Ant. I, John, am your companion in tribulation : and in the kingdom and patience of Jesus Christ. Alleluia.

Tierce.

Ant. I was in the isle that is called Patmos : for the word of God, and for the testimony of Jesus Christ. Alleluia.

Chapter as at Lauds.

Ry. I will speak of Thy testimonies also, even before kings : Alleluia, Alleluia. Vy. And will not be ashamed. Ry. Alleluia, Alleluia. Vy. Glory be to the Father, and to the Son, and to the Holy Ghost. Ry. I will speak of Thy testimonies also, even before kings : Alleluia, Alleluia.

Vy. Lo, I will not refrain my lips, O Lord.

Ry. And that Thou knowest. Alleluia.

Sexts.

Ant. I heard a great voice, as of a trumpet, saying, I am Alpha and Omega, the first and the last : and, What thou seest, write in a book, and send unto the seven churches. Alleluia.

CHAPTER. Is. l.

HE wakeneth mine ear to hear as the learned. The Lord God hath opened mine ear, and I was not rebellious, neither turned away back.

Ry. Lo, I will not refrain my lips, O Lord : Alleluia, Alleluia. Vy. And that Thou knowest. Ry. Alleluia, Alleluia. Vy. Glory be to the Father, and to the Son, and to the Holy Ghost. Ry. Lo, I will not refrain my lips, O Lord : Alleluia, Alleluia.

Vy. I will hearken what the Lord God will say concerning me.

Ry. For He shall speak peace unto His people. Alleluia.

Nones.

Ant. I, John, saw these things and heard them : and he saith unto me, Seal not the sayings of the prophecy of this book ; for the time is at hand. Alleluia.

CHAPTER. Wisd. vii.

ALL such things as are either secret or manifest, them I know. For wisdom, which is the worker of all things, taught me: for in her is an understanding spirit.

Ry. I will hearken what the Lord God will say concerning me : Alleluia, Alleluia. Vy. For He shall speak peace unto

His people. Ry. Alleluia, Alleluia. Vy. Glory be to the Father, and to the Son, and to the Holy Ghost. Ry. I will hearken what the Lord God will say concerning me : Alleluia, Alleluia.

Vy. Thou, O God, hast taught me from my youth up until now.

Ry. Therefore will I tell of Thy wondrous works. Alleluia.

Second Vespers.

Ants. of Lauds.

Psalms of the Common of Apostles, p. 216. The rest as at First Vespers.

———

[May 7.

FESTIVAL OF S. JOHN OF BEVERLEY.*

All of the Common of an Abbot or Monk, p. 225.]

———

May 19.

FESTIVAL OF S. DUNSTAN, ARCHBISHOP AND CONFESSOR.*

All of the Common of a Confessor Bishop, p. 222.

———

[May 21.

FESTIVAL OF S. HELENA, MATRON.*

All of the Common of a Matron, p. 233.]

———

[May 25.

FESTIVAL OF S. ALDHELM, BISHOP AND CONFESSOR.*

All of the Common of a Confessor Bishop, p. 222.]

———

May 26.

FESTIVAL OF S. AUGUSTINE, APOSTLE OF ENGLAND.

All of the Common of a Confessor Bishop, p. 222, except the

COLLECT.

GOD, Who didst give blessed Augustine the Bishop, to be the first teacher of the English people: by his help grant that our sins may be forgiven, and that with him we may come to the fruition of heavenly joys; through Jesus Christ our Lord. Amen.

May 27.
FESTIVAL OF VENERABLE BEDE, PRIEST.*

All of the Common of a Confessor not a Bishop, p. 228.

FEASTS OF JUNE.
[On the first day unhindered is said the Office of the Dead.]

June 1.
FESTIVAL OF S. NICOMEDE, PRIEST AND MARTYR.*

All of the Common of a Martyr, in Easter tide, p. 214, or, if after Trinity, p. 217.

June 5.
FESTIVAL OF S. BONIFACE, BISHOP AND MARTYR.*

All of the Common of a Martyr, in or out of Easter tide, as the case may be.

[June 10.
FESTIVAL OF S. MARGARET OF SCOTLAND, MATRON.*

All of the Common of a Matron, p. 233, except the Collect; the Second Vespers being superseded by the First Vespers of S. Barnabas (with Memorial of S. Margaret).

COLLECT.

O GOD, Who madest blessed Queen Margaret marvellous in her exceeding love for the poor: grant that by her pattern and her prayers, Thy love may continually increase in our hearts; through Jesus Christ our Lord. Amen.]

June 11.
FESTIVAL OF S. BARNABAS, APOSTLE AND MARTYR.

All of the Common of an Apostle in or out of Easter tide, as the case may be, except the

COLLECT.

O LORD GOD Almighty, Who didst endue Thy holy Apostle Barnabas with singular gifts of the Holy Ghost; leave us not, we beseech Thee, destitute of Thy manifold gifts, nor yet of grace to use them alway to Thy honour and glory; through Jesus Christ our Lord. Amen.

[June 14.
S. BASIL, BISHOP, DOCTOR, AND CONFESSOR.*

All of the Common of a Confessor Bishop, p. 222, except the

COLLECT.

O GOD, who didst vouchsafe to choose blessed Basil, Thy Confessor, to be a chief doctor and preacher of the Catholic Faith; grant, we pray Thee, that, he interceding for us, we may be delivered from the evils due to our sins, and may serve Thee, O Lord, with pure minds; through Jesus Christ Thy Son our Lord, Who liveth and reigneth with Thee and the Holy Ghost, ever one God, world without end. Amen.]

June 20.
TRANSLATION OF EDWARD, KING.*

All of the Common of a Confessor not a Bishop, p. 228, except the

COLLECT.

O GOD, Ruler of an eternal kingdom, mercifully look upon Thy family who celebrate the translation of King Edward; and grant that, as Thou didst vouchsafe to glorify him with celestial gifts, so his intercession may avail to obtain eternal happiness for us; through Jesus Christ our Lord. Amen.

June 22.

Festival of S. Alban, Proto-martyr of England.

All of the Common of a Martyr, p. 217.

June 24.

Festival of the Nativity of S. John Baptist.

First Vespers.

Psalms of the Feria.

Ant. The Angel of the Lord came down to Zacharias, saying : Receive a son in thine old age; and thou shalt call his name John Baptist.

Chapter. Jer. i.

BEFORE I formed thee in the belly I knew thee : and before thou camest forth out of the womb, I sanctified thee, and ordained thee a prophet unto the nations.

R̶7. Among those that are born of women : there is not a greater prophet than John the Baptist. V̶. The voice of one crying in the wilderness, Prepare ye the way of the Lord. R̶7. There is not a greater prophet than John the Baptist. V̶. Glory be to the Father, and to the Son, and to the Holy Ghost. R̶7. Among those that are born of women : there is not a greater prophet than John the Baptist.

Hymn. *Ut queant laxis.*

OH that once more, to sinful men descending,
Thou from polluted lips their chains wert rending,
So, holy John, might worthy hymns ascending,
Tell of Thy wonders.

Lo! from the hill of heaven's eternal glory,
Comes a bright herald to thy father hoary,
Gives thee thy name, thy birth and wondrous story
Truly foretelling.

But, while the heav'nly word he disbelieveth,
Lo! all his power of ready utt'rance leaveth,
Till by thy birth his tongue again receiveth
Power of speaking.

Thou, while thy mother's womb was thee containing,
Knewest thy King, in secret still remaining,
Thus was each parent through her child obtaining
Knowledge of mysteries.

Father and Son, to Thee be adoration,
Spirit of Both, to Thee like veneration,
Praise to the One true God of our salvation,
Ever and ever. Amen.

V̶. There was a man sent from God.
R̶7. Whose name was John.

Ant. to Mag. When Zacharias went into the temple of the Lord : there appeared unto him an angel of the Lord standing on the right side of the altar of incense.

Collect.

ALMIGHTY God, by Whose providence Thy servant John Baptist was wonderfully born, and sent to prepare the way of Thy Son our Saviour, by preaching of repentance; make us so to follow his doctrine and holy life, that we may truly repent according to his preaching; and after his example constantly speak the truth, boldly rebuke vice, and patiently suffer for the truth's sake; through Jesus Christ our Lord. Amen.

[*Or this, at this Office only,*

GRANT, we beseech Thee, Almighty God, that Thy family may walk in the way of salvation, and, following the counsels of blessed John the Forerunner, may safely come to Him Whom he foretold, Thy Son Jesus Christ our Lord. Amen.]

Compline.

As in the Psalter, p. 67.

Lauds.

V̶. There was a man sent from God.
R̶7. Whose name was John.

Psalms of Sunday.

Ant. 1. Elizabeth brought forth a son : John Baptist, the forerunner of the Lord.

Ant. 2. They made signs to his father, how he would have him called : and he wrote, saying, His name is John.

Ant. 3. Thou shalt call his name John : and many shall rejoice at his birth.

Ant. 4. His name is John; he shall drink neither wine nor strong drink : and many shall rejoice at his birth.

Ant. 5. This child shall be great in the sight of the Lord : for His hand is with him.

CHAPTER. Is. xlix.

LISTEN, O isles, unto me; and hearken, ye people from far: the Lord hath called me from the womb; from the bowels of my mother hath He made mention of my name.

R̸. Thanks be to God.

HYMN. *O nimis felix.*

O SAINT thrice happy, merit high attaining,
    Whose snowy pureness no foul spot is staining,
Mightiest Martyr, home in deserts gaining,
    Greatest of Prophets.

He who bare thirty-fold bright garlands weareth,
He who bare sixty double glory shareth,
His triple chaplet who an hundred beareth,
    Holy one, decks thee.

Come then, thou mighty Saint, of worth past telling,
All stony hardness from each breast expelling,
And in each rugged, crooked pathway quelling,
    Roughness and windings.

So this world's gracious Author and Salvation,
In each pure spirit, free from degradation,
Shall, when He cometh, find a fitting station,
    For His dear footsteps.

Now let celestial choirs, glad anthems pouring,
God, One and Trinal, praise Thee, while adoring,
We too, all prostrate, pardon are imploring:
    Spare Thy redeemed ones. Amen.

𝒱. Among those that are born of women.

R̸. There is not a greater prophet than John the Baptist.

Ant. to Ben. And the mouth of Zacharias was opened, and he prophesied, saying : Blessed be the Lord God of Israel.

The first words of the Canticle are not repeated, but it begins, For He hath visited.

Prime.

Ant. Elizabeth brought forth a son, John Baptist : the forerunner of the Lord.

Tierce.

Ant. They made signs to his father, how he would have him called : and he wrote, saying, His name is John.

   Chapter as at Lauds.

R̸. Thou hast crowned him : with glory and worship. 𝒱. Thou makest him to have dominion of the works of Thy hands. R̸. With glory and worship. 𝒱. Glory be to the Father, and to the Son, and to the Holy Ghost. R̸. Thou hast crowned him : with glory and worship.

𝒱. Thou hast set upon his head, O Lord.

R̸. A crown of pure gold.

Sexts.

Ant. Thou shalt call his name John : and many shall rejoice at his birth.

CHAPTER. Is. xlix.

AND now saith the Lord, that formed me from the womb to be His servant: I will also give thee for a light to the Gentiles, that thou mayest be My salvation to the ends of the earth.

R̸. Thou hast set : upon his head, O Lord. 𝒱. A crown of pure gold. R̸. Upon his head, O Lord. 𝒱. Glory be to the Father, and to the Son, and to the Holy Ghost. R̸. Thou hast set : upon his head, O Lord, a crown of pure gold.

𝒱. The righteous shall flourish like a palm-tree.

R̸. And shall spread abroad like a cedar in Libanus.

Nones.

Ant. This child shall be great in the sight of the Lord : for His hand is with him.

CHAPTER. Is. xlix.

KINGS shall see and arise, princes also shall worship, because of the Lord that is faithful, and the Holy One of Israel, and He shall choose thee.

R̸. The righteous shall flourish : like a palm-tree. 𝒱. And spread abroad like a cedar in Libanus. R̸. Like a palm-tree. 𝒱. Glory be to the Father, and to the Son, and to the Holy Ghost. R̸. The righteous shall flourish : like a palm-tree.

𝒱. The righteous shall grow as a lily.

R̸. He shall flourish for ever before the Lord.

Second Vespers.

Ants. of Lauds, with Psalms of the Feria.

Chapter, R̷., Hymn. Ut queant laxis, V̷. and R̷., as at First Vespers.

Ant. to Mag. And it came to pass, that on the eighth day they came to circumcise the child : and they called him Zacharias, after the name of his father. And his mother answered and said, Not so; but he shall be called John.

The Office of S. John Baptist is kept through the Octave; except as hereafter noted, and on Sunday, when the Office is of the Sunday, with Memorial of the Octave.

June 29.

Festival of SS. Peter and Paul, Apostles and Martyrs.

First Vespers.

Ant. Whom say men that I the Son of man am? said Jesus to His disciples; and Simon Peter answered and said, Thou art the Christ, the Son of the living God : And I say also unto thee, that thou art Peter; and upon this rock I will build My Church.

Psalms of the Feria.

Chapter. Acts xii.

PETER therefore was kept in prison; but prayer was made without ceasing of the church to God for him.

R̷. Cornelius the centurion, a devout man, and one that feared God, saw evidently an angel of God, saying to him : Cornelius, send and call for Simon, whose surname is Peter : he shall tell thee what thou oughtest to do. V̷. While Cornelius was praying, as yet unregenerate in Christ, an Angel appeared unto him, saying. R̷. Cornelius, send and call for Simon, whose surname is Peter : he shall tell thee what thou oughtest to do. V̷. Glory be to the Father, and to the Son, and to the Holy Ghost. R̷. He shall tell thee what thou oughtest to do.

Hymn. *Annue Christe,* V̷. *and* R̷., *as in the Common of Apostles, p. 214.*

Ant. to Mag. Blessed Peter, the Apostle, saw Christ coming to meet him : he worshipped Him, and said, Lord, whither goest Thou? I go unto Rome, to be there crucified afresh.

Collect.

O ALMIGHTY God, Who by Thy Son Jesus Christ didst give to Thy Apostle Saint Peter many excellent gifts, and commandedst him earnestly to feed Thy flock; make, we beseech Thee, all bishops and pastors diligently to preach Thy holy word, and the people obediently to follow the same, that they may receive the crown of everlasting glory; through Jesus Christ our Lord. Amen.

[*Or this,*

O GOD, Who hast consecrated this day by the Martyrdom of Thine Apostles Peter and Paul; grant that Thy Church may in all things follow their precepts, from whom it received the first principles of the faith; through Jesus Christ our Lord. Amen.]

No Memorial of S. John Baptist at any Office of this day.

Compline.

As in the Psalter, p. 67.

Lauds.

V̷. Thou art Peter.

R̷. And upon this rock I will build My Church.

Psalms of Sunday.

Ant. 1. Now Peter and John went up together into the temple at the hour of prayer : being the ninth hour.

Ant. 2. Silver and gold have I none : but such as I have give I thee.

Ant. 3. And the Angel saith unto Peter : Cast thy garment about thee, and follow me.

Ant. 4. Peter, lovest thou Me? Feed My sheep : Lord, Thou knowest that I love Thee.

Ant. 5. Thou art Peter : and upon this rock I will build My Church.

Chapter. Acts xii.

PETER therefore was kept in prison; but prayer was made without ceasing of the church unto God for him.

R̷. Thanks be to God.

HYMN. *Exultet cælum laudibus,*
℣. and ℟., p. 215.

· *Ant. to Ben.* Whatsoever thou shalt bind on earth, shall be bound in heaven: and whatsoever thou shalt loose on earth, shall be loosed in heaven, said the Lord to Simon Peter.

𝕻rime.

Ant. Now Peter and John went up together into the temple at the hour of prayer : being the ninth hour.

𝕿ierce.

Ant. Silver and gold have I none : but such as I have give I thee.

Chapter as at Lauds.

℟℣. *of the Common,* p. 216.

𝕾exts.

Ant. And the angel saith unto Peter : Cast thy garment about thee, and follow me.

CHAPTER. Acts xii.

AND behold, the angel of the Lord came upon him, and a light shined in the prison; and he smote Peter on the side, and raised him up, saying, Arise up quickly. And his chains fell off from his hands.

℟℣. *of the Common,* p. 216.

𝕹ones.

Ant. Thou art Peter : and upon this rock I will build My Church.

CHAPTER. Acts xii.

AND he went out and followed him; and wist not that it was true which was done by the Angel; but thought he saw a vision.

℟℟. *of the Common,* p. 216.

𝕾econd 𝖁espers.

All as in the Common, p. 216, *till the*

Ant. to Mag. The glorious princes of the earth, as in life they loved each other : so in death they were not divided.

June 30.

COMMEMORATION OF S. PAUL, APOSTLE AND MARTYR.

[*If the Church be dedicated to S. Paul, this festival is kept as follows : at First Vespers, instead of the Office of S. Peter, as above, Psalms of Sunday, Ants. and Chapter as set down below at Lauds, Hymn, ℣. and ℟., and Ant. to Magnificat, of the Common of Apostles, p. 215; Collect as at Lauds; Memorial of S. Peter, as follows :*

Ant. Blessed Peter, the Apostle, saw Christ coming to meet him : he worshipped Him, and said, Lord, whither goest Thou? I go unto Rome, to be there crucified afresh.

℣. Thou art Peter.

℟. And upon this rock I will build My Church.

COLLECT.

O GOD, Who didst give to blessed Peter, Thine Apostle, the office of binding and loosing souls, conferring on him the keys of the heavenly kingdom; grant, we pray Thee, that his intercession may avail to deliver us from the chains of our sins; through Jesus Christ our Lord. Amen.

No Memorial of S. John Baptist at these Vespers, nor at Lauds. Lauds and the other Hours till Second Vespers, as below. At Second Vespers, Psalms of the Common, Ants. and Chapter as at Lauds; all the rest as at Second Vespers of the Common of Apostles, with these two Memorials :

MEMORIAL OF S. PETER
as at First Vespers.

MEMORIAL OF THE OCTAVE OF
S. JOHN BAPTIST.

Ant. When Zacharias went into the temple of the Lord : there appeared unto him an angel of the Lord, standing on the right side of the altar of incense.

℣. There was a man sent from God.

℟. Whose name was John.

COLLECT.

GRANT, we beseech Thee, Almighty God, that Thy family may walk in the way of salvation, and, following the counsels of blessed John the Forerunner, may safely come to Him Whom he foretold, Thy Son, Jesus Christ our Lord. Amen.]

Lauds.

℣. Thou hast given an heritage.
℟. Unto those that fear Thy Name, O Lord.

Psalms of Sunday.

Ant. 1. I planted, Apollos watered : but God giveth the increase. Alleluia.

Ant. 2. Every man shall receive his own reward : according to his labour.

Ant. 3. Most gladly therefore will I rather glory in my infirmities : that the power of Christ may rest upon me.

Ant. 4. When I am weak : then am I strong.

Ant. 5. His grace which was bestowed upon me : was not in vain.

CHAPTER. Gal. i.

I CERTIFY you, brethren, that the gospel which was preached of me is not after man, neither received I it of man, neither was I taught it, but by the revelation of Jesus Christ.

℟. Thanks be to God.

HYMN. *Exultet cœlum laudibus,* ℣. and ℟., p. 215.

Ant. to Ben. I am now ready to be offered, and the time of my departure is at hand. I have fought a good fight, I have finished my course, I have kept the faith : henceforth there is laid up for me a crown of righteousness, which the Lord, the righteous Judge, shall give me at that day.

COLLECT.

O GOD, Who didst teach the multitude of the Gentiles by the preaching of blessed Paul Thine Apostle ; grant that we, who celebrate his nativity, may profit by his prayers; through Jesus Christ our Lord. Amen.

MEMORIAL OF S. PETER.

Ant. Peter, lovest thou Me ? Feed My sheep : Lord, Thou knowest that I love Thee.

℣. Thou art Peter.
℟. And upon this rock I will build My Church.

COLLECT.

O GOD, Who didst give to blessed Peter, Thine Apostle, the office of binding and loosing souls, conferring on him the keys of the heavenly kingdom ; grant, we pray Thee, that his intercession may avail to deliver us from the chains of our sins ; through Jesus Christ our Lord. Amen.

MEMORIAL OF S. JOHN BAPTIST.

Ant. Among those that are born of women : there is not a greater prophet than John the Baptist.

℣. There was a man sent from God.
℟. Whose name was John.

COLLECT.

O GOD, Who hast made this day honourable to us by the nativity of blessed John ; grant to Thy people the gift of spiritual joys, and direct the minds of all the faithful in the way of everlasting salvation ; through Jesus Christ our Lord. Amen.

Prime.

Ant. I planted, Apollos watered : but God giveth the increase. Alleluia.

Tierce.

Ant. Every man shall receive his own reward : according to his labour.

Chapter as at Lauds.

℟℣. *as in Common,* p. 216.

Sexts.

Ant. Most gladly therefore will I rather glory in my infirmities : that the power of Christ may rest upon me.

CHAPTER. Phil. i. and Gal. vi.

TO me to live is Christ, and to die is gain. But God forbid that I should glory, save in the cross of our Lord Jesus Christ, by Whom the world is crucified unto me, and I unto the world.

℟℣. *as in Common,* p. 216.

Nones.

Ant. His grace which was bestowed upon me : was not in vain.

CHAPTER. II Tim. iv.

I HAVE fought a good fight, I have finished my course, I have kept the faith. Henceforth there is laid up for me a crown of righteousness, which the Lord, the righteous Judge, shall give me at that day.

R̸/R̸. *as in Common,* p. 216.

Vespers.

The Office is of S. Paul, until the Chapter, where it is superseded by the Office of S. John Baptist.

Ant^s. and Psalms of the Common of Apostles, p. 216. *Chapter and the rest as at First Vespers of S. John Baptist,* p. 294, *with this*

MEMORIAL OF SS. PETER AND PAUL.

Ant. The glorious princes of the earth, as in life they loved each other : so in death they were not divided.

℣. Thou art Peter.

R̸. And upon this rock I will build My Church.

COLLECT.

O GOD, Who hast consecrated this day by the Martyrdom of Thine Apostles Peter and Paul; grant that Thy Church may in all things follow their precepts, from whom it received the first principles of the faith ; through Jesus Christ our Lord. Amen.

FEASTS OF JULY.

[On the first day unhindered is said the Office for the Dead.]

July 1.

OCTAVE OF S. JOHN BAPTIST.

Lauds, and all the Offices till Vespers, are said as on the Feast of S. John Baptist, p. 294. *At Lauds is said this*

MEMORIAL OF SS. PETER AND PAUL.

Ant. Peter the Apostle, and Paul, teacher of the Gentiles : these have taught us Thy law, O Lord.

℣., R̸., *and Collect as at First Vespers of the Octave.*

July 2.

FESTIVAL OF THE VISITATION OF THE BLESSED VIRGIN MARY.

First Vespers.

Psalms of the Common of the Blessed Virgin Mary, p. 209.

Ant. 1. Who is this that cometh out of the wilderness like pillars of smoke : perfumed with myrrh and frankincense, with all powders of the merchant?

Ant. 2. How beautiful upon the mountains are the feet of him that bringeth good tidings : that publisheth peace!

Ant. 3. Who is she that looketh forth as the morning : fair as the moon, clear as the sun?

Ant. 4. Her ways are ways of pleasantness : and all her ways are peace.

Ant. 5. To-day is salvation come : unto this house.

CHAPTER. Is. xlv.

VERILY, Thou art a God that hidest Thyself, O God of Israel, the Saviour.

R̸. The ark of the Lord continued in the house of Obed-Edom three months : and the Lord blessed all his house, because of the ark of God. ℣. And Mary abode with Elizabeth about three months. R̸. And the Lord blessed all his house, because of the ark of the Lord. ℣. Glory be to the Father, and to the Son, and to the Holy Ghost. R̸. And the Lord blessed all his house, because of the ark of the Lord.

HYMN. *Quem terra, pontus, sidera,* ℣. *and* R̸., p. 210.

Ant. to Mag. Joy is come unto me from the Holy One : because of the mercy which shall soon come unto you from the Everlasting, our Saviour.

COLLECT.

O GOD, Who didst cause the most holy Virgin Mary, Mother of Thy Only-begotten Son, to visit blessed

Elizabeth for mutual consolation; mercifully grant to us, Thy servants, that we may be consoled continually by His visitation, and protected by Thy power against all adversities; through the same Jesus Christ our Lord.   Amen.

Compline.

As in the Common of the Blessed Virgin Mary, p. 210.

Lauds.

℣. I will praise the Name of the Lord with a song.

℟. And magnify it with thanksgiving.

Psalms of the Common, p. 210.

Ant. 1. His blessing covered the dry land as a river : and watered it as a flood.

Ant. 2. Open, open now the gate : God, even our own God is with us, to shew His power yet in Jerusalem.

Ant. 3. Praise, praise God, praise God, I say : for He hath not taken away His mercy from the house of Israel.

Ant. 4. Blessed be the Lord God of Israel : which sent thee this day to meet me.

Ant. 5. The friend of the Bridegroom which standeth and heareth Him : rejoiceth greatly because of the Bridegroom's voice.

CHAPTER. Job x.

THOU hast granted me life and favour, and Thy visitation hath preserved my spirit.

℟. Thanks be to God.

HYMN. *O gloriosa Virginum,*
℣. and ℟., p. 210.

Ant. to Ben. Whence is this to me : that the mother of my Lord should come to me ?

Prime.

Ant. to Psalms as in the Common, p. 210.

Ant. to Quicunque. Thee duly praise, Thee adore, Thee glorify : all Thy creatures, O blessed Trinity.

The ℟. is said with this ℣., Thou Who wast born of the Virgin Mary.

Tierce.

Ant. Open, open now the gate : God, even our God is with us, to shew His power yet in Jerusalem.

Chapter as at Lauds.

℟. The voice of joy and health : is in the dwellings of the righteous. ℣. The right hand of the Lord bringeth mighty things to pass. ℟. In the dwellings of the righteous. ℣. Glory be to the Father, and to the Son, and to the Holy Ghost. ℟. In the dwellings of the righteous.

℣. Lord, lift Thou up the light of Thy countenance upon us.

℟. Thou hast put gladness in my heart.

Sexts.

Ant. Praise, praise God, praise God, I say : for He hath not taken away His mercy from the house of Israel.

CHAPTER. Joel ii.

I WILL pour out My spirit upon all flesh ; and your sons and your daughters shall prophesy.

℟. Lord, lift Thou up : the light of Thy countenance upon us. ℣. Thou hast put gladness in my heart. ℟. The light of Thy countenance upon us. ℣. Glory be to the Father, and to the Son, and to the Holy Ghost. ℟. Lord, lift Thou up : the light of Thy countenance upon us.

℣. My soul shall make her boast in the Lord.

℟. The humble shall hear thereof, and be glad.

Nones.

Ant. The friend of the Bridegroom which standeth and heareth Him : rejoiceth greatly because of the Bridegroom's voice.

CHAPTER. Wisd. vii.

WISDOM entering into holy souls, maketh them friends of God, and prophets.

℣. My soul shall make her boast : in the Lord. ℣. The humble shall hear thereof, and be glad. ℟. In the Lord.

℣. Glory be to the Father, and to the Son, and to the Holy Ghost. ℟. My soul shall make her boast : in the Lord.

℣. O magnify the Lord with me.

℟. And let us exalt His Name together.

Second Vespers.

Antiphons of Lauds. Psalms of the Common, p. 92.

CHAPTER. Ecclus. iv.

HE that holdeth wisdom fast shall inherit glory; and wheresoever she entereth, the Lord will bless. They that serve her shall minister to the Holy One : and them that love her the Lord doth love.

℟. Thanks be to God.

HYMN. *Quem terra, pontus, sidera,* ℣. and ℟., p. 210.

Ant. to Mag. The glory of God did lighten it : and the Lamb is the light thereof.

———

July 3.

Office of the Visitation until Vespers, the Psalms at Lauds being said under the first Ant., with Memorial of SS. Peter and Paul at Lauds. But if the Octave of the Visitation be not kept, the whole Office is of SS. Peter and Paul.

Ant. Peter the Apostle, and Paul, Teacher of the Gentiles : these have taught us Thy law, O Lord.

℣. They have declared His honour unto the heathen.

℟. And His wonders unto all people.

COLLECT.

O GOD, Who hast consecrated this day by the martyrdom of Thine Apostles Peter and Paul: grant that Thy Church may in all things follow their precepts, from whom it received the first principles of the faith; through Jesus Christ our Lord. Amen.

———

July 4.

FESTIVAL OF THE TRANSLATION OF S. MARTIN, BISHOP AND CONFESSOR.*

See Rubric of Observance, July 3.

All of the Common of a Bishop and Confessor, p. 222, except the

COLLECT.

O GOD, Who didst make blessed Martin to be a minister of eternal salvation on earth; grant, we beseech Thee, that as he fulfilled Thy commandments upon earth, so he may alway intercede for us in heaven; through Jesus Christ our Lord, Who liveth and reigneth with Thee and the Holy Ghost, ever one God, world without end. Amen.

MEMORIAL OF SS. PETER AND PAUL *at both Vespers.*

Ant. The glorious princes of the earth, as in life they loved each other : so in death they were not divided.

℣. Their sound is gone out into all lands.

℟. And their words unto the ends of the world.

Collect as in Lauds Memorial.

MEMORIAL OF THE VISITATION *at both Vespers.*

Ant. The glory of God did lighten it : and the Lamb is the light thereof.

℣. Full of grace are thy lips.

℟. Because God hath blessed thee for ever.

COLLECT.

O GOD, Who causedst the most holy Virgin Mary, Mother of Thy Only-begotten Son to visit blessed Elizabeth, for mutual consolation; mercifully grant to us Thy servants, that we may be consoled continually by His visitation, and protected by Thy power against all adversities; through Jesus Christ our Lord. Amen.

Memorial of SS. Peter and Paul at Lauds, as on July 3.

MEMORIAL OF THE VISITATION
at Lauds.

Ant. Whence is this to me : that the
Mother of my Lord should come to me?
℣. Thy name shall be called of God
for ever.

℟. The peace of righteousness.

Collect as at Vespers.

July 5.

See Rubric of Observance, July 3.

*Memorials of SS. Peter and Paul at
Lauds as before.*

July 6.

OCTAVE OF SS. PETER AND PAUL.

*All as in the Common of Apostles, p. 214,
except that which follows :*

First Vespers.

CHAPTER.   Ecclus. xliv.

THESE were merciful men, whose
righteousness hath not been forgotten.
With their seed shall continually remain
a good inheritance, and their children
are within the covenant.

COLLECT.

O GOD, Whose right hand upheld
blessed Peter, walking upon the
waves, that he might not sink, and delivered his fellow-Apostle Paul, thrice
shipwrecked, from the depths of the sea;
mercifully hear us, and grant that their
help may avail to bring us to eternal
glory; Who livest and reignest with
the Father and the Holy Ghost, ever
one God, world without end.   Amen.

This Collect is said throughout the day.

*Memorial of the Visitation as on July 4
at Vespers (if the Octave of that Feast
be kept.)*

Compline.

As on Festivals, p. 67.

Lauds.

Chapter and Collect as at First Vespers.

*Memorial of the Visitation as on July 4
at Lauds (if the Octave of that Feast be
kept.)*

Tierce.

Chapter as at First Vespers.

Sexts.

CHAPTER.   Ecclus. xliv.

THEIR bodies are buried in peace;
but their name liveth for evermore.

Nones.

CHAPTER.   Ecclus. xliv.

THE people tell of their wisdom, and
the congregation will shew forth
their praise.

*If the Festival of the Translation of S.
Thomas is not kept, Second Vespers are
said as in the Common of Apostles, with
Memorial of S. Thomas, and of the
Visitation, as at First Vespers.*

[July 7.

FESTIVAL OF THE TRANSLATION OF S. THOMAS OF CANTERBURY.*

*All of the Common of a Martyr, except
that which follows :*

First Vespers.

CHAPTER.   Heb. v.

EVERY high priest from among men
is ordained for men in things per-
taining to God, that he may offer both
gifts and sacrifices for sins.

COLLECT.

O GOD, Who grantest us to celebrate
the translation of blessed Thomas,
Thy Martyr and Bishop; we humbly
beseech Thee to hear the prayers of
Thy Church, and bring us from vice to
virtue, and from prison to the kingdom;
through Jesus Christ our Lord, Who
liveth and reigneth with Thee and the
Holy Ghost, ever one God, world without end.   Amen.

MEMORIAL OF THE OCTAVE OF
SS. PETER AND PAUL.

Ant. In the regeneration, when the
Son of Man shall sit on the throne of
His glory : ye also shall sit upon twelve

thrones, judging the twelve tribes of Israel.

℣. They have declared His honour unto the heathen.

℟. And His wonders unto all people.

Collect as at First Vespers of the Octave.
Memorial of the Visitation, as on July 4.

Compline.

All as on Festivals, p. 67.

Lauds.

Chapter as at First Vespers.
Memorial of the Visitation, as on July 4.

Tierce.

Chapter as at First Vespers.

Sexts.

CHAPTER. Heb. v.

NO man taketh this honour unto himself, but he that is called of God, as was Aaron; as He saith, Thou art a Priest for ever after the order of Melchisedeck.

Nones.

CHAPTER. Ecclus. xxiv.

WISDOM shall praise herself, and shall glory in the midst of her people. In the congregation of the most High shall she open her mouth, and triumph before His power.

Second Vespers.

Chapter as at First Vespers.
Memorial of the Visitation as on July 4.]

July 15.

FESTIVAL OF THE TRANSLATION OF S. SWITHUN, BISHOP AND CONFESSOR.*

All of the Common of a Bishop and Confessor, p. 222.

[July 16.

FESTIVAL OF THE TRANSLATION OF S. OSMUND, BISHOP AND CONFESSOR.*

All of the Common of a Bishop and Confessor, except the

COLLECT.

O GOD, Who didst call blessed Osmund Thy Bishop from earthly to heavenly warfare: grant to us, that having cast away earthly desires, we may attain to the good things of heaven; through Jesus Christ our Lord, Who liveth and reigneth with Thee and the Holy Ghost, ever one God, world without end. Amen.]

July 20.

FESTIVAL OF S. MARGARET, VIRGIN AND MARTYR.*

All of the Common of a Virgin Martyr, except the

COLLECT.

O GOD, Who on this day didst cause the blessed Virgin Margaret to enter heaven by the palm of martyrdom; grant us, we beseech Thee, that following her example, we may attain unto Thee; through Jesus Christ our Lord, Who liveth and reigneth with Thee and the Holy Ghost, ever one God, world without end. Amen.

July 22.

FESTIVAL OF S. MARY MAGDALENE.

First Vespers.

Ant. to Psalms. Behold, a woman in the city, which was a sinner: when she knew that Jesus sat at meat in the Pharisee's house, brought an alabaster box of ointment.

Psalms of the Feria.

CHAPTER. Prov. xxxi.

WHO can find a virtuous woman? for her price is far above rubies. The heart of her husband doth safely trust in her, so that he shall have no need of spoil.

R̸. Verily, great was the love of Mary Magdalene : who outstayed the disciples at the tomb of the Lord. V̸. Glowing with the fervour of love, and believing Him to be taken away, whom she had seen laid in the sepulchre. R̸. Who outstayed the disciples at the tomb of the Lord. V̸. Glory be to the Father, and to the Son, and to the Holy Ghost. R̸. Verily, great was the love of Mary Magdalene : who outstayed the disciples at the tomb of the Lord.

HYMN. *Collaudemus Magdalene.*

SING we now of Mary's trial;
　Joy and sorrow let us tell,
Both uniting in one rapture,
　Heavenward in one note to swell,
When the dove's glad note was mingled
　With the dirge of Philomel.

Nought the number of the feasters,
　Seeking Jesus, did she fear;
She her Master's feet anointed,
　Washed them with the falling tear;
With her flowing hair she wiped them,
　Made them ready for the bier.

Lo! the cleansed doth wash the Cleanser;
　On the Fount doth fall the rain;
Lo! the flower the raindrop sheddeth,
　Which returns to wash her stain;
Heaven to earth in dew descendeth,
　Earth gives back her dew again.

Spikenard in the alabaster,
　Offers she as tribute there;
In the pouring of the unguent,
　She a mystic sign doth bear :
Sick, anointeth her Physician,
　Her own healing to prepare.

Gazed the Lord in deep compassion
　Down on Mary bending low :
Much she loves : her sins are many;
　They are all forgiven now.
On the Resurrection morning,
　Mary first her Lord shall know.

Glory to the Paschal Victim,
　To our God all praise and might :
For the Lamb by death hath conquered,
　Lion, Victor in the fight;
Rose He on the morn of triumph,
　With the spoils of death bedight. Amen.

V̸. Mary hath chosen that good part.
R̸. Which shall not be taken away from her.
Ant. to Mag. And she stood at His feet behind Him weeping : and began to wash His feet with tears, and did wipe them with the hairs of her head, and kissed His feet, and anointed them with the ointment. Alleluia.

COLLECT.

GRANT to us, we pray Thee, most merciful Father, that as blessed Mary Magdalene, loving Thy Only-begotten Son above all things, obtained forgiveness of her sins, so she may ask for us from Thy mercy, everlasting blessedness; through the same Thy Son Jesus Christ our Lord, Who liveth and reigneth with Thee and the Holy Ghost, ever one God, world without end. Amen.

Compline.

As on all Festivals, p. 67.

Lauds.

V̸. Mary hath chosen that good part.
R̸. Which shall not be taken away from her.

Psalms of Sunday.

Ant. 1. Mary saw Jesus standing, and knew not that it was Jesus : Jesus saith unto her, Woman, why weepest thou? whom seekest thou?

Ant. 2. She, supposing Him to be the gardener, saith unto Him : Sir, if thou have borne Him hence, tell me where thou hast laid Him, and I will take Him away.

Ant. 3. Jesus saith unto her, Mary : she turned herself, and saith unto Him, Rabboni; which is to say, Master.

Ant. 4. Jesus saith unto her, Touch Me not : for I am not yet ascended to My Father.

Ant. 5. Go to My brethren, and say unto them : I ascend to My Father and to your Father, and to My God and your God.

Chapter as at First Vespers.

HYMN. *Æstimavit Hortolanum.*

AS the gardener Him addressing,
　Well and rightly she believ'd :
He, the Sower, gave His blessing
　To the seed her heart receiv'd :
Not at first His form confessing,
　Soon His voice her soul perceiv'd.

She beheld, as yet not knowing,
  In the mystical disguise,
Christ, that in her breast was sowing
  Deep and heavenly mysteries :
Till His voice, her name bestowing,
  Bade her hear and recognise.

She to Jesus, Jesus weepeth,
  Of her Lord remov'd complains ;
Jesus in her breast she keepeth ;
  Jesus seeks, yet still retains :
He that soweth, He that reapeth
  All her heart, unknown remains.

Why, kind Jesu, why thus hiding,
  When Thyself Thou would'st reveal?
Why, in Mary's breast abiding,
  From her love Thyself conceal?
Why, true Light in her residing,
  Can she not its radiance feel?

Oh! how strangely Thou eludest
  Souls that on Thee have believ'd;
But eluding, ne'er deludest,
  Nor deceiv'st, nor art deceiv'd;
But including, still excludest;
  Fully known, yet not perceiv'd.

Laud to Thee, and praise for ever,
  Life, hope, light of ev'ry soul!
Through Thy merits may we never
  Be inscrib'd in death's dark roll,
But with Mary's true endeavour
  All our sins, like her, condole! Amen.

℣. Her sins, which are many, are forgiven.

℟. For she loved much.

Ant. to Ben. Jesus appeared first to Mary Magdalene, out of whom He had cast seven devils : And she went and told them that had been with Him, as they mourned and wept.

Prime.

Ant. Mary saw Jesus standing and knew not that it was Jesus : Jesus saith unto her, Woman, why weepest thou? whom seekest thou?

Ant. to Quicunque. Thee duly praise, Thee adore, Thee glorify : all Thy creatures, O blessed Trinity.

Tierce.

Ant. She supposing Him to be the gardener, saith unto Him : Sir, if thou have borne Him hence, tell me where thou hast laid Him, and I will take Him away.

Chapter as at First Vespers.

℟. O God, Thou art my God : early will I seek Thee. ℣. My soul thirsteth for Thee, my flesh also longeth after Thee. ℟. Early will I seek Thee. ℣. Glory be to the Father, and to the Son, and to the Holy Ghost. ℟. O God, Thou art my God : early will I seek Thee.

℣. I sought the Lord, and He heard me.

℟. Yea, He delivered me out of all my fear.

Sexts.

Ant. Jesus saith unto her, Mary : she turned herself, and saith unto Him, Rabboni; which is to say, Master.

CHAPTER. Prov. xxxi.

SHE girdeth her loins with strength, and strengthened her arms. She perceiveth that her merchandize is good : her candle goeth not out by night.

℟. I sought the Lord : and He heard me. ℣. Yea, He delivered me out of all my fear. ℟. And He heard me. ℣. Glory be to the Father, and to the Son, and to the Holy Ghost. ℟. I sought the Lord : and He heard me.

℣. In the multitude of the sorrows that I had in my heart.

℟. Thy comforts have refreshed my soul.

Nones.

Ant. Go to my brethren, and say unto them : I ascend unto My Father, and your Father, and to My God and your God.

CHAPTER. Prov. xxxi.

A WOMAN that feareth the Lord, she shall be praised. Give her of the fruit of her hands; and let her own works praise her in the gates.

℟. In the multitude of the sorrows that I had : in my heart. ℣. Thy comforts have refreshed my soul. ℟. In my heart. ℣. Glory be to the Father, and to the Son, and to the Holy Ghost. ℟. In the multitude of the sorrows that I had : in my heart.

℣. Lo, I will not refrain my lips, O Lord.

℟. And that Thou knowest.

Second Vespers.

Antiphons of Lauds, p. 304.

Psalms of the Feria.

Chapter as at First Vespers.

Hymn. *O Maria, noli flere.*

WEEP not, Mary, weep no longer,
   Nor another seek to find;
Here indeed the Gardener standeth,
   Gardener of the thirsty mind:
In the spirit's inner garden
   Seek that Gardener ever kind.

Whence thy grief and lamentation?
   Lift, faint soul, thy heart on high,
Seek not memory's consolation:
   Jesus, Whom thou lov'st is nigh;
Dost thou seek thy Lord? thou hast Him,
   Though unseen by human eye.

Whence thy sorrow, whence thy weeping?
   True the joy thou hast within;
Lives within thee what thou know'st not,
   Balm to heal the wounds of sin:
'Tis within, why wander vainly,
   Seeking languor's medicine?

Now I wonder not, thy Master
   If thou know'st not while He sows;
For His seed, the word eternal,
   Unto fulness in thee grows;
"Mary," saith He,—thou, "Rabboni,"—
   And the soul her Saviour knows.

Glory be to God the Giver,
   That His grace is given free,
To the humble sigh of Mary
   Summoned by the Pharisee;
Grace's foretaste to the sinner,
   Then life's full feast giveth He.   Amen.

℣. Her sins, which are many, are forgiven.

℟. For she loved much.

Ant. to Mag. My heart is joyful in Thy salvation : I will sing of the Lord, because He hath dealt so lovingly with me.

July 25.

FESTIVAL OF S. JAMES, APOSTLE AND MARTYR.

All of the Common of Apostles, p. 214, *except the*

COLLECT.

GRANT, O merciful God, that as Thine holy Apostle Saint James, leaving his father and all that he had, without delay was obedient unto the calling of Thy Son Jesus Christ, and followed Him; so we, forsaking all worldly and carnal affections, may be evermore ready to follow Thy holy commandments; through Jesus Christ our Lord.   Amen.

Memorial of S. Anne, at Second Vespers, Of a Matron, from Common Memorials, p. 206.

July 26.

FESTIVAL OF S. ANNE, MOTHER OF THE BLESSED VIRGIN MARY.

All of the Common of a Matron, p. 233.

FEASTS OF AUGUST.

[*On the first day unhindered is said the Office of the Dead.*]

August 1.

FESTIVAL OF S. PETER'S CHAINS.

First Vespers.

Psalms of the Feria.

Ant. 1. I will make thee unto this people a fenced brazen wall : and they shall fight against thee, but they shall not prevail against thee.

Ant. 2. Fear thou not, O My servant, neither be dismayed : for, lo, I will save thee.

Ant. 3. I will deliver thee, I will surely deliver thee : and thou shalt not fall by the sword.

Ant. 4. In that day I will break his yoke from off thy neck : and burst thy bonds.

Ant. 5. I will go before thee, and make the crooked places straight : I will break in pieces the gates of brass, and cut in sunder the bars of iron.

CHAPTER. Jer. i.

I HAVE made thee this day a defenced city, and an iron pillar, and brazen walls against the whole land, against the kings of Judah, against the princes thereof, against the priests thereof, and against the people of the land. And they shall fight against thee; but they shall not prevail against thee; for I am with thee, saith the Lord, to deliver thee.

℟. Thou shalt be as My mouth : let them return unto thee, but return not thou unto them : for I am with thee to save thee and to deliver thee, saith the Lord. ℣. Jesus saith unto Peter, When thou wast young, thou girdest thyself, and walkedst whither thou wouldest; but when thou shalt be old, another shall gird thee. ℟. For I am with thee to save thee and to deliver thee, saith the Lord. ℣. Glory be to the Father, and to the Son, and to the Holy Ghost. ℟. For I am with thee to save thee and to deliver thee, saith the Lord.

HYMN. *Annue Christe*, p. 214.

℣. O Lord my God, in Thee have I put my trust.

℟. Save me from all them that persecute me, and deliver me.

Ant. to Mag. The Lord God will help me : and I know that I shall not be confounded.

COLLECT.

O GOD, Who didst cause blessed Peter the Apostle to be loosed from his chains and to depart unhurt; break, we beseech Thee, the bonds of our sins, and mercifully put away all evil things from us; through Jesus Christ our Lord. Amen.

Compline.

As on Festivals, p. 67.

Lauds.

℣. I will call on the Lord Who is worthy to be praised.

℟. So shall I be saved from mine enemies.

Psalms of Sunday.

Ant. 1. The Angel said unto Peter : Arise up quickly.

Ant. 2. The Angel said unto him : Cast thy garment about thee, and follow me.

Ant. 3. And he went out, and followed him : and wist not that it was true which was done by the Angel.

Ant. 4. When they were past the first and second ward, they came unto the iron gate that leadeth unto the city : which opened to them of his own accord.

Ant. 5. The Lord hath sent His Angel : and hath delivered me out of the hand of Herod. Alleluia.

CHAPTER. Acts xii.

P ETER therefore was kept in prison : but prayer was made without ceasing of the Church unto God for him.

HYMN. *Exultet cœlum laudibus,* ℣. and ℟., p. 215.

Ant. to Ben. Whatsoever thou shalt bind on earth shall be bound in heaven : and whatsoever thou shalt loose on earth shall be loosed in heaven, saith the Lord to Simon Peter.

Prime.

Ant. to Psalms. The Angel said unto Peter : Arise up quickly.

Ant. to Quicunque. Thee duly praise, Thee adore, Thee glorify : all Thy creatures, O blessed Trinity.

Tierce.

Ant. The Angel said unto him : Cast thy garment about thee, and follow me.

Chapter as at Lauds.

The Responsary at Tierce and at all the Hours as in the Office of the Common of Apostles, p. 214.

Sexts.

Ant. And he went out, and followed him : and wist not that it was true which was done by the Angel.

CHAPTER. Acts xii.

A ND behold, the Angel of the Lord came upon him, and a light shined in the prison; and he smote Peter on the side, and raised him up, saying, Arise up quickly. And his chains fell off from his hands.

Nones.

Ant. The Lord hath sent His Angel : and hath delivered me out of the hand of Herod. Alleluia.

CHAPTER. Acts xii.

PETER went out, and followed him; and wist not that it was true which was done by the Angel.

Second Vespers.

Antiphons of Lauds, p. 307.

Psalms of the Common of Apostles, p. 216.

Chapter as at Lauds.

HYMN. *Annue Christe,*
℣. and ℟., p. 214.

Ant. to Mag. And when Peter was come to himself, he said; Now I know of a surety that the Lord hath sent His Angel: and hath delivered me out of the hand of Herod, and from all the expectation of the people of the Jews.

———

[August 4.

FESTIVAL OF S. DOMINIC, FOUNDER OF THE ORDER OF FRIARS PREACHERS, CONFESSOR.*

All of the Common of Abbots and Monks,
p. 225.

———

August 5.

FESTIVAL OF S. OSWALD, KING, AND MARTYR.*

All of the Common of a Martyr, p. 217.]

———

August 6.

FESTIVAL OF THE TRANSFIGURATION OF OUR LORD.

First Vespers.

Psalms of the Feria.

Ant. 1. The earth was full of His praise: and His brightness was as the light.

Ant. 2. The sun shall be ashamed: when the Lord of hosts shall reign in the mount before His ancients gloriously.

Ant. 3. They shall see the glory of the Lord: and the excellency of our God.

Ant. 4. Ye shall have a song and gladness of heart: and the Lord shall cause His glorious voice to be heard.

Ant. 5. Thou art fairer than the children of men: full of grace are Thy lips.

CHAPTER. Is. iv.

IN that day shall the branch of the Lord be beautiful and glorious, and the fruit of the earth shall be excellent and comely for them that are escaped of Israel.

℟. They shall be satisfied with the plenteousness of Thy house; and Thou shalt give them drink of Thy pleasures, as out of the river: for with Thee is the well of life. ℣. Peter said unto Jesus, Master, it is good for us to be here. ℟. For with Thee is the well of life. ℣. Glory be to the Father, and to the Son, and to the Holy Ghost. ℟. For with Thee is the well of life.

HYMN. *Cælestis formam gloriæ.*

A TYPE of those bright rays on high
 For which the Church hopes longingly,
Christ on the holy mountain shews,
Where brighter than the sun He glows:

Tale for all ages to declare:
For with the three disciples there,
Where Moses and Elias meet,
The Lord holds converse, high and sweet.

The chosen witnesses stand nigh,
Of grace, the law, and prophecy:
And from the cloud the Holy One
Bears record to the only Son.

With face more bright than noontide ray,
Christ deigns to manifest to-day
What glory shall be theirs above,
Who joy in God with perfect love.

And faithful hearts are raised on high
By this great vision's mystery;
For which, in yearly course, we raise
The voice of prayer, and hymn of praise.

Thou, Father, Thou, Eternal Son,
Thou, Holy Spirit, Three in One,
To this same glory bring us nigh,
That we may see Thee eye to eye. Amen.

℣. My soul is athirst for the living God.

℟. When shall I come to appear before the presence of God?

Ant. to Mag. Since the beginning men have not heard, nor perceived by the ear, neither hath the eye seen, O God, beside Thee: what He hath prepared for him that waiteth for Him.

COLLECT.

O GOD, Who by the testimony of the Fathers didst confirm the sacraments of faith in the Transfiguration of Thine Only-begotten Son, and didst wonderfully prefigure by the voice from the bright cloud, the perfect adoption of sons; grant, we beseech Thee, that we may be co-heirs of the King of glory, and partakers of the same glory; through the same Thy Son Jesus Christ our Lord, Who liveth and reigneth with Thee and the Holy Ghost, ever one God, world without end. Amen.

Compline.

As on Festivals, p. 67.

Lauds.

℣. They shall walk in the light of Thy countenance.

℟. Their delight shall be daily in Thy Name.

Psalms of Sunday.

Ant. 1. Be glad then, ye children of Sion, and rejoice in the Lord your God: for He hath given you a Teacher of righteousness.

Ant. 2. This voice which came from heaven we heard : when we were with Him in the holy mount.

Ant. 3. A voice came out of the cloud, saying : This is My beloved Son; hear Him.

Ant. 4. Him shall ye hear : in all things whatsoever He shall say unto you.

Ant. 5. Every soul, which will not hear that Prophet : shall be destroyed from among the people.

CHAPTER. Baruch v.

GOD shall lead Israel with joy in the light of His glory : with the mercy and righteousness that cometh from Him.

℟. Thanks be to God.

HYMN. *Lux alma Jesu mentium.*

LIGHT of the soul, O Saviour blest!
Soon as Thy presence fills the breast,
Darkness and guilt are put to flight,
And all is sweetness and delight.

Son of the Father! Lord most high!
How glad is he who feels Thee nigh!
How sweet in Heaven Thy beam doth glow,
Denied to eye of flesh below.

O Light of light celestial!
O Charity ineffable!
Come in Thy hidden majesty;
Fill us with love, fill us with Thee.

To Jesus from the proud concealed,
But evermore to babes revealed,
All glory with the Father be,
And Holy Ghost eternally. Amen.

℣. O Lord my God, Thou art become exceeding glorious.

℟. Thou deckest Thyself with light as it were with a garment.

Ant. to Ben. Give unto the Lord the honour due unto His Name; bring an offering, and come before Him : worship the Lord in the beauty of holiness.

Prime.

Ant. Be glad then, ye children of Sion, and rejoice in the Lord your God: for He hath given you a Teacher of righteousness.

Tierce.

Ant. This voice which came from heaven we heard : when we were with Him in the holy mount.

CHAPTER. Is. iv.

IN that day shall the branch of the Lord be beautiful and glorious, and the fruit of the earth shall be excellent and comely for them that are escaped of Israel.

℟. This God is our God : for ever and ever. ℣. He shall be our guide unto death. ℟. For ever and ever. ℣. Glory be to the Father, and to the Son, and to the Holy Ghost. ℟. This God is our God : for ever and ever.

℣. Thy seat, O God, endureth for ever.

℟. The sceptre of Thy kingdom is a right sceptre.

Sexts.

Ant. A voice came out of the cloud, saying : This is My beloved Son; hear Him.

CHAPTER. Acts xii.

MOSES said unto the children of Israel, A Prophet shall the Lord your God raise up unto you of your brethren, like unto me; Him shall ye hear.

Ry. Thy seat, O God : endureth for ever.   Ⅴ. The sceptre of Thy kingdom is a right sceptre.   Ry. It endureth for ever.   Ⅴ. Glory be to the Father, and to the Son, and to the Holy Ghost.   Ry. Thy seat, O God : endureth for ever.

Ⅴ. His honour is great in Thy salvation.

Ry. Glory and great worship shalt Thou lay upon Him.

Nones.

Ant. Every soul, which will not hear that Prophet : shall be destroyed from among the people.

CHAPTER. I John ii.

IT doth not yet appear what we shall be : but we know that, when He shall appear, we shall be like Him; for we shall see Him as He is.

Ry. His honour is great : in Thy salvation.   Ⅴ. Glory and great worship shalt Thou lay upon Him.   Ry. In Thy salvation.   Ⅴ. Glory be to the Father, and to the Son, and to the Holy Ghost. Ry. His honour is great : in Thy salvation.

Ⅴ. Lord, to whom shall we go?
Ry. Thou hast the words of eternal life.

[*The Second Vespers are superseded by First Vespers of the Holy Name, unless the Transfiguration be the feast of the place.*

Second Vespers.

Antiphons of Lauds, p. 309.

Psalms of Sunday.

The rest as at First Vespers, except

Ant. to Mag. Behold My Servant, Whom I have chosen : My beloved, in Whom My soul is well pleased.

MEMORIAL OF THE HOLY NAME OF JESUS.

Ant. But I will rejoice in the Lord, and I will exult in Jesus my God : for He that is mighty hath done to me great things, and holy is His Name. Alleluia.

Ⅴ. All the world shall worship Thee, and sing of Thee.
Ry. And praise Thy Name.

Collect of the Holy Name.]

August 7.

FESTIVAL OF THE MOST SWEET NAME OF JESUS.

*If this Office be used in devotion through the year, it may be said on any day unhindered by a Vigil or Double Feast, except in Advent and Lent. Alleluia is not said, except during the Octave of the Feast and in Easter tide. At all other times, in the RyRy. the repetition is from the *.*

First Vespers.

Ant. 1. The Lord's blessed Name of Jesus be praised : from the rising of the sun unto the going down of the same. [Alleluia.]

Psalm cxiii. *Laudate pueri,* p. 46.

Ant. 2. Whosoever shall call on the Name of the Lord : shall be saved. [Alleluia.]

Psalm cxvi. *Dilexi,* p. 49.

Ant. 3. Thou hast broken my bonds in sunder : I will offer the sacrifice of thanksgiving, and will call upon the Name of the Lord. [Alleluia.]

Psalm cxvi. 10. *Credidi,* p. 49.

Ant. 4. For thither the tribes go up, even the tribes of the Lord : to testify unto Israel, to give thanks unto the Name of the Lord. [Alleluia.]

Psalm cxxii. *Lætatus sum,* p. 52.

Ant. 5. Before the gods will I sing praise unto Thee : I will worship toward Thy holy temple, and praise Thy Name, O Lord. [Alleluia.]

Psalm cxxxviii. *Confitebor tibi,* p. 59.

CHAPTER. Phil. ii.

HE humbled Himself, and became obedient unto death, even the death of the Cross. Wherefore God also hath highly exalted Him, and given Him a Name which is above every name : that at the Name of Jesus every knee should bow, of things in heaven, and things in earth, and things under the earth.

Ry. O praise the Lord with me, and let us magnify His Name together : for our heart shall rejoice in Him, because we have hoped in His holy Name. ℣. Tell of all His marvellous works, sing praise to His holy Name. ℟. For our heart shall rejoice in Him, because we have hoped in His holy Name. ℣. Glory be to the Father, and to the Son, and to the Holy Ghost. ℟. For our heart shall rejoice in Him, because we have hoped in His holy Name.

HYMN. *Exultet cor precordiis.*

O LET the heart exulting beat,
  When Jesus' holy Name resounds;
Above all other it is sweet,
And in all gladness it abounds.

Jesus, Who comforteth in woe,
Jesus, Who heals the wounds of sin,
Jesus, Who curbs the fiends below,
Jesus, Who routs Death's arms within.

Jesus! it soundeth sweetest, best,
In every measure, hymn, and song;
And with its comfort soothes the breast,
And lifts us up, and makes us strong.

Let that great Name of Him the Lord,
Jesus, from tongues of all men peal;
And let the voice and heart accord,
That every ill its sound may heal.

Jesu, Who savest sinners lost,
Be present as we kneel in prayer;
Guide Thou the erring, tempest-tost,
And us, Thy guilty servants, spare.

O let Thy Name be our defence,
In every peril guard and stay,
And purging us from sin's offence,
Perfect us in the better way.

O Christ, all glory be to Thee,
Who shinest with this Name above,
Honour, and worship, majesty,
Be Thine, O Jesu, Lord of love.

O Jesu, from the Virgin sprung,
All glory be ascribed to Thee,
Like praise be to the Father sung,
And Holy Ghost eternally. Amen.

℣. All the world shall worship Thee, and sing of Thee.

℟. And praise Thy Name.

Ant. to Mag. But I will rejoice in the Lord, and I will exult in Jesus my God : for He that is mighty hath done to me great things, and holy is His Name. [Alleluia.]

COLLECT.

GOD, Which hast made the glorious Name of Jesus Christ Thy Son our Lord most dear to Thy faithful people, and most terrible to evil spirits; grant, we beseech Thee, that all we, who worship this Name on earth, may receive in this life the sweetness of Thy holy consolations, and in the world to come, the joy of exultation, and of eternal blessedness in heaven; through the same Jesus Christ Thy Son our Lord, Who liveth and reigneth with Thee and the Holy Ghost, ever one God, world without end. Amen.

MEMORIAL OF THE TRANSFIGURATION.

Ant. Behold My Servant whom I have chosen : My Beloved, in whom My soul is well pleased.

℣. My soul is athirst for the living God.

℟. When shall I come to appear before the presence of God?

Collect of the Transfiguration.

Compline.

Ant. to Psalms. Have mercy upon me, O Lord : as Thou usest to do unto those that love Thy Name.

The Office Hymns, except at First Vespers, all take the Christmas Doxology, as at Lauds.

Ant. to Nunc Dim. O King, glorious among Thy Saints, Who art ever to be praised, and yet art ineffable : Thou, Lord, art in the midst of us, and we are called by Thy Name : leave us not, O our God; and in the day of judgment vouchsafe to number us amongst Thy Saints, O blessed King.

Lauds.

℣. Our help is in the Name of the Lord.

℟. Who hath made heaven and earth.

Psalms of Sunday.

Ant. 1. His Name was called Jesus, which was so named of the Angel : before He was conceived in the womb. [Alleluia.]

Ant. 2. O praise the Name of our Lord Jesus Christ : because it is lovely, and His mercy endureth for ever. [Alleluia.]

Ant. 3. As long as I live will I magnify Thee, O Lord Jesus : and lift up my hands in Thy Name. [Alleluia.]

Ant. 4. The righteous spoiled the ungodly, and praised Thy holy Name, O Lord : and magnified with one accord Thine hand, that fought for them. [Alleluia.]

Ant. 5. Young men and maidens, old men and children, praise the Name of the Lord : for His Name only is excellent. [Alleluia.]

CHAPTER. 1 Cor. i.

TO all that in every place call upon the Name of Jesus Christ our Lord, both theirs and ours: grace unto you, and peace, from God our Father, and the Lord Jesus Christ.

℟. Thanks be to God.

HYMN. *Jesu auctor clementiæ.*

JESU, Thou source of pity blest,
　Thou hope and gladness of the breast,
O stream of beauty, source of grace,
Delight of every heart and place !

Jesu, the beauty Angels see,
The ears' ecstatic minstrelsy,
The nectar of the Heavenly Home,
The lip's delicious honey comb !

Flower of Virgin Mother blest,
Jesu, true sweetness, purest, best,
Of man the honour and the head,
Thy light of lights upon us shed.

More glorious than the sun to see,
More fragrant than the balsam-tree,
My heart's desire, and boast, and mirth,
Jesu, Salvation of the earth.

Jesu, Who highest bounty art,
And wondrous joyance of the heart,
Of goodness the infinity,
Constrain us with Thy charity.

O King of Virtues, King renowned,
With glory and with victory crowned,
Jesu, by Whom all grace is given,
Thou honour of the courts of heaven !

Let choirs of Angels sing Thy Name,
And echo all Thy matchless fame,
Jesus on joyful earth hath smiled,
And us with God hath reconciled.

All honour, laud, and glory be,
O Jesu, Virgin-born, to Thee ;
All glory, as is ever meet,
To Father and to Paraclete. Amen.

℣. Blessed be the Name of the Lord Jesus.

℟. From this time forth for evermore.

Ant. to Ben. Joseph, thou son of David, fear not to take unto thee Mary thy wife; for that which is conceived in her is of the Holy Ghost : And she shall bring forth a Son, and thou shalt call His Name Jesus ; for He shall save His people from their sins.

Prime.

Ant. His Name was called Jesus, which was so named of the Angel : before He was conceived in the womb. [Alleluia.]

All the rest as on Christmas Day, p. 91.

Tierce.

Ant. O praise the Name of our Lord Jesus Christ : because it is lovely, and His mercy endureth for ever. [Alleluia.]

Chapter as at Lauds.

℟. I will praise the Name of the Lord * with a song : Alleluia, Alleluia. ℣. And magnify it with thanksgiving. ℟. Alleluia, Alleluia. ℣. Glory be to the Father, and to the Son, and to the Holy Ghost. ℟. I will praise the Name of the Lord with a song : Alleluia, Alleluia.

℣. Praise the Lord, O my soul.

℟. And all that is within me praise His holy Name.

Sexts.

Ant. As long as I live will I magnify Thee, O Lord Jesus : and lift up my hands in Thy Name. [Alleluia.]

CHAPTER. Col. iii.

WHATSOEVER ye do in word or deed, do all in the Name of the Lord Jesus, giving thanks to God and the Father by Him. .

℟. Praise the Lord * O my soul : Alleluia, Alleluia. ℣. And all that is within me, praise His holy Name. ℟. Alleluia, Alleluia. ℣. Glory be to the Father, and to the Son, and to the Holy Ghost. ℟. Praise the Lord, O my soul : Alleluia, Alleluia.

℣. Not unto us, O Lord, not unto us.

℟. But unto Thy Name give the praise.

Nones.

Ant. Young men and maidens, old men and children, praise the Name of the Lord : for His Name only is excellent. [Alleluia.]

CHAPTER. II Thess. iii.

NOW we command you, brethren, in the Name of our Lord Jesus Christ, that ye withdraw yourselves from every brother that walketh disorderly, and not after the tradition which he received of us.

Ry. Not unto us, O Lord; * not unto us : Alleluia, Alleluia. Ꮴ. But unto Thy Name give the praise. Ry. Alleluia, Alleluia. Ꮴ. Glory be to the Father, and to the Son, and to the Holy Ghost. Ry. Not unto us, O Lord, not unto us : Alleluia, Alleluia.

Ꮴ. Blessed be the Name of the Lord Jesus.

Ry. From this time for evermore.

Second Vespers.
Antiphons of Lauds.
Psalms of First Vespers.
Chapter as at Lauds.

Ry. But these are written, that ye might believe that Jesus is the Christ, the Son of God, and that believing ye might have life through His Name. Ꮴ. O give thanks unto the Lord, and call upon His Name; tell the people what things He hath done. Ry. That believing ye might have life through His Name. Ꮴ. Glory be to the Father, and to the Son, and to the Holy Ghost. Ry. That believing ye might have life through His Name.

HYMN. *Exultet cor precordiis,* Ꮴ. and Ry., p. 311.

Ant. to Mag. Then Joseph being raised from sleep, did as the Angel of the Lord had bidden him, and took unto him his wife : and knew her not till she had brought forth her firstborn Son : and he called His Name Jesus. Alleluia.

August 10.
FESTIVAL OF S. LAWRENCE, DEACON AND MARTYR.

All of the Common of a Martyr, p. 217, except that which follows :

Ant. to Mag. Thou art My servant, fear thou not, for I am with thee : when thou walkest through the fire thou shalt not be burned.

COLLECT.

O ALMIGHTY God, Who didst enable blessed Lawrence to withstand his fiery torments; grant, we beseech Thee, that we may extinguish the flames of our sins; through Jesus Christ our Lord, Who liveth and reigneth with Thee and the Holy Ghost, ever one God, world without end. Amen.

Ant. to Ben. Blessed Lawrence said, My night has no darkness : but all things shine with glorious light.

Memorial of the Holy Name, at both Vespers and Lauds.

[August 12.
FESTIVAL OF S. CLARE, VIRGIN.

All of the Common of a Virgin, p. 233, with Memorial of the Holy Name.]

August 14.
OCTAVE OF THE HOLY NAME.

[*If the Feast of the following day be not observed, all as on the Festival. Otherwise, all as on the Festival until Nones, inclusive, except that at Vespers the Ry. is not said. At Lauds is said this*

MEMORIAL OF THE VIGIL.

Ant. Thy loving kindness is better than the life itself : my lips shall praise Thee.

Ꮴ. My soul is athirst for the living God.

Ry. When shall I come to appear before the presence of God?

COLLECT.

O GOD, Who didst deign to choose the virginal womb of Mary wherein to rest : grant to us, who look forward to the feast of her Repose, that we may prepare a fit dwelling in our hearts for Thy majesty; Who livest and reignest with the Father, and the Holy Ghost, ever one God, world without end. Amen.]

[FESTIVAL OF THE REPOSE OF THE
BLESSED VIRGIN MARY.

First Vespers.

Ant. I sleep.   Alleluia : but my
heart waketh.   Alleluia.

Psalms of the Common, p. 209.

CHAPTER. S. Luke i.

BLESSED art thou among women;
for thou hast found favour with
God.

℟. One thing have I desired of the
Lord, which I will require : even that
I may dwell in the house of the Lord
all the days of my life, to behold the
fair beauty of the Lord, and to visit His
temple. ℣. For to me to live is Christ,
and to die is gain. ℟. Even that I
may dwell in the house of the Lord all
the days of my life, to behold the fair
beauty of the Lord, and to visit His
temple. ℣. Glory be to the Father,
and to the Son, and to the Holy Ghost.
℟. One thing have I desired of the
Lord, which I will require : even that
I may dwell in the house of the Lord
all the days of my life, to behold the
fair beauty of the Lord, and to visit His
temple.

HYMN. *Quem terra, pontus, sidera,*
℣. and ℟., *of the Common,* p. 210.

Ant. to Mag. At our gates are all
manner of pleasant fruits, new and old :
which I have laid up for Thee, my
Beloved.

COLLECT.

WE beseech Thee, Almighty God,
grant that we, who commemorate
the holy Repose of Blessed Mary, ever
Virgin, may attain to participation in
her eternal joys; through Jesus Christ
our Lord. Amen.

Compline.

As in the Common, p. 67, *except*
Ant. to Nunc Dim. I sat down under
His shadow with great delight : and His
fruit was sweet to my taste.

Lauds.

℣. O magnify the Lord with me.
℟. And let us exalt His Name together.

Psalms of Sunday.

Ant. 1. O that I had wings like a
dove : for then would I flee away, and
be at rest.
Ant. 2. My beloved spake unto me,
Rise up, My love, My fair one : and
come away.
Ant. 3. My soul thirsteth for Thee :
my flesh also longeth after Thee.
Ant. 4. I am come into My garden,
My sister, My spouse : I have gathered
My myrrh with My spice.
Ant. 5. The king's daughter is all
glorious within : her clothing is of
wrought gold.

CHAPTER. Is. lxii.

THOU shalt also be a crown of glory
in the hand of the Lord, and a royal
diadem in the hand of thy God. For
the Lord delighteth in thee, and thy
God rejoiceth over thee.

℟. Thanks be to God.

HYMN. *O gloriosa Virginum,*
℣. and ℟., *of the Common,* p. 210.

Ant. to Ben. They blessed her, and
said unto her, Thou art the exaltation
of Jerusalem : thou art the great glory
of Israel, thou art the great rejoicing of
our nation.

The Little Hours are of the Common,
with Ants. 1, 2, 3, *and* 5, *of Lauds.*
The ℟. *at Prime is said with*

℣. Thou Who wast born of the Virgin
Mary.

Second Vespers.

Psalms of the Common, p. 211, *with*
Antiphons of Lauds.

Chapter, ℟., *and Hymn, as at*
First Vespers.

Ant. to Mag. He hath regarded the
lowliness of His handmaiden : for behold, from henceforth all generations
shall call me blessed. For He that is
mighty hath magnified me.]

[August 20.

FESTIVAL OF S. BERNARD, ABBOT AND CONFESSOR.*

All of the Common of an Abbot or Monk, p. 225, except the
COLLECT.

O GOD, Who didst cause blessed Bernard the Abbot, kindled with the fire of Thy love, to be a burning and a shining light in Thy Church; grant, by his intercession, that we may burn with the spirit of love, and walk before Thee as children of light; through Jesus Christ our Lord, Who liveth and reigneth with Thee and the Holy Ghost, ever one God, world without end. Amen.]

[August 22.

OCTAVE OF THE REPOSE OF THE BLESSED VIRGIN MARY.

All as on the first day, except that at Second Vespers the R̂. is not said.]

August 24.

FESTIVAL OF S. BARTHOLOMEW, APOSTLE AND MARTYR.

All of the Common of Apostles, p. 214, except the
COLLECT.

O ALMIGHTY and everlasting God, Who didst give to Thine Apostle Bartholomew grace truly to believe and to preach Thy Word; grant, we beseech Thee, unto Thy Church, to love that Word which he believed, and both to preach and receive the same; through Jesus Christ our Lord. Amen.

August 28.

FESTIVAL OF S. AUGUSTINE, BISHOP, CONFESSOR AND DOCTOR.*

All of the Common of a Confessor Bishop, p. 222, except the
COLLECT.

O GOD, Who didst raise up blessed Augustine to be a doctor of the Church, and to unfold the mysteries of Holy Scripture; grant that we may always be instructed by his teaching, and assisted by his prayers; through Jesus Christ our Lord, Who liveth and reigneth with Thee and the Holy Ghost, ever one God, world without end. Amen.

August 29.

BEHEADING OF S. JOHN BAPTIST.

First Vespers.

Ant. He shall turn the heart of the fathers to the children : and the heart of the children to the fathers.

Psalms of the Feria.

Chapter and R̂. of the Common of a Martyr, p. 217.

HYMN. *Sanctorum meritis,*
V̂. and R̂., p. 220.

Ant. to Mag. I say unto you, that Elias is come already, and they knew him not : but have done unto him whatsoever they listed.

COLLECT.

O GOD, Who didst vouchsafe to blessed John Baptist to be in birth and death the forerunner of Thy Son; grant that as he was slain for truth and righteousness' sake, so we may fight unto death for truth and righteousness; through the same Thy Son Jesus Christ our Lord, Who liveth and reigneth with Thee and the Holy Ghost, ever one God, world without end. Amen.

Compline.

As in the Psalter, p. 67.

Lauds.

V̂. I will speak of Thy testimonies also, even before kings.
R̂. And will not be ashamed.

Psalms of Sunday.

Ant. 1. Lo, He doth send out His voice : yea, and that a mighty voice.

Ant. 2. Behold, I will send My messenger : and he shall prepare the way before Me.

Ant. 3. Thou, therefore, gird up thy loins, and arise : and speak unto them all that I command thee.

Ant. 4. If ye will receive it : this is Elias, which was for to come.

Ant. 5. I will make thee unto this people a fenced brazen wall : and they shall fight against thee, but they shall not prevail against thee; for I am with thee to save and to deliver thee.

The rest of the Common, p. 218.

Ant. to Ben. Herod sent, and beheaded John in the prison : and his head was brought in a charger, and given to the damsel, and she brought it to her mother.

Prime.

Ant. to Psalms. Lo, He doth send out His voice : yea, and that a mighty voice.

Tierce.

Ant. Behold, I will send My messenger : and he shall prepare the way before Me.

The Chapter and R꜏R꜏. at Tierce and the other Little Hours, of the Common, pp. 218, 219.

Sexts.

Ant. Thou, therefore, gird up thy loins, and arise : and speak unto them all that I command thee.

Nones.

Ant. I will make thee unto this people a fenced brazen wall : and they shall fight against thee, but they shall not prevail against thee; for I am with thee to save and to deliver thee.

Second Vespers.

Antiphons of Lauds.

Psalms of Sunday.

The rest of the Common, p. 219, *except the*

Ant. to Mag. John bare witness unto the truth : he was a burning and a shining light.

[August 31.

FESTIVAL OF S. AIDAN, BISHOP AND CONFESSOR.*

All of the Common of a Confessor Bishop, p. 222.]

FEASTS OF SEPTEMBER.

[*On the first day unhindered is said the Office of the Dead.*]

September 1.

FESTIVAL OF S. GILES, ABBOT AND CONFESSOR.*

All of the Common of an Abbot, p. 225.

September 7.

FESTIVAL OF S. EVURTIUS, BISHOP AND CONFESSOR.*

All of the Common of a Confessor Bishop, p. 222.

SEPTEMBER 8.

FESTIVAL OF THE NATIVITY OF THE BLESSED VIRGIN MARY.

As for the Conception, p. 273, *except the* COLLECT.

O GOD, Who in Thine own good pleasure wouldest reconcile the world unto Thyself; grant, we beseech Thee, that we, who celebrate the birth of Blessed Mary, may, assisted by her prayers, attain the salvation wrought out by her Son, our Lord Jesus Christ. Amen.

September 14.

FESTIVAL OF THE EXALTATION OF THE HOLY CROSS.

First Vespers.

Ant. Behold, I will lift up Mine hand to the Gentiles : and set up My standard to the people.

Psalms of the Feria.

CHAPTER. Ez. xvii.

I HAVE exalted the low tree, and have made the dry tree to flourish: I the Lord have spoken and have done it.

℟. Now is the judgment of this world; now shall the prince of this world be cast out : and I, if I be lifted up from the earth, will draw all men unto Me. ℣. Make thee a fiery serpent, and set it upon a pole : and it shall come to pass, that every one that is bitten, when he looketh upon it, shall live. ℟. And I, if I be lifted up from the earth, will draw all men unto Me. ℣. Glory be to the Father, and to the Son, and to the Holy Ghost. ℟. Now is the judgment of this world; now shall the prince of this world be cast out : and I, if I be lifted up from the earth, will draw all men unto Me.

HYMN. *Vexilla Regis prodeunt*, p. 147.

℣. Tell it out among the heathen.

℟. That the Lord reigneth from the tree.

Ant. to Mag. The tree of the field shall yield her fruit, and the earth shall yield her increase, and they shall be safe in their land : and they shall know that I am the Lord, when I have broken the bands of their yoke.

COLLECT.

O GOD, Who makest us glad to-day by the feast of the Holy Cross; grant, we beseech Thee, that as we acknowledge its mystery on earth, so we may attain the rewards of its redemption in heaven; through Jesus Christ our Lord, Who liveth and reigneth with Thee and the Holy Ghost, ever one God, world without end. Amen.

Compline.

As in the Psalter, p. 67.

Lauds.

℣. For God is my King of old.

℟. The help that is done upon earth, He doeth it Himself.

Psalms of Sunday.

Ant. 1. Blotting out the handwriting of ordinances that was against us, which was contrary to us : He took it out of the way, nailing it to His Cross.

Ant. 2. Thus it behoved Christ to suffer, and to rise from the dead : and that repentance and remission of sins should be preached in His Name among all nations.

Ant. 3. Thou smotest the heads of Leviathan in pieces : and gavest him to be meat for the people in the wilderness.

Ant. 4. The Lion of the tribe of Judah, the Root of David : hath prevailed.

Ant. 5. In the midst of the street of it was there the Tree of Life : and the leaves of the Tree were for the healing of the nations.

CHAPTER. 1 Cor. i.

WE preach Christ crucified, unto the Jews a stumbling block, and unto the Greeks foolishness; but unto them which are called, both Jews and Greeks, Christ the power of God, and the wisdom of God.

℟. Thanks be to God.

HYMN. *Lustra sex qui jam peracta*, p. 148.

℣. All the world shall worship Thee, sing of Thee.

℟. And praise Thy Name.

Ant. to Ben. Worthy is the Lamb that was slain to receive power, and riches, and wisdom, and strength, and honour, and glory, and blessing.

Prime.

Ant. to Psalms. Blotting out the handwriting of ordinances that was against us, which was contrary to us : He took it out of the way, nailing it to His Cross.

Tierce.

Ant. Thus it behoved Christ to suffer, and to rise from the dead : and that repentance and remission of sins should be preached in His Name among all nations.

Chapter as at Lauds.

℟. The stone which the builders rejected : the same is become the head of the corner. ℣. This is the Lord's doing, and it is marvellous in our eyes. ℟. The same is become the head of the corner. ℣. Glory be to the Father, and to the Son, and to the Holy Ghost. ℟. The stone which the builders rejected : the same is become the head of the corner.

℣. He is our God, even the God of Whom cometh salvation.

℟. God is the Lord, by Whom we escape death.

Sexts.

Ant. Thou smotest the heads of Leviathan in pieces : and gavest him to be meat for the people in the wilderness.

CHAPTER. Heb. ii.

FOR it became Him, for Whom are all things, and by Whom are all things, in bringing many sons unto glory, to make the Captain of their salvation perfect through sufferings.

℟. He is our God : even the God of Whom cometh salvation. ℣. God is the Lord by Whom we escape death. ℟. Even the God of Whom cometh salvation. ℣. Glory be to the Father, and to the Son, and to the Holy Ghost. ℟. He is our God : even the God of Whom cometh salvation.

℣. Great is our Lord, and great is His power.

℟. Yea, and His wisdom is infinite.

Nones.

Ant. In the midst of the street of it was there the Tree of Life : and the leaves of the Tree were for the healing of the nations.

CHAPTER. Eph. iii.

THAT ye may be able to comprehend with all Saints what is the breadth, and length, and depth, and height; and to know the love of Christ, which passeth knowledge, that ye might be filled with all the fulness of God.

℟. Great is our Lord : and great is His power. ℣. Yea, and His wisdom is infinite. ℟. Great is His power. ℣. Glory be to the Father, and to the Son,

and to the Holy Ghost. ℟. Great is our Lord : and great is His power.

℣. With the Lord there is mercy.

℟. And with Him is plenteous redemption.

Second Vespers.

Psalms of Sunday.

Antiphons of Lauds.

CHAPTER. Heb. xii.

LET us run with patience the race that is set before us, looking unto Jesus the Author and Finisher of our faith; Who for the joy that was set before Him endured the Cross, despising the shame, and is set down at the right hand of the throne of God.

℟. Thanks be to God.

HYMN. *Vexilla Regis prodeunt*, p. 147, ℣. and ℟., *as at First Vespers.*

Ant. to Mag. Then shall appear the sign of the Son of man in heaven : and they shall see the Son of man coming in the clouds of heaven with power and great glory.

———

September 17.

FESTIVAL OF S. LAMBERT, BISHOP AND MARTYR.*

All of the Common of a Martyr, p. 217.

———

September 21.

FESTIVAL OF S. MATTHEW, APOSTLE, EVANGELIST, & MARTYR.

First Vespers.

Ant. to Psalms. He pleased God, and was beloved of Him : for grace and mercy is to His Saints, and He hath a care for His elect.

Psalms of the Feria.

CHAPTER. Ez. i.

AS for the likeness of their faces, they four had the face of a man, and the face of a lion, on the right side : and they four had the face of an ox on the left side; they four also had the face of an eagle.

℞. The living creatures ran and returned as the appearance of a flash of lightning : their appearance was like burning coals of fire ; and out of the fire went forth lightning. ℣. It went up and down among the living creatures. ℞. Their appearance was like burning coals of fire. ℣. Glory be to the Father, and to the Son, and to the Holy Ghost. ℞. And out of the fire went forth lightning.

HYMN. *Annue Christe,* ℣. and ℞. *of the Common of Apostles and Evangelists,* p. 214.

Ant. to Mag. I John looked, and behold a door was opened in heaven; and behold a throne was set in heaven, and One sat on the throne : and in the midst of the throne, and round about the throne were four living creatures full of eyes before and behind.

COLLECT.

O ALMIGHTY God, Who by Thy blessed Son didst call Matthew from the receipt of custom to be an Apostle and Evangelist; grant us grace to forsake all covetous desires, and inordinate love of riches, and to follow the same Thy Son Jesus Christ, Who liveth and reigneth with Thee and the Holy Ghost, one God, world without end. Amen.

Compline.

As in the Psalter, p. 67.

Lauds.

℣. My heart is inditing of a good matter.

℞. I speak of the things which I have made unto the King.

Psalms of Sunday.

Ant. 1. How beautiful are the feet of them that preach the gospel of peace : and bring glad tidings of good things!

Ant. 2. Thy watchman shall lift up the voice; with the voice together shall they sing : for the Lord hath comforted His people.

Ant. 3. The first shall say to Sion, Behold, behold them : and I will give

to Jerusalem one that bringeth good tidings.

Ant. 4. And He declared unto you His covenant, which He commanded you to perform : and He wrote the words.

Ant. 5. The mystery of God shall be finished : as He hath declared to His servants.

Chapter as at First Vespers.

HYMN. *Exultet cælum laudibus,* ℣. and ℞., *as in the Common,* p. 215.

Ant. to Ben. In the midst of the throne, and round about the throne, were four living creatures, having each of them six wings, and full of eyes within : and they rest not day and night, saying, Holy, holy, holy, Lord God Almighty, which was, and is, and is to come.

Prime.

Ant. How beautiful are the feet of them that preach the gospel of peace : and bring glad tidings of good things!

Tierce.

Ant. Thy watchmen shall lift up the voice; with the voice together shall they sing : for the Lord hath comforted His people.

Chapter as at First Vespers.

The ℞. *at Tierce and the other Little Hours, of the Common.*

Sexts.

Ant. The first shall say to Sion, Behold, behold them : and I will give to Jerusalem one that bringeth good tidings.

CHAPTER. Ez. i.

A S for the likeness of the living creatures, their appearance was like burning coals of fire, and like the appearance of lamps.

Nones.

Ant. The mystery of God shall be finished : as He hath declared to His servants.

CHAPTER. Ez. i.

IT went up and down among the living creatures; and the fire was bright, and out of the fire went forth lightning. And the living creatures ran and returned as the appearance of a flash of lightning.

Second Vespers.

Antiphons and Psalms of the Common, p. 216.

Chapter as at First Vespers.

R̷. When the living creatures went, the wheels went by them : whithersoever the Spirit was to go, they went : and the wheels were lifted up over against them. Ẏ. When those were lifted up from the earth, the wheels were lifted up over against them. R̷. Whithersoever the Spirit was to go, they went. Ẏ. Glory be to the Father, and to the Son, and to the Holy Ghost. R̷. And the wheels were lifted up over against them.

HYMN. *Annue Christe,*
Ẏ. and R̷. *of the Common,* p. 214.

Ant. to Mag. Levi leaving all things, followed Jesus : and made Him a great feast in his house.

———

[September 23.

FESTIVAL OF S. THECLA, FIRST VIRGIN MARTYR.*

All of the Common of a Virgin and Martyr, p. 230.]

———

September 29.

FESTIVAL OF S. MICHAEL AND ALL ANGELS.

First Vespers.

Ant. to Psalms. The heavenly host adore the Son of the great King : Cherubim and Seraphim proclaim Him holy.

Psalms of the Feria.
CHAPTER. Rev. i.

GOD signified things which must shortly come to pass; by His Angel unto His servant John : who bare record of the word of God, and of the testimony of Jesus Christ, and of all things that he saw.

R̷. Thee, Holy Lord, all Angels praise in the highest, saying : To Thee be praise and honour, O Lord. Ẏ. Cherubim also and Seraphim proclaim Thee holy, with all the orders of heaven, saying: R̷. To thee be praise and honour, O Lord. Ẏ. Glory be to the Father, and to the Son, and to the Holy Ghost. R̷. Thee, Holy Lord, all Angels praise in the highest, saying : To Thee be praise and honour, O Lord.

HYMN. *Tibi Christe Splendor Patris.*

THEE, O Christ, the Father's Splendour,
  Life and virtue of the heart,
In the presence of the Angels
  Sing we now with tuneful art :
Meetly in alternate chorus
  Bearing our responsive part.

Thus we praise with veneration
  All the armies of the sky;
Chiefly him, the warrior Primate
  Of celestial chivalry :
Michael, who in princely virtue
  Cast Abaddon from on high.

By whose watchful care, repelling,
  King of Everlasting grace !
Every ghostly adversary,
  All things evil, all things base ;
Grant us of Thine only goodness
  In Thy paradise a place.

Laud and honour to the Father ;
  Laud and honour to the Son ;
Laud and honour to the Spirit ;
  Ever Three and ever One :
Consubstantial, Co-eternal,
  While unending ages run. Amen.

Ẏ. In the presence of the Angels I will sing praise unto Thee.

R̷. I will worship toward Thy holy temple, and praise Thy Name.

Ant. to Mag. When He bringeth in the First-begotten into the world, He saith : And let all the Angels of God worship Him.

COLLECT.

O EVERLASTING God, Who hast ordained and constituted the services of Angels and men in a wonderful order ; mercifully grant, that as Thy holy Angels alway do Thee service in heaven, so by Thy appointment they may succour and defend us on earth ; through Jesus Christ our Lord. Amen.

Compline.

As in the Psalter, p. 67.

Lauds.

℣. The smoke of the incense ascended up.

℟. Before God out of the Angel's hand.

Psalms of Sunday.

Ant. 1. I beheld, and lo, in the midst of the throne, stood a Lamb as It had been slain : and I heard the voice of many Angels round about the throne.

Ant. 2. The number of them was thousands of thousands, saying with a loud voice : Worthy is the Lamb that was slain, to receive power and riches.

Ant. 3. They fell before the throne on their faces : and worshipped God.

Ant. 4. The accuser of our brethren is cast down, and they overcame him : therefore rejoice, ye heavens, and ye that dwell in them.

Ant. 5. All heard I saying, Blessing, and honour, and glory, and power, be unto Him that sitteth upon the throne : and unto the Lamb for ever and ever.

CHAPTER. Rev. i.

THE revelation of Jesus Christ, which God gave unto Him, to shew unto His servants things which must shortly come to pass; and He sent and signified it by His Angel unto His servant John : who bare record of the word of God, and of the testimony of Jesus Christ, and of all things that he saw.

℟. Thanks be to God.

HYMN. *Christe sanctorum decus Angelorum.*

CHRIST, of the holy Angels light and gladness,
Maker and Saviour of the human race,
O may we reach the world unknown to sadness,
And see Thy face.

Angel of peace, may Michael to our dwelling
Down from high heaven in mighty calmness come,
Breathing all peace, and hideous war dispelling
To hell's dark gloom.

Angel of might, may Gabriel swift descending
Far from our gates our ancient foes repel,
And, as of old o'er Zacharias bending,
In temples dwell.

Angel of health, may Raphael lighten o'er us,
To every sick bed speed his healing flight,
In deeds of doubt direct the way before us,
Guide us aright.

Mary, the harbinger of peace supernal,
Mother of God, with all the Angel train,
All Saints be with us, till the bliss eternal
In Christ we gain.

Be this by Thy thrice holy Godhead granted,
Father and Son, and Spirit ever blest;
Whose glory by the Angel host is chanted,
By all confest. Amen.

℣. Praise the Lord, all ye Angels of His.

℟. Praise Him, all His host. Alleluia.

Ant. to Ben. God wrought His mighty power in Christ, and set Him at His own right hand : far above all principality, and power, and might, and dominion.

Prime.

Ant. I beheld, and lo, in the midst of the throne, stood a Lamb as it had been slain : and I heard the voice of many Angels round about the throne.

Tierce.

Ant. The number of them was thousands of thousands, saying with a loud voice : Worthy is the Lamb that was slain, to receive power and riches.

Chapter as at Lauds.

℟. An Angel stood at the altar : Alleluia, Alleluia. ℣. Having a golden censer. ℟. Alleluia, Alleluia. ℣. Glory be to the Father, and to the Son, and to the Holy Ghost. ℟. An Angel stood at the altar : Alleluia, Alleluia.

℣. The smoke of the incense ascended up.

℟. Before God out of the Angel's hand.

Sexts.

Ant. They fell before the throne on their faces : and worshipped God.

CHAPTER. Rev. xii.

AND there was war in heaven : Michael and his Angels fought against the dragon; and the dragon fought and his angels, and prevailed not; neither was their place found any more in heaven.

Y

R̷. The smoke of the incense ascended up : Alleluia, Alleluia. ℣. Before God out of the Angel's hand. R̷. Alleluia, Alleluia. ℣. Glory be to the Father, and to the Son, and to the Holy Ghost. R̷. The smoke of the incense ascended up : Alleluia, Alleluia.

℣. In the presence of the Angels will I sing praise unto Thee.

R̷. I will worship toward Thy holy temple, and praise Thy Name.

Nones.

Ant. All heard I saying, Blessing, and honour, and glory, and power, be unto Him that sitteth upon the throne : and unto the Lamb for ever and ever.

Chapter. Rev. xii.

THE accuser of our brethren is cast down, and they overcame him. Therefore, rejoice, ye heavens, and ye that dwell in them.

R̷. In the presence of the Angels will I sing praise unto Thee : Alleluia, Alleluia. ℣. I will worship toward Thy holy temple, and praise Thy Name. R̷. Alleluia, Alleluia. ℣. Glory be to the Father, and to the Son, and to the Holy Ghost. R̷. In the presence of the Angels will I sing praise unto Thee : Alleluia, Alleluia.

℣. Praise the Lord, all ye Angels of His.

R̷. Praise Him, all His host. Alleluia.

Second Vespers.

Antiphons of Lauds.

Psalms of Sunday.

The rest as at First Vespers, except the

Ant. to Mag. Michael, Gabriel, Cherubim and Seraphim, continually do cry : Worthy art Thou, O Lord, to receive glory. Alleluia.

Memorial of S. Jerome,
from Common Memorials, p. 204.

September 30.

Festival of S. Jerome,
Priest, Confessor, and Doctor.*

All of the Common of a Confessor and Doctor, p. 225.

FEASTS OF OCTOBER.

[On the first day unhindered is said the Office of the Dead.]

October 1.

Festival of S. Remigius,
Bishop and Confessor.*

All of the Common of a Confessor Bishop,
p. 222.

[October 2.

Festival of the Holy Guardian
Angels.

First Vespers.

Psalms of Sunday.

Ant. 1. Behold, I send an Angel before thee : to keep thee in the way, and to bring thee into the place which I have prepared.

Ant. 2. If thou shalt indeed obey his voice, and do all that I speak : then I will be an enemy unto thine enemies. For Mine Angel shall go before thee.

Ant. 3. I will bring you away peaceably, saith the Lord : for Mine Angel is with you, and I myself caring for your souls.

Ant. 4. He had power over the Angel and prevailed : he found him in Bethel.

Ant. 5. The Lord heard our voice, and sent an Angel : and brought us forth out of Egypt.

Chapter. Is. lxiii.

IN all their affliction He was afflicted, and the Angel of His presence saved them : in His love and in His pity He redeemed them ; and He bare them, and carried them all the days of old.

R̷. There shall no evil happen unto thee; for He shall give His Angels charge over thee to keep thee in all thy ways : they shall bear thee in their hands, that thou hurt not thy foot against a stone. ℣. The Angel said unto me, I am thy fellow-servant, and of thy brethren the prophets ; worship God. R̷. They shall bear thee in their hands, that thou hurt not thy foot against a stone. ℣. Glory be to the Father, and to the Son, and to the Holy Ghost. Ṛ. There shall no evil happen unto thee; for He shall give His Angels charge over thee to keep thee in all thy ways : they shall bear thee in their hands, that thou hurt not thy foot against a stone.

HYMN. *Eterne Rector siderum.*

ETERNAL Ruler of the sky,
  Whose might hath made and governs all;
Beneath Thy care and loving eye,
  All things Thou hast created fall.

Hear Thou the cry of sinful man,
  As spread the gloomy shades of night;
Our souls enlighten Thou anew
  Who gav'st the word, "Let there be light."

Send Thou the Angel Thou didst set
  To be our guardian and our friend;
May He from taint of sin and death
  Our soul and all its powers defend.

The wily serpent's envious craft
  May his angelic might destroy,
Lest Satan's net and snares unseen,
  Our heedless souls with guile annoy.

Far from our land may he repel
  Alarm of war and bloody fray,
Give tranquil peace to Christian homes,
  Drive plague and pestilence away.

Glory to God the Father be
  Whose mercy sends the Angel-host,
To guard the souls by Christ set free,
  And hallowed by the Holy Ghost. Amen.

Ẏ. The Angel of the Lord tarrieth round about them that fear Him.

Ṛ. And delivereth them.

Ant. to Mag. O Lord of heaven, send a good Angel before us : and through the might of Thine arm let those be stricken with terror, that come against Thy holy people to blaspheme.

COLLECT.

O GOD, Who by an ineffable Providence hast vouchsafed to send Thy holy Angels to guard us; grant to Thy suppliants, that we may be defended by their protection in this life, and in the next, be gladdened by their companionship; through Jesus Christ our Lord. Amen.

Compline.

As in the Psalter, p. 67.

Lauds.

Ẏ. O praise the Lord, ye Angels of His.

Ṛ. Ye that excel in strength, and hearken unto the voice of His words.

Psalms of Sunday.

Ant. 1. God, Which dwelleth in heaven, prosper your journey : and the Angel of God keep you company.

Ant. 2. The Lord, before Whom I walk, will send His Angel with thee : and prosper thy way.

Ant. 3. Blessed be God that hath sent His Angel : and delivered His servants that trusted in Him.

Ant. 4. The Angel of the Lord answered and said, O Lord of hosts : how long wilt Thou not have mercy on Jerusalem and on the cities of Judah, against which Thou hast had indignation?

Ant. 5. I have set watchmen upon thy walls, O Jerusalem : which shall never hold their peace day nor night.

CHAPTER. II Kings vi.

AND when the servant of the man of God was risen early and gone forth, behold, an host compassed the city both with horses and chariots. And his servant said unto him, Alas, my master! how shall we do? And he answered, Fear not: for they that be with us are more than they that be with them.

HYMN. *Laus angelorum inclyta?*

WHERE the angel hosts adore Thee,
  Thou, O God, in heaven dost reign;
At Thy Word they rose around Thee,
  And Thy Word doth them sustain.

Thousand times ten thousand bending
  At Thy throne, their homage pay;
Flames of fire in strength excelling,
  Swift Thy pleasure to obey.

Fashioned in a wondrous order,
  Thee they serve, their Lord and King;
Grant that, in our cares and dangers,
  They to us may succour bring.

Praise to Thee, Who hast created
  Earth and heaven with all their host;
Praise to Thee, O God most mighty,
  Father, Son, and Holy Ghost. Amen.

Ẏ. He bowed the heavens also, and came down.

Ṛ. He rode upon the Cherubim.

Ant. to Ben. Their Angels do alway behold the face of My Father : Which is in heaven.

Prime.

Ant. God, Which dwelleth in heaven, prosper your journey : and the Angel of God keep you company.

Tierce.

Ant. The Lord, before Whom I walk, will send His Angel with thee : and prosper thy way.

℟. Rise up, O Lord : and let Thine enemies be scattered. ℣. And let them that hate Thee flee before Thee. ℟. And let Thine enemies be scattered. ℣. Glory be to the Father, and to the Son, and to the Holy Ghost. ℟. Rise up, O Lord : and let Thine enemies be scattered.

℣. Let their way be dark and slippery.

℟. And let the Angel of the Lord persecute them.

Sexts.

Ant. Blessed be God that hath sent His Angel : and delivered His servants that trusted in Him.

CHAPTER. Zech. ix.

I WILL encamp about Mine house because of the army, because of him that passeth by, and because of him that returneth : and no oppressor shall pass through them any more : for now have I seen with Mine eyes.

℟. Let their way be : dark and slippery. ℣. And let the Angel of the Lord persecute them. ℟. Dark and slippery. ℣. Glory be to the Father, and to the Son, and to the Holy Ghost. ℟. Let their way be : dark and slippery.

℣. O Lord my God, Thou art become exceeding glorious.

℟. He maketh His Angels spirits, and His ministers a flaming fire.

Nones.

Ant. I have set watchmen upon thy walls, O Jerusalem : which shall never hold their peace day nor night.

CHAPTER. Eccles. v.

SUFFER not thy mouth to cause thy flesh to sin; neither say thou before

the Angel that it was an error : wherefore should God be angry at thy voice, and destroy the work of thine hands ?

℟. O Lord my God : Thou art become exceeding glorious. ℣. He maketh His Angels spirits, and His ministers a flaming fire. ℟. Thou art become exceeding glorious. ℣. Glory be to the Father, and to the Son, and to the Holy Ghost. ℟. O Lord my God : Thou art become exceeding glorious.

℣. The chariots of God are twenty thousand, even thousands of Angels.

℟. And the Lord is among them.

Second Vespers.

Psalms of Sunday.

Ant. 1. Take heed that ye despise not one of these little ones, for I say unto you : That in heaven their Angels do alway behold the face of My Father Which is in heaven.

Ant. 2. I say unto you, There is joy in the presence of the Angels of God : over one sinner that repenteth.

Ant. 3. And He shall send His Angels: and they shall gather together His elect.

Ant. 4. Are they not all ministering spirits : sent forth to minister for them who shall be heirs of salvation ?

Ant. 5. They fell down before the Lamb, having every one of them harps : and golden vials full of odours, which are the prayers of Saints.

CHAPTER. Gen. xxxii.

AND Jacob went on his way, and the Angels of God met him. And when Jacob saw them, he said, This is God's host.

HYMN, ℣., and ℟., *as at First Vespers.*

Ant. to Mag. One of the Angels shewed me the great city, heavenly Jerusalem : and it had twelve gates, and at the gates twelve Angels.]

[October 4.

FESTIVAL OF S. FRANCIS,
FOUNDER OF THE ORDER OF FRIARS
MINOR, CONFESSOR.*

All of the Common of Abbots and Monks, p. 225.]

October 6.

FESTIVAL OF S. FAITH, VIRGIN AND MARTYR.*

All of the Common of a Virgin Martyr, p. 230.

[October 9.

FESTIVAL OF S. DENIS, BISHOP AND MARTYR, AND HIS COMPANIONS.*

All of the Common of many Martyrs, p. 219.]

[October 10.

FESTIVAL OF S. PAULINUS OF YORK, BISHOP AND CONFESSOR.*

All of the Common of a Confessor Bishop, p. 222.]

October 13.

FESTIVAL OF THE TRANSLATION OF S. EDWARD, KING AND CONFESSOR.*

All of the Common of a Confessor, p. 228, except the

COLLECT.

O GOD, Who hast crowned blessed king Edward, Thy Confessor, with the glory of eternity; grant to us, we pray Thee, so to venerate him on earth, that we may reign with him in heaven; through Jesus Christ our Lord, Who liveth and reigneth with Thee and the Holy Ghost, ever one God, world without end. Amen.

[October 15.

FESTIVAL OF S. THERESA, VIRGIN AND DOCTOR.*

All of the Common of a Virgin, p. 233.]

October 17.

FESTIVAL OF S. ETHELDRED, VIRGIN, QUEEN, AND ABBESS.*

All of the Common of a Virgin, p. 233.

October 18.

FESTIVAL OF S. LUKE, EVANGELIST.

All as on the Festival of S. Matthew, p. 318, except the

COLLECT.

ALMIGHTY God, Who calledst Luke, the Physician, whose praise is in the Gospel, to be an Evangelist, and Physician of the soul; may it please Thee, that, by the wholesome medicines of the doctrine delivered by him, all the diseases of our souls may be healed; through the merits of Thy Son Jesus Christ our Lord. Amen.

At Second Vespers,

Ant. to Mag. His praise is in the gospel : throughout all the churches.

October 25.

FESTIVAL OF SS. CRISPIN AND CRISPINIAN, MARTYRS.*

All of the Common of many Martyrs, p. 219.

October 28.

FESTIVAL OF SS. SIMON AND JUDE, APOSTLES AND MARTYRS.

All as in the Common of Apostles, p. 214, except that at First Vespers, Lauds, Tierce, and Second Vespers, is said the following

CHAPTER. Rom. viii.

WE know that all things work together for good to them that love God, to them who are the called according to His purpose.

COLLECT.

O ALMIGHTY God, Who hast built Thy Church upon the foundation of the Apostles and Prophets, Jesus Christ Himself being the head corner-stone; grant us so to be joined together in unity of spirit by their doctrine, that we may be made an holy temple acceptable unto Thee; through Jesus Christ our Lord. Amen.

FEASTS OF NOVEMBER.

*[On the first day unhindered is said the
Office of the Dead.]*

November 1.

FESTIVAL OF ALL SAINTS.

First Vespers.

Ant. 1. The Saints of God in the
company of the heavenly citizens : are
praying for us.

Psalm cxiii. *Laudate pueri*, p. 46.

Ant. 2. O how glorious is the kingdom where all the Saints rejoice with
Christ : they are clothed in white robes,
and follow the Lamb whithersoever He
goeth.

Psalm cxvii. *Laudate Dominum*, p. 50.

Ant. 3. The righteous shall shine,
and run to and fro like sparks among
the stubble : they shall judge the nations,
and have dominion over the people.

Psalm cxlvi. *Lauda anima mea*, p. 63.

Ant. 4. A holy and very and marvellous light, shedding brightness on
those who endured in the strife of the
battle, they shall receive from Christ :
everlasting splendour wherein they shall
be glad and rejoice.

Psalm cxlvii. *Laudate Dominum, quoniam*, p. 64.

Ant. 5. All the elect of God remember
us before God : that we may be united
to them by the help of their prayers.

Psalm cxlvii. 12. *Lauda Hierusalem*,
p. 64.

CHAPTER. Rev. vii.

AND I saw another Angel ascending
from the east, having the seal of the
living God : and he cried with a loud
voice to the four Angels, to whom it was
given to hurt the earth and the sea,
saying, Hurt not the earth, neither the
sea, nor the trees, till we have sealed
the servants of our God in their foreheads.

R̷. Praise our God, all ye His servants, and ye that fear Him, both small
and great : for the Lord God Omnipotent
reigneth : let us be glad and rejoice,
and give glory to Him. ℣. Chosen
generation, royal priesthood, peculiar
people, shew forth the praises of God.
R̷. For the Lord God Omnipotent
reigneth. ℣. Glory be to the Father,
and to the Son, and to the Holy Ghost.
R̷. Let us be glad, and rejoice, and give
glory to Him.

HYMN. *Jesu salvator seculi.*

O JESU, Saviour of the earth,
  Help Thy redeemed ones in their need,
And let the Maid who gave Thee birth
For hapless sinners ever plead.

Let Angel armies kneel to Thee,
And Patriarchs in shining train,
And Seers in goodly company,
That we may full remission gain.

The Baptist, herald of Thy face,
The bearer of the mystic keys,
With all Apostles, ask Thy grace
To grant us prisoners release.

The Martyr-choir in heavenly seat,
The Priests who made confession bold,
The stainless Virgin ranks, intreat
That we be loosed from evil's hold.

The prayers of all Thy ministry,
Of all the dwellers in the skies,
Join with the vows we make to Thee,
To win us life's eternal prize.

All laud to God the Father be,
All laud, eternal Son, to Thee,
All praise for ever, as is meet,
To God the holy Paraclete. Amen.

℣. Be glad, O ye righteous, and rejoice in the Lord.

R̷. And be joyful, all ye that are true
of heart.

Ant. to Mag. Blessed are ye, O Saints
of God : who have been counted worthy
to become coheirs with heavenly powers,
and enjoy the brightness of glory.

COLLECT.

O ALMIGHTY God, Who hast knit
together Thine elect in one communion and fellowship, in the mystical
body of Thy Son Christ our Lord ; grant
us grace so to follow Thy blessed Saints
in all virtuous and godly living, that we
may come to those unspeakable joys,
which Thou hast prepared for them
that unfeignedly love thee ; through
Jesus Christ our Lord. Amen.

*No Memorial is said on this day at First
  Vespers, Lauds, or Second Vespers,*

unless it falls on Sunday, in which case Memorial is made of Sunday. If it falls on Saturday, Memorial is made of Sunday at Second Vespers.

Compline.

Ant. to Psalms. By the prayers of all Thy Saints, O Christ, restore health of body and soul to Thy servants.

The rest as in the Psalter, p. 67.

Lauds.

℣. The righteous live for evermore.
℟. Their reward is with the Lord.

Psalms of Sunday.

Ant. 1. After this I beheld, and lo, a great multitude, which no man could number : of all nations, and kindreds, and people, and tongues, stood before the throne.

Ant. 2. And all the Angels stood round about the throne, and about the elders and the four living creatures : and fell before the throne on their faces, and worshipped God.

Ant. 3. Thou hast redeemed us to God by Thy blood out of every kindred, and tongue, and people, and nation : and hast made us unto our God kings.

Ant. 4. Bless the Lord, all ye His Angels : make the day joyful and give thanks unto Him.

Ant. 5. All His Saints shall praise Him, even the children of Israel, even the people that serveth Him : such honour have all His Saints.

Chapter as at First Vespers.

HYMN. *Christe redemptor omnium.*

O CHRIST, Redeemer of mankind,
Thy servants here protect and spare,
Who hearest, with a loving mind,
The blessèd Virgin's holy prayer.

May those glad hosts which see Thy face,
The spirits of the heavenly home,
Away from us all evils chase,
Both past, and present, and to come.

The Prophets of the Judge most high,
The twelve Apostles of the Lord,
For us, with interceding cry,
Pray that Thou keep us in Thy ward.

God's Martyrs, who have won renown,
His Confessors, in bright array,
Ask that we too may win the crown
Which shines in everlasting day.

The choir of Virgins lily-white,
Thy Priests and all Thy ministry,
With every Saint in prayer unite,
Till we be joined, O Christ, to Thee.

Then purge away all unbelief
From every land where Christians dwell,
That unto Thee, our Victor Chief,
Our thanks and praises we may tell.

All laud to God the Father be,
All laud, Eternal Son, to Thee,
All praise for ever, as is meet,
To God the Holy Paraclete. Amen.

℣. Wonderful art Thou in Thy Saints, O God.
℟. And glorious in Thy majesty.

Ant. to Ben. Thee, the glorious company of the Apostles; Thee, the goodly fellowship of the Prophets; Thee, the white-robed army of Martyrs : Thee, all the elect with one voice acknowledge, blessed Trinity, One God.

Prime.

Ant. to Psalms. After this I beheld, and lo, a great multitude, which no man could number : of all nations, and kindreds, and people, and tongues, stood before the throne.

Tierce.

Ant. And all the Angels stood round about the throne, and about the elders and the four living creatures : and fell before the throne on their faces, and worshipped God.

Chapter as at First Vespers.

℟. Be glad, O ye righteous : and rejoice in the Lord. ℣. And be joyful, all ye that are true of heart. ℟. And rejoice in the Lord. ℣. Glory be to the Father, and to the Son, and to the Holy Ghost. ℟. Be glad, O ye righteous : and rejoice in the Lord.

℣. Let the righteous be glad, and rejoice before God.
℟. Let them also be merry and joyful.

Sexts.

Ant. Thou hast redeemed us to God by Thy blood out of every kindred, and tongue, and people, and nation : and hast made us unto our God kings.

CHAPTER. Rev. vii.

I HEARD the number of them which were sealed; and there were sealed an hundred and forty and four thousand of all the tribes of the children of Israel.

℟. Let the righteous be glad : and rejoice before God. ℣. Let them also be merry and joyful. ℟. And rejoice before God. ℣. Glory be to the Father, and to the Son, and to the Holy Ghost. ℟. Let the righteous be glad : and rejoice before God.

℣. The souls of the righteous are in the hands of God.

℟. And there shall no torment touch them.

Nones.

Ant. All His Saints shall praise Him : even the children of Israel, even the people that serveth Him. Such honour have all His Saints.

CHAPTER. Rev. vii.

A FTER this I beheld, and, lo, a great multitude, which no man could number, of all nations, and kindreds, and people, and tongues, stood before the throne, and before the Lamb, clothed with white robes, and palms in their hands.

℟. The souls of the righteous : are in the hands of God. ℣. And there shall no torment touch them. ℟. In the hands of God. ℣. Glory be to the Father, and to the Son, and to the Holy Ghost. ℟. The souls of the righteous : are in the hands of God.

℣. Wonderful art Thou in Thy Saints, O God.

℟. And glorious in Thy majesty.

Second Vespers.

Antiphons of Lauds.

Psalm cxi. *Confitebor tibi*, p. 45.
Psalm cxvi. 10. *Credidi*, p. 49.
Psalm cxxvi. *In convertendo*, p. 53.
Psalm cxl. *Eripe me*, p. 60.
Psalm cxlvii. 12. *Lauda Hierusalem*, p. 64.

Chapter as at First Vespers.

℟. The righteous live for evermore : reward also is with the Lord : and

the care of them is with the most High. ℣. Therefore shall they receive a glorious kingdom, and a beautiful crown from the Lord's hand. ℣. Their reward also is with the Lord. ℣. Glory, praise, honour, majesty, might, and jubilation be to the Father, and to the Begotten One, and to the Holy Spirit. ℟. The care of them is with the most High.

HYMN. *Christe redemptor omnium*,
℣. and ℟., *as at Lauds.*

Ant. to Mag. O Saviour of the world, save us all, and let Thy holy Virgin-mother pray for us, with the holy Apostles, Martyrs, Confessors, and Virgins : that we may be delivered from all evil, and be counted worthy now and ever to be filled with good things.

These Vespers of All Saints being ended, forthwith are begun Festival Vespers of the Dead, p. 260.

Compline.

As on the previous day.

[November 2.

COMMEMORATION OF ALL SOULS.

Lauds.

All as p. 264. [*But according to the Sarum use,* Eternal rest, etc., *is not said at the end of each Psalm, but only once at the close of all.*]

At Prime, and the other Hours, is not to be said, O God, make speed to save us, *nor any Hymn, but the Antiphon is begun immediately after the usual introductory Prayers which are always said in silence.*

Prime.

Ant. Eternal rest grant unto them, O Lord : and light perpetual shine upon them.

Psalm liv. *Deus in nomine.*
Psalm cxix. *Beati immaculati*, and *Retribue servo tuo.*

The Psalms end without Gloria, and the Antiphon is repeated. Then follows:

Lord, have mercy.
Christ, have mercy.
Lord, have mercy.

Our Father.

℣. And lead us not into temptation. ℟. But deliver us from evil. ℣. Eternal rest grant unto them, O Lord. ℟. And light perpetual shine upon them. ℣. From the gates of hell. ℟. Deliver their souls, O Lord. ℣. I believe verily to see the goodness of the Lord. ℟. In the land of the living. ℣. The Lord be with you. ℟. And with thy spirit.

Let us pray.

COLLECT.

GOD, the Creator and Redeemer of all the faithful, grant to the souls of Thy servants and handmaidens remission of all their sins; that the pardon they have always desired, by pious supplications may be obtained; Who livest and reignest with God the Father, in the unity of the Holy Spirit, God, throughout all ages. Amen.

After the Collect is not said, The Lord be with you.

℣. May they rest in peace.
℟. Amen.

Thus are said Prime, Tierce, Sexts, and Nones, on this day. Vespers are of the Octave. If the day falls on Sunday, the commemoration of All Souls is deferred till the morrow.]

[November 3.

FESTIVAL OF S. WINIFRED, VIRGIN AND MARTYR.*

All of the Common of a Virgin and Martyr, p. 230, except the
COLLECT.

ALMIGHTY and everlasting God, Who hast adorned blessed Winifred with the reward of virginity; grant we pray Thee, that we, assisted by her intercession, may despise the allurements of this world, and with her attain a throne of everlasting glory; through Jesus Christ our Lord, Who liveth and reigneth with Thee and the Holy Ghost,

ever one God, world without end. Amen.]

[November 4.

FESTIVAL OF S. CHARLES BORROMEO, BISHOP AND CONFESSOR.*

All of the Common of a Confessor Bishop, p. 222.]

November 6.

FESTIVAL OF S. LEONARD, DEACON, CONFESSOR, AND ABBOT.*

All of the Common of an Abbot or Monk, p. 225.

November 9.

FESTIVAL OF S. MARTIN, BISHOP AND CONFESSOR.

All of the Common of a Confessor Bishop, p. 222, except the
COLLECT.

O GOD, Who wast glorified in the life and death of blessed Martin, Thy Confessor and Bishop; renew in our hearts the same miracles of Thy grace, that neither death nor life may be able to separate us from the love of our Lord Jesus Christ, Who liveth and reigneth with Thee and the Holy Ghost, ever one God, world without end. Amen.

November 13.

FESTIVAL OF S. BRITIUS, BISHOP AND CONFESSOR.*

At First Vespers, Antiphons and Psalms of the Feria. Chapter and all the rest, of the Common of a Confessor Bishop, p. 222.

November 15.

FESTIVAL OF S. MACHUTUS, BISHOP AND CONFESSOR.*

All of the Common of a Confessor Bishop, p. 222.

November 17.

FESTIVAL OF S. HUGH, BISHOP AND CONFESSOR.*

All of the Common of a Confessor Bishop, p. 222, except the

COLLECT.

O GOD, Who didst greatly adorn blessed Hugh, Thy Confessor and Bishop, with singular merits and glorious signs; mercifully grant that his example may stir us up, and his virtues shine upon us; through Jesus Christ our Lord, Who liveth and reigneth with Thee and the Holy Ghost, ever one God, world without end. Amen.

[November 19.

FESTIVAL OF S. ELIZABETH OF HUNGARY, QUEEN AND MATRON.*

All of the Common of a Matron, p. 233, except the Collect, which is of S. MARGARET, June 10, with change of name.]

November 20.

FESTIVAL OF S. EDMUND, KING AND MARTYR.*

All of the Common of a Martyr, p. 217, except the

COLLECT.

O GOD of ineffable mercy, Who didst give blessed King Edmund grace to conquer the enemy by dying for Thy Name; mercifully grant to this Thy family, that assisted by his intercession, it may be made worthy to overcome and extinguish the ghostly temptations of the ancient enemy; through Jesus Christ our Lord, Who liveth and reigneth with Thee and the Holy Ghost, ever one God, world without end. Amen.

[November 21.

FESTIVAL OF THE PRESENTATION OF THE BLESSED VIRGIN MARY.*

All of the Common of the Blessed Virgin Mary, p. 209.]

November 22.

FESTIVAL OF S. CECILIA, VIRGIN AND MARTYR.*

All of the Common of a Virgin Martyr, p. 230, except the

COLLECT.

O GOD, Who dost gladden us with the feast of blessed Cecilia, Thy Virgin and Martyr; grant that while we venerate her birthday, we may also imitate her constancy in suffering; through Jesus Christ our Lord, Who liveth and reigneth with Thee and the Holy Ghost, ever one God, world without end. Amen.

November 23.

FESTIVAL OF S. CLEMENT, BISHOP AND MARTYR.*

All of the Common of a Martyr, p. 217.

November 25.

FESTIVAL OF S. KATHARINE, VIRGIN AND MARTYR.

All of the Common of a Virgin Martyr, p. 230, except the

COLLECT.

A LMIGHTY, everlasting God, Who didst cause the body of Thy glorious Virgin Katharine to be carried by Thy servants to Mount Sinai; mercifully grant that her prayers may help us to rise to the height of all virtues, where we may behold the glory of Thy presence; through Jesus Christ our Lord, Who liveth and reigneth with Thee and the Holy Ghost, ever one God, world without end. Amen.

COMMON OF VIGILS.

According to Sarum, Saints' Day Vigils are only noticed at Mass, contrary to the modern use, which supplies a Collect to be used from Lauds to Nones, inclusive. A common Collect is here supplied from the Sarum Missal for those who desire to follow the latter practice. The Vigil of the Repose, Aug. 14, is the only day thus provided for in the body of the book.

COLLECT.

GRANT, we beseech Thee, O Almighty God, that our service preceding the day of blessed *N.*, Thy *Apostle*, may more and more obtain for us the aid of *his* intercession; through Jesus Christ our Lord, Who liveth and reigneth with Thee and the Holy Ghost, ever one God, world without end. Amen.

PROPER OF SCOTLAND.

November 30.

FESTIVAL OF S. ANDREW, APOSTLE AND MARTYR.

As in the Proper of Saints, p. 271.

The Octave is kept as follows:

A Memorial is said daily at Lauds and Vespers till the Octave. At Second Vespers of S. Nicholas, the Ant. to the Memorial is that to Magnificat at First Vespers of S. Andrew. If the Feast of S. Nicholas is not kept, First Vespers of the Octave are said as on the first day, except that no R̷. is said. The five Psalms at Lauds are said under the first Antiphon. At Prime and at all the other hours till Nones inclusive, as on the first day, Vespers being of the Conception of the Blessed Virgin Mary.

December 4.

FESTIVAL OF S. DROSTANE, ABBOT AND CONFESSOR.

All of the Common of Abbots and Monks, p. 225, except the

COLLECT.

O GOD, Who didst adorn blessed Drostane, Thy Confessor and Abbot, by glorious miracles; grant, we beseech Thee, that we may attain to those eternal rewards which Thou hast bestowed on him in heaven; through Jesus Christ our Lord, Who liveth and reigneth with Thee and the Holy Ghost, world without end. Amen.

January 11.

MEMORIAL OF S. DAVID, KING AND CONFESSOR.

From Common Memorials, p. 205.

January 13.

MEMORIAL OF S. KENTIGERN, BISHOP AND CONFESSOR.

From Common Memorials, p. 203.

February 18.

S. COLMAN, BISHOP AND CONFESSOR.

All of the Common of a Bishop and Confessor, p. 222, except the

COLLECT.

GIVE us, we beseech Thee, Almighty God, continual perseverance in Thy service; and grant that (blessed Colman, Thy Confessor and Bishop, interceding,) we may come to Thee in glory; through Jesus Christ our Lord. Amen.

March 11.

S. CONSTANTINE, KING AND MARTYR.

All of the Common of a Martyr, p. 217, except the

COLLECT.

O GOD, Who didst glorify blessed Constantine, King and Martyr, in his triumphant passion; grant us, after his example, to despise earthly glory, and ever strive after the glory which is above; through Jesus Christ our Lord. Amen.

——

March 20.

S. CUTHBERT, BISHOP AND CONFESSOR.

All of the Common of a Bishop and Confessor, p. 222, except the
COLLECT.

O GOD, Who by an inestimable gift of Thy grace makest Thy Saints to be glorious; grant, we pray Thee, that (blessed Cuthbert, Thy Confessor and Bishop, interceding,) we may be found worthy to attain to the heights of sanctity; through Jesus Christ our Lord. Amen.

——

April 1.

S. GILBERT, BISHOP AND CONFESSOR.

All of the Common of a Bishop and Confessor, p. 222.

——

April 20.

S. SERF, BISHOP AND CONFESSOR.

All of the Common of a Bishop and Confessor, p. 222.

——

June 9.

S. COLUMBA, ABBOT.

All of the Common of Abbots and Monks, p. 225, except the
COLLECT.

WE pray Thee, O Lord, inspire our hearts with the desire of heavenly glory; and grant that we, bringing our sheaves with us, may enter that place where Thy holy Abbot Columba shineth like a star before Thee; through Jesus Christ our Lord. Amen.

July 6.

MEMORIAL OF S. PALLADIUS, BISHOP AND CONFESSOR.

From Common Memorials, p. 203.

——

September 16.

S. NINIAN, BISHOP.

All of the Common of a Bishop and Confessor, p. 222, except the
COLLECT.

O GOD, Who hast made this day honourable to us by the feast of blessed Ninian, Thy Confessor and Bishop; mercifully grant, that as we have received the light of Thy truth from his teaching, so, assisted by his intercession, we may come to the joys of eternal life; through Jesus Christ our Lord. Amen.

——

September 23.

S. ADAMNAN, ABBOT.

All of the Common of Abbots and Monks, p. 225.

——

November 16.

S. MARGARET, QUEEN AND MATRON.

All of the Common of a Matron, p. 233, except the
COLLECT.

O GOD, Who hast bestowed on the soul of Thy handmaid, blessed Queen Margaret, the rewards of eternal blessedness; mercifully grant that we who are burdened with the weight of our sins, may be assisted by her intercession before Thee; through Jesus Christ our Lord. Amen.

——

November 27.

S. ODE, VIRGIN.

All of the Common of a Virgin, p. 233.

Tu autem, Domine, miserere nobis.
Deo gratias.

The reader is requested to supply with a pen the following omissions:—

Page 63, *column* 1, *line* 2, *after* marvellous *add* , worthy to be praised.

Page 63, *column* 2, *line* 7, *after* ever *add* and ever.

Page 156, *column* 2, *after line* 2, *insert Ant. to Mag.* I have power to lay down My life: and I have power to take it again.